Praise for Shadows of the Apt

'The insectile-humans premise is inventive, shaping the world in all sorts of ways' *SFX*

'*Salute the Dark* impressed me no end . . . Mr Tchaikovsky showed he mastered the art of managing an epic almost to perfection . . . *Salute the Dark* fulfils the promise of the Apt series and brings its first part to an excellent conclusion, while starting new threads to be explored next. An A++ based on my three reads of the book so far and vaulting to the top of my 2010 fantasy novels' Fantasy Book Critic

'A good and enjoyable mix between a medieval-looking world and the presence of technology . . . I really enjoyed the novel and will certainly read the next novels of the series' Dark Wolf's Fantasy Reviews

Empire in Black and Gold

Adrian Tchaikovsky was born in Woodhall Spa, Lincolnshire before heading off to Reading to study psychology and zoology. For reasons unclear even to himself he subsequently ended up in law and has worked as a legal executive in both Reading and Leeds, where he now lives. Married, he is a keen live role-player and occasional amateur actor, has trained in stage-fighting, and keeps no exotic or dangerous pets of any kind, possibly excepting his son.

Catch up with Adrian at www.shadowsoftheapt.com for further information about both himself and the insect-kinden, together with bonus material including short stories and artwork.

Empire in Black and Gold is the first novel in the Shadows of the Apt series.

BY ADRIAN TCHAIKOVSKY

Shadows of the Apt

Empire in Black and Gold

Dragonfly Falling

Blood of the Mantis

Salute the Dark

The Scarab Path

The Sea Watch

Heirs of the Blade

The Air War

War Master's Gate

Seal of the Worm

SHADOWS OF THE APT
BOOK ONE

Empire in Black and Gold

ADRIAN
TCHAIKOVSKY

TOR

First published 2008 by Tor

This edition published 2012 by Tor
an imprint of Pan Macmillan
20 New Wharf Road, London N1 9RR
Associated companies throughout the world
www.panmacmillan.com

ISBN 978-1-4472-0860-0

9

A CIP catalogue record for this book is available from
the British Library.

Printed and bound by CPI Group (UK) Ltd, Croydon, CR0 4YY

Visit **www.panmacmillan.com** to read more about all our books
and to buy them. You will also find features, author interviews and
news of any author events, and you can sign up for e-newsletters
so that you're always first to hear about our new releases.

*To Annie, without whom many things
would not have been possible*

Acknowledgements

I owe a great deal to a great many people whose inspiration, aid and encouragement have made this book possible; more than can reasonably be named in such a short space. However I would like to thank: the support of my family and extended family; twice-yearly meetings of the Deadliners writing group in York; swordfights and archery practice in the wilds of Reading; late-night drinking sessions in the stews of Oxford; and the oldest and best of friends, Wayne, Martin and Shane, because they've been there from the start.

And I would like to thank especially my agent Simon Kavanagh, and to thank Peter Lavery, Jon Mitchell, Michael Bhaskar, and everyone else at Macmillan who collectively made all this possible.

A Map of the LOWLANDS and environs

• Hemesh · Alles •

One

After Stenwold picked up the telescope for the ninth time, Marius said, 'You will know first from the sound.'

The burly man stopped and peered down at him, telescope still half-poised. From their third-storey retreat the city walls were a mass of black and red, the defenders hurrying into place atop the ramparts and about the gates.

'How do you mean, the sound?'

Marius, sitting on the floor with his back to the wall, looked up at him. 'What you hear now is men braving themselves for a fight. When it starts, they will be quiet, just for a moment. They will brace themselves. Then it will be a different kind of noise.' It was a long speech for him.

Even from here Stenwold could hear a constant murmur from the gates. He lowered the telescope reluctantly. 'There'll be a great almighty noise when they come in, if all goes according to plan.'

Marius shrugged. 'Then listen for that.'

Below there was a quick patter of feet as someone ascended the stairs. Stenwold twitched but Marius remarked simply, 'Tisamon,' and went back to staring at nothing. In the room beneath them there were nine men and women dressed in the same chain hauberk and helm that Marius wore, and looking enough like him to be family. Stenwold knew their minds were meshed together, touching each other's and touching Marius too, thoughts passing freely back and forth between them. He could not imagine how it must be, for them.

Tisamon burst in, tall and pale, with thunder in his expression. Even as Stenwold opened his mouth he snapped out, 'No sign. She's not come.'

'Well there are always—' Stenwold started, but the tall man cut him off.

'I cannot think of any reason why she wouldn't come, except one,' Tisamon spat. Seldom, so very seldom, had Stenwold seen this man angry and, whenever he had been, there was always blood. Tisamon was Mantis-kinden, whose people had, when time was young, been the most deadly killers of the Lowlands. Even though their time of greatness had passed, they were still not to be toyed with. They were matchless, whether in single duel or a skirmish of swords, and Tisamon was a master, the deadliest fighter Stenwold had ever known.

'She has betrayed us,' Tisamon stated simply. Abruptly all expression was gone from his angular features but that was only because it had fled inwards.

'There are ... reasons,' Stenwold said, wishing to defend his absent friend and yet not turn the duellist's anger against himself. The man's cold, hating eyes locked on to him even so. Tisamon had taken up no weapon, but his hands alone, and the spurs of naked bone that lanced outward from his forearms, were quite enough to take Stenwold apart, and with time to spare. 'Tisamon,' Stenwold said. 'You don't know . . .'

'Listen,' said Marius suddenly. And when Stenwold listened, in that very instant there was no more murmur audible from the gates.

And then it came, reaching them across the rooftops of Myna: the cry of a thousand throats. The assault had begun.

It was enough to shout down even Tisamon's wrath. Stenwold fumbled with the telescope, then stumbled to the window, nearly losing the instrument over the sill. When he had the glass back to his eye his hands were shaking so much that he could not keep it steady. The lens's view danced across the gatehouse and the wall, then finally settled. He saw the black and red armour of the army of Myna: men aiming crossbows or winching artillery around. He saw ballista and grapeshot-throwers wheel crazily through the arc of the telescope's eye, discharging their burdens. There was black and gold now amongst the black and red. The first wave of the Wasp divisions came upon them in a glittering mob: troops in light armour bearing the Empire's colours skimming over the tops of the walls, the air about their shoulders ashimmer with the dancing of nebulous wings. For a second Stenwold saw them as the insects they aped, but in reality they were armoured men, aloft in the air, with wings flickering from their backs and blades in their hands. They swooped on the earthbound defenders with lances and swords, loosing arrows and crossbow bolts and hurling spears. As the defenders turned their crossbows upwards towards them, Stenwold saw the bright crackle as golden fire flashed from the palms of the attackers' hands, the killing Art of the Wasp-kinden.

'Any moment now,' Stenwold whispered, as though the enemy, hundreds of yards away, might overhear him. From along the wall he heard a steady thump-thump-thump as Myna's huge rock-launchers hurled missile after missile into the ground troops advancing beyond the wall.

'They're at the gate.' Marius was still staring into space, but Stenwold knew that one of his men was positioned on a rooftop closer to the action, watching on his behalf.

'Then it must be now,' Stenwold said. '*Now.*' He tried to focus the jittery telescope on the gates, saw them flex inwards momentarily and heard the boom of the battering ram. 'Now,' he said again uselessly, for still nothing happened. All that time he had spent with the artificers of Myna, charging the earth in front of the gates with powder, and *nothing*.

'Perhaps they got it wrong,' Marius suggested. Again

the ram boomed against the metal-shod gates, and they groaned like a creature in pain before it.

'I was practically looking over their shoulders,' Stenwold said. 'It was ready to go. How could they have . . . Someone must have . . .'

'We are betrayed,' said Tisamon softly. 'By Atryssa, clearly. Who else knew the plan? Or do you think the people of Myna have sold their own to the slaver's block?'

'You . . . don't know . . .' But Stenwold felt conviction draining from him. Atryssa, so expected but so absent, and now this . . .

'Spider-kind,' Tisamon spat, and then repeated, 'Spider-kind,' with even keener loathing. On the walls the vanguard of the Wasp army was already engaged in a hundred little skirmishes against the shields of the defenders. Tisamon bared his teeth in utter fury. 'I knew! I knew you could never trust the Spider-kinden. Why did we ever let her in? Why did— Why did we trust her?' He was white knuckled, shaking, eyes staring like a madman's. The spines flexed alarmingly in his forearms, seeking blood. Stenwold stared into his face but barely heard the words. Instead he heard what Tisamon had left unsaid, and knew not fear but a terrible pity. Spider-kinden, as Tisamon said. Spider-kinden, as subtle and devious as all that implied, and still Tisamon, with a thousand years of race-hatred between them, had let her into his life and opened the gates of his soul to her. It was not just that Atryssa had betrayed her friends and betrayed the people of Myna; it was that she had betrayed Tisamon, and he could not bear the hurt.

'It has been a long time,' Marius said quietly. 'A lot can happen that even a Spider cannot predict.'

Tisamon rounded on him, livid with anger, but just then with a great scream of tortured metal, a thundercrack of splintering wood, the gates gave way.

The ramming engine was first through, no telescope needed to see its great brass and steel bulk as it blundered over the wreckage it had created, belching smoke from its funnels. A ballista atop its hood hung half off its mountings, mangled by the defenders' artillery, but there were eyelets in its metal sides from which spat crossbow bolts and the crackling energy of the Wasps' Art. Swarming either side of it were their line infantry, spear-armed but shieldless. Clad in armour too heavy to fly in, they pushed the men stationed at the gate back through sheer force, whilst their airborne divisions were beginning to pass over the city. The guardians of Myna were a disciplined lot, shield locked with shield as they tried to keep the enemy out. There were too many of them, though; the assault came from before and above, and from either side. Eventually the defenders' line buckled and fell back.

'We have to leave now,' Stenwold said, 'or we'll never get out. Someone has to know what's happened here. The Lowlands have to be warned.'

'The Lowlands won't care,' said Marius, but he was up and poised, and Stenwold knew that, below them, his soldiers would be ready with shield and sword and crossbow. They went down the stairs in quick succession, knowing that, now their single trick had failed, nothing would keep the Wasps out of Myna. Their army had five men for every defender the city could muster.

What a band we are. The thought passed through Stenwold's mind as he took the stairs, bringing up the rear as always. First went Marius, tan-skinned and dark, with the universally compact build of his race: he had abandoned his people to come here, gone renegade so that he could fight against the enemy his city would not believe in. After him came Tisamon, still consumed with rage and yet still the most graceful man Stenwold had ever known. His leather arming jacket bore the green and gold colours, even the ceremonial pin, of a Mantis Weaponsmaster. Stenwold had never seen him without it and knew he was clinging to his grudges and his honour like a drowning man.

And then myself: dark of skin and receding of hair; stout and bulky, loud of tread. Not my fault my folk are so heavy boned! Hardwearing leathers and a scorched apron, a workman's heavy gloves thrust through my belt, and goggles dangling about my neck. Not at first sight a man ever intended for war. And yet here I am with a crossbow banging against my legs.

Down in the room below, Marius's soldiers were already alert and on their feet, Some had their heavy square shields out, swords at the ready, others had slung them and taken up crossbows. Two carried the baggage: a heavy leather bag containing Stenwold's tools, and a long wooden case. Even as Stenwold got sight of the room they were unbarring the door, throwing it open. Immediately two of them pushed out, shields first. Stenwold realized that he had paused halfway down, dreading the moment when there would no longer be a roof above him to keep off enemy shot. Tisamon and most of the soldiers were gone. Marius, however, was waiting for him, an unspoken urgency hanging in his gaze.

'I'm coming,' Stenwold said, and hated the shaking of his voice. He clumped on down the stairs, fumbling for his crossbow.

'Leave it, and just move,' Marius ordered, and was out of the door. Following behind Stenwold, the final pair of soldiers moved in to guard the rear.

And then they were out into the open air. The sounds of the fighting at the gate were very close, closer than he could have thought, but this street had seen no blood – not yet. There were citizens of Myna out and about, though, waiting in a scatter of anxious faces. Men and women, and boys and girls still too young to be here at all, they were clutching knives and swords and staves, and waiting.

At his unheard direction, Marius's soldiers formed up: shields before and shields behind, with Stenwold, the baggage and the crossbows in the middle. Marius was at point, already setting a rapid pace down the narrow street. His troop's dark armour, its single purpose, moved people quickly out of the way without need for words or action.

'I can't run as fast as your lot,' Stenwold complained. He already felt out of step and was just waiting for the men behind to jostle or stumble over him. 'Where's Tisamon, anyway?'

'Around.' Marius did not look back or gesture, but then Stenwold caught a glimpse of the Mantis warrior passing through the crowd like an outrider, constantly pausing to look back towards the gate and then move on. He wore his armoured glove, with the blade jutting from between the fingers, flexing out like a sword blade one moment, folded back along his arm the next. It was an ancient tool of his kind and a laughable anachronism, save that Stenwold had witnessed what he could do with it.

'What about your man, at the gates?' Stenwold called, trying desperately to fall into step with those around him.

'Dead,' was the officer's curt reply.

'I'm sorry.'

'Be sorry when you know the full tally,' said Marius. 'We're not out of it yet.'

There was a ripple among the people of Myna, and not from the passage through them of this little squad of foreigners heading for the airfield. Stenwold realized what it must mean. All around now, they were brandishing their swords or workman's hammers or simple wooden clubs. It would not be quick or easy to capture this city, but the Wasps would have it in the end. Their dream of a black-and-gold world would accept no less.

Stenwold was Beetle-kinden and in the Lowlands his people were known for their industry, their artifice, even, as he liked to think, for their charity and kindly philosophy. The people of Myna were his distant cousins, being some offshoot of Beetle stock. He could spare them no charity now, however. He could spare no thought or time for anything but his own escape.

A brief shadow passed across him as the first of the Wasp vanguard soared overhead in a dart of black and gold, a shimmer of wings. Three more followed, and a dozen after that. They were heading in the same direction that Stenwold was moving.

'They're going to the airfield. They'll destroy the fliers!' he shouted in warning.

Instantly Marius and his men stepped up the pace and Stenwold wished he had not spoken. Now they were jogging along, effortlessly despite their armour, and he was running full tilt within a cage formed by their shields, feeling his gut lurch and his heart hammer. Behind him there were screams, and he made the mistake of looking back. Some of the Wasps, it seemed, were not heading for the airfield, but had stopped to rake across the assembled citizens with golden fire and javelins and crossbow bolts, circling and darting, and coming back to loose their missiles once again. This was no ordered attack, they were a frenzied mass of hatred, out solely for slaughter. Stenwold tripped even as he gaped, but the woman closest behind caught him by the arm and wrenched his bulk upright again, without breaking stride.

A moment later his rescuer herself was hit. There was a snap and crackle, and the stink of burned flesh and hot metal, and she sagged to one knee. Stenwold turned to help but nearly fell over the man reaching to drag her upright. The Wasp light airborne troops were all around them now, passing overhead, or diving at the citizens to drive them off the streets. A crossbow bolt bounded past Stenwold like a living thing.

The injured woman was on her feet once more. She and the man beside her turned to face the new assault. Marius and the rest kept moving.

'Come on, Stenwold! Hurry!' the officer shouted.

'But—'

'Go,' said the injured woman, no pain or reproach in her voice. She and the man with her locked shields, waiting. Stenwold stumbled away from them, then turned and fled after Marius and the others.

Tisamon was beside him in an instant. He had a look on his face that Stenwold had never seen before, but he could read it as though the Mantis's thoughts were carved there. Tisamon wanted a fight. He had been betrayed. He had been broken. Now he wanted a fight that he could not win.

'Get a move on, fat-Beetle,' he hissed, grabbing one strap of Stenwold's apron and hauling him forward. 'You're getting out of here.'

'We are,' corrected Stenwold, too out of breath by now to say any more. He watched Tisamon snatch a Wasp spear from the air in his offhand and then the Mantis spun on his heel, launched it away into the sky behind them, and was immediately in step once again. Stenwold did not pause to look, but he had no doubt that behind them some Wasp soldier would now be dropping from the sky, pierced through by his own missile.

Myna was a tiered city and they hit a set of steps then, a steep, narrow twenty-foot ascent. Stenwold tried to slow down for it but Tisamon would not let him, grabbing his arm again and pulling him upwards, exerting every muscle in his lean frame.

'Keep moving,' the Mantis snapped at him through gritted teeth. 'Move your great big fat feet, you Beetle bastard!'

The sting of that insult got Stenwold to the top of the steps before he realized. There were more citizens up there, all trying to head in the wrong direction, directly towards the gates. Something in Tisamon's face or body language pushed them easily aside. Ahead, Stenwold could see Marius's squad taking the next set of steps at a run.

And Stenwold ran, too, as he had never run before. His toolstrip, and his sword and crossbow, all clattered and conspired to trip him up. His breath rasped as he dragged ever more of it into his lungs, yet he ran, because up beyond those steps lay the airfield. Then he would know if he could stop running or if it was already too late.

There were Wasp soldiers scattered across the airfield. At the far end, the great bloated bulk of an airship balloon was slowly settling into itself, gashed in a dozen places and deflating. Some half a dozen dead men and women were strewn like old toys between the flying machines, but a dozen more were putting up a final desperate defence, letting off their crossbow bolts at the circling Wasp soldiers from whatever shelter they could find. If the Wasps had been arrayed in military order they could have swept the place clean in a minute, but they were mad for blood, each one on his own.

Stenwold noticed one old man frantically stoking the boiler of a sleek orthopter that stood there like a tall ship, its slender wings folded together and pointing up towards the sky. A Wasp soldier passed close and caught him by the collar, hauling him ten feet away from the machine before touching down again and putting his sword through the old man once, twice, three times. A moment later a bolt caught the same soldier between the shoulder blades. He pitched forward, trying even as he fell to reach behind him and pull it out.

'That one!' wheezed Stenwold, stumbling towards the now deserted orthopter. It was stoked. It was ready to go. 'Come on!' he gasped.

In a moment Marius's men were around him, and then they were past him, deliberately moving away from the machine and making a brief wall of their shields with crossbows poised behind it, guarding the retreat as effectively as they could.

'Can you fly this?' Marius demanded. Stenwold merely nodded, because he had no more breath to speak, and no room left for doubt. The officer clapped him on the shoulder. 'Get it moving. We'll join you.' And then, as Stenwold hurried past him, 'Watch out for Tisamon. He does not want to leave this place.'

I know why. But Stenwold did not have the breath for it.

Tisamon was already at the orthopter, hand reaching for the hatch, then stopping. He looked back at Stenwold with an agonized expression. 'I— how . . .'

'The handle. Turn the handle.'

Hand on the lever, the Mantis shook his head, baring his teeth. One of Marius's men arrived just then, ducked neatly under his arm and hauled the hatch open, hurling Stenwold's toolbag inside. Stenwold reached the orthopter so fast that he bounced back off the scuffed wood of its hull. The soldier had already unslung his crossbow and was running to join his colleagues. Tisamon turned and went with him.

'Wait—' Stenwold got out, but the Mantis was already sprinting across the airfield with his blade drawn back ready for action. Even as Stenwold hauled himself up into the machine, the Mantis leapt and caught a passing Wasp by his black-and-gold boot, dragging the flailing man out of the sky and lashing the two-foot edge of his metal claw across the invader's throat. It would be a poor day for any Wasp who met with the Mantis just then.

Stenwold shouldered his way through the cramped interior of the flier towards the cockpit, there finding a single seat too small for him and unfamiliar controls. He was an artificer, though, and had lived with machines all his life. A moment's observation told him which glass bar indicated the boiler pressure, which lever unleashed the wings. A Wasp soldier darted across the large and wide-open ports that were mainly what Stenwold had between him and the fighting outside. Then the wings clapped down and outwards with a roar of wood and canvas and the soldier was sent spinning by the concussion of air. Stenwold's feet found pedals in the narrow confines of the footwell. The boiler pressure was now closing on the optimal. He put his head back, peering through the open hatch for any sign of his comrades.

Half of Marius's men were already dead, he saw, and this jolted his heart. They fought beautifully: even he, though no warrior, could see that. Each man knew by heart the thoughts of his fellows, so they moved as one. They were so few, though, and the Wasps swarmed all over the field. Shield and crossbow were no defence against their numbers.

'Come on!' Stenwold bellowed. 'Let's go now!' He could not believe that they would hear him over the din of combat but one of them must have, and so they all did. They began to fall back, shields held high. Even as he watched, another was lanced in the side by a crossbow bolt, falling awkwardly before rising to one knee. The others continued to retreat, and Stenwold might have thought it heartless of them had he not been so sure that the fallen man would be exhorting them to go, to leave him there. Stenwold realized that he knew none of their names, had not even heard many of them speak.

Ant-kinden, he would never understand them or their communal world. Or how Marius had managed to leave that world and not look back.

The hatch went suddenly dark. A Wasp soldier forced his way in, the dance of his wings dying behind him. One open hand still crackled with the fire of his sting but he was now leading with his sword. Stenwold was lurching backwards even as the man's shoulders cleared the entrance, hurling the first thing that came to hand, which happened to be a mechanic's hammer. It thumped into the Wasp soldier's shoulder and knocked him half out of the hatch. Then Stenwold was upon him, grabbing for his sword arm with one hand, lunging with the other. He never got hold of the man's sword, but his right hand somehow managed to draw his own, and he rammed it up to its narrow guard in his adversary's armpit.

The Wasp spat at him and he recoiled in shock, then recoiled again as he saw the blood stringing across the man's lips. Then the dying soldier was falling out of the flier, the weight of him taking Stenwold's sword from his suddenly nerveless fingers.

He had just killed another human being. *There's a first time for everything.*

One of Marius's soldiers now reached the hatch and cast the wooden case inside. Marius himself and three of his men were still inching their way back, painfully slow.

'Tisamon!' Stenwold called out. 'Tisamon!'

He saw him then, the Weaponsmaster, moving in and out of the Wasps as they tried to corner him. But he stepped through the golden energy of their stings, their crossbow bolts that fractured on the hard earth of the airfield. He caught their spears easily and hurled them back. His blade, twisting and darting too swift to see, was never still for a second. It moved as naturally as his wrist and hand and arm could, and there were always the spines of his arms to cut and tear at anything the metal missed. Tisamon was going to die, but he would have more company on his journey than he knew what to do with.

'Tisamon!' Stenwold shouted and the Mantis-kinden broke off from the fight, danced across to him, casually cutting down a Wasp that tried to put a spear in him.

'Get Marius inside and go!' Tisamon commanded. 'Go! Just go!'

Stenwold's face twisted up in anger and fear. 'You bloody-handed bastard! If you stay here then you're taking me with you! I'm not going without you!'

Even as he moved to meet the next attacker Tisamon's face showed how utterly unfair he felt that threat was. Even so, he was returning to the orthopter in the very next instant.

'Marius, now!' Stenwold shrieked, and at last Marius and his two survivors broke into a run, shields temporarily slung on their backs. Stenwold ducked away from the hatch and even as he did so a lance of energy blasted a smoking hole in the rim. Hands shaking, he squeezed himself back into the pilot's seat, and began to pedal fast. He felt the entire frame of the flier creak as the wings moved, first up and then down, powered by the steam-boiler but guided by his feet.

Someone vaulted into the flier, and Stenwold flinched in fear, but it was only Tisamon, face grim. He set on the wooden case immediately and tugged at the buckles, his bladed glove now removed. A moment later a woman belonging to Marius's squad climbed in too and turned to help her commander aboard. By now Stenwold had the wings working smoothly and felt the orthopter lurch as though eager to be gone from here.

Marius was halfway in when he arched backwards without warning and began to fall away. The female soldier caught his belt and dragged him to safety, but Stenwold caught a glimpse of the leather vanes of the crossbow bolt buried deep in the commander's lower back beside the rim of his shield.

'Any more?' He could barely keep the machine on the ground.

'No!' the woman yelled to him, and he doubled his pace

and the orthopter sprang into the sky, spinning a couple of Wasps out of their way with the displaced air.

Stenwold risked a single glance behind him to see what was happening. Marius was lying on his side, his skin turned from tan to ashen-grey, his sole remaining soldier investigating the wound. Tisamon had opened his case and was stringing his greatbow. Another relic of the Bad Old Days, Stenwold knew, but he would not have swapped such a bow in Tisamon's hands for the latest repeating crossbow. The Mantis crouched at the still-open hatch and nocked an arrow. A moment later he loosed it and Stenwold saw, as he circled the airfield, another Wasp go whirling downwards, sword spinning off separately, out-reaching him as he fell.

'Away would be good!' Tisamon snapped, reaching into the case for another arrow.

'I have to gain height first,' Stenwold told him, knowing that the Mantis would not understand. He was pulling the orthopter into a ponderously slow upwards circle of the airfield as the steam-driven wings worked up and down. None of the other Mynan flying machines had got off the ground. He did not want to think about what might be happening in the city below them. He just pedalled and steered, watching a rising circle of Wasps below them, flying men with swords and spears milling in a furious swarm. Tisamon leant far out, securing his position with one knee and one elbow, and drew back the string.

High enough. Stenwold decided, and wrestled the orthopter out of its curve. But he had misjudged the angle and ended up sending it straight out over the teeming city. Below him a dozen Wasp soldiers passed by, oblivious, but Stenwold's attention was by now somewhere else.

'Hammer and tongs!' he swore. 'Will you look at that!'

It was ugly as sin and it hung in the air as elegantly as a hanged man, but nevertheless it stayed up and there had to be some craft in that feat. A heliopter in Wasp colours, a monstrous, uneven metal box with three spinning blades straining to keep it from crashing to the ground. There must have been hatches in its underbelly, he realized, because there was a stream of missiles falling constantly from it onto Myna. He thought they were rocks at first but, on seeing the explosions, decided they must be fire-pots or firepowder grenades.

Why am I still flying at it? He wrenched quickly at the simple wooden stick and the orthopter veered away, the Wasp heliopter sliding out of his frame of vision as he cast his newly acquired vehicle across the city and out over the walls. The orthopter was a simple piece of machinery, and the artificers back at his native city of Collegium, hundreds of miles away, would have called it 'prentice stuff'. It was all Stenwold needed, though, for it could outpace the Wasp light airborne, and in only minutes their pursuers were dropping back, turning for the city again, and Tisamon could lower his bow.

The Wasp heliopter, however – that was a crude and primitive piece. Any self-respecting artificer would have been rightly ashamed of it. And yet it flew, and only five years ago the Wasps had possessed nothing like it.

'Marius . . .' he began. He could crane over his shoulder, but even while letting the machine glide on its canvas wings he dared not take his attention from the controls. 'Marius, talk to me.'

'He is sorry,' said the woman, and after a moment's blank surprise Stenwold realized that Marius must now be too weak to speak, but strong enough to send his thoughts into her mind.

'We have to tell them what has happened here,' Stenwold continued. 'Marius, we have to tell Sarn. We must warn your city.'

'He says we are considered renegades there,' the woman replied impassively. 'He says we can never go back.'

Beneath them the fields and small villages that were Myna's tributary settlements swept past. 'But Marius only left because he thought this was for your people's good,' Stenwold said stubbornly. 'He saw the threat even when they did not. You know this, and you have to tell them.'

'We can never go back there,' the woman said, and he realized she was speaking for herself this time. 'Once the bonds of loyalty are broken, we can never go back.'

'But Marius – Sarn isn't like the other Ant cities any more. There have been changes. There are even some of my own kin on the council there,' Stenwold insisted.

There was a lengthy silence from behind him, and he assumed that Marius must have died. He choked on a sob, but then the woman put a hand on his shoulder in a strong soldier's grip.

'He says you must do what you can,' she told him softly, and even her intonation resembled Marius's own. 'He says he regrets that things have ended this way, and he also regrets that the others, Atryssa and Nero, were not with us, but he does not regret following you from his city, and he does not regret dying in this company.'

Stenwold wiped a hand across his eyes and felt the first shaking of his shoulders. 'Tell him . . .' he managed, but then the woman's hand twitched on his shoulder, just once, just for a moment, and he knew that Marius was dead.

He let out a long, racked breath.

'We can tell nobody about this, because nobody will listen,' Tisamon said. 'We tried to warn your people at Helleron that the Wasps were coming, and what did they say? That nobody would invade Helleron. They claimed that the city was too useful. That Wasps needed to trade and deal in arms like everyone else. They look upon the Empire as just another Ant city-state.'

'And if we told your people?' asked Stenwold bitterly.

'Then they would simply not care. They have quarrels a thousand years old that they have yet to settle. They have no time for new ones.' And Stenwold heard, to his surprise, an equal bitterness in Tisamon's voice. The Mantis was hinging his metal claw forward and back, rolling his fingers about the crosspiece to lay the blade flat against his arm, then bringing it out to jut forward from his knuckles. It was not a threat, but just the man seeking reassurance in his old rituals.

'We saw their map,' Stenwold whispered. That one glimpse he had caught, of the Wasps' great map, had been a harsh education. A map of lands he had never seen, extending down to lands he knew all too well, the Lowlands of his home, and all sketched out with lines of advance and supply. A map of a projected conquest that stopped only with the Wasps' knowledge of their world.

'Nobody will care,' Tisamon repeated, and there was a rare wisdom in his voice. 'What is the Lowlands, anyway? A half-dozen feuding city-states, some hold-overs from the Days of Lore, when things were different, and perhaps a few men like yourself, trying to make sense of it all. The Wasps are a unity, we are a motley.' The gloom about him deepened, and Stenwold knew that his thoughts were turning inexorably towards Atryssa, towards the betrayal. Stenwold wished he could find some other way to explain her absence and their failure at the gates.

'What will you do,' he asked the Ant-kinden woman, 'if you cannot go home?'

'I will not be the first Ant renegade to go mercenary. If you now take us to Helleron I will sell my sword there,' she said. 'The market for us is good, and like to get better.'

'The same for me,' Tisamon confirmed.

'Tisamon—'

'No.' There was more finality in the Mantis's voice than Stenwold had ever heard from him. 'No return to Collegium for me, Stenwold. No debate and diplomacy. No society. No kind words, ever again. I followed you down that path once, and see where I am now.'

'But—'

'I will stay at Helleron and I will oppose the Wasps the only way I can.' With careful movements Tisamon replaced his greatbow in its case. 'You yourself have other means, Sten. You must go back to your college and your clever, machine-fingered people, and have them make ready. Of all of us, you were always the real hope of the future.'

Stenwold said nothing as, below them, the last of the straggling fields gave out, and a scrubby, dry landscape passed beneath them without so much as a whisper.

Two

I cannot even claim that I did not have time to prepare.

For they had not come, not then. He had fled to Collegium, returning home, and there had been no black-and-gold tide on his heels. The Empire of the Wasps had given him a stay of execution, it seemed. Instead of westwards, their armies had struck elsewhere: undertaking a brutal war of conquest against their northern neighbours. Oh, there had been merchants and travellers, and even the occasional diplomat sent by the Black and Gold, but no armies. Nobody could say that Stenwold had not been allowed all the time he could use.

Have I squandered it, or was there no more I could do than this?

'You're sure of this news?' he asked the messenger. She was a little Fly-kinden woman, barely more than three feet tall, standing in his comfortable study like a child.

'I'm just the voice, Master Maker, but the information's sure. They can't be long behind me,' she told him.

I knew this would come.

It would come masked. There would not be armies at first. The Wasps would come with smiles and open hands, promising peace and prosperity, but Stenwold's spies had told him of the march of thousands, the sharpening of swords. All the prescience in the world did not take the edge off the fear he felt. The fall of the city of Myna was flooding through his mind again, and no matter how long ago that had been. He knew the Empire had not been sitting idle. It had been keeping its blade good and sharp these past seventeen years.

Seventeen years? And what had Stenwold made of them, save to grow older and fatter, and to lose his hair? From artificer and idealist he had become politician and spymaster. He had his cells of agents established across the Lowlands, and he used them to wrestle with the Wasps' own spies. He had tried to spread the word of invasion to a people who did not want to hear. He had settled back comfortably in his home city, made himself influential, taken on the mantle of a master at the Great College. Teaching an unorthodox history, to the annoyance of his peers, he had fought with words against the conservative nature of his people, who just wanted to be left to their commerce and their provincial squabbles. He had stood before the Assembly of Collegium and made speeches and arguments and pleas of warning until they had begun to stay away whenever his name was listed as speaker.

'Go back to Scuto,' he now told the Fly woman. 'I will be coming to him with my latest crop. Have him get everyone under arms and ready.'

She nodded and ran to the open window, vaulting onto the sill. A moment later her Art had sprung shimmering wings from her back, little more than a blur in the air, and she was gone across the rooftops.

Stenwold stood slowly, looking about him. *If they had come straight on my heels, all those years back, I would have been more ready for them.* He had since become the College Master indeed. The more time they had given him, the more he had assumed he would have, and now the Wasp Empire was coming to Collegium at last and he was not ready for it.

At least the latest crop is ready. Or half-ready. Stenwold grimaced at the thought. He had been recruiting agents from among the College students for years. Now the time had come for him to foot the bill. This time it would not just be strangers that he would be sending into the flames.

Which reminded him. The wheels of Collegium did not stop turning just because an aging spymaster received a piece of bad news. He was needed at the duelling court, for his new blades were to be tested in the fire.

They called her Che, or at least she made sure they called her that as far as possible, because being named Cheerwell was an appalling burden to carry through life. Cheerwell Maker was the catch-up girl: she was always running to get where everyone else could walk to. It was all such a contrast to Tynisa, who was her ... what? The word 'sister' should have served well, save that neither of them was the daughter of Stenwold Maker, though he treated them both as such. Che was his niece, which was simple enough, while Tynisa was his ward, which was more complicated.

Che was always early for appointments. She had been waiting now for a half-hour at the door of the Prowess Forum, dressed up as a duellist without a fight. Here, at last, came Tynisa and Salma, and so at least she would not have to go in alone and feel even more foolish waiting friendless before an audience.

Looking at Tynisa she thought, as she always thought, *Such a difference between us!* Genuine sisters surely never had to suffer so. Che, like most Beetle-kinden, was short, somewhat plump and rounded, solid and enduring. She had tried her best with fashion, but it wanted little to do with her. Her hair was currently cut short and dyed pale – which was how people liked it last year – but this year the fashion, inexplicably, was for longer hair. How was she supposed to keep up?

Tynisa, of course, had long hair. She was fashionable

whatever she wore, and would look more fashionable still, Che was sure, if she wore nothing at all. She was tall and slender and her enviable hair was golden, and most of all she was not squat, ungainly Beetle-kinden at all. How in the world Stenwold had come by a Spider-kinden ward, or what strange dalliance had produced her, had always been a matter of speculation. Nobody held it against her, however. Everyone loved Tynisa.

'All ready?' She grinned at Che as she came to the Prowess Forum.

Che nodded morosely.

'Are we quite sure about that name?' asked Salma. As Che was dragged down by the name 'Cheerwell', in truth 'Salma' was the exotic Salme Dien. He was beautiful, as nobody was more aware of than himself. Golden-skinned and midnight-haired, he was a foreign dignitary from a distant land who, it always seemed, had just deigned to favour them with his presence.

'I like the name,' Che said. It had been her major contribution to their duelling team. 'Everyone's always "the sword of this" or "the flashing that", for duelling teams. "The Majestic Felbling" is *different*.'

'If I had known what a felbling was,' Salma said, 'I'd have had words.' Felblings were the flying furry animals that people across Collegium kept as pets. They were unknown to the Dragonfly-kinden of Salma's homeland, however, and he did not consider them dignified.

They passed on into the Prowess Forum, where a healthy crowd had already gathered, since Salma and Tynisa, at least, were always eminently watchable. Che started on seeing that the fourth of their number was already within. His name was Totho and he was as much of a catch-up as she was, she supposed. He was only here because she had been studying mechanics when they formed the group, and he had been the one helping her through the equations. He was a strong-framed, dark youth with a solid jaw and a closed, careful face that bore the stamp of mixed parentage.

'I think they assumed we weren't coming,' he said, glancing at the assembled watchers, as the others sat down beside him.

'The Majestic—'

The Master of Ceremonies, a greying, stocky man with a lined but otherwise deadpan face, re-checked his scroll, and decided to leave it at that.

'I told you they wouldn't go along with it,' said Tynisa. 'They're all about dignity, that lot.' She lounged back against the Prowess Forum wall, arms folded beneath her breasts, giving the Master one of her looks. He was an old, impassive Ant-kinden, though, and adroitly managed to ignore her.

'Well . . .' Che Maker started defensively, but before she could elaborate, the Master of Ceremonies called out, 'Who sponsors the Majestic?' and then her uncle Stenwold stepped forth to meet with him.

He was a big man, Uncle Stenwold. He was broad across the waist, and his belt wrestled daily with his growing paunch in a losing battle. He moved with a fat man's heavy steps. This hid from many people that his sloping shoulders were broad, purposeful muscle moving there and not just the aimless swing of his belly. He was an active sponsor of the duelling houses now, but he had been a fighter himself years before. Che knew in her heart that he could be so again, if he ever wanted. So much of his manner towards the world was calculated to put it off its guard.

He shook the hand of the Master of Ceremonies, while looking back towards them.

'Kymon,' Stenwold acknowledged. The Ant-kinden raised his hand to his mouth, a soundless cough that perhaps hid a small smile.

'My apologies. Master Gownsman and Armsman Kymon of Kes,' Stenwold continued formally, and the Ant granted him a fraction of a bow.

'Master Gownsman Stenwold Maker,' he replied. 'The Collegium Society of Martial Prowess recognizes your sponsored house and invites you to name your charges.' He flicked a finger at a Beetle-kinden scribe who had been staring, awestruck, at Tynisa, and the young man started guiltily and poised his pen.

'I give the Prowess the Prince Salme Dien of the Dragonfly Commonweal and Tynisa, a ward of my household. I give you Cheerwell Maker, niece of my family, and also Totho, apprentice artificer,' Stenwold announced, slowly enough for the scribe to copy down. The two score or so of idling spectators gave his foursome the once over, skipping over Che and Totho, giving their full attention to the elegantly lounging Tynisa, and Salma's foreign good looks. Stenwold stepped back as the Master of Ceremonies read from his scroll again.

'The Golden Shell?' he stated. 'Who sponsors the Golden Shell?'

Stenwold watched as another Beetle came forth. This was a good example of the way the affluent classes of Collegium were heading, he reflected sadly: a squat man with a receding hairline who was clad in robes of blue, red and gold woven from imported spider silk. There were rings cluttering his hands and a jewelled silver gorget beneath the third of his chins, to let the world know that here was a man interested in things martial. Each item of clothing and jewellery was conspicuously expensive, yet the overall picture was one of vulgarity.

I should use a mirror more often, Stenwold thought wryly. He might himself own only to the white robes of a College Master, but his waist was approaching the dimensions of this merchant-lord's, and the tide of his hair had receded so far that he shaved his head regularly now to hide its loss.

'Master Gownsman and Armsman Kymon of Kes,' said the newcomer with a flourish.

'Master Townsman Inigo Paldron,' Kymon acknowledged. Master Paldron pursed his lips and made an urgent little noise. Kymon sighed.

'Master Townsman *Magnate* Inigo Paldron,' he corrected. 'Forgive me. The new titling is but a tenday old.'

'I do think that, when the Assembly of the Learned spends more time debating modes of address than civic planning, something has gone seriously wrong with the world,' Stenwold grumbled, not quite joking. 'Just plain "Master" was always good enough for me.'

Master Townsman Magnate Paldron's expression showed that, in titles as in other ornament, he was unlikely ever to have more than he was happy with.

'The Collegium Society of Martial Prowess recognizes your sponsored house and invites you to name your charges,' Kymon told him.

'Well, then,' said Paldron with a broad smile. 'Fellow Masters, I give you Seladoris of Everis,' his broad hand singled out a slender Spider-kinden man, who stood slowly. 'Falger Paldron, my nephew.' A Beetle lad who seemed a year younger even than Che. 'Adax of Tark.' Adax remained seated. His narrowed eyes were boring into Totho across the width of the Prowess Forum. 'And . . .' Paldron's contented smile grew broader still, 'I present you with the esteemed Piraeus of Etheryon.'

Piraeus! The last name tore through the spectators like a gale through leaves. Not a name they would have expected at some little apprentices' house friendly. As if on cue he entered, pausing in the doorway nearest to his team-mates, a straight, slender stiletto of a man. He had been the duelling champion of the previous year with never a bout lost. So few of the Mantis-kinden ever joined Collegium's homely little duelling society – it was a frivolous thing to them; they were above it – and Piraeus was the exception.

'How much did you put out to catch him?' Stenwold asked Paldron softly. The magnate smiled beatifically at him.

'The poor lad misses his College friends, no doubt,' he said dismissively. It was, Stenwold reflected, just another problem with the great and good of Collegium today. Give them a famine, a war, a poverty-stricken district or a child shorn of parents and they would debate the symbolism and the philosophy of intervention. Give them some competition or empty trophy and they would break every rule to parade their victories publicly through the town.

'But fighting alongside Seladoris?' Stenwold said. '*Alongside* Spider-kinden?'

Paldron glanced back at his team. There was indeed a pointed distance between Piraeus and the Spider youth, and neither acknowledged the other. Theirs was a race-hatred with roots lost in the mists of time. It was remarkable that mere money had now built over it.

'Not such a problem,' Paldron told him. 'Who knows, he might even end up contesting against your . . . *ward.*' He said the word with a sneer barely disguised within the walls of polite conversation. Stenwold bore it stolidly, for it was hardly the first time. He glanced back at his team to see how they were taking the news. To his relief, rather than seeing them dispirited or alarmed, they were gathered in a close huddle, talking tactics.

'I could take him,' Tynisa was murmuring. 'You know how good I am.'

'We do,' Che acknowledged. 'And you're not *that* good. We saw him fight last year. I've never seen anything like it.'

'There's more to fighting than jabbing a sword about, little Che,' Tynisa said, casting another glance at the opposition. She had been pointedly staring on and off at Seladoris, and he was already looking ill at ease. In the cities of the Spider-kinden it was the women who pulled the strings and made the laws, and also the women who held the deadliest name in private duel, and he knew it. 'Let me have a chance to work on Master Mantis over there, and I'll have him,' she added.

'I don't think so,' Che said stubbornly. 'Look at him. Look how he looks at you.'

Tynisa had indeed gained Piraeus's attention, but he did not look at her in the way the spectators did. Instead there was a cold, bleak hatred there, dispassionate and ageless.

'So who do we put up against him, if not me?' Tynisa asked.

'He's really *that* good?' Salma had not been in Collegium last year.

'Better,' confirmed Totho, the apprentice, gloomily. 'He can beat any of us.'

'Che should fight him,' Salma decided.

'What?'

'With the best will in the world, Che, you're our . . . you're not our best fighter.' Salma shrugged, but without real apology. 'There it is. It means we can win by the numbers.'

'He'll go easy on you, probably,' Tynisa told her.

'He won't,' Totho said darkly.

'Look, this is all assuming that we even get to choose,' said Che hurriedly.

'Quiet now,' hissed Tynisa. 'Look, they're calling it.'

Kymon held out a fist from which projected the corners of two kerchiefs. Stenwold indicated that Master Paldron should choose first. The magnate squinted at the Master of Ceremonies' hand suspiciously, and then tugged at one corner. The kerchief that he drew out had one red-stained end.

'Now that's a shame,' said Salma, as the townsman waved the rag triumphantly at his team.

'Golden Shell, the first match is your choosing,' Kymon announced.

There was dissent in the ranks. Piraeus was arguing with his team-mates as to precisely who should have the honour of fighting him. From his jabbing finger it was clear that Tynisa would be his choice and, despite her earlier boasts, the Spider girl compressed her lips together nervously. The casting vote seemed to be with Falger, old Paldron's nephew. When the Mantis-kinden stepped forward he looked sullen and dissatisfied, pointing at Salma.

'Piraeus the Champion to fight the foreign prince,' announced Kymon, stepping forward. Stenwold and Paldron hurriedly found seats out of harm's way as the Master of Ceremonies strode to the very centre of the Prowess Forum. A circle of bare, sandy earth was there, raked level after every bout, contained within a square of mosaic whose corners boasted martial scenes picked out in intricate detail. No tile was greater than a quarter inch across and yet the vignette of a breach in an Ant city wall was as vibrant and clear as the two Beetle-kinden duellists that opposed it, forever saluting, across the circle. Beyond the mosaic, by a prudent distance, were the three tiers of stone seats, and beyond them the walls that, by ancient tradition, each had an open door. The roof above was composed of translucent cloth and wooden struts, as was the way with most of the public buildings in Collegium these days.

'No worries,' Salma said with an easy smile.

'Do you even have real Mantids where you come from?' Tynisa asked him. She seemed more worried for Salma than she had been on her own account. 'The man is good.'

'Oh, we have them,' Salma confirmed, sending his opponent a grin. 'We have more of them than you'll ever see around here. Up to our elbows in them, back in the Commonweal.'

Piraeus and Salma stepped forward until they were just beyond the circle. There was an excited whispering amongst the small audience, the knowledge that this would be a spectacle to earn drinks with in the tavernas afterwards. Stenwold was struck with the similarity of the two. Dressed as they were, in padded arming jackets and breeches tied at the knee, in sandals and one heavy offhand glove, they looked as if they could almost have been relatives. Piraeus was taller, of the angular Mantis build. His long fair hair was tied back, but what should have been a handsome face was marred with ill temper and harsh feelings. His arming jacket was slit to the elbow to accommodate the spines jutting from his arms. Salma was dark, his hair cut short and his skin golden, and he had been the ache in plenty of maidens' hearts since he arrived in Collegium from his distant homeland. He possessed a grace, though, that was not far short of the Mantis's. The two of them stood quietly and sized each other up, one with a scowl and one with a smile, and there was nevertheless a commonality about them.

Kymon took a deep breath and held out the two swords: each of them mere wood covered with a thin layer of bronze, but there was nobody in that room who had not discovered just how hard they could strike home.

Kymon looked from one to the other. Stenwold knew that the old man was still a military officer of the city-state of Kes, which could call him back from his prestigious civilian position at any moment. It had been twenty years from home for old Kymon, however. Here he stood, in a Beetle's white robes rather than armour, and he no longer missed the voices of his Ant-kinden people in his head.

'Salute the book,' Kymon directed. Piraeus and Salma turned to the north quarter of the room and raised their mock blades. The object of their salute was affixed to the wall: a great brass blade within the pages of a book carved from pale wood. On the open pages, one word to each, were scribed *Devotion* and *Excellence*.

'Clock,' said Kymon, and the mechanical timepiece hanging opposite the book groaned into life. The antagonists turned to one another as Kymon left the ring. The moment his back foot lifted from the arena they were in motion.

The first blow took place in the first moment of the match. Piraeus's strike had come with blinding speed, aiming to break the nose of the foreigner, at the very least. Salma swayed backwards without shifting his feet, and the champion's lash, at full extension, passed a few inches from his face. He had, indeed, seen Mantis-kinden fight before.

Then the fight proper was on and, to the thrill of the spectators, Salma was immediately on the offensive. He was fighting in proper Prowess style, leading with the edge of the blade, feet tracing a geometry of arcs and sudden straight advances. His free hand was up at chest height, leather gauntlet ready to deflect the Mantis's strikes. There was nothing that was not book-perfect, from the prints in the fencing manuals, until every so often he threw in something else. A lunge, a sweep, a brief discontinuity of footwork, that was his alone, some style of his own people. Though he knew how Mantids fought, Piraeus had never duelled a Dragonfly-kinden before. There was an edge there that let him keep up the offensive long after Piraeus should have wrested it from him, but the edge was eroding from moment to moment. Soon the Mantis would get the measure of him.

And, without warning, without anything in his stance or movement signalling it, Salma was far too close, virtually up the other man's nose, within the circle of his arms, and – they all saw it – there was a moment when Piraeus had his arm up, spines extended, about to gash across the foreigner's face. It would have maimed Salma, perhaps blinded him, but it would have seen Piraeus thrown out of the fight, his team disqualified, and of all things he wanted to *win*. In that moment of hesitation Salma brought his blade up to lightly tap the back of the Mantis's head.

They broke. Salma was at the edge of the circle, casting a bow to his team-mates. Piraeus stood, utterly still, with that anger peculiar to his kind that burned cold and forever. Salma and his team-mates would, everyone knew, regret what he had just done, and it might be now, or next tenday, or next year, but they would meet Piraeus again. Mantids were all about vengeance.

'First strike to the foreign prince,' Kymon declared impassively. 'Salute the book. Second pass. Clock!'

Things went downhill from there, of course. Piraeus was not one to let anger get in the way of skill and he had Salma's style now. Salma danced and ducked and swayed, but he never recaptured the offensive, nor could he hold his adversary off until the clock had wound down. The second blow of the match was a slap to his shoulder that he rolled with, barely felt, but it was a touch nonetheless. The third came when he blocked with his glove, and the Mantis dragged the rebound into a cut that bounced off his elbow and numbed his entire arm. Traditionally Mantis-kinden loved to fight, and loved a good fight too. They were supposed to respect a noble adversary, given all the old honour stories that they told. There was none of that in Piraeus, however. His look, as Salma clutched at his elbow, was one of sheer arrogance and disdain. None of it could disguise the truth. He might have won, but Piraeus winning a duelling pass was no news in Collegium. Instead, the taverna crowd would be telling each other how Salma had struck the Mantis *first*, and how the foreign lord had made the champion, for once, work for his fee.

Salma walked back to his comrades, still smiling despite

the pain. 'I've done better, I've done worse,' he admitted. 'So, you could have taken him?' he added for Tynisa's benefit.

For a second she grimaced, but then said, 'It's not my fault he was scared of me.'

'Speaking of which,' Totho said. 'They're waiting for us.'

'Can you take Seladoris?' she asked him. 'Or Adax?'

'Adax will choose me,' Totho said glumly, 'if he gets the chance. Frankly, I'd rather face him than the Spider. I've not got the speed for that.'

'Settled then,' Tynisa said, even as Che tried to get a word in. The Spider girl walked out to the edge of the circle and picked out her kinsman from the opposite team.

'Tynisa the Maker's Ward will now fight Seladoris of Everis,' Kymon dutifully announced, passing them the two swords. 'Salute the book.'

It was a short fight, half the length of the last bout. Since Seladoris had walked in, Tynisa had been working on him, fixing him with her stare, prying at his mind with her Art. All the while Piraeus and Salma had danced, Seladoris had never been free of her. Now, as he stepped forward, even Che could sense that she had unnerved him. It was not just Spider sexual politics – Spider-kinden made good duellists because they were so adept at reading others – but Tynisa was naturally quick, having quite a reputation amongst the little duelling houses. Seladoris was no novice himself and his technique was just as good as hers. What he lacked was her skill in disseminating a reputation. When he stepped into the ring he knew from her history that she was good and from her stare that she was better than he was. She had won even before their swords ever crossed.

Within two minutes she had scored two straight hits, the second of which jabbed his knee and toppled him out of the circle. Smiling a hard little smile, Tynisa bowed elaborately at Piraeus. *Look what you could have had*, she seemed to be saying. The spectators were vocal about her too. She was a favourite with the crowd.

Totho was already standing up as she returned, not even waiting for the Golden Shell's second choice. There was a heavy, set expression on his face, which was a serious one at the best of times. Across the ring, the Ant-kinden was standing. It was said, with good reason, that the people of the Ant loved nothing more than fighting their own kind, their brothers from behind different city walls. In truth, there was one thing they took even more joy in, and that was punishing halfbreeds. Totho attended at the Great College on an orphan scholarship and there was Ant-kinden and Beetle-kinden blended in his ancestry. Even on Collegium's cosmopolitan streets, a halfbreed had a hard life. In the harsher world outside it meant exile, slavery or, in the last resort, law-breaking.

'Adax of Tark to fight Totho,' Kymon noted, and even in his clipped pronunciation of the name there was censure.

'Here we go,' said Totho tiredly. 'Time for me to take a beating.'

Che touched his arm as he made to leave. 'You'll be all right.'

He managed half a smile for her. Only when he had gone to enter the circle did Salma say, 'He's going to get a beating, no two ways.'

'Oh surely,' agreed Tynisa.

'Can't you two have a little faith?' Che asked them.

Salma spread the fingers of his good hand in a lazy gesture. 'Dear one, I'm fond of the little halfway and I'm sure he does his . . .' Another vague gesture. 'His tinkering like a master, but he's not so good at this.'

Totho squared up against Adax of Tark. His Ant-kinden opponent was taller and as broad across the shoulders but leaner of build. He looked like a proper warrior as all Ants did. Every one of them was used to carrying a shortsword in their hands since the age of five, and they grew up inspired by all the martial minds around them.

Which means I can outthink him, Totho decided. He gave Stenwold a little nod as Kymon handed out the swords, for Totho was very keen to have Stenwold, of all people, see him in a favourable light, perhaps look past the accident of his birth.

'Salute the book,' Kymon intoned, stepping back, and then, 'Clock!'

Adax attacked, before Totho was quite ready, cracking him a swift blow on the shoulder. If he had reacted a moment later it would have been his head. Totho heard Kymon sigh.

'First strike to Adax of Tark,' announced the Master of Ceremonies. 'Clock!'

Totho got out of the Ant-kinden's reach quickly, because he knew his opponent would try the exact same move again, as indeed he did. There was no gap for a riposte in there, as Adax pressed and pressed at Totho's guard, but Totho was not looking for an opening. Totho could do little more than defend himself, keeping up a steady, curving retreat about the perimeter of the circle, with Adax following him step for step.

Outthink him, thought the halfbreed grimly, but there was precious little room for any planning. Adax was intent on keeping up a constant, efficient battering: only half a dozen different moves, but fast and always remorselessly on target. The Ant's face was set in an expression of dislike that had probably soured in place there as soon as the fight started. Totho realized that the next blow that landed on him would be delivered with all of the man's considerable strength. Still he managed to keep the Ant-kinden off him, by a hair's breadth. Always he was a step too far back, or his sword cut a parry with a only second to spare, and always the clock was grinding down, the ticks slower and slower, and Adax was a hit up, and not looking ready to give any points away.

To pull the match back Totho knew that he would have to do something spectacular at this point, and knew equally that he had nothing spectacular to give. Yet he was holding, holding. His parries were sloppy, but solid. His footwork was better, and Adax was getting frustrated.

Totho put an expression of unconcern on his face and kept up his guard. He had one thing that Adax did not, for whatever unknown parent had given him Beetle blood had passed on that breed's stamina. Adax had been battering at him full tilt for over a minute and there was now a sheen of sweat blooming on the man's forehead.

If only these matches went on longer. I could parry him to death. Totho grinned suddenly at the thought, and his opponent's calm collapsed.

'Fight me, slave!' Adax snapped angrily, his sword stilled for a moment, and Totho, without really planning to, hit him across the face for all he was worth, spilling the arrogant Ant-kinden to the ground.

He almost dropped his sword in surprise, because there was a great deal of blood and he thought for a moment he had maimed the other man for life. When Adax did look up from a wounded crouch, his nose was evidently broken, and Totho wondered about the state of his cheekbone, too. *I hit him bloody hard, I did.*

'Time!' Kymon called. The ever-slowing ticks of the clock had finally finished with the legendary solid 'clunk' that every duellist knew. The match was over.

'No!' Adax spat, voice sounding somewhat muffled.

'Time!' Kymon repeated. 'One strike apiece, so a draw, I'm sorry to say. And, for most of it, the dullest pass of fencing I have seen for many years.'

Totho couldn't help but grin, though. He didn't care much that Kymon didn't approve of him. He only cared that he had not actually lost. He looked over at his comrades for their reaction.

'Watch out!' Tynisa shouted in warning, and then something barged into him, knocking him out of the circle to stumble across the mosaic floor. He ended up amongst the spectators, almost in the lap of a middle-aged Beetle woman, craning frantically to see what had happened. Adax now lay sprawled right across the circle, one hand to his shin and the other to the back of his head. Kymon stood over him impassively, a mock sword in his hand.

Adax had tried to rush him once off his guard, Totho realized. Strictly against the rules, such behaviour, and had the victim been anyone but a lowly halfbreed, perhaps it would have even led to the whole team being disqualified. Inigo Paldron was already bustling up to make his unctuous apologies, however, and Totho knew it would not go any further. Kymon shot him a look, though, as he went to rejoin his colleagues, and it had a certain recognition in it. Adax was from the city of Tark, Totho reflected, and Kymon himself from the island city of Kes, and so perhaps the old man had not minded seeing a traditional enemy brought low.

'Not bad for a trainee pot-mender,' Salma conceded as he joined them. 'You had a plan, I take it?'

'Something like that.' Totho nodded to Tynisa. 'Thanks for the warning.'

She raised an eyebrow, shrugged slightly. He was not sure whether it was saying, *I won't be there next time*, or *You're one of us now*. Tynisa always made him feel especially awkward and ugly, and he had long-ago decided to avoid her attention as much as possible.

He sat down beside Che. 'Any good?'

She glanced at him distractedly. 'What?'

'Was I . . . all right?' He realized that she had not really been concentrating on his round. She was, of course, thinking all the time about her own fencing pass. Even now, Paldron's nephew was taking his place across the circle.

'He's, what, a year younger than you?' Totho said encouragingly.

'And no great shakes,' Salma added. 'He's yours, so just go and take him.'

'He's only in the team because of his uncle,' declared Totho before he could stop himself, and then he grimaced at the look of hurt that Che tried desperately to hide.

Because of his uncle, she was thinking. *Well, that's a broad net these days.* She glanced at her own uncle, in whose household she had been living for ten years. More than an uncle but less than a father, and she had certainly never been in a position to monopolize his affections. He could be hard work, Stenwold Maker: he expected so many things of his niece, and never quite acknowledged when she tried. Whether at scholarship, artificing or, of course, the fight . . . and here she was, now . . .

Just a game. A sport. True, the city was mad on sports just now, with the Games commencing in a mere tenday's time, but this duelling was still only an idle pastime for College students. It didn't matter whether she won or lost here. The taking part was the thing.

Except, of course, it was all on her shoulders now. If only Totho had lost his bout, then the best the Majestic Felbling could have managed was a draw. After drawing, the chosen champions of each team would then fight to decide it, and Piraeus would no doubt emerge victorious, and so, if she lost, it wouldn't matter. But now, after Totho's maddening stalemate, victory was apparently hers for the taking.

She took up her place opposite Falger Paldron. He was a little taller than she was, a dark-faced young Beetle lad, still slightly awkward in his movements. He was no fighter, she decided.

But nor am I. She was a girl with her hair cut short and

her physique cut broad. No Mantis-grace for her, no Ant-precision or Spider-tricks. She was just poor, lamentably named Cheerwell Maker, and she was no good at sports or swords or anything else.

'Salute the book!' Kymon barked out, and she realized that she already had a sword in her hand. Behind her, the others were clearly watching her every move.

Three

They muttered and moaned as he took the rostrum. These middle-aged merchants, the old College masters, men and women robed in white, reclining comfortably on the stepped stone seats of the Amphiophos. Some of them whispered to each other, scribbled agreements and concluded deals. One Master, stone deaf, read through the writing of his students and tsked loudly at each error he noted. Stenwold gazed upon them and despaired.

The heart of culture, he told himself. *The wonder of the civilized world. The democratic Assembly of Collegium. Give me a thousand Ant mercenaries, let me command where now I can only beg.* Then *we might get something done!*

Then I would be just like a Wasp indeed, in all but fact. That is why this is worth fighting for. He looked across their bored, distracted faces, writ large with their wealth and rivalries and vested interests.

'You know why I am standing here speaking before you, on today of all days.'

There was a jeering undercurrent of murmurs, but no outright mockery. *Just get on with it,* they seemed to say.

'I've stood here before,' Stenwold told them. 'You all know that. I have stood here often enough that all of you must have heard me at least once. I am no great musician. My tune remains the same.'

'Can we not simply refer to your previous speech and save ourselves an afternoon?' someone called, to a ripple of laughter.

'If I thought,' snapped Stenwold, loud enough to quash them, 'that one of you, even *one* of you, would do so, or had ever done so, then perhaps we would not be here, inflicting this ordeal upon each other!' They stared at him in surprise. He was being *rude*, and members of the Assembly did not shout at each other. He bared his teeth in frustration, wished for those Ant mercenaries again, and then pressed on.

'I do not think,' he said, 'that you're likely to endure many more of my speeches, Masters. I do not foresee a future where any of us will have liberty for such polite debate. I swear on my life that, when what I have foreseen comes to pass, I shall not stand here before you then and tell you I was right. I shall not need to, for there will be none of you who won't remember how I warned you.'

The resentful muttering was building again, but he spoke over it, muscling through it like the ram had broken the gates at Myna. 'Fourteen years ago,' he called out, 'I made my first speech here before you, not even a Master then, but just a precocious artificer who would not be silent. How long ago it seems now! I told you of a people in the east, a martial people, who were prosecuting war upon their neighbours. I told you of cities whose names were known to some of you, those of you who do business in Helleron perhaps. Cities such as Maynes, Szar, Myna. Not Lowlander cities, true, but not so very many miles beyond. Cities under the yoke of an empire, I said, and you listened politely, and said, 'But what is this to do with us?' Foreigners will fight, you said, and so the men and women of Maynes and Myna and Szar went with backs bowed, into slavery and conscription, and you shed not a tear.'

They sighed and fidgeted. The Speaker for the assembly, old Lineo Thadspar, made a 'hurry-up' gesture. He had allowed Stenwold this speech for old time's sake, and looked as though he now regretted it.

'Eight years ago I told you that the Empire was engaging in a new war, a war on a scale unprecedented; that the Empire was making war upon our northern neighbour, the great Commonweal of the Dragonflies. You heard from me how the armies of the Wasps had killed in their hundreds and their thousands, and no doubt you remember the answer that the Assembly thought fit to give me then.'

He gave them a chance, noticed defiance in some, disinterest in others. He remembered it keenly, that answer, though he barely recalled which of the fat, dismissive magnates had uttered it. In his mind the words echoed, still sharp enough to wound him.

'*Master Maker comes before us again to prate about the Wasps,*' they had said. '*He tells us they are fighting again, but that is their business. When the Ants of Kes land a force ashore and march on the walls of Tark, Collegium does not raise a voice. Why should we? Some kinden are warlike and therefore fight each other.*

'*Master Maker tells us that we should beware them because they are an empire, and no mere city-state, and so seeks to fright us with semantics. If the Mantids of Felyal decided to call themselves an empire, would we suddenly be tasked to descend upon them with sword and crossbow? I think not, for all the occasional provocation they give us.*'

There had been a murmur of laughter at that. Stenwold remembered it keenly.

'*And Master Maker also tells us they are fighting the Commonweal,*' the magnate had continued, all those years ago. '*And I say to that, so what and so let them!*' (They had cheered, back then, at this.) '*What do we know of the Empire, beyond Master Maker's ravings? We know that they are Apt and industrious, like us. We know that they have built a strongly governed state of many kinden, with none of the internal strife that beggars relations within the Lowlands. Are we, who claim to prize civilization, meant to despise them for theirs? We know that their merchants receive our goods avidly. Those of us with interests in Helleron and Tark know they will buy dear and sell cheap, when they know no better.'* (Laughter) *'And what do we know of the Commonweal? We know that they do not receive our emissaries, that they forbid any airship over their borders, that they have neither artificers nor engineers nor anything but a moribund and backward society of tilling peasants. We know that they will not even deal with our merchants, not at any price, that they would rather see grain rot in their fields than sell. All this we know, and can we really know the cause of the quarrel between these so-different people? What have the people of the Commonweal done to lay claim to our love, that we should turn on those that seem like our close brothers in contrast?'*

Looking now at these same faces, these same expressions of petulance, indifference, hearing those words echo in his mind, he thought, *I am wasting my time here.* It was pure spite that then made him go on, so that he could say, despite his promise, *I told you so.*

'Masters,' said Stenwold, and they hushed, for something in his voice must have touched them, some hitherto unmined vein of sincerity in his tone. 'Masters,' he said, 'listen to me now. I have come before you and I have spoken to you before, and always you have let my words fall at your feet. Hear me now: the Wasp Empire's long war with the Commonweal is done. They have swum in the blood of the Commonweal until even the vast Commonweal could bear it no longer. They have forced the signing of a surrender that places three principalities into imperial hands, an area of the Commonweal that would span a whole quarter of the Lowlands, were it placed here. Has the Empire put down the sword and taken up the plough? Has the Empire turned to books and learning, or the betterment of its poor and its slaves?'

He stared at them, waited and waited, until someone said, 'I'm sure you're going to tell us, Master Maker.'

'*No!*' he shouted at them. 'No, you tell me! You with your mercantile interests in Helleron, you tell me how many swords you have forged for the Empire! Tell me of the crossbow bolts, the firepowder, the automotive components, the engine parts, the flier designs, the tanks of fuel and the casks of airship gas that you have sold to them at your costly prices! Tell me of the men you have met with and talked money, and never asked why they might need such vast stocks of arms! For, I tell you, the Empire is not an Ant city-state where the citizens can all take up arms and fight if they must, be they soldier or farmer or artisan. The Empire is a great nation where every man is a warrior and nothing else. The work, the labour, the harvests and the craft, they leave for their slaves. There is not a man of the Empire who is not also a man of their army, and what can they do with such an immense force save to use it? Open your eyes, you merchants and you academics, and tell me where next such a force might march, if not here?'

'I think,' said the Speaker, old Thadspar, 'that I shall stop you at that question, Master Maker. You must, if you will riddle us so, give us a chance to respond. Well, Masters, it is a weighty gauntlet that Master Maker has cast down before us.'

'Yet again,' said some anonymous wit, but Thadspar held up a sharp hand.

'Masters! Respect, please. Will someone take this gauntlet up?' He drew back as one of the Assemblers stood and approached the rostrum.

'Master Maker makes a fine spectacle, does he not?' The man who took the stand was named Helmess Broiler, but it might equally have been any of them. He said no more until Stenwold had resumed his seat, smiling with infinite patience at the maverick historian. 'And I do wonder what we would do without him. These gatherings would lack their greatest source of wild imagination.' Polite laughter, which Broiler acknowledged and then went on.

'Yes, yes, the Empire. We all know about the Empire, if only because of Master Maker's two-decade hysteria about that realm. They are certainly a vital pack of barbarians, it's true. I believe they've made great inroads towards becoming a civilized nation recently. They have a government, and taxes, and even their own currency, although I understand their merchants prefer to deal in our coin.' More laughter, especially from the trade magnates. Broiler was grinning openly.

'Apparently they've had some trouble with their neighbours,' he said. 'But haven't we all? I remember well when the armies of Vek were at our gates, as do most of you. How many of you wanted to take a force of soldiers back to their city and teach them their place? I know I wasn't the only one, and perhaps we should have done it. The Empire did it. Faced with militant neighbours that threatened their emerging culture, they secured their own existence with force. Can we blame them? They would be in no position to send their ambassadors to us now if they had let their neighbours run roughshod over their borders before.' Broiler shook his head sadly. 'And the Commonweal, and their war – what do we truly *know* of those causes? We here do not have that great and silent state looming nearby to overshadow us, for geography intervenes. If the Commonweal, with all its vast resources, should take exception to us, what would we do? And their habitual sullen attitude gives us no clue that they hold us in anything but disdain. If the Wasps have clawed a victory and peace terms from such a mighty state, then surely we must congratulate them, and not castigate them. I have no doubt that if they wished to drive the Commonweal back, it was because such a brooding state on the Empire's very borders was cause for great concern.'

He put on an exasperated expression. 'And so,' he said, 'Master Maker insists that they are coming for us.' He was serious now, daring them to laugh. 'He tells us of the growth of their armies, the vast numbers of their soldiers, their strength of arms and their skill in battle. The fact that they have had to preserve their young state from so many hostile influences does not convince Master Maker that they might require these forces merely to defend themselves.' Broiler slammed his hands down on the lectern, looking angry.

'And now they come for *us*, we are told!' he cried out. 'The dreaded Wasps come for the Lowlands? Well, yes, yes, they do. Of course they do. They come with ambassadors. They come with trade, and an open hand. These last three years there has been a treaty standing between the Empire and the Council at Helleron, and everyone has profited by it. In only days their people will be here to formalize relations between their Empire and our great city, in just the same way. They recognize the central role we play in our turbulent Lowlands. They wish to know us better, to trade and prosper alongside us. Perhaps they will seek our guidance, like a young student come to learn from the old master.' His face, his hands, begged them to understand. 'Have any of you read the Treaty of Iron? There are copies in our libraries, so I encourage you to read one. This document happily recognizes the autonomy and friendship of both Helleron and Collegium. It sets down in clear type how their military strength is to protect what they have, not to gather more than they could possibly need.'

'Yes, they do,' Stenwold snapped, despite Thadspar's frantic gestures at him. 'And all the while they mass their armies and, on the strength of their empty signature on a scroll, we let them!'

'Oh they have their soldiers and their armies, Master Maker,' Broiler retorted. 'but there is only one possible reason they should turn them against us! It is because some fool here fires us up into a warlike fury against them! It is because we greet them with swords, and not friendship! Master Maker wishes to make his own prophecies come true by turning us against men who want only our recognition and support!'

Stenwold stood abruptly, leaving Broiler with his mouth open, bereft of words. He approached the rostrum, and for a second the man shrank back as though Stenwold would strike him.

'The Masters will excuse me,' Stenwold said. His tone was quiet, but there was no sound to compete with him. 'I must leave you to your talk, but for some reason I feel suddenly ill.'

Four

Salma was writing a letter. It was something he was out of practice with. This was not because the people of Collegium were not accustomed to writing letters. On the contrary, the literate middle classes were constantly penning each other missives, jokes, invitations and political pamphlets. Rather, the sheer fecund exuberance of it put him off. In the Commonweal of his birth one spent time in the writing, even in scribing the very characters themselves, but most especially in the thought that was behind it. Besides, for Salma, a letter home was no mere matter of sending a servant a few streets, or having someone take it to the engine depot or the airfield. It was going to cost a pretty price to get this where it was going.

He looked down at what he had written.

Most Highly Respected Prince-Major Felipe Shah of the Principality of Roh at his court in Suon Ren.

In the name of our most gracious Commonweal and the Monarch thereof, and by the love and affinity that I bear you by the Obligation of my Birth and the honour in which I hold your family.

Fortune prevailing I have found in this place of strangers one of a like mind and aims to my own, who sees with our same clarity in the dawn's light where others may turn their heads against the glare, and so have taken him for a Mentor.

He is a man for enquiries, especially where the sun rises, and there are many who answer the questions he poses. I myself am to be set an examination of questions, and some others with me, that I have leagued with.

Meaning that the wily old man knows what is brewing in the east, and perhaps he's the only one in Collegium to fathom it. And meaning also that he wants me for an agent, and that suits me. And I thought, and they all thought, that when I took this place at their vaunted College, that I would be going to sit around in the muck with a pack of coarse-grained primitives. But if Master Maker can find it in his heart to give me a blade and point me at the Empire, then I'm all for it.

Look for me in dark places. You will recall the gloom that fell when our cousin Daless lost her way. There you may find me, in the dawn's light.

Salma remembered Felipe Daless. She had been what he had always wanted to be: a Mercer warrior elite, in her shell and steel armour. It had been four years now since the Principality of Prava fell. He had heard, from survivors, that she had made a good showing at the end.

He re-read his missive, noting with a frown that he had been using the metaphors of dawn and darkness for the same thing. For poetic logic perhaps someone should persuade the Wasps to invade from the west for once. Ah well, nothing that was worth writing was worth writing simply.

In exile, this token of my esteem I send to you.
Prince-Minor Salme Dien

He finished the name with a flourish of his shard pen. He knew that the Beetle epistlers would have found this quaint, but he had no comprehension of their complex reservoir pens. A stylus of chitin was good enough for the Monarch of the Commonweal, and so it would be hubris in Salma himself to desire more.

'I'm ready,' he said, and the diminutive figure by the door stepped forward. She had been waiting for almost an hour while he wrote, without fidget or complaint, and he had a lot of respect for that in a place as bustling and assertive as Collegium.

'You are sure that you are capable of this?' he asked her. 'Most everyone in this town seems to think my homeland belongs in a storybook.'

The Fly-kinden stood about eye to eye with the seated Salma, a lithe young woman with blue-grey skin, and the circular badge of their Messenger Guild on her plain black tunic. 'Actually, sir, there are Guildhouses in both Drame Jo and Shon Fhor, and I can find my way from there to Roh.'

Salma folded the letter and sealed it with a disc of putty, using a thumbnail to press in a stylized little crest. It looked deceptively simple, but he knew any forger would go mad trying to imitate his precise style.

'No reply is expected,' he told the Fly. 'Odds are, anyway, I won't be where you might look for me.'

The Fly-kinden messenger took the sealed scroll from him and bowed minutely. A moment later she was at the window, and then gone: a flurry of briefly glimpsed wings and a small figure receding in the sky.

Salma took a deep breath. The moment the letter had left his hands, he had cast himself off on a journey of no return. At least his would not be a lonely one; the thought quirked his lips into a smile. He determined that he would now indulge in one of his favourite pastimes, and go and annoy Tynisa.

She knew from the boldness and the pattern to his knock that it was Salma, come to call on her because he was bored. Tynisa paused before her glass, debating whether to play dead or to call out to him. It was a shame, she thought, that he usually did seek her out from ennui. She kept a fair number of young men at any given time who would seek her out with gifts, with flowers or some trinket of jewellery, a good poem stolen or a bad one written. Salma sought her out merely because her company amused him, and that was not the same thing after all.

But it was why he interested her so much, she realized. It was because he was proof against all her looks and smiles and subtle words. *And* he was a prince. There were tacticians' sons aplenty in Collegium, and the heirs of industrialists, lords of commerce or of learning or strategy. None of them was a *prince*, though. The Lowlands did not possess any with that kind of cachet.

She was wearing her favourite silks, that swept down from her throat and left her shoulders bare: clothes suitable for a lady's private chamber. So many men would have given so much, she thought proudly, for the privilege of seeing her thus adorned, but Salma would just come in and throw himself straight on the couch, and not really care all that much about her looks.

'Oh come in then, if you have to,' she said, trying to sound annoyed by the intrusion. She supposed that she should at least be glad that it was always her he sought to alleviate his routine, but the thought didn't help that much. It was not that he did not have an eye for girls. He had his choice, almost, of the female students, and choose he did. Towards her, though, he was . . . different.

He sauntered in, pausing in the doorway to pass his robe to Stenwold's long-suffering servant. 'Well now, a work of art half-done,' he commented, leaning against the doorframe. 'Don't let me stop you. I'm always one for watching an artist at work.'

She gave a wry smile and turned her face towards him, seeing just the barest start of surprise break his poise.

'Careless,' he said. 'How did that happen?'

She touched the bruise which extended from cheekbone to chin on the left side of her face. 'You're the clever foreigner who knows all our ways inside out, Salma, so *you* tell me.'

He rolled his eyes. 'You didn't.'

'Didn't I? Then how else did I get it, your royal principalness?' She turned back to the glass. It was a Spider-made artefact. All the best ones were. It was not that the Spiderlands craftsmen had superior skill, more that they knew what to look for. *Being so fond of their own image, as I am.*

'Piraeus.' Salma stepped into the room at last, casting himself down on the couch.

'I told you what I wanted with him,' she confirmed. There was a whole alchemy of make-up spread out before her, Spider-harvested and prepared, all of it. She made several delicate passes across her face, first with one brush and then another.

'And?'

'And I told him I wanted to fight him, a duel, and he laughed at me. He looked at me down his nose, like the Mantids always do. I was beneath his notice, for I was a Spider. I was a thing of contempt, not fit to draw blade against.'

'He said all that?'

'Oh, posing, posing. You know how it is. I was talking too, though. When he finished speaking he had no more to say. When I finished he had agreed to meet me at the Forum.'

'And that must have gone well,' Salma noted dryly. She looked straight at him, over her shoulder.

'He beat me. He beat me by two strikes to none,' she admitted. 'I've another bruise on my side that's a little short of this one for size, but lovely for colour, like a flower bouquet. You can see it if, you want?' She tilted her head, mockingly coquettish.

He shrugged indifferently, one hand tracing patterns on the wall. 'I'm no chirurgeon,' he said with a blithe smile, 'but if you want. So what, then? Or did you really think you could beat him?'

'I wanted to see if I could make him *fight*, Salma. That was the object. This . . .' she passed another brush over the bruise. 'This is a medal for the sort of wars I'll be fighting in.'

'Spider wars.'

'Your people don't play that game, Salma?'

She had him there, and he laughed. 'Well, perhaps, but nobody plays as well as the Spider-kinden. Even one, it seems, brought up by Beetles. It must be in the blood.'

'In the blood and in the Art,' she agreed. 'And I needed to know. Now that Stenwold's come clean with me, with us, I needed to be sure of myself.'

'For a woman with a bruise the size of Lake Sideriti you certainly sound sure of yourself.'

She turned from her paints and powders again, a face now unmarked, devoid of blemish. 'What bruise?' she asked sweetly. 'And besides, I'll have him again sometime, and that time I'll win. It's not just the Mantids who remember a grudge.'

Cheerwell Maker, Che, was meditating. There was a room for that in any decent-sized house in Collegium, while in the poorer areas of the city there were civic buildings set aside just for this silent communion. If she had gone into the Ant city of Vek, miles down the coast, she would have found great echoing halls filled with men and women, and especially the young, each seeking to communicate with the infinite. In the Mantis holds of Etheryon and Nethyon, deep amidst the trees, there were glades and groves where no sword was ever drawn, where only the mind was unsheathed.

This was not about gods. Well read, she knew the concept. Even in the Bad Old Days before the revolution, this had not been about gods. Long ago, when her people had been no more than gullible slaves to charlatan wizards, there had been no idols or altars. The imaginary spirits and forces that the Moth-kinden rulers had believed in were invoked and commanded and harnessed: religion but not worship.

Meditation was different to that old quackery. Nobody doubted how important it was. The tactile evidence was all around them. Meditation was the Ancestor Art, the founding basis of all the insect-kinden. Whether it was meditation to make the Fly-kinden fly, and the Ants live within each other's minds; to make the Mantids swift, the Spiders subtle, meditation was the Art that lived within them all, waiting to be unlocked.

Cheerwell Maker was very bad at it. It was not that she was slow, for being slow would probably have helped. She had a quick mind, and it chafed too easily at inaction. No sooner had she approached some contemplative plateau than it buzzed off after some other trail and instead left her uncomfortably aware of her surroundings. Such as now.

The duelling match hadn't helped. It might even haunt her for the rest of her days. When she closed her eyes, trying to find tranquillity, what she saw instead was the inside of the Prowess Forum. Falger again was standing across from her, sword gripped too tight in one hand. He was a gormless-looking youth, Falger, and none too fit. She had realized that she really should be able to beat him.

All eyes had been upon her, and she had hated that. It was Tynisa, not her, who basked in the public regard. Che had felt herself becoming flustered, though. It was not the spectators: it was her comrades behind her, their eyes drilling her back full of holes. Most of all it was Uncle Stenwold, because she so wanted to prove to him that she could actually *do* this.

But meditation? She recaptured her train of thought and placed it under close arrest. This was not something that should be a challenge to her. Most children started this at eight or ten and took to it without trouble. All over the world Beetle-kinden men and women, and all the other races of mankind, sat cross-legged as she was now and opened themselves up to their ideal. Primitive peoples might have gods, and the Bad Old Days had their totem spirits, but sensible Beetle thinkers had conjectured the Ideal Form. All ideas, they said, possessed a most perfect theoretical expression, and what she bent her mind towards was the Ideal Beetle. Her people, all of them, across the Lowlands and beyond, had imagined and explored and refined the Ideal, drawn strength from it, for thousands of years, since long before the first word of history was written.

Now all she had to do was to prise open her mind sufficiently to allow the enveloping perfection of that Ideal into her life, and to accept its gifts. And yet her mind still battered against the recent past like a fly at a window pane.

Had this been easier when she was younger? No, she had always lived with too many expectations of her and under that kind of pressure she could never concentrate. She had always been the fifth wheel, passed from hand to hand. Nobody had really known what to do with her. Even her natural parents had been quick to get shot of her. True, it had been a wonderful opportunity offered, but for her or for them? Her father was a small-time trader in one of the Agora-towns tributary to Collegium. Theirs was a large family and everything had always been scarce. In retrospect Che wondered whether it had all been scarce because her father had his image to maintain among his mercantile friends and contacts. Certainly he had never gone without a good coat ornamented in the latest fashion.

And then he had got in touch, after rather a long period of mutual silence, with his brother who was now a Master at the Great College. Che suspected he had got in touch with that brother *because* he was a Master at the Great College, and her father was a socially ambitious man. Shortly thereafter she had found herself, at the age of eight, waiting at the depot with her bags packed for the engine to arrive.

Oh it had surely been a blessed opportunity for her, to grow up in the house of a College Master. She now had her education, her social standing, everything to be thankful for, and yet . . . And yet, of course, it had not been merely kinship that had won her the chance. Stenwold had motives. Stenwold always had motives. Stenwold, of course, had a young ward already, and he was delighted to find for her a companion of her own age.

A young, female ward – and what was the gossip there? She could only imagine how the respectable people of Collegium had babbled to each other when Stenwold Maker returned home with a Spider child.

But she was supposed to be meditating, not counting over old hurts like a miser.

The Ancestor Art, it so eluded her: had her ancestors proved as incapable as she was, then the human race would have perished. In the way-back, before steam engines and metalwork, the world had been a savage place. With nothing but fire and flint, her distant forebears had faced creatures that had no fear of man: hives of ants as large as children; spiders that strung webs thirty feet across; scorpions in the deserts that could rip up iron with their claws; praying mantids lurking in the darkest woods that would feed on man by choice and preference. Against these perils there was only the Ancestor Art. It bred a link, a kinship, between naked, helpless man and the great armoured beasts that ruled his world. A kinship first, and later a bond of communication, the opening of a whole chest of treasures.

All of which lore she had learned, of course. She had received excellent gradings from her history and metaphysics teachers but none of that helped her actually put such wisdom into practice.

And she would soon need it, so very soon. With very little time to prove herself, here she was, like a guilty student just a day before the examination, trying to rush through her neglected studies.

Stenwold would train a new batch of special students every few years. Her childhood in his house had been punctuated by them. They had all gone away, and later Che realized that this was because Stenwold had *sent* them. For Stenwold, mild College Master and historian, deployed a string of agents working for him in far places. Boring old Uncle Stenwold thus became a man of mystery.

And it was easy enough to decipher where his eyes were fixed. 'History', to the College, meant the history of the Lowlands, that great flat expanse of land lying between the sea and the Great Barrier Ridge, considered the cradle of civilization. Except that, during his classes, Stenwold would talk of other places, for human civilization did not stop when you passed the Barriers or came to the Dryclaw Desert, he explained. Che might have thought this was a wondrous thing but for the tone of voice which implied Stenwold alone had seen a storm on that distant horizon, and nobody around him would go home for their coats.

Concentrate, concentrate, concentrate. But it was like trying to will herself to sleep. Instead of lulling herself into a deep contemplation she was wide awake and excruciatingly aware of everything around her, with the word 'concentrate' branded on the inside of her skull.

'I've got to get this *right*,' she told herself in a desperate little whisper. The Art, the Ancestor Art, was all important, and she didn't know *anyone* who was as hopeless with it as she was. There were youths of twelve who had acquired a better mastery.

The Art was common to all the kinden, yet unique to each. It grew the spines on Mantis arms and gave the Mantids their prodigious speed and skill. It was the silent voice with which the Ant-kinden spoke to each other, mind to mind, to coordinate their battles. It made some strong, others resilient. It could cloud enemy minds, or climb enemy walls. It could make the earth-bound fly . . . Oh, she would so like to fly. Alas, Beetle-kinden were proverbially bad at it, clumsy and thunderous, but to be able to *fly*, to just soar into the air without a machine or a mount to carry her. Fly-kinden and Moths and the others might sneer at her, but she would not care how ungainly, how slow.

I think too much, she decided. *I'm too much of a rationalist.* Not that the Art was irrational, not like the old spurious magics the Moths still clung to. It was just poorly understood and utterly beyond her grasp.

She sighed. It was hopeless. It was all still getting away from her. She had no need, right now, to feel any more of a failure.

She wondered if it might have changed things if she had won her bout against Falger. She had made the first strike, too, a stinging rap to Falger's ungloved hand, and it had then seemed a foregone conclusion. He was as inexperienced as she was, and he seemed frightened of being hurt, and he had his fat uncle in the background growling and unsettling him, and she had him. He was hers for the taking.

And then she had started *thinking*. It was always such thinking that tripped her up. If she had been a dull girl, as Falger was a dull boy, then none of this would be a problem. Instead of concentrating solely on her next move, she had started thinking, and he had clipped her shoulder with a narrow blow. And then she had been thinking even more about how to stop him doing it again, and so he had done it again. His blade, with a horribly clumsy lunge, had poked her in the stomach, and so he had won. And his fellows had won, and his uncle had won, and she had lost, not only for herself, but everyone else. They had tried to tell her it didn't matter, but she knew in her heart that it did, and that she had let them all down. Again.

When, two years ago, Stenwold had opened his latest duelling school, he had started it around Tynisa and then set about looking for recruits. How Cheerwell had badgered him, morning, noon and night, practising ostentatiously outside his study window, breaking a vase in the hall with her practice parries, nagging at him and distracting him until he had let her join. And now his initial caution had proved to be so well founded.

That must be why, she thought. *That must be why he isn't taking me, too.* Because she knew his plans now. Something was happening far off that he wanted to see for himself, something in Helleron away to the east. He was departing in just a few days, and he was taking Tynisa and Salma to act as his agents there.

He was leaving her behind.

She stood up. Clearly meditation was not the order of the day. He could not begin to know how much he had hurt her, when he had come in to ask Tynisa to join him and said nothing to Che, even though she was right there in the same room. Some way or other she would make him take her too because staying here at home with the rejection would hurt her far more than anything that might happen to her in Helleron.

She tidied her crumpled robes. She could not give up now. She would just have to find him and *tell* him. There was no more to it than that.

*

Traditionally the houses of Collegium's richest and most privileged citizens were ranged up against the Great College itself. Perhaps it was considered inspiring to watch the students prepare for the governance of tomorrow's world. Besides, many of the great and the good were current or past College Masters, and probably felt at home close by.

There was, however, one straggle of buildings not favoured by either the great or the good, and that was the wing housing the Halls of Artifice. For the furnace burned day and night, and the air above was ahaze with smoke and steam, while the immediate neighbourhood smelled of oil, molten metal and burning chemicals. Anyone trying to sleep anywhere near the Halls would need earplugs, and few of Collegium's industrialists relished being reminded of the source of their wealth when they opened their shutters. Instead the housing round about was home for lowly College staff and students who could afford no better.

Stenwold arrived at the main portal leading to the Halls of Artifice and gazed at the curving line of workshops and smithies stretching away in front of him, remembering. They had added two new buildings since he had made his own prentice pieces here. Meanwhile two decades more of grime had settled on the hard-edged stonework around him. Forget the politics, the arts martial, the philosophy and history, here was the engine that had driven Collegium since the revolution which had ended the Bad Old Days. This was the hub that made the Beetle city great: not fighters, not schemers, not tatty mystics, but *makers*. And Stenwold was not alone in possessing this surname. Amongst his industrious nation the names of Maker, Smithy and Wright were as common as dirt.

He went inside, his clean robes already flecked with soot and ash, and swept past the porter with a nod, passing on through clamouring hall after hall, lit glowing red by furnaces, clogged with steam, until he finally located Totho.

With the excitement and distraction of the Games so close no ordinary student could be expected to be working today. But artificers were an odd breed. Totho was not the only one of them at work in the machine-heavy confines of the workshop. The few others were all true-bred Beetle-kinden, with a single Tarkesh Ant standing out bleach-pale amongst them. They were all bound together by their dedication to their craft. Among them Stenwold recognized an artisan's son and the daughter of a prominent silk merchant hard at work, each absorbed in some private mechanical dream. Totho was no different, as he stood hunched over a pedal-lathe, staring through dark goggles and sheets of sparks, as he machined a section of metal into shape.

Stenwold approached him, but did not distract the youth from his task. There were half a dozen mechanisms already lying on the bench beside him, all seemingly versions of the same artefact, and all meticulously detailed. Stenwold had heard how good Totho was at his chosen business. It was a shame, then, that the lad was a poor halfbreed and an orphan. If he had come with a finer provenance the word his masters would have used of him was 'great'. Collegium had spent centuries in the pursuit of freedom for all, opportunity for everyone, and if Totho had been in any other city he would have been a slave at worst, or at best an unskilled labourer. Here in Collegium he had acquired scholarship and skills, but the weight of his ancestry was like a chain about his ankles. He had all the written rules on his side, and all the unwritten ones working against him.

Stenwold picked up one of the finished items to inspect. It was a tube about as big as his fist, and he could see there was some manner of pump within it, but the precise purpose of it eluded him. Totho glanced at him briefly, then stopped pedalling and stepped away from the lathe. With the goggles, the gauntlets, the apron and the leather cap, he could have been any apprentice artificer in that busy little group, but Stenwold had recognized him instantly from the inward hunch of his shoulders, the slight downturn to his head.

'Did you want me, Master Maker?' the youth asked. His voice was an artificer's through and through: not loud but specially pitched to carry across the machine noise.

'I trained in this very hall,' Stenwold told him, unconsciously slipping into the same register. 'But it's been a while since I had to weld a join or fix a spring. What *is* this thing?'

'It's an air battery, Master Maker.'

'You don't need to be formal with me, Totho,' Stenwold told him, then added, 'I don't recall air batteries being part of the syllabus.'

'Just a personal project, sir,' Totho said. 'Only, with everyone else away at the Games, it seemed a chance to . . .'

'I know, yes.' *Nothing I didn't do myself, at his age. I thought I was going to be an artificer for life, when I was young.* 'I feel embarrassed to ask, because I'm sure I should already know, but what exactly is an air battery?'

The change in the youth was remarkable. The animation in him built momentum like a machine itself as he explained, taking his creation apart with gloved hands. 'You see, sir, there's a chamber here with air in . . . see the one-way valve I've put in here . . . now it's full and . . . you cock it like a repeating crossbow, with this lever here – just with your thumb, though, three or four times . . . and then you've put the air under pressure, lots of pressure . . . and then, with this lever here, you can release it all at once . . . and you produce almost as much force as a firepowder charge.'

'Hammer and tongs,' Stenwold murmured, impressed. 'And what were you intending to use it for?'

Totho pushed back his goggles, revealing two lighter circles in his grime-darkened face. 'Weapons, sir.'

'Weapons?'

'Projectiles, sir.' The life that had taken hold of him began to ebb a little. 'That's . . . what I want to go into. If they'll let me, sir.'

'No worries there, Totho. If not here, then Sarn, perhaps. A Collegium-trained weaponsmith commands a high price there.' The words rang a little hollow. Stenwold toyed with the air battery and put it down. 'Ever fancy going to visit Helleron?'

The youth's eyes went wide. 'Yes, sir, of course.' He probably dreamt about it longingly. In a warlike world, a fair proportion of the Lowland's weapons were made in the foundries of Helleron, ranging from swords by the thousand to land-ironclads and siege artillery. The city of Helleron was the acknowledged queen of the industrial age, and produced almost everything that could be manufactured, but it was the arms trade she was best known for.

'Well,' said Stenwold, and let things hang there for a moment as he considered further. Tynisa and Salma he had absolutely no qualms about: they could look after themselves if things went wrong. But Totho here was an unknown quantity: a halfbreed, a quiet lad who kept very much to himself. He had only come to Stenwold's attention at all because Cheerwell had needed to take some lessons in things mechanical, and it had been through Totho's quiet help that she had passed her examinations. Still, Stenwold had been impressed by his conduct in the duel with Adax. Kymon might dismiss it as tedious, but Stenwold privately thought that Totho, who possessed little and had done better than he should, had proved rather more than Piraeus, who possessed a lot and had done worse than he might.

'I'm travelling that way in a few days' time,' he informed the youth, as idly as he could. 'I might have some work there that a few young hands could help me with. So do you want to come?'

He had expected an instant, eager affirmation, but Totho squeezed just a little more respect out of him by weighing up the offer carefully.

'Sir, will Che – Cheerwell – be going as well?'

Stenwold frowned a little. 'I hadn't planned it—'

'Yes. Yes, I will,' Che told him, from the doorway behind. 'I don't care what you say, you can't keep me here.'

When Stenwold spun round he found her standing there with clenched fists, her courage screwed up to the hilt, more evidently ready for a fight than she had ever seemed in the Prowess Forum.

Five

Stenwold closed his eyes resignedly. For all her shortcomings, the girl had *timing*. 'Totho, would you—?'

'You can say what you've got to say in front of him,' Che told him. 'I want to go. I want to do whatever it is you're doing.' She was standing there fiercely in her best white College robe amidst the sparks and grime.

Stenwold turned on her. 'Absolutely not,' he said, his face leaden.

She confronted him defiantly with her hands on her hips, a solid young Beetle-kinden girl. A College scholar. *My niece.*

'I am a *part* of this,' she insisted.

'Cheerwell, you don't even know what "this" is,' he said reasonably. 'I am just going east on business, nothing more.'

'Business that includes Toth and Salma, and ... and Tynisa, but not me?' She had wanted to be so calm about this, to pick him apart with clever words, but now he was here, now he was here talking with *Totho*, like some clandestine recruiting officer. She found that she was losing it. Quietly, the studious artificers were creeping out of the room. Only Totho had not moved, staring somewhere at the ground behind Stenwold.

'What I'm about, it's best you don't know,' he tried.

'But you can tell everyone else? All my friends, but not me?' And suddenly she realized it was all going to come out. All of it, that she had been stewing, was just going to vomit out of her. 'Not me, though, is it? Never me. Please, Uncle Sten, I want to go. I want to do what you're doing. I know it's important.'

'Cheerwell, listen,' Stenwold said, still with a hand on reason, 'I don't want you to get hurt. I don't know exactly what to expect, but, worst to worst, it could be dangerous.'

'Yet you always claim the whole world's dangerous,' she insisted. The whole of the last few days was crashing in on her, the failed meditation, the bitterness of humiliation in that duel.

'Very dangerous,' he said. 'Helleron, points east . . . and there are things happening out there I don't want you involved in. It's not safe for you.'

'I don't care,' she told him. 'I can look after myself.' Looking at him there she could not stop herself. 'I'm not some . . . Well I'm not an old . . . fat man. What makes you think—?'

He moved then, just a little motion, a tug at his cuffs, but it changed his stance and cut her off, because there was something more than history books in his personal history. His face was mild still as he spoke. 'I'm sorry, Cheerwell, I don't want to put you in danger. What would I be able to say to your father?'

'You don't care. When did you last speak to him? Or write?' She actually stamped her foot. 'Why *not*? Why not me, Uncle Sten? Go on, say it. Just say it. What's wrong with me?'

'Cheerwell—'

'I'm never good enough, am I? I'm just stupid Cheerwell with the stupid name, and I'll just bumble along behind everyone else, shall I?'

'Will you find some calm?' he said, starting to lose his own. 'It's simple. There's no great conspiracy. You're my niece, my family, and I want to see you safe.'

'Blood, is it?' she said. She had thought it might come to this.

'If you want.' He gave a great hissing sigh. 'Cheerwell—'

'Only' – she choked on the words, reached desperately for her courage – 'from all that's been going on, I could . . . could have sworn that it was *her* you count as your own flesh and blood, and . . . and not . . . not *me* at all.'

And so it was said, and a silence fell on them, the three of them, like cinders from a pyre. Behind Stenwold, Totho was visibly cringing, hands clenched into fists over his apron. Che realized that she was shaking, not just a little but hard enough to make her teeth rattle. Her breath was coming out in short gasps and she knew that any moment she was going to break out in tears and make everything so much *worse*.

Stenwold was staring at her intently, and for a moment she thought he was really angry, angry enough to hit her, and she flinched away from him.

But he had never struck her before, and he was not going to do so now. The expression on his face was one she had never seen previously. He had gone pale and sick-looking, and very, very sad, and full of something else: some guilt or horror of his own making. All of this was evident in his face before he turned to leave them.

'I—' she said, but he was already going, walking out past her, away. 'Uncle . . . Please!'

He stopped, his back still towards her, broad with sloping shoulders.

'Totho,' he said, without looking round, 'nobody gains by any of this being repeated.'

Totho just nodded, which Stenwold couldn't have seen, but there was obviously an understanding between the two of them.

'Uncle . . .' Che said again. He turned, gently, slowly. His expression was still very sad, very thoughtful.

'You cannot come with me, Cheerwell,' he said. 'I have done a great many things that I regretted when the time came. This will not be one of them. I am sorry, though. Sorry for . . . I am *sorry*.'

Totho watched her dart into Stenwold's arms, still shaking, watched Stenwold's hurt, remorseful look. After a long while the apprentice cleared his throat, and the older man's eyes locked onto him.

'The . . . athletes will be arriving for the Games. We should . . . go and see.'

Stenwold's nod told of his gratitude for this diversion. 'So we should. Come on, Cheerwell. Dry your eyes.' He sighed again. 'Unless I'm mistaken, you'll see something of my purpose today. Let that something be enough for you.'

There was a crowd the length of the Pathian Way, the great northern avenue that led to the heart of Collegium. The wealthy and the more prosperous artisans rubbed shoulders unselfconsciously, sitting on the great tiered stone steps that lined the route. The ritual of the Games and the procession of the athletes were older than the College itself. These steps had been thronged like this when the city had still been called Pathis and the Beetle-kinden were second-class citizens and slaves, back in the Bad Old Days.

Before those comfortable steps thronged the poor, of course – standing room only – but they made up for it with noise and cheer. Being poor in Collegium was only a relative thing, for the poor of Collegium enjoyed ample work, and sewers and clean wells with pumps, and there was food to be had from the civic stores when times were lean. Governance by academics, philanthropists and the wealthy was hit or miss, but in Collegium it hit the mark more often than not. Most importantly, it had always been fashionable to be seen doing charitable work for the lower orders. Even the greediest magnate wanted to be *seen* to be generous, and even false generosity could fill bellies.

There was a roar moving along the crowd, a wave of sound making a steady progress matching the speed of the athletes themselves. People began craning forward, even pushing out into the Pathian Way, though there was a scattered line of the city guard to keep them in check, mostly middle-aged men in ill-fitting chain mail. Their presence was enough, though, and every tenth man was a Sentinel wearing the massively bulky plate armour that only Beetle-kinden possessed the sheer stamina to wear. The throng of spectators eddied back into place, but the cheering grew only louder and louder, for Collegium's own athletic best were the first band of heroes to enter the city by the Pathian Way.

Che stood up from her place on the steps, not because she was so very keen to see but because everyone else around her had. She tried to work out how many of the participants she could put a name to. In the lead, bearing the standard with Collegium's gold, red and white, was 'Dash' Brierwey, a slim, short-haired woman who was the only Beetle-kinden in living memory to win a short-run foot race. A pace behind, to one side of her, was a much older man whose name Che forgot, but who had contested in the long-run and the armour races before she ever came to the city. On the other side, balding and stout, was what's-his-name Pinser who had won the epic poetry recital the previous year. Behind these followed seventeen more stalwarts, some of them veterans and some of them hopefuls: runners, jumpers, warriors, musicians, wrestlers and poets, and she knew many of them had trained at the Great College itself.

Helleron's team came close behind, and Che glanced back at Stenwold to see if he might be thinking about their heated argument earlier. She would have given a great deal if Totho could invent a machine to take back hasty words. There were things that come to roost in the mind that should never be let out.

Stenwold was staring absently down the line, and she could tell he was tense, even though he was trying not to show it.

The Helleron team, marching under their bronze, red and black scarab banner, were fed a little less crowd approval than the city's home-grown heroes, but they received cheers nonetheless. They were mostly Beetle-kinden, and they and Collegium took the honour of that race with them to the field. Che could not hope to name any of them, but she knew that the big Beetle bearing their standard was a champion crossbow marksman, while the Ant-kinden just behind him was a renegade from Tark and known as a brutally efficient wrestler.

Traditionally, the Ant cities came next in the procession, and it was Collegium's dry humour to bring them in order of their victories in the previous year, to whet the fervour of a kinden already madly competitive. The cheers even picked up a bit, because the first platoon of neatly marching Ants hailed from Sarn, which in the last few decades of political reform had become Collegium's nearest ally. They were a uniform breed, tan of skin, regular of feature, and all equipped in dark armour, every one of them selected from that city's army. Che examined them keenly, for Ants were always competitors worth watching in any event. She felt a shiver pass through her as the block of perfectly disciplined soldiers passed by, each in step, looking neither to the left nor the right. She wondered what unheard words would be passing through their minds.

The cheering began to subside as the Kes team followed next, looking to Che much like their predecessors save for the coppery tone of their skins, and then the pale Ants of Tark following on their heels. After their passage, there was a distinct mutter of disapproval, for there was an ominous gap to represent the team from Vek, who had not attended yet again. There were enough still alive here who had fought to prevent Collegium becoming a Vek protectorate. Stenwold still remembered the scar of madness and confusion it had left on his childhood.

A showing from Seldis and Everis came next, a score of Spider-kinden, both men and women, and each of them as beautiful as heredity and cosmetics could conjure up for them. Che recognized a few from last year: duellists, gymnasts, exquisite poets, leaving the more brutal events for the coarser races to bicker over. Behind them was the combined Egel-Merro team of Fly-kinden, a jostling pack of little people casting looks at the crowd that were full of bravado and sly humour. They would take away most of the aerial races and acrobatics, of course, and, in all probability, a certain amount of the citizens' personal property.

And last, of course, straggled whatever the other two kinden of the Lowlands had managed to put together for a team this year. There were just eleven of them, far short of any of their competition, and nine of these were Mantids. They looked down their noses at the patronizing crowd, stalked with a killer's grace between the great packed masses of Collegium like hostage princes entering into captivity. They had come, though. No amount of disdain could hide it. They had come, and these would walk away with most of the sashes for single combat. The fact that an occasional champion was an Ant or a Spider only went to show how good the competition really was.

Amidst the Mantids were a couple of others, grey-skinned and grey-robed, shorn of any ornament, staring fixedly at the ground. These two were not official delegates from Mount Hain in the north, where the Moth-kinden had one of their few remaining strongholds. They were radicals, renegades. Like the few Moth teachers employed at the College, whose faces occasionally changed, but whose number somehow remained exactly the same, they were the exceptions to their race who had come to see the world beyond their insular homes. The Beetle spectators looked on them with amusement nowadays: these mystics from the mountains, these bugbears of myth, shakers of skulls and fetishes, clinging stubbornly to an age long consigned to the history books. There was no ire left, among the people of Collegium, for a race whose reach had once shadowed all of the Lowlands. That they had even held Pathis, the city of Collegium that was, before the revolution and the change of name, was near forgotten.

Che watched them, and wondered. She had never met a Moth-kinden, never even been close to one. Their lecturers at the College taught subjects that she would not dream of taking, reeking of stale mysticism and quackery. The city Assembly was always muttering about banning such anachronisms, but they clung on, in their dark little studies and dingy rooms, instructing a handful of students apiece.

There was now a murmur running through the crowd and she was broken from her reverie as Stenwold gripped her shoulder. She started, stared. For there was, this year, another team.

They brought up the rear, consigned there because the organizers had not known what to do with them. Her heart skipped when she saw their banner, their colours, repeated in their clothes, their armour, even the hilts of their weapons.

Black and gold. All of it black and gold.

They were men, every one of them. Some were pale and some were darker, and most were fair-haired, and handsome when they smiled. They smiled a lot, too, at the crowd, at the sky, at the city before them. Some of them wore banded armour and some simply cut clothes, and all of them had shortswords at their belts. They were not the rigid lattice of the Ants, but their step was close in time. If she had seen just one, she might have taken him for a halfbreed of some kind, one she could not instantly have assigned any special ancestry to. Seeing them, all of them together, the people of Collegium understood that a new race, a new power, had entered fully into the Lowlands.

They smiled openly, and the people of Collegium smiled back, but nervously. Everyone knew, though many thought little of it, that there were other kinden settled beyond the mountains and the Barrier Ridge, to the north and to the east. But the Lowlands had spent a long time looking inward: the squabbling Ant city-states and the reclusive Mantids and Moths. The people of Collegium should have been better aware, but the doings of foreigners beyond the Lowlands interested them little. They knew that in eastern Helleron their kin traded with all kinds of other kinden who came seeking out the legendary Beetle industry and artifice. They realised that Prince Salme Dien was proof of the Commonweal lying north, beyond the Barrier Ridge that so frustrated any serious travel, and they knew that down the silk road and across the sea extended the vast and enigmatic Spiderlands, realms of infinite wealth and cunning. They knew increasingly that, where there had been a scattering of little city-states not so long ago, now to the east of Helleron was a unified empire. Any serious trader with an interest in the east had been trying to grab a piece of the imperial business that had recently proved so lucrative. Fortunes had been made by holding a hand out to these people. Still, there was a ripple of unease that passed through the crowd, after the new-comers had gone by. That insistent black and gold, the brisk military step, the fierce energy, was something they had not seen here before. Enough people had business in the east to know that these Wasp-kinden were *soldiers*, just like the Ants were soldiers. Many had perhaps found that there were an awful *lot* of them, and all of them with smiles and swords and uniforms. A few had actually listened to the speeches of a certain Master Maker. In the wake of the Wasp athletes, and only when their backs were turned, people looked to their neighbours and wondered, *Are we sure about this, then?*

Che could not have said what her thoughts might have been otherwise, but Stenwold's grasp was tight on her shoulder, and she had been to his classes: his histories, which were not the histories of the other Masters, and which went further and deeper. These, in their resplendent livery, represented the Wasp Empire, and Stenwold had been warning his students about them for ten years.

On the night before the Games it was all Collegium's duty to celebrate. The tavernas would be thronging with men and women debating the merits of both the foreign and the local favourites. Bets would be made casually with friends and unwisely with strangers. Fights would start. In the houses of the middle classes private parties would be thrown, each grading itself according to which of the athletes and performers they had managed to attract.

Che's cadre of duellists had been invited to the villa of a prospering grain magnate, although it was no secret that it was Tynisa who had been in the man's mind when the invitation had been issued. It was a middling affair, as the social strata went. Their host had managed to bag a brace of Fly-kinden racers who left after the first turn of the hourglass – and took several silver spoons with them. Then there was the champion poet, Pinser, whose epic verse had been found subjectively excellent by the home-grown judges, but whose everyday persona and conversation made him the most atrocious bore. This party might have been doomed to a brief and frosty life had not their host also secured the presence of one of the Mantis-kinden duellists. She was a poised, sharp-featured woman, pale of skin, fair of hair. Her expression suggested that she was not entirely sure what she was doing there, but she was undoubtedly an attraction. The well-to-do of Collegiate guests came along eagerly to look at this strange, fierce warrior in their midst.

All the hosts across the city had vied to secure one of the Wasp newcomers, and failed. They had marched through Collegium down the Pathian Way and vanished into the College itself, where they were being billeted as guests of the Assembly. The city was alive with speculation: the words 'Wasp-kinden' frequently employed. Everyone had a question about them for his or her neighbour, but nobody had a sure answer.

Che had so far spent the evening avoiding people. Pinser had tried to corner her with some new verse of his, somewhat (he claimed with alarmingly wide eyes) *racy*, but perhaps a young lady would find it of interest . . .? This was one encounter that Che wished had gone, as they usually did, to Tynisa. Then she had been busy avoiding Totho, who obviously wanted to speak to her. She knew she was being unfair, and that he would be having an even worse time than she was, but he had been *there* and had heard all those stupid, stupid things that she had said. She did not feel that she could face him just yet.

Finally the four of them convened on the roof garden. It was a mild night, though stuffy inside. There was a cool breeze off the sea, and all around them the air sang with the city's debauchery. Tynisa sat at one edge of the roof like a lady holding court, and Che, worn down by the day's misadventures, sat docilely at her feet.

'So they're here now,' Che said. 'Not just a merchant or a single diplomat or a soldier of fortune, but a whole pack of them. Or a swarm of them, whatever.'

'And you're surprised?' Tynisa snorted. 'Stenwold kept saying they'd make their move sooner or later.'

'I suppose I just thought it would be later,' Che murmured. Totho was looking at her, or perhaps at the two of them. She avoided his gaze.

'How dangerous can they really be, if it's taken them this long to get here?' the Spider-kinden said airily.

Salma had meanwhile been playing some obscure game with the fist-sized moths that came to batter at the lanterns, catching them and letting them go, over and over. Now he gave a short laugh. When he turned, there was a decidedly superior look on his face.

'You Lowlanders amaze me.'

'It's easily done, O foreign flytrap. Why so this time?' Tynisa said.

'You'd barely even know that the Dragonfly Commonweal existed, if I hadn't made this trip.' He held his hands cupped together, the insect's wings fluttering within. 'There are people just beyond your own borders shouting at you, and you just turn away and close the shutters because it's rude to shout, and because you'd rather not hear. It's not as if the Wasp-kinden were hiding all these years. It's not as though they haven't been making good use of what the Lowlands will offer.'

'You've always known about the Wasp-kinden, haven't you?' Che said. 'I mean, before you came here and met Uncle Sten.'

'And your uncle knows I know.' He spread his hands suddenly and the bewildered moth bustled off back to the lamps. For a moment he had been something hard-edged, the enigmatic foreigner, filled with secrets. Then he was just Salma again with his customary smile, leaning back with his elbows on the garden wall. He would not be drawn further by their questions.

Stenwold's best robe, brought out of storage and newly re-tailored to accommodate a larger waist, felt crisp and sharp on him. Keeping him on edge, he reckoned, and perhaps that was for the best. It was his formal Academy Master's gown, with all the folds and creases that implied. He normally slung on any old garment but this time he felt he was here in a more formal capacity, and he knew everyone else would rather he stayed away.

Back to the Amphiophos then, that he had so recently walked out of: the circular chamber that the Assembly of the Learned met in, that had been used for the city governance before the revolution. The wall tapestries had been renewed since then, and the central stone of the ceiling had been replaced, with great artifice, with a geometric stained-glass window that cast red and gold and blue shards of light across the circular tiered seating which radiated out from the speaker's dais. Stenwold had found himself a seat at the back and was moodily watching the doors to the antechamber. About half the Assembly were present, too: Masters of the College and magnates of the town.

I knew there would come a day . . . But not this way. He had expected the sword first, in truth. He had expected the black and gold to show its true colours. Not through an embassy, not with this subtle cunning.

Seventeen years ago they would have come straight to the gates of Tark or Helleron with an army. *Seventeen years of war and conquest for them, and they have still found time to learn cleverness. I wonder who their agents have been, here, that I have not detected.*

The murmur of conversation waned and the Assembly waited as footsteps approached from the anteroom outside the hall. Two sentinels strode in, faceless in their helms, their heavy armour giving them a rolling gait. And there, behind them, were the Wasps.

Oh they had clearly learned a lot. Stenwold had seen the delegation sent to Myna, all armed threat and demands. Here, however, they wooed the Assembly with a show of imitation, for what else would best feed Collegium's ego? Their leader, square-jawed and fair, wore a decent approximation of the College's own ceremonial robes, with an intricate design of black and yellow interlocking along the folds. He even carried the hem of it partly slung over one arm, as a native would. There were three behind him, and one was obviously a guard: no sword at his belt, but there were barbed spurs of bone jutting forward from the backs of his hands. He held himself in a casual, relaxed pose that Stenwold recognized from watching alert military the world over. Unlike his master he wore a plain white tunic, almost the garb of a simple servant or slave. The man next to him wore the same garment, but held himself quite differently. Stenwold was a better observer than most, for he had been taught by a Spider-kinden long ago, and realized that this other man, for all his standing in the shadow of his fellows, was the one in charge. Stenwold saw it at once, from the way he watched his fellows closely, and the way they did not dare look at him.

The fourth ambassador was their master stroke. He wore a pale yellow tunic with a black sash, and he was a Beetle, a man of middle years and benign expression who could have made a home in Collegium without anyone turning a sidelong glance at him. This was no local, though: he was clearly an Imperial. *We are like you*, the Empire was saying, and only Stenwold knew how untrue it was.

Old Lineo Thadspar came forward with his hands clasped before him, a gesture of welcome that the lead Wasp copied smoothly.

'Noble visitors from distant lands,' he began, 'may we show you as much honour in our welcome as you have shown us in attending our Great Games.'

'What more honour could any wish than to be permitted to show our mettle against the best of this city and its neighbours?' The lead Wasp smiled about him at the curious onlookers. 'May I humbly present myself as God-ran, ambassador designate from our lands to your august Assembly. Thalric here is my chief aide, and able to speak my heart as well as I myself.' He indicated the man whom Stenwold had already picked as the true commander. *Of course he can*, the historian thought. *Better, even.*

'However, I suspect you may be more inclined to speak to my friend Honory Bellowern,' continued the smoothly smiling Godran, as the Beetle-kinden stepped forward. Stenwold, watching for it, saw the glance the Beetle gave to Thalric as he did so. *'My friend', is it? Master Bellowern had best be word perfect*, he judged, *or his diplomatic career shall be a short one.*

'Noble councillors of Collegium,' said Honory Bellowern in a rich, pleasant voice, 'I bring you greetings from the Consortium of the Honest, of which I am a factor. Already we have profited greatly from such dealings as we have had with Collegium, and I hope your brothers in Helleron have had no cause for complaint either. While men of more athletic stature shall take to the games, I hope there shall be those amongst you who will spare me the time to talk of such matters as trade agreements, diplomatic ties, terms and treaties and the like. Now that we find ourselves reaching out into the world, we are keen to formalize the bonds of friendship and prosperity between your Lowlands and the Empire.'

And Stenwold noticed a twitch in Thalric then, and realized that word, 'Empire', had not been spoken before, just 'our lands' and similar terms. A mis-step for Master Bellowern, then, but not a fatal one, for the mere mention of trade had the townsmen Assemblers' mouths watering. Ambassador Godran then put a comradely hand on Bellowern's shoulder and the two of them shared a rehearsed smile.

Stenwold watched as other members of the Assembly came up to make their names and businesses known. Not all, it was true: some sat back because they did not deign to meddle in the affairs of outlanders, while others, Stenwold thought, were reticent because they were not overly quick to give their trust. Indeed there was the look in some faces, of men who had over-eaten on a dish they now found slightly bitter. Heads turned in his direction and he sensed a tremor of anxiety there, as all of Stenwold's dusty warnings began turning over in their minds. Even the greediest of merchants would have seen enough, and heard enough, to know that Stenwold was no mere fantasist when he spoke warningly of the Empire, and now the Empire was *here*, standing in the Amphiophos itself, smiling and talking. But their eyes were very cold.

'Pray!' old Thadspar called out, to attract the general attention, and then, 'Pray, shall we not have . . . refreshment?' He mugged at his fellows and, at the word, a thing of glittering brass and steel came in from the antechamber. It was formed in the image of a robed Beetle man bearing a tray in its hands, and it resounded hollowly with the sound of gears and levers. Its course took it straight towards the ambassadors and Stenwold was pleased to see them start away from it in alarm. *Something your own artificers haven't done yet, then?* He saw Thalric's hand twitch, not moving to an absent sword, but the fingers flexing, clearing the palm. The Assemblers were laughing a little at the foreigners' confusion as the construct paused in the centre of the hall with its drinks ready for plucking, and after a moment the visitors awkwardly joined in. Old Thadspar was attempting to take the Wasp Godran gently to one side, now that the first rush of well-wishers had abated, and Stenwold shouldered through the crowd to hear.

'. . . remarkable indeed, Master Godran,' Thadspar was murmuring as Stenwold drew closer. 'Your empire's achievements have been instructive for us all, that you have done so much from such small beginnings, and grown so very prosperous.' His eyes sought out Stenwold, unexpectedly, just a sideways flicker over Godran's shoulder. 'We understand that war can be the fire that forges a great state ... but war, of course ...' The old man smiled apologetically. 'We value philosophers, here in Collegium. You know how they must always think about *everything*.'

Godran's smile was quick and easy. 'Oh, Master Thadspar, we have only just torn ourselves free of the Commonweal's ruinous war. We have a great deal to rebuild and repair. Simply feeding and clothing the Empire is a monumental task. We are like the man who fights all night with his wife, and in the morning does not feel like going off to work.'

There was a ripple of laughter at that, and Stenwold thought, *He even knows Collegiate jokes.* Stenwold would have spoken then, perhaps, but one of the College's other historians was heading towards him, a hand held up to catch his attention. The historian stepped aside to meet him, drawing back out of the Wasps' earshot.

'Master Maker.'

'Master Linewright.'

The younger man raised his hands. 'Master Maker, the Assembly has asked me to relay a request.'

Stenwold smiled a little. 'Pray relay, Master Linewright.'

'It is no secret what you think of our new guests,' said Linewright testily.

'I have done my best to tell it at every opportunity,' Stenwold said flatly.

'There was talk of banning you from here today, but that we could find no precedent. Maker, this is perhaps the most important embassage to come to Collegium in a generation.'

'No argument from me,' Stenwold said reasonably.

'The Assembly does not accept your view of these people,' Linewright snapped. 'How could we believe in civilization if such a monster as you foretell was even possible? And ...'

'And?'

Linewright glanced over his shoulder at the Wasps. 'And just say you were right – I don't believe it, of course, nobody does – but just suppose you were right . . .'

He's terrified, Stenwold realized. *Hammer and tongs, he knows I'm right and he's scared to death.*

'Just suppose you're right,' Linewright said, his voice suddenly hoarse. 'What could we *do*? Don't you think it's still better to befriend them than provoke them?'

'You're worried I'm going to denounce them openly as monsters and murderers. Believe me, I have no intention of provoking these people, or even speaking with them. Go back and join the festivities,' Stenwold added with heavy irony. 'Enjoy yourself.' Past the man's shoulder he could see the controversial visitors. Whilst Godran and his Beetle-kinden henchman were clasping hands and speaking homilies, Thalric was staring directly at Stenwold. He felt a shock as their eyes met. Had he seen this man before, as one soldier amongst many? Thalric seemed almost too young to have fought at Myna. The Wasp nodded, though, a private and personal nod for Stenwold alone.

I know you. That nod spoke volumes. *Don't think that I, that we, don't know all about you.*

Past midnight, and the windows of Collegium were darkening one by one, leaving the streets picked out in a web of gas lamps. Tynisa and Che were heading for home, bidding Totho good night where he turned away for the Charity Hall where he kept a room. He had spent the entire evening wanting to speak with Che, and she knew it. Now he had on him such a mournful expression that she wished she had not avoided him, but too late for that.

Salma was not with them, of course. Salma, to Tynisa's annoyance and derision, had left the party arm in arm with that Mantis-woman athlete from Nethyon. 'I hope she eats him,' Tynisa had said dismissively, but she was surprised to find how it rankled. When Salma took his pick of the local girls, adoring Beetle-kinden maids that she knew he felt nothing for, then she did not mind. It was not as though she had not romanced her share of industrialists' heirs, or young Ant officers away from home for the first time. Some she bedded and some she did not, but all of them gave her gifts and did as she wished. She was a Spider by birth, if not by upbringing. She cultivated her webs as a warrior would practise his swordplay, because it might be needed in earnest, come the time. This Mantis-kinden, though – Salma had bowed low before her, some elaborate ritual from his people, and she, who had seemed bored and alone only a moment before, had bowed back and taken his hand. And Mantis-kinden were not rumoured to be *casual* about their partner or anything else.

When they got back inside, Stenwold was waiting for them. They could smell his pipe on the air, so they peered through his study doorway. He was sitting in his favourite chair, ornate Mantis-carved work, and staring into the fire.

'Uncle?' Che said. 'I . . . we didn't think that you would still be up at this time.'

'Come in, both of you,' Stenwold said, not taking his eyes from the fire. 'Are the rest of the Majestic with you? No, I see not. Well I'll speak to you two now, and to them in the morning.'

'This is about the Wasp-kinden, isn't it?' Che guessed.

'It is. Tynisa, could you be prepared to leave for Helleron with me tomorrow?'

'And miss the Games?' Tynisa replied instantly, and then: 'Well, yes, I could . . .'

'Get together what you need. Travel light and travel armed.' There was a great purpose in Stenwold's voice. 'Years, I've waited – and now it's on me faster than I thought. Some "Dancer" I am.'

Tynisa understood that, although she didn't like the sound of it. Dancing was the Spider word for the politics beneath a city's skin. She had then wanted to ask more, prise more from him, but that one word made it all real and immediate for her. She left for her room upstairs.

'Don't say it,' Stenwold cautioned after she had gone, so Che clenched her fists and held her peace.

'You won't be idle here. You'll have things to do that I can't do if I'm away. You won't feel much better hearing this, but I need you here. And I don't want you to come to harm, Cheerwell. I want you to believe this.'

And the others? What about them? But Che knew that the others, even Totho, would have a chance to save themselves from the sword, from the bolt. Stenwold had judged her, and found her wanting. He wanted to keep her safe but still it hurt.

No more arguments now, not if he's leaving tomorrow. That was a strangely calming thought. She would now play the dutiful niece for him, and in that way he would have less to worry about, and perhaps that would keep *him* safe. Two could play at this game.

'If you're travelling tomorrow, you should retire to bed now, Uncle,' was all she said, to which he grunted an affirmative, levering himself up from the chair.

'Come on,' he offered, starting up the stairs. 'We'll have enough to say to each other in the morning.'

There was a window on the landing which looked out onto the Siplan Way and the sea, and though Stenwold stomped on past it, Che paused, for it was open.

'Uncle—' she began, in warning, and then Stenwold roared in outrage.

In the passage right in front of him there was a man, wrapped in dark cloth. A shortsword glinted. He must have been sitting in the shadows of the landing, waiting silent and patient, but he was all movement now.

Six

Stenwold went reeling backwards as the intruder's blade passed before his chest and then the Beetle's heavy hand lashed out and slapped him across the head, sending the assassin reeling into the wall. Stenwold went for him barehanded but the man was quicker, lunging with the blade and slicing a gash across Stenwold's arm. The Beetle fell away with a hiss of pain and hit the door of his own bedroom, slamming it open and tumbling backwards inside.

Che did not hesitate. Even as the dark figure turned she was on him, having instantly drawn the knife she carried everywhere for protection. It was a tiny thing, barely four inches of blade, but she raked it savagely across his back. At the same time someone else could be heard on the stairs, and that surely did not bode well. Stenwold's attacker had swiftly rounded on her. For the moment he held her off at his sword's length because in the dark he had not realized that she was just a teenage girl with a tiny knife. But heading up the stairs was a man wrapped in black, slender, grasping a long blade in one hand and a short one in the other. Before he could use either against Che, suddenly Tynisa was there too.

She had been doing as instructed, packing for a dangerous journey, so in her hand was her own rapier, a slim blade to match the new assassin's own. She started back as he ran at her, but her guard was up when he lunged, and she deflected both blades aside. He was quick, light on his feet and striking at her from all angles. She could fend him off satisfactorily but he had his offhand blade always ready for an opening, so bind and parry as she might she could not press the attack.

Meanwhile, in the very stance of the man she was facing, Che recognized his realization of the meagre opposition he faced. Determinedly she went straight for him even as he made up his mind. His blade was just drawing back as she lunged and slammed into him low down, shoulder to his chest, even as his blade passed inches over her head. The collision knocked the breath from her and she bounced off him and would have fallen had she not grasped the folds of his tunic. She had cut him again, a shallow line across one side. Gripping his belt she clumsily grappled for his sword, hanging on tight as he tried to cast her away. She was so close she could smell the sour taint of beer on his breath, even the blacking that he had used to dull the glint of his blade. He kept trying to throw her out to arm's length to get a chance at impaling her but she clung on stubbornly, trying to get her knife to him in turn.

Tynisa waited for her own opponent's next attack. Already she had gained a little measure of him. He was quick but unimaginative, his strikes were textbook. The next time he lunged for her, she passed under his blade. His offhand darted in, as she knew it would, but she was already past it, suddenly faster. As she passed him, she tried to bring the razor-sharp edge of her rapier across his throat, but he was pushing forward. The curved guard jagged off his chin and his feet tangled with hers. They were both off balance in a moment.

She felt the balcony rail at her back, and then a moment later it was snapping under their combined weight, pitching them both into the hallway below. But she had a free hand and he did not. She hauled at him as they went over, trying to thrust him ahead of her.

As his comrade vanished, the first assassin swore and

hurled Che away from him. She hit the passage floor hard, but kept hold of her knife, desperately turning to menace him with it. He paused, catching his breath for a heartbeat, as swords scraped and rattled below them.

'You!' bellowed Stenwold, from the doorway of his room. The assassin turned swiftly, and froze.

The reason was that Stenwold held a weapon levelled. It was a crossbow without the arms, a great, heavy four-barrelled thing with a quartet of broad metal bolts jutting aggressively out at the world, resembling javelins more than anything else. Che knew it as a piercer, and that there was a prodigious firepowder charge just waiting for the touch of a lever to explode.

The assassin remained poised, and Stenwold studied him levelly, despite the blood soaking his own arm. 'Sword on the ground, and perhaps—'

Che noticed the man about to spring, hoping to catch Stenwold in mid-sentence, and she stabbed down with the knife hard enough to pin his foot to the floor. At that moment Stenwold pulled the trigger. It was as if the sound swallowed up every inch of the house, as a double charge of firepowder erupted in the confined space of the piercer. The assassin was punched off his feet, flung all the way down the landing and pinned to the far wall by three of the bolts. The fourth, without any human obstacle to travel through, rammed itself so far into the bare wall itself that its tip must have been visible from outside.

The quiet that then descended, laced with the acrid smell of the spent powder, was absolute.

'Where's . . . Tynisa?' Stenwold asked heavily. Che pointed mutely downwards.

They got to the broken rail and looked down to see her standing with the second assassin splayed like a doll on the ground before her. As she stood, head bowed, looking at the first man she had ever killed, the blood-shiny rapier was still in her hand.

Che heard her uncle suck in his breath. 'Hammer and tongs,' he murmured. 'It's *her*.' Che caught a glint in his eye, some token of recognition that had nothing to do with Tynisa. The surroundings must be different, as must the dead man below, but this very tableau, this moment of stillness and contemplation, had caught him off guard. For just a second he was twenty years younger and elsewhere, seeing and wondering about some event long past.

And then Tynisa looked up at him, pale and staring. He hurried down the stairs and took her in his arms. *The first death*, he thought. There came to him the image of an orthopter's cabin in Myna with that Wasp soldier falling back. *The first death by our hands is always hard*. She would survive it, though, he knew. *It's in her blood*.

A moment later Tynisa pushed away from him and went over to Che, taking her foster-sister's hand.

'You're not hurt?' she said. 'I thought he had you.'

Che blinked at her. 'Uncle Sten killed him.' She had not expected such sympathy.

'I need you to do something for me,' said Stenwold to them both. He was now sitting on a nearby couch, the dead man at his feet. 'One of you go and get Doctor Nicrephos for me, quick as you can.'

'Doctor Nicrephos?' Che asked in surprise. 'But you want a proper doctor, surely?'

'He's an old charlatan, that one,' Stenwold agreed. 'But he knows his poisons, though. These killers . . . weren't using clean blades.'

Tynisa was out of the door in an instant, leaving Che gaping at him, feeling suddenly cold.

'But you . . . You can't . . .'

Stenwold managed a smile. 'Oh, I'm an old Beetle, remember, Cheerwell. My insides are made of leather. Take more than some street-corner thug's blade-spit to floor me. Still, maybe you should reload the piercer. Spare bolts and powder are in my room.'

She fairly flew back up the stairs, leaving him for a moment with his thoughts. He peeled the cloth from the face of the assassin there, recognizing the stamp of a halfbreed's features: a blend of Spider, Beetle and Ant-kinden. The other one had been pure renegade Ant, so Cheerwell had done well to even stave the man off. 'Local talent, these two,' he said to himself. Not Wasps, and nobody the Wasp Empire would either own or be connected to. The game had clearly changed.

Che came back down the stairs, stuffing heavy bolts into the piercer's muzzles. 'Will Salma and Totho be in danger too?' she asked.

'Tonight? I don't think so – but tomorrow is anyone's guess. Cheerwell, I'm changing my plans.'

'Changing them how?'

'I have four seats reserved on the *Sky Without* for tomorrow. You're going to be on it too. All of the Majestic will.'

'But you said—'

'Plans change. Now I need to stay here long enough to close my books, so I'll join you when I can.' Seeing her about to protest further he held up a hand. 'And I don't mean that as some kind of euphemism for "I'll never see you again", Cheerwell. I never was a death-or-glory boy. I'll catch up with you all in Helleron, but for now, as I said, I want to keep you safe. It's a mad thought, but I think you'll be safer with my people in Helleron than here alone with me.'

Tynisa was back now, pulling in her wake a stooped, grey-skinned figure. Che stood back as the old Moth-kinden entered. She recognized him from the College but he taught the sort of disreputable classes that sensible young Beetles did not choose to attend. He was the very picture of a storybook wizard, with his long hair gone a dirty grey, and his slanted eyes blank-white, without iris or pupil.

'Master Nicrephos,' Stenwold began. 'I have need of your services.'

The Moth laughed between his teeth. 'A believer at last, are you?' he replied in almost a whisper. 'No? Well, no matter. This morning I was your debtor. Tomorrow I shall not be, hmm?'

'Just come and shake your bones or whatever,' Stenwold grunted. 'And then consider all debts paid.'

Stenwold had gone out somewhere before Che was even up, leaving her with a clutching feeling of anxiety. The events of the previous night came back with a jolt at the sight of the ruined banister.

The world has gone mad.

She had watched while Nicrephos had ostentatiously tended to Stenwold's wound, and had ground her teeth in frustration at it. This was no doctoring. Nicrephos had muttered charms over the wound, burned a few acrid herbs and tied a little bag of something about the Beetle's arm. Stenwold had just sat there patiently, his dark features gone grey with pain or poison, leaving the quack to go about his mummery – even thanked him when he had finished.

After the Moth had gone, Che had rounded on her uncle. 'What was that all about? You can't tell me you believe in that nonsense, like some . . . credulous *savage*?'

Stenwold shrugged. 'I can't pretend it makes any sense to me, but I've seen Doctor Nicrephos bring back from death's doorstep a man that all the real doctors in this town had given up on.'

'But he barely even touched the wound!'

Stenwold shrugged – then winced. 'It's easy, once the lamps are lit, to scoff at shadows,' was all he said, and then he had retired to bed.

And this morning he was gone already to bustle about the town, but at least he had scribbled Tynisa and Che terse instructions.

The back room of the Taverna Merraia, third hour after dawn. Be packed. And that was all it said.

The girls walked there together, and close together, for there were a lot of foreigners about on the streets during the Games. Some were simply merchants and artisans but others had a darker look. More was bought and sold during the tenday of the games, of all commodities, than in the entire month beforehand. As was their way, Beetles never let such a gathering go to waste. In the simple walk from Stenwold's villa to the taverna they encountered a band of renegade Vekken mercenaries, all swagger and glower. They saw a Tarkesh slavemaster in conference with two Spider buyers, because whilst one could not own a slave within Collegium's walls, one could sell them on paper – a neat distinction. There were men who looked like brigands here to tout their loot, Spiderland nobles and their cadres of followers, Mantis-kinden killers-for-hire with their bleak stares . . . It was a relief to simply reach the taverna without some new assailant dashing at them from the crowds, and both of them had hands close to sword hilts. Tynisa might have her customary rapier, but this time Che wore a proper shortsword, Helleron made. When the killers next came hunting her, she would provide them with a real fight.

The Taverna Merraia was done up in a half-hearted Fly-kinden style, with low-set doorways they had to stoop through, and an interior walled with packed earth and carved wooden columns on three of its sides, while open shutters extended almost the whole of the fourth. The moment they entered, the miniature owner bustled out to them. 'Ladies, ladies, pray let us not expose you to all these rude gapers. Come, I have a private room for you, yes?' He raised a bushy eyebrow, and Che nodded slowly. It seemed that Uncle Stenwold had indeed been busy.

The back room was the real Fly-kinden thing, rather than the basic tat displayed out front for the tourists. The table stood barely more than six inches off the ground, and there were cushions instead of chairs. Most importantly, should they need it, there was an escape hatch in the ceiling that would take them out to a street running behind the taverna. Flies were known for such fallbacks.

'He must have sent word to the others too,' Che guessed.

Tynisa merely nodded. She had been oddly quiet today, hardly a word from her since they got up at dawn. Che examined her companion's face, but the deftly applied make-up hid any clue as to whether the girl had slept well or not.

'So? Last night?' she said finally.

Tynisa looked at her, captured her stare. 'Have you . . . *you* haven't ever . . . killed anyone, have you?' the Spider-kinden asked quietly.

Che shrugged, trying to look casual. 'I could have killed that one that cut Uncle Sten. I got him . . . a couple of times.'

Tynisa continued to hold her eyes until eventually Che admitted, 'But no. I haven't. I just *fought*, like we do at Prowess Forum. Till then I don't think I really realized it could be . . . for real.'

'I killed him.' Tynisa looked down at her hands. 'He was good, but I killed him.' With great care she drew the rapier from its slim scabbard, and Che could remember being very jealous when Stenwold had bought it for her. It was a beautiful Spider-forged piece of work. They were not great smiths by and large, but certain skilled crafts held their interest, and sword-crafting was one of them. This one was done as a copy of the Mantis style, the back-curving guard that protected the hand was formed into sharp, curving leaves and the blade was ground to a slightly uneven taper that nonetheless left both edges keen. True Mantis-work was rare and expensive as weapons came, and Stenwold had not been able to find the genuine article for sale. They might be tree-living savages in so many ways, without comprehension of all the great things the revolution had brought to the Lowlands world, but when the Mantis produced a sword, or a bow, or anything else they turned their craft to, they made it with the skill of ages.

'You *had* to kill him,' Che said solemnly, her eyes still on the blade. 'He would have killed you otherwise. Don't feel bad.'

'I felt . . .' Tynisa pursed her lips together. 'I felt so *alive.*'

'Alive?'

'In that moment, when I was past his guard, it was . . . Help me, Che, but it was wonderful. I forgot everything else. At that moment I didn't care about you, or Sten. I just knew that I had *won*, and it was good. It was so good.'

Che remembered the girl's sudden concern after the fight, Tynisa trying to make up for the remorse she should have been feeling. 'I don't know, I—' she started, and just then, blessedly, Totho and Salma were being ushered into the room by the taverna's owner. Totho was bundled into a shapeless long coat, a canvas bag slung over one shoulder, so it was Salma who must have drawn any looks all the way across Collegium. He was known for dressing well, but understated, always fashionable, never gauche. Now he was hidden somewhere within a hugely elaborate, high-collared robe and the garment was – as the saying went – almost splendid enough to be offered its own department at College. Blue and green and red, iridescent like mother of pearl, its curling hems were lined with plates of gold.

'What exactly are *you* got up as?' Tynisa demanded, recovering her customary cool. 'Or did Sten's note actually say you should look like a mad foreigner?'

'It's not my fault that nobody in this forsaken backward little town ever dresses properly,' said Salma. 'What was I supposed to do with my robe? Leave it behind?'

'Don't you have any . . . bags?'

Salma opened the robe to reveal an inner garment of simply cut turquoise cloth lined with numerous pockets. There was even a sword scabbard sewn into it containing a short-bladed weapon of odd design.

'You do realize that someone tried to kill us last night?' Tynisa told him, although there was no reason he should know. 'I suppose at least it won't be me now drawing the arrow-shot.'

'Tried to kill you?' Totho asked, shocked.

'Tried to kill Uncle Sten,' corrected Che, 'only we got in the way. The killers, they're . . . dead, both of them.' She remembered how the city guard had finally been called, and Stenwold had sent them on their way with the bodies and no questions asked, a clink of coin. Everyone, even Stenwold, seemed to be pretending that nothing had happened, and she suspected this was the way of it for those with secrets that too many questions could compromise.

Stenwold came in just then, without ceremony. 'Good,' he said, on seeing them all present. He settled himself on the floor across the table from them, making sure he had the door on his right hand and not to his back. 'Time for some truths,' he began. 'Although if you're half the people I take you for, there'll be no surprises. Che and Tynisa know the histories I've been teaching by heart now, and Salma's Commonweal has first-hand experience of the Wasp Empire's ways. And Totho . . .'

The artificer swallowed. 'I listen, sir.'

'So what is it you want to do?' Che asked Stenwold. 'About the Wasps, I mean.'

He nodded. 'The Lowlands has not changed – its political balance anyway – has not for perhaps five hundred years. It's incredible to think it, but if you discount the usual jostling rivalry between the Ant city-states it's much the same as it has been ever since the revolution. Perhaps conditions are better, in some places, but there has been a balance struck that has lasted, and that has had little to do with outside pressures and everything to do with our self-made isolation.' Try as he might he could not keep the College Master out of his voice. 'The world beyond our boundaries has contrived to assist us. The Spiderlands beyond Everis have always seen us as a resource, an amusement and an oubliette. The Barrier Ridge cuts us off from the north so well that most Lowlanders know little or nothing about Salma's home except the name "the Commonweal". Luckily for us, they have never been of a mind to impose their civilization on us. Salma's people are more inward-looking than we. A fair assessment, Salma?'

'Both harsh and fair,' his pupil agreed.

'And to the east . . . Well, most of it's desert, and what's not is a patchwork of little cities and hill tribes, and none of them rich or sophisticated, or that's what the textbooks say. Well, in the last two generations all that has changed, and keeps changing, and it will change faster than anyone wants.'

He sighed. 'Looking at you, the lot of you . . . it takes me back. When I was not so much older than you are, I and some like-minds headed east, to see if the disturbing news from that quarter was true. It was indeed, for a new power has arisen. The Wasp-kinden, who are described in our oldest records as barbarians primarily interested in cutting each other's heads off, are an *empire* now. Their borders have since been pushed to not so very far east of Helleron and Tark. There is a city called Myna . . .' The memories swelled in him, and he closed his eyes. 'We witnessed the fall of Myna, and realized a little of the Wasp dream. One world, one empire: that sums it up neatly.'

'But this must have been . . . what, twenty years ago?' Tynisa objected. 'So where *are* they? Why aren't they all over Helleron? Why aren't they at Collegium's gates with an army?'

'As to Helleron, they are familiar with the Wasps. Indeed, the merchants of Helleron have been doing well out of importing the spoils of their war, and they sell them the latest in Beetle-made arms in return. They want to see the Wasps as just another city-state that is constantly fighting, never really changing. There was a time, during the Empire's war with Salma's people, when enough of Helleron suddenly woke up to what was brewing on their doorstep. But the Wasps came in with their treaties and their promises, and signed lots of comforting pieces of paper about the Empire going no further than Myna and, so long as the trade revenue keeps coming in, the Helleren magnates overlook just what it is they're trading in. And perhaps those that don't overlook it don't get to live very long. And as for what their army is up to . . . Salma, you're best placed to answer that one.'

Salma's smile widened a little, but lost its warmth. 'I did wonder what you knew, when you took me as a pupil so easily.'

The other three were staring at him dubiously, and he shook his head. 'When I first came here, it had been only a year since the Twelve-Year War ended. Twelve years' conflict between my people and the Wasp-kinden.'

Their expressions had become intense as they tried to assimilate this, to stretch their minds around the periods of time involved.

'The Wasps only stopped their march forward when they became overextended. There was a rebellion behind their lines, conquered people trying to cast off the yoke. The Wasps then offered us a chance at peace, and by that time we had no choice but to take the terms they gave. They demanded three border principalities. Over here, in extent, that's from about Lake Sideriti right to the west coast, taking in all of Collegium and Vek along the way. The Wasps then turned round to crush the rebellions as we sat there with our Treaty of Pearl. We're still waiting for them to come back. So that explains where their army has been, all those years. Not sitting idle, believe me.' Salma sat back, watching them.

'And my agents in Helleron, who keep an eye and ear open for me, lead me to believe that the Lowlands will be next to feel the rod,' Stenwold finished. 'If nothing else it will mean that, when the Wasps move on the Commonweal again, they'll come at it from both east and south, and with Helleron's foundries supplying their army.'

'So what can we do?' Che asked the question in all of their minds.

Stenwold sagged. 'I had hoped that this would go differently, but time's a wheel that crushes better plans than mine. I'd wanted to take you ... take some of you with me to Helleron, to introduce you and gather a little information there. Once you were ready, and when I knew enough about the Wasp plans, I would put a question to you.' He paused, aware that he was turning a page in their lives, and his, that could not be turned back. 'I am putting the question to you *now*. Will you help me against the Wasp-kinden? I want you to be my agents in this. Think very carefully before you answer. Now, Totho.'

The halfbreed had been very quiet, very still. He watched Stenwold warily as the old man pulled a scroll case from within his voluminous robe.

'I had to fight for these, but they're yours. I know that the Master Artificers have been stinting you, so I've made sure you've got everything that's due to you. Your College accredits, Totho. As of now you're confirmed as a journeyman artificer.'

Haltingly, the youth took the case from him, not even daring to open it. 'Thank you, sir.'

'I'm giving these to you now so that you'll have them, whatever you decide,' Stenwold explained awkwardly. 'Just so you know I'm not a blackmailer.' *Though only I know all the things this business has had me do.*

'What would we need to do for you?' Tynisa interrupted.

'Difficult to say, right now,' he admitted. 'But go to Helleron and ask questions, meet my people there. Collect word as it comes in from the east, and find out what the Wasp foothold in Helleron amounts to. Sound simple enough? Then remember that the Wasp-kinden have agents as well, or can hire them. Our late-night guests were just such an example. You'll need to keep a blade and a fallback escape plan handy.' He grimaced. 'As I said, this isn't how I wanted it but right now, with what happened last night, I want you safely out of Collegium. Just now it's more dangerous for you to be with me here, than alone in Helleron. So even if you don't want to take me up on this suggestion, you should still leave the city.' He looked from face to face. 'Any thoughts yet?'

Salma stretched luxuriously, making it all seem like some minor matter, barely worth his attention. 'Of course,' he said. 'I've already written to my Kin-obligate in the Commonweal. I'll be a servant of two masters, Master Maker. Two masters with a common enemy.'

'I can live with that, and you won't be the first in that position,' Stenwold said.

'I want to help, too,' Che added quickly. 'I'll do whatever you need me to.'

Stenwold felt a stab of sadness. *I had wanted to keep you from this.* But he had no safe place to keep her now, and if the Wasps marched on the Lowlands there might be no such place anywhere.

Tynisa still held her own counsel, but Stenwold saw Totho nod slowly, though not looking too happy about it.

'I'll go, sir,' he said simply, and Stenwold wondered if

it was the accredits just received that had made up his mind. Or maybe it was the lure of Helleron's machines and factories, or something else.

'Tynisa?'

She smiled at him. 'Uncle Sten, there are things you aren't telling us.'

And he thought, *Blood will out*, because *she* had seen through him just as sweetly. He was playing a blindfold game that all Spiders knew in their hearts from their earliest years. Here she was in his city, raised amongst his own resolutely practical kind, yet she could still have been a Spider-kinden princess.

'And some of it I *will* tell you, if and when you agree, and some of it is not safe yet for you to know.' *And let them brood on why that is.*

Tynisa was still looking at him keenly, considering carefully. 'And you're going to join us in Helleron?'

'As soon as I can. When I have closed my business here.'

Her smile changed from the penetrating to the blithe. 'Why not, then? Let's all go.' He wondered how much she had guessed at. Still, he now had their agreement, although he wondered if any of them had given it for the right reason. He was not even sure he would know what that right reason was.

'So what's the plan, Uncle Sten?' Tynisa prompted him.

'Well,' he said, 'before all this blew up I made arrangements for four of us to take the rail as far as Sarn, and go overland from there to Helleron. Sound good?'

'If there's no other way of travelling,' Salma said. The idea of the rail automotive obviously did not sit well with him.

'As it happens, there is,' Stenwold confirmed. 'If all of this was happening a month from now, we'd have the Iron Road to take us direct to Helleron, and damn the expense.

However, the promised last hundredweight of track is slow to be laid, and we need to shift promptly. Because of this, by midday you four will be on board the *Sky Without*, which is leaving for Helleron today.'

'The *Sky Without* being some manner of flying boat, as I recall,' Salma remarked.

'An airship,' Totho breathed. 'Very new. Very large.'

Salma grimaced. 'Even better.'

'I will send one of the Messengers Guild to Helleron. It's about the only way to cover the distance before the *Sky* does. I'll let my people know you're coming. They should be meeting you at Benevolence Square, which is close on the airfield. My chief ally in Helleron goes by the name of Scuto, but the man you'll meet will be Bolwyn.'

'Well, Bolwyn's a good Beetle name. Is Scuto maybe Fly-kinden then?' Tynisa asked.

'I'll . . . let Bolwyn introduce you,' said Stenwold non-committally. From inside his robes he fished out a square of folded paper. 'Here. Keep this safe. This is Bolwyn.'

It was a portrait, a pencil sketch done with a minimum of lines and shading, but still giving a clear picture of a heavy-jawed middle-aged Beetle-kinden man. The signature, in spiky writing at its foot, read 'NERO'.

'Any questions?' Stenwold asked, after they had each taken a turn examining the portrait.

'Yes, what about you?' Che asked.

He smiled at her fondly. 'You're worried about me?'

'I am, Uncle Sten, yes.'

'Why shouldn't you be?' he said. 'A man past his prime, like me? Too great at the waist, too small of strength. A historian better suited to books than the blade. That's what you think, is it?'

'Well—'

'Because that's what the Wasps think too, I hope.' Stenwold put on a smile for their benefit, but inside he was thinking, *That Thalric, though. I can't see him falling for it*. 'I'll be with you in Helleron before you know it,' he assured them.

He took a good look at them, though, before they all left the taverna by the back entrance. His last agents. His ward, his niece. His chips were on the table now, and he had nothing held back. It was win-all or lose-all on this hand.

I wish I had Tisamon here. Stenwold used to fear nothing when walking in Tisamon's shadow.

He tipped the Merraia's owner handsomely for use of the room, and more for telling skewed stories later, about who had come in and who had left where. Those four young people had walked in free and innocent but left with his mark on them. He could make a list of those others who had taken that mark to early graves. Not a great list, true, but he had no more of them he could afford to lose.

He hurried off into the brightening morning light, wondering just how many eyes were fixed on him, how many of the busy crowd were marking his steps.

Seven

The airfield lay eastwards and seawards of Collegium, beyond its walls, although smaller airstrips had sprung up within the city wherever the rich magnates could find space for them. The earliest flying machines had been erratic things. The accepted way of getting them off the ground had been to launch them off the promontory beside the harbour, and hope the wind took them before the sea did. The science of aviation had advanced a little since then, of course.

Collegium boasted the largest airfield in all the Lowlands, with Helleron a close second. Beetles and artifice, Beetles and industry, they always went hand in hand. When Ant-kinden built fliers or automotives, they were intended for war. Beetles built them for all purposes, for freight, for exploration, for the sole sake of the mechanics, for simply travelling faster between two points.

Even so, air travel by anything other than Art-wings or a mount was a new thing to the Lowlands. The first reliable flier had been tested here four generations ago, but regular air travel was one generation old at best, and expensive too. Collegium's airfield had some four dozen fliers arrayed across its hard-packed earth. Each was different, the individual peculiarities of inventor and smithy making their mark. Orthopters, heliopters, even a few fixed-wings, but towering over them was a pair of dirigibles with their inflated gasbags, and towering over *them* floated the *Sky Without*.

'I've read all about her,' Totho was saying. 'She's the first of a new generation of lighter-than-air fliers. Most of the others of her size use hot air, you see, which means half the weight you actually lift is due to the boilers and the burners.'

Tynisa, walking behind him, had never seen him so animated. He was a real hermit crab of a man, she mused. What emerged infrequently out of his shell was nothing you'd guess at from the outside.

'But the *Sky* doesn't use air at all,' Totho went on. 'The bag's filled with precipitate of mordant aquillin, which is actually lighter than the air, and so you can free up so much more space for the freight and passengers, and the engines—'

'Toth, will you take a moment to think about who you're talking to here,' Salma said to him. 'Old news to Che, I'm sure, and, well . . .'

Totho craned back at him. 'I don't understand.'

'No, *I* don't understand – not a word. You're wasting your explanatory talents on me.'

'Oh.' Sudden comprehension came to Totho. 'But even if you don't, you must have seen—'

'We don't have air ships in the Commonweal, Toth,' Salma said patiently. 'Think about it. We don't have artificers. We don't have automotives or engine-mills or even *crossbows* in the Commonweal, now, do we?'

'But . . .' Totho floundered for a second. 'Amongst *all* of you?'

Salma grinned. 'You ever see a Mantis mechanic, Toth?'

'I . . . No, of course not.'

'You'll not see one amongst the Dragonfly-kinden, either. Nor anyone from the Commonweal.'

'Sorry, it's just . . . hard to grasp. Tynisa?'

She shook her head. 'Sorry, Totho. All machinery bibble-babble to me.'

'But you were brought up here in Collegium!' he protested. 'Surely . . .'

'Sorry. You ever see a Spider-kinden crossbow-woman? Being Apt to machines isn't something you can just pick up. You're born to it or you're not.'

'Don't worry.' Che patted Totho's arm. 'I was listening. Tell *me*.' Privately, though, as Totho's enthusiasm waxed again, she was considering what it must be like being Tynisa, or Salma, in Collegium. Or Doctor Nicrephos, or Piraeus, or any of them: all those who had lost out in the revolution, those centuries before.

She had seen Tynisa with a crossbow, once. It had been when they were both around twelve, and Tynisa had been determined to become good with it, as she had been with everything else she put her hand to. That day lingered in the memory because it was the first time Che had found something she herself could do, that her foster-sister could not.

But it's not hard, she remembered saying patiently. *You just point it at the target and pull the lever.* And the staggering weight of her understanding that Tynisa just *could not* grasp the notion, could not understand that the action led to the result. She almost shot Stenwold when she finally clutched the weapon so hard she mistakenly triggered it, and she could not even begin to reload or re-cock it. It was not just that she had never been trained, or taught. It had all been there for her, if only she could adapt her mind to take it in.

Persistent myth related that the crossbow was the first tool of the revolution. Almost certainly there had been something else, something less warlike and more practical. The crossbow was what won the battles, though. Any fool could pick up a crossbow and kill a man with it, any Beetle-kinden, or Ant, anyone *Apt*. Bows were an art-form, crossbows but a moment in the learning, in the making. The world had been turned upside down within a generation by men and women armed with the crossbow and the pulley, the hand-pump and the watermill. All the old masters of the Lowlands had been unthroned, their slaves prising mastery of the world from their impotent hands. There were a few exceptions, as always. She had heard of itinerant Beetle scholars going native deep in the forests of the Mantids, propitiating spirits and painting their faces, and fifty years ago there had even been a Moth artificer at Collegium, brilliant and half-mad. The old races of the superstitious night were waning, though. Only the Spider-kinden held on to their power, and that because they could play the younger races like a musical instrument. The world belonged to the Apt: Beetles, Ants, and most Fly-kinden these days, the races of the bright sun that drove out the shadows.

And also the Wasps: an entire Empire of the Apt. That was not a comforting thought.

'Salma,' Che began. Nobody was going to like this question, and she knew the answer would be less popular still. 'Your people fought the Wasps for twelve years?'

'They did,' he confirmed.

'How . . . Don't take this the wrong way, but how did they hold out for twelve years, with no artificers, no machines or modern weapons?'

He laughed at that, although his laugh was hollow. 'We are archers without peer, Che, and the Wasp-kinden are clumsy in the air when we fight them. We are quick and skilled and stealthy by turns.' Something lively went out of his voice. 'But, most of all, we sent our soldiers against them in wave after wave after wave. We sold each inch of Commonweal land to them for ten times its weight in blood, mostly. That is what we did when the Wasp Empire came.' He had suddenly stopped walking and they turned back to him, Che desperately wishing she had some way of taking her question back, of not hearing the answer.

He was still smiling at them and that was the worst part.

It was Salma's couldn't-care-less smile that they all knew well, and it clung on even when he said, 'At the battle of Shan Real the ground was so soaked in blood that their machines sunk in and could not be moved, and we flew over them and shot them as they tried to climb out.'

'You were there?' Che said. The other two were leaving this particular pitfall conversation to her, and quite right too.

'No, I wasn't there. I was too young, and far away,' he said, and shook his head. 'I do apologize, really. Tasteless stuff this early in the morning. Sometimes you . . . Lowlanders, though, you just don't understand how things are.'

'I know, we're all barbarians really,' said Tynisa wryly, 'scratching ourselves in public and sleeping in the same room as the dirigibles.'

His smile regained its stability. 'Bunch of savages, the lot of you,' he agreed. 'Now let's get on board this wretched flying machine before Totho explodes with impatience, shall we?'

The designer had fitted three decks into the gondola of the *Sky Without*, although without allowing much headroom on any of them. Relieved of the machinery that a hot-air dirigible required, the staterooms took up the top tier, where the view was marginally grander. Below that were the common room, the kitchen and the cramped crew quarters, and below that again those areas of the ship that the passengers would prefer not to see: freight storage holds and the mechanics' walkways that led to the ship's three engines.

As soon as his companions were ensconced in the common room, Totho made his apologies and found his way below with unerring instinct. He remembered when the *Sky Without* had been originally commissioned, designed in Collegium the same year as Totho had begun his studies, and with its major parts cast in the foundries at Helleron and then hauled at a snail's pace overland during the best part of eleven months. The *Sky* was now due to make the return journey in a little over a tenday because, for such a gargantuan vessel, she was fast.

Up on an exposed gantry Totho found the secret of that speed soon enough. Out from the body of the gondola, but still in the shadow of the airbag, two engineers were testing the starboard steering propeller. They glanced at him as he climbed hand over hand up to them, and one of them said, 'No passengers here. Go back to the decks.'

'Excuse me, but . . .' It was the first time he'd been able to say it. 'I'm an artificer from the College and I just wanted to have a look at the engines here.'

The effect was all he could have wished for. Their closed faces opened up instantly, and the fact that he was a halfbreed, which had caused their noses to wrinkle a moment before, was now forgotten.

The *Sky* had three engines, but the big central one, mounted in cast iron over the stern, was just a standard oil-burning propeller that gave the ship her speed. Totho was far more interested in the guiding props set out on pontoons. They were something quite new, quite different. He watched with fascination as the two engineers hauled chains and levers to bring heavy, dull-looking blocks into place around the propeller vanes, and saw the blades start to spin, first slowly and then faster and faster, all with no more sound than a faint hum. Soon the speed was enough to tug and swing the *Sky* about as she hung still anchored to the airfield. The engineers then exchanged a few satisfied words and began changing the configuration of the blocks to reverse the angle and direction of the blades.

Magnets, all done with magnets, the cutting edge of the artificer's trade. This took the sort of precision engineering that would not have been possible ten years earlier, but magnetic force could do almost anything with metal components. A few years ago one of the College Masters had produced the first magnetic crossbow, simple induction sending an all-metal bolt further and faster than any tensioned string. Totho had coveted that weapon, or any of the expensive copies that trickled into the arms market afterwards, but the price had been vastly beyond his wildest dreams.

'You'd better go within now,' said one of the engineers. 'I reckon the master's going to have us aloft any moment.'

But before Totho could ask to remain, to watch the airfield and Collegium dwindle, the scrubby countryside become like a tattered map, the other engineer put in, 'No chance. Always someone that has to pitch up late. You'd think it'd be different on a ship as swish as this, but look.'

And Totho looked, and there, practically beneath his feet, were the Wasps.

There were a half-dozen of them, a couple in gold-edged tunics that passed for civilian dress, but the rest in their banded armour, and they were stepping onto the winch-platform to be lifted aboard.

A jolt of alarm went through him, and he nearly lost his grip on the gantry, but a moment later he was going hand-over-hand as fast as he dared towards the far end hatch. His Ancestor Art came to his aid, making his feet sure, his hands cling tight, but still he knew that he would not get to the others before the Wasps had seen them. When he finally made the common room, the Wasps were just entering, and he was able to see, in all the detail he could have wished, his companions' reactions. Che twitched and stared at them helplessly and, though Salma's smile did not slip, even Totho could see how tense he was. Tynisa, however, seemed all ease as she reclined back in her seat, even sending the Wasp leader a smile of invitation. After that, Che's evident panic went unnoticed.

The Wasps were clearly searching. They were foreigners here, and doing their best to be restrained, but from the way their soldiers passed about the common room it was clear that they were looking intently at every face. The other passengers frowned at them or ignored them. They were mostly Beetle-kinden merchants whose business activities were strung between Collegium and Helleron, and the bustling Wasp soldiers attracted a lot of comment on how outlanders did not know how to behave. Of the other passengers, a well-dressed Spider with his small entourage fixed them with a narrow look that did not invite questioning, and the trio of card-playing Fly-kinden remained hunched over their drinks and bets and did their best to remain undisturbed. In the corner a Fly musician picked at a dulcimer, making a great show of ignoring everyone else.

The leader of the Wasps, a tall and lean man with a face that smiled both readily and shallowly, stopped by the table that Tynisa and the others had picked out. Across the common room Totho hung back in the shadows, trying to envisage some desperate rescue he could assay. There were just a few words exchanged, though, with Tynisa, and then the man moved on. Totho saw one of his soldiers come to him and point very obviously at Salma in his finery, but the officer had a harsh word for that kind of talk, whatever it was, and the soldier slunk back, his barbed fists clenched.

As soon as the way was clear Totho made a hasty journey of it over to their table. 'What happened?' he demanded. 'Why didn't they—?'

'They didn't because we weren't looking as guilty as a rich Fly, which is exactly the way you're looking right now,' Tynisa reproached him. 'Sit down, Toth.'

Totho did so, hands folded together in his lap. 'So what—?'

'We think they must be looking for Uncle Sten,' Che explained. 'They certainly had a very good look at all those traders over there, all Beetles and all around his age.

They'll have his description, but obviously not ours. Uncle Sten must have done his best to make sure there was nothing linking him to us. He must even have got someone else to make the bookings.'

'But one of them was . . . pointing at Salma.'

'Must be a veteran,' Salma said carelessly.

'We should be all right now. We'll just keep our heads down by staying in our stateroom,' said Che.

'Why?' Tynisa countered. 'If they're not looking for us, they're not.'

The floor beneath them, indeed the walls around them and the ceiling above them, flexed a little, and began to vibrate gently. Just at the edge of hearing there was the heavy, cavernous sound of the main engine. The *Sky Without* was now underway.

'It's going to be a long trip,' said Salma, rubbing at his forehead, the vibrations obviously bothering him.

'And I'm certainly not going to spend it in hiding,' Tynisa replied firmly. 'In fact, I'm going to start, right away, what we'll all be doing in Helleron. If we're spies, let's be spies.'

Che's face twisted. 'I'm not sure . . .'

'What did you have in mind?' interrupted Salma.

'That Wasp officer seemed like the talking type,' Tynisa said idly. 'You could see it in his face. He's been posted down here, miles away from anywhere he knows, with nothing but a pack of dull blades for company. I think he'd be glad of a little diversion.'

'But . . . he's the *enemy*!' hissed Che.

Tynisa laughed at the horror on her face. 'I've got his measure, Che. I can keep him strung out until we reach Helleron, and anyway, he looks the type who likes to impress. How better to impress a lady than to boast about the size of your empire?'

★

After she had left them, Salma leant over to Totho and said, 'I assume you're going to burrow right into this vessel's organs, or whatever they're called.'

'Engines,' Totho corrected. 'But yes, I had thought . . .'

'I may not know much about this boat-thing, but I see how you might get to see a great many places on board by simply going where the servants go. So go keep an eye on her, if you can.'

Totho looked over at Tynisa, who was now approaching the Wasp officer. 'Depends where she decides to go, but I'll try.'

His name was Halrad and it was easier than Tynisa had imagined. Here was a captain who should, in his opinion, have already been a major, which she gathered was a higher rank. He considered himself a clever man, a strategist and a sophisticate, and he was annoyed at being dragged away from Collegium before he could fully learn and understand it. He had wanted to see the Games and watch the (undoubted) victories of the Wasp-kinden team (the Wasp *race* as he put it). He disliked and disdained his underlings, who were never far from him, and she could see clearly how they disliked him right back. In short he felt misused and under-appreciated and within a brief while, she could play him like a kite in a good breeze.

The captain was interesting company, she could not deny: not so much for himself, but for what he was. At first she had thought of him as just like any of the self-important grandees of Collegium she had met with, for where was the difference between this soldier and an Ant commander or Beetle officer of the watch? To begin with, she thought she had the measure of his type. As their conversation progressed, however, as he opened up and they drifted from the common room towards his chambers, she sensed a jag of iron there. He spoke a lot of the world, the Empire, his family's status back home, his future plans. The word he spoke most was 'mine'. Tynisa was already quite used to her beaus boasting of their material possessions, their clothes, their investments and their property, but Halrad spoke exactly the same way about people, about cities, about concepts. He spoke in proprietary terms about literally everything, and when he said 'my future' he did not mean just the future in store for him, but the future that he would eventually own and control. In this way, she realized, he spoke for his entire people. He was the Empire in microcosm and she was fascinated.

And then they drank wine: he more than he realized and herself less than he thought. She asked him how he liked the Lowlands. 'Potential,' he decided. 'You have many things here that we do not.' His meaning, even in the words left unspoken, was clear. Some of those things would be cast aside by the Wasps, others possessed. Possessed as he *possessed* his rank and the soldiers who obeyed him because of it. Possessed as he had villas now in two conquered cities, and possessed the slaves who served in them.

Tynisa herself had not grown up, as most Spider-kinden would, with slaves at her beck and call. Beetle-kinden were resolutely proud about not keeping slaves: the trade was immoral, they said, and besides, paid servants worked harder. Even so, she knew that her own heritage was built on slaves' backs, that Ants still bred slaves in their cities, that the concept of slavery was hardly new. She would certainly not have wished Halrad for a master, and he seemed milder than most of his breed. One night, deep in his cups, he told her about a rebellion in Myna, the same town Stenwold had named. His slaves, he explained, had been implicated in the revolt. He had to have them killed, he said casually, but there were always other slaves available. Ants and Spiders would kill their slaves for the same reason, she was sure, but they would at least have been executing those they considered human beings. For Halrad it was just casting aside a piece of broken property, nothing more sentimental than that.

They were now five days and five nights into the *Sky Without*'s voyage, passing over rivers, hills, bandits and badlands with the ponderous grace of an aging matron. He had wanted to sleep with Tynisa, of course, but she was adept at putting *that* off: the effect of the drink, the lateness of the hour, and her own ineluctable talent for finding good cause to slip away. She kept him lusting, but even so, she was beginning to feel herself come under his proprietary aegis, realizing that she herself was, in his eyes, already *his*. That could cause problems later, unfortunately.

She had not ventured anything so crass as, 'So what are your plans?' but she had always kept a deft hand on the tiller of the conversation. She knew that he had been sent to find a certain man, a Beetle-kinden from the College, and that Halrad had already dismissed this mission as futile, blaming his superiors for the waste of time, for sending him too soon back to grimy Helleron. He assured her that the Wasps were in Collegium simply because it had been marked for them as the cultural centre of the Lowlands. In matters of learning and understanding, everyone looked to Collegium, and the Wasps wished to *understand*. He never completed this thought with, '. . . because we are going to invade you,' but it was there on his face, shining like a star, when he thought he had so cleverly hidden it.

Stenwold had been right in all particulars, and he had escaped the net as well. She found she was impressed and now she wondered, how much of her own string-pulling was inherent in her blood, how much she might have picked up, unknowing, from her foster-father.

*

Salma had been waiting, knowing it would happen. It could have happened anywhere, even in the common room. He knew they were not subtle, and that they had made plans the moment they had seen him.

In the event, it was a corridor on the stateroom deck, two of them suddenly blocking his path. They still wore their armour, with metal plates alternating in black and gold from throat to knee, tapering down from the waist. These were the light airborne, and his eye quickly noted each place where they were exposed: arms, legs, sides, face. These Wasps were equipped strictly for speed and flight.

Yet, they were bigger than he was, and there were two of them.

'Didn't think we'd see your kind here, Wealer,' the first one began.

Salma raised an eyebrow politely.

'On the run? Sinking ship? Is that it?' the soldier pressed on. His comrade said nothing, just watched him. His fists were barbed, two bony hooks curving from their backs.

Salma just smiled. He had only his under-robe on, but he keenly felt the weight of his sheathed sword inside it. He was poised, taut as wire within, yet outside he seemed without a care.

'Or maybe he's a spy,' the soldier said to his comrade. 'Wealer spy, where he's not wanted.'

'*Never* wanted,' the other man said.

'Don't think it'll do them much good,' the first said. 'Spies or no spies, we're coming back here, Wealer.' He stepped in close, trying to bulk out as large as he could before Salma, but the Dragonfly stayed put, his smile one of utter unconcern.

'I myself killed a lot of your kind,' the soldier continued, low and slow. 'Not proper war, though. Your lot don't even know how to fight a proper war. Ants, Bees, even Flies put up a better fight.'

Still smiling, Salma glanced brightly from him to his colleague. 'Sorry, gentlemen, do you have a point?'

'Yes we've got a point!' the soldier snapped. 'Our point is, that if you think this is far enough to run, think again! We're coming, Wealer. We're coming to your lands and we're coming here too!'

There was a silence then, in which Salma's smile only broadened. It was quiet enough to hear a scuff of feet from behind, as the two Beetle merchants who had appeared in the doorway of their stateroom backed off a little, staring.

The soldier who had been speaking backed away from Salma instantly, teeth bared and fists clenched so hard the knuckles were white. The other just went for him, though – scoring the barbs on his hands through the air where Salma had just been. The Dragonfly was already two steps further back and turned side on, waiting. He had not drawn his blade, but his hands were up, palms out and ready. He saw a flicker in his opponent's eyes: clearly he had seen Dragonflies fight unarmed before.

Even so the Wasp would have tried his luck, but his comrade, so talkative before, was now dragging him away. They had seriously broken orders, Salma guessed, but then he had heard it from a hundred throats that the one thing one could do so easily with the Wasp-kinden was provoke them.

Those engineers were a pragmatic lot. Where the metal met, as the saying went, there was little room for politics. When Totho had convinced them that he knew his trade they had let him in readily, his birth notwithstanding. He had always known how mechanics and engineers, all the grades and trades of artificers, kept an occult and inward society hidden away from laymen. This was his first taste of it: a dozen grimy, cursing men and women who regarded their human cargo as no more than freight that complained, and the airship's master and crew as mere ornament, but who themselves worked every hour each day sent, and kept the *Sky Without* aloft as surely as if they were carrying it on their shoulders.

For these few days he was one of them, and for the first time in his life nobody was looking askance at him because of his heredity – or being pointedly virtuous in ignoring it. If he could fix a piston, weld a joint and clear a fuel line then he was one of the elite, with the privileges and responsibilities that earned him. They were not all Beetle-kinden there, after all. A renegade Ant was lord of the main engine, having grown tired of war machines. There was a brace of Fly troubleshooters whose small frames and delicate fingers could fit into places the larger folk could not reach. There was another halfbreed, too, her ancestry being like his, Beetle and Ant conjoined. Her Ant parent had come from pale-skinned Tark, though, so she and Totho looked less like each other than anyone else on board.

A tenday into the voyage, with Helleron close on the horizon, Totho and a handful of the other engineers were called to the very belly of the ship, where he had never ventured before. Here, between the freight holds, gaped an open wound in the *Sky Without*'s underside. A broad rectangle of open sky was being winched open, with the dusty countryside appearing in a dun haze, far below, as they slowly lowered the *Sky*'s huge loading ramp into empty space.

'What's happening?' Totho asked.

'Incoming,' explained an engineer. 'New visitors, messengers probably. Look, there she is.'

Squinting, Totho made out a dark dot that closed, even as he watched, until he could identify it as a fixed-wing flier. Fixed-wings were new, quite the fastest things in the sky but expensive to build and easy to break. Totho watched its approach with interest. He had seen the design before, two stacked wings set back of the mid-point, the hull itself curving forwards and down like a hunched insect's body, with stabilizing vanes like a box-kite thrust forward. The single propeller engine, the drone of which came to them even at this distance, was fixed at the back, below a mounted ballista.

The hull of the fixed-wing was dark wood, and it was only as the craft was jockeying for position, trying to match speeds with the *Sky Without*, that Totho noticed the hurried repainting that had taken place: gold and black in ragged bars across the sides and the wings.

The flier swayed and darted, trying to meet up with the sloping runway the loading ramp had now been turned into. The engineer next to Totho swore. 'Bloody stupid, bringing a flying machine in like that. Had one once, an idiot who decided the best way to make the hatch was to come in at full speed. Went through three walls, punched out of the bows and dropped like a stone 'cos he's shorn his wings off doing it.'

At last the pilot managed the task, wings wobbling uncertainly, and the moving plane rolled up into the hold with the crew hauling the ramp closed as soon as it did. It was left sitting on the closed hatch with its propeller slowing gradually.

There were five Wasp soldiers in total packed into the flier, but one was very obviously in charge. He was standing up even as the engineers secured the ropes and clasps that ensured the loading ramp stayed closed.

The Wasp leader surveyed them all coldly, his gaze passing over Totho as easily as the rest. To him they were clearly all menials.

'Send a runner to Captain Halrad,' he ordered them, 'and tell him that Captain Thalric wants his company.'

The chief engineer folded her arms. 'Sorry, sir, I didn't hear you. Did you say you wanted to speak with the ship's master?' Her tone was profoundly unimpressed. If this Thalric had four armed soldiers at his back, she didn't even seem to have noticed.

The Wasp officer regarded her narrowly, and then mustered a tight smile. 'Of course that is what I meant,' he said, stepping out onto the *Sky*'s deck. 'Shall I bring my men along, or would it be possible for them to be billeted with their compatriots?'

Totho stepped back as the arrangements were made. As soon as it was possible, without catching the Wasps' notice, he was out of the hangar and running.

Eight

Captain Halrad had a professed fondness for Beetle-grown wine, Tynisa had soon discovered. He made a great show of sipping it, savouring the bouquet as he had undoubtedly seen the sophisticates do. He would tell her what a good blend this particular vintage was, when her own palette informed her it was what they called 'orchard wine', inferior stuff from the westerly vineyards.

She politely agreed with him. He was meanwhile telling her about life in the Wasp military. Or life in the Empire. It seemed to equate to the same thing.

'But you can't *all* be in the army,' she protested. 'How would that work?'

'A Wasp is a warrior. A male Wasp, I mean. There's no other livelihood,' he told her.

'What about artificers? Scholars?'

'Warriors,' he confirmed. 'Warriors first. If you're not a warrior you're less than a man, like our subject peoples.'

'But what about people with skills you need. *They* can't all be in the army too.'

'But they have to be,' he said. 'Let's say there was someone from outside whose particular assets,' he smiled at her, 'could be useful to the Empire. We'd *make* them army, army auxillian anyway, give them a rank. Without that, they would be nobody. No more than a slave, even.'

'You're looking at me as though *I* might be useful to the Empire,' she said, disarmingly coy.

'We'll make a general of you yet,' he promised, and then hissed wine through his teeth as someone suddenly hammered on the door of his stateroom.

'What is it?' he demanded, flinging the door open. One of his soldiers stood there at attention, and Tynisa saw something new, something urgent in his expression.

'You're to come right away, Captain,' the soldier announced, and when Halrad made to dispute this, he added, 'Captain Thalric says it.'

The change in Halrad was marked. Instantly he turned from being a man in control to a man being *watched*. Tynisa was fascinated. She stepped up behind him, asking, 'What is it?' In the doorway the soldier stared back at her with patent loathing.

'You just stay here,' Halrad told her shortly. 'I have to go. For your own safety you had better not leave this room.'

A moment later he was out of the room, and to her amazement she heard the key turn in the lock.

Che had tried her best to make herself useful on the voyage, but instead she had found herself without place, without purpose. Tynisa was off being either devious or indiscreet with the Wasp officer, Halrad, Totho had disappeared into the ship's bowels, and Salma seemed to be playing some dangerous game with the Wasp soldiers. He could always be found somewhere in their line of sight but usually somewhere public. He kept smiling at them in that strange way of his. She feared he was going to get himself killed, but somehow he was still alive each morning.

She therefore spent the voyage browsing the few books on the common room's shelves, or meditating in her own cabin. She had found that the constant soft revolution of the airship's engine was in some ways an aid to concentration. Well, at least she was able to enter something approximating a trance, although the Ancestor Art remained conspicuous in its absence.

Totho practically kicked the door open in his haste to find her, startling her into diving for her sword, which was all the way across the room.

'Trouble!' he told her.

'Wha—?' She gaped at him.

'More Wasps,' he explained. 'Turned up on a flier. New orders, I reckon.'

'That means the game's changed.' She stood, brushing her robes down. 'What do you think?'

'We can't take chances, because that makes eleven of them on board now.' His eyes went wide. 'With that many they could overpower the crew.'

'Where's Tynisa?' she asked him.

'I can go and find her.'

'Then I'd better look for Salma. We have to plan.'

Tynisa had discovered that, short of breaking a porthole and somehow squeezing herself through it onto the sheer hull beyond, the cabin door was the only way out, and the door was locked.

Now if she had been a Beetle, that would have been different. She was quite sure that if she had been a Beetle-maid then a few quick jabs with a piece of wire would see her out of the door and away as fast as her stubby legs would carry her. She even began to try that, kneeling before the lock and peering into the narrow keyhole, trying to imagine the pieces of metal inside that, in some way beyond her imagining, controlled whether the door would open or not.

She simply could not do it: there was no place in her mind to conceive of the lock, the link between the turn of the key, the immobility of the door. Of all the old Inapt races, the Spider-kinden still prospered as before, but that was only because they found other people to make and operate machines for them. Spider doorways were hung with curtains, and they had guards, not locks, to keep out strangers.

And so, due to the limitations of her mind, she was trapped, left to curse Halrad's name and pick over his belongings until he should choose to return for her. She found nothing of use, no sealed orders, no secret maps. He was, as she had already guessed, a dull creature of habit, and little more.

It seemed a very long time indeed before he returned, but up here the passing of time was difficult to gauge. Tynisa was instantly ready, though, a hand close to her rapier hilt as the lock clicked and the door opened. She had expected a bundle of soldiers to come pushing in to grab her, but it was just Halrad himself, conspicuously alone, his eyes wide.

'Come with me,' he ordered.

'Why? What's going on?'

'Don't question me, woman. Just come with me.'

He reached out and took her wrist. By the moment he touched her she had decided to play along, or he would have found her with steel drawn already. Instead she let herself be led, almost dragged along the corridor, down the spiralling wooden steps at the far end. Every time she asked him what he thought he was doing with her he just shook his head. She began to wonder if he had gone mad. He was acting like a man trying to escape a monster that only he could see. His feet skidded on the steps in his haste, and when they reached the common room deck he dragged her even further down, into the *Sky Without*'s guts, pushing past startled crew and engineers.

'Captain Halrad,' she protested, 'tell me what is going on!'

He turned on her with sweat shiny on his brow. 'You've been very clever with me,' he said. 'Yes, you have – and perhaps it's worked. You knew all along I was looking for Stenwold Maker. Don't try and deny it.'

She was sure that no hint of guilt touched her face, but still she turned cold within. *Exactly what did he know?* 'Master Maker?' she said awkwardly.

'You know him. I know that now. You were seen with him, in Collegium. Captain Thalric knows all about you. Still, does that really make you a spy? Not necessarily, you don't *have* to be.'

She saw it in his face, that he could not believe she was anything other than some innocent girl, caught up in something beyond her. If he chose otherwise then he would have been fooled by her, and he could not accept that. She had a moment for wry thought: *Spider-kinden, my race, we already have such a reputation for lies. Yet, individually, who can we not convince?*

She had an uncomfortable feeling that he was becoming less and less convinced as the minutes ticked by. Whatever was in his mind, he was making it up as he went along, and coming to fresh conclusions as he did so.

'What about my friends?'

Halrad shook his head angrily. 'Forget them: they're as good as caught. Thalric will have them and let him be satisfied with that. You, though, you're *mine*. He can keep his hands off you.'

'Who is this Thalric?' she asked, but he just tugged at her arm harder, hustling her onwards through the innards of the *Sky Without*. So she tried, 'But if he's just a captain and you're a captain—'

He stopped, just for a moment, to stare back at her. 'You don't understand. Thalric is from the *Rekef*. Every-one knows that.'

'The what?'

'None of your concern,' and he was hauling her off again. He barrelled his way past another engineer and abruptly they were in a larger space, not any longer the cramped warrens of the engine rooms. There was some kind of machine, of the winged variety, sitting innocuously in the middle of the floor.

'What are you trying to do?' she demanded.

'Oh well now, I'm just staking my claim,' he hissed. 'You see, Captain Thalric thinks he can take possession of just anything he pleases, but you're *mine*. We're almost at Helleron and he can't hope to search every corner of this ship before then, even if the crew would permit it.' He was now pulling her across the great hangar, towards an open doorway in the far wall. 'The cargo hold is through there,' he explained. 'And as of now, you're my cargo. I'll find somewhere safe for you, to keep you out of Thalric's way, but I'm going to have to lock you up there. We can't have you running around the ship any more, and besides . . .' His eyes were wild. 'If you do turn out to be something more than you seem, well . . .' His face was suddenly cold and she found it hard to believe he had ever smiled at her. 'Well then why should Thalric get all the credit for handing you in, when I can do that myself? And if you *are* just a Spider girl who's walked into more than she can handle, then you're mine, so you should get used to staying where you're put and doing what I say.'

They had come to the open doors leading into the next chamber, which was packed with crates all neatly tied down. Halrad's gaze raked it, and she realized he must mean to put her *in* one of the boxes to avoid this mysterious Thalric's search. 'Get in the hold, woman!' He tried to push her in, but she squirmed out of the way and then retreated from him along the partition wall.

'Don't make me force you,' he warned. He held one hand up now, and she started as bright worms of light writhed and danced about it. Ancestor Art, she realized, but like none she had ever seen before.

She took stock of the situation, of the room itself. At no

point did the thought of actually cooperating with him tempt her.

'Two things, Captain,' she said. 'Firstly, I won't abandon my friends. Secondly . . .' She swallowed, put him from her mind. 'Now would be a good time.'

'What?' Halrad's puzzlement turned into a shriek of agony as Totho stabbed him in the back. He arched towards her, and she threw herself aside, twisting out of his grip. For a second he remained standing, propped against the wall, just staring. Then he fell backwards and sideways, through the doorway and into the hold.

She turned to Totho, who was still staring at the corpse with wide eyes. Whatever he felt on this occasion, the first time he had taken a human life, it was not the exultation that had gripped Tynisa herself in the hall of Stenwold's townhouse.

'You've a gift for timing,' she told him calmly. 'How did you get here so fast?'

'What?' He looked at her, and visibly coloured. 'Oh, I . . . told some of the engineers I was . . . I, ah . . . liked you . . . so they kept an eye on you for me.' He avoided her gaze.

'That's sweet,' she told him, which only made his embarrassment worse. 'Look, did you hear what he said, about this Thalric person hunting for us?'

'Che's already gone to fetch Salma,' he explained. 'What should we do now?'

'Bring them here,' she told him. 'If nothing else, below decks is probably the last place they'll look. I'll hide the body in the meantime.'

Che found Salma lounging in the common room, but the news she had was not news to him. He indicated the trio of Wasp soldiers who were lurking along one wall. 'The ugly one in the middle came in just now, and since then they've obviously been on watch-and-wait. Something's changed, all right.'

'This new officer,' confirmed Che, who had put on something more action-worthy, tunic and breeches, with her possessions slung over her shoulder and her sword at her hip.

'They're onto us.' He shrugged. 'Whether they know for sure we're in service or they just think we can lead them to Stenwold, it doesn't really matter.'

'But what can we do now?' Che asked. 'We can't just sit here forever, and besides, if they get impatient, Totho says they could take over the whole ship and just fly us to the Empire, or something.'

'By the customs of my own people, there are two things we can do,' he told her, his customary sardonic expression creasing further. 'Firstly, I can get my steel out and hunt them down all across the ship, shadow to shadow. Kill them in ones and twos until they're all dead, or I am. That would be one option.'

She stared at him, wide-eyed. He sounded as serious as he ever could be. 'You've done that, before?'

'No,' he admitted. 'But it's a done thing, where I come from. Happened a lot during the war, I'm told.' He stretched. 'That, then, is the right hand. However there is always the plan of the left hand.'

'Which is what?'

'Watch and learn, O scholar.' He stood up abruptly and she saw a sudden shifting of stance amongst the Wasp soldiers, but he ignored them contemptuously. Instead, his meandering path took him over to a table occupied by a group of Beetle merchants, and before her eyes he proposed to them a game of chance.

It was a short while, minutes only, before the table was scattered with coins. Gambling was one of those frowned-upon pastimes that the poor were dissuaded from indulging in by a middle class that could not itself resist the lure, turning many a member of the latter class into one of the former in the course of a single profligate night. In short order Salma was matching cards happily with three cloth merchants and a brace of Fly-kinden, including the formerly aloof dulcimer player. Betting was fast and fierce, and Che kept having to remind herself that their lives were on the line here, because she had never seen Salma play cards before. He played as though he could not lose, and when he lost he was careless of it, but mostly he won.

The Wasps were watching even more closely now, suspecting some device, but Salma paid them no heed whatsoever, seeming utterly absorbed in his game. They barely glanced at Che, meanwhile, and she realized that they must be working on very limited information, second-hand descriptions. Salma was the only Dragonfly-kinden within a hundred miles, but she, a Beetle amongst Beetles, was safe in her anonymity.

Even as she thought this, there was a shout from the table and all chaos broke loose.

In the first few seconds of furious argument Che tried to piece together what was going on. Someone had been caught cheating, or suspected of it, and she soon realized that it was Salma. He, for his part, was outraged at the very suggestion, knocking his chair back and standing up, and then simply flipping the entire table over. Cards, money and angry gamblers were suddenly all scattered about the common room.

She saw Salma moving fast, but one of the merchants still managed to bounce a fist off him before himself sprawling over a chair. The Wasps were trying to move in but everything was now in an uproar. A pair of stewards were trying to restore the peace, for there were at least three private fistfights going on, and one large one to which everyone was invited. In the midst of all of this,

Salma grabbed her wrist, and a moment later he had extricated them both from the room, and they were running for the stairs.

'Where to?' she asked.

'No idea,' he admitted. The shouting from behind them was picking up in volume. She glanced back and saw a flash of black and yellow.

Without any warning, a whole panel of wall beside them was open, and they saw Totho framed in it, wreathed in cloud with the chill air plucking at him.

'I've been looking for you,' was his understatement. 'Out this way, quick,' he said, and then disappeared from sight. Che peered through the hatchway and saw Totho descending the *Sky Without*'s very hull, hand over hand on iron rungs. Below was an open walkway that must surely connect to the lower deck.

Che did not want, under any circumstances, to be out there with nothing but the strength of her grip to save her from a dive into infinity. The Wasp soldiers were coming, though, so her preferences seemed irrelevant.

'You first,' she said, and Salma simply dived straight through the hatch. As soon as he was clear of it, his Artwings blurred into life about his shoulders, catching him in the air, where he hovered and spun while waiting for her.

She bundled herself through the hatch and hauled it closed behind her, balancing precariously. A moment's extra thought showed her how to secure it, and by the time the Wasps had reached it, there was no obvious way for them to follow.

The wind tugged at her, seemed to get between her fingers and the slick chill of the metal rungs. She concentrated only on her hands, trying to make her descent as mechanical and unerring as an automaton's. Salma kept pace with her, and she knew he would try to catch her if she slipped, but she was not altogether sure whether he could.

And then there came another hatch, at last. Totho was holding it open for them, practically hopping from foot to foot. She shouldered past him into the cramped walkway.

'Where now?'

'Tynisa's waiting in the hangar.' He bared his teeth nervously. 'They're after us and I'm not sure there's anywhere we can safely hide. Maybe amongst the freight.'

Che closed the hatch after Salma, who said, 'Run,' remarkably quietly. The walkway stretched the length of the airship's gondola, but at the far end they could see movement: black and yellow yet again. Wasp soldiers were now forcing their way along the narrow space with their hands outstretched before them.

Totho took off at once down the walkway, with an engineer's practised hunch, and then almost immediately dropped through another hatchway. By the time Che had caught up, he was in the cavernous space of the hangar, where Tynisa was already coming out of hiding to greet them. As soon as Salma was clear of the hatch Che slammed it shut and threw the bar.

'No time!' she warned. 'They're coming!'

Salma looked about them. 'Where do these other doors go?' he asked.

'Engine room, a dead end,' Totho explained. 'And the other leads to the freight holds.'

'But we don't need to run anywhere on board!' Tynisa interrupted them. 'If we stay here they're bound to find us. So let's use this thing and just go.' She was pointing at the fixed-wing. 'Totho, start it up, make it go.'

Totho goggled at her. 'I can't pilot a flier.'

'But you're Apt, you're an artificer. You *like* machines.'

'I could repair it, yes, if it was broken.' He kept shaking his head at her, and Che saw a whole bucketful of hope drain from Tynisa's expression.

'But . . . that was my plan,' she said weakly.

'I can fly it, maybe' Che announced, to disbelieving

stares. 'I can try, at least,' she amended. 'I did a course on aviation at the College.'

'Then let's do it!' Salma said. Totho was already running for the loading ramp wheel, unlocking it and spinning it so that the ramp descended into its full slope with a shriek of abused metal. The fixed-wing flier shifted a foot downwards against its rope restraints, pointing backwards down the ramp, about to re-enact its arrival in reverse.

The first impact by the Wasps on the door they had entered by almost splintered it out of its frame. There was a fraught second of looks anxiously exchanged and then Che made the decision. Half-sliding down the ramp, she clambered awkwardly across the fixed-wing's hull to squeeze herself into the pilot's seat. The controls were simple: levers to steer the vanes, a crank to start the propeller. She began cranking straight away, just as the hangar door flew off its hinges, tumbling the first Wasp soldier into the room.

'In!' Tynisa decided, and she sprang into the seat behind Che, with Salma following close behind. Totho rushed to join then, thudding down onto the ramp and skidding dangerously on its metal slope. He reached for the lever that would release the ropes to free the flier, but before he could even touch it there was a crackle of fire and something bright struck sparks from near his hand. Totho fell backwards and had a gut-wrenching understanding that he was about to fall between the ramp and the hatch and then slip out into space. Salma and Tynisa both snagged him at the same time, and hauled him into the flier.

'I can't get the engine going!' Che said in a panic, and Totho was explaining that he had to release the snagging ropes or the flier would be going absolutely nowhere.

'Simple,' Tynisa said, and flicked out her rapier. Totho howled for her to stop, but a moment later she had severed the ropes just on one side. The fixed-wing pitched left and hung for a second as another bolt of energy burned into the deck above them. Then Tynisa had severed another two strands and the flier slid helplessly down the ramp and away into space.

But they were not flying. They were barely gliding, mostly falling, with Che repeating, 'The engine won't start! Someone look at the engine!'

That someone, Totho realized, would have to be him. He squirmed towards the aft end of the flier, where the dark bulk of the engine was set well back. He dived through the space between the upper and lower wings, dodged about the mounted ballista, and off the back of the craft.

His Art kept him there, clinging to the smooth side of the flier with feet and knees, whilst the air dashed past him and the world towards him. Totho had very little time in which to make a diagnosis. Perhaps less than he thought. There were figures above him, diving from the *Sky Without* with their Art-wings extended.

I can fly it. The words were rattling around in Che's skull, faster and faster. She had the flaps all the way back, so that if the engine had been functioning then the fixed-wing would be looping the loop. Instead it was dropping straight out of the sky, its nose gently tilting lower. 'Any time, Toth!' she called out. By now she had the levers pulled so far back that they were creaking in her hands.

Energy crackled across one of the wings from a ranging shot of the Wasps. Hanging almost upside down by his Art and his knees, Totho's hands searched frantically. He heard Che shout his name despairingly, but he could not be rushed now.

There. And just in time. There were clamps on the fuel lines intended to stop just this kind of theft. None of the Wasps had been an artificer or else something more sophisticated, harder to find, would have been used. Swiftly he plucked them off and shouted for Che to fire up the engine one more time.

There must have been quite a head of fuel waiting in the lines, because the engine seemed to explode, a flash of heat that scorched Totho's face, and great clouds of smoke were falling away behind and above them. A moment later the engine was running, propeller turning at first slowly, then fast enough to blur. The fixed-wing struggled in the air, Che wrestling with the sticks. Clinging to the engine casing, which in a very short time was getting uncomfortably warm, Totho feared the little craft was going to slide sideways, slipping through the air and then simply plummeting into a mad spinning dive. Che put all her weight on the controls, though, and the flier swung level, pitched the other way and then righted, dashing through the air with the engine still coughing and smoking.

She glanced behind her, and was rewarded with the sight of Tynisa and Salma actually clinging together from pure fear, and she gave out a great whoop of glee, for in that moment she was suddenly enjoying herself.

Then out of the smoke the Wasp soldiers came arrowing down on them with swords and fire.

Nine

'Get to the ballista! Salma! Tynisa! Someone get to the ballista!' Che yelled, and realized that neither of them would know what to do with it. Totho was now clambering, exhausted, up onto the flier's stern and so she shouted it at him instead. He gave her an aggrieved look but struggled over to the weapon.

A burst of energy impacted squarely on one wing, punching a hole through the light wood frame. The fixed-wing bucked dangerously and Che had to turn her attention back to keeping the craft level.

Behind her, Totho reached the ballista. It was nothing more than a glorified heavy crossbow, but double-strung with two sets of arms to give the single bolt more range and force. There was a two-handled winch at the butt end and he cranked it over and over to drag the string back against the resistance of the sprung steel.

'Pass me a bolt!' he called over his shoulder. For a moment he thought that they would prove incapable even of that. He began to curse all Inapt peoples, but then Tynisa nearly rammed a quarrel in his ear as the flier pitched and he snatched it from her and slotted it into place.

The first Wasp soldier appeared, darting past the fixed-wing on its far side. There was energy dancing about his hands, something that Totho could recognize as Ancestor Art, but of some Wasp variation he had never previously encountered. The man sent a bolt of energy straight at

Che, who flinched, pulling the fixed-wing into a long curving turn back towards the lagging Wasp soldiers.

'Get him away! Someone get him away from me!' Che shrieked. Totho tried to swivel the ballista about, but its angle of fire would not permit it. Instead he wrenched it back to face the other Wasps, two of them now almost on him, and one flew straight into the weapon's path without spotting it. Totho glimpsed a second's worth of abject horror as the man suddenly realized, then he released the trigger and the bolt rammed into its target at no more than ten yards' distance. The very force of impact hurled him away, end over end over end, somersaulting towards the earth. Totho hurriedly began winching the ballista's arms back again.

Another crackle of energy struck the side of the hull, just beyond the pilot's seat, and the entire flier rocked as Che ducked. There was nowhere to hide, though, nowhere to dodge. 'Hammer and tongs, someone do something!' she shouted, looking angrily back at the others.

Salma was standing up even as she looked, and a moment later he parted company with the fixed-wing, and his own wings unfurled into being. He launched into the air in a blaze of silver. His sword was already out, a wicked short punch-blade that thrust straight out from the knuckles, and he kept pace with the limping flier effortlessly, dancing in the air before diving beneath it. Che caught her breath. She remembered him saying that the Wasp-kinden were clumsy in the air but this had not been true until he took flight. She spotted him again a moment later, soaring up under the Wasp who was targeting her. The man had little enough chance to notice him before Salma had slashed across him, and in his wake the Wasp was left clutching a bloody wound in his side, tumbling over himself and falling out of the sky.

Salma paused, treading air while flying backwards as he kept up speed, and then he flung himself along the entire length of the fixed-wing, cutting a curve around its doubled wings and lunging at the closest Wasp with blade outstretched.

Che peered straight ahead and blanked her mind of anything now but flying the machine to safety. She forced herself to keep the flier level and would worry about Salma later. Still, that sight of Salma, vaunting in the air with his sword gleaming in the sunlight, was something that would not readily leave her.

Salma toyed with the other Wasp, darting in and out, hovering where the soldier could only lumber after him through the air. Then the Dragonfly was gone and past him. As the Wasp turned, spitting a bolt of sting-energy at his taunter, Totho shot the man in the back with enough force to slam the steel head of the bolt right through his chest.

There were three further specks in the sky out there, insignificant now beside the receding bulk of the *Sky Without*. For a moment Salma wanted to go after them too, to dance amongst them in the sky and to take them if he could. His ancestors and his fallen kin were calling for him to do so, urging him to test himself.

But he was not a man alone. He had others he was responsible for. Stenwold had known, when he gave them this task, that Salma was no callow youth but had experience enough not to indulge himself.

Fast though he was, he had to push himself to catch up with the fixed-wing, and that meant the Wasp pursuers would never overtake it. He caught hold of a wing, pulled himself forward into the arms of Tynisa and Totho as he released his Art and his wings flickered and vanished from his back. He discovered that he was panting heavily after the brief flight, shamefully out of practice. Tynisa was giving him a wondering look. Totho's expression was just relief that it was all over.

'Which way to Helleron?' he called. 'Can we get there in this thing?'

Che glanced back and grinned at him. 'I've taken a compass reading already,' she said. 'If we've got enough fuel we'll make it. Otherwise it might mean a bit of a walk.'

She brought the fixed-wing down still some distance from Helleron because, from the noise the engine was making, it would not have been able to carry them much further. Landing was, she now discovered, distinctly the trickiest part of the flight. Or at least the flier itself did not enjoy it. When it finally ground to a halt while traversing the furrows of some farmer's field, it had lost half a wing and the stabilizers from the front.

On solid ground at last, Che took a deep breath. That had been a harrowing experience, white knuckles clamped on the sticks, staring into the blue while trying to coax as much distance out of the craft as it could give her. She was glad to be travelling on nothing more challenging than her own two feet once again. Still . . . in a strange way she had enjoyed it. Beetles might possess the grace of stone blocks when the Art allowed them wings, but their artifice could make up for that sometimes.

'Everybody in one piece?' she called back, to a chorus of grumbles as her passengers began to extricate themselves from the mortally wounded flier.

The wronged farmer, whom they encountered shortly thereafter, told them that they were still about a day's journey from Helleron, further away than they had hoped. He was not the coarse-handed rustic that they had been expecting. This close to Helleron even the sons of the soil saw a great deal of the Lowlands culture passing by. They offered him the salvage rights to the fixed wing and Tynisa haggled languidly with him until they had secured transport to the nearest thoroughfare, as well as a few provisions and clothes. The latter, she explained, would be important since the *Sky Without* would doubtless be at berth at Helleron's airfield by the time they reached the city, and the Wasps would be out in force looking for them. Disguise would therefore be crucial, as they waited for Bolwyn at Benevolence Square.

'Why do we think the Wasps are all over Helleron, then?' Che asked.

'Their agents will be,' Tynisa said confidently. 'The Wasps have had a good while now to put them in place. We need to find Bolwyn as quickly as possible, and then step well out of sight.'

Helleron crept up over the horizon like a looming black tide. The road they were following was a jostling two-way stream of travellers feeding the city's eternal hunger for buying and selling. There were hand-carts and travelling tinkers laden with their packs; there were wagons drawn by horses or by great insects, mostly slow and patient beetles that could muscle along all day if need be. A few mounted wayfarers passed by too, either horse-borne or on bug-back. Much of the traffic was mechanical though, they noted, for Helleron was the centre of the artificing world, and its wandering children would return there in droves.

They watched the city come near from their perch on the hood of a great grain-hauling automotive trundling along on six metal legs – looking more like a beetle than those insects themselves. None of them had fully appreciated the concept of Helleron as the Lowlands' epicentre of industry. They had envisaged something like Collegium but with a few more factories and without the elegant white buildings of the College.

But Helleron was vast, extending half again Collegium's size, the greatest single city in all the Lowlands. It sprawled and it was dirty: whether its buildings had been raised of dark stone or not, they had been overlaid, day after day, with the grime of the city's foundries and workshops. There was a pall in the very air, as though the visitors were gazing on the place through smoked glass. A hundred hundred chimneys gouted it out continually, their narrow windows aglare with forge-fire.

It was built on two scales, the city. The factories were huge grubs, extended and extended, comprising mazes of workrooms, storerooms and vehicle yards. Up on the western hills, where the air was clearer, there were mansions built as grandiose statements in stone, telling about their owners' profits and losses. Between these hulks, however, swarmed the masses. The buildings that housed the workers of Helleron were crammed together, squeezed tight, beside and under and over, as though jostling for position beside the mighty flanks of their masters. The whole complexity was shot through with silver: the rails that were Helleron's breath and blood, shuttling men and machines, crew and commodities, across the breadth of the city, north to the mines or south part-way to the Ant city of Tark. It seemed at first glance that the rails' silver lacework was the only passage through the city. The walls of the buildings seemed so crammed together that surely not even the smallest insect could have crept between them.

They watched the sheer enormity of it grow and approach them across the distance. Even Totho, that champion of industry, was humbled.

'Are we even going to be able to find this Benevolence Square?' he asked.

'Uncle Sten said it was near the airfield – which is over there.' Across a cleared area of land the pale blister of the *Sky Without* was clearly visible. Che shaded her eyes, thinking for a moment that she might be able to discern some details, some dabs of black and gold, but she had forgotten the *Sky*'s great bulk. It was still further away than she realized.

Closer still, and they at last saw that there was indeed breathing space, even open space, in Helleron, but none of it had been left alone. There were squares, but they were roofed by the canvas of countless traders' stalls, or else thronging with swarms of citizens. There were alleys and roads, but half of them were concealed under over-arching buildings, the opposite sides of streets leaning in to turn a thoroughfare into a tunnel for the sake of a few extra square yards of living space in their upper storey. And where there were gaps between the buildings, these gaps were filled with people.

'No outer walls,' Salma said quietly. They turned to look at him in puzzlement and he gestured. It was plain to see, when you looked out for it. Helleron's very commerce apparently made it proof against invasion – or so went the theory writ large in its streets. Helleron free was of greater use to all the rest of the world than Helleron chained would be to anyone.

Tynisa recalled the ill-fated Captain Halrad's manner, his possessive attitude. If all Wasps thought that way then they would seek to pluck Helleron and hold it close, crush it in their grasping hands until it was good for nothing and nobody. The Wasp Empire, by Halrad's own words, was no respecter of mutual benefit. The Wasp Empire saw only property to be possessed and enemies to vanquish.

The four of them had dressed themselves up as local peasantry, and Salma and Tynisa had hoods up to shade their faces. If the mysterious Thalric was waiting for them in Helleron, as seemed almost certain, then they were determined to make it harder for him. The city's daunting size would become their unexpected ally.

Helleron finally fell across them like a shadow. The buildings rose abruptly high on both sides, the air thickening with smoke and the stench of people. Here on the outskirts were those seeking to mimic the commerce of the inner city: little amateur markets selling goods of dubious provenance for small change, itinerant entertainers and charlatans, beggars everywhere. A squad of Ant soldiers drilled in an open space before the city, their masters or employers no doubt tending their business within. Stake-fenced pens advertised the wares of slavers: even though Beetles kept no slaves and allowed none within their towns, more lives were bought and sold in Helleron every day than anywhere else in the Lowlands.

'Where do you stop?' Che inquired of the driver of their automotive. He was sitting one level down from them, exposed to the open air just like any real beetle driver.

'Chancery Street Station,' he rasped back. 'Got a big depot there, they have.'

'Excuse me, but do you happen to know Benevolence Square?' she continued. It seemed the easiest way, although she was sure an experienced agent would have had a more subtle way of doing it.

He did indeed, and although the way was long, they had only to follow one of the outer circula, as he called Helleron's ringroads, in order to come to it.

'You can't miss it,' their driver assured them. 'The old Benevolence place has got two great big skeletons all over it.'

That sounded unlikely, but they disembarked as instructed, having no directions to trust save his. The tide of busy humanity that was Helleron immediately engulfed them, and in the first moments Che was nearly ripped away from her companions and hauled off down the street by the simple crush of people, each one a slave to his destination. The four of them huddled together, feeling cowed by such a press. Great vehicles, beasts and wagons crawled past them to one side, the walls leered down to the other. A succession of short-tempered people buffeted them as they stood in the way, a stone in the course of the human stream.

Tynisa signalled that they should move on, and they

found their way into the flow, bustled along at an undignified pace. The people around them seemed mostly workers and small traders. They looked close mouthed and sullen, minding their own business and never looking at each other. Passing on, the wall to one side gave way to a succession of small workshops: a cobbler, a piece-maker, a sharpener, a leatherworker, men and women hard at work with solid, uncomplaining, joyless faces.

Salma's face, too, was wrinkled up. 'I can't understand how they live with the smell of themselves,' he complained. 'The smell of the air . . . it's like it's been burned and then sweated out.'

'Let me guess, they don't have . . . factories or anything like that, where you come from,' Totho said.

'And how thankful I am for it,' said Salma. 'We may have our vices but this mayhem isn't one of them. I don't even know if there's a name for what vice this is.'

'Helleron,' Tynisa suggested. 'There's your name.'

Totho shrugged, as best he could in the crush. 'Well, I think it's . . . it's got promise. I'd like to work here. Everything ever manufactured is made here. What do *you* think, Che?'

She felt rather guilty in the face of his enthusiasm, but she replied, 'Collegium for me, every time.'

'And that must be the Benevolence,' Salma said suddenly. Ahead of them, past a line of near-identical inns and stables, lay a square. The largest building fronting it was facing them as well. The driver had been wrong, however: there was only one skeleton patterned in pale bricks amongst the darker stone. The other figure depicted a woman, austerely offering her hand to the same cadaver. The 'old Benevolence place' had been an almshouse once, offering succour to the needy, the destitute, the sick and the mad. Now it was a workhouse, where any succour was bought with a hard day's labour. There was little enough going free in Helleron.

Salma struck without warning, his fingers pincering the wrist of a boy even as the child was putting a hand into his pocket. There was a fraught moment, for the child produced a blade, and then Che saw it was not even a child, but a Fly-kinden adult got up in child's clothing. A long look passed between Salma and the wretch, and then the Dragonfly let him go, and the man was immediately lost in the crowd.

'You should have called the watch,' Che said.

Salma gave her a bleak look. 'Just having to live here seems punishment enough.'

'There are an awful lot of people here,' sighed Tynisa. 'How are we going to find this Bolwyn individual?'

'We've missed him,' Salma said. 'He'd be expecting us off the *Sky Without* which must have got in . . . Totho?'

'Yesterday,' Totho guessed.

'We have to hope that he'll come here again to look for us. So let's get up on the steps of the big place over there, and watch for him. And if he doesn't come today, what's left of it, we'll try it again tomorrow. If that doesn't work then we'll make other plans. What other plans, though, I don't know.'

'I've got some relatives in Helleron,' Che suggested. 'I can probably remember their name, given a minute. *Someone* must know where they live.'

'It's a fallback, possibly,' Salma confirmed. 'Now, eyes on the crowd, and try not to look suspicious.'

There was no Bolwyn that day, or if he was there at all, they missed him. They ate unpalatable food from even less palatable vendors, and when the smoggy gloom deepened into night they sought refuge at one of the inns, only to find its prices unheard of, so that their communal wealth would barely buy them enough space on the common-room floor. Che then remembered that they had passed a Keepers' wayhouse coming in, and they tangled back through the gaslit streets trying to find it. They were not the only ones abroad after sundown, for at first they encountered guardsmen with oil-burning lamps and cross-bows, but only in those areas where the residents had wealth worth protecting. The other nocturnal pedestrians were involved in darker trades, either practising them or seeking to buy. The four soon had plenty of offers in their short journey, from the pleasures of the flesh to drugs and potions to small valuables whose current owners were anxious to part with them.

The wayhouse, found at last, promised no better accommodation than any of the inns, but it was to be had for the price of a reasonable donation, and they could rest easy there without the fear of getting their throats cut. The Keepers were a charitable order, originally from Collegi-um, which had spread throughout the Lowlands as part of the great upswell of humanist philosophy a century ago, when good deeds had been fashionable, and the wealthy competed in funding public works. The benevolent way of life still endured in Collegium, but apart from the grey-robed Keepers there was little enough of it to be seen in Helleron.

The next day, halfway to noon, Salma spotted their man.

They had been taking it in turns to stand up and stare, the others meanwhile sitting on the steps of the Benevo-lence, as many did. No beggars there, though. From time to time a pair of Ants with clubs dangling at their belts came out from inside, and anyone who could not show them at least a coin or two was thrown off roughly. The Benevolence provided only one form of charity for the poor, which was earned with hard graft.

Salma nudged Che with the toe of his sandal, startling her out of a light doze. When she stood up, as they all did, he murmured, 'Far end, on the right corner. What do you think?'

Che saw only a bustle of people there and it seemed impossible that Salma could have recognized any face at that distance.

'Give me the picture,' the Dragonfly demanded. He glanced quickly from the sketch to the crowd. 'It's him, I'm sure of it. Look, he's coming this way.'

It took the others longer to pick him out from the crowds, even with Salma muttering constant directions. Then the face leapt out of the mob at them. A man with a heavy, unshaven jaw, hair already receding a little from the time that picture was drawn. He wore the open, sleeveless robe that seemed to be the fashion for artisans and middle merchants here, but the under-robe below it was supplemented with a buckled leather cuirass. A man undoubtedly expecting trouble, and this impression inspired a kind of trust.

'We have to approach him. He won't know us,' Che said.

'Allow me,' Tynisa said, and sauntered casually down the steps of the Benevolence. They tracked her progress through the crowd, moving with no obvious direction or urgency, until she was within arm's reach of Bolwyn. He twitched as she passed, turned to look, and they guessed she must have snagged his sleeve. She spoke to him, simply an apology rendered, then apparently interest expressed by a male Beetle of middling years towards an attractive young woman of another kind. Interest repaid, as she smiled at him, and a moment later the pair were walking away together, making for one of the roads leading out of Benevolence Square.

'Off we go,' Salma said, and the other three descended into the crowd, trying to remain as inconspicuous as possible as they intercepted Tynisa and her newfound friend.

Once out of sight of the square, the two of them ducked under the awning of a clothier's shop and mulled over fabrics until the stragglers caught up. Bolwyn glanced around guardedly. He had a long knife sheathed at his belt, and one hand constantly plucked at the robe over it.

'Where have you been?' he demanded. 'Why weren't you on the *Sky*?'

'Due to mutual friends who wanted more of our company,' Tynisa told him. He grunted.

'So you're Stenwold's new people,' he remarked. 'He said to expect a Commonwealer and I'm not sure I believed him. Nice of him to pick his people so they're just about as conspicuous as possible.'

Salma looked at him levelly. 'I can't believe you saw through my disguise. Besides, I've seen a half-dozen of my kinden so far in Helleron. We get everywhere, apparently.'

Bolwyn shrugged. 'So, you know me but I'm not sure I need to know you, yet. We'll let the chief decide on that. When's the Old Man himself expected?'

'We don't know,' Che admitted. 'He said he'd meet us here as soon as he could, but there were ... problems back home.'

'Even in Collegium now? Well, how the world turns,' Bolwyn said, scratching his stubble. 'Let's get you off the streets as soon as, shall we? Come with me and just try to keep up.'

He looked each way down the street before hurrying out into the crowd, obviously used to Helleron's human press. For them, however, it took a fair deal of shouldering and elbowing to keep pace with him.

'Friendly sort, isn't he?' Che muttered.

'I don't think this business of ours breeds friends,' Tynisa told her.

Bolwyn got them off the street fairly quickly, heading down a narrow alley that was backed onto on either side by a row of small shops. Nobody else had much reason to go there, and only very few were out to watch them pass: an old Beetle sitting at a window, smoking a clay pipe cupped in his hands; a limping Fly in old rags scavenging through newer rags. There was a sour, rotting smell here over and above Helleron's customary reek.

Their guide kept glancing back at them, stopping and then starting again. Che thought that he could not look more suspicious if he tried, but then she was beginning to think that her breed was definitely not made for espionage. That led her to wonder just what her uncle had ever experienced that had led him into the trade. Or Bolwyn either, for that matter. What course had ended up in him turning down this alley on this day, with four amateurs in tow?

'Wait up, Bolwyn,' Salma snapped. 'Who's that up ahead?'

Che had not even noticed anyone, but she was beginning to realize that Salma's eyes were far keener than her own. Ahead, she saw, were a handful of figures, muffled in cloaks.

'Don't you worry about them,' Bolwyn's voice came back to them. 'They're mine, to make sure nobody comes after us.'

They hurried towards the waiting men, who looked tough and mean: an Ant, a Beetle and some kind of halfbreed. Their eyes, passing across Bolwyn's four young followers, remained devoid of emotion.

Is this the sort of person I'll be dealing with, from now on? Che wondered. She was beginning to feel homesick for Collegium, where unpleasant things, when they happened, were at least the exception.

Salma almost punched her in the mouth, and she had a second of utter confused hurt before she realized he had merely flung out an arm to halt her.

'*Run!*' he shouted, and she had a sudden sense of motion. She lost vital seconds trying to understand whilst the others were already reacting. Tynisa, her rapier clear of its scabbard, was skittering back down the alleyway.

Totho had already turned, running off back the way they had come and trusting that the others were following him. His artificer's bag jostled and bounced awkwardly on his back.

There were men now coming at them from a side alley, and as the first one's cloak twitched aside she caught a flash of black and gold.

'Bolwyn!' she cried, seeing even as she did that his three men were starting to move forward. They were not coming to her rescue, though. They were coming to join in the ambush.

Bolwyn turned, and for a moment his face was just an expressionless mask, without any life or feeling . . . and it seemed to *blur* even as she looked, a smearing of the features in some way that knotted her insides with horror. Then the Beetle's face was as before, but she still felt that something else was watching her through those mild eyes.

'Run!' Salma yelled to her again. He had his punch-sword now in hand, lunging forward as the first Wasp soldier cleared the alley's mouth. The man deflected the thrust but Salma pushed close, whipping his elbow up to crack into his opponent's jaw.

Che stumbled back, hands still groping for her own blade.

'*Run!*' Salma bellowed once more, and she ran.

Ten

Tynisa pelted down the alleyway, seeing the street at the far end, with all its life and its busy throng. There was a figure appearing in the way, though, then two of them: nondescript men who could have simply been out-of-work labourers, save for the shortswords they were now drawing from within their jerkins. She saw Totho, ahead of them, skid to a halt, about to turn and help.

'Go!' she shouted at him. 'Go! I can take them!' And he went, and she was running full pelt with her rapier extended, and there were still only two of them.

They were not skilled. Even as she was almost on them something in her read them, the way they stood, the way they held their swords. These were cheap hoods, and she was better than that.

She feigned left, went right at the very last moment. The man to her right had gone along with her first indication. Now he was in the way of his fellow. She buried the rapier in him, through the leather of his jerkin, his shirt, under his ribs. She held firm to the hilt and ran on, letting the force of her charge drag him around by the wound, letting it pull her around to face him, and slide the blood-slick rapier clean of him even as he fell. He got in the way of his fellow even then, the wretched man help-lessly stumbling over the convulsing body. She could see herself as though she was watching an actor in some awful, mock-tragic opera. She watched as she put the blade effortlessly into the back of the man's neck as he tripped past her, ramming it home with brutal efficiency and then whipping it out again.

She felt a keen and terrible sense of her own prowess, some possessing force that guided her hand, that hissed triumph in her ear. Her face, unknown to her, was smiling.

Totho was gone and she looked back for the others. Instead she spotted two Wasp soldiers coming for her. Their swords were sheathed but they had open hands outstretched to unleash the fire of their Art. She heard Salma shouting for her to run.

She skipped backwards into the crowded street. The people eddied about her, some staring at her reddened sword, some into the alley at what she had done with it. There were now screams, shouting. She watched the Wasps coming.

Then there were more than Wasps coming. From further down the street a half-dozen guardsmen were pushing. They had shields, armour. She cast a desperate look back down the alley. There was a lot going on there, and she could not see how her friends were faring.

The guard were almost here and she decided that she had no wish to answer questions. She would find some-where to hole up, come back as soon as things allowed. Without putting her blade away, she ran for cover.

Che had her sword out and, when the Wasp grabbed her other wrist, the decision to slash at him was taken entirely on reflex, following her training at the Prowess Forum. The Wasp flinched back from it but she still laid open the back of his hand. Somewhere behind her Salma was fighting, steel ringing on steel amid the curses of his opponents.

The Wasp reached for her again, sword up now to deflect her own. She retreated from him, knees bent and stance textbook-perfect. 'Salma!' she called.

'Run!' she heard him urge her once again.

'Can't!' She watched the Wasp as she spoke and knew, before he moved, that he would take advantage of the word. He came in, weapon high but still trying to grab her with his wounded hand. Her blade darted forwards at his chest, and then under his parry, sliding along his side. It cut only armour, though, scoring along the metal beneath his cloak. He snagged the collar of her tunic and she brought the pommel of her blade down across the raw wound on his hand.

He snarled and his control snapped. He hit her clumsily across the face, which must have hurt him more than her, and then he was no longer trying to catch her, but to kill her.

His sword stabbed forward and she rolled with it, sensing the blade pass her by. The hilt jarred into her shoulder. He was too close for her to stab, but she punched him in the side of the head with her own hilt as hard as she could. He reeled half into her, and she cast him past her, slashing him across the back. Again her sword rang on armour, but the force of the blow sent him to the ground.

'Onto the roof! Che!' She heard Salma's voice, but from overhead now. He was hovering above her holding out a hand.

Part of her was already saying *I'll never make it*, but there was a new part, a part that was fighting for her life and was not about to give up now. She took a great run at the nearest shop-back. There was a barrel there that she sprang onto, feeling it topple and give way even as she did so, but she was jumping again, in a great ungainly extended stumble. She caught a window ledge with her other foot and pushed off into space. And there was nowhere else for her to go.

Salma caught her outstretched hand and heaved. He could not have lifted her from the ground, but she was

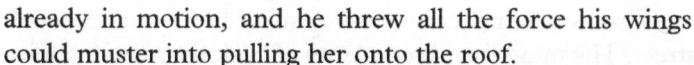

already in motion, and he threw all the force his wings could muster into pulling her onto the roof.

She shrieked as her arm nearly came out of its socket, but a moment later they were up there, all of two storeys up, and he was still pulling, forcing her to run.

There was a Wasp coming after them, the one she had wounded. He was fighting mad, his wings a blur, and she and Salma had nowhere to go but over other exposed roofs.

'What now?' she demanded – and he shoved her off.

She fell onto a shop awning on the other side of the roof, and ripped through it immediately, landing with enough force to knock the breath out of her.

The shopkeeper, a Fly-kinden, was glaring down at her angrily. 'Beetle-kinden!' he spat. 'You're never going to learn that you just don't belong up there!'

She got to her feet, looking up, watching out for the Wasps. There were none to be seen yet. She looked along the street: there was no sign of Tynisa, or Totho either.

A hand fell on her shoulder and she whirled round, her sword up ready. Salma caught her wrist in time, and for a moment they just stared at each other.

She let her breath out from under bruised ribs. 'The soldier . . .?'

'No more.' She was pleased to see that even he, even Salma, seemed shaken by the episode. 'Come on. We have to find the others before the enemy does.'

As soon as he reached the next alley mouth Totho turned, expecting to see Tynisa coming after him. If she was there, the crowd hid her. Eyes wide, he stared, trying to find one friendly face amid so many.

He found something, but not what he wanted. There were two serious-looking men, cloaked and hooded, forging their way towards him. The glimpse he caught of one's face suggested Wasp-kinden to him.

What were they going to do, stuck here in a crowded street? His mind furnished plenty of options. A swift knife-blade, a sagging body. The heedless citizens of Helleron would not pause in their steps to tend to an ailing halfbreed foreigner.

They were closing in now, like fish through shallow water, and Tynisa was nowhere to be seen. With a cold feeling in his heart he turned and began running again. He heard the commotion behind him as they picked up speed as well, while he had a heavy bag to haul and knew that he was no great runner.

And he did not know Helleron well, but he did not let that stop him. He took the first street left, hurtled down it as fast as he could manage, ignoring the shouts, the curses, the occasional drawn blade, as he barged past anyone who got in his way. He left a trail of confusion that any fool could follow, but his followers had to wade through it too.

'Stop, thief!' one of them shouted, and abruptly the crowd ahead of him was turning, all eyes fixed on the halfbreed and his bag. Totho gritted his teeth and tried to pick up speed, but his legs were already giving it their all. A solid-looking Ant-kinden tried to bar his way, and Totho ducked low, rammed a shoulder into the man's chest and knocked him flat. Totho stumbled over the falling man, somehow kept his feet and took a right turn the moment it was offered him. Another dirty little alley, and a short one too. Then there was a crossroads with one even smaller so he turned left.

At first he feared there was no way out. Then he spotted an even narrower passage, roofed over by the overhanging walls of houses. It was now his only way out.

There was someone lurking in the mouth of it, a twisted figure shrouded in a cloak. Totho lowered his shoulder again. At the last moment the figure fled on before him, and he saw that it was now beckoning.

What have I got myself into? There was still the pounding

of feet behind him, and he hurtled into the gloomy alley-way bag-first, pushing it ahead of him and unable to see a thing. Someone was shouting, 'Come on, boy! Come on!' from up ahead, the cry echoing madly, jangling with his own breathing, the echo of his boots, the cries of his pursuers.

'Duck, boy, duck!' the voice yelled, and without thinking he went down, jarring his chin on the tools in his bag as he landed in an inch of filthy water.

Something sped over his head. He looked back quickly to see his two pursuers silhouetted against the tunnel mouth, one halted and one already falling. When the black shadow of his body hit the ground, Totho recognized the sharp spine of a crossbow bolt standing proud of it.

The second man charged forward, and the tunnel was suddenly lit by the fire spitting from his hand. He must have guessed he could get to the mystery assailant before the crossbow was recocked, but another bolt struck him straight in the chest even as he loosed his sting. The harsh impact told Totho that the victim had been wearing armour and that it had not helped. Another two missiles zipped overhead, taking the Wasp in the shoulder and the gut, and he staggered back, sword falling from his fingers. At last he fell.

Totho's own sword was in his hand, and he crouched behind his bag and waited, peering into the darkness.

'Who are you?'

'Good question,' rasped the voice of the stranger. 'I'm the one who just saved your life. That good enough for you?'

'No,' Totho said firmly.

'Does the name Stenwold mean anything to you?' the stranger asked.

'And if it did, why should I trust you? I've . . . relying on the word of strangers . . . hasn't turned out so well recently,' Totho finally got the words out. In truth he was terrified because he could not see the man at all, but he himself would be silhouetted, just as the Wasps had been.

'Founder's mark, boy!' the stranger snapped impatiently. 'All right, moment of truth. Blink and you'll miss it. The name's Scuto. Did Stenwold at least tell you that much?'

'Scuto?'

'Ringing a bell, is it?'

It was, but there was more to consider than that. *Founder's mark*. It was an oath Totho had heard from artificers at Collegium who had arrived to study there from Helleron. In truth it meant nothing, for a native Helleren might have been working for either side in this conflict. It was an artificer's oath, though, and he decided to let its familiarity carry the vote.

'All right,' he said, standing up wearily. 'I've got a sword here. I'm not giving it up. If you've got somewhere . . . a bit drier to go, then . . . well . . .' Wearily he shouldered his dripping bag.

'Good boy,' came the voice of the stranger. 'Now you just follow me.'

'I can't see you.'

'Then just walk straight. Ain't no way out of this alley but the way we're both going.'

The taverna went by the name of the Merraia, just like the one in Collegium where Stenwold had outlined this ill-fated errand to them. Inside it were three low-ceilinged storeys, with a central open space for the airborne and a rope ladder for the rest. The bottom storey was open to the street on one side, and there Che and Salma took a table where they could watch the traffic.

Unlike the Collegium place, which had been a haunt of the locals, a good half of this taverna's clientele were Fly-kinden, as though they really had set up a little slice of their warren-city of Merro here in Helleron. Most of the surrounding buildings also seemed to be adapted to that diminutive people's stature and practices, with ground-floor doors and windows boarded up, high windows added into walls, and probably fallback hatches opening in the roofs.

The other patrons of the taverna were not the sort to ask questions of a pair of fugitives, lest they themselves become the subject of questioning in return. Che saw Beetles, Spiders, halfbreeds, and a few others who must have belonged to kinden she had never encountered before. Each table was the hub of a little business deal, over food and wine and the music of a zither.

'What are we going to do?' she asked. Salma shrugged. His customary smile was absent.

'We have to look for the others,' she insisted.

'It's a big city,' Salma said. 'I didn't even realize cities this big existed. Shon Fhor, heart of the whole Common-weal, isn't this big. I could fly over this place every day for a year and I'd not see them if they were on a rooftop waving a flag.'

Che opened her mouth, shut it again immediately.

'Not that I won't,' he said. He downed the shallow bowl of wine and refilled it from the jug their host had provided.

'We need help,' said Che. 'Uncle Sten has people here, so if we can only make contact . . .'

'Stenwold's friends are compromised,' he said seriously. 'As you saw, they already managed to turn Bolwyn.'

A shiver went through Che's stomach as she remem-bered what she had seen, and she put down her own bowl. 'Salma, I'm going to say something very strange.'

That brought a hint of his smile back at last. 'That's something *new*?'

'Salma, when I saw Bolwyn, just before everything went wrong, he . . .' She put a hand to her forehead, feeling abruptly tired and frightened. 'He . . . I thought he . . . He seemed to . . .' She pursed her lips in frustration at her inability to get the thought out. 'He wasn't Bolwyn – just for a moment. I know that sounds mad. I just . . . I can't explain it. It wasn't make-up or a mask, and it wasn't some new Art thing, because . . .'

'Because you always know Art when you see it,' Salma put in for her. 'Like that thing the Wasps do, with their lightning. *That's* Art.'

'And this wasn't. It . . .' She shuddered. 'It was horrible. I don't know what it was.' Reviewing her last few words she felt abruptly disgusted with herself. 'I'm sorry, I must have imagined it. There are more important things . . .'

'It must have been magic,' Salma told her.

She laughed. 'Of course, that's just what it was. Magic.'

He continued to look at her, his slight smile still there, until she realized that he was being quite serious.

'Magic?' she asked him. 'Salma, no offence, but there's no such thing as magic. That's just something that primitive people believe, or at least that people believed in before the revolution. Moth-kinden and that kind of thing, I mean. Come on now, magic?'

'Primitive people, is it?' His smile widened. 'Like my people?'

'Your people are sophisticated people, civilized people. Or that's what you're always telling us.'

He placed a hand on hers across the table, not as a gesture of intimacy but to impress on her the import of his words. 'I believe in magic, Che. I've seen magic done. My Kin-obligate – in the place where I grew up, the prince there had a seer in his privy council who could see into the future.'

'Salma, it's easy enough to take a guess at what might happen. It's a trick for the credulous, really.'

'I saw him conjure up the soul of a dead man, and question it.'

Now it was her turn to smile. 'I'm sure that there was a

rational explanation. Smoke and mirrors and that kind of thing.'

'The dead man was my father.'

She stopped whatever was about to come out of her mouth, and instead emptied her bowl of wine.

'I heard him tell me about the Battle of Shan Real, where he had died. When I later heard the story from a soldier who had been there, it was all absolutely as my father's shade described it.'

'But Salma, that old wizard could already have heard it from a soldier as well – maybe someone fleeing the battle, ahead of the rest.'

Neither his gaze nor his smile faltered.

She took a deep breath. 'I don't want to offend you, Salma. You're a friend – the best friend anyone could ask for. You saved my life and my uncle put his trust in you, but I don't believe in magic. I'm sorry.'

He shrugged. 'Of course. I won't tell you about the Silver Faces then, because that wouldn't change anything.'

'And why would it change anything?'

He was openly grinning at her now, so that she still could not tell whether he was making fun or not. 'Oh it's just a legend, in any case, from long ago. It was said that they could capture your reflection in a mirror, you see. It was said, that way, they could get to look like anyone.'

Che's stomach twisted again, seeing in her mind's eye Bolwyn's shifting face, but she fought it down. *I do not believe in magic.*

'They were the very first spies, apparently, and the best,' Salma continued, voice low like a man telling a ghost story. 'A secret order of intelligencers. No man could tell them apart from those they copied. They were just a myth, you'll say, and I'm sure you're right. True, they're reported as fact in the chronicles of the Commonweal: from when we used them against our enemies, when our enemies used them against us. But this was long ago, before your revolution, and many strange things are reported in the earliest annals, that no one today, no young Beetle-kinden lass, anyway, would ever credit.' He laughed at her expression that, behind its attempted defiance, now had a small child's wide-eyed awe at the inexplicable. 'Remember, your revolution never reached us, so we're just ignorant primitives.'

'It's impossible to tell if you're being serious.'

'I hope so,' he agreed. 'Now, how are we going to track down Tynisa and Totho?'

'Well, unless you can just magic them out of your robe,' Che said, a little archly, 'then I had better hunt down my relatives in Helleron, because they'll know this city so at least they can help us look.'

It was a slum that Totho was led to. There was no other word for it. The skyline was dominated by the smokestacks of a factory whose long, uneven bulk rambled from here all the way down to the river. There were no windows in the pitted expanse of wall that now faced them, though huddled up to that blind countenance were hundreds of crooked little homes. Each had been built from whatever was ready to hand: wood, stone, brick and pieces of metal made each one an individual eyesore. There was no plan to them, either individually or in their general arrangement. The pathways between them were crooked, in-turning, shadowed both by the shacks and by the looming factory. The ground was little more than mud, under which fragmented cobbles occasionally shifted enough to twist an ankle.

Totho guessed that much of the slum's populace must be out working, perhaps in that very factory, but there were still plenty of people about to watch him pass. Many were children, all thin and dirty, all staring at him. He had expected to be accosted, asked for money, but they kept their distance. He realized this was because his sword was still in his hand and, after that realization, it stayed there.

Depressingly, a large number of these people were halfbreeds. Most were Ant–Beetle crosses, just like himself, but there were some he could not even begin to identify, the mongrel results of a succession of taboo unions, or perhaps the get of kinden he did not yet know.

The adults he saw were evidently not interested in legal employment. One and all they gave him a level, assessing stare, but they had seen his guide and let him be. His guide was well known, even in shrouded outline.

Totho himself had already been given enough chance to study that uneven form. The man made a great show of his awkward, rapid shambling gait, but Totho noticed the way the cloak was pushed up and outwards by whatever was hidden underneath, and guessed this man was wearing armour, something outlandish and irregular, like some flashy prize-fighter. None of this made Totho happy about the present deal but if he stopped following now he would be lost, and then he would rapidly be prey.

His guide turned abruptly aside and went over to a door in one of the sloping shacks. A quick fumble with a key and he was inside, holding the door open and gesturing for Totho to follow him. Follow he did, but not without qualms and a close grip on his sword.

There was precious little light inside, and his benefactor seemed to have instantly disappeared. It was only when the back wall started to glow softly that he realized it was only a drape, with a lamp now lit behind it. He pushed his way carefully past the curtain.

'Nine,' said the voice of his guide as he did so. 'Nine separate buildings.' It answered his question.

From the outside this small terrace of ramshackle huts had looked no different from the others. On the inside it was revealed as all one, a single dwelling. The contours were, of necessity, irregular, and there were no internal walls, just posts to keep the undulating ceiling where it should be. More hanging drapes of hessian and wool were all his host had to differentiate sleeping quarters from kitchen, storeroom from workshop. *Workshop?*

Totho stared. Of all the things he had thought of on entering that door, it was not this, and yet here was something as familiar to him as his own name. Most of the floorspace was given over to benches on which half a dozen mechanisms had been anatomied for repair. Between the benches he recognized a big upright grinder, a bandsaw, a set of optic lenses and a punch-press. It was almost like coming home.

'I took you for the type,' his host remarked, and Totho snapped from his reverie. In his fascination he had almost forgotten the man existed.

'Thank you for . . .' He had decided to trust this man, and then, turning to look at him, he choked on his words. Scuto had cast his cloak back and he was indeed wearing armour, but it was an old leather breastplate that had been crudely cut to fit him. The rest of his shape was entirely his own.

As a child back in Collegium, Totho had watched puppet shows on occasion, and even then he had been more interested in how it was done than in the stories and jokes. There had been one puppet that turned up in most of them which was known as the Malefactor and existed to get other puppets into trouble and so start off the plot. It had a great hooked nose that almost met its upward-curving chin, and Scuto looked just like that long-remembered manikin. Between nose and chin his mouth appeared as a crooked line in skin that was nut-brown and slightly shiny, and above the nose his eyes were small and suspicious. He was frankly hideous. It was not even the face that made him so, or the hunched back, for he bristled everywhere with curving spikes. There were small ones the size of fish hooks, and others as long as knife blades, and they sprouted from him at random and all over. His breastplate, his very garments, were roughly cut to avoid these, but still his tunic was darned a hundred times over, and ripped even so. It was a wonder, Totho thought helplessly, that this man had not cut himself to ribbons.

'Yeah, well,' Scuto said sourly. 'You ain't a picture yourself, halfbreed.' He shuffled over to one of the benches and put down his crossbow. It was a sleek repeater with a high magazine at the top, holding ten quarrels at least.

'I— I'm sorry but . . .' Even the sight of the crossbow could not keep Totho's attention off the man himself.

'But what, halfway? I'm a pureblood, me.' Scuto's smile showed barbed snaggle-teeth. 'You don't get so many of my kind down here, but the Empire knows us. They can't stand us. Wonder why. Thorn Bug-kinden, that's me, so live with it.'

'You mean there's . . .'

'More of us?' Scuto actually cackled, which improved his appearance not one bit. 'Way north of here, boy, there's more of us than anyone could sensibly want. And you know the real killer? There ain't one of us quite like the other. You look on me, and you see a real ugly bug. Well that's what I see in the mirror, boy, and that's what I see when I look at all my folk.'

Totho nodded. 'I think I can . . . understand that.'

'Bet you can, you being a hybrid boy and all.' Scuto looked him up and down, from a vantage point focused around Totho's chest. 'So, you going to admit to being one of Stenwold Maker's little helpers?'

'I suppose I am.' At this point it didn't seem that there was much point denying it.

'That bag there says you're an artificer, boy. You just carrying it for someone else, or can you do something useful with your life?'

'I've received my accredits from the Great College,' Totho said with pride.

'Don't mean squat to me, boy. Till you show me you can do something, you ain't no artificer to me.'

'Oh really?' Totho heaved his bag onto a bench and began rifling through it. 'How do you keep all this stuff here anyway? You couldn't keep it secret. They'd . . . hear you milling through the walls. Why hasn't it been stolen or something?'

Scuto spat, not as an insult, Totho guessed, but some local way of showing emphasis.

'Listen, boy, in this neighbourhood I'm the man. That means half the eyes and spies out there are on my books. That means there are swords and crossbows out there that point where I tell them, and when I ask it, I can get a real doctor to come out here who knows he'll be safe and get properly paid. It all adds up, because anyone out there who means me ill will run foul of the locals unless he's got a damn army, believe you me. What with all that and your man Maker's work to do, it's a wonder I find time for my actual occupation.'

'Which is artificing.' Totho pulled a device from his bag and handed it over.

'That it is.' Scuto took the air-battery in his thorny hands and squinted at it. His look was suspicious at first, then surprised and at last appreciative. 'Not bad work, boy. Very neat, very small. You've got good hands there. Pistons, is it? For powering engines?'

'I was going to use it for a weapon. I . . . like weapons,' Totho said awkwardly.

'Not a lad your age that doesn't,' said Scuto, grinning. 'This has potential. If Stenwold's work leaves you any time free, I'd like to see what you do with it.'

'Stenwold's work?' Totho's instant smile suddenly soured. 'What happened with your man?'

Scuto grimaced. 'You don't want to know.'

'I do! Three of my friends are still out there, if they haven't already been caught.' He bit his lip. 'I should never have left them. I thought they'd be right behind me. And all because your man sold us to the Wasps!'

'No he didn't,' Scuto said, but he was looking down at his hands as they toyed with the air-battery.

'Then how do you explain what happened? He led us right into an ambush!'

'No he didn't,' said Scuto again. 'On account of this morning I fished his body out of the reagent vats in the factory right behind us. Someone had dumped the corpse for a quick get-rid-of job, but picked the wrong vat.'

'This morning? But—'

'Oh I know, boy.' When Scuto shrugged, the spines rippled across his shoulders and back again like grass in the wind. 'I was watching at Benevolence Square, and I tracked you from there. I *saw* the bastard, and for sure, it was Bolwyn, a man I've known for three years. And yet his body's in the poorgrave five streets from here, and has been since near dawn.' The Thorn Bug bared his teeth again. 'Beats me, boy. Beats me.'

Eleven

It was one of the better tavernas of middle Helleron. Well appointed, its upper windows at least gave a view of the slopes where the gleaming white villas of the wealthy held sway. The service was known to be good, the host friendly and the watch were slipped enough coins to have them come running at the hint of any trouble. Most of all, though, the Grain Shipment Taverna was discreet. When Thalric entered, tipping his broad-brimmed hat to the host, the wide-waisted Beetle-kinden just nodded. Thalric was able to find a table, lean back in his chair, and in a short while the host's boy was at his elbow with a bowl of watered wine and the murmured message that the back room would be ready for him any time he wished.

Thalric felt no desire to hurry, though. He was not looking forward to this meeting. Behind him his two bodyguards had taken up positions beside the wall, keen eyed and, regrettably, looking like nothing so much as a pair of on-duty soldiers. They knew, of course, that if they got it wrong, if they chanced to be looking left when the action went right, then there would be no excuses. Not with Captain Thalric. He had a reputation that put men on edge all the way up and down the ladder of rank. In fact he was the very terror of the outlander Wasp war effort just now.

He looked at his reflection in the wine, wondering how much the dark liquid was hiding of the lines the last few years had put on his face. The final year of the Dragonfly war had been a tough assignment: Thalric and his picked men behind enemy lines, and fighting a cat-and-mouse war with the Commonweal's own Mercers, their heroes of covert war. When the word had come about rebellion flaring in Maynes, he had been relieved to be recalled to deal with it. Then the Empire's eye had turned west, and he had been sent to Helleron.

He felt as though he was already at war with Helleron, for the call of duty fought a nightly battle with his own desires, and did not always come away the utter victor. Imperial cities were simply not like this. Firstly, imperial cities were actually governed. Helleron had its council of the fat and wealthy, it was true, but Thalric had seen the city from all sides and he knew that, if it was governed at all, it actually governed itself. It was ruled through a thousand small concerns, ten thousand petty greeds, by gangs, factory magnates, artificer-lords, black marketeers and, of course, foreign agents. More, this was accepted, and even intended, by its people. It was all a great, sprawling, grasping chaos, the absolute anathema of the Empire's iron rule, and Thalric found he rather enjoyed it. His line of duty, the sinuous line he was reeling through the fabric of Helleren society, had led him to many places that the Empire had not shown him. He had been to the theatre to watch a riotous play that openly derided the very people paying for the privilege of watching, and yet was applauded for it. He had gone to dinner with Beetle magnates and Spider slavemongers and renegade Ant weapons dealers and made polite conversation with them. He had talked business in exclusive clubs and richly decked chop houses and brothels that offered girls of every kinden he could name. For a military man with an active mind he was required to remind himself of his duty at least once a day.

He was going to miss it all. He knew that the Empire's rule, when brought to this place, would crush much that made it what it was. His trembling subordinates would never have guessed that his iron reputation would allow for such regret.

Or for worry, come to that, but Thalric was a worrier by nature and that was why he was so good at his job. By worrying about everything, he allowed very little past him, and right then he was worrying about his contact. His contact had worried him for twenty years now, ever since they had started their unnatural association.

Thalric stood up, tipped the wink to the host's boy and went up the stairs to the back room. It would be dark, he knew, since Scylis did not like being seen, and anyway Thalric had decided it would be better not to see whatever face the man might present to him. *A master of disguise* he had told himself. A clever man with masks and cosmetics. As the history of their dealings had been written, such assurances to himself had begun to ring hollow.

He had a particular fear – for fear was another thing he owned that his men would not guess at – that, should he suddenly unveil a lamp or light a candle at one of these meetings, the face he would see facing him would be his own.

He could see the dark shape of the man by the open window. Always cautious, was Scylis. Thalric took his time, sitting down, getting comfortable, sipping the last of his wine.

'So,' he said, 'what went wrong?'

Scylis made an annoyed sound. 'What went wrong is that you might as well employ clowns and circus freaks as your soldiers, and your local talent is even worse.' The voice was crisp, sarcastic, accentless. 'They closed the trap too soon, and your children meanwhile made their fare-wells and left. I'd advise you to discipline your men but there aren't that many of them that even managed to walk away alive.'

Thalric nodded. His four errant 'scholars', as he had

been briefed, were turning into quite the death squad. 'Afraid for your life, Scylis?'

The hidden man made a hiss of disdain. 'If you had really wanted them dead, I would have killed them. As it was, I played my part. Do not think you will now withhold payment.'

'Ever the mercenary.'

'I could argue quite persuasively that being motivated by personal wealth is nobler than by imperialistic conquest,' replied Scylis's dry, amused voice. 'However, my rates for scholarly debate are the same as those for my other services, so I doubt you would want to retain me as a pedagogue.' He loved the sound of his own voice, Thalric knew. Not that he talked too much, but each word came out finely crafted and with relish. Yet he could sum up what he really knew about Scylis in seconds, and spend days over what he did not. From the shadow's build, and the voice, he had decided that his catspaw was Spiderkinden, but Scylis could be Scyla for all he knew, and neither of those need be the agent's real name.

'You'll be paid,' Thalric said, 'but could you impersonate any of them? Did you get a good enough look?'

'It would be by appearance only,' said Scylis. 'I didn't speak long enough to get to know them. Not like I did with Bolwyn.'

Thalric considered Bolwyn. He had no doubt that Scylis had questioned him most persuasively, before the man's death, in order to assume that role. He felt no regrets about him. It was for the Empire.

'It may yet come to that,' he told the shadow. 'In the meantime, here is your price.' A bag of coins, gold Helleron Centrals, clinked on the floor. 'I'll have work for you soon enough. Word by the usual route.'

'A pleasure as always, Major Thalric,' came Scylis's reply.

'*Captain* Thalric,' the Wasp corrected.

'Come now, would you respect me if I could be fooled by your games? We have danced, you and I, and I know you.'

A characteristic Spider expression, and Thalric decided it was genuine, rather than a part the man was playing.

'You know me, do you?'

'I know your subordinates fear you, which is no strange thing in an officer, but your superiors fear you even more. Shall I utter the dreaded name and see what it conjures?'

'Best you don't,' Thalric advised, as it came unbidden into his mind: *Rekef*. The army held a blade to the throat of the world, but he stood with his blade at the throat of the army, for the Emperor would tolerate no resistance, within or without. 'Much more talk of that, Scylis, and even you might outlive your usefulness.'

Scylis made a dismissive sound, but he obviously gave some weight to the warning, because he changed the subject smoothly. 'Did your men tell you about the Spider-kinden duellist? Quite the fencer to watch.'

Thalric nodded. 'Yes they're a proper bag of surprises.' He stood up, feeling abruptly weary. Scylis always seemed to be mocking him, and he wished that he had some other agent who could do what this man appeared to be able to do, however it was that he managed it. 'If you come across any information, any leads, you know I'll pay for it,' he said, as he left the room.

For the Empire. That was the rod at his core. No matter how much Helleron might tempt him with its decadent, delectable pleasures, when it was *for the Empire* he put all that aside and knew neither regret, worry nor fear. He was not a bad man, in his own estimation. No, he was a loyal man, and for an imperial citizen that was the crowning virtue. When the order had come to him, during the last war, to kill the three infant children of Prince Felise Dael, he had carried the knife himself to end the noble line, and known no remorse.

This thought stopped him on the stairs, for he had children himself, hundreds of miles away, whom he had barely ever seen since they were born. A wife he no longer wrote to. The fear of his underlings and the loathing of his superiors. Coded orders on scrolls scheduled for burning.

Their mother had been there, when he killed those three children, held restrained between two of his men. It was not that he had forced her to watch, simply that she had been in the nursery when he arrived. Standing on the stairs in the Grain Shipment Taverna he found that he wished she had been taken away.

For the Empire. It made him feel stronger, just saying the words to himself, but sometimes he felt as though he was turning into something like Scylis: masks and masks and masks, until he could hold them all up before him, and not know which was truly his own face.

Tynisa awoke slowly, but cautiously. She was somewhere she did not recognize. She could feel it from the bed, the sounds around her, the very smell. It could mean many things, from a kidnap to a successful liaison. She stayed quite still, allowing herself to come to without the world becoming aware of it.

A lumpy straw mattress and a sour, stale smell. If this was a liaison then she was certainly slumming it.

Bolwyn's betrayal! It was all she could do not to open her eyes, to leap off the mattress. Bolwyn's betrayal, then dashing for the alley mouth, two dead Wasps on her slope-shouldered conscience that seemed to be able to shrug them off so easily, but where was she now?

Her head ached abominably. She must have struck it on something.

She had got out into the street. More Wasps had been coming, cutting furrows through the crowd. Her bloody sword had been like a talisman to clear the way for her. She had tried to cut her way back, find Che and Salma, but there were Wasps and town militia approaching, and she had been driven further and further.

She had been exhausted. She had run and run and Helleron had always been there. In the end she had been running to escape the city itself, and failed.

It had consumed her.

So, she was in its bowels. With the most careful of movements, eyes still tight shut, she felt for her blade. Gone. She wore nothing but a shift. Where had she run to? Her mind simply did not have the answers.

It was time. She finally opened her eyes.

On a filthy mattress, covered by a stained sheet, in some tiny room with one slit window.

There was a chair across from her, near the doorless doorway. A small man was dozing in it, and carelessly slung over its back—

She was on her feet before she could stop herself, but silently, silent as her kind could be. In two steps she was within reach, and she had the hilt in her hand. She slid it from its scabbard.

That woke him, the whisper of steel on leather beside his ear. Even as he jumped she had the blade beneath his chin, drawing a bead of blood as he started. He was a halfbreed, she saw, looked like Beetle and Fly-kinden in there and perhaps more. He stood very still. He only had a knife himself but kept his hands far from it as if to reassure her.

'Where am I?' she hissed.

'Malia's house,' he croaked, eyes flicking from her to the blade.

'And who's Malia that I should know her?'

'She's my chief. She's important. You don't mess with her.' His voice shook as he said it, though. She smiled cruelly.

'Well maybe I want to give this Malia a message. Maybe

you're the message, what do you think? So tell me something useful.'

'I – I – I – I don't know. What do you—? You were just brought in. I don't know. I just got told to watch you,' he stammered.

'Why?'

A woman's voice, from the doorway: 'Why talk to the little finger when the face is here?'

Tynisa jumped back, rapier extended in a duellist's guard. The newcomer was a woman of beyond middle years, greying, but lean and solidly built. She wore the under- and over-robes that the Helleren favoured, but she was Ant-kinden and still retained that race's warrior stance. Her shortsword stayed in its sheath. Given the confidence in her, it was obviously a pointed statement.

Tynisa slowly lowered the blade until the tip was close to the floor. She could bring it up at a moment's notice, but for now she wanted to talk. 'And you're Malia?'

'That I am.' The woman surveyed her dispassionately. 'You bounced back quickly, child.' Her voice still had a little of the Ant formality about it.

'I'm no child.'

'That remains to be seen. You owe me.'

'For bed and board?' Tynisa said contemptuously. 'What, didn't you have any stables you could sling me in?'

A quirk at the corner of Malia's mouth. 'This is Helleron. Here this is luxury accommodation. You owe me because you killed one of my people.'

'When?' Tynisa grasped at those parts of the previous day that still eluded her. 'When did I?' *Is she with the Empire?*

'Oh, he went for you first, but that makes no difference.' Malia folded her arms across her chest. 'He always was a fool, and when you ran in, sword all red, he clearly decided you were for target practice.'

A thought, an image, the scattered shards of the previous day now drifting ever closer. A man pointing a shortbow at her, letting loose an arrow. It had passed across her back, ruffling her cloak, and she had gone for him. She had been moving without thought by then, reflex to reflex.

'I killed him.' She had cut the bow in half as he raised it to defend himself, and a twist of the wrist had turned the move into a lunge that had opened his throat.

'And you injured four others of mine,' Malia said. 'They went to help the man you killed. You bloodied them all before one of them got a club against your head. And here you are with your sword pointed at Auntie Malia, to whom you owe so much.'

'They're not debts I recognize.' Another dead man. Tynisa barely felt the weight.

'If you think I can't draw sword and kill you, then you had better think again,' Malia said, in all seriousness. 'I might be a matron now, but I was a duellist and assassin in my time, and I never gave up the sword habit.'

Tynisa slowly, deliberately, raised the sword until it was directed at her. 'But?' she prompted.

Malia's twitch turned into a full, grudging smile. 'But I might have other uses for you. Sword's point, child! Who are you? You raise a stink around Hammerstake Street. You leave a neat set of dead men for the guard to puzzle over. You cross three separate fiefs trailing your bloody sword, and you end up on my back porch brawling with my men. And brawling well, for there's not one of them who shouldn't be grateful for the lesson in swordsmanship.'

'I need to find some friends of mine,' Tynisa said levelly.

'As I said, you owe me,' Malia told her. 'Now, you can add to your credit, if you want, and I can have people keep an open eye. But you owe me, and I have a use for you.'

Here it comes. 'And what might that be?' The slit

window would not have fit a Flychild. If she wanted to get out of here the hard way it would have to be through Malia. The woman could have been lying, of course, but Ants were warrior-bred from birth.

'You owe me,' Malia repeated. 'I owe other people in our fief and you'd make a fine gift for them.'

'Slavery?' spat Tynisa, and Malia raised a hand to quiet her.

'You don't understand where you are or how things work, child, so keep your anger until you can use it. If I had a choice I'd find work for you myself, put you on my books. Teaching sword, perhaps. Or using it. As it is, I think I'll send your talents up the ladder. I'll be quits, and you'll have a better chance to do whatever you need to, so long as you remember that you owe. And when you owe, you do what you're told.'

'What's to stop me just running, as soon as I get the chance?'

Malia nodded. 'Intelligent questions, good. Firstly, you'd be hunted. Secondly, I'm guessing you are already hunted, and the fief will be able to shelter you if you keep faith with us. Thirdly, if you want to find someone in Helleron, there are a lot of doors to knock on if you're on your own. Fourth and last, you never know, you might actually like it in the fief. You seem just the type.'

Tynisa lowered the sword again. 'And what is a fief?'

'It's like a family, and a city, and a factory all in one, child,' Malia said. She turned and began to descend the stairs, and without options Tynisa sheathed her blade, slung the baldric over her shoulder, and followed.

'A family because you do what your elders tell you, and they take care of you,' Malia called back to her. 'A city because there are rulers and subjects, and territory that must be defended. A factory because we're all so very, very busy making things. Although most of what we make is what other people would call trouble.'

'You're a gang then? Criminals!' Tynisa started.

'That we are, child. One of a few hundred spread across Helleron, and neither the least nor the greatest. We're the Halfway House, and I think you'll fit in just perfectly.'

A rain had swept down off the mountains to attempt the futile task of trying to wash Helleron clean. After it had filtered through the smog of the factories it was greasy on the skin, stinging in the eyes. Che and Salma sheltered in the townhouse's doorway, and she hung on the bell-rope again, hearing the distant tinkle from within the house.

The slot beside her head flicked open. 'I told you to go away,' said the appalled voice of the servant. 'I shall call the watch.'

'Please tell Master Monger that I'm here,' she said. 'I am his cousin.'

'Master Monger is not at home to vagrants,' the servant told her – and this after she and Salma had changed back into their proper clothes. She reflected that if Salma was a vagrant, he was the best-dressed one in the world.

'But I'm *family*!' she insisted.

'Master Monger is too wise to fall for such a ploy, urchin,' said the narrow piece of servant she could spy through the slot. 'I swear that I shall call the watch. Be off with you.'

'I . . .' A stubborn streak took hold of Che. 'Hammer and tongs!' she swore, just like Uncle Stenwold. 'I am not moving off this doorstep until you fetch Master Elias Monger, and when he finds out how you have treated me, then by all the coin in the mint, he will have you thrashed!'

The silence that followed this outburst was broken at last only by Salma's quiet chuckle.

'I should do as she says,' he confirmed quietly. '*I* would if I were in your shoes.'

The slot slammed shut and they could hear the man pattering off into the house. Elias Monger's townhouse was not one of the villas on the hill itself, though it was practically at the hill's foot. Cousin Elias had clearly been doing well for himself, even if his hospitality left something to be desired.

'Well,' said Salma after a moment, 'I don't know if they're going to let us in or set the watch-bugs on us, but you've certainly made an impact.'

'I . . . don't know what came over me,' she said, feeling a little giddy. A moment later they heard the sound of feet approaching, several pairs of them. They took a step back from the door and Che smoothed down the front of her tunic.

When the door opened there were two armed men standing there, not soldiers but solid Beetle-kinden nonetheless with studded clubs and a couple of shields that had probably been adorning the wall until a moment ago. To Che's credit they looked nervous. Behind them was a lean, pinch-mouthed man she recognized as the servant, and beside him a shorter, fuller-figured individual with a thunderous frown on his face. He had a scroll in one hand and a reservoir pen in the other, obviously called to the door from the middle of his book-keeping.

'Now what is this? Grace and favour, but I can't be doing with these interruptions!' he snapped. 'I suggest the pair of you make yourselves scarce before my men give you a richly deserved beating.'

'Master Monger?' Che said meekly. 'My name is Cheerwell Maker and I have come here from Collegium. Uncle Stenwold sent me.'

Monger made to give some derisive reply, but then paused and squinted at her. From a chain about his neck he brought up a monocle to his eye. 'Cheerwell?' he said suspiciously.

'My father is Dorvy Maker, sir, but Uncle Stenwold took me in. I've been studying at the Great College.'

'Oh, Dorvy's child.' There was no great love in the

words, but Che was already aware that her parents were from the less reputable end of the family. 'Cheerwell,' Monger mused. 'That does sound familiar. Who's this other fellow?'

'Oh, this is Salma—' Che started, and then stopped herself. 'Excuse me, this is Prince Salme Dien of the Commonweal. He would also like to guest at your house, cousin.'

Salma, on cue, executed an elaborate genuflection, something exotic from his homeland. Monger's mouth picked up.

'Well, a Commonwealer.' Whatever he had heard about Salma's people, it obviously included something good, or at least profitable, because his reserve was fast diminishing. 'A prince of the Commonweal and my own dear cousin Cheerwell? Remarkable days indeed.' He gave the snide servant a look of exasperation. 'Really, I can only apologize for the zeal of my staff. You must understand that we have a great many callers of a less than savoury nature. Please come in, do come in.'

She had walked a fine line in telling Elias their story, and did not want to compromise him by naming names and allegiances. So it was that she patched together something close enough to the truth to resemble it at a distance. She and her friends had been sent to Helleron on some unde-fined business by Stenwold. They had been attacked in the street, although she did not know by whom, or why. They had been scattered in the fray and two were still missing. She and Salma needed a place to stay until Stenwold arrived, and they needed their host's help.

Despite her obfuscation she guessed that Elias had read between the lines well enough. He seemed to understand that, under the circumstances, Totho and Tynisa would not be making it easy to be found.

'I'll send the word round to my foremen and factors to

look out for them,' he promised them over dinner. 'I'll post up a bit of a reward, as well. There are a whole breed of people in this city for whom finding other people is a way of life.' *Finding other people who don't want to be found.* The words hung unsaid in the air.

'Do you think it's wise, to just . . .' Che squirmed, knowing that whatever word was now put out would reach their enemies soon enough.

'My dear girl,' Elias told her. 'What else can we do? Otherwise it's like looking for someone in a crowded plaza by blindfolding yourself and whispering their name. Don't worry. I'm not without influence in this city. I have seven factories and a mining concern, and that means that when I speak, people listen. We'll have your fellows safe within these walls before you know it. Just give it a few days.'

Che toyed with her food, glanced at Salma and saw her own concern mirrored in his easy smile. Helleron was vast, her friends were small, and the Wasp Empire that had taken such an interest in them would not rest. She could not imagine Elias Monger's connections working faster than the Wasps' implacable malice. Hour by hour a dreadful cold feeling was growing in her chest, as she thought of Tynisa and Totho.

Twelve

There was a Fly-run eatery on Bleek Street where Sinon Halfway, leader of the Halfway House cartel, held court. Court it was, too, Tynisa realized at once. Malia brought her into a long room decked out in Fly style, with a low table taking up much of the floor. Some half-dozen Fly-kinden staff were serving three dozen men and women, and it was evident to Tynisa from first glance that there was a right end and a wrong end of the table to be kneeling at. The right end was closest to the enthroned figure of Sinon Halfway himself.

He was a lean man just turning to fat around the middle, due to the few years now when he had not personally taken up a sword to defend his empire. He was dressed like a man about to flee the city with all his wealth upon him, but she saw that all of them were, more or less, for aside from a few who looked ostentatiously spartan, the gangsters sported chains and rings, amulets and jewelled gorgets, even in one case a mail shirt made from coins, good silver Standards of Helleron mint. Sinon would have been worth, in gold and gems alone, as much as half the table, and she understood that it was a status thing. A wealthy man who hid his light under a bushel would gain no respect for that here.

The name told true. Sinon was a halfbreed, and she guessed that he was Moth-kinden interbred with the pale-skinned Ants of Tark. What should have been an unpleasant mottling had instead left him with milky skin traced with veins and twists of grey, like marble. It was an exotic, oddly attractive sight. His hair was dark, worn long over his shoulders in a Spider style. His eyes were just dark pupils circled in white, without irises. The melange of his ancestry had conspired to make a man at once unnerving and compelling.

'So Malia has brought me a gift,' he said, and the conversation about the table immediately stopped, each gangster looking across or craning over to see her. Malia left her side then, taking her place at Sinon's right hand.

'Delightful,' said Sinon. His mouth and voice were amused, his eyes unreadable. 'But I'm told that you're not just here for ornament. Malia says you can fight. What's your name, Spiderchild?'

'Tynisa, Master Sinon.' She hadn't meant the honorific. Some holdover from childhood had brought it out of her.

'And well-mannered too, such a rare combination. And you understand that you owe me a debt, a debt that Malia here has passed on to me.'

'I've been told it,' Tynisa replied. A murmur of laughter passed through the gangsters at her attitude. Only those closest to the head of the table were untouched by it.

'And *can* you fight?' Sinon asked her politely.

'I can.'

'Well, then, there may be a place for you at my table,' Sinon said. 'But I understand you need my help, Spider-child. Malia's already told me your little story. Help me and then perhaps I can spare some help for you.'

She realized that she was reacting too much, taking too little control. She narrowed her eyes, clenched her fists, stared at Sinon. 'So,' she demanded. 'Where do I sit?'

There was a ragged murmur of approval from the gangsters, but Sinon held up a hand for silence, and got it. 'Don't get too fond of her,' he warned his people. 'She doesn't know our traditions yet. You sit, Spiderchild, where you want, but be aware that for you to have any elbow room everyone moves down a seat. Now you tell me where you sit.'

Tynisa let herself pause. She would not jump as soon as Sinon cracked the whip. *Has it come to this?* she thought. *What would Stenwold say?* Sinon was talking about fighting for blood, just to join in his little clique. The fiefs of Helleron had harsh and simple rules. *At what point do I become one of them? When I draw their blood? When I take their place?*

She wondered if she could still refuse now, if she could flee – a sudden dash down the hall, out of the building, onto the unknown streets of Helleron. *And then what?* She would never find Che or the others on her own. She needed help, and this thief, this killer, was apparently the only help she had.

And beneath all that was another dark voice, telling her that they had questioned her skill, that they wished to see her blade drawn. *It is your duty and your pleasure to oblige them . . .*

She walked down the line of the table, seeing who met her gaze, who avoided it. There were a lot down the far end of the table that she knew she could beat, humiliate even, without worry. They were the rabble, the desperate hangers-on just clutching at the edges of Sinon's favour. But if she was going to do this, she was going to do it properly.

She paced back towards the table's head, feeling the hum of appreciation as they began to ask themselves just how daring she was going to be. The gangsters were a motley lot: Beetles, Ants, Flies, Spiders, plenty of half-breeds, and a few she could not name. Whatever their race, towards the head of the table they met her stare levelly. They had scars, most of them, amidst the jewellery, so it had been a fight for them to get where they were, and it would be a fight for her to take it from them. The few of them who did not seem to be warriors looked at her without fear, and from that she guessed at the presence of some stand-in or bodyguard to protect their useful talents from needless harm. Artificers, accountants, intelligencers and the like, no doubt. Sinon would have need of those.

She looked up to the very head of the table, at Sinon himself. He was watching her with great interest and she sent him one of her best smiles to show him she was not afraid of him.

To his right was Malia, of course, and Tynisa felt that to challenge her would be bad grace, and she was also not sure she could win. The woman had held onto her place at Sinon's right, where anyone could call her out for it. That bespoke a truth behind her boasts earlier.

On Sinon's left sat a giant. Standing, he would be at least seven feet tall, his head brushing the ceiling. His skin was dead white, not the translucent pale of an albino but a waxy blank whiteness she had never seen before. Strange as that was, it was nothing to his lower jaw, which jutted out in a snarl of upwards-pointing fangs, or his hands that sported great bone blades curving from thumb and forefinger, eight inches long at the least. His eyes, above a flat nose and that grotesque jaw, were small and calm, and he cupped the wine bowl in his palm and three fingers with great care. He was more, she decided, than a simple brute. His yellow eyes were keenly picking her apart, evaluating her, and she decided that he would be too much, too soon.

Remember Che and Salma. Remember who you are shedding blood for. Or, if the worst came to the worst and the Empire had beaten her to it, at least Sinon's people could become her tool for revenge. The thought brought a sudden fire to her. *So I draw a little criminal blood today, and how much Wasp blood tomorrow?*

She had her blade out in a moment, startling those nearest to her, but she was pointing across the table, to the giant's left-hand neighbour. He was a pale Ant from Tark, and he stood right away with an eagerness that spoke of a few tricks she did not know about. He looked like Adax from the College duelling society, and she decided that she had always wanted to take that particular man down a peg. Even his image here would do.

'Where do we fight?' she asked.

'Why, right here, where we can all see, but try not to tread on the food,' Sinon said with a lazy gesture.

With deliberate ease the Ant-kinden drew a pair of shortswords from beneath the table. He grinned at her, and then glanced at his comrades. There were three other Tarkesh Ants here for dinner, and he singled them out especially. She saw it then: his mind and theirs would be as one during this fight. Whatever he missed, they would see on his behalf. There would be no surprising him.

'Two-sword boy, are you?' She felt proud of the calm humour in her voice, though inside she had begun to think that she had made a serious mistake. With a swift dart she snatched an eating knife from the nearest diner and balanced it in her left hand. 'I suppose that evens the odds a little.'

The spectators gave her a scattered laugh. She took three steps back and settled into her stance, rapier extended, blunt knife held back and high as though she would make the killing stroke with it.

Their fighting space was a strip three feet wide and twenty long, and she hoped that her longer blade would tell in it. He did not seem to be worried, though, standing still down the length of their battlefield, relaxed and eager.

'First blood,' Sinon warned them. 'It's been a quiet day so far. I don't want a body spoiling it for me. Of course, if first blood is last blood, well, what can you do?' The halfbreed licked his lips, obviously a man to enjoy a little dinner entertainment. 'Well off you go then. Don't keep us in suspense.'

Tynisa moved first, and almost had him then, a quick step, step and lunge and he was almost on the end of her sword. His spies in the audience called him to it just in time, though; and then he was on her.

He fought left and right, attacks from either side coming in without pattern, a constant driving dance of swordwork. His face, behind it, was set, without clues for her. He drove her back and back until her instincts told her the wall was just an inch behind her back heel. As he came in at her again she bounced backwards, got a foot on the wall and pushed. His left sword went past her, close enough to snag her tunic, and her rapier lanced over his head. She followed it, diving part-over, part-past him, trying to crack his nose with her elbow as she did. He swayed back, though, warned again by his collaborators, and she landed past, rolling just once and coming up on her feet.

He was already at her, driving in through a storm of applause from the crowd. She had his measure now. He came from left and right but his stock of moves was limited, the same strikes mirroring each other every time. She began to fend him off, sliding his blades off her own and then turning parries into ripostes, until they were in the middle of their narrow slice of arena, and he was no longer driving her before him. All the while she kept the eating knife poised, glinting in the light, always in his eyeline, always on his mind.

She realized that she had already made up her mind how to end this, perhaps even before she started. Even as she kept him at the length of her rapier, outside his reach, the plan she had not even known about was made plain to her, and she saw that it was good.

She went on the attack, seemed to mis-step. Abruptly she was too close, playing into the range of his blades. He took the chance she offered, by accident or not. She dragged her sword in, moving it like light and shadow, both of his blades skittering off its hand-guard and quillons. The eating knife darted in.

It came from above him for the top of his head, but the

voices in his head were shouting for him to watch for it. He twisted faster than she had thought, his blades coming up to catch the blunt knife. She was already a step back and the rapier was inside his guard. With utter delicacy, she struck.

She had intended to pink his shoulder, first blood as Sinon had said, but her blade laid open the side of his neck, and he went down in a startling abundance of red. For a moment she thought he might get up again, leaning on his sword and spitting at her, but then he fell forward, and she knew that he was dead.

Looking down now, with the heat of the moment cooling on her, she realized that she had absolutely no right to beat him. She was, after all, merely a good duellist for the College circuit. With a wood and bronze blade she had been better than most, but worse than some.

With a live blade in her hand, where death was at her shoulder and not just the gain or forfeit of a game, it seemed she had a talent for reddening her blade with other people's blood. She had not drawn this blade in anger without having a man die over it and yesterday it had taken four of Malia's men to catch her, even exhausted and confused as she must have been. *And she had blooded them all.*

She had a talent, for sure. If Sinon had his way, she might even have a vocation. The thought did not sit well with her, but a moment before, with the fierce fire of victory on her, she would have welcomed it.

What am I becoming?

She looked at Halfway. There was a commotion all along the table, some applauding and some cursing her, but in her mind it was just her and the gangster chief here now. She met his strange eyes and her smile, however forced, challenged him.

'Malia didn't exaggerate a word of it,' he said, his followers quieting even as he spoke. 'In fact, I think she even played it down a little.' He glanced at the Ant woman, who was looking ever so slightly concerned. Tynisa thought back to their first meeting, and wondered just what might have happened had she herself pushed it to a fight.

Better not to know. They were right when they said she needed them. Everything had gone wrong and her comrades were scattered to the winds. If this gang of murderers and blackguards was her only tool, then she would grasp it by the hilt.

Smiling so sweetly, she cleaned her blade and went to sit beside the giant, just a seat away from Sinon himself.

Elias Monger was a busy man. Rather than leave them in his house to fret, he had suggested that they come to see the leading sights of Helleron with him, such sights consisting of his commercial holdings and factories. Che wondered if he was trying to impress Salma the prince with his wealth and productivity. If so, that plan had fallen at the first hurdle.

Around them, the cavernous space boomed and thundered, as though what they were making here was not crossbow bolts but elemental weather. It was order on a grand scale: the ranks of great forges and presses and tooling machines that were never still, the constant onward progressing, each pair of hands only a tiny part of the grand scheme. The sheer industry of it, the fact that someone had worked all this out, this machined sequence, and then made it real as one of Elias Monger's factory floors, was beyond Che's ability to conceive.

'What do you think?' she asked.

'I thought you Beetles didn't keep slaves.' Salma's bleak gaze took in the long, gloomy, toiling room and found little in it he liked.

'Slaves?' Che said blankly. 'These aren't slaves.'

'Aren't they?'

She put her hands on her hips. 'No, they aren't. They're here to earn a wage. They're here of their own free will. You're just saying that because you don't understand what they're working *at.*'

'Free will?' Salma saw, in that long room, more people than he could readily count. They were almost shoulder to shoulder at the benches, each repeating some action over and over. Some were tending pole-lathes, others shaping shards of chitin. Some at the back fed a row of forges whose red glow shed more light than the grime-covered windows. Others poured molten metal into moulds, and others still honed the edges of the tiny pieces resulting, or freed them from the casts. Each man or woman had a fragment of a job, performed over and over. Each was utterly absorbed by it, working as fast as they could, passing over forever to the next pair of hands in line. Salma wondered what would happen if, in their same free will, they decided not to work.

'Oh, lose the long face,' Che snapped at him, annoyed. 'So they don't do things this way in the Commonweal. This is industry, Salma. This is how things happen in the Lowlands. We can't all spend three years making the perfect sword or whatever.'

'I don't think I can stay in here,' Salma said. 'I'm going to wait over by the door where there's light and air.'

'Suit yourself,' she said, nettled. He caught her gaze as he turned, though, and something must have communicated itself to her. Looking back across the room there was a moment, just a moment, when she saw the hundreds of labouring bodies and wondered: free will, yes, but how many of them had a family an eighth of an inch from starving? How many had come to Helleron to make their fortunes and now could not afford to leave?

At the far end of the factory were stacked bundles of crossbow bolts being carefully counted by an overseer. Each day this one factory shipped hundreds of them, made for a price nowhere in the Lowlands could match. Business was not good enough for Uncle Elias, though. Clearly some part of his grand machine was not keeping pace with the rest.

'I don't care how you do it,' she heard him complain as she approached. 'Hire more workers or get this lot to work faster, but we're down almost five parts per hundred, and the orders just keep mounting up. I want next tenday's turnover to be the same as the last, and the tenday after to be even better.'

The Ant foreman nodded glumly. 'It will be done.'

'Good.' Elias turned to see Che. 'How do you like my factory?'

'It's very impressive, uncle.' She had begun calling him that, rather than cousin, because he was Stenwold's age.

'What does your friend think?'

'I don't think he's really used to it,' she said.

'Well, the Commonwealers never were good customers. A bit snobby about their own craftsmanship, if you ask me.' Elias shrugged. 'It's always the same with the Inapt: they want everything handcrafted to thousand-year-old techniques that take forever, and then wonder why everyone else has a bigger army.'

'Did you ask the foreman about Tynisa and Totho?'

'He's seen nobody, but Helleron is a big place . . . Excuse me.'

A messenger had just flown into the factory, a young Fly-kinden with wings glittering red in the forgelight. He landed at a run and virtually threw himself at Elias's feet.

'Master Monger?' The youth was quite out of breath.

'That's me. Is it from Tarhaven's delegation?'

'No, Master. From Officer Breaken at the north-west shaft.' The Fly handed over a scroll and retired, chest still heaving.

Elias cursed quietly to himself and read the scroll by firelight. His face, when he looked at the messenger, was brutal, and Che thought he would strike the unfortunate man. 'Is this it?' he demanded. 'Is this all the report Breaken knows how to make?'

'He . . .' The messenger flinched back. 'He asks for you to come at once, with—'

'I see what he asks for. Does he have any idea how much this *costs*?' Elias's hands wrung the scroll and the Fly-kinden stepped further back from him.

'Uncle Elias?' Che asked, as much to distract his attention from the wretched messenger as anything else. Staring at her, Elias forced on a smile for Che's benefit.

'Is something wrong?' she prompted him.

'Just . . .' He let out a shuddering sigh. 'Just business. Cousin Stenwold has no idea how . . . delicate things can be, here in Helleron.' He looked past her at Salma, standing pale and wan in the forgelight. 'Do you think your friend would enjoy a little mountain air, Cheerwell?'

She nodded cautiously. 'Perhaps.'

'This . . .' He shook the mangled scroll at her. 'I have some business north of the city, one of my mining concerns. Perhaps some clearer air would do you good. I'm told our local brand can have an effect on strangers.'

Che dearly hoped that Salma would find some more solace in the mountains, but, knowing what she did about the Helleron mines, she had an uneasy feeling about how he would react. She nodded cautiously, but it was to Elias's back as he was already marching for the factory doors. The messenger scurried after him, and Elias called over his shoulder. 'Get me another twenty men. I don't care who you hire them from so long as they're good for the work. Flares, crossbows. And a repeating ballista – make it two. I'm going to cut the heart out of this *now*.'

Che and Salma exchanged surprised glances. It seemed Uncle Elias was going to war.

★

Helleron had been founded where it was because of the mountains. The Tornos range was a miner's delight, and most of all it was shot through with the richest iron deposits in the Lowlands. What had started as a small foundry town four centuries ago was now the hub of all the Lowlands' trade and mercantile ventures. Iron and steel were the body and bone of the city, consumed by it in vast quantities, refined in its organs, cast forth in a thousand shapes, and most of them warlike.

Salma had made a rough journey of it, a rigid passenger in the jolting convoy of steam automotives that clattered out from Helleron. It was the motion. It was the smell, it was, Che realized, the very fact of it. He had experienced none of this back in his distant home. Even in Collegium he had always flown or walked. Now he was travelling on a conveyance from another world, and it was making him ill. His golden skin had gone verdigris green by the time Elias called a halt in the shadow of the mountains.

It was not exactly the clear mountain air and scenic views that Elias had promised them. Salma still wore his smile like a shield against the world, but she could see the strain telling in his eyes. They had disembarked in a great quarry, where the stone of the foothills had been scooped away over decades. Gaping, propped-up holes in the sheer rock were the shallow mines, and above them a vast winch-and-pulley system creaked as its steam engine laboured to bring up the next load of men and ore from the utter depths. The quarry floor was laced with rails, and one wall formed the support for a lean-to as large as a castle, where the ore smelting took place. Elias had explained that it was cheaper to smelt it here and then ship the metal over to the city, or at least it had been ten years ago. In the light of recent developments he was having to rethink the profitability of his enterprise.

Elias had begun trying to explain the mine to them but

there were a dozen different people with claims on his time, and in the end Che and Salma were left like two baffled islands in the middle of all the bustle. Something had gone wrong here, she saw, spotting a pair of big drilling engines that were obviously out of commission, and one of them blackened and burned. A team of artificers was furiously stripping them both, arguing over what had been done and how best to fix it. There were soldiers here, too: Beetle-kinden guardsmen in Elias's employ, wearing chain mail and breastplates, and with crossbows to hand. They kept watching the sky, Che noticed. They were clearly nervous.

'What do you think is going on here?' she asked Salma.

'Do you think I can guess? This is a world I have no dealings with,' he told her, a little more life returning to him. 'I was about to ask *you*.'

'I'd guess some competitor of Elias,' she mused. 'I get the impression they take their business very seriously in Helleron.'

'Never a truer word spoken,' said Salma, heartfelt.

There was a hauling engine just setting off for the city, she noticed, with crates of iron taking up most of the flatbed behind the stacks of its wood-burning furnace. But it carried three long, shrouded burdens as well, surely nothing other than the corpses of miners or guardsmen. She had heard Elias giving orders to the driver a moment before, issuing instructions to bring back some artillery. Whatever had happened here, nobody believed it was over.

At last Elias turned back to them, still with a half-dozen menials waiting anxiously to report. 'This is a wretched business,' he said, twisting the rings on his fingers. 'I sometimes wonder why I ever got into it.'

'What happened here?' Che asked him. 'Who attacked them?'

Elias sighed. 'This was going on when I first took to the factories, but then we made the treaty and everything went quiet. Ideal time to get into the mining game, you'd have thought. So look at me now: two days behind on deliveries and I don't even want to think about the repair costs. It's not as though Helleron's ever packed with tramp artificers kicking their heels for want of work, and now there'll be a half-dozen other mine owners bidding against me.'

'But who did it? Someone wants to force you out and take over?'

He gave a bitter laugh. 'Force me out is right, but not the rest of it. If they even wanted the workings here, then at least I'd understand. There'd be a basis for negotiation. I'd even sell up, for a price. But these bastards – excuse my language, Cheerwell – these wretches, they just want us gone.' He saw her confusion and said, 'It's the Moth-kinden from Tharn. Just because they like to mooch around up there in their caves chanting and mumbling to themselves, they take offence if anyone actually wants to make use of the place.'

'Moth-kinden?' Che couldn't quite grasp it. 'But I thought they were—'

'A gaggle of hermits minding their own business?' Elias suggested. 'Think again, Cheerwell. We've always had problems with this lot because they're as militant as they come. They just don't want us anywhere near their precious sacred mountain, and every time we come to terms about our mining operations, give it just a few years and they're back. Raids, thefts, murder, and sabotage! Don't start me on the sabotage. Just because they don't know what a cog does or how a lever works, it doesn't mean they can't find a way to break the most sophisticated equipment when they put their bloody minds to it.'

'What are you going to do?' she asked. 'Are you going to send a messenger to parlay with them?'

'They'd probably kill anyone I sent to them,' Elias growled. 'They only talk when *they* want to. They come down to us when they've had enough. No, if I had my way, I'd get together with the other mine owners and put an airfleet together, sort them out once and for all. For now, though, I'm going to get some repeating ballista, some flarecasters and a squad more crossbowmen, and we'll see if they're stupid enough to come back tonight.'

He stormed off, still with a trail of anxious clerks and foremen shadowing him.

Che turned to Salma. 'You heard that?'

'Every word,' he said. 'And I wondered, once these veins are exhausted, and if the Helleren started looking to the north of here, coming along with their rails and their engines – I wondered what my people's reaction would be.'

'You can't be condoning this!' she hissed.

He held a hand up, and took her aside to somewhere the miners and their watchmen could not overhear.

'Until you have heard it from all sides, don't be so quick to judge. My people could not endure to live with this on our borders, and if we refused them, how long before the Helleren found some excuse to come anyway.'

'Salma, you're talking about my people, my *family*.' His words hurt her more than she would have thought, and she wondered if that was because she knew there was some truth in them.

'Well,' he said with a shrug, 'it's moot, as north of here isn't Commonweal any more anyway.' His smile cut her with its bitterness. 'It's Empire all the way.'

Thirteen

Scuto shambled back into his workshop. It had been the best part of an hour since he stepped outside for a whispered conversation with a young Fly-kinden, clearly one of his agents. Totho had spent the time disassembling one of his air-batteries and planning a few improvements to it. He could never just sit idle. His artificer's hands needed work, to stop his mind from worrying. He jumped up as the Thorn Bug returned.

'Well,' Scuto said. 'Whatever else happened to your friends, the Wasps didn't get 'em. Looks like all three made a run for it. Shame they didn't follow you.'

'Any idea where they ran to?' Totho asked.

'In Helleron it's like leaving tracks in water,' Scuto said. 'Still, I have my eyes and my ears, and looks like your girl, the Spider one, went places even I'd not go without an escort. She must have cut through two fiefs at least. People that way don't like answering questions, but I'll see what I can do.' He shook his head. 'You people, you're such a mix of craft and cack-handedness. I can't make you out.' He settled himself across the workbench from Totho, who heard the scrape of his spines against the wood. 'You give the Wasps the slip, which is good form, but then you got no fallback arranged, so the four of you just go gadding off through the city. What were you thinking?'

'We weren't expecting there would be trouble,' Totho said. He tried to state it as a reasonable point, but it sounded weak even to his own ears.

'You must always plan a fallback,' Scuto told him. 'Last year Sten sent me and some lads to Sarn. Safe enough, you'd think, what with the Ants there behaving 'emselves these days, but we fell real foul. If we'd not had some rendezvous arranged in advance I'd still be there looking for 'em all. Mind you, that was just pure bad luck and accident, 'cos we ran bang into some Arcanum business that had nothing to do with us.'

'What's an Arcanum?'

'If you don't know, you don't need to know,' Scuto told him, and promptly added, 'Moth-kinden stuff, anyway. Loose cogs, the lot of 'em.' He put a thorny finger into the workings of the air-battery.

'Master Scuto, shouldn't we be . . . doing something?'

Scuto raised a thorny eyebrow. 'Like what, boy? Want to go onto the streets and hand out fliers? Stand on a roof and shout their names?'

'But—'

'Sten really did send you out not knowing the half of it,' the Thorn Bug continued sadly. 'Boy, a good agent's got to learn how to wait. My people are asking questions. All we'd do ourselves is get in the way, and maybe get you caught by the Wasps. Founder's mark, boy, do none of you know anything about the trade? Who are you clowns anyway, really?'

'Just College students.' Totho shrugged. 'Master Maker, I don't think he meant it to come to this. Not this soon.'

'That man uses the Great College like his own personal militia,' grumbled Scuto. 'You *all* artificers?'

'We're all duellists, I suppose. That was the link. Tynisa and Salma were good at it, anyway. And then there's Che – Cheerwell, rather. She's Stenwold's niece.' Totho looked at his hands. 'I hope . . . I hope she's all right. She's not as tough as the others.'

Scuto made an unpleasant noise that Totho realized

was laughter. 'Sounds as though you're after the foreman's daughter,' he said. A suggestive leer from the Thorn Bug-kinden was worth three from anyone else.

'I . . . well . . . A little.' Totho did not know where to put himself. 'But, I'm a halfbreed, you know, so . . .'

'So much for that,' Scuto agreed. 'Don't need to tell me, boy. I couldn't get myself into the worst brothel in Helleron even if I was made of solid gold with platinum clothes.' He looked Totho over, sympathy sitting awk-wardly on his nightmare face. 'Let's change the subject, take your mind off things, shall we? Let's look at this air-battery of yours. Weapons, you reckon?'

'Once the air pressure is high enough it can be *directed* out. The force of it is quite remarkable.' Totho, too was glad to settle on less uncomfortable topics.

Scuto nodded. 'You ever get your hands on a nailbow?'

'Only models at the College, but I've seen them used. They did a demonstration.' Despite the hollow, sick feeling in Totho's stomach when he thought of Che all alone in Helleron, this simple talk of mechanical things was work-ing to calm him.

The Thorn Bug grinned. 'I love 'em. They work basic-ally on the same principle as this toy of yours, only instead of air pressure they use a firepowder charge to send a bolt as long as your finger through steel plate. Bang! Noisy as all get out, and they jam often as not, and firepowder's just asking for trouble. I heard that if the nailbow gets too hot, then it just blows itself apart and takes matey the operator with it. So you were thinking of using your bottled air to send a crossbow bolt?'

'A smaller missile would be better, though. I see what you mean.'

'Right, tell you another thing.' Scuto's grin broadened. 'Last year this fellow Balkus came to me, kind of an off-and-on friend. Ant renegade from Sarn. He's a nailbow-man. Used to be in their army squad down there until he went rogue. He wanted me to make the thing more reliable. What I did is, I lengthened the barrel that the bolts come out of, and I machined a groove down it, in a spiral. Still jams like a bastard, but when it fires he can get half again as far, without much worry of missing. You reckon this business of yours here would benefit from the same deal?'

Totho turned the idea over in his mind. He could see the reasoning behind it falling into place, and felt strangely excited by it. Nobody at the College had ever taken his ideas seriously. 'I do,' he said. 'I absolutely do.'

'Well, then, while Scuto's little army is out tracking your friends down, why don't you and I have a little brainstorming session and see if we can't make this thing a reality?'

The Halfway House had been quick to accept her. She had been surprised, as she had expected reprisals for the man she killed. There was no comeback, though, even from his countrymen. The moment he had hit the ground he was nothing.

She could easily have forgotten him herself. In the round of greetings, introductions, boasts and invitations that followed, nobody seemed to recall that her new place at the table was still warm from another's body. Sinon Halfway kept no empty seats. There were always hopefuls, coming off the street, wanting to sit at his table.

Later, he gave her two gold rings and a clasp in the shape of a centipede eating its own tail. 'You should have these,' he said laconically.

'Some girls just expect flowers.' She examined the pieces critically: heavy and crude, like most of the affectation the Halfway House favoured.

Sinon relaxed back on the pillow next to her. 'They're not love tokens, my devious lady. They're your share of Pallus's stake, after I took what he owed me.

She tried to see the trinkets in a different light, to attach some emotional significance to them, the estate of a dead man, but she could not. They were also worth more money than she had personally ever held before, even at black-market prices.

Since sitting at his table she had been waiting for the other shoe to drop, for Sinon to discuss her alleged indebtedness to him. She knew the moment was coming, but it was a day and a night now since she had killed the Ant – Pallus, as she had just discovered. She had taken her chances then, sitting high at the table, turning her College games to a deadly serious business. *And I did it for Che, and the others*, and she could tell herself that as often as she liked.

And Sinon had asked her to his bed. He had not demanded: it was not some tithe he exacted from all the women of the Halfway House. He simply let her know that he had an interest, and in the end she had agreed. She needed to cement her foothold within the fief, and she would have more leverage with him after she had lain with him. Also she had wanted to *see* him, see the whole of that marbled skin spread out before her. He intrigued her, so unlike the pariah halfbreeds she had previously known. He was a more exciting lover by far than those – fewer than most thought – that she had taken at the College. Exciting because he was older than her, and sly, and exciting because he was dangerous. He was a gangster and a killer and his will now shadowed her life. In lying with him she took hold of some of that power and controlled it. It was an old game.

And yet, as they grappled, the thought had come to her, *Is this what it would be like with Salma?* and she had tried to see that storm-sky skin for a moment as bright daylight gold.

Now they lay together in the room of a taverna Sinon had picked out, with a dozen of his heavies on watch in the common room below, and he tilted his head back and closed his eyes, the dead man's gold now off his hands. She could have slit his throat there and then, or perhaps he was secretly tensed, just waiting to see if she would turn on him. Spiders, after all, had a certain reputation.

'You owe me,' he said.

'And was that part of the payment?'

His eyes flicked open. 'That was something between us, was it not? A mutual benefit?' To her surprise he sounded just a little hurt. *Men and their egos.* She smiled at him.

'So I owe you?'

'Tynisa, dear lady, you're someone who gives the impression that you won't be with us for long, one way or the other. You have your own path and I'd not begrudge you that.'

She raised a quizzical eyebrow.

'No,' he said. 'But you owe me and debts must be paid. If I do not enforce that rule, I'm nothing. You owe me for Malia's dead man, and you owe me for the help you've asked of me. But it's your choice whether you pay that off all at once, or break it up into pieces.'

'All at once, if I can,' she said instantly. 'No offence.'

'Honesty never offends me,' he told her. 'Which is not to say that I haven't had men killed for it.' His expression was infinitely mild, infinitely truthful. 'I will have a job for you, I think, that will make us quits, and once you've done it I already have a lead on your friends.'

Her heart leapt. 'Stenwold's family?'

'No, we tried there but they've seen nobody. Another lead, but a good one – only when we're quits.'

There was a gentle knock on the door.

'Chief,' said the voice of the white-skinned giant. 'It's starting to move down here.'

'We'll be there,' Sinon called back, and slid out of bed, slipping into his clothes. Tynisa followed suit, taking one more look across the streaked skin of his muscled back before it disappeared beneath his tunic.

'So what's this job you want from me?' she asked.

'It will depend on how *this* goes now,' he said, but from his tone she guessed there was little argument about it.

Down below, his men were all on their feet, tense. The white giant was marshalling them with curving gestures of his huge claws. He was Scorpion-kinden, she understood, exiled from the Dryclaw Desert south of Helleron. They called him Akta Barik.

'All ready to go, chief,' he said. His voice was quiet and he spoke slowly and with great precision, to avoid mumbling through those jutting fangs. 'Just got word: their man's on his way.'

'So what is this?' she asked.

'Just a formal way of settling the disputes, so that everyone can see how it falls out.'

'Sounds a bit above board for your types,' she said. He threw her an amused look.

'I didn't say it was the only way, or even the final way.' He surveyed his men and addressed them peremptorily. 'Fighters, do me proud.' No more speech than that. When the door was opened, there were eight of them went stepping into the street, and neither Sinon nor Barik was amongst them. The street was clear, or at least clear in front of the taverna. A safe distance either side, quite a crowd had gathered.

'Did Barik say their *man*?' Tynisa asked. 'Just one?'

Sinon nodded. 'That was the arrangement.'

'But . . . eight on one?'

He gave her a look that was not filled with optimism, and went to the doorway to watch.

A disturbance in the crowd showed people pressing away very hurriedly. Someone was coming who parted them just by word of his approach. Tynisa saw the eight

Halfway House combatants tense, spreading out into a loose semi-circle to await his approach.

He stepped clear of the crowd at last: a tall Mantis-kinden, strangely dressed. She saw a green-dyed arming doublet, slit from wrist to elbow for his forearm spines; breeches and boots of darker green; a brooch pin of gold, a sword through a circle, ringing vague bells in her memory. He had no rapier, such as she would expect of a Mantis duellist. Instead there was a metal gauntlet on his right arm with a two-foot blade projecting from the glove.

He walked, very deliberately, until he was at the very centre of the circle his opponents had half-made. He stood with his arms by his sides, feet close together, looking slightly down.

'A Weaponsmaster,' she identified at last. 'I didn't think there were any left.'

Sinon just grunted, watching, and she still could not understand it: eight men against one, even a Mantis, even a Weaponsmaster, for what that was worth. They had shortswords, maces, offhand daggers; one even had a spear. She looked at them and saw they were not confident. Each was waiting for another to make the first move. The crowd had settled into a rapturous hush.

The Mantis drew his weapon arm up, crooking it across his body with the blade pointed downwards, folded back along his arm. He finally looked up.

One of the men shouted at him, a wordless yell, and they descended upon him at once, six coming at him from three sides, and two bursting into flight to take him from above. In the instant before he was eclipsed from her sight Tynisa did not even see the man react.

But react he did. Even as she lost sight of him two men were already reeling back. In a flash of green he wove between the remainder. The metal claw of his hand danced and spun in the air around him. She saw swords spark off it and the spear lopped in two. In an instant the Mantis had whipped it across the closest swordsman's face, guiding a mace blow away, and slashed the wielder's chain mail open, laying his chest raw. The blade lanced upwards to stab into the groin of a Fly-kinden arrowing down with sword and dagger. The short blade moved like a living thing, a flying thing itself. It led and its wielder followed, and he was not touched. His steps were so graceful, so sure, that it was as though he and his enemies had rehearsed this fight for the audience, performed each move a thousand times before this one bloody performance. He walked through the storm of their attacks and they did not so much as tear his clothing.

He put the spines of his arms down past the collarbone of a Beetle-kinden, twice and thrice before the man could react to the first blow. The blade lashed behind him, where the final assailant had been lunging. It cut aside the sword that came for his back, bounded around it, letting the attacker's own momentum bring him straight onto it.

Seconds. It had been only seconds. Tynisa found that she had her hand clutching white knuckled on her sword hilt.

Eight men lay dead on the cobbles, who had been living and breathing moments before as they filed out of the taverna. The face of the Mantis-kinden was icy, no cruelty there but a bleak detachment. She fell back before he could look in her direction. His was a gaze she did not want to meet.

'Well, that's that,' said Sinon unsympathetically. 'Now the Gladhanders get the protection business all along Skulkacre.' He came and sat beside her in the common room, with those others of his men who still walked.

'Who is he?' she asked.

'Tisamon. They call him Tisamon.' Sinon steepled his fingers. Outside in the street, agents of the Gladhanders were already carting off the bodies for stripping and disposal. 'Now, dear one, I need you.'

She looked at him levelly. 'You want me to kill the Mantis?'

She had caught him out. That she could see what she had seen and still make the offer, it was more than he had expected of her. He looked up at Barik and the others. 'To the door, lads. Nobody else hears this.'

The Scorpion shepherded them away, leaving the lord of the Halfway House and his new recruit alone.

'Not him, dear one. He's just a mercenary. I want you to kill his employer. I've taken your measure, dear lady. Your face has two advantages over the faces of my regulars, namely that it doesn't look like a bent boot, and that it won't be recognized. Now, if you truly want to pay me all you owe, kill the chief of the Gladhanders for me.'

'I thought this was how you sorted things out.' She indicated the bloodied cobbles of the street outside.

'As I said,' he told her, 'it's not the final solution.'

After sundown, the attack picked up where it must have left off the previous night. Instead of being mute witnesses to its after-effects, Che and Salma were there this time: not at the mine site, but Elias, like most mine owners, had another house away from Helleron. Close by the mountains and just a few hundred yards from the rock face and shaft, it was a simple affair compared to his townhouse, just a single-storeyed, flat-roofed lump of a place with a stable block for messengers. It was barely staffed and not intended for visitors, but Elias had turned a servant out of his room to accommodate his new guests. Che felt somewhat guilty about that.

She had been deep in meditation, attempting once more to find the Ancestor Art within her, when she had heard the first explosion. It was a big one, too, for a faint tremor reached her even through the walls. Instantly Che was on her feet and even as she was running for the window she guessed that something had set one of the fuel sinks off. A lot of the mining machinery ran on mineral oil so there was a good sized cache out by the works, and now . . .

She caught her breath as she got to the window, because there was a jet of flame a hundred feet high lighting up the walls of the quarry and the foothills of the very mountains themselves. Its faint roaring reached her, eclipsed anything else that might have been audible. There must have been a fearful alarm going on out there. She strained her eyes, looking beyond the dancing column of fire. Sure enough, she could see movement, a great panic of movement. Elias's guards on the ground would now be swinging their repeating ballista round this way and that. Others would be loosing crossbows. She saw flecks and shimmers in the sky, airborne figures briefly silhouetted before the flames. The Moth-kinden were out in force.

They were barbaric raiders, she reminded herself. They were enemies of progress. As a good Beetle, that was how she should see them. If they had not been so fanatic, they would have been ludicrous, a pack of old mystics lurking in their caves.

She thought of Salma. He was her friend and she respected his opinions. Yet he did not see things as she did.

The door burst open behind her and she whirled round, hand to her sword, half-expecting some mad Moth assassin. Instead it was one of Elias's two domestic staff.

'You're to stay inside the house, miss,' the man said, as though she had been contemplating jumping out of the window.

'They're not going to come here, are they?' she asked.

'Nobody knows, miss,' said the man, plainly himself in the grip of fear. 'They could do anything.'

She returned her gaze to the window. The flames were lower now, the oil stocks burning dry. She thought she could see the shadowy bulk of one of the repeating ballistas being cranked round, spitting out a man-length bolt every few seconds. There would be guards out there with good crossbows, perhaps even piercers. They had strong armour there and she wondered what weaponry the Moth-kinden possessed to assault such a force with. Spears and stones, perhaps. Bows and arrows.

They had accomplished something already, though. Hundreds of Centrals' worth of fuel had now gone and the mine works would be set back for days, at least.

And what is the point? The industrialists of Helleron were not going to go away. They would only return with more soldiers, better protection. One day, perhaps, they really would muster a fleet of fliers and airships and attack the Moths at their very homes, if that was the only way to stop their raiding.

And would that be the answer? She had the uncomfortable feeling that she had been assigned a role in this conflict without ever being asked. There had been a few Moth-kinden at the College, she recalled: strange reserved creatures like Doctor Nicrephos. She had not spoken to any of them but she knew the history. Before the revolution the Moth-kinden had held most of the Lowlands in chains. With the Mantids acting as their strong right hand, they had terrorized the other races with their superstition and charlatanry, or so the history books now claimed. Then the revolution had come: the rise of the Apt, the fall of the old ways before the forge-fires of innovation. It had all started in Collegium, which had been called Pathis when the Moths ruled. The revolt had then burned its way to every corner of the Lowlands, leaving only a few Moth haunts and Mantis holds untouched.

Surely they can see progress.

She thought of the way Salma had reacted to the factories, the mine workings, how it had struck him almost like an illness. He had kept his smile hoisted for all to see, but she knew the sight had appalled him. After all, they were not enlightened people in his Commonweal. They still thought magic existed. No factories, no artificers, no machines.

And, of course, to the east the Wasp-kinden were stoking their own furnaces to turn out weapons of war. Those they had not bought from the clever smiths of Helleron, that is.

After such thoughts she could not watch any longer, and went to join Salma in the main room of the house. Elias had locked himself in his study, so as best they could they played a few hands of cards with the trembling servants, everyone endeavouring to ignore the continuing sounds from outside. Even when the commotion was right at the outer walls, with soldiers running past, the harsh clack of crossbows loosing, they shuttered the windows and pretended not to hear.

In the morning it was all over. She awoke and spent a moment regarding Salma, in the next bed, still smiling slightly even in sleep. She rose, dressed, and went into the dining room to meditate again.

And she then remembered the previous night, sleep falling from her fast like a veil. Opening the shutters showed that a plume of smoke still twisted from the mine workings.

She wondered how many had died. Then she wondered how many had died on both sides. The thought shocked her. At the College she had learnt that the Moth-kinden, for all the faults laid at their door, were not a warlike race, quite the reverse.

There were evils everywhere in the world, Che supposed, and, once she had admitted that, she would have to allow that her own race was responsible for some of them.

There was a well out in the house's yard, between it and the stables. Taking up her sword for good measure, she wandered outside and drew a bucket of water up, feeling the chill of morning on her. The ground was flecked with ash, and she wondered what else had burned in the night. Perhaps they had set fire to the winch or the smelting shed? It was all like prodding some great beast with a stick, one of the big hauling beetles or something. You would annoy it and annoy it, and sooner or later it would turn round and you would discover it was far, far stronger than you had ever imagined. The Moth-kinden could not know what they were inviting down on them.

There was a squad of guards, five of them, poking about the perimeter of the yard, perhaps totalling up all the damage done during the night. They paused expectantly to watch her, and her original idea of washing there, in plain view, became suddenly less attractive.

She gave them a hard stare and an imperious gesture, for she was the cousin of their employer, after all. Reluctantly they went about their business, and for good measure she carried the bucket of water into the stables for her ablutions. A pair of messengers' horses would make more bearable spectators.

She closed the stable door behind her and heard a soft whisper of sound from deeper within. Steel on leather, a blade being unsheathed. Her reaction, without thought, found her dropping the bucket and dragging her own sword half out.

There was a man in the shadows at the far end of the stables. He was slight, grey-skinned, a Moth she realized, and even in the gloom she saw the glint of a knife.

Fourteen

Markon Crosthwaite, who revelled in the name Markon the Friendly, rose from the table and made encouraging gestures to his men until they cheered him to the echo. The kneeling man before him, one of Sinon Halfway's more expendable specimens, crouched even lower. The man was some kind of Fly-kinden halfbreed, an insult in itself, but Markon was feeling glutted with his own success. Besides, if he cut this man's ears off and then hung him out of the window, who would be able to go to Sinon and tell that piebald freak just how happy Markon was?

He reversed his hands and his men faltered to an expectant silence. 'Now, creature,' he said. 'On your feet, if those lumps on your legs' ends are feet.'

The halfbreed got up, head still held low, waiting for the blow or the lash or the knife in the back. *And so he should, the filthy little mixed-blood*, Markon thought approvingly. 'Want to go, do you? Business taken care of?'

There was a barely perceptible nod.

Markon beamed at his people. 'But my friend, you haven't thanked me for my hospitality. If there's one thing I can't abide it's bad manners.'

The little man flinched and muttered something. Without needing the nod, one of Markon's men balanced a dagger on his shoulder.

'Thank you, Master Markon,' the Halfway House man got out, in a shaking voice.

'Master Markon what?' Markon snapped at him.

'Markon the ... the Friendly.' The halfbreed's shoulders were up by his ears, waiting for the strike. Markon's lip curled with contempt for him.

'Your good friend Markon the Friendly,' he told the man. 'And if your uncle Sinon is wise, you'll tell him that he should do a little more business with his good friend Markon the Friendly. It doesn't do to forget one's friends when the money's going round. You tell him that, you hear?'

The halfbreed nodded frantically and Markon spat on the ground in disgust. 'Get out, you vermin. Tell Sinon to send someone of better blood next time, or I'll have your boss's ears.'

Once Sinon's man had bolted from the taverna, Markon let his men cheer him a little more before waving a dismissive hand at them. 'Has the Mantis called for his pay?' he asked.

'Been and gone a long time back, Master,' one of his men reported. 'Not too friendly, that one.'

'And cursed expensive at that,' Markon agreed absently. 'For all that, better to have him hired than let him onto the market. You all saw the fight. How many do you think he could take? Ten? Twelve?'

'At least.'

Markon nodded. 'And if he failed ... well, good enough to be rid of one like that, than risk him changing who his friends are.' He shook himself, business done for another day. 'Enjoy yourselves, my friends,' he told his men. 'You've earned it all. I shall go upstairs and seek my own enjoyment.'

They whooped and called at that, and he paused halfway up the stairway to acknowledge them once again. They had found a particular prize for him to celebrate upon, a young girl fresh to the city. It was time for Markon to become friendlier.

He pushed into the room, seeing her already laid out on

the bed, waiting for him. One of the staff brought him a jar of wine and two bowls before backing out, bowing deferentially.

'Today,' Markon declared, 'shall be long remembered in this fief.' He favoured the girl with his best smile, as white as any artifice could make it. She was Spider-kinden, his special prize, and as handsome as they came.

'Unrobe me,' he told her, and she came forward, standing behind him to free his robes and tunic with deft, careful motions of one hand. Her fingers were cool, steady. He flexed his shoulders, still muscled despite a decade's easy living, and turned to her.

'Now, girl,' he said – and she ran him through the stomach and opened his throat as though they had planned it together.

Tynisa watched his blood soak into the counterpane and contemplated her life to date. She felt a desperate need to laugh at it, at the sheer folly. Had she spent all those years in the College learning philosophy, history and the humanities, just to find her true vocation here on the streets of Helleron? And such a vocation! A player in the games of princes, a tool of statecraft, the unspoken and the unacknowledged shadow that every man of power used and feared.

All simple enough, as Sinon Halfway had predicted. She had not believed it would work, but here she was.

She had wondered, in a scholarly way, whether she could actually kill a man who was not trying to kill her. She had prepared all manner of arguments to strengthen her purpose. He was a gangster, after all. He was a killer and an employer of killers. She had seen his handiwork out on the bloodied street. She would be, if not quite doing the world a service, then at least be doing it no great harm.

The chief of the Gladhanders was dead.

And how simple it was, once armed with one piece of

knowledge: that the portly Beetle-kinden gang boss had a weakness for Spider-kinden women. A weakness well known, and therefore his subordinates were careful to check each momentary concubine. Her face was new to them, though, and she was unarmed. One of Sinon's better sneaks had made sure her sword would be there in the room before she ascended the stairs. Markon had died without a sound.

Now she went to the window and opened the shutters, looking out on an unsuspecting day. With a sense of drama, she waved her kerchief in the morning air, knowing it would be noted.

She then transferred her attention to the door and waited.

Within moments she heard shouting from downstairs and outside: the Gladhanders' sudden shock as Akta Barik and a score of toughs from the Halfway House charged the building. She imagined the huge Scorpion-kinden kicking down the door, swinging in with his monstrous great sword that was as long as he was tall. Behind him would be swordsmen, spearmen, crossbowmen, whatever Sinon had chased up.

The door to the room was flung open by a panicked-looking Ant-kinden.

'Chief! It's the Halfways—' he got out before she killed him.

In all she killed seven of them, one at a time, as they piled into the room seeking guidance. Hers was the highest headcount of the day. When one of Sinon's men finally ascended the stairs, he stopped halfway because the sight of Tynisa and her mound of corpses was too much for him. He backed away quietly and decided to let her come down when she was ready.

When she did descend the stairs she felt like a battle-queen standing before her army. The footsoldiers of the Halfway House cheered her for a saviour. Only Barik was silent, favouring her with a respectful nod that, taken in context, meant much more.

A half-hour later it was all done, and those members of the Gladhanders still free and living were taking any shelter they could, or thinking very hard about changing their colours. Tynisa meanwhile sat in the same taverna before which Tisamon had performed his feats of carnage, only two streets away from the scene of her own bloodletting, and watched the ordinary people pass by.

'You've a talent,' Sinon told her, 'and I like you. You're an original.'

She watched his face cautiously.

'If you want,' he said, 'you can stay on. You've more than earned your place here. I'll make you the equal of Malia and Barik, and neither of them will mind. We're expanding, so: room for another lieutenant.'

She opened her mouth to refuse straight away, then closed it, feeling a strange cold creep across her. She had been reborn in blood, this day. What would Che say if she knew what her not-sister had done? What would *Stenwold* say? And she was good at the work, certainly. Another few jobs and she would have worn her conscience entirely away, and then she might even start to enjoy it.

The thought roiled in her stomach, queasy and thrilling all at once. She thought of the Mantis, Tisamon. How much respect could one person gather? Lords and magnates would beggar themselves to possess that much awe and adulation.

She thought then of a life that was just fight after fight, betrayal after betrayal, and exactly how much that adulation would mean. And how long would they still cheer her, once the blade was dulled?

'I can't stay,' she said. 'Part of me wants to, it's true, but I have obligations.'

'Understood,' said Sinon, without acrimony. He fished

in his tunic, brought out a folded sheet of paper. 'Go to this address, you'll find your contact: Scuto. He's a known man of your Stenwold's, according to my spies. And he's well protected, so best go openly and peaceably. It's even possible he's already found the rest of your company. Tell me, though,' he eyed her with a faint smile, 'are all your fellows as accomplished as you?'

'No,' she said, and it was not boasting but a fact.

'Then trust to hope, for this Scuto's a rough creature, his friends and his surroundings worse. If your friends went in there unwary, things may have gone the worse for them.'

Tynisa thought of poor Che, as unwary a victim as Helleron could ever claim. *But patient and politic,* she instructed herself. Che would not be here, in Tynisa's shoes, because Che would not have attacked half the staff of the Halfway House in her flight. This was a Beetle city and Che would blend in, would stay safe and out of trouble. *I know she would. What else could she do?*

They were both frozen in the moment. Che had her sword mostly unsheathed, eight inches of bared metal, and was now poised in the duellist's bent-kneed stance into which she had dropped. The Moth had a long dagger in one hand, the other wrapped about his ribs. His face was pointed, grey-skinned, dark hair cut close in a widow's peak. His eyes were slanted and blank white, like a blind man's. After a moment Che decided he was only a little older than she was. If he had not been threatening her, if she had not been threatening him, he would have seemed handsome.

It impressed her most, in that moment, that he did not instantly discount her. After all, she was a young female Beetle-kinden, a little overweight, an expression of shock almost certainly on her face, caught halfway through unsheathing her sword. He must have been a warrior taking part in their raid and he could have the blood of her own kind all over his hands. Still, he watched her cautiously and, in his eyes, she was a fighter and something to be wary of.

He was small, she saw, as Moths often were, and slight of build. He held himself with a rigid concentration, and she decided he was going to be very fast when he moved. She saw his lips twitch, wondered if this was it.

His pale tunic was stained. His offhand was slick where it held his side. She understood, then, why he was here.

There was a heavy thump on the door behind her. In that moment she and the Moth very nearly killed each other as the tension snapped back like a cut cord. In that brief moment he was two paces closer to her, dagger held up. Her sword had meanwhile cleared its sheath. He locked eyes with her.

'What?' she called out. Her voice, to herself, sounded understandably strained.

'We're checking the whole place in case any of those bastards got in, miss,' came the voice of one of the guards. The Moth's eyes widened.

'I . . .' She started. He was staring at her, and abruptly she found it hard to answer. There was something in her head, plucking at her, trying to turn her mind. 'I don't . . .'

She stared into those white, depthless eyes and felt the pressure of his will upon her, desperately trying to stop her speaking. His teeth bared slowly as the strain told on him. It was an Art of the Moths, she realized, some Ancestor Art of theirs.

She summoned what resolution she could manage. She could feel his grip slipping. He was weakened by injury, or she was stronger than he thought, but she shook her head abruptly and she was free of his mind.

'Miss?' asked the guard doubtfully from outside, and she opened her mouth to answer. The Moth's face was very composed and he settled onto his back foot, dagger held out. She realized that he was going to fight, and that she would see him die the moment the guards came in.

She thought of Salma.

'Well, there's certainly nobody in here,' she said, sounding terribly false in her own ears. 'Now let me wash, will you?'

The voice came back: 'Right, miss,' incredibly, and there was the scuff of their feet as the guards tracked off.

In all that time her eyes had not left those of her adversary. There was no gratitude there, but perhaps curiosity.

'If you want to fight, fight me,' she told him quietly. 'Otherwise . . .' And her words tailed off, because she could not think of one.

'Otherwise what?' he asked. His voice was soft, with precise consonants.

She stared at him. Her sword was beginning to weigh in her hand.

He took a deep breath, and she saw that it pained him. He tucked the dagger back in his belt. 'It would seem that I am your prisoner.' His look was challenging, uncompromising. 'What do you intend to do, Beetle-girl?'

She disposed of her own blade, wondering what precisely she *was* supposed to do now. She found that she was more frightened of him now than when he had his knife out. He was something that had stepped in from another world, from some story of past times. 'I . . . never really met a Moth before.'

His look was bleak. 'Now you have.'

'Do you want me to look at that for you?' She uttered the words almost automatically, sprung from some reflexive humanitarianism that the College had taught her. He was instantly suspicious, hand reaching back for his knife, but she told him, 'Look, if I wanted to hurt you, I'd have called the guards in.' A stray thought gave her some justification, for herself or even for him. 'A Moth doctor at Collegium once helped my uncle Stenwold. Let's put it against that, shall we?'

He sat down heavily on a bale of straw, taking his left hand from his side. It came away glistening with strands of blood, and she swallowed hard. She had learned medicine at the College, at least a little. She took up her bucket, still half-full, and knelt beside him.

It was a crossbow bolt that had caught him, but he had been lucky. It had grazed his side close to the skin and the heavy missile, designed to ram through armour, had left two gashes that tracked the diagonal course of a missile shot from the ground up into the air. The wounds left were ragged with the path of the chitin flight. She felt him wince as she dabbed off the blood, seeming almost black against his grey skin.

'I can . . .' Her hands shook at the very thought. 'I can try to stitch this . . . if you want. And I can get some alcohol to clean it.'

'A fire. Hot water,' he rasped. And then, 'Please.'

He clasped his hand to the wound again and she stood.

I should not be doing this. Elias Monger would be so very angry.

But Uncle Stenwold would approve.

'You hide here,' she told him. 'I'll see what I can do.'

It was easier than Che had expected. The two house servants were overworked, and still jittery after last night's events. She absconded with a needle, some gut thread, a bottle of Elias's best brandy and an iron pot of hot water.

She thought he had fled when she first got back into the stables, then that he had been caught, but he reappeared, stepping out of the shadows when he was sure it was her. She considered the strange, fragile trust that they had built between them.

He sat down and she cleaned the needle and thread in the scalding water, then doused them in the brandy.

'Why are you doing this for me?' he asked suddenly. She started at the sound of his voice, so close.

'I already told you—'

'Don't tell me about your uncle Stenwold,' he said. 'The truth.'

She hurriedly got on with the stitching then, to avoid his probing. She felt him stiffen as the needle first went in, his hand burning paler as it gripped.

'I am a student at the Great College,' she said, as she oh so carefully closed up his wound. 'And at the College they teach us that words, not violent acts, are the best way to settle any dispute. To settle through swords is to settle only until tomorrow, but to settle through reasoned debate is forever. Or at least that's what they tell us.' She began tying off the thread at the first wound, not exactly a neat job but it would serve. 'I'm not afraid of you.' It was not entirely true. 'You are not my enemy.' She was quicker with the wound over his ribs, where he must have twisted as the bolt seared across him. She felt more practised now and he sat in silence as she worked, as she bandaged him inexpertly with strips torn from the sleeve of her own robe. *I'll have to say I just snagged it on something.* Only when she finished did she realize he had been gazing down at her, his grey face expressionless.

'I have never met a Beetle before,' he began. Still kneeling by him, she suddenly felt very uncertain, awkward. 'I hope they are not all like you.'

'Why?' she asked, but he had turned to the cooling water and dropped something into it, some sharp-smelling herbs. He had his dagger to hand, she noticed, and for a second her heart froze, but he was just using it to stir the pot.

He could have killed me at any time. The moment she had finished, he could have thrust the knife into her neck. She felt furious with herself for not thinking of it, and pitifully relieved that he had not struck her.

'Because I have fought your kind, I have killed your kind, but I would not wish to kill someone like you.' His voice was level, emotionless. He tore a swatch of cloth from his already tattered tunic and dipped it in the pungent water before pressing it to his wound, saturating the bandages.

'Killed my kind . . . ?'

He looked at her sharply. 'Those who would have killed me,' he said simply. 'You must have guessed it.' Whatever he had put in the water obviously stung his wound sharply and he winced as he removed the cloth. 'Do you have a name, Beetlechild?'

'Cheerwell,' she said. 'Cheerwell Maker.' He arched an eyebrow at that. 'It's a perfectly good name,' she continued, giving him a frown. 'People call me Che.'

He paused a long moment, the reply slow in coming. 'I am Achaeos and you have my thanks. The omens warned me that our work of last night would not end as I expected. I am grateful that you have found a way to fulfil that.'

'Omens . . . ?' she said helplessly. 'You took part in that raid because of omens?'

'No, despite them.' He slung the cloth back into the water. 'What will *you* do now?'

'Go back into the house and try to forget this ever happened,' she said firmly, though she knew that she would remember Achaeos for a very long time. She realized that she was on her knees, which were starting to hurt. She began to shift, and he put a hand out to help her up.

Standing, she held on to it for a second longer. It was calloused in strange places, and she guessed it was an archer's hand.

'I cannot fly, not until I have rested further. I will leave here tonight, I think, if I can.'

She nodded. 'I . . . I think that would be best.'

As she left the stables she paused a moment to lean against the closed door. She felt strangely detached from the real world, as though it had all been some dream. *How could something so unusual happen to someone like me?* Still, the tingle of his hand in hers remained to vouch for it.

She could see a party of men from Helleron, either on their way to the house or the mines. More soldiers for tonight's defence. She hoped that Elias would have finished his business here by then. She did not want another night of bloodshed on her conscience, not now she had met the enemy.

'You really do surprise me sometimes,' was Salma's response to the whole business.

'You mean you think I was wrong?'

'I didn't say that. I'm just surprised. What happened to all that march-of-progress rhetoric of yours?'

'I . . .' If he was going to be so mocking about it, she wouldn't give him the satisfaction of letting him know it had been his own views that had swayed her. 'I just felt it was the right thing to do and . . .'

He raised an eyebrow, waiting.

'He's still out there, waiting for dusk,' she explained. 'It's . . . strange, knowing that.'

'Well now.' His smile was merciless.

'It's not like that. It's just . . . strange,' she said heatedly. And it *wasn't* like that. *It isn't!* But Achaeos still lingered in her memory: strange, dangerous, ephemeral. From another world.

And then she thought back to the revolution of the Apt, five centuries gone, when her people had thrown off the yoke. A Spider historian had once described it as the 'revolution of the ugly': the solid-built, strong-shouldered slaves, the Beetle-kinden and the Ants. *We do not have their grace*, she admitted to herself. She knew it more than most. Growing up alongside Tynisa would teach anyone that.

Salma was watching her carefully, and she wondered how much her expression had let slip.

'I think it was the right thing too, whatever may come of it,' he said softly.

'Thank you.'

There was a rap at their door, and Che opened it on one of the servants.

'Excuse me, miss, sir, but Master Monger wishes to speak with you. He's waiting in the dining room.' There was a slight edge to the man's voice, and she felt a chill descend on her. *They've found him!* She couldn't tell whether her fear was for Achaeos or for herself.

She glanced at Salma, who put a comforting hand on her shoulder. Together they went across the main room of Elias's house into the dining room that occupied one corner. It was a simple affair, as was all of the house compared to the comforts Elias allowed himself in the city. Just a table and half a dozen chairs, and a door into the kitchen for the servants to shuttle food through.

'Uncle—' Che started, and then stopped, because Elias, sitting at the table, was not alone. There was a man with him and for a moment Che thought she should know him, but could not place him. It was only when Salma's punch-sword cleared its scabbard that she realized the newcomer was a Wasp.

'Wait!' she cried. 'Uncle Elias, what's going on?' She herself still had not drawn. Beside her Salma had turned, and she heard movement in the main room behind them.

'Please tell me.' Che stared at Elias. His look was uncomfortable. He would not meet her eyes.

'This is Captain Thalric,' he said. 'He was ... very quick to answer the notice I put up, about your friends. It seems you've been meddling in things you shouldn't, girl. You should never have left Collegium.'

Che had stepped into the room, giving Salma a chance to stand back to back. She heard the Dragonfly murmur, 'Seven here,' just as the kitchen door opened and another four Wasp soldiers, in full armour, stepped through.

'But I'm family! Your blood!' she protested. 'Uncle!'

'*Blood?*' Elias looked up at her with a sudden flare of anger. 'Because you're the brat of that brainless oaf Dorvy, the wastrel of the entire family? Or the ward of that obnoxious eccentric Stenwold? This is Helleron, girl. We don't have time for your charity or philosophy. We're all trying to earn an honest living here and Captain Thalric represents some of my best customers, whereas you ... you're just an inconvenience. Now tell your outlander friend to put his sword down and do the decent thing.'

That did it. Her blade was out in a moment and she was up onto the table in another, charging down it point first at an aghast Elias. Behind her, chaos broke loose as the soldiers rushed Salma, but she knew the intruders at the kitchen door were not close enough to stop her.

Thalric was, however. Che had written him off as the typical officer type, one to stand about and watch others do the dirty work. Instead he lunged forward, caught her wrist and turned it, her blade's point passing from Elias, across Thalric's chest and then past him. She rammed into him with some speed and the two of them took the entire table with them as they collapsed to the floor.

Salma was meanwhile doing his best, and two Wasp soldiers were already reeling back with bloody wounds. There was no room for him, though. He could not take flight and they were crowding all about him. A fist caught his jaw, another slammed into his side. He got his short blade into a third man, deep this time, a fatal wound. The soldier hunched about it, clutched at Salma's wrist as he tried to free the sword. Salma elbowed the nearest Wasp in the face, still wrenching at the trapped blade. One of them was behind him, dragging at him, an arm round his neck. He went down, losing his blade, letting the backward momentum pull him from the soldier's grip. His hands lashed out, breaking one man's nose, knuckling another in the eye. In a moment, maybe just for a moment, he was free of them, diving for the hilt of his sword.

Che wrestled furiously with the Wasp officer, Thalric.

He had her sword wrist pinned to the floor and was grimly trying to catch her offhand with his own. His face, close enough for her to smell the wine on his breath, had a set, determined expression. Even when she managed to get a solid fist into the side of his head he just grunted. Then he had her, and was casting himself backward and up, dragging her with him. She discovered that he was much stronger than he looked, certainly a lot stronger than she was.

'Take her!' he shouted, and without much option she rammed her forehead into his chin. He cursed, and for a second his grip loosened, and she was out of it. Then two solders had grappled her to the floor again. Thalric wiped blood from his lips.

Salma got two fingers on the sword before one of the soldiers kicked him in the gut. He twisted about the blow and put the heel of one hand solidly into the kicker's knee, sending him to the floor with a crunch of the joint. Another soldier piled on top of the Dragonfly, knocking the breath out of him. Then two of them were hauling him up, a knee jammed in his back. The man with the broken knee had his fist raised, already burning with golden light.

Salma closed his eyes.

The sound was more violent than he expected in the sudden silence of the room, a hissing crackle of violated air. He opened his eyes. The injured man was lying on his front, the back of his head now smoking and charred.

'Alive!' snapped Thalric at them. 'Alive, I said! Not so difficult, is it?'

Salma saw that Che was a captive too, and knew that would complicate matters.

'Bind him. Use the Fly manacles,' Thalric instructed. His lip was still bleeding and he wiped at it absently.

'And the Beetle?' one of his men asked.

'Just tie her hands. She won't be flying anywhere we can't follow.' Thalric took a deep breath. 'Master Monger, your assistance is most appreciated and will, of course, be rewarded.'

'You're taking this man's *money?*' Che exploded. 'You're selling your own cousin for money?'

'For contracts, Cheerwell,' said Elias, as if that made it all right.

'But they're invaders! They're going to come here and take over everything!' she shouted at him.

'You obviously have not heard of a little something called the Treaty of Iron,' Elias said airily. 'The Empire has no interest in us. And besides, nobody takes over Helleron.' He settled back in his chair. 'Helleron serves everyone best by remaining as a free city. Everyone has always known that. Here we do business with every city, every general, every merchant. Captain Thalric's people are no different. In fact, they are some of the best customers Helleron now has.'

'A lot of good that'll do you,' she snapped, 'when they invade your city using your own weapons!'

'Enough!' Thalric was not loud, simply extremely authoritative. 'I can have you gagged, Miss Maker. Don't force me.'

Salma had been securely tied, his arms pinioned tightly behind his back, contorting him enough so that he would not be able to summon his Art-wings. He caught Che's eye momentarily with a look that said, *Be strong.*

'Take them outside. We'll be heading east tonight,' Thalric ordered his men, and they bundled Salma and Che out of the dining room, twisting their arms painfully at the first sign of resistance.

'Well, I'm glad that's over,' said Elias primly, looking around the devastated room.

'We will pay for any breakages, of course,' said Thalric. 'And I think I will leave half a dozen men here, as well.'

'I . . .' Elias eyed him, for the first time with a little suspicion. 'I'm not sure that will be necessary.'

Thalric smiled sardonically. 'For the Empire's love, Master Monger, do you think I'm going to garrison Helleron house by house, starting with yours? You forget, Stenwold Maker has arrived in Helleron, and doubtless he will come here, and soon. I have a great respect for his abilities to follow a trail of information, especially information I have planted for him to find. When he does, my men will seize him and then he will cease to trouble you.'

Fifteen

Achaeos lay back on the hay bale and closed his eyes. He was not sure what was happening, but he knew it was bad.

The Beetle-girl, Cheerwell, had just been dragged out of the house as a prisoner, along with some unknown Commonwealer. There was a whole pack of soldiers about them, their black-and-gold striped armour gleaming. Even now they were hauling the Dragonfly about by his bonds, jeering at him, boasting of how many of his race they had killed.

Achaeos tried to recall the wars the Commonweal had fought. He could have listed every major conflict of his own people in the thousand years before the revolution, but more recent history was hardly their strong point up in Tharn. *Always fighting old battles.* He cast the saddening thought away angrily.

He had a dagger but he was injured. He did not know whether he could even fly. He had lost his bow and quiver in the fighting last night. The one had leapt from his hand when the crossbow bolt found him over the mine workings. The other he had cast off himself, for more speed, as he had fled – fled here, and some sanctuary it had turned out to be. Still, he had successfully evaded Beetle soldiers before and he would do so again if he must. They were clumsy things and even if a very few Beetles could see in darkness almost as well as the Moth-kinden, none could see so well as to see him.

He peeked through the crack of the stable door and saw

that the Dragonfly had fallen to his knees and been jerked roughly up again.

There had been a war just recently. The Moths had seen some of it, by scout and by distant divination. There was some new tribe on the march in the east, but that had not been important to the Moths of Tharn, who had their own battles to wage. *Battles lost a long time ago . . .*

He wanted to dash airborne from the stable, to put his blade to use and get the debt he owed off his shoulders. Moths were not bound to honour as the Mantids were. They would break a promise or let an insult slide if circumstances suited. Still, they never did so without knowing it was a choice they had made deliberately, to turn their backs on something significant. Achaeos *wanted* to act but his back was being turned by his very situation. He was in no condition to help the girl.

And she's only a Beetle. But that thought didn't help. Strangely, he felt even more moved to help her, to show her that her people had no monopoly on good deeds. In some strange way his race's reputation was now at stake.

There were more soldiers than ever out there and one who seemed to be in charge was giving them orders. One squad went back into the house, the rest were moving off elsewhere.

Achaeos bared his teeth. *If I act now, then what?*

As always, he fished in his pouch for the bones. It was a habit for him, especially when cut off from his own people. Good or bad, the omens never ultimately decided his actions. Bad omens just made him more careful.

He dropped to one knee and cast a handful of these shards of bone onto the floor, noting which sigil fell where, which of them touched another, which were alone. It was a bad spread but, unlike some of his comrades, he did not then try for a second opinion. The bones were warning him that he would not succeed if he ventured out now. Had he been already determined to go, this would not have stopped him, but here it merely confirmed his opinion. He let his hand stray from his dagger.

Good fortune, Beetle-girl. I cannot help you. The bones spoke of the future. He hoped that meant she would have some chance to free herself before she fell victim to the fate of so many female prisoners. The thought did not sit well with him. *But there is nothing I can do!*

He told himself that he would fly at nightfall, if he could. He could then look for her, even – if he felt his indebtedness stretched so far. Or he could simply go straight home and forget about Cheerwell Maker and her fate. No doubt his mentors in Tharn would find his quirks of conscience on this matter ridiculous. Five centuries ago their rule of the Lowlands had been shattered, defeat after defeat at the hands of their slaves' new weapons. In the Moths' minds a battle line had been drawn with the revolution, and they had been engaged in ideological warfare ever since.

So he waited, patiently, after the soldiers and their captives had gone. He waited and he watched. Every so often a patrol of Beetle soldiers came round, but none thought to look in the stables, nor would they have spotted him now his strength was back.

In the fullness of time the sky faded towards evening, the silhouetted bulk of the mountains bringing a premature sunset as the sun clipped them. Achaeos stretched, felt his side tug. He thought he could make it, fly at least part of the way, hole up somewhere in the foothills, as far away from these mine workings as he could find. In the first shallows of gloom he slipped from the stables, and froze.

There was a figure crossing the yard before the house, another Beetle. Achaeos waited, very still, very quiet, and the man did not see him. This was a large, broad-waisted Beetle-kinden, clad in hard-wearing leathers, like many of their machine-priests, and he rapped at the door tiredly. Then he glanced around, almost looking straight at

Achaeos. The Moth-kinden was a friend to shadows, and besides, he sensed the Beetle was looking for something else, had been expecting something more. Certainly, before the door was opened, he cast a searching glance back the way he had come.

'Sir?' came the thin voice of the servant.

'Is Elias Monger within? I need to see him,' said the big man.

'I shall check for you, sir. Are you here from the mines?'

'No, I am not. Tell him Stenwold Maker's here to see him.'

The servant obviously knew the name, stiffening briefly at it, and was already retreating as he said, 'I shall let my master know.'

The door closed. Stenwold Maker glanced around again. He was clearly on edge, Achaeos saw. Something promised or hoped for had not happened as expected.

Stenwold Maker? The memory came to the Moth belatedly but forcefully. Of course, *she* had mentioned the name: that of her uncle, whom some other Moth-kinden had healed once. And her name had also been Maker, had it not? Achaeos found the Beetle clan-names very similar: Maker, Monger, Shaper, all of a piece. *But it was something like Maker . . .*

He had another choice, now and flexed his shoulders again. If he could fly, and this turned out to be a bad idea, he would be away before they could catch him, but if he could not fly . . .

The door opened and the burly Beetle was heading inside. Achaeos would be detected now, if he moved: seen by the servant, by the guards.

He moved anyway, swiftly, opening his mouth to speak.

A hand was suddenly twisting his collar, choking him backwards. There was the twinkling point of a blade under his chin.

★

It was a poor place that Sinon had sent her to, and not a safe one either, as he had warned her. Tynisa had her hand to her rapier at all times, and all around there were eyes, watching her. She was an intruder, unwanted, and they were all making that clear.

Eventually she had slowed and held a coin in the air until a Fly-kinden boy of about twelve had run up to her. He had a knife in his belt, and his hand cockily on the hilt in imitation of her own stance, and he stared at her boldly.

'What you want, miss?' he asked. His eyes kept flicking to the coin, for all that it was just a ceramic three-bit.

'Scuto,' she said, and saw the name was recognized. 'I'm here to see him. Where is he?'

He licked his lips, and then pointed over at one shack, almost indistinguishable amongst the masses. She dropped the money into his hand and then stayed him with a gesture as he made to go.

'Same again if you tell him I'm here. Tell him Stenwold's ward is here. Got that?'

He nodded and she favoured him with a smile.

'Good lad, we'll make a regular Messenger of you yet. Now off you go.'

She watched as he pelted for the shack. There were still eyes on her, people in the shadows between buildings, in the overhung alleys. They were sizing her up, working out whether it was worth the risk to see what she carried. She kept her stance disdainful, not bothering even to return their scrutiny.

A moment later the boy was out again, beckoning to her. *Here goes.* Sinon might have decided she was best swept under the carpet, now that she was out of his service. He might even have regretted it but it would be just business to him, and he was as much a businessman as Helleron's greatest magnate. Tensed inside, relaxed to the outside world, she strode forward as if she had no care in the world.

A *thing* of some sort came out of the shack. It was mostly shrouded in a cloak, but looked as though the man beneath was smuggling insects under it. A face she took for a theatre mask, until it moved, looked at her balefully. There was a crossbow in this apparition's malformed hands. She started wondering whether she could dodge a bolt and get to him before he had recocked it, and decided that she could.

Behind him was . . .

Behind him was Totho, staring at her. The sight of him brought an unexpected rush of relief to her. That even one of her friends was still alive on his feet in this greedy city seemed amazing to her. She had not realized, until now, how little hope she had been husbanding.

'Totho!' she called and began to run forward, but the ugly man raised his crossbow threateningly.

'You stay right there,' he called. 'Not a step, or you'll have this beauty here to deal with.'

'Totho, what's going on?' she demanded. Her hand was already tight on the rapier grip and, without meaning to, she had stepped forward. Instantly the crossbowman loosed, the bolt diving neatly into the dirt before her. She tensed, but the bow was already recocked somehow, another bolt gleaming there.

'Ask her,' the ugly man snapped at Totho, who swallowed visibly.

'Tynisa,' he called. 'What was the name of the man you fought in our match against the Shell?'

'What? Totho, what is going on?'

'It's really, really important that you answer me,' he said. 'Tynisa, please.' She could see the man with the crossbow getting tense. Her calculations on reaching him had gone to tatters.

'I fought Seladoris,' she said, frowning. 'You fought Adax of Tark, and drew. You broke his nose. What is going on?'

The relief in the pair of them was visible. The ugly man lowered the crossbow and took the tension off the string. She approached carefully, and Totho came forward to meet her. She thought at first he was going to embrace her, lost friend to lost friend, but his nerve failed and they just clasped hands instead.

'I'm so happy you're safe,' he said. 'I felt terrible . . . leaving you there.'

'We all left each other,' she said. 'Let's just hope Che and Salma left us as well as we left them.'

He hung his head, although she had not meant it as a reprimand. 'This,' he said, pointing at the ugly man, 'is Scuto, Stenwold's man.'

Scuto looked even worse close-to than at crossbow's point. He leered. 'Come on in,' he invited her. 'You've got some catching up to do.'

'I don't understand,' she said, when confronted with the story of Bolwyn's death and apparent rebirth.

'Shame. What with you being a Spider-kinden, I thought you might,' Scuto said. 'Seemed like your kind of thing, running off with other people's faces.'

She gave him a sour look, which was like spitting into the tempest. 'I have lived most of my life in Collegium, so I'm not up on the latest cosmetic fashions in Seldis this season.'

Scuto shrugged. 'So it's a worry, but not one we can do anything against.'

'But you see why I had to ask,' Totho put in.

'I suppose so.' Tynisa frowned at the array of incomprehensible mechanics around her. 'This must be home away from home for you. You've landed on your feet.'

'So what happened to you?' he asked, and for a second she was about to tell him: the Halfway House, the gangsters, the deaths. For just a second she was proud of it all.

Then she looked at his face and remembered who he

was, and who she was, and where they had come here from. In Collegium criminals did not boast about their deeds but kept them secret. In Collegium there was a rule of law, and murderers did not swagger about openly in the street.

'Just surviving,' she said. 'Just making my way. So where are Che and Salma?'

'Best information suggests they took refuge with some of Stenwold's family,' Scuto said.

'But I tried there and they said . . .' But of course it had been Sinon saying it. She had not asked them herself. What if he had betrayed her, after all?

'That they ain't seen 'em,' Scuto agreed. 'That's the line they took with my boys as well.'

She nodded, relieved.

'Thing is,' the Thorn Bug continued. 'I got definite witnesses who saw some fellow in a real fancy robe and a yellow hide go into one such townhouse. Now I ain't sure myself, but I reckon that sounds like your man, 'specially when he's got a Beetle-girl with dyed hair alongside him. Only now everyone's claiming they ain't seen 'em.'

'Maybe they're just scared the Wasps will find them,' Tynisa suggested.

'Stenwold'll get to the foot of it, though.' The prospect did not seem to delight Scuto.

'Stenwold? He's here?'

'He got to Helleron today,' Totho confirmed.

'Some of mine met him at the usual place, told him the state of things,' Scuto explained. 'Wanted him to come here, but he's always got to do things his own way. The only reason he keeps me around is he ain't invented a way of being in two cities at once. No, he's gone off asking questions himself, so cobblers knows where the bugger is now.'

'But . . . the Wasps, they're hunting him,' said Tynisa.

'Think I don't know?' Scuto said balefully. 'Think I

want him beetling off across the city? And it's not as if *he* don't know either. But there you have it. You just can't tell a man his own business these days.' He grimaced, exposing his yellowing fangs at them. 'He'll just have to deal with it himself, whatever it is.'

There was a hurried hammering on the door. A boy, the same Fly-kinden boy Tynisa had spoken to earlier, called in, 'Scuto, someone's coming. Someone real big and heavy.'

'Stenwold?' Tynisa asked.

'I'll tell him you said that.' Scuto picked his crossbow up again and cocked it. 'No. They already know ol' Sten, around here.' He peered through one of the shack's half-boarded windows. 'Hell. Scorpion-kinden, and he's big all right.'

'Scorpion?' Tynisa gingerly peered over his spiked shoulder. 'I know him.' It was Akta Barik from the Half-ways. For a moment she wondered if he had been sent after her, but if Sinon had wanted her dealt with, he had been given far better chances than this. 'Let me speak to him.'

'He's all yours.' Scuto kicked the door open for her, keeping the crossbow handy.

Barik stopped when he saw her, waited for her to approach him. He had his monstrous sword over his shoulder, its scabbard-tip almost dragging in the earth. She knew she could draw before he had even got both hands on it, but his hands were weapons in themselves.

'Hello, Barik,' she said cautiously. Behind the fence of his teeth, his expression was unreadable.

'Got news for you. Came in after you left.' His quiet voice just carried to her. She decided she would have to trust him more than this, or she would miss whatever he was saying. She stepped closer, well within the reach of his sword, still outside the reach of hers. He gave a small nod of acknowledgement.

'Slave deal going on, north-east camp. I was shifting some merchandise for the chief,' he said. 'Only I saw one there, in a gang they were shipping out. He was a Commonwealer, Dragonfly-kinden. Not been many Wealers in Helleron since they had that big war in the northlands.'

'A *slave*?' she said, appalled.

'Might not be your man but' – he waved a taloned hand – 'Sinon reckoned I should tell you.'

'Thank him for me,' she said earnestly. 'Tell him, when I'm back this way, I owe him, just a little.'

He nodded. This was the proper way of doing business.

As Barik stomped off, she slipped back into Scuto's lair. 'We have another problem,' she announced.

Sixteen

'Ah, Stenwold,' Elias said, as his visitor came in. 'One moment, will you?' He made an ostentatious show of checking some figures on his scroll, adding them up, underlining the total. Only when he had replaced the reservoir pen in its gold holder did he look up, smiling. 'I confess, I had no idea you were expected in Helleron, let alone out here. Have you perhaps cultivated an interest in mining?'

'No more than in anything else,' Stenwold replied. He looked oddly out of place in Elias's study, even amongst the reduced facilities of this simple house near the mines. The dust of the road was still on him and he wore his artificer's leathers like armour, proof against sparks and metal shards. Even with a sword at his belt he was hardly cousin to the lord of the manor.

'So, tell me,' Elias prompted, leaning back in his chair.

'I may need your help, Elias,' Stenwold said simply.

'If I can, but what's the problem?'

'My niece, Cheerwell, and some companions of hers, they appear to have gone missing.'

'In Helleron? A College field trip, was it?'

Stenwold gave him a narrow look. 'They entered the city a few days ago and were attacked, got separated. Cheerwell's got a good head on her shoulders so she'd have thought of family.'

Elias shrugged. 'Well you must try some of the others rather than me, although I would have heard, I think, if any errant cousin had come to town.'

Stenwold nodded solemnly, a man confronted with what he had most feared. 'You haven't seen her, then? No sign at all?'

'I'm sorry.' Elias stretched out another scroll of accounts. 'But I'll do all I can, obviously, to find her. Just say the word.'

'Well.' Stenwold took a deep breath, reflecting that a man of his age and position should not find himself in such a situation. 'The word is that Cheerwell and a companion came to the very door of your townhouse. Her companion was a Dragonfly prince in full regalia, so he would have been hard to miss.'

Elias frowned at him. 'What are you implying?'

'That they came to you, cousin Elias. Cheerwell was running from her attackers and, like any sensible girl, she went to her own family for protection.'

'Stenwold, I've already told you, I haven't seen her.' But Elias's expression revealed a thin smile creeping up on it. Stenwold's heart sank. A disappointment, perhaps, but equally not a surprise.

'What's going on, Elias?' he asked softly.

Elias steepled his fingers, elbows planted on the desk. 'My dear Stenwold, you have always been, shall we say, a maverick. The way you blunder about waving warnings at people, you're the family embarrassment, really. Perhaps they may put up with it in Collegium, where I hear eccentrics are considered one of their greatest resources, but it's different in Helleron. Here you can't just charge about like some Ant-kinden pugilist looking for a fight. What precisely do you want?'

'I want my niece, who is also your cousin,' said Stenwold, his face now stripped of all warmth or humour.

'You've made enemies here, Stenwold,' Elias said, 'and they hate it when you pry into their business. If you've got your niece involved in that, it's your own fault.'

'Yes, yes it *is* my fault,' Stenwold admitted. 'Although I

had thought to keep her from danger by sending her here. So much for that. What exactly did you do to her, Elias?'

'I?'

'Shall we dispense with the dissembling? I can see that you're desperate to gloat, and here am I, a willing audience. So tell me how clever you've been, Elias. What has happened to Cheerwell?'

Elias clasped his hands together, the essence of a merchant concluding a deal. 'Your enemies heard about her, Stenwold, and they tracked her down.'

'They tracked her to you.'

Elias's smile dried up. 'And if they did? The girl was blundering from trouble to trouble. She would have ended up in their hands eventually.'

'You could have sheltered her.'

'Why should I?' Elias stood up, angry. 'You bring your rantings to my door and expect me to put myself out for you? You've *invented* a war, Stenwold, and *you* can fight it. You're the one who has been agitating all over Helleron about the best clients this city has seen in a hundred years.'

'What have you done with my niece?' Stenwold said, still the soul of reason.

'I handed her over to them, Stenwold. And why not?'

'Because she was your cousin? Ah no, we've been there.' Stenwold's hands were fists. 'And how much did you get?'

'If the Empire was kind enough to render a reward, then so be it,' Elias told him.

'You sold her then,' said Stenwold. 'Have you any idea what they'll do to her? Torture her? Execute her?'

'Oh, don't be so melodramatic, they're a just people,' Elias replied. 'They'll probably make a slave out of her.'

'Is that all?' Stenwold hissed. 'Just a slave, is it?'

From elsewhere in the house something thumped, and Elias's thin smile broadened just a little.

'She was a wanted criminal, in their eyes. As are you.'

'Enough of this!' Stenwold was right up to the desk, two feet of wood all that was between them. 'Where have they taken her?'

'I have no idea.'

'Tell me!'

'I have told you. Why should I care where she's gone? She's gone, and that's enough for me.' Elias leant forwards across the desk until he and Stenwold were nose to nose. 'However, you'll find out, and sooner than you might want.' Abruptly he broke off and took a bell from beside the penholder, ringing it loudly. His expression was triumphant when he added, 'In fact, you can join her.'

The echo of the bell fell away into the walls. Stenwold had his hand to his sword hilt, a step back from the desk now, waiting. After a moment of looking at the room's single door, he cocked an eyebrow at Elias.

'And?'

Elias rang the bell again, and then a third time, so hard that it bounced from the desk top. The high sound sang out, fell silent. Nothing.

'Guards!' Elias shouted. 'Guards! To me, now!'

There was the smallest of smiles on Stenwold's face. 'It can be so difficult,' he commented, 'hiring reliable staff these days.'

'Guards!' Elias bellowed again, and this time the door finally opened, and a man, a single man, entered, stalking into the room like death. A tall Mantis-kinden in green, a claw-like metal blade jutting from his right hand.

'Tisamon,' Stenwold said, and despite Cheerwell's plight, despite his cousin's betrayal, he could not suppress a grin. 'I didn't know if you'd got my message. I didn't know if you'd come.'

The Mantis smiled back, or as much as he had ever done. 'Ten years since you last called for me. How could you think only ten years would keep me away? I am no fickle Beetle-kinden, Stenwold. *We* remember.'

'Who is this?' Elias demanded. 'What is going on?'

'You have made use of my talents in the past, Master Monger, in matters of business,' Tisamon told him mildly. 'My name is Tisamon of Felyal.'

Elias's eyes bulged. He had missed the name the first time but now it came to him in full force. 'I will pay you twice what this man is offering,' he croaked. 'Five times.'

Tisamon's lips twitched and he shook his head.

'He takes money,' Stenwold explained to his cousin, 'but he fights for honour, and that's a currency I fear you're not good for.' He was round the edge of the desk in a moment, his sword out while his free hand grasped Elias's robe at the front.

'Stenwold, please—'

'You sold my niece to the Wasps,' Stenwold hissed through clenched teeth.

'Please, I can—'

'You have nothing worthwhile to offer me,' Stenwold said. He found that his sword arm was actually shaking with the effort of restraining it. 'You have betrayed your own family, your city and your race. What should I do with you?'

'Stenwold, I'm sorry—'

'But you're not. Or you're sorry you've been found out. If a squad of Wasps turned up now, you'd sell me for as much as the market would bear. *Shut up*!' He slammed the babbling merchant back against the wall. 'You have no idea how much, how very much, I want to kill you, Elias. Every base and violent part of me is baying for it.' He mustered all the control at his command and released the trembling man, stepped back. 'I will not compound your betrayal by making myself a kinslayer, however. I do not think I could live with that.'

He sheathed his sword, unblooded still, and turned to go.

'Stenwold, cousin . . . thank you . . .' Elias gasped.

His back turned to the merchant, Stenwold paused in the doorway. 'Tisamon, however, has no such qualms, I wager.'

'What?'

Stenwold stepped out of the study and closed the door behind him, then went to sit on a chair in the hall, feeling utterly drained and disgusted by the world. Through the closed door behind him he heard Elias shrieking out his desperate offers to buy Tisamon's soul. A fitting thing for him, Stenwold decided: dying with numbers on his lips.

After a moment Stenwold glanced round to see the Mantis emerge from the study, cleaning his blade meticulously with a piece of cloth cut from Elias's robe. 'Did you really think that I might turn my back on you?' Tisamon said quietly.

Stenwold approached the Mantis-kinden wonderingly. 'Look at that. You haven't aged a moment in ten years.'

'You have,' Tisamon said uncharitably. 'Older and balder and fatter. Mind you, you were never slim or well-haired.'

'And young?'

'It seems to me we were neither of us ever that young, even then.'

Left hand to left they clasped, and Stenwold noticed that the other man had aged, even so. The patches of white might be lost within his fair hair, but there were new lines on his face that bespoke a less than happy life.

'What would you have done,' the Mantis asked lightly, 'if your message had not reached me?' He did not say *if I had not come.*

Stenwold felt a lurch within him, at what would befall them both shortly. Himself and his oldest friend. 'I would have fought,' he said simply.

'I think you would,' Tisamon agreed.

'How many would I have been fighting, then?'

'Half a dozen of your locals, the same number of Wasp

light infantry.' Tisamon shrugged, as though to suggest it was nothing much to think about. Stenwold reminded himself: *Barely a sound, all the while I was talking to Elias.* Tisamon had earned his bread as assassin as well as duellist, even back then. He had treated the trade as the continuation of the duel by other means. There was not even a single spot of blood on his clothes.

'We have a lot to catch up on,' Stenwold said.

'Less than you think. The past has been just keeping place for the future, hasn't it? They've finished playing with the Commonweal and now they're coming for us, at last.'

At last? But yes, of course Tisamon was looking forward to the Wasps' next move. 'You keep yourself informed?'

'Helleron's a hive of rumours, for those who will listen.'

'And yet nobody will listen.' Stenwold shook his head as he walked out of his dead cousin's house, and had his sword immediately to hand. There was a man standing there, right outside the door: a Moth-kinden, Stenwold noted with surprise. No servant or creature of Elias's then. 'Who are you and what are you doing here?' Stenwold asked him.

'Not an assassin, as I had first assumed,' came Tisamon's voice from behind him. 'In fact, something of a benefactor. He was creeping up on you even as you went in the door. He'd seen the Wasps, you see, and wanted to warn you,' Tisamon said, 'but sadly I was creeping up on him.'

Stenwold glanced back at the Moth. 'You didn't kill him then?'

'Moth-kinden,' said Tisamon. 'Old habits die hard.' Like the rest of the past, the ancient fealties of his people ran deep. 'Old loyalties, we have,' and he was smiling at Stenwold again like a ghost from seventeen years ago.

Stenwold turned back to the waiting Moth, who had not moved or made a sound all this time. He noticed the stranger was wounded and bandaged messily. He could not make the connection. 'So where do you come in? What are the Wasps to you?'

'I care nothing for them. But I wanted to warn you.'

'Warn me?'

'I saw your niece being taken,' said the Moth without much inflection, keeping his expression guarded.

'You saw Cheerwell?' Suddenly Stenwold came alive. The Moth backed off smoothly as he approached.

'She . . . helped me,' he said.

Stenwold stopped before he forced the man out of the door. 'You have nothing to fear from me,' he said, and then: 'I understand now. You must be from Tharn. A raider, are you?'

The Moth nodded cautiously. 'My name . . . is Achaeos.'

'Well, right now Helleron doesn't have much claim on my loyalty,' announced Stenwold. 'The master of this house, my cousin Elias Monger, lies dead in the next room, and I imagine your grand high potentates or whatever they're called are going to be rubbing their hands over that.'

'They will shed no tears,' Achaeos agreed.

'Tell me about Cheerwell. Where is she?'

Achaeos related all that he had witnessed without emotion. He had a trained eye for detail, Stenwold noted: here was a man used to spying out the enemy. The thought that he, Stenwold, might be one of that enemy was a strange one. With a very few exceptions the Moth-kinden were a race he had never had much to do with.

'They took them where?'

'South and east. I know the city has slave camps located at its edge,' Achaeos reported. Stenwold had no idea whether Moths kept slaves these days, and nothing in the man's tone enlightened him.

Stenwold rubbed at his chin, feeling the stubble grown

there. 'You have no idea how hard I pushed in order to make the time I did. If all this had happened in a month's time I'd have had a completed railroad to carry me straight here from Collegium. As it is, this last tenday and more, I've hopped on at least five different forms of transport, and still I'm too late. Too late by a single day.'

'You'll go after her.' For Tisamon it was a rhetorical question.

'She's my niece, and she's with another of my students. I'll go after them both.' Stenwold bared his teeth in something like a smile. 'I shall not lack for help, though. Do you remember Scuto the Thorn Bug?'

'Remember him?' said Tisamon. 'I've turned down three contracts to kill him.'

Stenwold maintained the semblance of a smile. *These histories we do not ask about.* 'I shall go to him now. He's bored into this city like a grub. For information or material, I shall not lack for help.'

'My blade is yours,' Tisamon said, so simply that Stenwold stared at him.

'I had not thought . . .'

'I told you.' The Mantis looked down. 'I have been marking time all these years. Did you think I would turn from you now?'

They had met perhaps three times, after the siege at Myna. Sometimes Tisamon had helped in Stenwold's intelligencing, at the start. As the work changed, and watching and waiting became more important than a swift blade, there had been less need to call upon him. Meanwhile College work had claimed Stenwold more and more and they had gone their separate ways. It had been ten years since they had last seen each other.

'I . . . don't know what to say,' the Beetle stammered. A terrible feeling of doom hung over him: *We will both regret this.* 'At least take time to think.' *Before burdening me with your promise.* Mantis promises were harder than steel, and heavier to bear. 'You have a life, here . . .'

Tisamon was staring at his feet again. It was a sight so familiar that for a second it was twenty years ago, Tisamon unable to answer some cutting observation one of the others had made.

'I have no life, here,' the Mantis whispered. 'Seventeen years, Sten – You know what I mean.'

Time has not passed for him. He knew that the Mantis-kinden were loath to let go of hurts, or wrongs, or old friends either. He had never quite appreciated how alien the feeling would be, to become involved with such a mind.

I am so sorry, my friend.

They had made arrangements to meet that evening, Stenwold and Tisamon. They had almost spoken the name of the place together, their old haunt from the old, old days. The moment of coincidence had brought a brief wash of nostalgia to Stenwold, but the emotion had only driven in the jagged-glass thought of what was to come that much more deeply.

He had set off for Scuto's slum den, resolutely keeping his mind on the task to come. Beetles were a practical folk, he told himself. They did not spend their lives worrying about things they could not be sure of.

Scuto's neighbours spotted him way off, but he had no worries about that. Many of them would even recognize him as the Thorn Bug's friend. Here, of all places in Helleron, he did not fear assault.

Which thought turned sour very fast when Scuto's door was kicked open just in front of him, revealing the spiky grotesque levelling a crossbow at him.

Stenwold froze, thinking, *Ah no. Don't say they've turned Scuto now as well. Not the man I sent them all to.*

'What was I doing when you first met me?' Scuto asked, squinting suspiciously.

Stenwold stared at him. 'What?'

'What was I doing when you first met me?' the Thorn Bug demanded, jabbing the crossbow towards him forcefully enough to make the bolts in its magazine rattle.

Stenwold goggled at him. 'I don't think I can remember precisely. I do remember that you had a sideline in truly awful poetry, if that's any help. I could even recite some for you.'

'No need,' said the Thorn Bug hastily. 'Come on in. We've had mixed news.'

He backed into the shack, setting the crossbow down, and Stenwold followed.

'I've had news too,' he said, 'mostly bad—' before he was almost knocked off his feet by Tynisa.

'I'm so glad you're safe.' She was hugging him as hard as she could. 'We thought you were walking right into a trap.'

'Oh I was,' he confirmed, and when she gave him a startled look he added, 'What, you think old Stenwold can't look after himself?' He held her at arm's length, seeing beneath her skin the shadow of the last few days. 'It's good to see that you can survive a little, too,' he said gently.

Beyond her, amidst the clutter of Scuto's artifice, he spotted Totho lurking. 'You made it too, then? Good lad.'

'Yes, Master Maker,' replied Totho dutifully, at once as though he was still back at the College.

'Good pair of hands, this one,' Scuto put in. 'If you was thinkin' of posting him here, I could use him.'

'Who stays and who goes,' said Stenwold soberly, 'well, that's the question, isn't it? Cheerwell and Salma haven't been so lucky, it seems. They've been handed over to the Wasps.'

'We know,' Tynisa said. 'A Wasp slave convoy has

already left the city, heading east, and it sounds as if they were both in it.'

Stenwold let out a long breath. 'You've been using your time well. East, is it?'

'The Empire,' Scuto put in helpfully.

'Oh, I know that. It's been a while, though, since I was out that way.' *Seventeen years, and why did I ever think I could escape this moment.* 'I wish we had more time.' *I wish I had more time.* 'Nobody needs to come with me, and I mean that.'

'That's good, 'cos I certainly ain't going,' Scuto said with finality. 'They don't like most anyone in the Empire, but they really don't like my kind.'

'And I need you here anyway,' Stenwold confirmed. 'Totho, you can stay here, if you wish. Scuto would be a good teacher.'

'I . . . would rather come with you.' Totho gave Scuto an apologetic look. 'Sorry, but . . . they're my friends.'

'If things go badly for us . . . well, in the Empire they're harsh on those of mixed blood,' Stenwold warned him.

Totho shrugged, as though to say it was not so different even beyond the Empire's borders.

Stenwold gathered himself. 'Tynisa . . .'

'Of course,' she said firmly. 'Of course I'm with you. You don't even need to say it,' but when she saw him nod, and fake a smile, she thought that perhaps he had been going to say something else.

'Scuto, you find us what we need for our journey. I'll meet the pair of you by the old Draywain spoil foundry just east of the city. I have a reinforcement to fetch.'

Seventeen

It was not at all as she had envisaged, but in retrospect she supposed that her beliefs about her own importance had been misplaced.

She had fully expected to be rushed into Helleron, thrown into some dungeon, questioned, even tortured. She had been ready, in her defiance, to spit in their faces.

The sun shone bright on her and the air was full of dust. No secluded oubliette was set aside for her or Salma – at least she still had Salma. When she glanced at him now he was still able to muster a smile for her benefit.

There were a dozen of them now as prisoners. Thalric's soldiers had joined up with another squad guarding a single line of roped-together captives, and they had promptly set out across the scrublands east of Helleron. There was to be no talking between the prisoners, a rule enforced by the fists of the guards where necessary, but Che was not sure that they would have had much to say. They were Ants of some unfamiliar city, Beetles who did not look Helleron-born, a couple of Fly-kinden, a lanky, sallow creature with a distinctive high forehead that she could not place. Most were men, only a couple were women, and uniformly they looked even more dispirited than Che herself felt. They bore their captivity with a sense of inevitability.

The first evening, the soldiers built a staked palisade about them, as crude a piece of handiwork as Che had ever seen. The prisoners were kept roped together, and watched over at all hours. Some of the Wasps carried crossbows, but she knew that none of them was without a means to punish their prisoners at range. Thalric kept himself separate from his men, having found a flat rock to perch on some distance away, and was intent on reading from a scroll whilst he ate.

She had thought that she would be somehow special after they had gone to such lengths to take her and Salma into their custody. Now it seemed she was considered just another slave.

She was woken past midnight by the approach of another group, but it turned out to be more of the same. Her eyes settled first on the string of listless captives and only then shifted to their captors. These latter were Wasps of a different stripe to Thalric's soldiers: a half-dozen men in open-sided tabards, lean and muscled and bestial. They seemed almost faceless in full helms, T-shaped slots showing narrow slices of hard faces, and they had clubs and whips fastened at their belts. Slavers' weapons, Che quickly realized: enough to keep the livestock in order, yet nothing too dangerous should it fall into the wrong hands.

There was a shifting among the Wasp soldiers as they arrived, and she saw that these newcomers were not exactly well loved. Her fellow prisoners plainly recognized them, and a tremor ran through them at the sight.

Thalric came pacing over. 'Someone light a lantern,' he directed, and a soldier obediently struck the flint on an oil-lamp. The glow it cast across the rough ground was anything but cosy.

'Captain Thalric.' The foremost slaver gave him a half-hearted salute. 'This season's harvest.'

Thalric looked over the new prisoners, about twenty in all. 'More runners, Brutan?'

'Why not?'

The officer gave the slaver a narrow look. 'You're sure you haven't been exceeding your brief?'

'You think they'll care?' replied the man Brutan. 'A slave's a slave. In the long term, what difference will it make?'

Thalric shrugged. 'I'm sure you know your business. Nineteen bodies added to your tally then, Brutan. I'll see the count is passed on.'

'We're coming with you, Captain. I'll pick the bounty up myself.'

There was a definite murmur of distaste amongst the Wasp soldiers, but Thalric shut them up with a glance. 'As you will, Brutan. I'll put the whole lot of them into your care, then. As I said, you know your trade.'

The new prisoners were much of a muchness with the others, plus a scattering of half-breeds and a single man that Che decided could even be a Wasp himself. This realization came paired with the fact that two of Brutan's slavers were clearly Ant-kinden, possessing the pale skins of Tark. These slavers obviously either operated by different rules, or they paid little heed to whatever rules they were given.

The regular soldiers were only too glad to give up their charges to the newcomers, and quickly left to huddle round their fire. The palisade was soon being widened, and the new slaves packed in so there was barely room for them all to sit. The slavers kept a close watch on them, but many of the prisoners seemed to sense that the regime had now changed. A low, cautious murmur was struck up, a halting exchange of names and places. *Where did they take you? How far did you get?*

'Salma,' Che whispered. 'I'm frightened.'

'I think you're allowed to be,' he encouraged her, squeezing her hand. 'Just be calm. Stay calm and wait.'

She tried to be calm, but it was like meditating. She simply could not concentrate. The Beetle-kinden man sitting next to her turned and asked, 'Where did you break from?' in a hollow, weary voice.

'Break from? They caught us just outside Helleron,' Che replied.

'No, no, where did you escape from, to reach there? How far did you manage?'

She understood, then. 'This is the first time. I've never been a . . . a slave before.'

He nodded in sudden understanding. The man looked about Stenwold's age, but Stenwold made thin by a very harsh life. 'I'm sorry,' he said.

'Well, I'm sorry for all of us,' she replied.

He shook his head, would not look at her. The tall, sallow man beside him took up the slack. 'His meaning: we are escaped slaves and the Empire has harsh lessons for those who attempt to flee. You are with us now so you will suffer as we do. We are sorry for you because by being with us we have included you in our future suffering.'

'You were *slaves*,' Che said. 'You can't blame yourselves for escaping.'

'You will learn.' The sallow man of unknown race shook his head. 'We are blamed. We are the lesser race.'

Che stared at him. In the dark it was hard to tell how he meant this fatalism, but she had a feeling that it went deep, that it had long been pounded into him.

'I am not a slave,' she announced stubbornly. 'I will *never* be a slave. Not in here.' She pointed at her forehead. 'No matter how often they tell me it.'

None of them seemed able to look her in the eyes. She singled one out, a ruddy-skinned Ant-kinden woman. 'You're a warrior? I thought all Ants were warriors. Tell me you don't think like this.'

The woman's agonized expression implored her to keep her voice down. 'I took part in the rebellion at Maynes,' she replied. 'We were warriors then – for the space of two tendays. Then their army returned from the front and they crushed us. They crucified four hundred men and women around the walls of the city. Not revolutionaries, just anyone – anyone they didn't like the look of. They took hundreds of our children away to become slaves in other cities. The survivors, any who had fought, they branded in the face. I ran away. I am not a warrior any more. I have seen what misery it brings. Now they will kill me when I am taken back to them. They will kill me where the whole city can see it.'

'Then why not fight?' Che demanded. 'What have you got to lose?'

'You do not understand,' the Ant woman said flatly.

The man of unknown race hissed suddenly, and they fell quiet as one of the slavers passed alongside the palisade. After he had gone, the high-browed prisoner leant over towards Che.

'Tomorrow, if you still live, you will learn how to be a slave,' he said, almost as though he was encouraging her.

'If I live? You may not have heard, but we Beetles are tough.'

'Tomorrow one of us will most certainly die,' he said simply. 'It is the Empire's way.'

Most of the slaves woke at dawn, from long habit. Those who did not, exhausted from the previous day, were allowed a single whip-crack in which to wake themselves. After that the whip itself came down.

The dawn had woken Salma, and he shook Che into wakefulness before the slavers could get round to her. The prisoners were being hauled up and roped together again for walking. He looked about him, trying to gauge if this was their chance to make a break for it, but there were too many slavers posted all about. He might have given it a try, on his own: a lightning strike to get a knife in his hands, to cut his bonds and into the air. He was not optimistic about his chances, though, and Che would never make it.

Salma had never been the responsible type: he had always taken being a prince frivolously. This had given him a light-hearted outlook on life. At home he had played the games of court, wooed young women or sparred and flown with his peers. Even when war and the Empire had come to the eastern principalities, he had not taken it seriously enough.

Thereafter he had been sent to study at Collegium, where Stenwold had broached to him the subject of the Empire. It had all still seemed a game, a bit of excitement for him to intersperse amongst his studies and casual seductions. Of course the Wasps were his enemies, but that was all so far, far away.

In the Lowlands, though, they had developed so many wondrous means of transport, so that same *far away* could become *here* very quickly indeed. Salma found himself learning all about responsibility now.

'Come on.' He helped Che stand up, and a blank-helmed slaver tied them together and set them moving. Back in Collegium Salma had always found Che tremendously amusing, in a fond way, of course: how she bustled about and was always so *serious* about everything. Her studies, her ethics, her desperate attempts to break into the Ancestor Art. Everything was a crisis on which her personal world hinged. Privately he had found such endeavours hilarious, just as so much else of Beetle society appeared risible to him.

Now here she was, tied to him by three feet of rope, and he felt such a burden of responsibility for her that he wanted to thrust her behind him and strike out at any Wasp who even looked at her. This emotion surprised him: he did not know where it came from. He had never seen Che as a candidate for one of his idle conquests. Nor was it because he felt a responsibility to Stenwold to keep his niece safe. This was something entirely new: he wanted to keep her safe because she was all he had.

And thinking about her safety allowed him to ignore the ignominy of his own bondage.

The slaves had been lined up now in a single row and everyone was clearly waiting for something to happen. It came when one of the slavers removed his black-and-gold helm, revealing heavy-jawed features and a shaven scalp. When he spoke, his voice identified him as Brutan, their leader.

'You are all slaves!' he shouted at them.

Che glanced off to one side at Thalric and his soldiers, who were studiously ignoring what was going on. Instantly a whip cracked towards her, sending her reeling into Salma.

'*Look at me, you bitch!*' Brutan bellowed, the cords of his neck standing out. 'Slaves look at their masters when they're spoken to. Not in the eye, but you look!' He cracked his whip again. 'You are all slaves!' he repeated. 'Worse, you are all escaped slaves, slaves twice over. That makes you lowest of all slaves!' Brutan was glaring at them all with an abiding and personal loathing, enough to make his eyes bulge and veins throb in his forehead. 'You are the worst kind of scum because you have made the Empire waste my precious time in fetching you back!' he almost screamed. 'I only wish the Empire had more slaves to spare because then I would have the lot of you executed. However, a lesson must now be taught, so that you do not try wasting any more of my or the Empire's time.'

He stalked forward, proceeding to one end of the line, then strode along it, looking at each face in turn. 'The only thing left now is to make my choice.'

His progress past them was agonizingly slow. He stopped often, while each slave stared down at his own feet. Many were shaking and somewhere down the line someone was weeping in desperate sobs that no amount of effort could muffle.

Brutan stopped in front of the lanky, sallow man, considering. He was now only a few bodies down the line from Salma and Che. He moved on, passing a Beetle-kinden, then the female Ant that Che had spoken to last night. He stopped again.

'Commonwealer,' he remarked. 'Slavery too good for your kind, is it?'

Salma stared at his feet and said nothing.

'I've got a villa in Dras Hesha, boy. You know where that is?' And when Salma said nothing, he shrieked, 'Slaves answer their masters! Do you know where that is?'

'Yes, sir,' Salma said quietly. 'Yes, master.'

'I keep my villa well stocked, boy. In fact I've got a Dragonfly girl there: she could just about be your sister.' He watched carefully, his eyes flicking about Salma's bowed face, waiting for the first rebel spark. The words passed the Dragonfly by, though. He felt them strike him, strike where his pride was and then course to either side like the waters of a stream. His responsibility protected him. He could not indulge in mere pride, now he had Che to look after.

Brutan's lip curled in disgust, and he passed on down the line of prisoners.

At the very end he turned suddenly and pointed with the handle of his whip. 'You!' It was one of the Ant-kinden he had selected. Instantly the man braced himself to resist but a pair of slavers descended on him from behind. One of them struck him a glancing blow with a club and then they had cut him free and were grappling him away from the rest.

'Don't look,' said Salma in Che's ear and she frowned at him.

'I've seen death before.' She was so desperate to put on a brave face.

'Not this death. Don't look.' Salma knew what was

coming. It had been mentioned in dispatches from the war front: the favoured Wasp way of execution, especially for their own.

Two of the slavers carried long spears, tipped at each end with a skewer-like point, and with a crosspiece halfway down, like a hunting spear. Che stubbornly watched them as the first spear was firmly grounded in the earth at an angle, and it was only when the slave was dragged towards it, and she understood, that she closed her eyes and turned her head away. Then all she had were the sounds, the hideous shrieks of the man that went on and on, weaker and weaker.

And when she opened her eyes, he was still alive, only just, too weak for any further sound. He hung off the crossed spears that passed through his body, emerging under the armpit to lance into his spread arms so that he was splayed like an unattended puppet. She hoped, she fervently hoped, that he would die swiftly. It was all the hope she could offer him.

She had believed that she was so special, and that Salma was special, considering how much trouble Thalric had gone to to track them down. And yet here they were, and how close had Salma been to providing that grotesque example?

'All right!' Brutan bellowed, as the line of slaves was made whole again. 'The Captain wants to leave now. Time for you to start moving!'

Even before the slaves could begin stirring, the whips were in motion. To the east their path would take them beyond the shadowy fastnesses of the Darakyon Forest, through hill country and off all the maps, into the Empire itself.

Stenwold had been bracing himself against all manner of things recently, but he was not prepared for the sheer onslaught of memories on seeing Tisamon seated at the usual table at the Taverna Egelitara. It had been their old gathering place, of course, where they had always met in Helleron, all five of them together. The place was still here after all those years, though the family that owned it had changed generations in that time. And there was Tisamon himself, leaning back in his chair at the corner table outside the taverna, as though any moment Marius or Atryssa might cross the square to greet him.

But there was nobody save Stenwold left of that world now and the Beetle walked over with a heavy heart.

It was only when he was almost at the table that he noticed the Moth, Achaeos. The small man sat as though he were not here in the very citadel of his enemies, a quiet shadow at Tisamon's table. Nobody paid him any heed beyond the occasional puzzled look. Perhaps it was Tisamon's lean figure that discouraged them, but Stenwold rather thought it was the simple difference in the way his own race and the Moths viewed each other. To the Moths of Tharn, Helleron represented evil on earth, come to rape their sacred mountains and infect their culture. To the industrial barons of Helleron, the Moths were a small annoyance in a larger world. They lost more sleep over fluctuations in the price of tin.

With a nod to Tisamon Stenwold took a seat. 'I see you're still here,' he said, turning to the Moth.

'Apparently,' said Achaeos. His tone made it clear that Stenwold was still a Beetle, despite it all. 'I intend to make good on my debts.'

'You're beginning to sound like *him*,' said Stenwold, with a glance at Tisamon.

'Masters of the Grey, Servants of the Green,' said Achaeos, a little litany that Stenwold knew referred to the way things were before the revolution. 'Who is to say we cannot learn from our brothers?'

'Right, enough wordplay. I am about to go and rescue my niece from Wasp-kinden. So what do you want?'

The direct question at last scratched the composure of Achaeos, just slightly. 'Your niece helped me,' he said. 'I was unable to help her later, and I wish to redress that.'

'I'm going to speak very bluntly now,' said Stenwold. 'Are you Arcanum?'

The Moth's white eyes widened at that name, at the fact that Stenwold even knew it. The pause stretched across the table. Tisamon watched impassively.

'I am not,' Achaeos said at last. 'But . . . there are agents in the city, of course. I have spoken to them. They agree that the matter of the Empire of the Wasps may concern them, so I am to report to them.' Inwardly, Achaeos cringed at the true memory, how he had nagged and nagged his uncaring contact within the Arcanum until he had finally secured the woman's permission. The backwards-told story for Stenwold sounded so much better. He had not told the Arcanum about Cheerwell or his debt to her, for such things would not be understood. The secret society that passed for the Moth foreign service was not in a tolerant mood these days.

Stenwold, though, had taken this news strangely. 'You believe that your people could be persuaded that the Wasps are a threat?'

Achaeos's eyes narrowed, trying to judge his angle. 'It is possible.'

'They *are* a threat,' Stenwold confirmed. 'I've been saying it all along from here to Collegium and back, and nobody's been listening. It's about time though. After we get Cheerwell and Salma back, you and I should talk.'

Achaeos nodded, privately resolving that, once that rescue was accomplished, he would be gone.

'I suppose we should join the others.' Stenwold felt the oppressive weight of the near future settle on him with the words. 'They're waiting just outside the city.' He stood, unable not to stare at Tisamon. *Here it is, the moment.* He had been gifted with so many years in which to ready himself for this, and how he had wasted all that time.

'Do you know where they're taking her?' Tisamon asked.

'East, either to Asta or deeper into the Empire.' Stenwold shuffled, wanting to be gone now, to get it over with. Achaeos was standing, waiting, but Tisamon had other things on his mind.

'I've hunted men east of here these last few years. I've tracked Wasp convoys. They're creatures of habit. Do you want me to go ahead and scout?'

Stenwold paused, the doom on him suddenly staved off a little further. 'Scout?' No, it would not be fair on Tisamon. The inevitable would wait and wait, but it would always be there. Far better to face it right away. Even as the thought came to him, though, his voice was betraying him: 'That would be good. In which case, I'll trust you to find us by . . .' And how long could this be put off, really? 'By nightfall?'

'Nightfall it is.' Tisamon rose, and Stenwold wished they had more time together, there and then, with no rescues to perform. He did not know if he would still have a friend when he and Tisamon met again.

Scuto had secured transport for them, although Stenwold suspected they might have been better off walking. It was a rickety-looking automotive: a simple open cab balanced on a set of eight rusty legs.

'Is it fast?' he asked.

'Faster than walking? Just about,' was the Thorn Bug's reply. Stenwold peered underneath the contraption's high-stepping legs. Walking automotives had gone through a period of taking short cuts a generation ago and, as he feared, this one was very much a victim of its times. Instead of eight separate legs there were just two projecting from the engine, so the vehicle would be lurching along on two four-pronged feet.

'It'll go fine,' Scuto assured him, 'so long as you wind it each morning. Two-man job, but you've got Totho there to help you. Don't forget, if you're complaining, any fuel east of here's going to have black and yellow stamped all over it.'

'I suppose that's true.' A decent clockwork engine had a lot of advantages over steam or combustion. It would never run dry and it was easy enough to repair if it broke down. Stenwold had whittled cogs from wood before now to set one aright.

'What's troubling you?' Tynisa asked him suddenly. 'It's not just Che, is it?'

He smiled at her, though his heart sank. 'It's . . .' But he could not say it. Anything he said now would be too much of a lie. 'I'll tell you later,' he added. *When I have to. When I'm forced to it.*

It had been a long day of walking. What rest stops the Wasps had allowed them were overshadowed by the slavers, who never allowed their charges to forget their presence. Water was rationed with a parsimonious hand. Hard bread and stale cheese was their only food. On the march, if any slave faltered he was whipped back into line without hesitation or mercy. Che had begun the day full of pity for her broken-spirited fellows and ended it thanking providence only that she was in better physical shape than most of them.

Towards dusk it became evident that they were approaching something at last. Some things, in fact: two structures that could not be made out clearly against the darkening sky.

'Farmstead?' Che suggested. Salma peered ahead, his eyes much better than hers in the gloom.

'Not buildings,' he confirmed. 'But I can't see just what

they are.' Then a slaver passed close to them and they knew well enough to be quiet.

It was near dark when they arrived, but Che recognized them by then, because she had seen similar constructions before. They were automotives, but monstrous huge ones. She had seen them used for bulk transport of stock, and stock, she realized, was just what she and the others had become.

For a score and a half of slaves, even one of these machines would have been too capacious, but the cages that made up the back half of each were already mostly full. It was more of the same, Che noticed, but she could not believe that *all* of these unfortunates were supposed to be escapees. Even as they approached the two great engines, another column of prisoners was moving up – from the south as far as she could judge. Hairless men with dead white skins, jutting jaws and pincered hands, the slave-runners of the newcomers loomed head and shoulder over their charges. Che watched numbly as their leader met with a delegation of Wasp slavers and began to haggle over the price of his wares.

'From the Dryclaw,' she guessed. 'Or even the Spider-lands. It depends how far they've come. The Empire must provide a ready market.'

'Oh it does,' Salma confirmed. 'The Empire is built on their shoulders. Slaves work in their fields and build their houses. Slaves go down their mines and attend their every need. The Empire is built on slaves' backs and on their bones, Che. And as for the Wasps themselves – fortune forbid they should take up any work but soldiering.'

Che glanced up at him. 'Does the Commonweal have slaves?'

His smile grew wry. 'We don't call them that, but I suppose if *you* have paid slaves in your factories, then we have slaves in all but name working our land. What an open-minded man the College has made of me.'

Their column was now stopped and she saw Brutan and Thalric, a careful distance between them, go and speak to the leader of the automotive-riders. The big, pale southerners were concluding their business. Their hands looked so vicious, made for nothing but fighting, that Che stared at them in awe. In the flickering firelight there was nothing about them that did not speak of casual violence. Their clothes were a mishmash of leather, hide and chain mail. They had axes at their belts or else huge swords slung across broad shoulders. They looked at the Wasps with brash and measured expressions.

Brutan had returned to his own men and was giving out some orders. Che caught only the occasional word, but enough to understand that they would be camping here for the night, and would be moving on with the machines in the morning. She looked around for Thalric but he was still with the machinists, discussing something in close detail with their leader. Apparently in the absence of any other instructions, the convoy crew winched down the cage doors of the automotives and began to herd the slaves out.

There was another palisade, two in fact, but this time pitched in a semi-circle about the rear of each of the automotives, where the only place to go freely would be the inside of a metal-barred cage. The convoy drivers secured all the slaves to the palisaded stakes, their human bounty now numbering over seventy souls.

The slaves stayed hugging the perimeter, not venturing into the central space for fear of calling the slavers' notice, until the Wasps decided to feed them, long after they themselves had eaten. With a practised swing one of them hurled a cloth bag into the very centre of the pen, and immediately sheer chaos erupted. Che herself stood no chance. If she had even moved it would have been into a maelstrom of elbows and knees and fists as the slaves fought over the meagre fare.

I always did want to lose a little weight, she reflected as she pressed back against the palisade until the melee broke up, leaving only a few scuffling bodies locked in combat over the remaining crusts and crumbs. With a weary sigh, Salma dropped down beside her. She had not even realized he had joined in. Wordlessly he handed her a mangled handful of broken biscuit, hard waybread, a ragged fragment of cheese.

'You've got some for yourself?'

'Enough.'

'Then thank you.'

A shadow fell across them. Expecting a slaver, Che looked up to find a burly Ant-kinden looming over them.

'Yes?' she asked, and he lunged for her, or rather for the food in her hands. Even faster, Salma was in the way, lurching up from his sitting position to put a shoulder in the man's hip, toppling him to the floor. Salma remained standing as the Ant got to his feet. He looked about twice as broad as the young Dragonfly, whip-scarred and well-muscled. The slaves on either side of Che were shuffling sideways, hastily trying to get out of the way. Salma shifted his footing, waiting for the Ant to make a move.

'Oh now, listen!' Che shouted, or at least she intended to shout, but it came out more as a squeak. 'There's no need for any of this. We're all slaves here. Why fight amongst ourselves?'

Everyone was gaping at her as though she was mad, slaves and slavers both. She even caught sight of Thalric, ten feet beyond the gamblers, staring at her.

'We're better than that,' she told the slaves, turning her back on the Wasp captain. 'We might be in chains, but we don't have to amuse them by behaving like animals.'

The Ant made his move then, because Salma had been

distracted by her outburst, but he underestimated the Dragonfly's speed. Salma was in the air at once – for the four feet of extra height his leash allowed him, and he savagely kicked the big Ant across the face twice before coming down on the other side of him. Furious, the Ant rounded on him, and then made a dash for Salma's leash as it stretched taut across the pen. Even as he yanked on it, Salma was already moving for him, and got an elbow into the side of his head and then a fist into his chin. The Ant swayed but he still tugged viciously down on the leash, almost dragging Salma off his feet, and then got a hand on the Dragonfly's wrist and twisted, hard.

Salma grimaced as his arm was bent back. He hit the Ant twice, three times with his free hand, but the Ant absorbed the blows stoically. Che looked around at the slaves nearest her but it was obvious nobody was going to step in.

She jumped up and hurtled in herself. No sword here, and she had never fought bare-handed before. That was not an art the College taught. Still, she threw her entire weight forwards in a lunge for the big Ant.

She had been hoping to strike him in the side or the waist, to topple him and break his grip on her friend by sheer momentum. In the dark, though, he was further away than she had guessed. She felt herself falling short, had a frantic impression of the ground rushing towards her, and then her shoulder, and her weight behind it, slammed into one side of the man's knee.

The Ant howled in sheer agony and rolled onto his back, twisted into a ball. Che found herself sprawled at Salma's feet, staring upwards. He did not even look at her at first, eyes on his fallen opponent, but the Ant's howls of pain were now fading into wretched sobbing. There would be no more threat from that quarter any time soon. Salma finally extended one hand and then the other, and with a wince helped her up to her feet. Both of them feeling bruised, they retired to their little patch of earth.

The rest of the slaves were watching them narrowly, in case they would make themselves the new tyrants of the dispossessed. Che and Salma ignored them, huddling together for warmth as the chill of the night descended.

Eighteen

Tisamon was waiting for them at nightfall, just as promised: a whipcord-lean figure caught in the sun's last rays at the crest of a low hill, angular even under a cloak. His travel habits had not changed. There was a long bag slung on his back that must be his bowcase, and he wore a rapier alongside it that Stenwold had never seen him use. He might have been waiting there for ten minutes or for a hundred years.

Stenwold screwed the fragments of his courage together, halting the awkwardly lumbering automotive just before the hill's incline and clambering down. It had not exactly been the most amicable of journeys so far. The machine itself was clumsy and long overdue for scrapping, while Totho and Achaeos had instantly developed an intense dislike for one another, making any conversation difficult.

'They're picking up company.' Tisamon's voice reached him as Stenwold ascended the hill. 'Another half-dozen soldiers. Another score of slaves. It's going to be interesting when we come to extract them.'

Extract them? Like a barber pulling a tooth? Stenwold looked at the mess of tracks Tisamon showed him, that held no secrets for his eyes.

'I can go on tracking all night if you want,' Tisamon offered, and briefly the spectre of hope, of another stay of execution, raised itself.

'No,' said Stenwold, more firmly than he had intended.

'I don't think our transport could manage to keep up in any event. There are parts of it that definitely need tightening before we go further.'

'What is that monster, anyway? We've shared some grotesque mounts in our time, but that thing deserves some sort of award.' Tisamon was never exactly merry, but there was a lightness to his tone that cut Stenwold to the bone.

'Tisamon. I have to . . . I have to . . .' How long had he been given to prepare the words, and now they were nowhere to be found. 'I have to tell you something.'

They were fast approaching the automotive and its three silent passengers. Tisamon's pace did not slacken, but something changed in his posture, his breathing, as Stenwold's anxiety jumped across to him.

'What's wrong?' he asked. They were now so close. The setting sun was behind the machine so that they were standing in its long shadow.

'I . . .' But like a well in the desert, the words had dried up since he last visited them. 'I have to . . . show you something.'

Tisamon stopped at last. His face was blank.

'Time to make camp,' Stenwold called out to the automotive's passengers. 'Achaeos, can you make a fire?'

'Are you suggesting that I might need Beetle ingenuity for that?' said the Moth acidly, flitting down from the machine with obvious relish.

'Tisamon, this is Totho,' Stenwold said as the artificer climbed down. Tisamon barely spared him a nod. 'Totho,' Stenwold added, 'would you take a look at the machine, make sure everything's still in place.'

'Good idea,' agreed Totho, and he unslung his tools and crouched down between the automotive's legs, but not without a backward glance at his mentor.

'And . . .' *Here we are.* 'This is Tynisa.'

'Tynisa?' Tisamon said, but it was the name alone, the

Spider-kinden name, that had caught his ear. He was staring at her as she let herself down the ungainly machine's side, and his eyes were fixed on her face when she turned to him.

Tisamon made a wordless sound, deep in his throat, like an animal at bay. In a moment he had dropped into his fighting stance, and his claw was raised and drawn back. Stenwold had not even noticed it on his hand a moment before. What surprised Stenwold was that Tynisa was already out with her rapier, and clearly every bit as ready to fight.

'Tisamon,' he shouted, 'listen to me!'

'*What is this?*' the Mantis cried in a tone of pure horror. 'What have you *done?*'

'Tisamon,' Stenwold began again. 'I can explain.'

'*Explain?*' Tisamon's eyes were like a strangled man's. His teeth were bared, every muscle in his body bowstring-taut. The last rays of the sun touched the blade of his claw, caught the long line of Tynisa's rapier. Achaeos and Totho remained utterly motionless, utterly at a loss.

'Stenwold, what's going on?' Tynisa said tightly.

There was a moment in the very near future, seconds away only, when Tisamon would snap, and then blood would be shed. Stenwold could foresee it with complete clarity. In a normal fight this man was ice, but his own emotions were fiercer enemies than he could ever face down. He heard a hiss escape through the enraged man's clenched teeth, and knew that the clock's hands were down, the strike was here. He lunged forward between them, almost onto the point of Tynisa's sword, seeing Tisamon dodge behind him and the claw sweeping down. He closed his eyes.

He heard Tynisa scream and felt a stabbing pain in his shoulder, and something very cold, the thinnest of thin lines, against his throat. Everything seemed to have stopped.

He opened his eyes very slowly. The first thing he saw was Tynisa before him, her face stricken, and for a moment he thought she must have stabbed him. Her arm was extended, and he followed its line as best as his current situation would allow. There was the hilt of her sword and the narrow blade . . . and Tisamon's hand was flat against it, and the rapier's length caught between his palm and the spines of his forearm. Its point was frozen over Stenwold's shoulder, trapped on its way directly towards Tisamon's face.

Tisamon's other arm, his right, was across Stenwold's shoulders, the spines digging straight through the hardened leather and into his flesh. The folding blade of the Mantis's claw was closed about Stenwold's throat like a clasp-knife, and it was impossible for him to tell whether it had drawn blood or not. Beyond Tynisa he glimpsed Totho with a spanner in his hand, mouth hanging open; and there was Achaeos, somewhere further off, his dagger clear of its scabbard but pointedly not part of the conflict.

Stenwold heard his own ragged breath mixed up with that of the two duellists.

'Let him go,' said Tynisa, and Stenwold reckoned that making demands just then was not for the best.

'You're going to fight me?' Tisamon asked her, and his tone, that clipped precision of speech Stenwold knew of old, indicated a man whose blood was up.

'I've seen you fight and I know what this is about,' she declared. 'So I worked for the Halfway House. So what?'

'For the Halfway . . . ?' A frown passed over Tisamon's face. 'What are you talking about?'

'The fiefs, in Helleron . . .' Now Tynisa was looking uncertain. 'You were fighting for the Gladhanders. We destroyed them after . . . Isn't that . . .' His baffled stare was getting to her. 'What is this about?'

'Yes, Stenwold, what *is* this about?' asked Tisamon, and that dreadful coldness of diction was still there.

'I will tell you everything, but only you,' Stenwold finally got out. 'Let's go up the hill and I will spare nothing of the truth. You have my word.'

'That would have been a golden thing, only a moment ago,' said Tisamon sadly, but his arm uncoiled by degrees. Stenwold winced as the spines withdrew from his back.

'Someone had better tell me what's going on,' Tynisa suggested.

Stenwold nodded. 'Let me talk to Tisamon first. This is going to be difficult.'

He began to trudge back the way he had come, though this time Tisamon did not walk beside him as a comrade, but with the wary distance of an antagonist.

Tynisa watched them go. 'What?' she said, to the night air as much as to anyone. 'What is it?' Tisamon had looked at her as though she had killed his own brother and danced on his grave. She turned round for some kind of support, but Totho was edging himself underneath the automotive, and there was precious little warmth to be gained from the Moth's slyly superior façade.

To the pits with the pair of them, she decided. In fact, to the pits with all of them. There was something going on, and it had led to a notable duellist drawing on her, and that meant she had a *right* to know what was going on.

As softly as she could, she began to follow in Stenwold's path, letting darkness be her cloak.

On the other side of the hill, out of sight of the automotive, Stenwold suddenly stopped. It was a calculated risk, for if Tisamon's temper broke again, he would be dead without the others even knowing. It showed a trust, though, and he so desperately needed to regain this man's confidence. It also put them far enough from the camp that quiet voices would not carry, and harsh words might sound jumbled enough not to be understood.

Tisamon was watching him, blade still by his side, tucked back up the length of his arm.

'Speak,' he hissed.

'I . . .' Stenwold grimaced. 'It's difficult for me. It really is. Give me a moment to put my words in order.'

Tisamon bared his teeth. 'Let me help you. Let me prompt you. She's *her* very image. Souls alive! *She's her very image!*' Again it was not anger but a ragged horror that twisted him. 'How . . . How . . .' His stark frame was shaking, and Stenwold wondered if there was even a name for the emotion that had taken hold of him. 'She's *her* daughter. She must be.'

'Yes, Tisamon. Tynisa is Atryssa's daughter,' Stenwold admitted wearily. Now the moment was upon him, he wondered if he had the strength for it.

'How did you come to . . . No!' Tisamon's eyes narrowed. The blade of his claw flexed, hinging out and back in. 'She betrayed us, Stenwold – at Myna. You know this. They knew your plans. They sabotaged your devices. *She* told them.'

'Atryssa, Tisamon. At least speak her name.'

'You think I can't?' Tisamon spat. 'Atryssa *betrayed* us. Happier with that? She sold us to the Empire, and she left us to die there in Myna. And don't forget that not all of us escaped alive.'

'Oh, I remember Myna. I've never stopped thinking of it,' Stenwold said. 'But she didn't betray us, Tisamon.'

'She—'

'Hear me out!' Stenwold snapped. 'Hammer and tongs, hear what I've got to say, and then if you still want to kill me, well, I'm all yours.'

Tisamon regarded him in silence.

'You see, while you stayed in Helleron, I hunted her down. I wanted to confront her with what she had done. Only she wasn't easy to find – no, let me finish – she was in hiding, yes, but not from us.'

He closed his eyes, calling back seventeen years in order to picture the scene.

'Nero found her in the end. He was always a good man for the tracking. When we got there she was . . . hurt.'

There was the merest twitch in Tisamon. It gave Stenwold hope.

'She had been trying to get to us, to keep the rendezvous, but the Wasps intercepted her – or some of their agents did. She had to fight them.'

That was too much for Tisamon. 'So she would *fight* them! She was a skilled duellist. A handful of Wasp agents would not have slowed her down!'

'Listen!' Stenwold realized that he himself was finding it difficult to stem the anger he felt. This was an injustice long gone unsettled, and he now had it in his hands to put history right. The knowledge gave him the strength to say it: 'She beat them. She did beat them, but she was badly injured, because of her condition.'

'Her . . . condition?'

Stenwold actually mustered a smile, as hard-edged a piece of work as any he had known. 'She was with child, Tisamon, when she fought them. It slowed her down.'

The Mantis stared at him blankly.

'When Nero and I finally found her, she was near her time, but she was weak, very weak. She had been keeping low. The Wasps were still hunting her. She was in a Merro slum. There was no one else with her.' He watched expressions fight to make themselves known on Tisamon's face. 'When she bore the child, she died, but the child lived.'

And he left it at that, let Tisamon's unsatisfied questions fall into the pit of silence between them, then waited and waited.

'What . . . ? But who . . . was the father?' A mere whisper.

'I don't know. Who might have shared her bed last, do you think?'

Tisamon stared at him. 'No . . . no.'

'She spoke only of you, those few days we had. She had put aside her protections. It was her choice.' Stenwold was aware that he was simply putting the knife in now, but it was a knife he had carried for a long time, which had weighed on him every day of it.

'She's . . . that girl is . . .'

Stenwold nodded.

'But she looks . . .'

'Oh, the looks she gets from her mother. There's no doubting that. What she gets from her father has yet to reveal itself.'

'She's a halfbreed?'

'I suppose she'd have to be,' said Stenwold. 'That's how it works.'

Tisamon reached out as if to grab hold of his collar, stopped with his arm outstretched, head shaking slightly. 'Why didn't you tell me?'

Stenwold now held his gaze without flinching. 'And what would you have said, at the time? What would your exact reaction have been, if I had sent a messenger with the word that the woman you hated most in all the world had borne you a child? You would have killed the messenger, I can tell you that for sure. And by anyone mad enough to take a message back, you would have given the order to have the infant destroyed.'

'No . . .'

'*No*, is it?' Stenwold demanded. 'A halfbreed, Tisamon? A *Spider–Mantis* halfbreed? That most vile of all abominations? That's what you would have thought, isn't it? Or can you deny it?'

'You had no right,' the Mantis said.

'No right to keep her from you, or no right to let her

live? What's it to be? *I* had a choice then. Poor Atryssa was dead, and I could take the child as my own, my responsibility, or I could let her die, as you no doubt would have wished. I'm afraid that with a choice like that, mere Mantis pride doesn't enter into it.'

'Pride? How dare you—'

'Pride! Is it *not* pride – the curse of your whole wretched tribe?' Stenwold was aware he was going too far now, but unable to stop himself. 'Hammer and tongs! In the College, you know, there's an exercise they put students through: to decide why each of the kinden is great in its own way and what makes them special. Well here's a new hoop for them to jump through. Why are we all such bloody broken things? You and I, Tisamon. Beetle complacency and Mantis bloody pride!'

'You had no right to take that choice!'

'Nobody else was going to take it!' Stenwold got as far as reaching for the man's arming jacket to shake him, but stopped himself fast before he made the mistake.

'She's an abomination.' Tisamon sounded stunned. 'She's a halfbreed. A shame upon my race and family.' His mouth formed the words very slowly. 'My daughter?'

'Yes, your daughter. And now you have to decide if you're going to do now what you would have done then, or if you can – just possibly can – widen your mind enough to accept that she exists. And I warn you, if you act against her, not only will you not find it so bloody easy, but you'll also have me to deal with, probably Totho too.' He saw a harsh look come over the other man's face and interpreted it as best he could. 'Oh, I know, you wouldn't break into a sweat over it, but don't think that would—'

'I would not . . . harm you.' Tisamon sounded and looked a hundred years older in that moment, ashen and fragile as no Mantis that Stenwold had ever encountered had looked before.

'And?'

'I will not harm her.' Something was building in Tisamon, and Stenwold saw that it was not even the shock of having a daughter that was crippling him. *Atryssa*. It was that Atryssa was dead, had died without him, had died with him believing her a traitor. It was an unwelcome conclusion that Stenwold should have come to a long time before, but he saw now that Tisamon had stayed in Helleron because he had never wanted to see Atryssa again – because he did not want to be the one to end her life. For a Mantis, he supposed, that was love. Stenwold stepped back, suddenly fearful that he had gone too far.

'I need to think.' Tisamon turned away, hiding his face.

'I'm sorry. I should have ... I should have told you before. Sooner.'

'You are right in all you said,' Tisamon stated. 'I would not have understood, and it remains to be seen if I ever shall. I will ... I will rejoin you at dawn, I hope. I need time and space to ... I need to be alone.'

He made a slow progress away from that place, heading into the hills. Stenwold stood and watched him until darkness and the land put him out of sight.

He did not notice Tynisa's expression, as he returned to camp. He was too concerned with his own woes.

It had been a sour day's journeying. Stenwold sat hunched at the controls of the limping, lurching automaton wrapped in a dusty silence that nothing had relieved. Achaeos and Totho's silent enmity seemed to somehow be growing in the vacuum of their mutual ignoring. At first Stenwold had thought it was because Totho was a half-breed. After the lad went to tinker with something in the back, making Achaeos's disdain only increase, he realized it was because Totho was an *artificer*. This was a clash of world-views.

Tynisa, however, Achaeos seemed to regard with a wary

respect. That reaction had sprung up after she had drawn on Tisamon. No, Tynisa's problem was with Stenwold himself, for she had not said a word to him all day. She had glared at him if he even chanced to look her way. He supposed that she was still waiting for an explanation of Tisamon's reaction to her, but he was wretchedly unable to give it. Tisamon himself had not returned. Until he spoke to Tisamon again, until Tisamon had sorted out precisely how he felt, Stenwold could not bring himself to explain to her. It just was another betrayal. He owed her more than he owed to the Mantis, and yet he could not wrench himself free of those bonds formed two decades ago.

The entire sorry business had gone from bad to worse, and he now was in danger of losing everything by it. He thought back to that moment of choice, by Atryssa's deathbed, and wondered what he could have done differently that might have made this moment bearable.

He pictured coming to Tisamon with an infant and a story – or even a child of, say, six or ten. He pictured the wrathful reaction of the man. In seventeen years, time had dulled it a little, built over it like a coral, so that the shape of it remained but not the edges. Even so it had been a close-run thing between Tisamon's self-control and his blade's temper. No, if Stenwold had tried this trick ten years earlier, Tisamon would certainly have killed him, and killed the child.

Would he? Was Tisamon a man to kill an infant, his own daughter still in swaddling? *Is that what I really believe of my old friend?*

With a heavy heart Stenwold acknowledged that, yes, Tisamon *was* the man to do it. It would have been done in rage, and perhaps he would have later mourned the loss, but his pride would have spurred him to it, even so.

★

At least Stenwold had been able to encourage himself by the fact that they were gaining on their quarry, even though he had no real plan for tackling the reinforced Wasps when he found them. Before dusk, though, the ground ahead changed, and it did not take a tracker to tell him that the slavers had new transportation. The land before them was scuffed and scarred with a great reticulated trail. Some large tracked vehicle, or more than one of them, was now shipping the slaves eastwards. Stenwold feared that, whatever this conveyance was, it would travel faster than their own jolting relic.

That night he faced the prospect of a joyless camp. He turned to Totho instead, as the only one of his companions he still felt comfortable talking to.

'We need to go faster,' he said.

Totho cast a sidelong glance at their automotive. 'It's not going to be easy, sir,' he said, 'and it might not survive it. I needed to tighten every joint as it is.'

'I'll help you,' Stenwold suggested. 'If the two of us work through the night, we might be able to wring a bit of extra speed out of this contraption. And you don't need to keep calling me sir. We're not at the College now.'

Totho shrugged. 'Well, s— Well, Master Maker—'

'Totho?'

'Well.' Totho cut the honorific by dint of extreme effort. 'I'm game if you are.'

It had been a good idea of his, Stenwold allowed, but he had not anticipated the problems with its execution. The chief problem was that Stenwold had been teaching history and busying himself with politics for the last decade, and Totho was fresh from the College and sharp with it. It was a short while before Stenwold realized that he simply did not understand some of the more technical points the boy was making. After that, he became reluctantly convinced that he himself was just getting in the way. Still a stubborn pride that would have befitted Tisamon kept him sweating and slaving away by the sputtering gas lamp that Totho had rigged up, until eventually the youth said, 'If we both work . . . if we both work all night, sir, then neither of us will be in any shape to . . . to drive it in the morning.' This awkward display of tact was shaming. Stenwold had never ceased to think of himself as an artificer, despite his lack of practice, but it seemed the rest of the world had stopped considering him one a long time ago.

When I get back to Collegium, I will have to brush up, he vowed. He slid himself out from under the automotive, confessing openly that this was a good idea, and in that case why didn't he get some sleep now. He felt old and wretched.

When he approached the fire he found Achaeos was asleep, but Tynisa was not. Whether she was keeping watch or just waiting for him he could not say, but her hard stare fixed him as he approached the circle of firelight. Her gaze was filled with a slow-burning anger that, he reflected sadly, she must have inherited from her father. Faced with that, he paused at the edge of the camp, knowing that it was his duty, as her guardian, as a human being, to say something, to explain.

He could not. Wordlessly he turned away, and built up a meagre fire on the other side of the automotive. That was where Tisamon eventually found him.

He heard the tread before he saw the man, and then the lean, tall figure was striding out of the night to sit, silently, across the small fire from him. The guttering light chased shadows across the Mantis's angular face. For a long time neither man trusted himself to speak.

'We are neither of us the things we would have wanted to be when this day came,' Tisamon said softly at last, without looking at him. 'Look at us. What are we? You have become the meddling intelligencer, sending the young to their deaths. I am a sell-sword who has not cared, these last years, whose blood was on my blade. You said to Monger that I fought for honour, but until you called for me that had not been true for a long time.' A heavy pause. 'We did not think, when we were young, that we would end up here.'

'We did not,' replied Stenwold, heartfelt.

'I . . .' Tisamon stopped, stirred the fire with a stick. His lips moved, but for a long time there was nothing. Stenwold gave him his time. It was not as though he himself had anything to say.

'Thank you for raising my daughter,' said Tisamon, and seemed visibly relieved to be rid of the words. Stenwold stared at him, not quite sure he had heard them.

'I have been thinking,' the Mantis said. 'At first, I decided that you had done me a great wrong, but then I could not describe to myself, precisely, what that wrong was. We believe, my people, in defining our grievances. How else could we hold on to them for so long? And so I realized that if you had not done me a wrong, then the whole of my world must turn inside-out, and so instead I find that I owe you a debt. Such a debt that a man can never truly repay.'

And your people take your debts just as seriously as your wrongs, Stenwold reflected. Tisamon would still not meet his gaze, had still not wholly come to terms with it all, but he had found a way to paint the past in colours that he could at last understand. It was a matter of *honour*, and he could live with that.

And at last the Mantis looked up, and the corner of his mouth twitched up too. 'Do you remember, all those years ago, when you would talk and talk, and I would say nothing at all? How we have changed.'

And Stenwold laughed at that, despite himself, despite it all. He laughed and laughed.

And afterwards he said, 'I'll have to tell her, now. I'll have to speak with her. You know that.'

'Then tread carefully,' said Tisamon, still smiling sincerely. 'If she's her father's daughter, she might not take it well.'

Nineteen

She danced for them the next night. It was like nothing they had ever seen.

The slavers had put the two huge vehicles with the caged backs facing one another, and strung a wide fence around both to make a single big oval enclosure. They were all gathered around one end or the other, and most of the soldiers as well. Che was nervous. Something was going on, and the only thing she could think of was a blood-fight. Death-fights were not common in the Lowlands. In Collegium, for instance, they thought of themselves as far too civilized, and while the Ant cities loved a gladiatorial match they watched it for the skill and not the blood. The practice was known, though. The Spiders did it, in their southern fastnesses, and it was rumoured that Helleron had underground fighting dens, for the connoisseur of death as entertainment.

They had banked up fires either side of the palisade, with another burning in the very centre of the pen. Looking around, Che spotted Brutan, the slavers' leader, and a fair number of the automotive crew, but not Thalric. Presumably he felt himself above whatever was going to happen.

And then *she* stepped forward. They had not noticed her before. She must have been caged on the other vehicle, or even kept separate entirely. Che felt Salma twitch as he saw her, tense for a moment. Che glanced from him to the woman uncertainly.

She was . . . for a moment Che thought she must be a Moth-kinden, because she possessed their featureless white eyes. When the firelight caught her, though, Che started in surprise, because her skin was moving.

She had been grey as grey a moment ago, a Moth indeed. That was plain enough to see. She wore only the briefest of clothes, a loincloth, a band of cloth tied across her breasts. Now something was happening to her. Shadows were chasing themselves across her flesh. No, not shadows: colours. The ruddy firelight tried to hide it, but as they watched, a fleeting patchwork of reds and purples, dark blues and pale pieces were flitting and skipping over the contours of her body.

A pipe and drum struck up from somewhere. Che twisted round to see it was the lanky, sallow-skinned man playing, keeping time on the drum with his foot. And then *she* danced.

It was a wild thing, and she led where the pipe only followed. It was not like the carefully orchestrated Collegium terpsichoreans or the rustic folk dances Che had previously seen. This was not the lewd invitation of a brothel. It was like nothing in the experience of a Lowlander. It was furious and angry, it was beautiful, it was sad. Every man's eye was on her, most women's as well. When Che tore her gaze away, she passed it across the yearning faces of the prisoners, to the guards beyond. The Wasp soldiers were lost in it, utterly. There was something stripped from their faces that she had never seen them without, as though some buried knife had been sheathed for this moment only. The impassive helms of the slavers showed nothing, of course, but many of them had taken them off to see better, and the same bereft, gentle look was on them. There was lust there, certainly, and all the ugly baggage that it brought, but it was shackled, in those men of chains, by something wholly other.

And she danced, to the skirling wail of the pipe, the

skittering of the drum. The music spoke not of her but of the desperate, hopeless need of her audience as it chased and chased and never caught her.

Che glanced aside to make some comment to Salma, but his face was stricken with amazement, all of his haughty smiles and hidden laughter cut away from him.

She danced, and then she was done, a bitterly scornful obeisance to those who watched from beyond the palisade, leaving the pipe to squeal to a close along with her. She stayed there, motionless, bending forward so that her forehead almost touched the sand, one arm flung forward, one leg straight and the other folded beneath her. The dead silence the pipe had bequeathed stretched on and on.

And when she raised her head it was to Salma that she looked and that outflung arm became a desperate entreaty, her obeisance a plea. *Help me. Save me.*

At last it was Brutan who said, 'All right, feed the bastards,' and the Wasp-kinden picked up the vices they had, for an instant, put away, and remembered they were conquerors and warriors.

The dancer stood, looking uncertain now, and drained, and so very sad. Che felt a movement beside her and realized that Salma was standing. The dancer saw him, flinched back a moment and then looked again. She was making a first step towards him when three slavers muscled into the palisade and took hold of her, leading her off. She did not resist but she cast a last glance back at Salma that made him flinch too.

'What was that?' Che said. 'I mean . . . Salma, are you listening to me?'

'Of course I am,' but he still seemed preoccupied as he sat down again.

'Salma, did you recognize her or something?'

'I don't . . . No, not her. I know what she is, though.'

'And?'

'There are a few communities in the Commonweal – "In" meaning within, rather than a part of. They are . . . different. Butterfly-kinden, you know. I'd never seen one before. Only heard people talk about them. And it's true, all they say. For the love of lords and princes!' he exclaimed.

Che had never seen him so shaken. 'So she danced well. So what?' she said, feeling a little ill disposed to this dancing Butterfly already.

'What?' he asked her, trying for jovial. 'You think I'll abandon you and go off with her?'

'I do know everyone seemed to be turned into a drooling idiot the moment she appeared, but you were king of the idiots, if you ask me,' she grumbled.

His smile was coming back, and very much at her expense. 'Cheerwell Maker, don't tell me that's jealousy I'm hearing? I didn't know that we two were handfast.'

She coloured a little, knowing that in the firelight his eyes would spot it easily. 'No, of course not. I was just worried about you, that's all.'

Salma was about to reply when his eye was caught by two slavers approaching. He tensed, ready for them to single him out.

It was Che, however, who had their attention. 'You! On your feet.'

'Why?'

He hit her so fast that even Salma could not put himself in the way, slapping her across the face with an open palm. The blade of his hand had a bone hook jutting from it, Art-grown, and, even with her head ringing, she realized he could have done a lot worse.

'No questions, slave. On your feet.'

She didn't need to be told a third time. Salma was half on his feet too, but the second slaver directed a hand at him that crackled with energy.

'No more heroics from you, Wealer,' he warned. 'Don't think anyone would miss you.'

'Where are you taking her?' Salma demanded.

The energy blazed up in the man's hand, and Che cried out, 'I'm going with them. It's all right. Don't hurt him.' It was anything but all right, but Salma was leashed to the pen and they would have been able to kill him at their leisure. 'Please, I'm going.'

The soldier severed her leather with the spurs on his hands, and the two of them virtually dragged her from the pen, not giving her time to get her feet underneath her.

'What have I done?' she asked, but they just dragged her out through the palisade and let other slavers reset the stakes.

She repeated the question and one of the soldiers raised a hand to strike her again. She quailed away, tried to hide her face, but they had her arms secure. The man gave a guttural laugh.

'Full of questions, this one,' he said.

'Shouldn't be asking 'em,' said his companion. 'She won't like the answers.'

And they dragged her off into the dark. She had one last glimpse of Salma's agonized face before the pen was way behind her, and she was being hauled alongside the looming bulk of one of the automotives. She had a brief glimpse of a Wasp-kinden artificer tinkering with it, glancing at her with disinterest and then returning to his work.

'What's this?' She recognized the gruff tones even as her escorts slowed and stopped. The broad-shouldered figure of Brutan the slavemaster had intercepted them. 'What's going on, lads?'

'Orders, Sarge,' said one of them.

'You take *my* orders, lads,' said Brutan. He took Che's chin between his thumb and forefinger, yanked her head up. She could see almost nothing of him within his helm.

'Someone got a taste for Beetle flesh, is it? I don't recall giving you any orders, lads, so who's been meddling in my operation.'

'Captain Thalric, sir,' said the other slaver awkwardly.

'Well Captain Thalric can kiss my arse,' Brutan declared. 'If he wants a whore he can speak to the pimp.'

'I don't know, sir—' began one of the slavers.

'Mind you,' Brutan said, ignoring him completely, 'it's a poor pimp that hasn't dipped his wick in all the bottles.' The blank mask of his helm was very close to Che's face, and there was nowhere she could pull away to. 'Not exactly a prizewinner, is she? But I'm not feeling choosy so bring her over here.'

He strode off, but the two slavers had not moved. 'Sarge,' said one unhappily.

Brutan rounded on them. 'Did I or did I not give you an order?'

'But it's Captain Thalric, sir.'

'You don't seem to know who's holding your chain in their hands,' said Brutan, coming back with hands open, fingers splayed.

'They say he's Rekef, sir.'

Brutan stopped. 'So what if they do?' he asked, but there was a slight change in his tone. 'Think I'm scared of that? Think I'm scared of him?'

The silence of the slavers suggested that *they* were, but they were also scared of their leader. When Brutan barked 'Bring her!' they did.

She was pulled off to a secluded dip beyond the main camp, slammed onto the ground on her back hard enough to put the breath out of her. Until that moment she had not quite appreciated what he intended.

'You can't— You're not going to—'

'Shut her up,' said Brutan, sounding bored. He was undoing his belt with practised fingers.

Che screamed, and when a slaver put a hand over her

mouth she bit him savagely. He cuffed her and her head rang with it, and the other was already stuffing a rag or somesuch into her mouth. She fought and fought, and it took the both of them to hold her down as Brutan dragged at her breeches.

'Do you really think—?' one of the slavers was saying.

'Yes, *I* think,' Brutan snapped at him. 'You just do as I say.'

'But if he *is* . . .' the other whined, casting a look back towards the camp. Che's frantic struggles and muffled cries might not have been going on at all for all the notice they took of them.

'Shut up, the pair of you.' Brutan had begun to sound harried. Now he lurched across Che. She felt his bare flesh on hers. Then there was a pause. It was such a pause that she stopped fighting, trying to work out what was going on. Brutan was still suspended above her on his hands and knees. She could see only darkness within the helm that he had not even taken off.

She glanced down and saw more than she wanted to of the man, but saw, moreover, that he was going limp.

'Sergeant?' one of the slavers asked nervously. After a moment Brutan rolled off her and cursed.

'Pox-rotten Rekef bastards.'

There was another pause. Given this small opportunity, Che pulled up her breeches and did her best to tie them with the broken cords left to her, still not quite believing what was happening.

'Sergeant?' asked the slaver again.

'You'd better take her to him,' Brutan muttered, sounding furious with them, with her, with Thalric, and with himself.

The big automotives obviously transported more than slaves. Thalric had a tent now, pitched out of sight of the slave pens. When she was hustled inside, the man was sitting before a folding desk, looking for all the world as though he were in his study somewhere civilized. A hissing white-flamed salt-lamp gave an unhealthy pallor to his skin.

He looked up, at her and at the two slavers. He must have heard her screaming just moments before but his face admitted nothing of it.

'You may go,' he told her escorts, and they left gratefully. There were two of his soldiers at the door so she knew that this did not offer an escape attempt. It remained to be found out just what it did mean.

'Sit, if you want,' he told her. She regarded him curiously. It was impossible to place his age, save that he was neither young nor old. He was regular of feature, without being striking in any way. He would have been equally fitting as a College registrar or at the winch of a rack. In fact his bland features could have placed him anywhere.

'Why did you send the slavers to fetch me, if you don't like them?' she asked him, watching for a reaction.

'Because it's their job,' he replied simply. 'You're a slave. They're slavers.' After a moment he relented. 'It's no secret that the regular army doesn't get on with the Slave Corps. The army doesn't like them because taking slaves is no true profession for a man of the Empire, and I don't like them because they're greedy and self-interested.'

'Do you ... do you know what ... ?'

'I can guess.' His face was without guilt or pity. 'Our Brutan is a lusty fellow, or so they say.'

'And are you going to punish him?'

'Why should I? What has he done wrong?'

She gaped at him. 'I don't think you know what that word means!'

'Miss Maker.' Abruptly he was stern, standing. She flinched back from him. In that instant response she realized that she really was a slave.

'Miss Maker,' he said again, 'it remains to be seen whether you will enjoy any protection from Brutan and his like, and before you say a word, his like includes plenty who wear the chains, as well as those who wield the whips. I can have you separated from your Commonwealer friend in an instant, and after that you'll be just one more victim's victim.'

She tried to face up to him boldly but the crawling horror of the thought was overtaking her, as he knew it would.

'We are going to Asta,' he told her. 'It's a little outpost of ours but it has sufficient facilities for my purposes, which are to learn what you and your fellow know.'

'You mean torture.'

'Do I? Well, let that be what I mean then. However, it is possible for you and I to keep our questioning artificers idle for an hour or so. Sit and talk to me.'

She tried to read his face, his posture, but there was nothing. 'I won't . . .' It was harder to say it than she had thought, with his threat still hanging in the air. 'I won't betray my uncle.'

'Then simply sit and talk,' he said. 'A few words, a little wine perhaps. Let us find out where the borders of your betrayal are. Let us visit them together, look into that forbidden country.'

'You think you can trick me,' she said.

'You think I can't trick you,' he countered. 'Why should we not see who is right?'

She regarded him suspiciously, saying nothing, and he smiled. It was such a frank and open expression that it took her off her guard.

'We tried to kill your uncle. We hunted you across the Lowlands. We tried to trap you in Helleron. We caught you. We enslaved you. We nearly raped you. We threaten you. With all of that on the account, some people might quite have taken against us.'

A strained laugh escaped her, his humour was so unexpected.

'Perhaps tonight I should talk and you should listen, and tomorrow or the next night you may feel like talking to me,' he suggested.

'I – I don't think that I'll ever—'

'Don't . . .' His voice stopped her, in that one word was a world of warning. 'Don't say anything that you cannot take back. You think you're special, yes?'

'I . . . Not so special your bully boys mightn't have killed me just like anyone else, as one of their nasty little examples.'

The smile again. So very genuine and wry, and yet the things he smiled at would have appalled any rational person. 'But you were in no danger, Miss Maker. I had already made sure that you would live through the experience. It was just an object lesson.' He leant forward over the desk. 'But if you are overly stubborn, then next time it may be for real. You think I am an evil man, yes?'

'That we can agree on.'

He sat back, poured two goblets of wine as he spoke. 'Taken as a whole, I would say that I am no more virtuous nor vice-ridden than any other, save for one overriding virtue. Do you know what that virtue is? True, it is a virtue rare in the Lowlands, in my limited experience. It is loyalty. I will do anything the Empire asks of me, Miss Maker, and I will do anything for the benefit of the Empire. I will destroy villages and lives, I will cross deserts, I will . . . kill children.' She noticed the minute hesitation there and filed it for later use. 'I will do all of this, and I will account it no evil, but instead a virtue, the virtue of *loyalty*, the Empire before everything, my own desires included. Do you understand how this relates to our little talk right now?'

She shook her head slowly.

'It means that if the best use I can put you to is to offer

you wine,' and he did so, 'and treat you kindly and have a conversation or two within this tent, then I shall serve the Empire that way. If the best use I find is to put you to the question, or gift you to Brutan, then I shall do that. It is nothing personal, Miss Maker. Do I make myself clear?'

'I suppose you do.' She took the wine cautiously, sipping. It had a dry, harsh taste, somewhat unfamiliar.

'Then tonight I will talk to you, and thus try to make it easier for you to talk to me,' he told her. 'I will tell you about my people and my Empire, and in that way hope that you will understand why we do what we do.'

At that moment the most delicious aroma entered the tent, preceding a soldier bearing a platter. There was dried fruit on it, and nuts, and what must be honey, and a half-dozen slices of steaming meat that must surely be horse. She found that she had taken two steps towards the table as soon as it was set down.

'Help yourself,' he offered, as the soldier left. She was instantly on her guard, but he shrugged. 'Or not? You will profit nothing from abstaining. A moral victory on this small point would be an empty one, would it not?'

And she had to concede that. She had to concede that, because she had eaten slave food for two days and she was unable to take her eyes off the plate. By awkward stages she sat and took up a piece of meat, bolting it even as it burned her fingers. She saw Thalric's expression then, and recognized it as that of a man who had won the first battle of a campaign. She hated him for that, but did not stop eating.

'You must have a very skewed picture of the Wasp-kinden,' he told her. 'If you think of us at all, you must think that we're savages.'

She nodded vigorously, still eating.

'Not so far from the truth,' he admitted, and she raised surprised eyebrows. 'The Empire is young. Three generations, three Emperors.'

She frowned at him.

'No, we don't live for hundreds of years. Nothing like that. Our Most Revered Majesty Alvdan the Second is not thirty years of age. His grandfather was one tribal chieftain in a steppeland full of feuding tribes, but he had, as the story goes, a dream. He took war to the other tribes, and he subjugated them. He brought all the Wasp-kinden together under his banner. It took a lifetime of bitter fighting and worse diplomacy. His son, Alvdan the First, built the Empire: city after city brought into the fold, the borders pushed ever outwards. Each people we made our own, we learned the lessons they taught us. We honed the tool of war until it was keen as a razor. Our Emperor now, Alvdan Two, was sixteen when he came to the throne, and since then he has not rested in furthering the dream of his father and his grandfather. We have fought more peoples than the Lowlands even knows exist. We have defended ourselves against enemies who were stronger than us, or wiser than us, or steeped in lore we could not guess at. We have conquered internal strife and we have done what no other has ever done before us. The Empire is physically near the size of the entire Lowlands, but all under one flag and all marching to one beat. The Empire represents progress, Miss Maker. The Empire is the future. Look at my people. They have a foot in the barbaric still. They must be forced into discipline, into control, into civilization! But they have come so very far in such a short time. I am proud of my people, Miss Maker. I am proud of what they have brought about.'

'So why inflict their regime on other people?' she demanded.

'Because we must grow lest we stagnate,' he replied, as though it was as very simple as that. 'And because those who are not within the Empire remain a threat to it. How long before the Commonweal takes arms against us, or some Ant general similarly unifies the Lowlands? How long before some other chieftain with the same dream raises the spear against us? If we were to declare peace with the world, then the world would soon take the war to us. Look at the Lowlands, Miss Maker: a dozen city-states that cannot agree on anything. If we were to invade Tark tomorrow, do you know what the other Ant-kinden cities would do? They would simply cheer. That is the rot of the Lowlands, Miss Maker, so we will bring them into the Empire. We will unite the Lowlands under the black-and-gold banner. Think what we might accomplish then.'

'All I can think of is that you would turn my race, and all the Lowlands, into slaves within your Empire.'

'There are many Beetle-kinden in the Empire, Miss Maker. They do very well. The Emperor trusts most of the imperial economy to them, as far as I can make out. The Empire needs slaves to do a slave's work, but we would not enslave the Lowlands. The people of the Lowlands would simply discover that their best interests lie in working with us.'

'Tell me, Captain, what is the Rekef?'

The question caught him quite by surprise, but in the next moment he was smiling again, as though she had, at last, proved a promising student. 'Well, how has that word come to you?'

'Brutan, amongst others.'

'The Rekef, Miss Maker, is a secret society.'

She had to laugh at that. 'But everyone seems to know you're in it so how can it be secret?'

'Well, that is rather the point.' His smile looked a little embarrassed. 'Why, after all, would you be part of a terrifying secret society that strikes fear into the hearts of men, if nobody even knows that you're in it? In actual fact, if I was Rekef Inlander then the first anyone would know about it would be when they found themselves hauled in and being put to the question, with a list of their crimes before them.' His smile became self-mocking. 'To tell the truth they even frighten me. I, on the other hand, am Rekef Outlander. My place is dealing with people like you.' He paused, searching her face. 'Have I reached you, Miss Maker? Have you heard what I have said?'

'You've given me a lot to think about.'

'And?'

'I remember . . . when I was in Helleron with Salma – the Dragonfly-kinden, although I'm sure you know that – when we were there, we saw a factory, and he said he had thought that we Beetle-kinden didn't keep slaves. And I told him not to be so ridiculous, because they weren't slaves. They were working for a wage. They were there of their own free will. But I couldn't persuade him. Whatever I said, I couldn't make him see that they were free. Perhaps that was because he was right.'

Thalric's smile was still there, but bleak, very bleak. 'Your point is elegantly made, Miss Maker.'

She put down her goblet, composed herself. 'What will you do with me?'

He looked down at the scroll before him and ticked off a few items carefully with a scratchy chitin-nibbed pen. She thought at first he was only trying to make her squirm, but then realized that he really was thinking what might be done with her.

'I will call you for another conversation – at Asta perhaps. Another chance for you to talk to me, before the artificers become involved, or your Dragonfly friend is hurt. Until then . . . let us hope the dreadful reputation of the Rekef suffices to stave off Brutan's advances.'

'You're . . .?' She didn't want to ask it. She knew it would make her look weak. 'You're not going to . . . ?'

He looked up at her, face quite without expression. 'Guards!' he called suddenly, and then, more softly: 'No, Miss Maker. I cannot see how that would serve any purpose. Not yet.'

He was so very smug behind that bland façade. He was

so very in control that, as the soldiers came in, she did something very unwise, knowing it to be so even as she did it.

'Whose children did you kill?' she asked.

His nib snapped, its tip leaping across the tent. For a second he held himself very still, while she could see the great shadow of his anger pass across his face, and something else, too, some other emotion his features were not designed for. The soldiers had paused halfway towards her. She thought even they were holding their breath.

At last he let his anger out in a long sigh. 'Take her back to the pens,' he instructed, not looking at his men. The shadow of that other emotion was still there on his face.

Twenty

Stenwold walked carefully into the firelight, and let her see him coming. Totho was still clattering about beneath the automotive, and the Moth's eyes were closed in what Stenwold hoped was sleep. He sat down, not across from her, not next to her, but at an angle, a no-man's land. She stared at him sullenly.

'I think it's time,' he said, 'that I told you some things. About yourself.'

'You obviously know nothing about me,' she told him coldly, 'or you would have realized that I would follow you – you and . . . and him – when you went away to talk.'

The world seemed to die around him in that moment, like autumn arriving all in one day.

'You followed?'

'Yes.'

'And you heard?'

'Everything.'

'This isn't how I wanted it, Tynisa.'

'I'm not sure you even know how you wanted it,' she told him harshly. 'Why, Stenwold? Why didn't you tell me? Why did I have to find out this way? Why not ten years ago? Why not five years ago? Or even two?'

He felt terribly old now. 'Tynisa, I didn't tell you because I had not yet told Tisamon.'

'But you . . .' Her face twisted. 'So you'd rather . . . So I . . .'

He held his hand up, and to her credit she let him

speak. 'If I had told you at twelve or fifteen that your father was a Mantis-kinden hired sword working out of Helleron, then I know you would have wanted to meet him, even if it was just to see the man who abandoned your mother. I would have forbidden it, but I *do* know you, and I know you would have found a way. And if you had confronted him, looking like you do, so like her, he would have killed you. That is nothing more than the truth.' He rubbed at his forehead. 'And so I made the resolution to say nothing. I might have broken that resolve, but . . . but you never asked. *Never*. You never asked who your parents were.'

Her expression showed pure betrayal. 'I didn't *need* to ask who they were. I thought . . .' Her voice was starting to shake. 'I thought that you . . .'

'No,' he said quickly, 'you couldn't have thought that.' Because, of course, that was the gossip when he had arrived at Collegium with a motherless child in his arms: that she was the fruit of some indiscretion of his. It had been a minor scandal. The child's pale skin had told its tale, though, and when the child grew, it became obvious to all that nothing so heavy and down-to-earth as Beetle blood was flowing in her, and the questions multiplied but the speculation died away, and he had thought *that* particular rumour must have been put in its grave long before now. But here it was again, and he was confronted with it from its very source.

'What was I supposed to think?' she demanded. 'You raised me. You looked after me.' The firelight showed tears of pain and frustration tracking down her cheeks. 'You're my father. Until last night, that was who you were, to me. I never thought . . .' A sob, choked back. 'Or if I did, I stopped myself thinking. And now you're just . . . I'm just . . .'

'I did everything I could for you,' he told her sadly. 'I did bring you up as if you were my own. It was my promise to Atryssa. I gave you the best start in life that I could think of, in Collegium. I even found a sister for you, so that you would always have company. I did everything but tell you the truth.'

She was silent, it seemed to him, forever, staring into the fire. He felt like a man walking a tightrope, Tisamon to one side and Tynisa to the other. *I was never meant for such juggling*.

'Tell me about her,' she said at last. 'How did it happen? What could have possibly gone wrong, to put me in the world?'

'Please—'

'Tell me.'

He settled back. 'It's a story you should recognize. We met in Collegium – at the College itself. I know it seems absurd that *he*,' a nod towards the solitary Tisamon, 'could ever have been a student, but he came to Collegium hunting I know not what, something he could not find at home. We were the strangest group. We fought in the Prowess. They were all so good and I was a liability, but they carried me with them.' The memory hurt more than he would have thought: the sweetness of those innocent days stuck in his throat.

'What was *she* like?' That question, coming from the very mirror of Atryssa? This night did not feel real to him any more.

'She stepped off a boat into Collegium with nothing but the clothes she wore. Everybody loved her and the city never knew what had hit it. She got everything she asked for. I think she was from one of the great Spider houses, the Aristoi they call them. But they had fallen on hard times, lost their footing in the dance. She didn't speak much about it, never looked back. She was Spider-kinden, after all. She could do all the things that they do, intrigue with the best of them, but . . . she had a heart, and she was a friend, and I think we all loved her, just a little. Your mother.' The sun had been so much brighter then, in his memories. It had shone every day. Debates in the chambers, duels at the Prowess, learning artifice from the masters. As a young man, with the world ahead of him and no worries, none.

'As for Tisamon, he came from Felyal, where the real fanatics live. He hated her race. He hated her, at first. Even then he was the best fighter anyone had ever seen, but she herself was close on the second. They would duel together in the Prowess Forum all the time. Each one could find no other to challenge their skills. She gave him something no other could, and he came to love her even as they fought. Mantis-kinden! And when they love and hate, it is with all their being. And he hated himself, at first, because he thought he was betraying his own race. Oh it was a difficult business. And yet your mother worked on him, and broke his defences down.' He reached around for his pack, opened it up. 'I've something I should show you, I think, at this point. It's been a long time waiting for you to see it. I've carried it to many places. Coming to Helleron, I thought . . . well, there was always a chance.' He withdrew a flat leather wallet and opened it to reveal a canvas perhaps a foot across. With great care he folded it out so that she could see.

Two decades ago the fashion in painting groups was to have them surprised in some domestic scene. So it was that the five figures here were in a taverna somewhere, turning to look at the viewer as though suddenly interrupted in some drinking discussion. The paint had scuffed, in places, flaked and chipped, but the picture was still clear. Tynisa stared.

Seated left of centre was a young Beetle who could have been Stenwold's son, save that he had never had one. Still stocky, slightly round at the waist. She looked from that cheerful, smiling face to the solemn one the fire now danced on, trying to bridge the chasm time had made.

Standing behind his chair was Tisamon: there was no doubt of that. The artist had caught him perfectly, down to the hostile expression on his sharp features, a threat to the intruder. His right hand, almost out of sight behind Stenwold's chair, wore the metal gauntlet of his folding claw. In the far left of the picture, a bald, knuckle-faced Fly leant back in his chair, a bowl of wine tilted in one hand, seemingly on the very point of overbalancing. Across from him was a darkly serious Ant-kinden man, his back turned three-quarters to the viewer, the links of his chain-mail hauberk picked out in minute detail.

In the centre of the picture, sitting on the table with her legs dangling, was a girl whose face Tynisa had herself watched grow from a child's to a woman's, in daily mirrored increments. At that point – in the frozen piece of time the artist had preserved – it was as though it was she herself amongst those strangers.

The picture was signed, 'Nero', in small strokes.

'Tisamon – and me, of course,' Stenwold said, seeing even as he said it that there was no 'of course' about his younger image. 'That's Nero himself, the one with the wine. He had a trick with mirrors, to paint his own image in. Nero lives still, usually trawling around the south, Merro, Egel and Seldis. The Ant is Marius. He . . . died. And of course, that's Atryssa. The most beautiful woman I ever knew.' He found himself looking from the painted likeness to the living one. 'I had thought that your father's blood would show but, as you grew, year by year, you were more like her. No mother could give her child a greater gift.'

'Except to stay with her,' said Tynisa sadly. 'Tell me the rest, Stenwold. I have to know.'

'And we went our ways. Marius went back to Sarn and the army. I stayed at Collegium. Your mother and father made a living as duellists, out Merro way. I was early, perhaps even the first, to discover what was raising its head up east of the Lowlands. I followed my researches and they led me to the Empire. I called for my friends and they came, even though Marius had to leave his beloved city for me. We agreed to work against the Wasps. We saw some of their plans, and we knew that the Lowlands were just another point on the map for them, another place to conquer. You've heard of the city of Myna, and you know what happens next. It seemed destined to fall beneath the Empire's boot, so we agreed to regroup there and see if the Wasps could be stopped before its gates. Nero dropped out – Fly-kinden always know the best time to make an exit. The rest of us . . . When we met, Atryssa wasn't there. And then we were betrayed. The defenders of Myna were betrayed. It seemed that only one of us could have done it. And Atryssa wasn't there. It broke Tisamon, or nearly. Because he had loved her, in spite of everything he believed about her people.'

For a moment Stenwold could not go on. The sound of a city dying was still in his mind. He remembered the citizens of Myna out in the streets, Wasp soldiers coursing overhead, the breaking of the gates: the bitter taste of failure and betrayal. He remembered the desperate fight on the airfield. Marius's soldiers retreating, shields held high. Marius calling. Marius, dying in the orthopter. The grief and rage and loss that had become Tisamon's whole world.

'Marius died as we fled Myna, and if I hadn't stopped him, Tisamon would have got himself killed as well.'

'But she didn't betray you?'

'To this day I do not know who did, save that, after all this time, I know it was none of my friends,' Stenwold replied. 'But it was too late, then. Too late for Marius. Too late for Atryssa. Too late for all of us.' The end of his golden days. The shadows gathering. Tisamon was right: Stenwold had become what he had despised. He had gone on to set himself against an Empire, and he had made his students his pawns, and some of them had suffered, and some of them had died.

'What am I supposed to do now?' Tynisa asked him. 'Knowing this, with *him*? Help me, I feel like I'm losing my world.'

He reached out and she took his hand gratefully. 'Please,' she said, 'what am I? I thought I was yours, and now I'm just some . . . mistake? Some cast-off?'

'No!' he said quickly. 'Tynisa, listen to me. Don't ever think that you were not meant. She told me, close to the end. She told me of her last night with Tisamon, before we split up. Before Myna. She had her precautions, like any woman in her position, but that last night – she felt it might really be their last night. She let it happen. She loved him, and she wanted to bear his child.'

When she folded herself into his arms, he held her and wondered if it would feel different if she had genuinely been his daughter.

'And what now?' she whispered.

'He will not come to you,' he told her, 'because he does not know how. But that still means you can go to him when you are ready.' And in response to her half-heard correction, 'Yes, *if*. If you are ready.'

He had expected some burden to lift from him at this point, but the crushing weight of his responsibilities piled higher on him, and he knew he would never be free of them.

His place was always away from the fire. Moth-kinden were born and raised in cold places, and he did not need its light. Achaeos's eyes, the blank white eyes of all of his people, knew neither night nor darkness.

The others were still arguing, the fat Beetle and his Spider girl. Achaeos had not even tried to follow their conversation. It was clearly some tawdry domestic business that had sprung up between them and the Mantis, and it was therefore beneath his notice. The other one, the loathsome machine-fumbler, would be either asleep or worshipping the stinking, groaning monster they were forcing him to ride in. Achaeos shuddered at the thought. The motion of it made him feel ill, the sight of its moving parts turned his stomach.

After the distraction of their bickering gave way to a need for sleep he reached for his bones and crouched down to cast them, as was the old habit. What did it matter what they said, when his destiny was out of his hands already? They had looked at him as though he was unsound, the Arcanum back in Helleron. He was drifting from them, from what they expected of him.

The bones fell amongst patchy grass. He grimaced and poked about, moving the blades aside to try to determine what pattern they made, but it had no sense to it. It seemed to be promising absurdly catastrophic things, far beyond 'yes' or 'no', or even 'life' or 'death'. He decided that the uneven ground had fouled the divination and gathered them up again. With care he cleared a decent patch of ground, plucking the grass away, rubbing the ground flat. He was going to far too much effort now, just to satisfy his habit, but it had become a point of pride. He took a breath and cast the bones again.

For a long time he remained very still, studying them. It was a pattern he had never seen before, outside the books – the old books, that was. If he had not researched his pastime so keenly, he might never have recognized what the world was telling him.

They gave one word to it, in those old books, and that word was 'Corruption.' To the Moths it had its own meaning, as everything did. It did not mean the bribery and material greed of the Beetle-kinden. It meant the rotting of the soul, the very worst of the old dark magics.

He shook himself. He was a poor seer, no great magician he. He was in no position to make these dire predictions. *I have misread the sign, or miscast the bones.* He reached for them again, to gather them up, and drew his hand back with a startled hiss. They had burned when he touched them and, as he watched, they were blackening, pitting. The scent of decay came to him, and he finally knew what they had been trying to say.

He almost fell into the fire, he was so desperate to reach Stenwold Maker. The man was asleep, but Achaeos did not care. He took hold of a heavy shoulder and shook it, and heard a whisper as Stenwold began groping immediately for his sword.

'What ... What is it? What?' he muttered. 'Are we under attack?'

'I have to speak to you, now,' Achaeos almost spat at him.

'What?' Stenwold paused and then stared at him. 'I know it doesn't bother your people, but it's the middle of the night.' He looked haggard, ten years older.

Achaeos looked around at the others, most of whom were at least half awake by now. Tisamon, truly on watch, was staring at him keenly, blade already bared. 'Come away from the fire and talk,' Achaeos insisted.

Stenwold cursed and got to his feet, bulging blanket wrapped around him, and his sword still in his hand. He looked just like a bad actor playing a comic hero. They removed from the fire enough that their talk would not disturb the others, though still under Tisamon's harsh gaze.

'You're going east,' Achaeos said.

Stenwold rubbed his eyes with the forearm of his sword hand. 'Achaeos, that's not exactly news.'

'You do not know what is east, of here.'

'The Empire's east, Achaeos. Asta's east. Szar's east, and Myna, and then Sonn, and eventually you get to Capitas and you meet the Emperor. Of all the Beetles in the world, you don't need to tell *me* what lies east.'

'The Darakyon is east. East and close,' Achaeos said urgently.

Stenwold just looked at him. 'You mean the forest? What's that to you? Your people don't live there, do they? I didn't think even the Mantis-kinden lived there.'

'*Nobody* lives there. Nobody travels there who has any sense. The Darakyon is evil.' Achaeos clutched at Stenwold's blanket-cape. 'Terrible things were done there.' He sensed, rather than heard, Tisamon's stance shift.

Stenwold continued to peer at him, tired and irritable and mired in his own difficulties. 'I'm sorry,' he said shortly. 'I have other things to worry about than the beliefs of your people.' He shook off Achaeos's hand and returned towards the fire. The Moth watched him go with bared teeth.

So fly! he thought. *Fly away from this fool and his mission.* But he could not, and he almost wept in frustration at it, at the invisible chains that were keeping him here.

There was a seat for the driver at the front of each automotive, and room for just one more sitting beside him, beneath the shade of a rough canvas roof. Thalric was the extra one in the lead vehicle but he was reflecting that it was a remarkably uncomfortable way to travel even so. His own men and the slavers were sitting along the open sides of the vehicle, exposed to the dust, and he was beginning to wonder if the slaves, confined in their cage, didn't have the better deal of it.

He considered his earlier conversation with Cheerwell Maker, and decided that he had lost control of it. It was not just her jibe at the end, however well aimed. He had indulged himself: he had wasted time in boasts about the Empire that he felt so fiercely about. *Strutting before a young woman, honestly!* Still, perhaps he had given her sufficient food for thought. They were nearly at Asta now.

If she decided to stick, then there were people there who would loosen her.

Or perhaps he could pass her over to Brutan. He considered the slaver's likely response to the gift and realized that he found it distasteful, but that was not for any reason that would have satisfied Miss Maker. As an individual, the slavers' habits irked him primarily because they were running their operation for their own sordid enjoyment, and that was not the Empire's way. As a servant of the Empire, however, he knew it all served, in the end. The Brutans of this world were most slaves' first introduction to imperial policy, and that was a hard but necessary lesson. They had to be shown that they had no right and no appeal. Any slave who could say, 'You can't do that to me,' was not a slave.

There was a thump on the roof of the cab, and a moment later someone put their head down into Thalric's field of vision, annoying the driver beside him. It was a Fly-kinden man in the uniform of the Scout Corps.

'Message for you, sir,' the Fly reported.

'Well?'

'Care to join me up top, sir?'

Thalric narrowed his eyes, but the Fly was silhouetted against the outside glare and his expression could not be read. With a hiss of annoyance Thalric pushed himself out of the side of the cab, grabbing at rungs while flickering his Art-wings to keep him stable. The Fly was sitting cross-legged atop the wagon when Thalric reached him, forward enough that he was out of earshot of the other men.

'This had better be important.'

'You're summoned, Major. Report to the quartermaster's in Asta after sunset tonight.'

'Summoned? Who by?' Thalric caught up. 'Major, is it?'

'Yes, Major. I'll look for you there, sir.' In an instant

the Fly kicked off into the air, letting the passing breeze catch him. His wings sparked to life and he was off.

Major? Major meant Rekef business. Thalric was a captain in the Imperial Army, but the Rekef gave out its own ranks. Despite the dust and the heat he felt a queasy chill inside him. Rekef Inlander seemed most likely – investigating him? He had done nothing wrong. He had been telling the truth when he professed to Cheerwell Maker his unbending loyalty. Still, he knew that, to catch all treason and malfeasance in the Empire, the Rekef machine had to grind small and thorough, and innocents would always get caught up in the teeth of the wheels. Of course he would make the sacrifice willingly, if the Empire demanded it. It was just that he would rather not have to.

Che could no longer dispute that they were approaching somewhere. Where there had been scrubby wildland, now there was a packed-dirt road that the slave wagons were churning up with their tracks. Che and Salma had been given some time now to watch the other travellers, those passing in the opposite direction and those the slave convoy overtook. The sight was not encouraging.

They saw squads of soldiers, mostly. Many were heading west. Others were returning patrols, slogging wearily through the dust with spears sloped against their shoulders. Occasionally a messenger would thunder past on horseback, or the shadows of flying men would pass over the prisoners' cage.

'Where is there, out here?' Che wondered. The Lowlander cartographers had never been much for going beyond the borders of the lands they knew. It was part of the inward-looking mindset that was now giving the Wasps such free rein.

'Commonweal maps don't go into much detail here. Just "wildlands", that kind of thing,' said Salma. 'Mind you, they're mostly about a hundred years out of date at the least. It's been a while since the Monarch's Nine Exploratory Heroes were sent to the four corners of the world looking for the secrets of eternal life.'

'The who sent for what?' she asked incredulously. He grinned at her. She had noticed a difference in him, after her return from Thalric's tent, and after his concern for her had been allayed. When she had pressed him on it, he had eventually admitted this gem of knowledge that he had mined in her absence.

'Her name,' he had revealed, 'is Grief in Chains.'

And she had stared at him, and then remembered the Butterfly-kinden dancer who had so fascinated him. 'What sort of a name is that?' she had asked, nettled. She had always had a chip on her shoulder about her own name.

'Oh, they change their names a lot, Butterflies,' he admitted. 'Still, don't you think it's nice?'

And there had been a little extra life in him, from then on, something his own chains could not drag down. Now he was grinning at her and she could not tell whether he was being truthful or not. 'Three centuries ago the Monarch was very old, and he sent the nine greatest heroes of the Commonweal out into the unexplored parts of the world, because his advisors and wizards had told him that the secret of life eternal was out there to be found. Some went north across the great steppe, through the Locust tribes and the distant countries of fire and ice, and the ancient, deserted mountain kingdoms of the Slugs. Some went east where the barbarians live, and where the broken land is studded with cities like jewels, or to where the great forests of the Woodlouse-kinden grow and rot all at the same time. Some went west, and sailed across the seas to distant lands where wonders were commonplace and the most usual things were decried as horrors not to be tolerated. And some,' and here his smile grew mocking, 'went south across the Barrier Ridge, and found a land where no two people can agree on anything, and the civilized comforts of a properly measured life were almost completely unknown. And five of the Exploratory Heroes returned, with empty hands, but with tales enough to keep the Regent's wise men debating for centuries.'

She was agog, just for a moment, waiting. 'And? What about the others? Did they find it?'

He laughed at her. 'Nobody knows. They never came back. Some people still say, though, that the last of the Heroes still wanders distant lands, living eternally, eternally young, trying only to get his prize back to a Monarch who died just two years after the Heroes set out.'

Che tried to appear unimpressed. 'Your people are very strange. Are all those places real?'

He shrugged carelessly. 'They're on the maps, for what it's worth. What about *your* maps?'

'Oh, commerce. Merchants go everywhere and sell to everyone. Our maps have the caravan routes picked out in red. We have treaties and trade deals. We like pieces of paper with signatures on them. But most of all we expect people to come to us, since Collegium is the centre of the world as far as we're concerned. I'll tell you about Doctor Thordry,' she said. 'That should explain the Collegium attitude to explorers, anyway.' And she did so, spinning the tale out for as long as she could, aware that the other slaves in the cage, piqued by Salma's dismissive words, were all listening now.

Thordry had been an artificer of a century ago, around the very beginnings of man-made flight. He and his man-servant had set out in a flying machine of his own invention and they had gone south, across the sea. It had been an ingenious piece of work, his machine. Che had seen it, even run her hands along the brass-bound wood of its hull in the Collegium Museum of Mechanical Science. An airship with a clockwork engine that Thordry and his companion had wound each day by letting out a weight on a cord, which they had then hauled in by hand.

Thordry had been gone and almost forgotten for five years when he had surfaced again. He came back with maps and stories of lands across the sea, none of which were believed and some of which were simply unbelievable. He had spent two years wandering as a self-appointed, itinerant ambassador for Collegium, and then set sail for home. His navigation skills, and ill winds, had landed him up in the Spiderlands, and he had spent a further year there as a fashionable talking point before seeing that his popularity was on the wane, and setting off for home.

But on his arrival, the triumphant explorer had not received the reception he had been expecting. He had not been laughed at, quite, but the Great College virtually ignored him, and to the populace he was a celebrated lunatic. His stories of distant lands were treated as just that, stories. When they were printed it was as *The Marvellous and Fantastical Adventures of Doctor Thordry and his Man*. His maps, that connected with no land known, were quietly shelved.

'And that,' Che finished, 'is how Lowlanders treat explorers. Which is why we have an Empire on our doorstep that's sharpening its swords as we speak, and yet everyone's talking very loudly amongst themselves to block out the sound of it.'

'Helleron can't exactly fool itself. Helleron must have sold half the weapons that were used against my own people in the war,' Salma said, and she snorted.

'Oh, I think we've seen quite enough of Helleron and the Empire in bed together,' she said bitterly, and to her surprise there was a current of agreement among the other slaves.

There might even have been a dialogue, then, the start of community between them. The reminders of their state were never far away, though. Even at that moment the slaver automotive passed another string of luckless captives. It was a caravan of the taloned, white-skinned race that someone identified as Scorpion-kinden. They had a string of pack-mules, and a pair of mule-sized scorpions loaded with baggage, but the pick of their trading stock was trudging along, tied to the end of their chain of animals. They were gaunt, malnourished, coated with dust, their clothes gone to rags that could not hide their lash-marks. Che tried to decide if they were escapees or criminals or honest men and women, but she realized soon enough that all they were was slaves.

Twenty-one

Two lamps, turned low, lit the quartermaster's quarters, and the quartermaster had prudently agreed to absent himself. It was only a fraction after dusk when Thalric made his entrance, and yet there they were, already waiting for him. Four of them, all Rekef, no doubt, though he only recognized the one.

'Colonel Latvoc.' He saluted, which was something he had not needed to do for some time. The greying Wasp-kinden, dressed in loose and nondescript civilian clothes, gestured for him to find a seat.

'Major Thalric,' he said, his face giving no hints, 'this is Lieutenant-Auxillian Odyssa.' His moving finger picked out a Spider woman lounging against a sack of dates, which she pillaged occasionally. 'And Lieutenant te Berro,' the Fly-kinden who had summoned him. The Rekef, particularly the Rekef Outlander, made much use of foreign recruits. Their promotion prospects were limited.

The fourth man was a Wasp, thin faced and patient looking. He watched Thalric carefully. The fact that he had neither been named nor referred to was not lost on Thalric.

'You seem nervous, Major,' said Latvoc.

'Not at all, sir.' Thalric sat down, feeling his heart stutter. He was sure that his veneer of calm was fooling nobody.

'Very well, in accordance with our charter I declare that we, in this room, are the Rekef presence in Asta, and that our decisions made here shall bind the Empire, and be for the Emperor.' The formality brushed aside, the old man smiled. 'We have a problem, Major, that you can help us with.'

'Of course, sir.' *And is it me, this problem?* He had seen what happened when the Rekef got its sting into someone. There was no mercy or kindness. He had himself been its agent, and he had known Rekef officers to fall from grace in the past. The Rekef watched the Empire and the army, and the Rekef also watched the Rekef.

But I have done nothing! And he knew it would not matter.

'You are familiar with a Colonel Ulther, are you not?' Latvoc had let him stew for long enough, it seemed.

'*Colonel* Ulther? I knew a Major Ulther, some years ago, sir.'

'The very man. You knew him well, did you not?'

'He was my commanding officer. In the regular army, that is.' Thalric's first promotion: it had been in Myna, after the taking of the city, and it had been just before the Rekef had decided he would best serve the Empire from within their cloak of secrecy. 'I haven't seen him for some years, but I would say that I knew him well. I heard that he had governance of Myna some while back.'

'Just so, in which position he remains.' Latvoc looked over to the Spider, Odyssa, who took up the thread.

'Would you say that you respected Ulther, Major?' she asked.

'Yes, when I knew him.'

'Did you like him?' He felt her Art at the edges of his mind, trying to draw him out, seeking weakness.

'I respected him. As an officer. This was years ago and—'

'That is understood, Major. When you were raised to the Rekef, you did not note any concerns about him?'

'I had no concerns.' He felt a sheen of sweat start on

his forehead. Something had gone wrong with Ulther, apparently. What remained to be seen was whether someone had decided that his, Thalric's, time in the Rekef's favour was over, and was using his past association to hammer in the spike.

'There will be war with the Lowlander cities soon,' said Latvoc slowly. 'This is not news to you, I am sure. You have been faithfully ensuring that the path to victory for the armies of the Empire will be as smooth as possible.'

'Yes, sir.'

'It has come to the attention of the Rekef that others are not so dedicated to their duty,' Latvoc explained.

Odyssa glanced at Latvoc, and then at the unnamed, silent man, who nodded ever so slightly. Thalric found that he was flexing his fingers as if freeing his palms for battle, and forced himself to relax.

'We have received some reports from agents in Myna that the governance of that city is subject to certain irregularities,' said Latvoc. 'Supplies and manufacture that is required for the Lowlands campaign is slow in coming and short in measure. It may seem trivial, and no doubt to the perpetrators it is intended to seem so, but an army cannot march without rations, cannot fight without weapons. Small acts mount up and become large ones, so an army that should have been in readiness at Asta is behind schedule, missing everything from boots to hard tack to spare parts for the fliers.'

He seemed to be waiting for Thalric to comment, but Thalric had nothing to say, was waiting still for the catch.

'When a man is appointed a governor of a city by the Emperor, Major Thalric,' Latvoc continued at last, 'he is put into a position of responsibility and power beyond even that of an army general. It has been known for such power to turn an officer's head. There is a temptation to consider those resources, the money and the goods that the Empire requests of him, and to hold them back and stint us with excuses. Such things are known, and it is unfortunate that Colonel Ulther has now become the target of some of these rumours. Do you understand me?'

'I understand you, sir,' said Thalric wearily.

'Although you are technically Rekef Outlander,' and there was a slight admonition there in him appearing to be content with the lesser wing of the service, 'your past association makes you the obvious man for us to send. Lieutenant Aagen of the Engineering Corps is heading to Myna to collect supplies in the morning. You will go with him, investigate the situation with your old friend Ulther. Take what action you feel appropriate. Resolve matters. Report to us.'

Thalric permitted himself a breath.

'Any questions, Major?'

'I have two prisoners. I had hoped to interrogate them here.'

'Aagen is already transporting livestock. Take them with you, if you must. The facilities in Myna are superior. You could give that to Ulther as the reason for your presence. Any further questions?'

'No, sir.'

'Dismissed.'

Thalric stood, saluted, and left. It was a good twenty yards before he permitted himself to relax, and even then the thought remained. *Not this time. Maybe next time. Or the time after that.* He had never scrupled about taking the Rekef's reputation by the hilt and using it. He never put that weapon down, though, without knowing that, the next time it was raised, it could be at his own throat.

Why do I do this? The question surprised him, because he already knew the answer. He loved the Empire. Still, inside his head, where even the Rekef could not catch a treasonous thought, he wondered what sort of Empire they were building, where even the watchmen must fear being watched.

It was not yet dawn when the voices came from above them. Asta had an uncompromising system for the keeping of slaves. Che and Salma, along with some dozen others, were confined in a sheer-sided circular pit. Salma and any others who looked as though they might take to the air were hobbled, chains drawing their elbows tightly behind their backs. They had not bothered with Che, so she had spent much of the night trying to free him, with no more success than she would have had flying out of the pit herself.

If only I had concentrated more, dreamed less. That Art still escaped her and, besides, Beetles were poor fliers and everyone knew it. And now it was too late.

The first voice she heard from above was Thalric's. She had listened to him talking long enough to know it. 'Attention!' it called, then, 'And is this Aagen of Dinas I see before me.'

'Spit me, but it's Captain Thalric,' said another voice, a Wasp with more of an accent than Thalric himself. 'Well, that's a five-year spell of good luck broken.'

'*Lieutenant* Aagen of the Engineering Corps, I see,' came Thalric's unseen voice. All of the slaves were awake now, but only she and Salma seemed to be really listening.

'Battlefield promotion during the Maynes rebellion. What can I do for you, Captain?' asked the faceless Aagen.

'You're setting off for Myna?'

'Soon as it's light. You could build a whole new automotive out of the parts I'm missing here. I'm going to take my rank badge and shove it in people's faces back at the depot until I'm happy.' Despite the accent and the context, this was so like one of the College artificers speaking that Che felt dizzy.

'Good,' said Thalric. 'Are you heading there with an empty hold?'

'No waste in this man's army, Captain. Got a special delivery to make. I hear you might want in on that.'

'And two prisoners. You're set up to carry prisoners?'

'I'm carrying prisoners already. One prisoner, anyway.'

The noises from above now sounded like men moving large crates. There had been a ragbag of automotives up above, as the slaves were being housed, so Che guessed they were loading one of them prior to Thalric's mooted journey. That she and Salma would be unwilling travelling companions of the man seemed overwhelmingly likely.

Thalric had been silent a moment, and now he asked, 'Just one prisoner? I thought they didn't waste space in your army, Lieutenant?'

'Don't make the rules, Captain, just follow the orders. Special delivery, like I said.'

The artificial lights of the workmen above had given a little definition to their prison pit's mouth, but now Che saw that there was a growing greyness there. Dawn failed to enliven her. Her very recent life had made her long for the rest that night brought. At least in dreams she was not chained.

There was a shape silhouetted up there, cutting into the rim: a head looking down. When it spoke, she picked it as Thalric.

'Clear for the hoist,' he called down, and ducked out of the way as a wooden platform was winched across and began descending on them at some speed. There was a scatter of limbs withdrawn and bodies moved, and then the lift touched bottom.

'Cheerwell Maker and Salme Dien,' Thalric called. 'And don't make me go down and fetch you.'

Salma exchanged glances with Che. 'Later,' he whispered. 'We'll have our chance.'

She shrugged and wasn't sure she believed him.

They had to cling together on the platform, or rather, she had to cling to him as his arms were pinioned. The chance of escape remained conspicuously absent, too. The field above, of which the slave pits formed only one edge, was a bustle of activity. The Wasps rose early.

Salma started, and she followed his gaze across the field to see a ripple of halted motion as working Wasps paused to gawp. A figure was now being led towards them, and Che identified it as the Butterfly-kinden, Grief in Chains.

'So that's your special delivery, is it?' Thalric asked her handler as they approached.

'None other,' said the man leading her, who must be Aagen, from the voice. 'They told me she should get the hold all to herself, but your orders are over any other, Captain.'

Thalric clapped him on the shoulder, which surprised Che. It was such a casual, human gesture from this harsh man.

Grief in Chains was not pinned like Salma, but there was a collar at her throat for the slender chain in Aagen's hand. The Wasp artificer went to a vehicle nearby and was unlatching a hatch at the back. This machine was a squat, ugly-looking thing, large and brick-shaped, entwined with the swept funnels of a steam engine. It had a pair of propellers at the rear, and one huge prop underneath, only inches from the ground, almost clipping against its four stumpy feet. Che found it incredible that anyone would inflict such an ugly thing on the air.

The space within would clearly provide more room than they had been allowed for some time. Grief in Chains stepped in first, for all the world like a Spider-kinden princess escorted to her carriage, and then Aagen secured her chain to a ring on the interior.

'Good job you're coming with us, really,' said the

artificer. 'If it were just me and the stoker alone with her, who knows? She's quite a piece of work, isn't she?'

Thalric looked unmoved, or at least affected to be. At a signal from him, Che and Salma were bundled inside. The Wasp looked at them critically: the bound Dragonfly, the awkward-looking Beetle.

'Chain them anyway,' he told the soldiers. 'Necks to the wall, like the woman. I'm not a man for gambling.'

'Will you look at that,' Stenwold breathed, peering through his telescope. He had known, he should have known, what he would see here, but it still shocked and frightened him. All these years he had been preaching it, and now here was proof, but how much he would rather have been wrong.

'Is that Asta?' asked Tisamon, hunching over his shoulder.

'If they still call it that.'

'What's Asta?' Tynisa asked. Beside her, Totho stirred in his sleep. He had been working on the automotive the whole night through.

Tisamon went instantly quiet, and Stenwold sighed inwardly. To his knowledge neither of them had even tried to reach out to the other. Such reticence, at least, Tynisa had inherited from her father.

'When we passed through here last, this was a tiny village, little more than a caravan stopover point. It was fairly cosmopolitan, more Beetle-kinden than anything else, though the name's from the Scorpion. There's an oasis there, you see. Northernmost one of the Dryclaw. Now . . . well, just look at it.'

They were now at the very bounds of the Lowlands. Whilst to the south and the west the Lowland world was bounded by sea, and to the north by the great landslip of the Barrier Ridge, the eastern edge of its expansion had been checked by the desert. The great barren waste of the Dryclaw stretched for hundreds of miles, and there were only two ways round. South of the desert lay the narrow coastal Silk Road that led to the Spiderlands, and north . . . well, north was here.

Passage north of the Dryclaw was never easy, but it had been easier in the past. The land had left its people only two roads. One led south of the Tornos mountains and north of the Darakyon Forest, a rocky and unappealing path of steps and leaps. The other ran south of the forest, where the land turned from wood to scrub, from scrub to desert, and here was Asta, this little caravanning town, the oasis.

Except that Asta was no longer little, nor was it trade that drove so much traffic between it and the eastern world. The original mud-brick buildings of the village were now surrounded by a great host of sheds and long, low halls, all with the appearance of having been hastily constructed. Beyond them extended a veritable tent city and all of it was rendered in black and gold. The Wasps had come to Asta and it was no longer a village. It was a staging post.

'This is an invasion in the making,' muttered Stenwold. *If only the old men of the Assembly were here with me now! If they could see this then how could they doubt me?* He was suddenly afraid for his home city, for poor blind Collegium with all its flaws. Would realization come to the Assemblers only when the Wasps were at their walls?

He silently watched the automotives and pack trains coming in, the dash back and forth of the flying sentries, and the thunder of the orthopters, the drilling squads of soldiers. Even for the Imperial Army there was a huge concentration of troops down there.

'How are we going to find them, in all of that?' Tynisa asked.

'Nightfall,' said Tisamon. '*I'll* go.'

'You're sure?' Stenwold asked.

The Mantis nodded. 'In the meantime we have another problem. Any closer and they'll see us. Especially in this device.'

'We'll leave it here for now,' Stenwold confirmed. 'We can use the cover of the trees to get closer.'

He sensed a sudden change in mood behind him. Craning back to look, he saw that Tisamon was shaking his head slowly. 'You forget,' the Mantis said, 'this is the Darakyon.'

'Oh, not this again—'

'It is not a place that we should go,' Tisamon said implacably. 'Any of us.'

'I told you,' Achaeos had been silent all day, hunched in the rear of the automotive with his hood up. Now he pushed it back, eyes narrowing in the sunlight. 'My people know more of this than any of you, and they do not venture into the Darakyon without good cause.'

'That's because your people are superstitious,' Tynisa told him. 'It's just a forest.'

Tisamon did not look at her. 'My people once claimed the Darakyon: a hold of we Mantis-kinden. No longer. Now no man may live there, and only fools travel its paths unprepared. You are all unprepared.'

'What . . . what happened?' she asked him, but he just shook his head, still turned away from her.

'Don't just—' she started, but there was a sudden light touch on her arm. Achaeos's expression had lost some of its aloof distance.

'Crimes were done there,' the Moth said, 'by my people and his, together. After the revolution, when we feared to further lose our waning power. More than that is a secret held only by the Skryres, who know and see all. But this is known: those who did these terrible things, they have not left. They are still there and they do not receive visitors well. Why do you think the Mantis-kinden will not live here any more? Why do you think the Wasps or the Beetles have not already felled these trees for their furnaces? Time has been stilled within these trees for five hundred years.'

'I . . .' Tynisa wanted to mock him, but he so clearly *believed* what he said, and she could tell that Tisamon did as well. 'This is ridiculous.' She contented herself with that.

In the end, they made a compromise by clinging to the very forest edge. Even here the shadows lay heavily on them. Totho seemed oblivious to it all, but Stenwold cast a few anxious glances about him as it grew dark. Tynisa remembered his dealings with Dr Nicrephos in Collegium, and guessed that he was a Beetle of unusual experience.

They set the lowest of low fires, embers stoked merely to blunt the chill that seemed to hang about them. As the night approached, while the trees behind them seemed to draw the darkness to themselves like a mother summoning her children, Tisamon stood up.

'Don't take any risks you don't have to,' Stenwold warned him. 'That's not a town, it's a military camp and they're going to be watching.'

'Don't lecture me, O historian,' said Tisamon, and Tynisa guessed he was eager for his skills to be put to use again.

'I'm going with him,' she told Stenwold.

A chill descended between the two older men.

'I don't think that's wise—' started Stenwold, but she folded her arms.

'It's my sister we're going to find, near enough. She's not even going to know who . . . who this man is, so I'm going.'

Stenwold grimaced, glancing at Tisamon, whose shadowed face was unreadable. Then, after a moment, the Mantis nodded curtly. No words, no encouragement, but at least that. A moment later he was gone, buckling his claw gauntlet to his arm. Tynisa took one more look at Stenwold, who was looking unhappier than ever, and then followed him into the gathering dark.

'Well . . .' he began, and had nothing to follow it with.

'I'm sure that . . . Tynisa can look after herself,' Totho said awkwardly.

'I just feel there's an explosion waiting between those two. I didn't ever want to leave them alone.'

'She's right about . . . well, if the first thing Che saw was your man there . . . He's not exactly . . .'

Stenwold conceded the point. 'It's an imperfect world.' A moment later he frowned. 'Where's Achaeos?'

For the Moth had vanished.

Sitting with them in the shadow of those trees had taken courage he had not known he possessed. It had been the fat Beetle and the grease-fingered Totho that had been the spur. They had made their little camp, as happy as anything, and even Tynisa had joined in and had not cared. She was Spider-kinden and she should know better. It pained him to see how they had blinded her by bringing her up amongst the Beetles.

Oh, Tisamon knew, of course. This place must stir up more dread in Tisamon than even Achaeos could imagine. It was the cautionary story that Mantis fathers raised their children on – warning of the price of hubris, that ancient corruption. His hands twitched instinctively for his bones, but they were gone. He felt as though he had lost a sense.

Now the Mantis and the Spider girl had gone off, a ridiculous pairing, into the camp below to find Cheerwell Maker. *So let them find her, and let this be over with.* He took a deep breath to calm himself. *Prepare, magician,* he addressed himself. It was a title he had scant right to. He had never been a great champion of the lore of his own people. He knew enough of it, though, and it struck him now that if that same lore could do nothing to find Che, then the Beetles' scepticism might as well be justified.

I am a seer of Tharn, he told himself. *So let me see.* Away from the fire again, and yet not deeper into those appalling trees, he felt about for the strands of the world around him. He had touched Che. She even had his blood on her hands from the wound she had healed. There was a cord that ran between them – oh was there not! The cord that would not let him walk away.

His awareness cringed from the tangled mass that rose behind him, but the Darakyon seemed quiet at least. The ancient wrongs that had been poured into the place were sleeping.

There was a host of thousands of souls in Asta, but they were chaff. They were Wasps or the slaves of Wasps. Here and there was a spark of quality, some luckless scion of an elder race held in imperial servitude. If he had wished he could have found Tisamon and Tynisa easily enough, just by their heritage: Moths, Spiders and Mantids, the ancient rulers of the world.

Che had no such Inapt heritage, but he felt for the cord that must have tied his fate to hers, through her ministrations – *linked through more than that?* He stamped on such thoughts. He reached out towards the makeshift town of Asta, the grey deadness of its machines, the legion of sleeping soldiers and slavers and artificers. *Che!*

His powers were weaker even than he had thought. To find an acquaintance was surely not beyond them, not when he was as close as this. Was it all those machines that were confusing his magic? Or was he really such a poor seer after all and a burden on his people? He hunted, but there was no trail, not the faintest mark to lead him to her.

His heart lurched. *What is the first mark of the fool?* his people asked, and the stock answer came back, *That he listens to fools.* So it was that fools clustered together to make their plots and their machines, and so it was that Achaeos had been drawn into fools' company. *Stenwold says they have taken her to Asta, but she is not there. Tisamon will waste his stealth, while we all waste our time.* The answer brought a rush of relief to him, that at least his powers were not so atrophied – and then another of despair. *So she is further, further than I can reach her, and I shall not be free.*

As he stood and made to return to the fire, he felt the Darakyon at his back flex and stretch and come awake.

Oh we should not be here! and he hurried back towards the fire, and saw that he was not the only one.

'Maker! Halfbreed!' he called out. But he saw them already springing up from the fire and both reaching for their weapons. 'Get away from the fire, you fools!' Achaeos yelled sharply, and they blundered towards his voice, in the darkness that blinded them and was nothing to a Moth's sight. It was so clear to him: the trees and the buckled land, the fire and his two clumsy allies. Clear, too, the Wasp soldiers who had been silently approaching, drawn to the dim glow of the embers.

Stenwold and Totho were already into the pitch dark between the trees before the Wasps reached their fire. One of the intruders unshuttered a lantern instantly and cast the beam across the forest, till the others shouted at him to put it out. There were a half-dozen of them, Achaeos saw. One was kneeling to study the surrounding ground in the firelight. He heard, 'I told you I saw a fire out here,' and, 'Smugglers, you reckon?'

'Further into the woods,' Stenwold murmured, 'but quietly.'

'No, not further into the woods . . .' Achaeos began, but Stenwold and Totho were already retreating deeper into the Darakyon. All around them Achaeos felt the forest stir, not the trees themselves, but the blood that had been spilt there, the pain and terror of those who had died. He felt his breathing ragged, his heart racing. The Wasps were following after, though, creeping forward as silently as they could, listening for the crack of twigs.

'Lantern now, then, and rush them!' one whispered.

'Fall back!' Stenwold hissed, and they were ploughing deeper, running and stumbling away from the sudden light of the Wasps.

The light passed across Achaeos, the sharp beam of the lantern. There was a shout, and a sting crackled out, flashing fire past him. He fled, almost sobbing with the sense of the Darakyon stirring all around, and the Wasps gave chase with a savage cry.

He could see Stenwold and Totho ahead of him, staggering like blind men through a landscape Achaeos could see perfectly. He tried to catch them up. It should have been simple.

Achaeos tripped. Those vines had not been there a moment before. He staggered on, the Wasps shouting behind him, letting loose their stings and crossbow bolts. The dense, thorny undergrowth seemed always in his way. He tried to push through it, but it raked at his hands, tore his sleeves. He turned aside, searching for another way round. Stenwold and Totho were further off now, and he realized that their path was curving back towards the forest's edge whilst his own was only going deeper.

I woke it up. I caught its attention. A horrible sense of inevitability had caught him. *Better to be killed by the Wasps.* But it was too late to make that choice. The trees around him were vast and twisted, their bark creased and stretched tight about their bulging trunks. There were thorns and briars everywhere, whole nests of them. Wherever he turned, only the path leading into the centre of the wood seemed clear.

He heard a scream behind him, and he stopped running. He did not want to turn round, but something, some morbid curiosity, drew him to do it. There was enough of the forest to obscure his view, but the Wasps' voices were now rising in panic, in horror. He heard, *'What is it?'* and *'Kill it! Kill it before—'* For just a moment he saw a shape, one that was not quite insect, or human, or plant, but possessed thorn-studded killing arms that rose and fell with lethal speed.

Then there was quiet, and he thought of all the blood that was soaking into the soil of the Darakyon, and he closed his dark-seeing eyes and just waited.

And the Darakyon waited, and when he opened his eyes there was no monster, no terrifying chimaera rising before him. There was a darkness, though, between the trees, that his eyes could not penetrate. There were shadows, and the shadows were shapes, and once he had understood that, he did his best not to look at them.

'What do you want with me?' he asked, his voice little more than a rattle in his throat, and still they waited, until he realized that whatever it was was posing the same question to him. He had been so bold as to catch its notice, and it wanted to know why.

Nobody has spoken with the Darakyon for a hundred years.

His people forbad it, and for good reason. Time and dark deeds had clawed away at this place, festering in it for centuries.

There was a thought that was coming to him now, because he was standing, alive, in this ever-dying place, and it was waiting for his words. *Nobody has spoken with the Darakyon for a hundred years, so what do they know – what do they really know – about what this place might do?* The tales of his people regarding this place were all horrors to scare the children with, but the one thing they agreed on was that the Darakyon was *strong*.

I came here for a purpose. It was while looking for Che that

I felt the forest awake. I am a weak seer, unequal to the task of finding her, but I am standing at the heart of the greatest magic I have ever known.

The night had lost its reality. He was outside time, outside all rules. In that moment he felt that he could accomplish anything, that he could overcome the losses of his race and turn back the revolution. and who knew what else?

'Give me your power,' he told the trees. 'Loan me your power this night.' And he reached forth to take it.

And the Darakyon answered him back, *Who asks?* in a voice that was like a dry chorus of a hundred voices. He could not tell whether it came from the trees themselves or from between them, but the sound of it froze him. A voice like dry leaves and the dead husks of things, and the passage of five hundred years.

Who would draw upon what we have hoarded? gusted the voice of the Darakyon, and Achaeos could barely speak. His breath plumed in the air, as the temperature plummeted instantly away. His great pride, that a moment ago had seemed to hold the world in its palm, had withered within him, like leaves when the winter comes.

'I am Achaeos, a seer of the ancient paths of—' he stuttered out.

Hist! You are no more than a neophyte. What could persuade us to lend you our strength?

He fought in vain to summon an answer, and then they said, *What could save you from us?*

'I am a seer . . .' he tried again, but there was laughter now, and it was worse than the voice itself had been.

None would miss you. You are a stray leaf fallen far from your tree, little neophyte.

He felt himself trembling from fear and cold both. His arms were still outstretched, but the power beyond his fingertips was so vast and so *other* that he could no more compel it than he could command the sun.

Do you think the bearer of the sign can still ward you from us, you who have conjured us into wakefulness and come into our heart?

'No . . .' He choked, his fear was so high in his throat that he could barely speak. 'I only sought . . . I was only trying to find . . .'

Did you think these sacrifices would glut us in blood, little Neophyte?

Sacrifices? 'The Wasps . . . Yes, they are yours,' he stammered out. A dry crackle of laughter echoed around him.

And the other two, who now stumble within our borders, seeking a way out? The two slaves – are they also ours?

It was a moment before Achaeos understood, and when he did the temptation was painful. Buy the Darakyon with the blood of Stenwold and Totho, a Beetle and a half-breed? *If it were only that ill-favoured creature Totho . . .* but Stenwold was *her* family. More, Stenwold was the only one who could control the Mantis, and the Mantis surely would *know*.

'They are not for you!' he choked out, and that rustling laughter came again.

Such demands you make, who have so little power to stop us. Such dictation of what we may and may not do. What will you buy their lives with, little Neophyte? What entreaties have you for us?

He felt his stomach lurch at this abrupt change of direction. 'I just wanted to . . . to find her.' It sounded pitiful, even to him.

We shall see what you would do.

The shapes between the trees shifted, and something infinitely cold seared through the inside of his head from front to back, hissing like acid. His mouth snapped open, unable even to scream. Bent backwards, choking, he fell to the ground, his limbs pulled in, every joint locked.

And then it was gone, and he was left gasping, shuddering,

lying on his side amongst the tangled roots of the Darakyon.

You are pathetic, the phantom voice told him. *You will not even own to why you seek what you seek. But we have seen. We have seen all, and the pain that you will suffer for the road you take. We cannot be commanded to lend you our power.*

Achaeos lay and trembled, crouched into a ball, and waited for the axe to fall.

But we have seen through you, little neophyte. The shapes between the trees were more distinct now, though he knew that he did not wish to see them clearly. *You show spirit, and we have always valued spirit, courage. Always.*

In that last word, lingering over it, there was contained a window opening onto a centuries-old loss, a betrayal, the end of an era. He remembered how the Mantis-kinden had dwelled here and that, although they lived here no longer, yet they were not gone.

We cannot be compelled, by you or your betters, little neophyte, but we shall lend you what you ask. This forges a debt between us. We shall remember it.

He opened his mouth to protest that he did not want their gifts, but it was too late. He had asked and he was given what he asked for. The cold that before had shrieked in his skull now hammered into his chest, infused him. He keened with it, burned with it. It shattered its way into him.

He had so little time. On his back, in the bowels of that terrible place, he called out, not with his own voice, but with the vicarious power that filled him.

Cheerwell!

Twenty-two

It was as though a hand, chill as ice, had placed its fingers on her forehead, and Che awoke, or tried to wake. Something caught her, like a spider's web, halfway between sleep's abyss and the conscious heights of the waking world.

A voice was speaking to her. *Cheerwell!* A voice she should know from somewhere, and yet supported by a vast chorus of whispers, and all of them also saying her name.

'What . . . what is it? Who . . . ?' She knew she did not speak, and yet her words went out.

Listen to me. You must hear me. And again that half-familiar tone that she could not place.

'I hear you.'

Do not fear, Cheerwell, for I am coming for you, to repay what is owed. I am coming to free you.

'I don't understand . . .' She felt as though she was on some rushing, surging wave, being whisked away beyond her own control. She had no sense of place or time. The darkness was thick and absolute.

You must tell me where you are, Cheerwell, said the voice – or voices – to her. *Where are you? Let me find you.*

And at last the concept came to her and she trawled her mind, feeling even as she did that she was rising towards the waking world where things like this could not be.

'Myna. Going to Myna.'

And, even as she spoke, she felt a withdrawing, and she

was suddenly rushing on towards wakefulness, pelting pell-mell for it, and at the last moment the owner of that voice came to her.

Achaeos!

'Achaeos!' And she woke with her own voice and his name ringing in her ears.

She opened her eyes on the storage bay that was their cell. Salma was sitting cross-legged across from her and his eyes were open also, as though just this moment he had been snatched from sleep. The Butterfly, Grief in Chains, lay on her side, but she too had pushed herself up onto one elbow, her white eyes wide. 'Night brother . . .' she said quietly.

'Che, are you all right?' Salma asked.

'I don't know.' Che found she was panting heavily, as though she had been running. 'What just happened?'

'There was something here,' Salma said definitely.

'Something . . . what? Why did she . . . ?' She turned to the Butterfly. 'Why did you say what you just said.'

Grief in Chains just stared at her.

'I felt . . . Salma, tell me!' Che pleaded.

'I can't,' he said. 'I don't know enough, and you wouldn't believe me anyway.'

'Are you going to tell me it was . . . It was just a dream, that's all.'

Salma's habitual smile found his face at last. 'Of course.'

Grief in Chains sat up fully. 'You were touched,' she said. 'Darkness touched you.' She seemed visibly upset. She had spoken very little during the previous day's journeying, but when Salma reached a hand out to her she had clung to it.

'It was just a . . . a dream,' Che insisted. *A bad dream or a good one?* she asked herself, and received no answer.

Abruptly someone banged on the hatch. 'You keep it quiet down in there!' barked one of the two soldiers

Thalric had brought along. 'You don't want to wake the captain up, that's for sure.'

Che closed her mouth and then frowned. 'Wake? It's . . . it's already day . . .'

'Day?' Salma asked her, puzzled.

'It's light.'

'Che, it's dark.'

She goggled at him. She could see him so clearly. She could see Grief clearly, and also the bare walls of their prison. The light was strange, though. It was like strong moonlight, leached of colour. Even Grief's ever-changing skin and hair were just a motley of greys to her.

Salma pointed upwards. Lining two walls were a row of slits, and when she had bedded down for the night there had been a faint light there still, as the dusk passed into darkness.

The light was not coming from there, for they were no brighter than the rest of the room. The strange light was not coming from anywhere.

'Salma,' she said slowly. 'I think I've found the Art – the Ancestor Art. Or else it's found me. Salma, how did *you* first know that you could . . . ?'

'I could jump into the air and stay there,' he said blandly, but she was too excited to care about his sarcasm, because she could see clearly and it was still night. This was a Beetle Art, she knew, though not a common one, and why should it not finally manifest in this closed box of a place?

And yet there were others who could see in the dark from their very births, needing no Art for it, who were truly creatures of darkness and the night. She had met one recently and his blood had been on her hands.

Night brother, the Butterfly had said, and she had dreamt the voice of Achaeos, remembered somehow from that strange, brief encounter.

She leant back against the wall and discovered that

there was a patina of frost slowly melting across it. Yet the night outside had been overcast, not chill at all.

They crept back towards the camp before dawn, Tisamon padding silently in front, and Tynisa trailing behind. For her it had been an unreal night. Tisamon was a hard man to keep up with, and yet she had shadowed him all the way to Asta. Together they had passed through the ring of sentries, dodging the great lamp, the beam of which passed sometimes across the temporary streets of the muster town. All the while there had been not one word spoken between them. Tisamon had, at first, barely seemed to know that she was there, but as the night had progressed, something had grown between them, some wordless commonality. His stealthy poise and tread had slowly changed to include her in his progress. Where he had once looked both ways, silent in the shadows of a storehouse or barracks, now he would look left while she looked right. He had eased into a trust of her, a confidence that she was up to the task, and all still without ever acknowledging her. Then had come the slave pits, and he had stepped back and kept watch while she, who knew the pair, had sought out Che and Salma.

The two hunters had developed an understanding, it seemed, and, as they had come back through the forest fringe, perhaps more than that. The darkness within the forest was as dense as midnight, not the near-dawn they had left outside, but she could still see enough in the half-light to make out the trees.

And more than the trees. She stopped suddenly, and Tisamon halted at the same instant, looking straight at her.

'Yes,' he said, 'you see them too, don't you?'

She was not sure whether she really had until he said it, but there were figures there, amid the trees. Not close, not moving, and in the gloom even her eyes fought to distinguish their outlines. Then they became clearer, or perhaps closer, and she stopped trying to make them out. They were human, or might have been. They had the poise and stance of Mantis-kinden and yet, as she had glimpsed them, they seemed to be formed like praying mantids, with gleaming chitin and glittering eyes, and yet again there was gnarled wood and thorns worked into them.

Tynisa stopped then and turned her eyes away. 'I do not ... I cannot be seeing this.' A Collegium-raised girl, from a world of rationality and science, for all that she understood none of it.

'Your blood says otherwise,' was Tisamon's quiet reply, before they moved on in silence once more.

It took a while of tracking to locate Stenwold's new campsite. When they stepped into sight the Beetle looked up at them and she saw the brief hope dashed in his face.

'Any sign?' he asked quietly.

Tisamon shook his head and went to sit by the dying fire.

'They keep their prisoners in pits there, and we looked in every one,' Tynisa explained. 'No sign. They could have been in one of the buildings. There was no way of knowing.'

She went to sit next to Tisamon, but he looked up at her with a face utterly devoid of invitation, only his usual cold mask with which he confronted the world, the face of a man expecting a fight. Their shared silent communion of the night was gone, and in his eyes there was no admission that it had ever existed. Mere minutes before they had been moving as one between the trees. Now his eyes were unwriting it all, remaking each memory in his own image. She felt a bitter anger well up in her.

What was all that about, then? What did we share earlier, and where did we leave it? But she could voice no questions, and he would give no answers. Her fists clenched and unclenched and, not for the first time, she wished that she could talk to Che right now. Che was the only person she could unburden herself to.

All the more reason to rescue her.

She rose and went to sit beside Stenwold instead.

'Why did you move the camp?' Tisamon asked. 'Not that it was difficult to find.'

'We had some nocturnal visitors.' Stenwold shook his head heavily. 'A patrol chased us into the woods.' He saw Tisamon flinch and he frowned. 'They're just woods, Tisamon. Trees. You get them all over.'

'Are they indeed?' The Mantis regarded him. 'And so you two just crept into the Darakyon and crept out again?'

Stenwold shared an unhappy glance with Totho. 'Well . . . you can imagine me and the boy here at night in the middle of a forest . . .' A quick look at Tisamon showed the Mantis was not satisfied with that. 'What can I say?'

'I don't know. What *can* you say?'

'It was dark. There were sounds. Woods at night are . . . not my favourite place,' Stenwold said defensively. *There were sounds. Oh there were sounds all right.* He wondered if the last dregs of the panic showed again on his face, in that moment: he and Totho blundering in circles, trying to retrace their path. There had been no path. Behind them had been only briars, until they had found a pitch-black clearing by feeling with their hands, a clearing from which there was *no way out at all*. They had gone from tree to gnarled tree, lancing their gloves on thorns, leaving drops of their blood smeared on the bark, and they had gone around and around in the darkness until Totho had tried to light a lantern, and to the pits with the Wasps. Stenwold remembered that moment most of all, for the steel lighter would not catch, just sparks and sparks that illuminated nothing but themselves, and in the silence afterwards they had heard an almost musical sound, from all around and far away, that could have been the forest breathing.

'We had . . . all sorts of games running through the woods at night,' Stenwold finished weakly, and heard Tisamon's almost triumphant snort.

'Where is the Moth?' the Mantis asked.

'Achaeos?' Stenwold looked at his hands. 'He wasn't with us. I can't imagine the Wasps caught him. He can fly and see in the dark, after all. Still, if he's around, he's still keeping his distance. He never did want to go into the forest.'

Stenwold and Totho had sat down to wait for dawn, while the Darakyon creaked and rasped about them, lightless and bitterly cold. The time they had spent there, unable to sleep, nerves constantly fraying at each groan and snap, had seemed too long to possibly fit inside only one night.

Then it had come to them. They had heard it, the slow, careful approach of something very large. There had been the rattle of Totho trying to load his crossbow blind, and Stenwold had taken up his sword, hopeless in the darkness. *I do not believe in Tisamon's folk tales*, he had told himself, but traitor logic had grinned at him and said, *Why think of ghosts at all? There are many things belonging to the material world that can kill a man.* In his mind's eye he had envisaged that stealthy approach as a mantis, an insect ten feet long with huge night-seeing eyes and neatly folded killing arms. He had held out his sword invisibly before him, hearing Totho's fumbling grow increasingly desperate and hearing the *thing*, whatever it was, grow closer.

They had run, the pair of them. In the same moment, as if by agreement, they had bolted, and the clearing was suddenly permeable again. They had bolted through briars and needling thorns and not stopped, and they had run until, without warning, there were no trees around them and they were half a mile east of their original camp. They had then spent the scant time before dawn finding the automotive again.

'It's just a wood,' he said, voice sounding hollow to his own ears. 'In the dark, the imagination will always run riot. We were in no real danger, two armed men. It's Achaeos I'm worried about.'

'He might just have absconded,' Totho said darkly. 'This isn't his fight.'

'When he comes back . . .' Stenwold said, and paused. 'When he comes back, because if he doesn't we may have to make a different choice, we have to make a decision. We don't know whether Che and Salma are being held at Asta, or whether Achaeos now is, if things have gone really badly, or whether they've already gone east, deeper into the Empire. If they're being kept apart from other prisoners, well, that could prove good or bad.'

'What do you mean?' asked Totho.

'I mean that it probably suggests they've been set aside for questioning,' said Stenwold. 'I'm sorry. It could just mean they're being given special treatment, held more securely, I don't know, but . . . Tisamon and I know how the Wasps work.'

'Maybe . . . I should go in tomorrow night,' said Totho reluctantly. 'I mean, I'm not so . . . with the creeping around, but I've got the tools to force a lock.'

Stenwold grimaced. 'It may even come to that.'

And a new voice asked, 'Where or what is Myna?'

Achaeos had returned. He looked dead on his feet, his grey skin gone deathly pale, eyes narrowed down to white slits.

'Where in the name of reason have you been all night?' Stenwold demanded of him.

Achaeos regarded him coldly. 'Myna,' he said. 'Does this name mean anything to you?'

'It does.' Tisamon stood, his metal claw unfolding from the line of his arm.

'She is going to Myna,' the Moth said. 'They are not in the town down there.'

'How did you find this out?' Stenwold asked him.

'Old ways.' Achaeos shrugged. 'Ways you wouldn't understand.'

Tisamon and Stenwold exchanged looks in which their mutual memory of Myna was unearthed, and neither of them looked happy with it.

'This is ridiculous,' Totho said. 'He *can't* know that.'

'They are gone to Myna,' Achaeos insisted stubbornly.

'He could have . . . crept into Asta,' Tynisa said slowly, 'and overheard. But you didn't, did you?'

'There are ways,' said Tisamon. 'Masters of the Grey,' he added.

'Servants of the Green,' Achaeos completed, as if by rote. 'Yes, there are ways.' *If only you knew what I have risked, to take those ways.* 'So, Mantis, you at least believe me.'

There was a very swift movement that Achaeos could not follow, and a moment later the thin, cold edge of Tisamon's blade was pressing against his neck. He held very still, nearly swallowing his heart inside, but outside he managed to cling to his customary aloofness.

'I am no fool, nor am I quick to trust,' Tisamon told him. 'There *are* ways, yes, and one of them is to be in the pay of our enemies. Moths are subtle. It would not surprise me to find you playing such a game. Especially a game that led to Myna. What better place to lure Stenwold, in order to catch him?'

'I speak only what I have seen, Servant of the Green. If you know my kinden so well, you should know not to bandy threats against me,' Achaeos said defiantly, but the blade twitched against his skin, the faintest prick of blood welling.

'Don't think that you can frighten me,' warned Tisamon, although to Stenwold's ear, who had known him so long, there was a slight uncertainty to his voice.

'I was not an assassin the last time you drew on me,'

said Achaeos, 'and I am not a spy now. I could tell you one thing more that should convince you, but it is for your ears alone.'

Without moving his blade from its resting place, Tisamon leant close suspiciously. As he heard the Moth's whispered sentence, the others saw him flinch from it. At once the blade was clear of the Moth's neck, folding back along its owner's arm.

'He's telling the truth,' the Mantis announced.

'Just from a bit of mystic posturing?' Totho demanded. 'Listen, Che could be in one of those buildings right now. They could be about to actually torture her. And now we're supposed to . . . just go away to some whole other city, all because of some dream you had or something? Stenwold, you're not going to listen to this rubbish, surely?'

To his alarm Stenwold was not looking dismissive, only troubled. 'There is more in the world than we know,' he said quietly. 'I have been a long time trying to stave off that conclusion, but in the end I have had to admit there are things I have seen that I cannot account for. Tisamon, you truly believe this?'

A short nod was the Mantis's only response.

'Tynisa?'

She gave Tisamon a narrow look. 'I'm with Totho on this. We should at least take another turn around Asta first.'

'Well, in Collegium we abide by the vote, and it looks as though I get the deciding one,' said Stenwold. 'I'm out of my depth here, with this talk of arcana, but logic tells me that Asta is a staging post, a muster ground. If you had important prisoners, maybe you would indeed move them to the nearest proper city. Which is Myna – of unhappy memory. Tisamon . . .' Stenwold hesitated, biting his lip.

'Speak,' Tisamon said.

'I . . . find it difficult to hold to what I cannot understand.'

'You always did.'

'But I never had so much riding on a decision before. What did he say to you, the Moth? What did he say to convince you?' He glanced at Achaeos, who was impassive as always.

'I cannot think that it would help you to know.'

'Please tell me,' asked Stenwold, and the Mantis shrugged.

'He said that those who told him they had gone to Myna also said that they stayed their hands from us because of the badge that I bear.' He touched it for a moment, the gold circle-and-sword pin of the Weapons-masters. 'And I earned this, Stenwold. I earned it in blood and fire.'

For a long time Stenwold stared at him, before transferring his gaze to the others. Totho still looked rebellious but something in Tynisa's face, some recent experience, had changed her mind. He gave a great sigh. 'We'll go to Myna.' He had never thought that he would see Myna again, nor had he wished to.

It was a jumbled vision they had of it, landing at an airfield overflown by yellow and black flags. The cumbersome heliopter shuddered and groaned at the last, settling too fast and creaking with the effort, despite the repairs that Aagen had grounded it for last night.

The savagery of daylight, after the dimness of their holding cell, left the two of them staggering and blinking. Salma could not shield his eyes and so Che put her hands over them for him, knowing how much more sensitive they were than hers. Grief in Chains did not flinch or blink but gazed straight at the sun with her all-white eyes and glowed with it, drinking it in. She had paled and pined in the last day, but now she shone as though she had a piece of the sun inside her, and for a second the Wasp soldiers stepped back, and every head on the airfield turned to stare.

Then Thalric was hustling them, ordering the soldiers to take them in hand. They were rough with her and with Salma, but Grief they escorted with something more uncertain. She was beautiful, Che had to admit; she was perfect. Colours flowed across her skin like silk.

Che received only a confused, blurring impression of Myna. First the airstrip, where most of the traffic was military; then onto narrow streets and being hauled, tripping, down runs of little steps; brief glimpses of the citizens, men and women of a bluish-grey cast of skin, not quite Beetle-kinden, not quite Ant – another new race for her – who went about their daily lot with heads downcast. There were plenty of Wasps, too: most were soldiers, and others not in armour were probably still soldiers, judging from what Thalric had said about his people. Other kinden wore the imperial colours: plenty of Fly-kinden running errands, or sometimes watching from a high vantage point, with a bow and quiver on their backs. There were more, too: lean, long men and women resembling the musician who had been a slave with them in Brutan's convoy. These went barefoot but wore yellow shirts and black breeches, like some poor imitation of their Wasp masters, and they carried staves and odd, two-pronged daggers. From the brief glimpse she had, they looked like guards, city watch.

But of course, she realized, as the shadow of a great wall fell across her, *it would be considered menial for Wasps to police their subjects, unless there is some great need for it.* These strange sentries must be drafted in from some other imperial conquest.

And then she looked up at the edifice that loomed above them, and she choked, because it was ugly beyond belief. All around it the buildings of Myna conformed to a low and careful style, flat-roofed and spartan like Ant-city designs. This *thing* was so utterly alien here that it must have been Wasp architecture: a great tiered monstrosity that looked so out of place it might have been dropped from the sky. There was a broad flight of steps at the fore that narrowed upwards to a door that, even as they approached, still looked tastelessly oversized. They could have driven a fair-sized automotive through it, if they could only have got it up the steps. The door was flanked by two statues, which matched neither each other, the building nor the city. One of them was something abstract, the work of some madman or genius who had made the stone flow like water under his hands. The other showed a warrior in strange armour, and Salma missed a step when he saw it and almost fell back-wards. From that reaction Che realized it must be from his own people, war loot from the recent campaign.

Brief glimpses of the interior, where shafts of sunlight fell like spears, and there was a gallery hall like a museum that valued its exhibits by the amount of gilt they sported rather than their meaning, and then they were descending underground again. Grief was taken off one way by Aagen, with a final backwards glance at Salma, then Che's chin was seized, her head tilted painfully back to look up into Thalric's face.

'I have business,' the Wasp told her, 'and when I am done we have a conversation to finish, so think on it.'

She was still thinking on it when the cell door closed behind her.

On the other side, the free side, of her cell door, Thalric took a moment to consider his options. The Rekef Inlander had sent him to Myna to have a word with his old friend Ulther. Myna was one of the cities supplying the war against the Lowlands, the war that Thalric had been preparing for a long time, and apparently it was not pulling its weight. Was it really due to Ulther being greedy and corrupt? It only mattered that the Rekef thought it so. They did not trust Ulther, which meant that neither should Thalric.

On their way to the governor's palace he had been carefully watching the crowd. Still, he had nearly missed it, for Fly-kinden got everywhere, after all. That was why the Rekef made use of them. Because he had been watching, he had seen te Berro, watching him in return. The Rekef had sent Thalric, but they did not trust *him* either. There was clearly a choice coming up in the near future which he was loath to make.

Thalric liked life simple, which many would think was a strange attitude for a spymaster. The simplicity he craved was to know exactly what side he was on. This was why he had thrown himself into the Rekef Outlander so diligently. The Empire was right and the quarrelsome, disorganized and barbaric foreigners were wrong. Once you had that simple truth in your head, so many problems just melted away.

But the problems had just been waiting for their moment, he now saw.

Ulther and he, they went way back. Thalric had been aged fifteen at Myna, the most junior of junior officers. They had given him a squad of ten men and put him near the front when the gates fell. He had acquitted himself adequately.

There had been a colonel commanding the assault. At this remove Thalric found he couldn't remember the man's name. He had died, anyway. The Soldier Beetle-kinden of Myna hadn't done it. Some roving assassin with an anti-Empire brief had played that role. Rumour suggested it had been a Commonweal plot. Whatever the reason, Major Ulther had taken charge of the street-to-street fighting. The Mynans weren't as tricky as Ant-kinden, no mindlinks here to coordinate perfect attacks and defences, but every one of the bastards had been out fighting, even the children. It had been dealt with in the usual way – cause enough destruction and hold a knife to the leaders' throats. Ulther had caused the destruction and held the knife, and in Thalric's view he had done it brilliantly, so Myna had been taken in half the time, with half the loss of life.

And then of course the street-to-street patrols, rooting out the resistance and hunting down the ringleaders, had been the very action to test the young Thalric, so that by the time the city was firmly in Empire hands he had been made a full lieutenant and the envy of his peers. Ulther had then taken him into his confidence, his inner circle, so Thalric had learned a great deal about the Empire and how it worked.

Ulther had put forward his name to the Rekef, or so he always believed. The irony was not lost on Thalric. He could cling to the hope, he supposed, that the rumours were misplaced and that Ulther remained a pillar of imperial loyalty, but what were the chances of that?

A chill went through him. Even if Ulther had not put a foot wrong in seventeen years, if Thalric went back to the Rekef with that report what would they do? What would they think of him? Would they have sent him at all if they had not wanted a foregone conclusion? Who exactly was under the lens here, anyway?

Too many questions and too little solid ground. He went in search of Aagen and found him supervising the loading of his flier.

'Lieutenant Aagen.'

Aagen threw him a preoccupied salute, while leafing through a manifest.

'Lieutenant, I want you to arrange for another pilot to take this machine back to Asta.'

'Thalric?' Aagen turned quickly enough at that. 'I mean, sir?'

'I'm going to require your services here. Consider yourself deputized, Aagen,' Thalric continued.

'But—'

Thalric put a hand on his shoulder, guiding him to one side. 'Listen, Aagen, I've known you for a long time . . .'

'Yes?'

'I need someone here I can trust.'

Aagen glanced over his shoulder at the local soldiers supervising the loading. 'But the governor—'

'*Not* the governor or his men, understand?'

The artificer's face fell. 'Oh spit, like that, is it? Listen, I'm Engineering Corps. I'm not one of your sneaks.'

Thalric smiled. 'Who knows, Lieutenant, maybe you'll be promoted. By the way, you've done some interrogation work, haven't you, as an artificer?'

Aagen nodded, though his expression showed he was not happy about admitting it.

'You might want to revise your notes then,' Thalric said grimly. 'I may require your services.'

They were glad of the automotive in the end, with the exception of Achaeos, who would have happily abandoned it. The roads had become impossible for between Myna and Asta there was a constant traffic of black and gold. However the stilt-legged machine that Scuto had found for them was more than capable of making its stuttering way cross-country, with Totho and Stenwold winding the clockwork twice a day.

Are we inside the Empire now? When did we cross the border? But it was a false premise, of course. Stenwold knew that maps took boundaries that shifted like water and tried to set them in stone. The borders were where the Empire wished them to be, unless somebody took a sufficient stand.

And will they finally take a stand? When I go to the Assembly and tell them that the little stopover of Asta is now a nest of soldiers? Or will they just shut their ears again and throw me out?

The land lying east of the Darakyon was rugged, home to a few families of goat herders or beetle drovers. Off the road itself there was no imperial stamp to be seen. *What could they do to further oppress this poverty?* On one occasion, Stenwold and the others shared a fire with some of the locals: quiet, sullen men with blue-grey Mynan skin. There were many halfbreeds amongst them, mixing blood of Beetle-kinden or of Wasp. They seemed inheritors of an unhappiness that no shifting of political boundaries would change, but they asked no questions and they had fresh meat. This made them more than tolerable fireside companions.

When the imperial patrol did at last find them, they were prepared. Tisamon, Tynisa and the Moth had melted away, ready with sword and claw if matters turned difficult. Stenwold and Totho had meanwhile waited patiently as a half-dozen of the Light Airborne fell to earth around them.

This was when Stenwold had been sure that they were now inside the Empire. If they had been beyond its borders then there would have been blood, and in the confusion of ambush it would have been blood on both sides, likely as not, but clearly these men were bored, sent out from some convoy just to make work for them in conquered territory. They saw only a tramp artificer and his apprentice riding on their antiquated machine, the two of them looking for skilled work in Myna. Was there much work in Myna, Stenwold asked? The Wasp sergeant had shrugged, then made enough loose threats to justify a small offering of imperial coin. A moment later the patrol was airborne again, and receding into the distance.

'Why didn't they arrest us?' Totho had demanded.

'Arrest who? An old artificer and his boy?'

'But you're Stenwold Maker. They must know—'

'Know what? Who's Stenwold Maker? I doubt every imperial soldier carries a picture of me in his pocket, Totho. Besides, they wouldn't know we're coming, because . . .' He had turned to see Achaeos and the rest now approaching, the Moth's face invisible within his cowl. 'Because there is no way that we ourselves could have known,' Stenwold had finished awkwardly.

They halted the wheezing automotive within sight of Myna itself, counting on sufficient distance to hide them. Myna was built on a hillside with the airfield at its highest point, as Stenwold and Tisamon had good cause to remember, so they made their vantage point on another hill, looking across a lower rise to the city.

Stenwold had his telescope out from his pack, the dust of years brushed off it only recently, and was now squinting through it at their objective keenly.

'The walls are refortified. Looks like there's less artillery though. I suppose they're not so much worried about an actual siege as internal trouble. The Wasp stripes are flying from the towers . . .' he carefully moved his point of view across the city, or as much as he could see of it, 'and someone's built the world's biggest wart of a building where the old Consensus used to stand. Demonstration of power, I suppose. And the airfield looks busy, so I'd guess this is a major stopover on the road to Asta and the Lowlands.' He took the device from his eye and carefully folded it away. 'This is going to be difficult.'

'It always was,' Tisamon confirmed, and the two of them looked at their younger companions. A Spider, a Moth and a half-caste artificer – not the most inconspicuous of travelling companions.

'I'll get inside—' the Mantis started, but Stenwold cut him off.

'Not this time. This one's mine.'

'Stenwold,' Tisamon said reasonably, 'you've absolutely no gift for creeping about.'

'You forget my great advantage though. I'm Beetle-kinden and my race live all over the Empire. A tramp artificer can get work anywhere there are machines.'

'They'll be looking out for you,' Tynisa warned him.

'Probably,' Stenwold agreed, 'but in a city that sees such a lot of traffic, it's a job and a half to spot one man, and because they're expecting either one man or a whole group, I'll take Totho along with me as my apprentice. A tinker and prentice should be inconspicuous enough, all right, Totho?'

The young artificer swallowed nervously, but nodded.

'And what will you do once you're inside?' Tisamon asked.

'Start dropping names,' Stenwold said. 'There must be someone left that we used to know, and if there's any kind of resistance movement, they'll undoubtedly be involved.'

'Be very careful,' Tisamon warned him. 'You don't know for sure that they'll welcome you with open arms.'

'They've no reason to, but I don't see any other choice. We can't exactly break into the prisons of Myna on our own. When I've made contact there, we'll sort out the best way of getting you three in. If there's no easy way, then at least Totho and I – who, as you say, aren't built for the shadow stuff – will be inside the city. After that, you three can make your own way. Agreed?'

'And meet you where? I don't want the same mess as in Helleron,' Tynisa said. 'Especially in a city riddled with Wasps.'

'There are two plazas in Myna, or at least there were. At the east plaza there used to be a merchant exchange run by an old Scorpion-kinden named Hokiak. He might even run it still.'

Tisamon remembered. 'That was a low place.'

'I hope it still is,' Stenwold said. 'Hokiak was a black marketeer before the Wasps moved in, and if we're lucky he or his successor still is. That sort of trade is useful to all sort of malcontents and revolutionaries, so it's a good place to start looking. I'll leave word there for you, if I can.'

Twenty-three

It was a throne room. The design was copied from the imperial chambers at Capitas, and Thalric was uncertain whether this counted as honour or presumption. The long room had an arcade of pillars to either side, and shafts had been cut into the high ceiling above to make a further double row of columns composed solely of slanting sunlight. The pale stone was set off by the ochre of the pillars, while a mural running across the circuit of three walls was painted in a style that Thalric knew to be local.

A servant youth in plain dark clothes, also local, announced him at the doorway, and now Thalric began the long trek towards the seven seats at the far end. The Emperor held court at the centre of eleven thrones, of course, but this display in Myna was still something of a liberty.

Only five of these seats were occupied. Ulther lounged in the central throne with three other Wasp-kinden on one side and a Beetle on the other, all watching the newcomer's approach intently.

'Thalric!' Ulther's voice, though not loudly spoken, rang the entire length of the chamber, showing that the builder had done his work well. 'Captain Thalric, as I sit here! Now tell me, how well have you done for yourself, since we parted company?'

Thalric saluted smartly before the tiered dais, although it took considerable skill to keep his initial reaction to the man's changed appearance off his face. *It's been more than ten years*, he reminded himself sharply but, excuses aside, being governor of Myna obviously suited the old man too well. That his hair was white now, instead of grey, was time's due, but his belt now strained to keep his waist in check, and even the tailor's skill was not enough to have the fine gold shirt conceal the man's bulk. There were two chins resting above the topaz gorget, and a face that had been merely heavy when Myna had fallen was jowly now.

His hesitation was noticed. 'Oh sit, sit,' Ulther insisted without rancour. 'When you're my age even you will want to find a more sedentary way of serving the Empire – and then see where it gets you. The way I look at it, if I had simply gone home to my family and managed the farm, then I would look just as bad and nobody would mind. I don't see why things should be so different just because I'm on public display all the time.'

Thalric ascended the steps and found a vacant seat, eyes flicking across to the others there.

'Captain Thalric served with me during the conquest, and a fine officer too,' Ulther explained for their benefit. 'Thalric, these here are my advisors, at least for the present. Captain Oltan is Quartermaster Corps, and Captain Rauth is Intelligence.' The two Wasps nodded towards Thalric suspiciously. 'And then Masters Draywain and Freigen, who are with the Consortium of the Honest.'

The Consortium was the Empire's attempt to regulate trade but, from what Thalric had heard from his Rekef contacts, it was a narrow battle over exactly who was regulating whom. He gave the Beetle-kinden and the bored-looking, middle-aged Wasp a nod. *Perhaps it's one of these who is responsible for strangling the supply lines. Perhaps I can exonerate Ulther after all.*

And is that what the Rekef wants?

'What brings you here, Captain? Come seeking promotion?' Ulther grinned at him, and that grin, for all that aged and fleshy face, remained wholly familiar. Inwardly

Thalric twisted. He had wanted a private audience with this man, a chance to speak frankly.

'A change of pace, Colonel,' he said easily. 'It's been a long time on the front line for me. I've been asking for a chance to rest my feet for months. They sent me here. Do I get my wish?'

'We're always busy here, Captain,' Ulther said. 'However,' he added, avuncular, 'I'm sure I can find you a tenday to lick your wounds. Make yourself at home in my city.' When Thalric raised an eyebrow at that, Ulther's smile broadened. 'I've got Myna firmly in the palm of my hand, Thalric, and when it twitches I squeeze. It's a simple lesson, though they never do seem to learn it.' He clapped his hands and a moment later a dozen servants came in from a door behind them, bearing trays with flasks and goblets. 'Let me show you what Myna can offer, shall we?'

'I'm surprised, in a way, that you've not moved inwards, towards the capital,' Thalric said. The servants attending them were all women, he noted, and all of them young. Not one of them was Mynan, either, which was undoubtedly a wise precaution for body slaves. Ulther had obviously ransacked the Empire for servants pleasing to the eye, and there were even a couple of Wasp-kinden amongst them.

'Who would they get to replace me?' Ulther took a goblet and watched appreciatively as a Spider-kinden slave poured it full. 'I know Myna better than any, even better than the pestilential natives themselves. I keep a lid on the pot, you see, boil as it may. They would have risen up a few years back when Maynes did. They were all set, but I knew it in advance. Crucify a handful on the crossed pikes, arrest a few more, and then the families of the ringleaders packed off as slaves to Great Delve. A firm slap early on will stop a tantrum later.'

'Very creditable,' agreed Thalric. He helped himself from the tray of sweetmeats proffered to him, glancing up at the slave who served him. She was one of his own kinden, fair-haired and handsome, but she kept her eyes lowered, as slaves should.

'These two,' he said, indicating the pair of Wasp slaves. 'Objectors or Indebted?'

'Indebted, to the best of my knowledge. There's a lot of them on the market these days, especially from the capital itself. Terrible, terrible situation.' Ulther's sympathy was transparent. 'Still, I try to give 'em a good home, where I can.'

The young woman remained very still, and Thalric wondered what trauma she was now thinking back to: sold to pay her husband's debts, or her father's?

'I'll send her to your quarters later, if you want,' Ulther offered. 'We might as well make your stay here a memorable one.'

'I'll take you up on that,' Thalric said. He sensed the woman stiffen slightly: a Wasp's pride against being passed from hand to hand like a chattel. She *was* a chattel, though, merely a slave and a commodity. There was no more to it than that.

Thalric raised a goblet, and he and Ulther touched rims across the face of Captain Oltan.

'Here's to "memorable",' said Thalric, but he felt sad as he said it. *Memorable, yes, but for all the wrong reasons.*

Ulther settled more comfortably into his padded throne. 'Speaking of memorable, or so I hope, I have now a little entertainment for you: a new jewel in my collection. I even understand that you yourself escorted her to my city.'

Thalric raised an eyebrow, even as he filed the repeated *my city* away for later perusal.

In answer, Ulther clapped his hands once more and the serving slaves retreated several steps behind the crescent of chairs. A moment later two men walked in, of local appearance. One was white-haired and bearded, and he cradled a stringed instrument that Thalric did not recognize, something like a stretched lyre. The other was little more than a boy and carried a small drum. They made themselves unobtrusive amongst the pillars and sat waiting. Thalric had already guessed what would come next, for a pair of soldiers then led the Butterfly-kinden dancer into the hall. Aagen's special delivery. Inwardly, he made another note.

'Well at least take the chain off her,' Ulther directed. 'She's not a performing felbling.'

One of the soldiers closed the door whilst the other carefully unlatched the chain from the woman's collar.

Thalric sipped his wine, which was sweeter than his taste preferred, and settled in for a wait. He had never much appreciated dancers or the like. He had caught a glimpse of this one performing before and she was good, but it was not his choice of entertainment.

The woman, named Grief in Chains as he recalled, stepped out until she was within a shaft of sunlight. It fed her skin so that the shifting colours there glowed and burned. From their unseen niche the musicians struck up, a slow picking of the strings at first, the drum a low but complex patter.

Grief in Chains moved, and she took the sunlight with her. It sparkled on her skin and ghosted like mist in the air behind her. And she began to dance.

Thalric maintained his lack of interest until the music changed tempo, the pace quickening bar after bar until she was spinning and leaping across from sunbeam to sunbeam. Then she was in the air, the iridescent shimmer of her Art-wings unfolding about her, and his breath caught despite himself.

She had always been chained before, so the slavers had not seen half of what she could do. With the music soaring and skittering all around them, the plucked notes becoming hard as glass, the drum like a dozen busy feet, she danced and spun, coasting in space and swooping at the pillars' tops. She seemed to embrace the very air, to mime love to it, and Thalric had never seen the like before. Even he, for the moments of that airborne ballet, even he was touched.

Then she was in bowed obeisance again, and the music had struck its final moment, and Thalric shook off, somewhat irritably, the net that had been on him. Looking at his fellows, though, he saw a wide-eyed rapture, and nowhere more so than on Ulther's face. What had he paid, and what had he done, to catch this jewel? More, what would he have to do to keep her from his fellows?

A spark of insight came to Thalric then, and it cut him deeply, but it was the answer to a question he had not known to ask.

Memorable. He watched the Butterfly girl as they chained her again, studying her suddenly with renewed interest.

It was rare for Thalric to be able to mix business with pleasure but, still, he took his pleasure first, moving quickeningly atop the Wasp-kinden slave-girl, sourly aware that her responses were born of a need to appear willing, and that the pleasure, such as it was, was all his. Even this pleasure was a distant thing to him, a need that he could watch and analyse even as it was being fulfilled. As he reached his peak Thalric was thinking wryly of the fleshpots of Helleron, whose varied depravity he would now miss, and that this was the first time in some years that he had lain with one of his own kinden.

She went to leave then, sitting on the edge of the bed with her back to him, gathering up her clothes. When he touched her arm, she would not look at him – did not, in fact, until he told her, 'Stay.'

'I should be returning. They'll ask—'

'It wasn't a request.'

And that got her attention. When she looked at him

there was something left, after all, of the Empire in her face: a pride that had been battered but not quite broken down. She still possessed internal walls that her servitude had not breached.

'What's your name, woman?' he asked, sitting up. He saw her eyes flick from his face to the jagged scar that flowered beneath his right collarbone.

'Hreya,' she said quietly. 'They say you're with the Rekef.'

'Let them say what they want.' As Ulther had started him off on that road, it was only to be expected that rumour here would be rife. 'How did you come to this, Hreya?'

Her expression suggested that such questions would have been better asked before, but he lived his life to maxims of efficiency, in this as all else. At last she revealed, 'My father gambled. You know the laws, sir.'

They were harsh laws, carried over by the Empire from the days when there were nothing but three score squabbling hill tribes to call themselves the Wasp people. Women were property – of either father or husband – and as such they were prey for creditors, to be sold into marriage or into slavery. Thalric would never think to speak against imperial law, of course, but it was still a tradition he could have done without. The mothers of the Wasp-kinden deserved better, he thought. They might be women, but they were still of the race. They shared in the Empire's destiny.

'How many of you does Ulther keep to hand?' he asked.

'Almost thirty, I think, at last count,' she told him. 'For the use of himself and his guests.'

'Any locals?'

'Not yet, sir. Sir, I'm cold.'

The utter indignity of her having to seek his permission to clothe herself, and the fact that she said the words with a straight back, with the shame sloughing off her, touched him. 'Dress, by all means. I just want to talk a little. About the governor, if you will?'

As she gathered her gown to her she gave him a hooded look, and he added, 'None of this will reach him.'

'You're his friend, sir. From long ago.'

'And I'm interested in him as he is now. You can speak freely about him to me. Unless you'd rather I tell him you disappointed me.'

Her expression hardened. 'And if I tell him you were asking questions, sir?'

He smiled, because she had so very little but she was willing to make use of it. 'Perhaps I want him to know. Although he may not thank you.' He saw from her reaction that he was right. Ulther would not welcome his body slaves playing spy for him unless he had asked them to. 'Tell me about his guests, then.'

That was safer ground. 'They are officers, mostly, and merchants of the Consortium, sir. He entertains them.'

'Oltan and Rauth, that lot. Quartermaster and intelligencer, aren't they?'

'So they say.' He had been listening for that, the slight scorn in her voice.

'You are a good subject of the Empire, are you not?' he said softly.

'I am a slave.'

'But you know what serves the Empire and what does not, even so,' he pressed. 'So tell me, not what *they* say, but what *you* say.' He would have offered her money, perhaps, but slaves had no right to possess money. She could never spend it without raising suspicion. He would have to find a harder currency. 'Speak to me honestly and openly, and I will do what I can for you. This I promise.'

Her look revealed not one grain of trust at first, but he let her read his face, his eyes. She was desperate, although she herself had not known it until now. He had opened the slightest portal into the darkness where her life had gone. What choice did she have?

Salma's smile was wan and waning. The cell was dark, night creeping in through the high grille on one wall, but Che could still see his smile, as though through a sheet of dusky glass.

'It's that girl, isn't it?' she said, knowing that the words made her sound petty. 'I don't see . . . I mean, you've only known her for a few days, barely spoken to her.'

'Ah, but it's the gaps between the words that you can fall into,' he said. 'My people traditionally say that, but I never really appreciated it before. Perhaps it's just because she's a reminder of home.'

'She is?'

'The Butterfly-kinden . . . it's difficult to explain. Enclaves of them live within the bounds of the Commonweal, but they're not really a part of our world.' They came and went as they pleased, he recalled. He had never even seen one close to before, there were so few of them. They wanted for little, did not trade or toil. They had no need to. From the moment they were weaned from their mother's milk the sun and their Art were enough to sustain them. They lived to dance, to sing and rejoice. They were special, life's own chosen, and in the Commonweal they were respected. They went out into the world to perform, and for the love of performing, and they were gifted with fabrics and gems and applause. If they lived also beyond the Commonweal's borders, he had not known it.

Except that those borders had changed. Some band of Butterfly-kinden somewhere must have greeted the dawn only to discover they were under the Empire's shadow now.

He had heard others of his race speak about their fascinating beauty, their ethereal charms, but he had never credited it. Now he found his mind drawn back and back again to Grief in Chains. It was true she was new to him, so briefly arrived in his life, but as he sat here in darkness now, he felt the loss of her colours.

She had, he was beginning to realize, done something to him, touched him in some way. She had been trapped in chains, a slave. He had reached out to her. That had been consent enough for her to put her mark on him.

And Che was jealous, which amused him. His smile regained some of its life then, and Che remarked, 'Now you're laughing at me.'

'Not at all,' he said insincerely. 'You're right: we hardly spoke.' But they had spoken. Whilst Che had dozed, as only a Beetle could in that thundering machine, Salma and Grief had sat close together. She had tried to paint her home for him but, depicted in her colours, he could not place it. Nowhere in his Commonweal was as bright as that. Afterwards, he had told her about himself: his family and his Kin-obligate, and his service to Stenwold.

He had promised that he would help her if he could, when he could not even help himself. He had somehow the feeling that this was an oath the universe would exact on him to fulfil. His people believed in oaths just like the Mantis-kinden, with whom they shared many traditions. Oaths were magic.

There was a rattle at the door, and he heard Che start up suddenly. The light that came in was cold lamplight, and two soldiers were silhouetted against it.

'You,' said one, pointing at Che. 'Here, now.'

They took her to a room which had been some man's study once. There was a large window shuttered on the east wall, and there were bare shelves and patches on the walls where tapestries had hung. Any original finery had been pirated for other rooms until the one adornment left to it was an ornate table. Behind the table stood Thalric, dressed only in a long tunic, with a knife but no sword at his belt. Her brief moment of hope died as she recalled that the Wasp-kinden never went unarmed, that their hands alone were weapons.

'Leave us,' he directed, even as the guards thrust her within. They backed out and closed the door on her. Thalric remained standing, arms folded, and he eyed her vacantly for a moment, in her grimy and haggard state. There seemed something different about him, some new tension or edge. He was clearly in the hold of some crisis that had little to do with her.

'What do you want from me?' she said, trying to find some courage in herself. Her voice quavered. It had been a long journey, a long time spent in the dark cell. She was hungry and tired and frustrated, not in the mood for this encounter, not remotely ready. She had an uneasy feeling, even then, that she did not have the emotional reserves necessary to deal with him – nor he with her. Still, he did not seem to register her defiance.

'I'm here to listen to you,' he said shortly.

'Couldn't sleep then? Do you want me to tell you a story?' It was defiance born of a lack of any hope. Some part of her wanted it all over. She heard herself say the mocking words and braced herself, but he did not rise to them. He seemed curiously distracted, his mind partly elsewhere.

'A story? Quite,' he said. 'Don't tell me I haven't given you enough time to prepare.' He sounded annoyed, as though *she* had summoned *him* here inconveniently in the middle of the night.

She folded her own arms, unconsciously mimicking his stance. 'I have nothing to say. I've already told you, I won't betray my friends.'

'On the contrary, you have a great deal to say. Let's start with Stenwold Maker's plans, for example.' Now he was finally rising to her words, but his ire was fuelled from something within.

What's eating at you, Captain?

'He never told me any of them,' she said. 'For this very reason, I suspect. He didn't tell any of us and I wasn't even supposed to be leaving Collegium. If your thugs hadn't burst into our house that night I'd still be there.'

Still be whining about not going, too, I suppose. Oh, what I didn't know, back then.

'What a loss that would be. And your companions, those that are still free – the Spider wench and the half-breed – you have a great deal to say about them, I imagine.' He was leaning forward against the table, and she matched him across it, almost nose to nose. She had been a penned-up slave all day and she was not in the mood, whereas he was off balance already, and suddenly she found herself pushing.

'You've found out as much as I could tell you,' she said. 'Didn't you have agents at the College reporting back to you?'

'Listen, girl, this is your one remaining chance to exercise your own free will in this business. Tell me what you know.'

'What I *know?* I know some history, Captain, and applied mechanics, a little medicine and a bit of nature lore. I have nothing else to tell you.' She could sense the coiled spring of his temper.

'Miss Maker—'

'What? I know they're my friends, and they would help me if they could, and I hope they're all right, and I'm glad you haven't caught them because they're my *friends*, and that's how it is between friends. I care for them. I hope they care for me. That's *friendship*.'

Some barb, some unknowing dart in her speech made him flinch as though she had drawn blood 'Don't play games with me, girl,' he warned her. In a detached way she could see the anger rising in him was not anger focused on her, but had been in place before she was even brought in front of him. The entire conversation was taking second place to some other struggle in his mind. He had locked her up, then had her dragged here before him, and he wasn't even paying proper attention save when some chance word got in the way of his thoughts.

'Games? Who's playing games? What's this then, if not a game of yours?' she got out. 'I'm your prisoner. Am I supposed to forget that and just give you my life story? If anyone's playing games it's you, Captain. Your whole life must consist of them.' She was stammering a little, choking on her own boldness. Something she had just said had touched a nerve, made him pause to think. He stared at her with almost desperate loathing.

She had taken enough. She could not stop herself. 'What's the matter, Captain?' she asked, not quite believing that he was letting her get away with it. 'Maybe you should tell me about it. Maybe that would help, because I have nothing to tell you.'

'Now is a poor time to discover rebellion,' he said, his voice taut.

'Better now than not at all, I think—'

A muscle twitched in his face, and the table exploded. She was flung backwards across the room in a shower of wood shards, striking the wall hard enough to leave her breathless. She saw him stride towards her over the wreckage. The palms of his hands were black with soot, wispy with wood-smoke.

'Now look what you've made me do,' he said, each word through clenched teeth.

'You can't blame me,' she said, gasping, and knew he understood her but did not care.

'And if I chose to take it out on you, who would stop me?' he said. He was standing over her now, and his hands were still smoking.

'What use would . . . what good would killing me do for your Empire?' She had never been really afraid of him – not until now. He had spoken to her previously, and he had been civilized. Now that civility was gone from him. She peered into his Wasp soul with all its hard edges and hungry fires.

His eyes were so wide she could almost see his torment as a living thing. Sparks crackled across his fingers and she hid her face from them.

'The Empire needs a happy Thalric more than an unhappy Thalric,' he grated, each word snapped out with all the control he could muster. 'And right now I think it might make me happier to make a corpse of a Beetle maid who will not *talk*.'

But he did not and, after a pause, she cautiously looked up at him. His face was still stern, remorseless, and there was no humour there when he said, 'It is the scourge of my people, Miss Maker, this temper of ours. I have a stronger rein on it than most, but do not presume.'

With shaking hands she reached up, plucked a three-inch-long splinter from her hair. Her heart was still stuttering: he had been so close, was still so close to killing her. 'Captain Thalric—' She heard her voice shaking and hated herself for it, hated herself more for the next word. 'Please listen to me. I don't know anything you want to know. I don't know Stenwold's plans, or where he is now, or what he wants. I don't know anything that can help you. Can't you . . .' She got a hold on herself before she actually said it.

As he watched, she rearranged her clothes, brushed the sharp flecks of wood from them. 'Salma and I,' she went on, her voice now almost steady, 'we are just ordinary students of the Great College, and we have stumbled into something monstrous. What harm could we be to your Empire? You only . . . frustrate yourself, in this questioning. How would it hurt your Empire if you freed us, aside from saving it the cost of feeding us?'

He barked a laugh at that suggestion, but his face was still barren as the Dryclaw Desert, when she dared to look at it.

'Miss Maker, you are Stenwold's creature, and he is the Empire's enemy. Whatever meagre help you could render to him, you would. Rather than let you loose to cause trouble I would have you killed without a thought. In fact, if there were even fifty-one out of a hundred parts of you that opposed the Empire I would thrust a knife beneath your chin rather than set you free.' He turned away. 'You are lucky, then, that you are still useful to us as a source of information.'

'And after that?' she said, forcing herself to her feet. 'And what about after that? What hope have I then?'

At the word, 'hope' he laughed at her, shaking his head, half turning away, and the look on his face – of disdain, derision – was such that she attacked him.

She did not know how she did it, only that she believed him, then. She was a dead woman whether now or later, a woman totally without hope. Without any premeditation she went for his knife hilt and found her hand closed around it. Her other fist cracked against his jaw as she drew back to stab.

He had a hand on her knife wrist instantly, and for a second they swayed back and forth, as she used both hands to try and force the blade into him. He was far stronger than she was, however. She saw the muscles cord on his bare arms, and he was now pushing her back until she slammed into the wall. The knife fell from her fingers, ringing in her ears as it struck the floor, and he had a hand under her chin, where he had said he would stab her. She felt his thumb and fingers dig in there, and waited for the crackle and sear of the fire.

But it did not come. His temper, that had been only a scratch-depth from the surface a moment ago, had not stirred all this while. In fact, when she opened her eyes, he was even smiling slightly. She was horribly aware of how close he was to her, how strong.

'Very good,' he said, almost in a whisper. 'And what then? My guards are outside the door. My people are all over the palace. My Empire *owns* this city. And what *hope*, you say? No hope whatsoever, even if you had it in you to kill me.'

'Perhaps that's all I hoped,' she said, a whisper too, but there was something else in his eyes, now, and she wondered if she imagined that she saw respect there.

'Hope only,' he said, 'that when we are done with you, the Empire can use one more live slave rather than one more dead Beetle. There is your *hope*, Miss Maker.'

'Threats, still,' she murmured.

He released her suddenly, as simply as that, reclaiming his knife from the floor and scabbarding it. 'You're right, of course,' he said, the epitome of calm itself now. His demeanour admitted nothing of the smashed table, or her attack on him. 'Threats oft repeated become dull edged with overuse. Enough threats, then. I'll send you back to your cell now, and next time I call for you, I promise, there will be no threats.'

The guards took her back to the cell, where she found Salma sleeping fitfully, waking up and thrashing about, and then fighting for the blank respite of sleep again.

Tomorrow night they will do it, she told herself. *I must be strong.*

She wondered how strong she would have to be to resist the tortures of the Empire. *And I am such a very strong person, by nature. I have such famous reserves of strength and willpower*, she taunted herself bitterly.

She clutched at her knees and shivered, and could not sleep. When the tread of the guards outside signalled a new day, it gave her no joy, and when the vile food was passed in to them, she could not eat it. *When the night comes, they will come for me.*

Salma tried to comfort her, but he had only hollow words. What could he say?

And, of course, they came for her in daylight. This was the Empire, and torturers were not skulking figures of moonlight and darkness but working men for the working day. She was hauled from Salma's side in mid-morning, and she knew this time it would be different.

Salma must have known as well. He actually tried to obstruct them. His arms were still bound, even though he could have flown nowhere. They had only untied him for a short space each day so as to leave him the use of them. Salma had charged them with his shoulder and they had knocked him down and kicked him until Che, through her own struggles, forced them to turn their attention to her.

Previously she had always been taken up, towards the sun. Now they just hauled her further along the corridor. She had a glimpse of several other cell doors like theirs, each with a hatch and a grille. Some were open, some locked against other prisoners or perhaps against no one. She had a brief glimpse of an airier cell, its bars all the way from floor to ceiling, leaving the occupant exposed to all passers-by. A woman watched her pass, a local girl, hands gripping the bars.

There was a single room at the end there, but with no hatch on the door. Che began struggling, but the two soldiers raised her almost off the ground, twisting her arms, and the way they manhandled her inside was effortless.

She could not see, for a moment, what it was all intended for. She thought at first it was a workshop, for the room was dominated by a big workbench, pitted and scarred with the use of years, edged with fittings for tools and clamps and vices. To her it seemed innocuous, something familiar from the College machine rooms, until she was dragged to the table and rolled onto it. Then she looked up, and she screamed and screamed and fought them, so that another man had to come and pull the buckles tight while the two soldiers devoted their entire efforts to pinning her down.

Yet it was nothing so much, out of context. This was a workbench, after all and, just as she would have expected, there were tools up there above her on the jointed arms that artificers preferred. Drills and saws, clamps and pliers and files – really nothing one would not find in any ordinary workshop. But they were poised right above her and the soldiers were clamping her to the bench.

Twenty-four

Hokiak's Exchange was still there in the dingiest corner of the eastern plaza, just as Stenwold remembered it. Furthermore, so was Hokiak himself, although the intervening years had not been kind to him.

He was the oldest Scorpion-kinden that Stenwold had ever seen, perhaps the oldest there was. They were a ruthless, primal people in their desert home and a man did not live long amongst them once his strength began to wane, unless he possessed some edge over his fellows. Hokiak's edge was a self-imposed exile. Even when Stenwold had known him, he had been too old to go home. Now he was positively decayed, his waxy skin folded into sallow creases and his once-yellow eyes faded to a dim sepia. His throat was as creased as a discarded shirt and the characteristic large frame of his breed had slumped to fat now, and even that was ebbing like a low tide, leaving his bare chest an unsightly ripple of wrinkles and old scars. One of his foreclaws was a jagged stump that had not regrown, and his jutting jaws revealed a ghastly thicket of rotting spurs on protruding gums. He sat on a wicker chair and smoked, and occasionally skewered candied insects from a box with a thumbclaw.

The Exchange itself was clearly faring better than its namesake. Stenwold and Totho pushed into a small room made smaller still by stacks of heaped boxes. The air was thick with spices, and the pungent, dizzying tobacco that Hokiak still smoked. His staff was hard at work prising the lids off crates, cataloguing their contents and then nailing them back. There were three youngsters engaged at the work: a pair of Fly-kinden around Totho's age and a dark Mynan girl no older than thirteen. They were supervised by a Spider-kinden man who couldn't have been much short of Hokiak's own years. Spiders aged rather better, though. This one had long silver hair and a trace of an aristocratic demeanour, but was almost skeletally thin.

'Stenwold, are you sure about this . . . this looks like a pirate's den,' Totho whispered as he took a glance at the place. He was right, too. Most of the commodities that were hanging from the rafters, or being hurriedly boxed, were exotic plunder from far parts of the world, and Stenwold knew that there would be a back room with the real contraband in it.

'Our friend Hokiak,' he murmured, 'was a black marketeer – and is one still, unless I miss my guess. Now the sort of people we're looking for will have good use for someone who can smuggle goods in and out. It's all about contacts, Totho.'

'Don't just stand there letting the dust in,' Hokiak suddenly complained in a surprisingly deep voice. 'In or out, Master Beetle.'

Stenwold closed the door behind him. With Totho dogging his every step nervously. 'Well now, Master Scorpion, how's about finding a little work for a tramp artificer and his boy?'

'You any good?' Hokiak blinked rheumy eyes at him. 'Always can find work for a good 'un. You got references?'

'There's an old, old Scorpion-kinden I know who used to be able to vouch for me,' said Stenwold. 'His name's Hokiak. You might even know him.'

The Scorpion squinted at him. 'Windblast you! I don't know . . .' His voice tailed off, and he scratched his withered throat with his remaining claw. The Spider-kinden man was now looking over, Stenwold noted, with a hand on a dagger's hilt: not a threat, but just to be ready in case Stenwold turned out to be one.

'Stenwold Maker?' Hokiak said in a small voice. 'Can't be, surely. Stenwold Maker must be dead three times by now.'

'If any of us is guilty of living beyond his time, old man, it has to be you,' Stenwold told him. 'I didn't know whether I would still find you here.'

Hokiak had fumbled a stick to his hand, and it bent alarmingly under his weight as he heaved himself to his feet. He took a very close look at Stenwold, their faces only inches apart. 'Blast and blow me, if it ain't old Stenwold himself,' he concluded, and the Spider removed his hand from his blade. 'Didn't ever figure I'd see you again. Now, Gryllis, this old boy and I did a load of business before the conquest.'

The Spider nodded cautiously. 'Delighted to make your acquaintance, Master Maker,' he said, in a voice still sounding cultured. By now the three youngsters had stopped working in order to listen, and Gryllis turned and cuffed the nearest Fly boy irritably. 'Dirty your hands, you little parasites. Don't think the arrival of one Beetle-kinden's cause for a holiday!'

'So what in the wastes brings you all the way back here?' Hokiak asked Stenwold. 'I figured you'd made tracks once this place came under new management.'

'I thought you might have done the same.'

The old man shrugged. 'Ain't got nowhere to go, me. Besides, don't matter who you are, everyone needs the services of an importer–exporter now and then. Matter of fact, the Black Guild business is better than ever.'

The Black Guild was Lowlander parlance for smuggling, although it never approached anything like a genuine guild's unity. 'You're shifting goods for the Wasps now, are you?' Stenwold asked him, a little uneasily.

Hokiak grinned at him, an appalling sight. 'Now you know it ain't like that. I just shift for them that asks. I ain't never one to nail my heart to a flagstaff, and no mistake. So if you got some business you ain't keen for them stripeys to figure, you came to the right place.'

Stenwold nodded. It could be a bad mistake, of course, to trust this old villain. He could find himself in the cell next door to Che's in no time, if she was still even in this cursed city. Still, his options were fast running through his fingers like grains of sand.

'Let's just say,' he replied, 'that I want to meet some people the Wasps aren't too anxious for anyone to meet.'

Hokiak nodded sagely. 'Not dealings I'd want to see in an establishment like mine. You'd better help me hide my eyes.'

Stenwold placed two coins on a crate in front of him, gold, stamped each with a winged sword and the words 'Central Mint of Helleron'. Hokiak whistled when he picked them up.

'Centrals, no less. Your coin's good, Stenwold. These're harder than the Empire stuff these days. In that case, I'd advise you to go straight into the back-room bar and get yourself and your lad here a drink. I'll join you there presently. Gryllis, you can watch the shop for me.'

'I'm sure I can manage,' replied the Spider laconically.

As well as the hidden contraband store, there was a liquor house at the back of Hokiak's, and there had been long before the Scorpion had lent his name to this place. They found seven drinkers there already, and none of them looking the type to stare at too closely. Stenwold registered a pair of Ants of a colour he did not recognize and a trio of Fly-kinden gamblers with knives laid out on the table to indicate theirs was a closed game. There was a female Beetle with a tremendous scar down one side of her face and one hand on a big under-over double-armed crossbow, whom Stenwold thought was probably a game hunter. There was even a Wasp-kinden man in repainted armour, who must surely have been a mercenary or even a deserter. Behind the bar stood a Mynan woman, one of that local strain that seemed to be a stable half-breed of Ant and Beetle, and for a couple of small coins she handed out clay beakers of an acrid clear liquid.

'Don't drink it,' Stenwold warned Totho as they found a table.

'I have tried drink before, sir,' the artificer said stiffly.

'Not drink like this. The first time I tried this stuff I was left blind for a day.' Stenwold realized that he had chosen his seat to face the door. Old habits were coming back to him.

'How much do you trust that old man?' Totho inquired.

'I wish I knew.' Stenwold sighed. 'I wish I knew. I don't think he'd go out of his way to hand us in, but it'll be different if there's a reward out. Just be ready to jump if it all falls over.'

Totho nodded, and Stenwold looked up to see Hokiak poling his way over with the help of his stick. With a wheezing sigh the old man lowered himself into a chair at their table.

'Don't you look at me like that, Maker. I still got years left in me,' he said, between ragged breaths.

'You'll outlive the pair of us,' said Stenwold, hoping it wasn't true. 'Tell me, your deputy—'

'Partner,' Hokiak corrected. 'Old Gryllis is the soul of discretion. He ain't the kind to draw attention to himself. Used to be a player, way down south, and got enemies still on the look-out for him. He likes a quiet life now, same as all of us.' He produced a squat clay pipe and lit it, sending a worm of smoke that trailed across the width of the table. 'Mind, you seem to be looking for a mite more noise in yours. You're after the Red Flag lot.'

'Am I?'

'That's what they've gotten to callin' 'emselves these days – on account of what they leave behind at the scene. You sure you want to mix with them? Don't get me wrong. They're good customers of mine. Always on the look for me to get 'em things in, or people out sometimes. Still, they ain't what you'd call nice boys and girls.'

'Living under the Wasp boot will do that to you,' Stenwold observed. 'Anyone left over from my time?'

'A few, just a few,' Hokiak confirmed. 'Mind, it's the young bloods what run it now, mostly. You get me a handful of those Centrals and, sure, I can get you where you'll meet 'em. I just got to warn you, you mayn't like it when you do.'

'I'll take that chance,' said Stenwold. 'I need their help. Maybe I can even help them in exchange. How many's a handful, Hokiak?'

The old man gave him a carious smile. 'Blast me, but it's been a long while. You used to have always that madcap lot with you, din't you? That Spider-kin who was such a looker, and there was your Mantis feller what did the prize-fighting that year. I won a parcel and a half on him. If'n you was new, Maker, I'd have bigger hands, but seeing as you remember an old man after all this time, call it a dozen and we're happy.'

It was a lot of money; for Totho, more money than he had ever seen in one place. Still, he saw Stenwold count it out willingly and without regret.

The old Scorpion had made the arrangements and then given them directions, which had led them by moon-light to a dark square. Stenwold kept his gaze steady, his breath rising as a slight plume in the night air. There were many such faded locations, away from Myna's centre and its main thoroughfares and the grotesque wart of the governor's palace. This had been a rich area of the city before the conquest. The surrounding houses here were three-storeyed, many of them, and some still sported empty iron hanging baskets where flowers had once been kept, or the peeling traces of ochre or dark blue where the lintels had been painted about the doors and windows. Many windows were shutterless now, and others had them hanging precariously off one hinge. Stenwold guessed that half of these houses were abandoned now, and such occupants as remained were not those families that had originally held court here.

Hokiak had directed him here, though. They would meet *here*.

Totho, beside him, had Scuto's repeating crossbow in his hands, with a full magazine slotted into the top. Stenwold was beginning to wish he had brought a crossbow himself, and not just his sword. If the Scorpion had betrayed them this would be a poor place to get trapped by Wasp soldiers.

'Master Maker,' Totho whispered a warning.

Stenwold started and turned to see two tall men in yellow shirts and black breeches passing into the square. One held a staff, and the other a lantern. They pointedly paid no attention to the two foreigners, instead lighting two braziers with exaggerated care before moving on. The dim red light lent the scene little warmth, however. Stenwold and Totho had seen many such men – and women – in Myna, standing guard at markets or patrolling the streets. They were substitute soldiers, brought in for the inferior tasks that the Imperial Army disdained, having been conscripted from elsewhere in the Empire. Stenwold thought they were probably Grasshopper-kinden from Sa, which was far enough from Myna that they would not be tempted to rebel or defect. Auxillians, they were called: slave soldiers of the Empire.

The lamplighters passed on, but there was something so very private in their manner that told Stenwold they had been expecting him to be there. He began to feel nervous, or at least more nervous. There were too many shadows in this part of Myna and his night vision had never been of the best. That was part of the Art that had always eluded him. Closer into the city's hub there would have been gas lamps flaring, but out here there was only naked flame, primitive and unreliable against the darkness.

'Master Maker,' said Totho again, after a short while of waiting.

'Stenwold – call me Stenwold, please. Or even Sten,' the older man said.

'Sten' was clearly too much for the young artificer who, after a pause, began again: 'Stenwold, then . . . There's something I've been meaning . . . that is, when I had the opportunity . . .'

Stenwold kept his eyes on their surroundings, but he nodded to show he was listening. 'Go on.'

'It's only that . . . When we've freed Che . . . freed Cheerwell I mean. And Salma of course. But when we have . . .'

The boy was certainly taking a long time over this, whatever it was. Meanwhile Stenwold clutched his hand about his sword hilt. The night was getting colder, too, the sky above ripped clear of clouds, pockmarked with stars.

'It's just, I've never met her parents, you see,' Totho continued wretchedly.

Caught unawares, Stenwold could genuinely not think what he meant. 'Her parents?' he asked, turning a blank expression to the youth.

'Only . . . I haven't asked her at all. She doesn't . . . She doesn't even know, I think.' Totho's dark face twisted. 'But since you're her uncle . . .'

'Totho, are you talking about a *proposal*?' Stenwold asked, completely thrown by this, in this place and at this time.

'I . . .' Totho read in his face something that Stenwold would have hidden had he realized it was there. The young artificer lowered his head in humiliation. The thought etched on Stenwold's brow had been clear enough, even in the dull light. His plans for Che, whatever they might be, had not included welcoming a halfbreed artificer into the family.

Stenwold saw his reaction, divined it accurately. 'Totho, I don't mean to say—'

'It's all right, Master Maker.'

'You're a fine lad, but—'

'They're here, sir.'

Stenwold stopped, turned. They were, indeed, there.

Men and women were emerging from the shadows around the other end of the square. They were not as stealthy-silent as Tisamon was, but they moved with a minimum of fuss, only the occasional clink of metal or scuff of leather. Stenwold made a quick headcount, and by the time his eyes had passed back again to catch the stragglers there were fifteen of them.

Most were men and most were young. Almost all of them wore a scarf or some kind of cloth hiding half their faces. They had hoods, cloaks too. All of them had a blade out and ready, even if it were no more than a sharpened kitchen knife. A couple even had crossbows raised, bolts to the string.

Stenwold stayed very still. He noticed that Totho held his repeater aimed casually downwards, and he silently approved. There was an ugly mood amongst these new-comers, as Hokiak had warned him.

He studied the few exposed faces. There was one older woman whom he thought he should know, from way back. Another was a lanky Grasshopper-kinden, and he guessed that these young fighters had contacts in the Auxillians who would ensure they were not disturbed here.

Amongst the few bare faces was one who must be their leader, from the way he stood and the way the others gathered around him. He was young, five years over Totho at most, and he bore a shortsword of the old Mynan style that was no longer made. There was a peaked helm on his head, of black-painted steel, and the bulkiness of his tunic suggested a breastplate underneath. Their scarves and masks were coloured red or black, and Stenwold knew the hidden armour would be too. The thought brought back a flash of that final day in Myna all those years ago, his younger self watching by telescope as the defenders readied themselves. This man would have been only a child then.

With his offhand, the man drew a dagger from his belt, and Stenwold tensed absurdly, despite the fact that there were swords and knives and crossbows levelled at him already. Wordlessly the same weapon was cast at his feet to clatter on the flagstones. There was a ribbon tied about its pommel. This, Stenwold guessed, was the 'red flag' that Hokiak had spoken of, which they left behind as their sign.

'The old man said you were after meeting us,' the leader began. 'An old Beetle and a halfway? Why?'

Not so old, not yet. 'Because I need your help.'

'And what gives you the right to that?' The man stepped forward so that the dagger was immediately at his feet, and Stenwold within reach of his swordblade. 'I am Chyses, old man, and these are my people. We help ourselves and our city, but not foreigners.'

Stenwold kept himself calm, blotted out the sword, the implicit threat. 'My name is Stenwold Maker, and I have been here before – before the conquest, in fact. Does none of you here know my name? You,' he turned to the older woman. 'You would have known me, perhaps. I spent some time here.'

She frowned at him, then looked to Chyses, who signalled for her to speak. 'I remember a Stenwold Maker, a Beetle-kinden,' she said slowly. 'I can't tell if you're him. I won't vouch for you.'

Stenwold glanced around the semi-circle of resistance

fighters, seeking other heads with greyer hair. *Nobody else?* 'I did my best, then, to help your people.'

'I remember a Stenwold Maker,' rumbled another man. 'I was an artificer's apprentice when the conquest came. I remember a Stenwold Maker who talked us into some mad plan that didn't work. I remember how we were betrayed.'

Stenwold stayed very still, because one of the crossbows was now directed straight at his head. 'Not by me,' he said, and he could feel Totho as tense as a wire beside him. He realized that the current mood could not last: it would ebb or it would break in blood. 'I did not betray you. I did my best to help you and I'm sorry I couldn't do more.'

'I think this is a Wasp scam,' said Chyses, half to Stenwold, half to his followers. 'All too easy, isn't it? "Oh, I was here before the conquest", "Oh, I did my best for your people", and then we show you where we hide and what we do and, the next thing we know, the Rekef's down on us. Sound familiar, old one?'

Stenwold took a deep breath, but before he could even deny it, Chyses cut him off.

'I don't want to hear it. We've been tricked before – but not ever again. Kill them. Dump their bodies in the sewers.'

'Chyses!' It was a squeak more than a cry. The resistance leader turned to see that the crossbowman, so recently menacing Stenwold, was now himself held hostage.

'Tisamon,' said Stenwold, and the flood of relief was almost embarrassing. The Mantis had his off-arm lightly about the man's throat, his forearm spines in deep enough to draw pinpricks of blood. His right arm was raised, the claw of his gauntlet folded, ready to strike at any that came near.

'Kill him,' Chyses ordered, but something in Tisamon gave them all pause.

'Don't you know me?' the Mantis asked. 'Not you, Khenice?' he asked the older woman, whose name that instant returned to Stenwold's halting memory. 'I saved the life of your son once, in a brawl with two Ant mercenaries. Was that for nothing?'

Khenice stared at him, and Stenwold was reminded again how little Tisamon had changed compared to him, or any of them.

At last his name fell from her lips. 'Tisamon.' And then, 'Perhaps it *was* for nothing. He died fighting the Wasps at the gate, when your outlander plans failed. But yes, yes you did. I remember.'

The revolutionaries were in disarray now. Some still held close to Stenwold, some were trying to watch Tisamon. Now others saw that Tynisa, with her rapier drawn, had crept up unseen and unheard behind them. Stenwold guessed that somewhere in the gloom of the higher buildings he would find Achaeos, to whom night and shadow were no barriers.

'I have been a friend of Myna before now,' Stenwold persisted. 'And I have something I must do here. You may wish to help me, or not. I hope you may even gain by it, so will you at least hear me out?'

Chyses looked from him to the uncertain faces of his supporters, and the nodding of Khenice. At last, with obvious reluctance, he agreed.

For those three, entering Myna had apparently been easy, so easy that Stenwold wondered whether he should not have simply sent them in and himself stayed at home. As soon as night fell, Tisamon had made the decision. He did not see it as disobeying Stenwold's instructions. He had simply wanted to keep a personal eye on matters. It annoyed Stenwold to acknowledge that his friend had been right.

They had taken the wall swiftly and silently, with Achaeos aloft keeping watch as they climbed. Tisamon did not have the Art for it, to cling to the stones, but Tynisa did, and she let down a rope for him. It was mere minutes and one dead sentry later before they had invaded Myna.

After that it was a simple piece of work to locate Stenwold, for of course Tisamon remembered old Hokiak, and was remembered in turn. The old man had at first been reluctant to give details of his business but, between old acquaintanceship and Tynisa's charm, he had been persuaded. All this was still playing catch-up, of course, for Stenwold and Totho had already been on their way to the meeting. The painful fact was that Tisamon and his fellows were simply faster, more sure of themselves in the darkness.

I should be grateful, Stenwold told himself. Instead it just seemed to reinforce the fact that he was neither as young nor as good at this game as he seemed to have believed. Certainly Chyses would have killed him and Totho without a qualm, had Tisamon not been as fleet and decisive as he was.

The Red Flag had led them into ever more dubious parts of the city, quarters that the occupation had let go to rot. Stenwold guessed that the Wasps were now paying for that neglect. He saw enough lurking figures to guess that there were whole neighbourhoods here that the resistance had gained effective control over. He began to wonder just how strong Chyses' people might be.

Myna. He had seen the city fall. It had been his great failure, that had set him on this intelligencing path. He forced himself away from any thought that now he could save it. *I am here for Che and Salma. I cannot fight their wars for them. It's not as though I did a very good job the last time.*

And then the next thought: *If I cannot accomplish some-thing against the Empire here, then my next great failure may be Collegium itself.*

Telling the tale, Stenwold found that it was simpler than he had thought. Putting words to it brought home just what was at stake and what was important.

His niece and another student of his had been captured by the Wasps in Helleron. It was believed – and here he could not stop himself from glancing at Achaeos – that they had been brought to Myna for questioning. A rescue was urgently needed.

With good reason the resistance in Myna – the Red Flag – did not trust the sky. Wasps held airborne patrols and they employed enough Fly-kinden in their ranks as well. The stubborn heart of Myna had therefore gone underground. There were some thirty men and women in this resistance cell, which had tentative links to other cells across the city, and they were now in a rambling ware-house cellar near the river, heavy with damp. The walls were a history unto themselves. The upper stones were the pale, plain pieces that the Mynans themselves fa-voured, but the bottom three rows were crumbling carved masonry centuries older. Some other place had stood where Myna stood now, and had fallen and been forgot-ten long before the Wasps ever arose to trouble their neighbours.

The cross-section of Mynan life found here was a broader version of the group that had come so close to ending Stenwold's personal story earlier. Most of them were too young to hold any clear memories of the con-quest, but the occupation had scarred them all. They had grown up second-class citizens in their own city, but their parents, those whose parents still lived and were free, had nevertheless passed the city's pride on to them. They took this burden very seriously. Chyses was obviously their leader but Stenwold saw that it was a temporary arrangement. The man steered them by main force, and yet his orders were up for debate. They were debating now, turning over Stenwold's words and passing them back and forth.

Eventually it was Chyses who had come back to them, and brought along with him one of the foreign militia, a very tall woman with a long face and close-cropped dark hair.

'You're in luck,' the resistance leader told Stenwold shortly. 'You see, we have friends amongst the Auxillians.'

'I'd noted that,' Stenwold said. 'I was surprised to see it.'

'The Wasps've got no imagination,' sneered Chyses. 'There's a detachment of men and women from Myna serving as Auxillians far east of here, and instead they pass us a bunch of Sa'en Grasshoppers to keep the peace, as though it's just the same. They see us all as dirt. They don't make any distinctions.'

Stenwold nodded. He had never been to Sa but he had known a few Grasshopper-kinden. They could certainly fight, when they wanted to, but they were a peaceful people by nature, a thoughtful people: fighters, perhaps, but not warriors. Still, it was not in the Wasps' nature to make exceptions regarding the way their slave races served them.

'The more they tighten their grip on us,' said Chyses, 'the closer together they bring us.' It was obviously a slogan that he was repeating. 'This here is Toran Awe. She's a sergeant-auxillian in the militia. Tell him.'

The Grasshopper-kinden gave Stenwold a brief bow. 'There are not so many outlander prisoners being kept in the palace cells,' she said. 'Locals mostly, and anything else raises rumour. Three came in not long ago: a Beetle girl, a Commonweal Dragonfly and a dancer.'

'I don't know about the dancer, but the other two must

be ours.' Stenwold's gaze twitched unwillingly to Achaeos, who was sitting cross-legged on a displaced block of masonry and staring straight back at him.

'Then we can help you,' Chyses said. 'And you can help us. Because we need a rescue too.'

Twenty-five

They had both ankles pinned down now, and one wrist, and she turned frantically to the man tugging at the buckle. She knew him: he was the man they had come to Myna with, the one Thalric had spoken to. Desperation brought his name to her, when nothing else could.

'Aagen! You're Aagen, aren't you?' She tried to keep her voice steady, instead hearing the ragged mess she made of it. He glanced at her briefly and pulled the strap tight.

'Thalric said you were an . . . an artificer? Is that right? You're not a soldier? Please listen to me. I'm an artificer. I studied mechanics. Please . . .' She yanked at the strap but there was no give in it.

He was now giving her a pitying look. 'Of *course* I'm an artificer,' he said, and she went cold all over. Of course he was an artificer: for the Wasps, this was an artificer's job – the same as repairing an automotive or making a pump, and no more or less worth the attention of a trained professional.

'You're going to . . . to torture me?'

He looked unhappy about it, but it was too small a concession to common humanity to do her any good. He was a Wasp of the Empire, and he was going to do it anyway, unhappy or not.

'Good work, Aagen,' said that hateful voice, as Thalric strode in and admired the handiwork. 'I told you it would all come back to you.'

'Yes, Captain.'

'Oh cheer up.' Thalric seemed to have abandoned his angst of the previous night. Now he was all energy. 'You two can leave us,' he told the attendant soldiers. 'This is for our ears only.'

They looked a little put out at that. Perhaps they had been looking forward to the excruciation of a Beetle girl. Still, Thalric watched them stonily until they left, and then bolted the door behind them.

'Thalric,' Che's voice was a little hoarse from the screaming, 'you don't have to do this.'

He cocked an eyebrow at her.

'Thalric, *please*,' she said. She could feel tears springing to her eyes. Aagen was – she shuddered – laying out a medical kit beside her, unrolling the pocketed strip of cloth to reveal the gleaming points of the probes and the clips and the scalpels. 'Please don't do this. You're a . . . an intelligent man, a civilized man.'

Thalric was smiling at her now, in a terribly derisive way. 'Has all that spirit dissipated through the drain in your cell, Miss Maker? What a loss that will be to humanity.'

'Captain Thalric, this is . . . beneath you,' she told him, but still her voice quavered, despite her best efforts.

'So I shouldn't use this expedience to get what I want from you?'

'No . . . No . . .'

'So you're ready to talk?'

'I . . .' She swallowed. 'Yes. Yes I'm ready.'

'It's a shame then that I'm no longer ready to listen,' he told her. His eyes, above that smile, were ice. 'Fire up your machine, Aagen.'

The artificer hesitated, just for a second, and for Che that meant a second more of freedom from pain and she could have blessed him for it. Then he strode across the room and started pulling levers. Somewhere below them there was a boiler room, where a head of steam had been got up some time before. The metal arms above her shuddered into life almost immediately with a great hiss and a rattle.

'Louder!' called Thalric. 'I want to hear it roar!'

Aagen glanced at him wildly but did as he was bid, raising the pressure until Che would have had trouble answering any questions above it. *Maybe they just wanted to make her scream.*

But that wasn't Thalric's way. She narrowed her eyes, watching him. He was oblivious to her, now beckoning Aagen over.

'The time has come,' she heard him say, 'when I need your services, Aagen.'

The artificer glanced at their victim, but Thalric shook his head impatiently. 'Not as a professional but as a loyal citizen of the Empire.'

Aagen liked that even less, from his expression, but Thalric was beckoning him over to the far end of the room, and he came when called. With the rumble of the steam engine and the ringing of the suspended tool-arms filling the room, Thalric bent close to him and spoke carefully and clearly. There were patches that Che could hear, but patches only. It was enough to set her mind racing even so.

'I want you to find a place . . .' she made out, followed by, '. . . must know. Then go to the . . . waiting for you . . . in chains . . .' By now she was craning sideways, trying to squeeze every word she could from Thalric's murmuring.

'. . . no one, not even me . . . let you know, if I can . . . not then . . . self scarce.'

She realized that even if there was someone listening at the door, or even from behind some false panel in the walls, they would hear none of it. To the outside world it would seem that Thalric had a prisoner in the torture room, and the machines themselves were drowning out the sounds of whatever evils he was enacting.

Thalric was obviously asking for some confirmation, and Aagen was nodding, unhappy still, voicing some objection that Che could not catch at all.

Thalric grinned wickedly. '. . . say I share the attraction . . . never know . . .' He clapped Aagen on the shoulder, the same comradely gesture he had made before.

Finally, something Che heard all of, for all the good it did her. 'Now dispatch it straight,' Thalric instructed, and Aagen nodded, not a military salute but the nod of a friend with an errand to fulfil. Then he unbolted the door and left her alone with Thalric.

The Wasp captain wandered over to the steam engine and studied the levers. Che understood he was about to release the steam from the system and stop the noise, and that he was not entirely sure how to go about it. She saw the tool heads above her, shivering with steam-driven power, imagined a mechanized arm of one holding the drills dropping suddenly, unfolding like the sting of a scorpion, flicking its steel tip out into her . . . 'Thalric!' she yelled desperately. 'Thalric!'

He glanced over at her.

'The one at the end! The red band!'

His lips twitched, and for a moment she thought he was not going to comply at all, but then he pulled the lever up, and she heard the steam venting from the system somewhere above.

The roar of the machine died away and soon the quiet in the small room was deafening.

His footsteps, as he came over to the bench, sounded like thunderclaps. For a long time, far longer than she liked, he stared down at her wordlessly, though his expression spoke volumes. He was perhaps considering just how much at his mercy, his personal mercy, she was.

In the face of that look, which disturbed her more than she could tell, she had to speak up, if only to disrupt the moody train of his thoughts.

'So you're sending her away?'

He raised an eyebrow at her.

'Grief in Chains,' she continued, and his expression became briefly irritated. Quickly hidden again, but she saw it there nonetheless.

'You have keen ears, Miss Maker,' he told her dryly.

'I'm more used to having machines around me than you think, perhaps.'

He considered her again, but at least it was now an assessing look and not something darker. 'I shall have to remember that when next torturing Beetles,' he said.

'You trust Aagen a lot, don't you?' she said, and for a fragile second there was a genuine smile on his face. Erased, again, but visible, for that brief second, on a face which surely could not belong to that fiend Thalric, agent of the Empire.

'We go back many years, Aagen and I, so I can trust him with a great deal.'

'Even with Grief in Chains?' She could not entirely keep the bitterness out of her voice as she said it. 'She seems to have an effect on men.'

'I trust him even with her. He is a good servant of the Empire.'

'I don't understand you, Thalric.' She was still very much at his mercy, but her curiosity overtook her.

'I am not here to be understood,' he snapped, but she persisted.

'You can't just live for an Empire. Everybody must live for himself as well. Your man Aagen's not just a good servant of the Empire. He's a friend of yours.'

'Enough,' he said, 'or I'll work the machines myself.' Then he sighed and, with a few simple moves, loosened her straps, arm, leg, leg, arm. Wincing, she sat up, and let herself slide down to the floor.

'Let me guess, it's back to my cell now.'

'Until the next time.' He had obviously achieved whatever piece of subterfuge he had intended, and yet he still seemed less than delighted.

He escorted her back to the cell himself, and she guessed he did not want guards examining her too closely. She felt lucky because, if he had wanted to, he could easily have put enough marks on her to defy any scrutiny.

And she felt doubly lucky, in that case. While he was unbuckling her ankles, she had palmed a probe from the medical kit. She was no expert housebreaker, but the locks on Salma's bonds were big and crude, and she possessed an artificer's training, after all.

Outside her cell, Thalric turned to the guards – the same two he had brought all the way from Helleron. They took orders only from him.

'Nobody is to see the prisoners except me,' he told them. 'If anyone insists on it, and won't take my name as a warning, then you're to kill the prisoners first, no mercy.' *The girl knows too much just now, and I have no time to finish with her.* He left them abruptly, for he had an overdue appointment to keep.

He went to meet Ulther in the war room. The place was a suitable testament to the old man's sense of drama. He kept it on the same underground floor as the cells, to start with, away from the prying eyes of household servants, and it was coldly lit by blue glass lamps which put Thalric in mind of dark chasms beneath the sea. One end of the long table was choked with charts and logistics reports, while at the other was laid out a map, taking in all the terrain between Myna and Helleron. Wooden counters, like game pieces, picked out key locations across the intricately plotted countryside, whilst pinned-out ribbons showed marching routes and scribbled notes held down with tacks.

'Your area, this, I think,' Ulther said. 'To tell the truth, I let them get on with it. One city's quite enough for me to handle.'

Thalric nodded, welcoming this chance to update himself on where the Empire's plans had so far taken them. Just seeing those place names made him long to be in Helleron again, where it was all *happening*. He had only intended a brief side trip to Asta for the interrogations, and then Colonel Latvoc had got hold of him and he had found himself drawn into *this*. His agents in Helleron must now be wondering what was going on.

He moved around the table, trying to pick out details in the undersea light. Behind him, but extending overhead and blotting the finer details of the map, was the suspended carapace of one of the great forest mantids, an insect that could rend a horse. It had been posed as if in mid-strike, its raptorial arms outflung to shadow the paper landscape below.

'What do you think?' Ulther asked him. 'Another new acquisition. He's for the throne room eventually.'

'Is it really necessary?' Thalric asked, taking an irritated glance at it.

'You've never been to the North Empire, I take it? The hill tribes?'

'My line of work hasn't taken me there.'

'It's an education. The Empire hasn't changed them much in three generations, thataway. In between calls from the tax collectors, they're still cutting each other's throats and running off with each other's women.'

'I've heard they're still a pack of barbarians, if that's what you mean,' agreed Thalric. 'Still, good to recruit for shock troops, I hear.'

'They do have something we've lost, you know,' Ulther remarked, and Thalric glanced up in surprise. 'Oh yes,' the governor continued, 'they might be savages but they know how to *live*. Life is short and brutal there, so they take full advantage of it. You won't find a chieftain amongst them without some trophy, like this fellow, behind his throne – to give him strength, to give him courage.'

'Don't tell me you believe all that.'

'I don't need to. When people come in, they'll see my spiny friend here, and *they'll* believe. That's the point.'

Thalric made a noncommittal noise, but Ulther was smiling broadly. 'When you're done there, Captain, I have something else to show you. Another jewel in my collection. Perhaps *the* jewel.'

That caught Thalric's attention. 'Lead on,' he said.

It was a short walk. Ulther took him to the cells, and for a moment Thalric thought the trouble would start right then, but this was a different prisoner, another woman, a local.

'Her name,' said Ulther, as if savouring it, 'is Kymene. But they call her the Maid.'

Thalric was instantly struck by her, less by her appearance than her manner. She had been resting on a straw mattress when they arrived, but she stood up instantly, waiting in the cell's exact centre with a fighter's poise. Her skin was the familiar blue-grey of all Mynans, and her hair was dark, cut clumsily short. Ulther had dressed her in a simple sleeveless tunic and breeches, giving her an almost boyish look. Except for a row of bars her cell was open along one side. Despite being kept on display like a wild beast, she stared straight into Thalric's eyes. There was a challenge and a contempt there, and he felt something respond within himself. Defiance was a dangerous flag for a captive young woman to fly so plainly. Her eyes were steel, though. He felt a shock almost physical as he met their gaze. *No surrender*, they seemed to say.

'What's so special then?' he asked the governor, trying to keep his voice casual.

'Special? My dear Thalric, she *is* the resistance. She's their adored leader, and a merry chase she led us, too. She was top of the wanted list for all of a year and a season, running the poor Rekef ragged trying to trap her. We tried everything. We infiltrated her followers; she killed our spies. We tortured family members; they lied to us. I've never known the like. To capture her in the end I had to turn to freelancers, the wretched scum.'

Thalric frowned. 'You did well to catch her. When do you start her interrogation?'

Ulther laughed jovially. 'Not so hasty, old friend. We've had her here two tendays so far. We're breaking her down, piece by piece.'

'Two tendays, and you've not put her to the question?' Thalric heard the disbelief in his own voice, but Ulther blithely ignored it.

'I prefer to break them slowly,' Ulther told him. 'No sun, no air, no freedom – and no privacy. We'll rebuild her mind, my friend, piece by piece. Every dawn she is less the rebel and more . . . pliable. Soon, what will she not promise for a glimpse of the outside world?'

He wants her for his wretched collection, Thalric finally understood, and it was a sourly amusing thought. The old man had been wise enough, before now, to confine his tastes to imported vintages. To invite this woman into his bed would be a death sentence for him, like as not. The amusing thing was that she had not seen it either. She held on to her pride so hard that she could not grasp the escape being offered to her.

Still . . . on meeting Kymene's eyes, he could see what Ulther so desired there. She was not beautiful in any sense that Thalric usually understood. She was not the scintillating Grief in Chains, or even of the proper imperial proportions of the slave Hreya. In that look, so fierce with lancing disdain, she seemed unattainable, and that was somehow more attractive than mere beauty.

But Ulther was still playing a dangerous game. 'Should she not have been interrogated immediately, though, concerning her fellows in the resistance?' Thalric asked.

'Time enough for that,' Ulther replied vaguely.

Thalric saw the woman shake her head slightly with a cold smile, and he wondered, *Would she talk, even so?* Mere pain and the threat of it might be something she was proof against. She was armoured in her belief.

'Aren't you going to introduce me to your new sycophant?' Kymene spoke, and her voice was mocking. 'You do love to parade them past me.'

'My dear, this is Captain Thalric of the Rekef Outlander, and he was with me here when I first captured your city,' Ulther told her. 'You owe him a debt of gratitude almost as much as you owe me.'

She studied them both, and obviously found nothing to choose between them. 'Then it shall be paid. Do you want me to curtsey now?' she said. 'Or perhaps I should get on my knees, I'm so honoured.'

A soldier came in then, and stood waiting to one side until Ulther went over to him. Thalric watched carefully, thinking, *And here it starts.* He realized Kymene was watching too. She was kept underground and behind bars, but she was looking out for anything that would help her. He liked to think that in her position he would do the same.

'What do you mean, gone?' Ulther suddenly demanded, gripping the soldier by the shoulder strap of his armour. 'Who took her? Where?'

The soldier's reply was low, but his glance in Thalric's

direction told it all. Ulther let go of the man suddenly. 'Get out!' he snapped, and then turned to his old friend with an expression of forced good humour.

'Thalric, that fellow had a strange tale to tell me.'

'Really?' Internally, Thalric was bracing himself.

'He said that my Butterfly, my dancer, has been taken from her room, and now nobody knows where she is.'

'I know,' Thalric said. 'I ordered it.'

'You ordered it.' The governor let a slow breath pass before coming closer. 'Somewhat of a liberty, Captain. And why, if I may ask?'

'You're right, she's a remarkable specimen,' Thalric replied blandly, 'and it so happens that my future projects west of here could use just such an operative. You know how the Rekef Outlander needs all sorts, all skills. Helleron is in a delicate enough state just now, and she could tip it. I have therefore requisitioned her.'

Ulther's control was admirable, and he even managed a smile. '*Requisitioned*, is it? I am governor of Myna remember, Thalric. You know this. You are an old friend, but under whose authority, Captain, can you go about *requisitioning* my possessions?'

'I am a captain of the Imperial Army, but also a major of the Rekef. My work in the west is Rekef business.'

'I know you're bloody Rekef. I directed you at them, in case you've forgotten.'

'Then you should understand. Imperial needs come before personal ones, Governor.'

'But I hadn't even . . .' Ulther's meaty hands crushed the air impotently, and Thalric mentally provided *had her yet* to finish the sentence.

'I'm sorry, Governor,' he said, affecting to sound both businesslike and bored, 'but she's quite unique, as you've obviously noticed. If I'm to take Helleron it's a matter of hearts and minds as well as bodies and swords. You can see how she'd be of use to me.'

And he smiled. Ulther was staring at him as though he had turned into a venomous thing – which in a sense he had.

'I don't know you,' the other man said.

'Well, it has been a long time.' Thalric met his gaze levelly. 'You don't grudge the Empire this small thing, surely?'

And Ulther smiled, although it did not reach his eyes. 'Not at all, *Major*, although you . . . might just have asked. When, may I ask, shall she be returned to me?'

'Returned?' Thalric answered. 'Impossible to say, although I think it likely that, by the time I'm done with her, she will know more than it is healthy for a slave to know. We must all make sacrifices, Governor, for the Empire's good.'

Ulther nodded ponderously. 'Ah, well, that I can understand, Major.' And he kept the smile as he left to ascend again to the sunlit levels, but Thalric did not want to think what his expression might become after that.

And before he himself followed, he looked again at Kymene, who was studying him carefully. For a second, in her eyes, there was a look almost of complicity. *She enjoyed that scene.*

He made himself follow Ulther, but he was aware of her eyes following him all the way.

Twenty-six

'Her name is Kymene,' Chyses explained. Stenwold, who had heard a lot of Mynan names over the last half-hour, sensed from the way this one was said that it was special.

'She used to run your cell?' he guessed. *Che and Salma are the priority,* he reminded himself, but he was an intelligencer by habit, and thoughts were forming about Mynan resistance. The Empire's reach was as strong as the platform it reached out from.

'She is the beacon for the whole resistance,' Chyses told him. 'They were trying to catch her for well over a year. She invented the Red Flag: the symbol that strikes fear into the hearts of the Wasps. She is the best of us.'

'How did they catch her then?'

Chyses smiled sharply. 'Not with their thick-headed soldiers. The Bloat hired hunters from all over the Empire and one of them got lucky.'

Stenwold had gathered that the 'Bloat' was their name for the present governor. 'And she's been held for two tendays, now?'

Chyses nodded. 'And well guarded, deep in the guts of the palace. They think we can't get to her.'

'But you can?' *And you can get to Che and Salma* remained unsaid, and yet Stenwold felt the thought must be so apparent it must be branded on his face.

'They built that palace up so fast, just to show us we were conquered.' Chyses slapped the fist of one hand into the palm of the other, a habit he indulged in a lot. 'But they didn't think much on what lay underneath. See this?' He was indicating the decayed masonry, the lowest layer of stones of their sprawling cellar. 'There was some city here before we built Myna, before the revolution, and nobody even remembers whose, but they liked their tunnels. The sewers beneath us were their streets. They go right under the palace, under everywhere. That will be our way in.'

'Sewers?' Stenwold glanced at Tynisa and Totho, who were listening close by. 'Lovely.'

His sarcasm passed Chyses by. 'Our problem is that without Kymene we're vulnerable, fragmented. If the Bloat were to launch an assault on us now, if he got to know about enough of our safe houses and fallbacks, then we would . . .'

'You'd have a job to hold things together,' Stenwold finished.

'And at any attempt by us, right now, to make a rescue, the Bloat would clench his fist on the city like he did a few years back, when they had that uprising in Maynes.'

'So you can get to her, but your people would suffer for it,' Stenwold said. 'For a revolutionary that's a surprisingly responsible attitude.'

The look Chyses flashed him was savage. 'On my own, Master Beetle, I would set the fires myself, if the smoke from it would drive this city's people onto the streets,' he said flatly. 'However, *she* would not approve. I myself will not bow my head to either governor or emperor, but for Kymene . . .'

'I understand. And I see where your logic goes.' Stenwold felt a flash of dislike for Chyses but reminded himself, *We need this man.* 'Mynan resistance, red flags everywhere, and the administration comes down on you like thunder. But if a pack of foreigners is loose in the palace freeing prisoners, including your Kymene . . .'

'We understand each other.' Chyses took his hand off

his sword hilt, and Stenwold only then realized that the young man had been holding it. He still looked as if he wanted to kill people. Here was a man whose reserves of humanity had been drained. *They need this leader of theirs soon.* Revolution would not happen overnight in Myna, Stenwold divined, but neither would invasion happen overnight across the Lowlands. *Give me an audience with this woman, this undisputed leader of the resistance . . . Have we stumbled onto the weapon I have been looking for?*

'And you would provide . . . ?' he probed.

'Maps of the sewers, guides to go along with you, a few extra swords without livery to betray them. Hermetic lamps, an autoclef . . .'

'You're a well-equipped lot, aren't you?'

'Hokiak keeps us well supplied.' Chyses was humourless. 'Kymene is more important to us than any of it.'

'Well.' Stenwold settled back. 'I will have to canvass the others but I suspect we won't get a better offer.' He glanced up then, because Tisamon was approaching, and the Mantis looked sterner than usual. Tynisa stood up even as he arrived. The tension between the two of them was still there, the unresolved history, so much so that Stenwold could almost taste it.

'I have been talking to Khenice and those who remember the conquest, talking to them about your plans back then,' Tisamon announced.

'And?' Stenwold asked.

'They do accept that – that none of us betrayed them.' And only the briefest catch in Tisamon's voice revealed how recently he had been forced to accept it himself. 'We have been comparing memories. Totho?'

The artificer started. 'Yes, sir?'

'Tell them about Helleron. About the man you met there.'

Tynisa opened her mouth as if to speak, looked from Tisamon to Totho. The artificer glanced at her but Tisamon was waiting for his answer, and the Mantis plainly intimidated him more than Tynisa could. So, in his halting way, Totho gave the plain facts of what had happened to Bolwyn, and how it was that a dead man had met them in Benevolence Square. He could not keep the disbelief from his voice, but he spoke only the facts as he had witnessed them.

Chyses and the other Mynans appeared as sceptical as he himself was, looking to Tisamon for some explanation.

'We have named all those who knew about the original plan,' Tisamon said, 'many of whom died in the conquest. We can find no weak link, and yet our plan was betrayed. I think that there was a spy, indeed, but he might have been wearing the face of another.'

'But that's not possible,' Khenice said from behind him. 'We knew them all intimately and you couldn't disguise—'

'*This* man could,' Tisamon interrupted her. 'You heard the story: a perfect likeness.'

They still did not seem convinced, and Stenwold could not blame them. His own rational mind told him that such things were impossible. He had travelled more than most, though, and in stranger company, and had been forced, in the past, to accept that there were things in the world he could not account for.

'Where is this leading you?' he asked the Mantis.

'We may not be secure,' Tisamon warned. 'Even now we could be compromised.'

Stenwold put his head in his hands. 'Anything is possible, Tisamon, but I can't leave Cheerwell and Salma in their hands. I have to try.'

'Then let me scout the way first, that's all I ask. I will go now, with whatever directions our friends here can give me. There will be no time yet for a trap to have been set for me.'

Chyses stood up. 'And one more thing.' He and Tisamon

faced one another with a kind of generalized mutual dislike, two aggressive men confined in a small space. 'You can't trust us, is what you're saying. We can't trust you, either. When you do go to retrieve your friends, then Master Stenwold here will stay with us as surety. If you don't get Kymene back for us, then it will go badly for him.'

Stenwold sighed. Their relationship with the Mynan resistance was getting rockier by the moment. He nodded in response to Tisamon's enquiring look. *Besides, let them think I'm just a fat old man.* He might surprise them yet, if this went sour.

'Give me your best directions,' Tisamon instructed. 'I care nothing for your plans and drawings.' Chyses bristled at the tone, but nodded, went across the cellar for the maps.

When Tisamon departed, Tynisa followed him.

Problem after problem. Stenwold felt them weighing heavily on him.

'Master Maker,' Totho spoke at his elbow.

'I've told you, you don't need to—' The moments of his last conversation with the youth came back to him and he grimaced. 'Yes, Totho?'

'We still don't know how the Moth knew that Che and Salma were here, sir.'

Stenwold frowned at him. 'What are you saying?'

'That it could be a trap, like Tisamon says. A trap because *he's* set one.'

Stenwold glanced about the cellar, trying to find Achaeos. The Moth was almost hidden in the shadows across the room, sitting on his own in a nook of crumbling masonry.

'If he wanted to throw us to the Wasps, he has had ample chance. He even warned us of the ambush, before Asta. I cannot say precisely why he has linked his path to ours, Totho, but I feel sure it's not to sell us out, or not to the Empire.'

'But . . . I still don't trust him, Master Maker. I can't. Everything about him . . .'

Stenwold looked into the boy's honest face, that was itself stamped with a halfbreed taint others despised on sight. *Is this what they have taught you, by hating you?* But that was not the reason, he realized. Totho and Achaeos had loathed one another from the moment that they met, and Stenwold had no idea why.

Achaeos himself was finding it every bit as difficult to disentangle his motives. He had heard enough of Chyses' plans to find them fraught with danger. The time had come to ask himself whether he should even be here, let alone accompany the others on this lunatic's assault. The Mynan people – these Soldier Beetle-kinden as they called themselves – he found hostile and ill-favoured, and he had no faith in them or in their captured leader.

And yet he had the uncomfortable feeling that he was not able simply to sever his ties and fly away. It was not that he was already so deep within this Empire that the Wasp-kinden seemed to have built for themselves. He had no doubt he could find enough shadows between here and Tharn to cover his retreat. It was because he had, in his moment of madness, gone begging to the Darakyon. He had sought and received its help, and that had been for a purpose. He had told the things of the forest that he would rescue Cheerwell Maker. And, whilst riding their power, he had told *her* that he was coming for her. He had not meant to bind himself so irrevocably to this course but, now he came to recollect, he felt that he was indeed wholly bound.

Magic was a force that *pushed*: this he knew from his youngest days. What it pushed upon was a fabric that underlay the world, a weave beyond the weave. Perhaps the fabric was not so strong now as it once was, since the Apt minded and their machines were wearing it thread-bare. Still, it was there, and the cunning man learned to pull its threads and to twist the way it hung. That was the secret of their spy, of course: that had been an honoured calling back in the Days of Lore before the damned revolution. It surprised Achaeos to find that there was a practitioner left, but what other trade could so effectively hide itself from the world?

He cast his gaze, that knew neither shadows nor masks, across the assembled rebels and their uneasy guests. He felt there no tuggings at the weft of magic, but if such spies were as good as their legends, he probably would not anyway.

He saw the halfbreed artificer glaring at him. No love lost there and yet Achaeos was not entirely sure why. He had plenty of cause to hate back, of course. The Apt were driving his people into cultural, even physical extinction, so it should be he who nurtured a grievance. Instead, it was this young man with the world apparently in his hands, and Achaeos wondered what it was he was missing.

If he was honest with himself he felt he already knew, but he was not ready to be honest with himself. Honesty – now there was a wound that was slow to heal.

It was going just like before, and Tynisa was losing patience.

Within minutes of leaving the resistance cell she had virtually fallen into step with him, just like their scouting of the Asta slave pits, just like their entry into Myna and their ambush of Chyses' people. He had instantly adjusted to her and, without any signal, any conversation, they were become a hunting pair. Every move he made was informed by her own, as hers was by his. He did not need to look at her, to signal to her, to wait for her. Some part of him trusted her implicitly to be in exactly the right place, to do the right thing.

Yet when they were back with the others, she knew it would be gone again, this link she was now sharing with him. Not only gone, he would not admit of its existence. He would blot her out, refuse to deal with her.

She had a hook inside her now, and it had been pulling at her ever since she had discovered the truth. From the comfortable illusion of being Stenwold's daughter, however implausible that might have been, she had been thrust straight into another world. It was a harsh-edged world, and it gave her a mother long dead, and this man, this distant, impossible man, as a father. She needed to confront it, but he would not let her. Tisamon simply retreated from it.

He was a coward, she told herself. He was the great Mantis Weaponsmaster, of course. He could kill a hundred men just by sneezing. He was a coward, though. He had met something beyond his courage, and he was ignoring it.

They had followed the directions that Chyses had given. The sewers beneath Myna were ancient – ancient and huge. In places they had been more vast than some of the halls of the Great College, their monumental stones overgrown with algae, their sides slippery with grey moss. Sometimes from the broad walkway on one side to that on the other was a watery gap of ten feet. Myna was a city but by no means grand enough to warrant such extravagant plumbing. There had been carvings, too, but too effaced by time and the elements to be made out, no clue as to the builders of this fallen place that even the Mynans had mostly forgotten.

At one point they emerged into a square, as though these sewers had been a whole city in their own right once.

There was a broken-off stump of a statue there, just worn feet and the jagged lower edge of robes, but time remained mute and kept its secrets.

Things moved in the water that she did not get a proper look at, and roaches half the size of a man scuttled away from the dim light of the hooded lantern Tisamon bore. It gave out barely a gleam, but they both had eyes able to take that gleam and use it to best effect.

The directions had been good and Tisamon's recall of them perfect. The resistance movement had taken its time in plotting these sewers that had become its main thoroughfare. In less time than Tynisa had imagined they had found some more recent architecture. Before Governor Ulther had raised his great palace as a symbol of his supremacy there had stood here the Consensus where the senate and tribunes of Myna would meet to argue policy. Even a seat of government requires its sewers, and more than that. Though the structure above ground had been banished, the cellars remained, tucked down beneath the later cells and storerooms that the Wasps had excavated.

They had found the narrow stairs exactly where Chyses had indicated. Tisamon had padded up them first to reach the hatch there, which a sympathizer serving within the palace secretly kept unbarred. With no more fanfare than that they had slipped into the palace itself. Where they entered had been a mere grain cellar, but they now stepped where Wasp feet had recently trod, and the resistance's plan was thus vindicated. Tynisa had wanted to press on then, to find Che and Salma on their own. But a single exchange of looks with Tisamon had dissuaded her. They needed more hands, and they had made a deal with Chyses. Tisamon took his word as seriously as his life; it was a Mantis thing, but she could grasp it if she reached far enough.

And then they were on their way back, to report that

the plan was sound, that it could be accomplished, and she knew that as soon as they were done, their shroud of silence replaced with the need to speak, then she would be shut out by him again. It was like before, at Asta, or when they crept over the walls of Myna itself. He would take it back, take it all back, and then he would hate her again.

And she made up her mind then, *When Che and Salma are free I will force you to recognize me, you bastard. I will force you on the blade's point, or I shall make you kill me, because I cannot live with this indifference.*

Twenty-seven

Thalric returned to his chambers and methodically ensured that everything essential he owned was ready to take on his person. He laid out his sword and swordbelt, his pack with writing kit and paper and all the imperial documents he carried. He then took out his most valuable possession, for a man who travelled light. It was a short-sleeved shirt of copper-steel mesh, made somewhere far beyond the Empire's borders. They were highly sought after, far more in demand than could be satisfied by the thin trickle of supply that reached the imperial markets by the Silk Road. He had been lucky to find it, for copper-weave armour was normally a perquisite of generals and statesmen.

He stripped off his tunic and put the garment on. Its thin layer of cloth backing was cool against his chest. When he put another tunic on, with sleeves down to the elbow, no watcher would guess at the thin layer of metal next to his skin.

He then buckled his swordbelt, wondering how much time he still had. The thought that at the end Ulther might stay loyal did not occur to him. He had lived with treachery long enough to hear its tread on the stairs.

And such a simple net to catch a man who was governor of Myna: to take his toys away and wait for the tantrum. If Thalric had been sentimental he would have been bitterly disappointed. In fact, he now admitted, he *was* disappointed. He should not have had to do this, not to Ulther, who had once been his friend and patron.

But the story that Hreya had told him had been clear enough: Ulther was a man of appetites. The great warrior of two decades before had become today's petty tyrant. Myna was his city and he ran it for his personal delectation and that of his cronies, his *sycophants*, as the woman Kymene had called them. For a man of Thalric's trade it had not taken long to uncover the signs. The imperial tallies did not tally. There were goods and coin going missing, far more than the mechanical supplies that Aagen had come here to chase. The war that was being constructed in Asta was months behind schedule, stinted at every turn as Myna was made a chokehold in the imperial supply lines. What Ulther did not appropriate himself, his parasites soon made off with. The black market of Myna was growing fat on war supplies that the Empire could not afford to lose.

Ulther was grown drunk on power, and his henchmen were growing fat on the Empire's tax money and war funds. Meanwhile the city itself had been on the brink of explosion for years. Ulther had done a good job of keeping it from boiling over, but it was still seething, and Thalric had seen enough damaging reports. Even incarcerating Kymene had not been a real blow to the resistance because Ulther had seen her as a trophy and not an opportunity. The good man Thalric once knew had become a liability, had become a burden on the imperial war machine, a cancer that must be operated upon immediately, if the Empire was to exercise its full strength against the Lowlands.

So Colonel Latvoc had been right, in the end. He had even been right, in all probability, to send Thalric. That did not mean that Thalric had to like it, however.

He drew his blade, examined its surface for rust. It did not see as much wear as it should, but then a good Rekef agent seldom needed to fight in person. This time it would be different, though.

He looked up. 'You can come out now,' he said. 'You're fooling no one.'

He could not, in fact, have said where the watcher was, although he knew he was being watched. The shadow that moved was outside the window, someone crouched on the sill beside that narrow aperture. With an impressive display of dexterity a small figure squeezed through an opening never intended as an entrance, and descended to the floor in a glitter of wings. It was te Berro, Latvoc's man.

'How am I doing?' Thalric asked dryly.

'Why don't you tell me?' Te Berro dusted himself off. He was wearing a shapeless white robe, like many of the local Fly-kinden, but Thalric saw a bulge that must indicate a dagger hilt.

'The lines are drawn. They'll move against me soon,' Thalric said. 'Ulther will go and wrestle with his conscience for a while, but his greed will pin it easily. Then he'll send men after me.'

'Do you require help?' te Berro asked him. 'The Rekef Inlander have a few hands in the city, low ranked mostly.'

That would be a blessed abrogation of responsibility, to step aside and let the Rekef deal with his old mentor.

Thalric shook his head. 'I'll do it. If it's possible, I'll do it. But keep an eye on me, in case.'

'If so, we may be too late.'

'Then so be it.'

'Your prerogative, of course.' Te Berro nodded. 'Good luck, Major Thalric.' The Fly's wings blurred at his shoulders and he hopped to the window ledge.

'Lieutenant . . .'

'Major?'

Thalric took a deep breath. 'You've been on Colonel Latvoc's staff for how long, Lieutenant?'

'Over a year now, sir.' As te Berro crouched at the window, it was impossible to know whether the question made him uncomfortable.

'If he wants Ulther dead, why not just kill him?' The words dropped like lead. Te Berro stared, trapped suddenly in a conversation he had no wish to be a part of.

'Sir?'

'We are the Rekef, te Berro. City governors choke on their meat or fall out of windows or cut their throats shaving, same as everybody else. Why this charade?'

'You think he tells me anything?' te Berro said, hurrying the words out before they could be used against him. 'You've made your investigation. You've found a reason to convict him. Be happy with that, Major. Be happy that it will all look legitimate when Ulther's friends come calling.' His face twisted slightly. 'Besides, maybe it's not really Ulther they're interested in. Maybe it's you, Major?' His wings sprang dustily into existence, and a moment later he had contorted his way out of the narrow window and was gone.

By the sputtering, ghostly light of their artificial lamps Achaeos heard them whisper about the hands that built these ancient sewers. He rolled his blank eyes at it all but knew enough to stay silent.

There were enough of the lichen-overgrown and defaced carvings left for him to recognize the ancient structure as his own people's handiwork. So Myna had once been a city of the Moth-kinden, so long lost now that even Tharn was unaware of it. But no, somewhere high enough up in the echelons of his masters that knowledge would remain. There was precious little of the past that they did not know. Knowledge was a currency in Tharn, and it was guarded more jealously than gold, even from their own kin.

Achaeos wondered whether they ever thought of him, wished him luck or wondered if he still lived. By this evening that might be a moot point.

He, who had so often troubled the world for news of the future, now felt trapped by the strings of fate. A chain of happenstance had tethered him to this moment, as surely as if he had become a slave of the Wasps himself. He had not intended any of it. He had merely sought Elias Monger's stables as a brief hiding place. He would have been gone at nightfall, and nobody would have been the wiser – if not for that meddling woman.

And even her name was maddening. Only a Beetle would call a girlchild 'Cheerwell'. They had no grace or taste.

If only she had not intruded. If only she had not been too strong for the Art-trance he had thrown over her. If only, when she had broken free of him, she had not gifted him back his freedom by her silence. If only she had not treated his wounds, his blood glistening on her hands, or if only he had not let her do so.

Well, fate dealt me a poor hand, and I played it badly even so. No sense battering himself against the glass now. He had provided for himself as best he could, and Chyses' cell had provided him with a bow of cheap Fly-kinden make and a dozen short arrows. They would have to do.

He kept ahead of the lamplight, having no need of it. Even further ahead were the Mantis and the Spider-kinden girl, retracing their earlier steps. He could read the hostility between them clearly, although he had no interest whatsoever in their squabbles, save that the task would become easier if they were not at each other's throats. Behind him came the heavy tread of the Apt: the halfbreed artificer clutching a truly grotesque-looking crossbow; then the leader of the resistance, Chyses, and two of his fellows, hooded and masked like travellers on a dusty road. Behind them, on near-silent bare feet, was the turncoat Grass-hopper militiawoman, Toran Awe, with her staff. Achaeos put no faith in any of them.

He sensed they were approaching their destination, for Tisamon and Tynisa were slowing, waiting for the light to catch up with them. He padded to a halt beside them, looking at the hatch just above. Now the stones around him were no longer relics of his own people's fall, for which he was grateful.

The others soon joined them. Chyses unrolled a rough map of the palace's lower floors, which had been prepared with the complicity of servants working in the building. Achaeos had difficulty making anything of it.

'We'll need to head up from these storerooms,' the Mynan explained. 'There are several cellar systems and they don't link. The cells we're all interested in are right here. That's assuming the prisoners haven't been moved in the last few days. Who has the autoclef?'

'That would be me,' Totho said, displaying the toothy device for a moment. 'Do we know exactly which cells they're in?'

'Kymene's cell is open fronted, so I'm told, but as for your friends, just open every cell you come across. As far as I'm concerned, anyone who's been locked up by the Wasps deserves to go free,' said Chyses.

'The Wasps will realize we're there that much the sooner,' Tynisa warned him.

'And they'll have more to worry about,' Chyses said. 'And I would not be a true enemy of theirs if I did not set every last one of their prisoners free, whether they be friends of mine, or friends of yours, or even just criminals and murderers.'

Totho exchanged an uneasy glance with Tynisa, but Tisamon was already over at the hatch, listening intently. A moment later he levered the trapdoor open, took a second to peer around, and then pushed it all the way up and pulled himself through.

It was quiet in the storeroom itself, but there was movement enough above it. Large buildings like this palace never really slept, and there was a whole nightshift of servants preparing for the new day: cleaning and repairing, stoking fires, baking breakfasts. Chyses had said that the hated governor had a love of opulence. It all multiplied the number of eyes now abroad to see them.

Chyses had also been adamant that these servants were mostly locals and so would keep their mouths shut. Tisamon remained unconvinced.

He gathered himself and then took the stairs with a measured, silent tread. A faint lamp-glow came from above, and he crept to the door. It was barred from the far side, but he slipped the blade of his claw between door and frame. Behind him, he sensed Tynisa and the Grasshopper, Toran Awe, tense.

The bar lifted, and Tisamon eased the door open. A soft gleam of lamplight fell past him as he leant back into the shadow of the door. Toran Awe slipped by into the corridor. She was wearing her uniform: the yellow shirt and dark breeches that were the stamp of her conscription. They heard her murmur something, and then there was a sharp sound of wood on flesh, a muffled cry, and another blow.

Moments later the Grasshopper was back, dragging with her the body of a Mynan servant. Chyses' eyes – the only part of him visible between hood and mask – glared at her resentfully.

'Don't tell us,' Tisamon warned him, 'that every one of your people taking the governor's bread is just waiting to throw off their shackles.'

'He is stunned only,' Toran assured them, as she passed

the limp form back to them and Chyses' two associates laid it in the grain cellar.

'And this way, he may not suffer for what we're about to do,' Tynisa added. Chyses' angry look did not soften, but he nodded grudgingly.

'The sands are running now,' said Tisamon, 'until he's missed. Where does your map say we should go next?'

Achaeos could have told them, if only they would have believed him and if only they could have walked through solid earth and stone. The maze of the palace was unknown to him, but he could feel her heart beating, even through these cellar walls, feel the blood he had shed on her hands calling out to him.

Thalric had to wait until dusk before they came for him, and he would never know whether it was Ulther's conscience that had restrained him that long, or if they had needed the time to gather their courage.

He had made himself readily available. Wherever he had gone throughout the day, there had been servants watching who could report on his doings. It was important, at this point, that they find him easily.

His plan, which seemed to have come to fruition without his ever having to piece it together, was complete.

He had chosen a walled garden this time, situated on one of the higher tiers of the palace. The expense that must have gone into the hauling of the earth and the plants staggered him, let alone the constant attention needed to prevent such an artificial plantation from withering where it stood. It would be as suitable a place as any to confront what Ulther would send for him.

When he saw them he was instantly relieved. If it had been soldiers then he would have been out of his depth. Ulther had a great many soldiers to call on, and the Auxillian militia as well, but it was obvious he did not trust the garrison. The Rekef's reputation had done its work well. Ulther knew there must be Rekef agents in place, but could not know who, and so he could not even trust his own men in this. Instead, he had gone to his henchmen, his sycophants, and told them that the hour had come for them to repay him for all his favour.

Some half a dozen men came stalking carefully into the garden. Thalric had made sure he was seen going there, but he had chosen a vantage point concealed behind a stand of stunted fruit trees, so he had a good chance to see who he was dealing with.

He recognized first Oltan the quartermaster, surely a leading hand behind the embezzling of supplies that had brought Aagen here. The items he had taken as his due, intended for the war effort, instead went onto the black market, feeding into the lawlessness of the city and therefore the power of the resistance. Behind Oltan came Freigen of the Consortium of the Honest. Thalric, who disliked self-important merchants even when they did their job, would lose no sleep over his death. Draywain, his Beetle-kinden partner, was not present; either he was insufficiently martial or insufficiently reliable. There was the intelligencer, Rauth, as well, who must have found his own games to play with the Empire's resources, and there was a confidence to his walk that had Thalric pinning him as the most dangerous of the conspirators. There were another two as well, unknown to him, but evidently of the same stamp.

Then, muscling in from behind Freigen, came a figure looming head and shoulders over the others: a Scorpion-kinden, massively built and bare chested. Some hired thug or bodyguard, Thalric guessed, and he looked a capable one. He was not armed, and that in itself was worrying. It suggested that his scythed hands alone would be sufficient for his needs.

With Thalric not immediately visible, they paused at

the garden's entrance. Rauth was glancing upwards, evidently wondering if their quarry had made his escape skywards. Some brief argument went on between the others, and then Freigen took a step forward.

'Captain Thalric, are you there? The governor has sent us to . . . to talk with you. Will you come forth?' The hesitation part-way through made his speech ridiculous and Thalric saw an annoyed look pass over the faces of some of the others.

Now or never. He stretched out his hand, stepping forward to get a better look at them. His Ancestor Art coalesced in his mind and he sent it forth. His fingers spat golden light at them.

He had been aiming for the Scorpion hireling but, as luck would have it, Oltan had chosen that moment to step in to tug at Freigen's sleeve and the bolt of energy struck him instead. As Thalric had been aiming for the centre of the Scorpion's chest, Oltan took the blow full in his face, slamming back against the big mercenary and then collapsing to the ground, dead before he knew it.

'There!' howled Freigen, and launched a bolt of light at Thalric himself. It went wide and Thalric already had his sword out, still half hidden by the trees. Some of them were coming for him and others were seeking cover of their own. The Scorpion shouldered Freigen out of his way and ran at Thalric, claws out and held low. Thalric sent another bolt that scorched across the huge man's shoulder but barely slowed him, and then he kicked off into the air. Sting-bolts lashed left and right of him, but none of them close yet. He glanced down to see at least three of them coming after him, and wondered whether they were any good, whether their years of self-indulgence had left them room for training and practice.

He chose to alight on another tier quickly, for he was not the strongest flier of his people. Even as he touched down they were upon him.

The first man approaching was a face unknown, barrelling up with his sword foremost and his eyes almost closed. No warrior, this one. Thalric stepped aside neatly, ducking into a crouch as the man passed over him and stumbled into an awkward landing. Before he could recover, Thalric had kicked out into an extended lunge, his wings flickering for just a second to help turn a three-foot jump into a six-foot leap. His sword caught the man in the ribs. His victim had the armour of the light airborne on under his tunic, but that was open at the sides, and the man screamed in shock as the blade pierced him, rammed home almost to the hilt.

As the guard flexed against the man's ribs Thalric instantly let go of it and was snatching the man's own military-issue blade from the air. He whirled just as a thrust sliced across his shoulder, grating on the copper-weave armour beneath. His assailant's face twitched with surprise, either at Thalric's speed or his mail. Thalric elbowed him in the face, breaking his nose and spattering them both with blood.

Rauth was now standing on the very edge of the balcony, wings dancing in and out of existence to keep him balanced there. As the bloody-faced man staggered away Rauth took one step down and levelled his blade, his offhand raised high and directed forward. For Thalric it was a pose that brought back a lot of bittersweet memories.

He recalled that the girl Cheerwell had been part of some duelling circle at Collegium, for all the good it had done her, but the Beetle-kinden were not unique in their ritual combat; Thalric himself had done his time amongst the Arms-Brothers when he was a junior officer, learning the blade and practising his social contacts. Rauth had taken the stance of an Arms-Brother duellist, and he was waiting for Thalric to join him.

Old habits, however inappropriate, die hard. Thalric felt himself drop into the correct stance without really choosing to, and a moment later he was making his careful advance.

Rauth lunged first, kicking off into the air and reversing his blade, coming down point first towards Thalric's collarbone. Of course these were not the practice blades of dull bone usually seen in the sand circles of the Arms-Brothers. The steel flashed past Thalric as he swayed back, and his own stroke went wild, but he followed it up with three savage circular sweeps that Rauth dodged and ducked until he was on the very edge of the tier again. There was no parrying among the Arms-Brothers: the sword was for offence only, feet and wings were for defence.

Rauth was airborne again, passing straight overhead. Thalric spun as he passed, cutting across the man's flight-path and scoring a narrow line across his calf. The man with the broken nose ran in suddenly, half-blinded and charging like a mad animal. Thalric stepped left and low, his leading leg folded double, and as the man went past he opened him up below the sternum with a single slice, and then sent him over the side with a spinning kick, launching him screaming down twenty feet into the unsuspecting garden.

Rauth had tried to make use of the distraction but as he pounced again from above his doomed comrade's flight got in his way. He ducked back and Thalric drove up at him. For a moment they spun about one another in the air, swords drawing a complex web of lines about them, and then they were on the very balcony edge once again, back into their familiar stances.

Time to bring this to a close, decided Thalric. It was not a move from the Arms-Brothers manual but he launched a bolt of energy from his offhand at Rauth's chest. The other man jumped back, but the flash seared across him anyway, and he dropped from sight off the balcony, injured but by no means done for. A moment later he was soaring back and around to come up on the other side. Thalric turned – and came face to face with the huge Scorpion-kinden hireling.

How—? was all he had time to think, and *Bastard must have climbed up*, before one of the great clawed hands pincered into his left shoulder.

The pain nearly made Thalric drop his blade. The finger claw was deep under his shoulder blade and the thumb wedged in near his collarbone, and the big man was doing his best to lift Thalric off the ground by his grip. Over the Scorpion's shoulder Thalric saw Rauth arrowing in, sword forward. He flared his wings in a desperate flurry, gripping the Scorpion's wrist, and kicked off from the tier's edge. The movement spun the ungainly Scorpion about just as Rauth was coming in, and the assailant's blade slashed across the huge mercenary's back.

The Scorpion roared in pain and backhanded Rauth away, whereupon Thalric rammed his blade into the big man's chest, and gripped him by the throat for good measure before blasting forth with his sting. The shock knocked the great man flat, and Thalric was flung away. A moment later he was falling.

The pain of his pierced shoulder was almost all he could think about and he barely got his wings about him to catch him in mid-air. He was already below the level of the treetops in the garden when he stayed his mad plummet. As he laboured back up he knew that he would not have the strength to fly after this final effort.

Rauth was just getting to his feet, sword already in hand, and Thalric saw his glance flick from his approaching opponent to the sword still lodged in the Scorpion's body.

Thalric was feeling dead on his feet and every movement sent a jolt of pain lancing through him. Even so, he got to his sword first, hauling it from the corpse and bringing it into line with his enemy as Rauth bore down on him. Suddenly footsteps from behind brought the truth of the situation, though. He had forgotten Freigen the merchant, who presumably did not count flight as one of his assets. He had been all this time running up stairs, but now he was here and Rauth paused, waiting for the inevitable moment when Thalric's attention proved insufficient to split between them.

An expression of shock crossed Rauth's face in the very moment before Thalric, with the very last of his reserves, ran him through. The sword's tip grated on armour first, but found its way between the metal plates, biting through the leather backing and deep into Rauth's body. For the third time, Thalric felt the sword hilt slip from his fingers. He dropped to his knees, trying to even out his breathing, and it was a good many seconds before he turned round.

Freigen was lying face down with an arrow in his back, while the diminutive te Berro sat ten yards away at the far end of the balcony, calmly unstringing his bow. It had been, Thalric was forced to admit, an admirable shot.

He stood up at last, feeling a little strength return to him, and reclaimed his own sword from the first man he had stabbed. The Fly-kinden looked up with a diffident smile as Thalric approached to thank him.

'Don't mention it,' te Berro said. 'All suspicions confirmed now, of course. So, what about Ulther?'

'I should do it,' said Thalric.

'Forgive me, but you don't look in any shape for that.'

Thalric let out a harsh laugh: he felt about a hundred years old at this moment. 'I don't expect you to understand or approve, but I owe it to him to do it myself.'

'Your operation, your choice,' te Berro confirmed. 'He's in his harem, waiting to hear the news from his victorious assassins.'

Thalric nodded, still gathering his strength like an officer marshalling wavering soldiers. He wiped his blade off on dead Freigen's back, and carefully sheathed it. No sense in alarming the servants as he went on his way to murder their master.

Twenty-eight

Chyses' two men had remained in the storeroom to guard their retreat, in case anyone sought to bar it against them. Chyses himself had taken the rest where his map led, up stairs and through dim corridors lit only by the slanting moon. He carried a mineral-oil lighter which he struck up only when the map proved impossible to decipher in the gloom, and he led them with a kind of blind confidence.

Achaeos knew, though, even before they came to the large hallway, that Chyses was not entirely sure where they were.

The room itself quite obviously took him aback. The ceiling was two storeys high, with a grand flight of stone-faced steps taking up half the floor space. Chyses hissed to himself and took the map out again. Tisamon and Tynisa stood waiting a few paces to either side.

'I think . . .' Chyses said, trying to get the map angled towards moonlight. The windows were so high up on the wall behind them that their light slanted directly to the far end of the room, rippling up the stairs. Irritably, he struck up the lamp again, and tried to unpuzzle the map by its pale flame.

'Let me see.' Totho came forward, balancing the cross-bow in one hand. Chyses jerked the map irritably away from him – and at that very moment a Wasp soldier appeared at the top of the stairs.

He did not run for help. Instead he started down the steps towards them with an angry cry. Later, Tynisa guessed that all he had seen were Totho and Chyses. She and Tisamon, silent and still in the darkness, had escaped his notice.

She was a pace towards the guard, still unseen, when Totho let fly with the crossbow. The first bolt, by sheer luck, caught the man in the shoulder. He lost his footing on the stairs and clattered back onto them with a yell. The second shot, following hard on the first, shattered into pieces against the steps, while the third took him in mid-chest as he sat up, a perfect target-range hit, slamming him down again and cutting short his cry of warning.

There was no immediate uproar from around them, but they knew it would soon be coming. 'Which way, Chyses?' hissed Tisamon, and perhaps the threat implicit in his voice brought the man's judgment into focus, because he was now pointing back into the hallway they had just exited.

'Next door along,' he told them. 'Stairs down, should be.'

Tisamon was already past him and gone. Totho was still fumbling fresh bolts into the wooden magazine atop his bow. 'Come *on*,' Tynisa urged him, and then she realized that Toran Awe, was not following them.

'What—?'

'I will speak to them when they come,' the Grasshopper said calmly. 'I will send them the wrong way. After all, I am militia. I am supposed to be here.'

Tynisa gave her a quick nod, and then followed Totho along the hall.

This time Chyses was right, or at least his map was. The plain stone stairs took them into the earth again, and to another hallway with small doors to one side. Totho was already bustling towards one with the autoclef, a spiny device about a foot long which he fed into the keyhole and then adjusted. As it click-clicked to itself within the lock,

Totho gritted his teeth and continued to play with it, cycling through various combinations of teeth in search of the one that would move the tumblers. It did not look like a high-standard lock but something workaday and easily made. It should not be taking this long, surely.

Finally, it clicked, and the door pulled open as he removed the autoclef. Inside were two ragged Fly-kinden men, blinking sleepily up at them.

'Who are these?' one of them demanded of the other, but Tynisa just pointed to one side.

'Go. Get out and don't ask questions,' she said and, still not quite believing their good fortune, they fled.

They found three locals in the other cells, and then two empty ones. There was no sign of Salma or Che.

'Kymene's cell lies deeper than this,' Chyses announced. 'We have to move on.'

'What about our friends?' Tynisa demanded, and he shrugged.

'We don't know where they are. We do know where Kymene is and that's all we know.' The locals they had rescued had already vanished in the opposite direction.

There was a gasp from along the corridor, and they saw two servants standing there, having just come up from some deeper level. They immediately turned to flee and Tisamon was on them like an arrow, charging down the hall towards them.

'No!' Chyses yelled, and then the servants were rebounding at the far end of the hall, as a soldier suddenly appeared there. In an instant his hand was outstretched, energy crackling from it. Tisamon dropped to his knees, skidding along the smooth flags of the floor, and the bolt of fire lanced over his head even as he rammed his claw forward, taking the man in the side and then again across the throat as he fell.

They could hear a disturbance on the floor above, but seeming to get fainter as they listened. Tynisa hoped

Toran Awe would be successful in her subterfuge and keep them running, and that the Grasshopper would not suffer for it.

'Downwards,' Chyses hissed, and two turns later he at last found a stairway for them. By now Tynisa had lost all track of whether they were above or below the storeroom through which they had entered, but just as she was deciding that Chyses had lost the way again, Achaeos spoke from her elbow.

'This is it,' he said. 'We're getting closer.'

His face, grey and white-eyed, was unreadable.

Chyses was moving faster now, informed constantly by the sounds from above that their sands of opportunity were running out. He took less care now, he was almost running headlong. Tynisa and Tisamon could keep up with him, but she knew that Totho was clumping along increasingly far at the rear. Achaeos could be anywhere. She lost track of him from moment to moment.

Then, ahead of them, a door burst open and Wasp soldiers came out.

Chyses hit the first one head on. He could not have stopped if he had wanted to. He had a long dagger drawn and, as the two of them went over, he was already stabbing at the man savagely. The second man clear of the door tried to back away, almost tripping over Chyses and then righting himself with a flash of his wings. In that moment Tynisa was on him. Her first lunge merely scraped on his armour, giving him a chance to drag his shortsword clear of its scabbard. But before he could thrust it into her she was over his guard, the point of her rapier entering under his ribs and pressing forward until only inches of the blade could be seen between flesh and hilt. He stabbed at her anyway, even as his legs gave way, but she twisted out of the blade's path easily, pushing down on his shoulder to yank her sword free.

She turned to find Tisamon had felled two more,

Wasps without armour, and was lunging at another who was trying to back away from the doorway. The vicious claw slashed the man across the chest, but shallowly, and then a bolt of Wasp-sting energy lashed out to char the facing wall, making Tisamon duck sideways out of view. Tynisa made to lunge through the doorway past him but, while she was still thinking it, Achaeos put in a brief appearance, crouching low and already releasing his bowstring as she saw him. There was a cry from inside, and she and Tisamon went sweeping into the room in the next moment.

Instantly Tisamon was brought up short, snapping himself back into a defensive stance with his claw raised high to confront some great menace. She pushed past him, running her blade into the adversary whose chest Tisamon had already slashed so that he sprawled back across a great table.

There was a last Wasp there, at the far end of the room, and she registered his widening glance. There was an arrow in him, the shaft shuddering as he tried to remain standing. He had his hand held out towards her and, had he not been a Wasp, she might have thought it a gesture of supplication.

Tynisa froze: he was too far to take a run at. While she hesitated, another arrow seemed to flower magically beside the first, and a gush of blood burst from his lips. The Wasp fell back against the wall and slid to the ground.

That was it. There were no more of them. It came to her afterwards that, aside from the first two soldiers, the rest had not been in armour, had in fact been dressed in civilian clothes.

Tisamon was now advancing down the length of the table's far side, and at last she saw what had so startled him. The carapace of a gigantic praying mantis hung on wires, looming over the table. Tisamon stared up at it and then, with an angry sound, he vaulted onto the table, scattering papers, and sliced through the wires with three swift blows. In a moment the macabre display was tumbling down, chitin plates bouncing and cracking.

Tynisa saw that the table had some kind of map on it, and papers as well, closely written with numbers. She swept up as many of them as she could grab and folded them, stuffed them into her tunic. *Stenwold will like these,* she had decided.

Chyses was in the doorway with his bloodied dagger. 'We're wasting time,' he insisted.

'You led us here,' she replied sharply. 'Now lead us where we're supposed to be.'

Thalric did what he could with the wound. Ten years' worth of field surgery in yet more friendless places than this came to his aid. The Scorpion's claws had punched straight through his copperweave mail, leaving two jagged circles of broken links. He wondered, if he had not been wearing it, whether he might have lost his arm at the shoulder.

He took a moment, out of sight of the world, and even of te Berro, just to sag against a wall and close his eyes. It had been a rough night and the worst was still to come. Already he could hear running feet and he had left a pretty pattern of bodies in the garden and on the upper tier. Let them come flooding upwards. Let them start their search there on the terrace itself, or stare up at the skies for aerial assassins. He was already heading in the opposite direction.

Yes, quite. It seemed his whole career had reversed direction recently. He could not quite disentangle the pain in his shoulder from the feeling of defeat and despair that attended his mission. It should not have to be like this, a man turning on his friend, but Thalric was above all a loyal servant of the Empire.

He was also a loyal servant of the Rekef and, if he

strained his imagination just far enough, he could justify to himself that the two were the same thing.

He had run ragged his reserves of strength in that fight, so his sword would be his first resort now. Using the Art-made sting of his people – which had become the symbol of their conquest in the eyes of the conquered – was draining on one's physical reserves.

He knew he could have let te Berro and his agents deal with Ulther, but that would have been one betrayal further than he was willing to go. If things went badly, if Ulther had more sycophants to deploy, or even managed to kill him personally, then perhaps there would be some balance restored in that. He pushed himself away from the wall with a groan, and started off on his way to Ulther's harem. The thought that he might encounter Ulther in the throes of the old man's passions drew an involuntary, horrified laugh from him.

The servants he passed flinched away from him at the sight of his grim expression or his bloodied shoulder. There was a great deal of commotion on the upper floors that Thalric passed through like a ghost, and as he descended the stairs it was like going underwater, suddenly so quiet, but with a pressure in his head he knew was bred of doubt and guilt.

There were half a dozen guards in a sentry post near the cells, but Tisamon was running ahead of the pack now, and Tynisa got there just in time to put her rapier in the back of one who was trying to put distance between himself and the Mantis. Inside the sentry room Tisamon stood behind a table strewn with cards and small coins and the floor was scattered with bodies, like some Collegium woodcut depicting the evils of gambling. Despite her willing involvement in the venture the sight brought home to her just how much blood had been shed that night, and how much might yet be spilled.

Chyses joined them then, and Totho barrelled past him and began clicking away at the first locked door, not with the cumbersome autoclef but with a set of keys taken from one of the slain guards.

'No, further on,' the Mynan directed. 'She's down that way.'

'We'll do this my way,' Totho told him patiently. 'I'm not here for your leader.'

Chyses bared his teeth and Tynisa saw his knuckles whiten about his dagger hilt. She moved to stand beside Totho, where the Mynan could see her intent. At the same time, and somewhat to her surprise, she found herself seeking out Achaeos.

The Moth gave her a small head-shake. 'Further in,' was all he would say. Totho hunched his shoulders against the revelation and sprung the first door open. Inside there was a shabby-looking Soldier Beetle-kinden, a greying, careworn-looking man.

'Out,' Chyses told him. 'Out and get yourself a weapon from the guard room there.' The prisoner paused only a moment and then went to obey.

Without saying anything at all, Tisamon went to the foot of the stairs they had descended and waited. Tynisa knew that his instinct was right. There would be more soldiers coming soon. Their luck had held so far but the imperial garrison in Myna was large, and all within easy reach of the palace. As soon as someone realized just what was going on then they wouldn't be able to move for armed Wasps. She cast a glance at Tisamon, seeing how they were working together like a pair of hands now, just like before. She could hardly believe it. *Before tonight is out I shall shock you, father. You cannot ignore me forever.*

Totho was working feverishly on the fifth door now, and meanwhile they were accumulating more ragged, determined looking Mynan men and women, weighing

Wasp swords and daggers in their hands and waiting for further orders.

These had been a warrior people, Tynisa recalled, before the conquest. Not so belligerent as Ant-kinden or the Wasps themselves, but fighting to defend their own was ingrained in them. *Just as well, because they're going to need it.*

They had reached the end of this row of cells but the corridor continued, and Chyses was already hurrying down it. They all heard his shout of 'You're here!' and then he was running back towards them.

'I've found her!' he declared. 'Come on, man, hurry!'

A woman's voice from down the corridor called, 'Chyses, watch out!' and almost as the words echoed the first bolt of energy crackled past. Totho dropped to one knee and worked the crossbow's lever furiously, emptying the weapon as another sting-bolt exploded against the wall beside him, scorching his cheek. One of the Wasp soldiers ahead of them went down before Totho's barrage, but the way ahead was dark and he was not a good shot by nature. A second soldier had ducked behind his companion, and was now crouched flat against a wall. Tynisa dragged Totho into the shelter of one of the cells as he fumbled for another magazine.

'You're not a soldier,' she reminded him, but then there was the hiss of another bolt of energy zipping past the doorway, and she heard Chyses curse.

She tensed, because she knew, in spite of herself, that Tisamon was about to rush the man, and that she would go too, to back him up. Even with that thought there came a cry from where the soldier was, and the sound of a scuffle, metal ringing on metal. Tisamon dashed past their doorway and Tynisa followed suit but it was over before either of them got there. The soldier lay face down with an arrow in his back and several jagged wounds elsewhere, and Achaeos was standing over him, trembling. He held a dagger in his hand, his arm steeped in blood to the elbow. His offhand palm was wet with his own and he had a split lip, and from that Tynisa could reconstruct the past moments. Achaeos had crept up in the dark for a shot, but it had not been as sure as he hoped, and the wounded man had charged him. She wondered whether this was the first time he had killed a man close to.

'Good work,' Tisamon nodded, and the Moth nodded back wordlessly. Something twisted in Tynisa then, because that simple commendation from him was more than she had ever received.

'Kymene!' Chyses exclaimed, and Tynisa realized that behind the bars of the one open-fronted cell, in the shadows, stood a woman who was watching them keenly. As she stepped into the light, Tynisa was struck by the instant calming effect she seemed to exert on the Mynans there, each and every one of them.

'The door, if you please,' she said, as though all of this were her own plan and she had been expecting them. Totho hurried up with the keys and then, when none of these would fit, starting scratching away with his autoclef. Tisamon returned down the corridor to take up his post by the guard room, and Tynisa knew it would not be long before they heard the sounds of further fighting there.

'Who are these people?' Kymene asked Chyses.

'Foreigners,' he explained. 'They're here after two of their own.'

'Then we owe them a debt for their aid,' she said, and just then Totho opened the gate in the bars with a cry of triumph. As Kymene stepped out like a queen entering her kingdom, Tynisa decided that the woman could be no more than a year or two her senior.

She heard awed whispers from some of the freed prisoners. 'The Maid,' and 'The Maid of Myna,' they murmured.

'Whom do you seek?' Kymene asked her.

'A Dragonfly man and a Beetle-kinden girl.'

'A brown-skinned girl with dyed pale hair?'

'You've seen her!' Totho exclaimed instantly. 'Where—?'

'I don't know which cell is hers, but when they lead her back to it, they always take her that way,' Kymene explained. 'Chyses, you must stay and guide them.'

There was no argument from Chyses now as he bowed the head to his leader. Kymene laid a hand on his shoulder in thanks.

'Show me how you intend to leave this place,' she said, and he had the map out ready in an instant. She studied it for a moment, marked the route. 'I will take these,' she indicated the freed prisoners, 'and I will meet you on the outside. Be quick.'

If it had not been for the injured shoulder troubling him, if it had not been for the spectre of his confrontation with Ulther looming large, Thalric reassured himself, he would not have slipped as he did.

He was on his way to the harem, making the best speed he could without actually running. Ahead of him he saw some servants scattering at his approach, but he was used to that by now. Only a moment later, but far later than it should have, did the realization strike him. *Servants with swords drawn?* And these people had been dirty and ragged, not wearing the plain dark tunics that Ulther dressed his menials in. He swung round instantly, but they had already closed in and a hand grasped his collar. There was a sudden point of pain at his throat.

He was about to fight, to summon his energies for a final retributive sting, but the angle of the blade changed slightly, putting the razor edge against his flesh, and he felt a little blood welling up there, and he remained still.

They came up to him then, a half-dozen grimy Mynan locals holding Wasp swords and daggers like the very piece at his throat. Some soldier's diligence in keeping his kit in good order was now about to make an end to him.

He craned around, and his captor pushed him back against the wall, the blade cutting a little with the movement.

He found himself staring right into the face of Kymene and his heart went cold with it. She was unmistakable, the Maid of Myna. Caged, she had seemed too great for that space to contain. Here she was free like an impatient beast that had never lost the ways of the wild. She put him in mind of a great green hunting beetle, as large as a horse, that had once been brought to a gladiatorial match. Even pitted against mounted soldiers with spears, the monster had made a bloody accounting of itself, raising its great mandibles to the crowd and cowing them to silence.

'I know you,' she said softly. 'You're – don't tell me – Thalric. Captain Thalric, is it not? The political.'

'Your memory does you credit,' he said hoarsely.

'I'm sure you remember *me*,' she said with a wicked smile. 'It seems you've been in the wars, Captain Thalric. Or did you have an accident cleaning your crossbow?'

'It's been a busy night,' he confirmed. Her eyes held his, and he felt as though they were unravelling his mind, his entire past, piece by piece.

'It's liable to get busier before dawn,' she promised. 'Where are you bound, Captain, all bandaged up like that? The infirmary's the other way, they tell me.'

He tried a smile and found it came quite easily despite her, or even because of her. 'I'm going to kill Governor Ulther,' he said, and he knew she could see, in his eyes, that it was no less than the truth.

He had surprised her, though, and he treasured that moment, even though the blade wavered against his skin. She might be the Maid of Myna, but she did not know everything.

'The Bloat? You're going to kill the Bloat?' she asked, and it was a moment before that name made a connection.

'If you'll let me,' he said mildly, and watched his words ripple through her supporters, now a dozen in number. They were all staring at him, blankly or wonderingly.

'Captain Thalric, hero of the revolution, is it?' Kymene said slowly. 'Perhaps one good deed to balance out all the bad ones?'

He gave her a thin, bleak smile.

'Or is it just Wasp politics, like your little sideshow earlier?' she prompted.

'We take our politics seriously.'

The blade was gone from his throat, so suddenly that for a second he thought she must have rammed it home. 'I don't care whether it's politics or paid, whether he slept with your woman or muddied your name, or whether you just want to see what colour his fat liver is. I give you your life, Captain Thalric. Now let's see what you do with it.'

And with that she was off, her supporters dashing after her, leaving Thalric fingering the shallow graze on his neck.

There was a pressure building above them, they knew. It was composed of a large number of Wasps who, for now at least, were on the wrong trail, but would realize their error soon enough. As they left Kymene and her guard, their pace quickened and quickened. They had done everything save what they had come to do. The last sands were teetering in the hourglass.

'There!' Totho said, for there were more doors, more cells ahead. There were more guards, too. A pair of them had come out into the corridor, Wasps in light striped armour. One of them was so astounded by the sight bearing down on them that he just gaped, but the other one cried the alarm.

Tynisa was on them even with the release of their first

sting, and she felt the heat of the blast wash past her face. He had not drawn his sword, that man, falling back on Wasp-Art to save him, and she made him pay for that by slipping her blade around the side of his armour plates. The other man had a sword ready but, as he tried to use it against her, Chyses had slammed into him and the two of them grappled fiercely on the ground. Tynisa was about to finish the fight for him, but Totho's warning shout made her start back. A third man had come out by the same way, and this one was something more. He wore heavy armour of the sort called sentinel-mail, with plate and chain all over that her blade would not pierce, and a helm that left only a slit for the wearer's eyes. For all that metal weight he came out fast, and he had a long-shafted glaive in his hands, its swordhead lunging towards her. He almost took her, too. She misjudged the weapon's reach, and what had seemed a safe distance brought the weapon's point dancing right before her eyes the next moment, so that she had to fall backwards to avoid it.

She heard the harsh ratchet of Totho's crossbow, and saw the man twist at the next moment. One bolt stuck in, hanging limply from the chain mail, but two rebounded back from the man's curved shoulder-guard and helm.

There were other guards following behind him now, a pair of them emerging to pause and stare in shock at the fight. The sentinel drew back his glaive to spit her, and she scuttled back across the floor, seeing one of Achaeos's arrows break across the man's breastplate.

Tisamon!

But Tisamon was behind them, still covering their retreat.

The sentinel had now stepped right over Chyses and his opponent, driving for her with the polearm. Tynisa stepped aside and lunged, trying for his throat or else the eyeslit, but he swayed back and her blade bent dangerously against his gorget. Then the haft of the polearm slammed her into the wall, driven with all the strength of a man who has lived in such armour for many years.

Chyses meanwhile had finished his man, but was caught between the sentinel's back and the two new soldiers. They were in some quick debate, though, and even despite her bruised ribs Tynisa wondered why they were not attacking. Chyses took his chance, and lunged at the sentinel from behind, slamming his dagger into him with all the strength he possessed. It bit into the chain mail beneath the backplate and must have done some work because a muffled roar rose from within the helm.

Then Chyses suddenly had the iron-shod butt of the glaive across his jaw. He spun back against the wall, leaving his dagger in place, and Tynisa jabbed forward again. She got her opponent's throat, but there was chain mail even there, and leather beneath it. Her sword bit and then bowed, but she put all her strength into it with a desperate shout.

The blade skidded from the mail and she slammed into the man himself. The sharp curves of her own sword's guard scored a line across her face below one eye and the sentinel fell back against the corridor wall, driving Chyses' dagger inches deeper into the small of his back.

And then she saw the two soldiers come to a decision at last as they drew blades and headed off in the opposite direction, towards the cells.

They were going to kill the prisoners, and she knew without doubt that those same prisoners must be Salma and Che.

The sentinel roared and hurled her away with the shaft of his glaive as he struggled back from the wall.

Tisamon! she thought again, but there was no Tisamon. There was only her.

Twenty-nine

He tried to tell the first soldiers he saw that there were slaves loose, prisoners freed. The men backed away from him, staring at his face and his bloody tunic, enough to make him wonder what rumours had been spread about him to anticipate his demise. They would not even stop to listen to him. Deeper in, there were guards who tried to bar his way, heedless of his warnings. He stared them down. He did not need to summon up the name of the Rekef, for te Berro's agents had done their work well. He was *known*. It would be a loyal soldier that barred the Rekef's path and it seemed that Ulther himself no longer inspired such loyalty. The barriers that the governor had put up parted before Thalric: the guards continued staring straight ahead as though he was not there. He hurried on towards the harem.

And it was a harem: the word used amongst the servants and soldiers was not just hyperbole. Ulther had adopted his design and intent from the decadent excesses of the Spiderlands: a large, many-alcoved room at the deep heart of the palace, windowless and lit only by the leaping flames of sconces. The alcoves and the outer edges of the room were strewn with cushions providing the only resting place for the score or so of women Ulther had summoned there. Among them were the slaves that Thalric had seen before, Hreya included, and there were others, of whatever kinden had taken the old man's eye over the last few years: Spiders and Ant-kinden, Wasp and Grasshopper, even a sullen-looking Dragonfly maid, for Ulther had a roving and acquisitive taste.

He had made this place a Wasp place, even so. Here, amongst the shadows and the lounging women, against the pillared buttress looming dimly at the far wall, he had installed another carved throne as rich as the one in the great hall above. Enthroned, the governor of Myna reclined there and waited. He did not seem surprised when Thalric appeared at his arched doorway, rather than one of his assassins.

Thalric gazed across the assembled beauties, and then towards Ulther, whose reproachful gaze seemed to indicate that there was yet one beauty missing. There was an absence shaped like Grief in Chains, and it stood between them.

'Captain Thalric,' Ulther said, taking his time over the words, shaping the consonants with care. 'You seem to have undergone some recent reversals. A difficult night, perhaps?'

'I've had better.' Thalric took a few steps in, looking only at Ulther, but sensing the women draw back at the sight of the blood and the bared sword.

'What's this about, old friend?' Ulther inquired.

'You tell me.'

'Oh no, none of that. It's a little late to get coy, isn't it?' The big old man shifted himself on the throne, and only then did Thalric see through the gloom that there was a blade laid across his knees, something narrow and wicked looking. 'You dealt with Rauth and the others, I assume? All of them? A shoulder wound's a light enough price, for so many dead men.'

'They were amateurs.'

'I suppose they were. And why, you ask, did I have to send them?'

'Because your love of your appetites has become greater than your love of the Empire,' said Thalric, stopping far enough from Ulther that he would have a chance to duck if the old man loosed his sting.

'No, because you forced me to it. You made me gather them and give those orders. You know it, Thalric, so why? Not because you needed the Butterfly dancer. You wanted this, then? You're tired of my friendship? Was I not a good friend to you?'

'The Empire, Ulther. Always the Empire.'

'Oh but nobody thinks like that!' the old man snapped. 'You think the generals think like that? You think the *Emperor* does? We drive the Empire like a plough over earth, Thalric, and we do it so we may reap the harvest. You will not find a man out there who serves the Empire simply for the Empire's sake and no other.'

'But you will find one *here*,' said Thalric sadly.

Ulther's lip curled as if dismissing the notion. 'You may say so, Thalric, but I see your plan, nonetheless.'

'What plan is that?'

'What a show for the locals, eh? The governor and his old friend shed each other's blood, and over a woman! I'm sure your Rekef friends will ensure the story is spread.'

Thalric just shook his head, but Ulther chuckled indulgently.

'No false modesty, old friend. If you'd just cut my throat they'd smell the infighting all across this city, the wretches. Have me removed by decree and it weakens the Empire's colours here in Myna. The locals are desperate for any excuse to dig up their armour and wave their swords. But now . . . now it's personal. Is that what you wanted? Wave my head at the crowds to show that you won't be crossed, even by old Ulther? Show them that we're a bunch of hard lads even with our own kind? As if you and I would fall out over a woman, old friend.' Ulther's eyes pinned him. 'When did they make you Rekef Inlander, anyway?'

'I was Outlander, and I'll be so again, as soon as I can

– but for now . . .' Thalric managed a one-shouldered shrug. 'I don't need excuses, Ulther. You're guilty of what they say you are. The reason I haven't cut your throat while you slept is that I owe you this much. This much and no more.'

'So . . .' The old man levered himself up out of the chair, and the women drew back again, sensing the blood of the near future like a taint in the air. 'You'll secure yourself a nice promotion, old friend. See, I always was good for your career. Back to the Rekef Outlander? Don't fool yourself. Now they've taken you in, you won't look back. They won't let you. You're one of them now.'

Thalric said nothing, waited. Ulther held his blade to the light, let the fluid firelight shift across its length. It was not the army's short straight blade but a rapier, as much a Spider design as the room.

'You look tired, Thalric. Perhaps you came for an execution. To put an old man out of his misery?' Ulther mused. 'If that's so then I've a disappointment for you. I was an Arms-Brother myself. I remember the moves. Care to share a pass or two with me, for old time's sake.'

'If you kill me it will make no difference,' Thalric said softly. 'You're finished here. You know that.'

Ulther's gaze swept the harem's contours, symbolizing all he had built. 'So be it,' he said, and dropped into a ready stance. Thalric did the same, feeling the pull of his wound, trying to calculate, in that uncertain light, for the extra length of Ulther's blade.

He waited. He was in no hurry just then, so Ulther would have to come to him.

Ulther obliged. With surprising speed he came forward, and the point of his sword was flicking out, drawing a narrow line across Thalric's chest, scraping on the copper-weave even as Thalric danced back. In an instant Ulther had brought the point up, feigning at Thalric's face. His hand was quick, his footwork less so. When Thalric bounded past him and lunged, Ulther's retreat was hurried, awkward. Thalric harried him across the harem floor, hoping to pin him against the far wall, where his shorter blade would finally tell. He took it too fast and his shoulder shot fire through him, pulling him back halfway across. Ulther got to his distance again, eyes narrow. All expression had left his face, making it a jowly, hanging mask.

He barked out something wordless and lunged, moving from Arms-Brother style to something more suited to a rapier, some Spider duellist business, arm straight out before him. Thalric gave ground fast, the rapier's point dancing like a gnat before him, and Ulther matched his pace, his wrist dancing like a younger man's, his body lumbering to catch up. Then Thalric sidestepped, let the sword's point past him and stabbed.

He had made a clumsy job of it, signalled it too clearly to his opponent. Ulther had a chance to slip out of the way, but his momentum carried him close past the blade, a long gash tearing his fine clothes and bloodying the bulge of his flank. He gave an inarticulate yell and whipped the rapier across Thalric's face.

It was only the flat of the blade in that wild move, but it was so unexpected, so far from any school of duelling, that it connected. Thalric found himself on the floor, half from his failed evasion and half from sheer pain. He blinked. He had both eyes still, but one was gumming with blood from a gash across his brow that must continue across his cheek. Ulther was barrelling down on him with blade extended, and he scrabbled aside, slashing the old man across the leg as he slid out of the way. Another shallow wound, and bloody. All skill and art between them had fallen aside. Ulther was old and angry. Thalric was devastatingly tired.

They circled. Thalric had one eye sealed shut now. Ulther limped, but his narrow eyes were blazing with the fury of a trapped animal. The thought came to Thalric that he might lose this one, but it was a distant cold thought that barely touched him.

Ulther slashed twice to drive him back, and Thalric caught the second blow on his sword, turned it, though the old man was stronger than he had thought, and made another lunge. It was a leaden move and Ulther got his offhand in the way, trying for a palm-parry but taking the blade's keen edge across his forearm instead. At the same time he had drawn his rapier back to strike, but Thalric was within the point's reach, and instead the ornate guard punched into his ribs, pushing the two of them apart again.

Thalric knew it could not be long. Neither of them had the fight left in them. He was ceasing to care who won now. He just wanted it over.

Ulther's face was no longer the face of the man Thalric had known. He lunged, making his enemy stumble back, and then followed up the advance by making mad, random slashes, the narrow blade slicing the air before Thalric's face, nicking his leg, the point dancing across his copper-weave with a ripping rattle. Thalric tried to capture the rapier with his own sword, to bind it aside and close, but the fury that was driving Ulther kept the slim blade darting and passing, never still. Thalric sensed rather than felt the wall behind him, made a clumsy dive aside and just remained on his feet, the rapier whacking across his armoured back like a whip. He could feel the blood flowing beneath the bandage on his shoulder. His breathing was raw and ragged.

This is it. I've reached the end of it. I've no more left.

He lunged. An offensive was now his only choice because his defence was killing him. He caught Ulther unprepared. The rapier speared over his shoulder and he rammed home with the shortsword, but he had misjudged the distance, had come too close. The crosspiece of the hilt dug into Ulther's paunch, and the man roared and slammed his offhand, open-palmed, into Thalric's chin.

The world went dark for a second, spinning and wheeling about him, and he crashed to the floor. The sword bounced from his grip and, though stunned, he lunged for it, but Ulther tried to stamp on his hand, barely missed it, and then kicked the sword away. The old man's breathing was thunderous as an engine, Thalric himself wheezed like an invalid. He was completely done and he lay at Ulther's feet without the strength even to twist aside when the blow came.

Ulther drew the rapier back to skewer him, and then stopped, staring down.

'Oh Thalric, this is too bad,' he said softly. 'It should not end like this between us. It should not.' He seemed sincere in his unhappiness, even in his victory. Then his face hardened and he drew the rapier back again. 'But so it ends.'

There was a flash that was so white it was dazzling to Thalric's one good eye. He cringed away from it, covering his face. He should, he realized, be dead by now, yet no blade had found him.

He opened the one eye that he could to a narrow slit. There was a murmur amongst the women but no sound of combat. With infinite reluctance he sat up, clutching his head. Then he saw Ulther. The great bulk of the governor of Myna lay face down within arm's reach, and there was a charred hole burned into his back.

Then there were hands on him. Thalric fought them off at first but then found them helping him to his feet.

'I thought you were dead,' a woman's voice was saying.

'Me too.' He focused on her at last. Hreya? It was Hreya. The look on her face was more caution than concern, as in a woman uncertain what she has gained or lost. His eyes again found the body of the governor, the charred star across the small of his back. He glanced at her and she nodded. Thalric found that he was leaning on her more than he wanted to, but could not quite muster the ability to stand on his own.

'What now, Captain Thalric?' she asked.

He finally summoned his strength to him, all of it, all those reserves he almost never tapped, and stood alone, gently stepping away from her. The mound of Ulther's body drew him inexorably and he was bitterly glad he had not been the man to strike the death-blow.

'I have work yet to do,' he said hoarsely. 'Prisoners . . .' The thought came to him then of his own prisoners. He could see so much more clearly with Ulther dead and gone. 'Prisoners,' he said again, and with Hreya watching, with all the women watching, he made his halting way out of the harem.

Che's hands were raw by now. She had thought that this would be so much easier. She had an education, after all.

If her Art had not been able to banish the darkness for her then it would have been impossible. Even so, she was having to teach herself the craft of lockpicking from first principles. It was not something she had ever been called upon to do before.

She had studied mechanics. She knew how a lock worked. This was not exactly a masterpiece, either, the shackles securing Salma's arms. The Wasps always made solid, practical things.

She had been working at it for hours now. The sun had gone down on her as she scratched and fiddled with it. The medical probe she had stolen, its end bent to catch the tumblers, was awkward in fingers gone numb with the interminable fumbling. She was constantly dropping it and having to find it again.

She had three tumblers now where she reckoned they should be. There were only two left.

'I think you had better hurry, if that's possible,' Salma murmured.

'If you're getting cramp again, you can sit down. I could use the break myself.'

'I don't think that's an option.'

She had heard nothing of what was going on outside, as her concentration on the stubborn thing had been all-consuming, but now she listened. There was something happening beyond their door and it sounded fierce. She heard cries of pain and the sound of blade on metal.

'*Please*, Che. Any time now would be useful,' Salma urged her. The first thought that came to her had been *rescue*, but clearly Salma was not anticipating anything good.

She took up the pick and went at it again, fiddling and scratching, feeling out that fourth tumbler that was so stubborn. It was stiff: nothing a key could not turn, but her pick was a slim thing, scraping and sliding past the tumbler's catch.

'Che, *hurry*.' Salma was as tense as a drawn bowstring. The sounds without were louder now, some voice roaring in rage and pain amid racing footsteps.

She twisted the pick and felt it bend against the tumbler. If she kept up the pressure, she would either succeed or the pick would break. She must gamble everything on the quality of Wasp steel.

There was a key in the door then, the hurried fumbling of a simple task done under great pressure. *Concentrate!* She wrenched at the pick, waiting for the dreaded snap. She pushed until her wrist ached.

The door opened, pulled so hard it slammed against the wall outside. She started in shock and that extra twitch put the fourth tumbler in place. No time for the fifth.

There was no fifth. She had miscounted at the start. The shackles fell from Salma in that instant, and his wings blazed to life before her startled face, the force of them knocking her back across the cell.

His arms would be bloodless and numb, good for nothing, but he hit the soldier in the doorway with one shoulder, bearing the startled man over with the force of his charge. There was another man behind, also knocked out of the way. He had a sword but could not use it for fear of stabbing his fellow. Che ran at him, no war cry and no warning, and before he could put his sword between them she had hold of his sword arm and yanked at it with all her weight and strength.

Tynisa tried to force her way past the sentinel, gripping the haft of the man's glaive and pushing at him, but he shook her off contemptuously. Behind him the soldiers were opening one of the cell doors. She caught a brief glimpse of Totho coming closer with his crossbow raised, but he was not a great shot at the best of times, and the best of times were now long behind them. She thrust at the sentinel again with her rapier, scraping at his armour.

Then Achaeos was there. In truth she had forgotten about him. There had been no arrows for a while. He must have been gathering his courage.

He came in around ceiling height, his wings sparking from the stones, and he dropped onto the sentinel's shoulders, trying to stab through the eyeslit. The sentinel went berserk, swinging about like a beast, his glaive slashing left and right, up and down while Achaeos was trying desperately to hang on with one arm, his wings flashing in and out, the force of them wrenching at the man's neck.

And then he lost his grip, falling off, but he held on to the helm with one hand, dragging the sentinel's head up and back. Tynisa darted forwards, with the glaive stabbing blindly out at her, but she vaulted it, one foot bending the haft as she used it for purchase, and the narrow tip of her sword punched up under his chin. The chain mail there stopped it for an instant, and then the rings gave way, and he cried out and fell backwards, as dead as she could make him.

Beyond him . . . Tynisa's heart leapt when she saw all was not lost. Salma and Che were there, but they were still fighting. Even as she took the sight in, she saw Salma cast down by his opponent and the man's sword drawing back. Totho was beside her by then with a clear shot, and he cranked the crossbow's lever twice. One bolt was lost in the darkness beyond but the second found its mark in the man's ribs, sending him to his knees. Salma wrenched his sword off him at that point, and turned it against its owner, putting his whole weight behind it.

By that point the other man was done as well. Che had been grappling with him, losing ground as she tried to hang on to his sword. Then there was a dagger in his side and Che finally got the sword off him, but held off from using it. The dagger whipped out and thrust in again, Achaeos's white eyes and white teeth flashing in the gloom. Chyses was beside him at that point, reeling from the blow he had taken, but determined to do his part, and the two of them bore their enemy down and slew him.

Tynisa ran in and virtually caught Che as the girl staggered backwards. She looked utterly exhausted, bruised and battered, but completely overjoyed. She embraced her foster-sister hard enough to make her ribs creak.

'You came! Hammer and tongs, look at you! You came!' Che released her hold as she saw, past Tynisa's shoulder, the narrow-framed figure of Achaeos carefully cleaning the much-used blade of his dagger.

'You . . .' she said. There was a memory suddenly in the front of her mind: a dream she had swum through during the heliopter journey to Myna. There was a shock, a physical shock, as she met his featureless eyes – and she knew, outside reason, that he knew.

Then Totho was at her elbow, and she hugged him too for good measure, not noticing his surprise at the embrace. Behind her, Salma was telling Tynisa how every part of him above the waist had cramp.

'We have to leave,' Chyses insisted. 'We have to go, now.'

They made their hurried way, the best pace that Che and Salma could keep up with, to the stairs leading up from the cells. There they found Tisamon.

Tynisa spotted him first and, although she had known to find him there, she scuffed to a halt at the sight. He was positioned halfway up the stairs, gazing back down at them. The stairs themselves were visible only in uneven patches, and those were all slick with blood.

The bodies of eleven Wasp soldiers lay there, perhaps more, and from the way they were laid out, most of them had arrived together as a squad. He must have leapt into the midst of them to deny them the use of their stings, and the few lying near the top of the stairs had taken wounds in their backs as they had scrabbled desperately to get away from their untouchable adversary.

Or not quite untouchable. There was a thin line of red across Tisamon's cheek, almost a twin to the mark on Tynisa's own face, which had been made by the pointed guard of her own blade.

'We're ... going now,' Chyses told the Mantis, his voice catching a little at the sight of the carnage. Tisamon gave him a brief nod, and stood aside to let him lead the way.

The entire palace was in the throes of chaos. Thalric kept blundering into guards and demanding to know what was going on, but very few of them gave him a coherent response. To credit all of them there were a dozen separate attacks underway, all in different parts of the palace. Soldiers and Auxillian militia were running everywhere and getting in each other's way. If the Mynan resistance truly knew what was going on, he thought, and mounted an attack right now, they might actually force the Empire out of its own headquarters. As he passed on through, it was clear that there was far more confusion than actual conflict going on. Someone had clearly laid a few false trails, and his own activities of the night had hardly helped.

He knew exactly where he was going. The cells. Cheerwell Maker and her Dragonfly friend. He had not even considered them at the time, when he had run into Kymene and her escapees. Those had just been locals and, more, he had been under the burden of what he had to do that night to Ulther. Now it was done, however, his perspective was coming back to him.

And he almost ran into them. He heard the footsteps in time, though, and ducked back into a doorway, flattening himself against the wood and freezing, as instinctive to him as breathing after all his years in the field.

They were a ragged crowd. Only one Mynan local and a grab-bag of others, even a Mantis-kinden with one of their ridiculous hingeing claws. And near the back was the Dragonfly-kinden male, and there, behind him, was Cheerwell Maker.

They were off down the corridor and he raised an arm after them, feeling the Art-force of his sting stir in his palm and fingers. Cheerwell Maker had a broad back, a good target even in this light.

It would be a shame not to continue his interrogation. A shame not to have one more conversation with her.

It had been a long night, and he had to act now if he was going to seize this chance. There was a babble of voices in his head, though. He could hear Kymene's voice: *Perhaps one good deed to balance out all the bad ones?* and there was Cheerwell herself asking what harm the Empire would suffer if she were freed.

And he had told her that he would rather cut her throat there and then than stand the least chance of her impeding the Empire in any way. He remembered it clearly, after all of that weary night. He could hear his own flat words ringing in his ears.

He was not the master of his own mind in that moment, as Che's back retreated further down the corridor. The gates were thrown wide and anything could enter. *Ulther's last moments, both betrayer and betrayed. Aagen's distaste with the torture implements . . .*

The Dragonfly noblewoman screaming, screaming, as he killed her children for the Empire.

And then he told himself, he did not know whether he even had the strength in him to summon his Art. And he might yet recapture her, or even turn her, or find some use for her still alive. And a hundred other post-facto justifications.

He felt physically ill. He did not know whether it was because the shield of his loyalty had been chipped, or because of the lesson all those voices had been reciting in his head.

He reached for his Art, and felt his palm warm with it, and spark. It felt as though he were trying to lift a monstrous weight, to conjure the sting-fire into being, and all for the pittance reward of a dead Beetle girl. His breath caught with the strain of it.

It had been a long night. He was allowed one error of judgment.

He lowered his arm, and set off to find a bed to collapse into.

Every step and they expected the host of the Empire to descend on them. Even when they reached the storeroom the commotion above had not ceased, but was working its determined way down towards them. They dropped back into the sewers as fast as they could. Achaeos went first, descending gratefully into the dark, and flitting far ahead, beyond the lamp that Chyses had rekindled. Totho and Che were left to help the hobbling Salma, whose breath hissed with pain at every step, from the cramp that was still running up and down through his back and arms. Tynisa stared at Tisamon. She knew he expected her to go first, that he would play rearguard. She stepped down into the sewers but she was waiting for him when he followed, keeping pace with him, letting the others drift out of sight, out of earshot. Soon Tisamon lit his own lantern, a tiny low light that was enough to stop the dark defeating their eyes. It was as though the lamplight did not fall on her, though, for still Tisamon would not look at her, would not acknowledge her save that everything they did was linked, step for step, in a mutual understanding neither of them could deny.

Where else can I confront you, if not this dead and buried place?

It was time to force fate, to bring matters to a head.

She waited until they were long gone from beneath the palace. She gave him that leeway. Then she stopped and waited.

He had slowed even as she did so, that bond between them communicating, through her footsteps or her breathing, that something was wrong.

'Tisamon,' she began, and he had stopped, merely a grey shape and a black shadow.

'We've put this off for too long,' she told his back. 'We have to talk, please, Tisamon, let's talk.'

She almost held her breath then. The only sounds were the water of the sewers, the faint skitter of the roaches beyond the lantern's stretch.

She thought she saw him shake his head, though she

could not be sure. In the next moment he had started off again, as though she had said nothing.

'Tisamon!' she snapped. 'Or Father. Would you prefer that?'

She had stopped him, but she was running out of things to throw at his feet. Again he had paused, but it was only a moment. She had to run after him to avoid being left in the dark.

She had just one missile left. She had saved it until the last because, once loosed, it could not be taken back.

'Spite on you,' she hissed, and the whisper that followed was her rapier clearing its scabbard. And yes, he knew that sound. It stopped and turned him far more sharply than any of her words had.

'Look at me,' she challenged, and he did. In the lantern's uncertain light she could not name his expression, or even see if he had one. The claw buckled to his right hand and arm was now just a shadow amongst shadows.

'Put that away,' he said, his voice flat. 'This is no time to play.'

She dropped into her duelling stance, sword levelled at him. 'Oh, you're right,' she told him. 'And I've done playing.'

He lifted the lantern slightly. His eyes held only a look of disdain, and he made to turn away.

'If you turn your back on me now, I swear I'll kill you. And believe me, I take my oaths every bit as seriously as you do.'

With unhurried movements he placed the lantern on the walkway and turned the light up a little, narrowing his eyes against it. 'Don't be foolish,' was all he said.

'Foolish, is it? We have unresolved business, you and I.'

'Have we indeed?'

He would not even face it, nor did he look at her sword.

Nothing in his stance suggested he believed in it as a threat. He would not fight her, would not even entertain the idea. He would not take her seriously.

'I know what you're afraid of,' she told him.

'Do you indeed?'

'Oh, I know it's not this sword,' she said, inching closer. 'I know it isn't me. You're the great Tisamon and you fear no fighter under the sky or beneath the earth.' Even as she spoke she was in Collegium again, before it all started, baiting Piraeus into fighting her. Mantis pride, that was the key. They were all armour on the outside, but vulnerable, so vulnerable within.

And I myself am of them – half of them.

She made a sudden advance on him, but he contemptuously kept his distance. There was no fear in it, simply that he had no interest in fighting her. He would have taken the challenge of any wretch in the street, but not hers. She could chase him off into the darkness, but he would evade her and lose her.

She prepared her barbed dart. 'You are afraid,' she told him. 'You're afraid of this face.'

His stance changed, ever so slightly. Even now that same link worked between them, as though they were Antkinden of the same city, sharing thoughts.

'You're afraid of the past,' she told him, 'because you abandoned her. You wanted to believe she was a traitor, that she had seduced you and discarded you, rather than even go and find the truth. Much easier that way, wasn't it? But you know now. You know that it was you who betrayed her. And that's what you really can't face!'

And she lunged at him, but this time he did not give.

She thought for a terrible moment that she was going to run him through, but she had forgotten who she had drawn sword on. The moment before the tip of her rapier pierced his arming jacket, his blade had swept it aside. She felt it scrape across the claw, across the armoured gauntlet.

Then the claw unfolded and he was at her.

She almost fell over her feet, turning her desperate lunge into a stumbling backstep. She nearly fell over the lantern in her next step, kicking it so that it was lying at the very edge of the walkway. She fell back ten paces without being able to stop herself, but he had pulled his advance up short, something catching in his face, and she got to the length of her rapier and drove in again.

She had never fought like this before. It was not the Prowess Forum's formal style, nor the street brawling she had espoused since then. It took all of her skill in every stroke, blade flickering faster than eye could follow. It was every ounce of her youth and effort and instinct against a master.

Her thrust had been for his chest, but his blade was there before it. She bounded over it, driving forward, pressing on, keeping ahead of his circular guard, over and beside and under and always, always, pressing forward. The moment he took her blade aside she would be at his reach, and he within hers. His face, as he passed the lantern's light, was set and deadly.

She had forgotten his offhand. Even as she thought his blade was outmanoeuvred, he slapped her rapier out of line with his left palm, slinging her sword arm across her body, and the crescent of his blade was a bright line in the lamplight as it came to cut her throat.

She swayed back, so far as to almost overbalance. She heard the passing of his blade, just an inch away, yet she had not given up her advance. She dragged her rapier back, sending the razor edge across his stomach, under his guard. His offhand caught it, palm-to-flat, and he twisted away, pushing her blade aside but exposing his left side to her. She thought she had him then. She flicked her sword from his grasp, brought the pommel past her chin to put the length of the blade between them, and speared it at his flank. Her target was gone, though. He had turned about on the instant, and the scythe of his claw was sweeping for her head.

She kicked backwards, and this time she fell. The blade swept over her and she was scrambling to her feet as fast as she could. He feinted towards her, stopped. Or at least she had thought it was a feint. The lantern was between them now and she could see the catch again, something holding his blade back.

Her face. She should listen better to her own words. He had driven her back past the lamp so its light fell on her face. Each time it did there came that minute catch in his assault.

She reclaimed her feet. There was a slice of time in which he was poised, staring at her face – at dead Atryssa's face.

Then he went for her, and she knew her luck was used up.

The claw spun and swept, moving with all the fluid grace his wrist and arm could lend it, spiralling past her guard. Even so she got her blade in the way, hearing the two metallic sounds as she warded it off. Then she had lunged back at him, and he turned the thrust, but not effortlessly. For a second they were locked together, face to face, and then she dodged away and back before he could get his spines into her. He was dancing towards her again, a man who had fought since he was a boy, a man of forty years, and all bar six or seven of them spent with a blade in his hands. He was just a shadow now, the lantern light behind him as he forced her to back up, step after step.

He was death.

She swept away a lunge, tried to riposte into him. Her thoughts had ceased and she had no time for them. Her feet, her body, her blade, everything depended on her instincts, her reflexes, faster and faster. She took his blows and turned them into her own attacks, over and over. He was always there with a parry that led, as though some natural law compelled it, into another series of blistering attacks. He was faster still. He was picking his pace up, and her breathing was ragged. She had almost stopped using her eyes, long since stopped using her mind. The blows came out of blackness, and she heard them as much as saw them. She fended them off and fended them off. She had stopped attacking. He left her no room for it. Then her rapier blade was abruptly caught between his forearm and his claw, and as she tried to draw it back he rushed forward. She felt the hilt twist in her hand and held on to it hard, and he turned his arm and dashed it against the sewer wall, and her blade, her beautiful blade that Stenwold had bought for her, snapped at the guard, leaving not even a sharp stub.

He was going to kill her.

She cried out then. The link between them was enough, still, to let her know that he would strike.

She was braced for it, with a dignity that surprised her in the face of death at her father's hands. She felt the cold edge of his blade. It was at her throat, of course. He had his habits, as did any fighter. Her breath sobbed into and out of her lungs, and beyond it she heard his, too. She imagined him using all his control to hold back the killing stroke.

But it was not like that. He was now still as still, no struggle. Her eyes slowly grew accustomed to the light within the very grey periphery of their lantern. His face was merely a faint pale outline on which no expression could be discerned.

She did not trust herself to speak or make any sound at all, and he too was silent.

Then the blade moved, and she forced herself not to flinch. It did not slide away, though. Instead she felt the flat of it against her cheek, cupping her face more towards him, then this way and that, his eyes straining to see her.

And then it was gone from her, folding back along his arm. He turned, merely a silhouette, leaning against the sewer wall with one hand. She noticed the rise and fall of his breathing.

She could have killed him, though she realized this only later, so glad the idea had not then occurred to her.

'You are my daughter,' he said finally. 'And by my damned soul, you are *hers*.'

The words struck her almost physically, as he never had. Something wrenched inside her, and she let her sword hilt fall from raw fingers. She approached him with faltering steps, feeling her breath catch.

'Nothing you said was untrue,' continued Tisamon. 'I have lived with false betrayal for seventeen long years, and with the truth for only days.'

She wanted to say something to him then, some damning condemnation of him, or even some words of sympathy, but she could manage neither. Sobs began racking her so hard they hurt.

When he turned to her at last, she saw the kindred tracks of grief down his own face.

She thought he would not be able to bear to touch her. The wounds were freshly reopened, the blood still redly flowing. Still, when she approached him he put a hand on her shoulder, at first as tentative as a man reaching for a nettle, then stronger, as the man who grasps it.

Awkwardly he took her in his arms, his daughter, and she clung to him, her face pressed into his chest, with his golden brooch cold against her cheek.

Thirty

Che woke slowly, fearfully. There was the rustle around her of people moving about, a murmur of low voices. She was lying on a hard mat of woven straw and a cloak was laid over her. There was an echo, but not the familiar tight echo of a small cell relieved only by Salma's close breathing. This was some larger space, amid some multitude. She had no idea where she could be.

And then it came to her with a leap of joy that she only needed to know where she was *not*.

She was not in her cell. She was not in Thalric's power.

The pieces were falling into place.

They had come for her. Tynisa and the Moth and the others.

She was *free*.

At the thought, Che sat bolt upright with a gasp of breath. The darkness around her resolved itself, dimmed into grey shades more penetrable to her eyes. Her Art showed her a vaulted, subterranean roof, other sleeping forms. At the far wall, where her gaze was inevitably drawn, was the robe-wrapped form of Achaeos, with his head slightly bowed. She realized that only she could see his gleaming eyes from within the cowl. To her they almost shone, where there would be darkness for anyone else. A moment ago she had not even recalled his name.

She peered further around the room. There were almost two-score people sleeping here in rough ranks, and half a dozen standing watch, or perhaps just having woken before dawn as she had. Some crumbling cellar, this was. Probably she had seen it before when they came in but she had no memory.

'Che,' said a voice, soft from behind her, and she craned back to see Totho. He had been sitting at the head of her mattress almost like Achaeos's opposite number. Instinctively she reached out to him, grasped his wrist, just to be sure that he was real, that it *all* was real.

'I—'

'You should try to sleep more. There's a little while till dawn yet,' he said.

'I've lost all sense of time,' she told him. 'Where are we?'

'Some hideout of the resistance here. They got us into the palace to help you.' He glanced about, his face darkening. 'They didn't do much more than that. They were more keen on finding this leader of theirs.'

'I don't care,' she said. 'So long as it worked, I don't care.' She looked around suddenly, panicking. 'Where's Salma? Did he—?'

'He's got the sense to still be asleep,' said Totho pointedly. 'He's over there. He looked after you well, then?'

'We looked after each other. It was complicated. I think it might have gone worse for us but the man who took us prisoner had some other business to deal with and he never quite got around to us.' Her face hardened, enough to make Totho flinch. 'Are we going back to Helleron now, Toth?'

'No idea. Probably.'

'I've got a message for my Uncle Elias.'

He shook his head. 'No point trying to deliver that. Tisamon killed him, Stenwold told me.'

'Tisamon? The Mantis?'

Totho nodded soberly. 'He's . . . To tell the truth he frightens me. Che . . . ?'

'Yes?'

'I . . .' His face, as usual, gave no clue as to his mind. He had grown up with the weight of mixed blood on his shoulders, and he had learned to hide himself deep. 'I . . . I'm glad you're safe.'

'Not half as much as I am,' she replied with feeling. 'Totho, I want to see the sky again.'

'The sky?'

'I've been in wagons and in fliers and in cells for days and days now. I don't care if it's night. I just want to be outside. Just to stand in the doorway of this place will be enough. I'll come back in straight away if anyone's there.'

She stood up awkwardly, stretching, and bundled the dark cloak about her. After a moment he took her hand and guided her around the main body of the sleepers, nodding reassuringly to any Mynans who were already awake, and nervously to Tisamon, who was over in one corner, carefully sharpening and oiling the blade of his claw.

There were a couple of sentries outside, one lounging in the street like a homeless beggar, the other two floors up with a crossbow, watching down over the little square. The night was chill, the sky like pin-studded velvet, untroubled by clouds. They paused in the doorway, looking out, and in halting words Totho did his best to explain what had transpired since that fateful day in Helleron had separated them. He made most of it clear to her: Scuto's intervention, Stenwold's interview with Elias and the appearance of Tisamon, the hunt leading to Asta, and from there to the gates of Myna.

And there she stopped him. 'Tell me . . .' It was a question she could barely believe she was asking, but there was a hook lodged in her mind, and its barbs were troubling her. 'How did you know? How did you know where we were going?'

Totho looked stubborn. 'Tisamon and Tynisa went right into the Wasp camp there,' he said, but he could not hide from his tone that there was rather more to it than that.

She just waited in silence, trusting him to tell her the truth, and confronted with that trust he could do nothing else.

'The Moth, he . . . just knew.' Totho looked sullen. 'I still don't trust him. Either he's been speaking to the Wasps or else he was just guessing.'

Che shook her head. Her mind swam with the details of that inexplicable half-dream. *Inexplicable?* That was the very wall she was battering against. *There is no way he could have known. There is no way he could have called to me, or that I could have heard. Impossible. Inexplicable.* If the sun had been above them she would have shaken it off and found some glib sleight of mind to wish it away, but faced with the immensity of a dark and moonless sky, in this strange and intimidating city, she felt shaken by it, as if on the brink of some great irrational abyss.

In the hold of the heliopter, in her dream, that had been more and less than any dream that had troubled her before, he had asked of her where she was bound, and she had said. She had told him.

She should ask Totho about the precise times. She could then count the days back to that night when Aagen had grounded the flier within sight of Myna's walls in order to repair it. Surely that would dispel any coincidence.

Or strengthen it. She found now that she did not want to ask him. The possible answers lurked like childhood monsters in the shadows.

'Totho, I . . . need to think. Just a little time to myself.'

He had his stubborn look again. 'You should go back and try to sleep, really.'

'I'm as wide awake as I've ever been,' she said, and it was true. 'Please, Totho.'

Reluctantly he left her, but she heard him murmur to the beggarly sentry to watch over her.

After he had gone, she wondered about him. They had not been apart so very long, but Totho had changed. She supposed they all had. They had been young and naive when they stepped aboard the *Sky Without*, but they were growing up fast now. It had been a time of harsh lessons. Totho still had that awkwardness about him, that shyness born of a tainted heritage, but beneath it was developing a core of steel. She would never have guessed him for a fighter, but he had been there ready with crossbow in hand when she had needed him, as had they all.

'Come on,' she said abruptly. 'No sense skulking. I know you're there.'

There was an amused snort, and Achaeos fluttered down from the upper storeys on glimmering wings. Like the Ant- and Beetle-kinden they resembled, the people of Myna had never built for three dimensions. A deft, slight-framed man with Art-born wings had the run of the place.

She looked at him cautiously. He had come down out of arm's reach, and was regarding her with his arms folded within his robe.

'Why?' she asked him.

'Who can say?' She imagined there might even be bitterness in his voice. 'But here I am.'

'I'm glad of it. You . . .' She could not say it. 'I had a dream that . . . gave me comfort. At that time there wasn't much comfort for Salma and me.'

'A dream?' Noncommittally.

'Yes. A dream.' She was defensive about it.

He shrugged. 'You Beetles,' he remarked, but did not qualify it. 'No matter. We'll be back to Helleron soon enough, and then we two can be enemies again. I assume my debt to you is now paid?'

'Debt?' She took a step towards him. 'The bandage?

Those stitches? Your people need to fix a better rate of exchange, if this is all in return for that! You have done for me such ... things that you had no need to do. But you did, and I don't want to be your enemy *ever*.'

She wanted to reach out to him, then. Through all his masks, he looked so baffled, so unsure of why he was there. In the cold night he just looked so alone.

'We should not be enemies,' she said. 'If the Wasps come to Helleron, do you think they will not move against your people also? Believe me, their Empire makes no exceptions.'

He said nothing, but she could see he was thinking how his people might rejoice in the fall of Helleron, even if it meant their own homes burned.

'Take my hand.' She held it out beneath the moonless sky, her Art-sight, still so new to her, making a dark silver of her skin. 'Take it now, while you can.'

His own hand seemed only a lighter shade of the same colour when it finally ventured from within his robes. As it hesitated, she reached forward impulsively to grasp it. She had expected to find it cool, but it was surprisingly warm.

'I am Cheerwell Maker of Collegium. I do not speak for my family. I do not speak for my city or my kinden. I speak for myself, though, and I say that I owe you more than I can ever repay, for in my time of greatest need, you were there for me. I do not know why. I have no answers. Still, you were there, and you came into the place of our enemies and you shed their blood to free me.' The words were just tumbling out, and she had a strange feeling that they were only partly hers.

Certainly Achaeos's expression was stricken by them. 'Do not say such things so lightly,' he said, for a moment trying to pull away. 'You do not know how strongly oaths can bind us!'

'I say nothing lightly,' she told him, and he ceased resisting, staring into her face.

'You can *see* me,' he said, and she realized that, save for a guttering torch across the square, there was no illumination here but starlight. His blood and kinden gave him the eyes to see her, and her Art the eyes to see him.

'Yes, I see you,' she confirmed. 'I spent so long calling out to the Ancestor Art, but it was only your . . . only the dream that woke it in me.'

He did not know what to do with her now she could see. All masks were gone within that moment. She scared him, drew him, shocked him. Realizing that, she became scared herself, acutely aware of the warmth of his hand in hers, of how close he suddenly was to her.

'I—' she started, feeling the line between them – the line that had played out its length all the way from Helleron to Myna – draw tight. A moment later she had released his hand and was stumbling back, hurrying inside before whatever words now arising within her could escape.

A few ragged hours of the night were all Thalric was given to sleep in. Once Che and her compatriots had made their escape, there had been order to restore in the palace, and only then had he sought out a field surgeon of the garrison to attend his wounds. He could have summoned a doctor from the city, but Thalric's experience had led him to rate the hard-won skills of a field surgeon over the most educated physician in the world.

Now it was late after dawn, and the whole palace was up and about. Order, in a greater sense, was being restored to its pedestal. He knew that the Rekef would have things well in hand, that whispered voices would pass throughout the imperial staff in Myna informing them of the true state of things.

He had meanwhile sent for Aagen, and now met the man in a small anteroom set aside for waiting guests.

The artificer gave him a cautious nod. 'Still alive then.'

'Only just. Any trouble?'

Aagen shrugged. 'I heard that some soldiers were looking for her – the Butterfly girl. The locals round here
aren't exactly Empire sympathizers. Odd what counts in
your favour, sometimes, isn't it?'

'This city is working itself towards revolution,' Thalric
decided. 'Ulther didn't see it, he thought it was still tame
in the palm of his hand. He'd lost sight of the realities.'

'Let's hope we're both well clear before that happens,'
Aagen said, and Thalric nodded.

'I'm sorry I had to use you, Aagen. I had nobody else.'

'Well,' the artificer said with a sheepish grin, 'I'm not
complaining, you know?'

'She danced for you?'

Aagen tried to suppress the smile, but it spread regard-
less. 'She did, as it happens. Just danced, nothing else,
but . . .'

'I know. I've seen her.' Thalric stood, clapped his
comrade on the shoulder, feeling glad that here at least
was one friend that he had not been forced to turn against.
'I'm glad you came through this safely. I owe you, as a
comrade and as an officer. I'll remember.'

With dragging footsteps he made his way to the throne
room, for he knew there was bound to be a reckoning.
The doors were opened for him by fresh-looking soldiers,
and closed again as soon as he had gone through. The
room itself was almost empty. Much of Ulther's finery had
already been removed.

It did not surprise Thalric at all to see the central throne
occupied by the same nameless man who had been at
Latvoc's council. He now regarded Thalric keenly, his thin
face creased into calculating lines. Colonel Latvoc was
there, too, standing to one side of the throne, a scroll half
unfurled in his hands. Odyssa the Spider was absent, but

Thalric noticed te Berro lounging to one side, almost hidden behind a pillar.

'Colonel,' Thalric managed a salute, 'you've made good time.'

'I haven't,' Latvoc told him with a smile. 'In fact I haven't officially arrived yet and, indeed, will not for some time. The handing over of the governor's power will be as seamless as if Colonel Ulther himself had effected it. However, someone must oversee matters until then – in an unofficial capacity of course.'

'Of course, sir.'

'You appear to be one of those rare officers who delight in leading the charge, Major Thalric,' Latvoc observed. 'It is a mixed blessing but I can only congratulate you on your work here.'

'Thank you, sir.'

'It can't have been easy for you.'

Thalric blinked once, considering. The wise course was to disavow all personal feelings in this, but they were weighing him so heavily that he did not think he could. Not quite. 'I am loyal to the Empire, sir. I made my choice.' But his voice was not as steady as he would have liked.

'Good man,' Latvoc said. 'Of course, this resolution will not be entirely without benefit to yourself and—'

'That's not why I did it, sir,' said Thalric, more firmly than he meant. He was aware that after the previous night he was not as in control of himself as he would prefer.

There was a flicker of annoyance in Colonel Latvoc's face. 'I was not suggesting, Major, that you did. However, as far as the records show, you are ranking Rekef officer in this city. If you have any decisions to make, as de facto governor, then make them.'

It was a harsh question to put to a man unprepared for it, but Thalric guessed that he would be given no second chance.

'The Butterfly slave, Grief in Chains.' He looked keenly at Latvoc for a reaction.

'I hear she's quite the performer,' the Colonel said mildly.

'She belonged to Colonel Ulther. I would like to give her to Lieutenant Aagen, who was instrumental in aiding my work here.'

'Agreed,' said Colonel Latvoc without even a batted eyelid. 'Anything else?'

'Another chattel of the colonel's, a slave of our own kinden named Hreya, was of some assistance to me. I would like her freed.'

Latvoc coughed into his hand as though Thalric had made some error of etiquette at a social gathering. 'The Empire does not free its slaves, Major. It may gift them, reward them, treat them finely, bestow responsibilities on them, even suffer them to render advice, but never grant them freedom. What a precedent to set! However, the Empire will gift her to *you*, Major. If you, as an imperial citizen, wish to free her, well, I'm sure your eccentricity will be overlooked this once. Anything else?'

'Just that I would also like to mention Lieutenant te Berro's good work on my behalf.' Thalric saw the Fly flinch at the mention of his name, but then raise his eyebrows at the compliment.

Latvoc nodded approvingly. 'Recognizing the worth of subordinates is a good trait in an officer. It breeds loyalty. Duly noted.' From te Berro's unguarded expression Thalric had the impression that this was not a trait Latvoc himself possessed. 'Anything else?'

'No, sir.'

'Nothing, Major?' Latvoc frowned. 'Colonel Ulther had a great many more chattels than that – a whole palace full of them, in fact.'

'I leave them in the safe hands of the Empire, sir. I would like only to return to my work in Helleron. The plan must be nearly at fruition now and my agents will need my leadership.'

'Well.' Latvoc glanced briefly at the enthroned man. 'Major, there has been a proposal made concerning your future. General Reiner has noted your abilities and sensibilities and decided that they are just what the Rekef is seeking in its officers.'

Thalric stood quite still because, by the naming of that silent, enthroned officer, he had been admitted to some greater and more secret world. The generals of the Rekef were themselves almost never knowingly seen beyond the imperial court.

'Sir?' he said.

'You have done sterling work for the Rekef Outlander in your time, Major,' Latvoc said, as the general's eyes bored into him. 'However, your skills could also be of use to the Rekef Inlander. The Empire must be constantly guarded from within as well as without.'

This would be more than a promotion, Thalric knew: the Rekef Inlander, the older and more favoured sibling of his own service branch, answered to nobody but the Emperor. They were a law unto themselves. They feared nothing.

Except each other murmured a treacherous thought.

And everyone feared them. They were the shadows within the army. No man knew if his neighbour was writing reports on his ill-chosen words or if his slave had passed on his drunken confessions of the night before. Every man felt the eye of the Rekef on his back, whether he was an enlisted soldier or a great general of the Empire. No man was immune, and anyone could disappear without warning or trace.

This task here, with Ulther, was Inlander work. It had been a test, then? They had set him at his old mentor's throat to see if he were cold enough for it. He was cold, ice cold.

'I appreciate the honour, sir, but my plans in Helleron—'

'Can be completed by another, I am sure. Think it over, Major.'

And in the Rekef Inlander it would always be his own people who were under the knife. He would protect the Empire from treason like a surgeon saving a body from rot, by cutting out the infected part and everything close to it. Every day would be like last night then. And no doubt the call would come, one day, to set him against Aagen or some other loyal man he had once called friend.

'If the Empire orders it, sir, I will do as I am ordered,' he said, knowing that these next words could see the fear of the Rekef landing on his shoulders, could see him gone as surely as Ulther was gone. 'However, if I am merely offered an invitation, I must decline. My work in the Rekef Outlander is precious to me and it will falter without my guidance.'

There was a long silence. Latvoc glanced at General Reiner, and Thalric watched for a message to pass between them, but none came that his eyes could divine.

And at the last, 'That will be all, Major,' said Colonel Latvoc, and Thalric turned and left the room still not knowing what their thoughts were.

Thirty-one

Dawn had come slowly to Myna, as the sun told it, but there had been a starlit dawn that had swept across the city like wildfire. It said: *Kymene is free.* It said: *Ulther the Bloat is dead.* In the minds of the people of that city, these two events were inextricably bound.

In the cellar where Chyses' cell kept its headquarters there had been a steady influx of visitors, ambassadors arriving from other cells. Some were his old allies, others had opposed him, even fought against his people. Now they were here to see Kymene again because, of all the people in the city, she could unite them. Ulther had known it, too, but Ulther had been just as taken with her as her own people were, so had not done what he might to deprive Myna of its Maid.

Tynisa sat and watched the resistance come and go, or cluster in small groups to await their leader. Chyses went from one to another, shaking hands, clasping wrists like a soldier should. She could see he was working hard to bury old enmities, for the men he spoke most words of encouragement to were those who liked him least.

Che was taking a while to recover, or at least something was on her mind, and Salma was still sleeping despite the mounting fuss around him. He had been bound almost all the time he was imprisoned, Che had said. That must have stopped him getting much rest. She imagined him with arms dragged behind his back, sitting through the night and watching over Che. Idly she stood up and walked over to his pallet.

Tynisa had always prided herself on being independent, relying on no one. It was an easy thing to take pride in when she had never needed to do so. Her relationship with Salma had always been a joking, teasing one, underscored by an annoyance that her charms had never been quite enough to conquer him. Her relationship with Che had been, she admitted, a vain one. It had been a pleasant situation to have a plainer sister, one so earnest and good natured, and graceless.

Only when they were taken away from her had Tynisa realized how she loved them both, how they had become part of her. She knelt down beside Salma, seeing in sleep a face that he never usually presented to the world. Asleep, he looked five years younger, and it struck her that she had always assumed him older than her, and never known different. Absently she smoothed the dark hair from his forehead, and watched as his eyelids fluttered for a moment. *Dream dreams of freedom*, she urged him silently.

She heard no tread but suddenly felt Tisamon's presence beside her. He wore his usual grave, melancholy expression, and she wondered whether he ever relaxed it, even when sleeping.

'I have something to speak to you about,' he said softly. 'If you will.'

Where am I with him now? The fight in the sewers had broken down the wall surrounding him, but he was still exploring the new world that she presented for him. She sensed that he had now come to some decision.

She followed him over to the patch of floor that he had slept on, where his pack and few belongings lay.

'You have something of mine,' he said, and she did not understand.

Seeing her blank expression, he smiled bleakly. 'Nothing I would wish on another, but it is within you.

You have Atryssa's face, her clever mind, I think, her skill, but you have something also of mine.'

Something of the Mantis, she realized. 'I ... my Art shows nothing of your kinden, I think ...' she said. 'I cannot fly. I have no spines like yours.'

Mirth now, in that smile, of a wintry kind. 'And is all Art worn so openly? Tell me what races in your veins when you fight, Tynisa. Tell me the lust in your heart when you scent blood. Tell me of your *joy* when blade meets blade.'

His words felt like a blow.

'No—'

'But yes,' he said. 'I have seen you fight. With a Spider's poise, yes, but you have my people's Art behind you, and it makes you deadly and it makes you *alive*.'

She recalled that moment in Stenwold's house, standing over the slain assassin with her victory singing in her ears, and fighting the Wasps and the street thugs in Helleron, the men of the Gladhanders, the guards she cut through to get to Che and Salma. She could pin motives to all of those – to save herself, to save her friends, to pay her debts – and yet her heart had taken fire once the steel was out. Something had come to possess her then, that coursed through her like a fierce poison, that made her mad. It also made her brave and swift and fierce. She thrilled with the knowledge of her own skill even as she cut lives from bodies like a gambler shuffling cards.

'I ...' Her heritage, her Mantis heritage, was lurking behind this Spider face of hers, and with it all of its blood-greed, its oaths and promises, its ancient traditions and its long memory. All of this she was inheritrix to.

And it was terrible, to find that heritage inside her like a cancer, but when she met his eyes he looked as proud of her as nobody had ever been, and it was wonderful, then.

'That sword does not fit you,' he said. It was a Mynan shortsword she had borrowed, a heavy, inelegant thing.

'It's better than none,' she suggested.

He knelt by his gear and gestured for her to do the same. She felt an odd shiver as she did so. She stood now on the far side of some barrier or threshold that he had long kept her from.

'When we came to this city before, I had expected to meet your mother here, as you know,' he said, not quite looking at her. 'And I did not, and the truth of why that was so is recent for both of us. However . . .' He spread his hands, and she saw the spines on his forearms flex with this small motion. 'I had meant . . . I had thought, while we were apart. I wanted to make some gesture, to bind her to me, to bind me to her. Just something.' A faded smile. 'We could not wed. For my people it is a ceremony sacred, and they would slay me rather than see me united with her kind. For hers, however, their women may take many men, as they will. But I wanted to show what she meant to me. I am not good with words, as you can tell. So I found her a gift.' One hand made a movement towards his rolled blankets and his pack, but he withdrew it. 'And then she did not come. But I could not cast the gift away. It was . . . important, valuable, to me. I have carried it ever since, wherever I went. I have put it above my bed and hoped that some rogue would steal it, and rid me of it, for it has always reminded me of her. And every night, when I came back to whatever low place I lodged in, there it still was. And now you are here, in this city, her daughter and her very image – and my own blood as well. And you have lost a sword.'

At last he looked her straight in the eye. 'You don't believe in fate,' he stated.

'I do not.'

'You have a heritage. In truth you have two. You have been brought up by Beetles, surrounded by machines and ideas you cannot ever grasp. You try to think like them, but your blood says otherwise. My people believe in fate, and in many other things the Beetle-kinden do not teach, and your mother's kinden likewise. I believe this is *fate*.'

And he lifted from behind him a rapier such as she had never seen. It was scabbarded in iridescent green that shifted and changed as the light touched it, bound with what she thought at first was brass, but then saw must be antique gold. It was shorter than her old blade, but when he put it into her ready hands she found it was heavier. The guard was crafted into interlocking shapes that might represent leaves or elytra, all in gold and dark steel and enamelled green. Her eyes seemed unable to stay still on it without turning to follow its twining lines.

She had taken it by the scabbard, which seemed to be finely worked chitin shell, and now she reached for the hilt but Tisamon stopped her.

'There are formalities,' he told her. His hand touched the sword's tapered pommel, which ended in a curved claw. In an instant he had pressed his palm to it, drawing a raw red line beside the ball of his thumb. She saw a drop of his blood glisten on the gilt metal.

'Now you,' he said. She opened her mouth to protest and he told her, 'This is important. I do not ask you to believe, only to believe that *I* believe.'

She gripped the scabbard just below its neck and stabbed the same metal thorn into her hand. It felt like the sting of a small insect just before the poison starts, a tingling pain. *His blood, and my blood, both on my hands.*

'Now draw the sword,' he directed, and she did.

When her hand closed about the textured wood of the grip something went through her, a shock as though she had just been stabbed. Her heart lurched and for a second she felt the sword in her hands as a living thing, newly awoken. The feeling passed almost at once but her sense of wonder returned in force as she slid the blade from the scabbard.

It was shorter than she was used to, as she had guessed

from the sheath, and it did not seem to be of steel at all, but a dark metal lustreless as lead. It was thicker, too, than she had thought, tapering only in its last few inches. In her hands it was like an unfamiliar animal that might yet get to know her scent and be trained.

'This is . . . *old*,' she said slowly.

'There are perhaps six or seven amongst my people who still have the secret of making such blades, but this one dates back to the Age of Lore, as all the best ones do.'

'The *when*?' It was a term she had not heard in Collegium.

'Before the Apt revolution,' Tisamon informed her.

'But that's . . . not possible.' She looked at the weapon in her hands, gleaming only a little in the dawn light. 'That was over five hundred years ago.'

'And the forging itself occurred another hundred before that,' he said. 'Forged in an age before doubt. Forged in blood and belief and the purity of skill – all the things that make up my kinden. It is mine to hold and give because, though I prefer the claw, I have completed my mastership of this blade, which is the blade of your blood from mother and father both. I have undergone the rituals, stood before the judges of Parosyal and shed my blood there. One day, if you consent, I will take you there too.'

It took her a moment to realize what he was saying. The Island Parosyal was some kind of spiritual place for the Mantis-kinden, or so she had been taught. He did not mean some mere religion. He was speaking of the Weaponsmasters, the badge he wore, the ancient order so jealously guarded.

'They would never accept me,' she said. 'I am a halfbreed.'

'If I vouch for you, if I train you, and if you are sufficiently *skilled*, then there will be no human voice with the right to deny you,' he told her. 'It is your choice,

Tynisa. I am a poor father to you. I have no lands, no estate, no legacy from four and a half decades, save my trade. So it is all that I can give you.'

And before she could cloud her mind with 'but's and 'what if's she said, 'Yes.'

A silence fell almost the moment that Kymene entered the room. Even Stenwold, part-way through puzzling over the charts and accounts that Tynisa had given him, paused instinctively, looking up. He caught his breath despite himself.

He had seen her last night, of course, looking weary and dirty from the sewers. bruised from her captivity. More like a thin and underfed waif than the Maid of Myna.

She had used her time well since, and he had no idea if she had even slept, for now she presented herself to her faithful in the way they wished to see her.

She wore full armour, or a version of it. A conical helm and coif framing her delicate, unyielding features. A breastplate, a man's breastplate, painted black with two arrows on it in red. One pointed towards the ground, the other towards the sky, and Stenwold read that as *We have fallen. We shall rise again.* She wore a kilt of studded leather tooled with silver, high greaves patterned after the breastplate, and gauntlets the same. She wore no shirt, no breeches, though, as an ordinary soldier might. Her arms and legs showed bare skin of blue-grey to remind them that she was no mere spear carrier but the Maid of Myna. Her black cloak billowed behind her as she entered.

There was no cheer as she arrived, and Stenwold bitterly thought she deserved one until he realized what attention such noise might call down on them. Instead the cheer was in their eyes, in their faces.

'Chyses,' she began, and the man came forward almost

nervously. 'You are the one who gave me hope in the dark. I shall always remember you for it. You are dear to me, from now.'

She clasped him by the arm and Stenwold guessed that their history had not been so amicable in the past, and it was to erase that stain that he had mounted the rescue. Chyses made to return to his place, and Stenwold saw tears glint in his eyes, but then Kymene was catching at his sleeve, keeping him at her side.

'You have come here from all across the city,' she told her audience. 'I know most of you. I know that you are not all friends with one another, that each of you holds a revolution in your hearts that differs from your neighbour's. You are all come here under one roof, though, when before my capture I could not bring you together. Let us thank the Wasps for that, at least.'

A slight current of laughter, while Stenwold glanced from face to face. Old and young, men and women, Soldier Beetles of Myna and a few others, Grasshopper militia, Fly-kinden gangsters sympathetic to the cause, even a couple of ruddy-skinned Ant renegades from the conquered city of Maynes. All of them now watched Kymene and waited for her orders.

'You must probably expect me to set the city alight with a single brand, to call on every man, woman and child of Myna to rise up with staves and swords to drive the Empire from us.'

A few cries to the positive, but her tone had caught their attention, and they waited.

'You know that the Bloat is dead!' she called, to emphatic nods and savage grins. 'But who killed him?' she demanded of them, and that struck them dumb.

'I did not slay him, not that I would have stayed my hand. Neither did Chyses, nor any of our party. Yet we all know he is dead. So who slew the Bloat?' Her eyes fixed each in turn until one spoke.

'They say he crossed another Wasp over a woman, is what I've heard. I heard they executed some officer for it.'

'It was Captain Rauth, I heard,' another put in. 'The Bloat's sneak. We won't miss him either.'

'Is that what they say?' Kymene asked, killing the murmur of speculation that was beginning. 'The Wasps have been fighting each other? Even as Chyses was breaking the lock of my cell, they were killing one another in the dark? Myna will have a new governor, worse no doubt than the old, and look to that man for why the Bloat was killed. For now they have put the word out that the Bloat is dead, made it very public indeed. Why is that, though? Why trumpet the news from end to end of the city, so that we all know it and can take heart from it?'

She strode along the front row of her audience, her cloak unfurling behind her.

'Which one of us does not know that our enemy possesses cunning as well as force? We have all felt it, I most of all when their mercenaries caged me! So why have they let us hear so soon that the Bloat has fallen? They have let us hear because they are waiting for us to act. They know that we are growing strong, and they wish us to become no stronger before we strike. They are waiting for us to go to the ordinary people, and then they will put us down with fire and blood. Because we *are* strong but we must be stronger. The time for revolution will come, but it is not now, and the Wasps know that.'

She had them utterly. They stared at her and Stenwold stared with them.

'For many days, five tendays at the very least, there must be no murmur of resistance. They cannot stand waiting with sword raised forever. Some time they must lower the blade, and all that while we will grow stronger. Our time will come, but we must be more cunning than the Wasps in order to triumph. Strength alone will not avail us. This is why Chyses was wise to enlist these foreigners in my rescue. Those Wasps that saw them and lived, and there were few,' a murmur of grim satisfaction at that, and several glances at Tisamon, 'will say that it was merely some foreigners rescuing foreign prisoners. You shall pass the same story around, wherever the Wasps might overhear. Let them begin to doubt themselves. Let them lower their guard. Do nothing to hone their suspicions. You now all understand why this is?'

And they did. Kymene was a rare speaker, Stenwold decided. She cast her words into a room of disparate and divided people, and each one was drawn closer by them, until they were all standing together before her, and she was speaking to each one and all of them.

He still held out little hope for the Mynan revolution, but without Kymene he would have held out no hope at all.

After she had finished rallying her troops and had sent them back to their followers and their resistance cells with her instructions, Kymene still was not finished. With no visible sign that she had been locked in a Wasp cell until the small hours of that morning, she came over and sat before Stenwold, motioning for the other foreigners to join them. They filtered in slowly: Cheerwell sitting beside her uncle with Totho a little behind her; Tynisa and Tisamon sitting close together on his other side, she still holding the sheathed blade her father had given her; Achaeos a little further back, shrouded in his robes like a sick man on a cold day.

'You are a remarkable revolutionary,' Stenwold said, putting aside the stolen Wasp papers only with reluctance. 'I've known a few activists in my time, but we call them "chaotics" in Collegium, and that's as much a testament to their own lack of cohesion as their aim in causing chaos. I can't think of any who, in your shoes, would have counselled such patience.'

'I am just a woman who loves her native city,' Kymene said. 'I remember your name, Master Stenwold Maker. One still hears it on occasion. You fought the Wasps during the conquest. Or you ran from them, depending on the story.'

'A little of both, I fear.'

'Well, all records are rewritten now. I know you came here to rescue two of your own, and that freeing me was incidental to your plans, but because you have given me back to my city, to work for its freedom again, I owe you more than I can ever pay. What I can afford to give, though, you have only to ask for.'

Stenwold nodded tiredly. 'Well, it would be a lovely thing to shake hands and say we are replete with what we'll need, but I fear we must indeed call on you for help. No great demands, but help enough.'

'Ask,' she prompted.

'I need a messenger, the fastest you can get, to fly to Helleron.'

'It shall be done.'

'I'll have prepared a message in an hour's time that must be taken to a man of mine there.' He saw the worried looks of his protégés and continued, 'I'll explain all in a moment, but first let's deal with what we need. I assume a flier's out of the question.'

She actually laughed at that. 'To steal one from the Wasps would be to break my own instructions to my followers, and there are no fliers outside their hands. I can get you horses, though.'

Stenwold weighed that up. 'We ourselves have an automotive stowed outside town. Can you get us enough horses for a change of mounts halfway, and I'll trade you the machine?'

'Agreed,' she said. 'Your line of credit extends a while yet, Stenwold Maker. What else? Ask.'

'A man to go to the city of Tark and gather information.

I can brief him in detail. I have no agents there, and now I need some eyes.'

'Agreed, though you may have to pay him.'

'Not a problem. In addition we'll need supplies for our journey to Helleron, and a change of clothes for most of us wouldn't go amiss.'

'Agreed.'

'Then I think we'll be in shape to leave you.' He looked at his hands, bunched into fists in his lap. 'There is one more thing, though. Not something I ask of you, but something that you should know.'

She nodded, waiting silently, and he thought she guessed already at what he would say.

'The Treaty of Iron is rusting fast,' he said. 'The Wasps have recovered their losses from the Twelve-Year War and they are now ready to march again. I've seen their staging point at Asta, and I've read their logistics reports, and their next assault could be underway in a matter of tendays. Westwards – this time the might of the Wasp Empire will be concentrated west of here, their power brought to bear against the cities of the Lowlands.'

'It would be a logical step for them,' she agreed.

'You do not need me to tell you that, when our enemy most exerts his weight elsewhere, that is the time any revolution might have the best hope of success.'

She smiled thinly. 'I think we understand each other,' she said. 'My people are not ready yet to throw off the Wasps, but they will be. May that turn out to be to your people's good, as it will be to mine. Our revolution *will* succeed,' she said, and there was not the faintest smudge of doubt on her, 'but we may need allies in the west if we're to stay free.'

'I have one thing to ask, if I may,' said Salma. He had been fast asleep the last anyone was aware of him, and now he sat down beside them even as he spoke. Even in his prison-grimy tunic and breeches, he looked vastly more the young man they remembered. Even his smile was back.

'Ask it,' Kymene said.

'There was another prisoner of the Wasps. A Butterfly-kinden named Grief in Chains?' the Dragonfly pressed.

'I know of her.' Kymene looked at him oddly. 'Last I heard she was some kind of pawn in their little games.'

'She was passed into the hands of an officer named Aagen. Che overheard them discussing it,' Salma said. 'I need to know where she is. There's one rescue left to make.'

'Tynisa did better than she knew in bringing these to me,' Stenwold remarked. He had his fellows gathered before him like a class in Collegium, even Tisamon. Only Achaeos kept himself distant, as usual. 'Of course these are only a fragment, but I have grown used to reading fragments these last ten years.'

'I thought they must be plans. Invasion plans, perhaps?' said Tynisa. 'I had a look at them, on the way back. I . . . didn't understand them.'

'Nothing so dramatic. Just quartermasters' notes, logistics, accounts. The minutiae of an army's organizing,' Stenwold told her. When she looked crestfallen, he added, 'But dearer than gold for all that, for they tell me where the Wasps have gone to, and in what numbers, and also with what provisions and equipment. If you know how to read them, then they're as good as an annotated map of their progress.'

'And what is the news then?' Tisamon asked. 'The fighters here have been saying that a lot of troops have been moving through, going west. We've seen some of that.'

'They don't lie.' Stenwold nodded. 'And neither do these reports. Remember Asta? That was just a staging ground, and now I know where they were staging for.

Look here.' He turned one of the sheets over, and took a stylus from his toolbelt, dotting on the places as he named them. 'Myna here. Asta here. This,' a scribbly blur, 'is the Darakyon. Helleron here, beyond it. Here now is the Dryclaw.' A dotted line delineated the shifting boundaries of the desert. 'And here . . .' For a second he was indeed back in the classrooms of the Great College. 'Anyone . . . ?'

'Tark, sir,' Totho said.

'The Ant city-state of Tark, easternmost of the Lowlands cities. And what are the Ants of Tark best known for?'

'Slaves,' said Che distastefully.

'A little simplistic,' Stenwold said, with a scholarly wrinkle, 'but it represents the truth that, of all the Ant city-states, Tark can consider itself rich. It stands on the Silk Road leading from the Spiderlands, on the west road used by the Scorpion-kinden of the Dryclaw into the Lowlands, on the east road for the Fly warrens of Egel and Merro. But its trade harvest is so particularly rich precisely because it is the portal to the entire Lowlands. Only not even the Tarkesh think like that. And why? Because they are more concerned with maintaining their military strength against the other Ant cities, rather than in preparing against an outside threat.' He made an arrow with the stylus covering the march from Asta to Tark. 'Now there *is* a threat. Myna has seen a vast number of soldiers already shipped to Asta, and the majority of them are headed onwards for Tark. I would guess from these figures anywhere in the region of thirty thousand: Wasp soldiers and Auxillian support totalled. Together with field weapons, war automotives, fliers, of course. It's all in these papers, if you know how to read them.'

'What can we do then?' Che demanded, as though there could be some simple means by which to save a city.

'The Ants of Tark will have to manage their own

defence, not that they'd appreciate any offers of help from outsiders. The Wasps have moved ahead of us, but at least I will have eyes there to see what may be seen, and can report to me. We must go to those places in the Lowlands that will listen to us. Collegium, Sarn, even Helleron.' The stylus tapped the map. 'And there we have our next problem, for not all the soldiers mentioned in these reports are slated for Tark's walls.'

'Where else?' Che looked from his face to the map and back.

'Two armies, a forked attack. The bulk of the soldiers against the military might of Tark, but enough, perhaps enough, to take on Helleron. How many soldiers would it take to conquer Helleron? How many to persuade the Helleren that working with the Empire would be better than against it, or that the terms of the Treaty of Iron were now due to relax?'

'Send a few men and a large enough purse,' interrupted Achaeos's acid voice from beyond them. Stenwold nodded at him without acrimony.

'And they have sent more than a few men, and I have no idea of the size of the purse, but Helleron is where we must now go to do most good. If the magnates of Helleron can band their armies and their wits together, they have enough to resist a force of ten times this size. If they are divided, or blinker themselves to the truth, then the Wasps may take Helleron very easily indeed, and then the Lowlands will be open to them. Helleron, as I say, is where we can do most good. I have already sent my messenger off to Scuto there, warning him to prepare. We may not quite outstrip the Wasps but the messenger, and word of their coming, will do.' He sighed, paused a moment before continuing.

'So we come to it at last. I have made you my agents. I have sent you into danger, imprisonment. I have gambled with your lives, I who am a poor gambler at best. I ask you now to go to war with me, and any of you may still say no. I will not hold that against you, even my oldest friend or my closest relation.'

Those gathered close faced him with equanimity, not a face flinching, and so he looked beyond towards the Moth. 'This is not your fight, Achaeos.'

They all turned to look at him, and he glanced at Che for a moment before answering. 'None of this has been my fight, Master Maker, and I will not go to war to save Helleron.'

'And I cannot blame you. You have already done much for us—' Stenwold started, but Achaeos held up a grey hand.

'Your niece and I spoke, this morning before the sun. We spoke of many things. She told me that the Wasps would eventually come to my people as to yours, and I have seen their works, and I believe her. And whilst you Beetles may chip, chip, chip at our mountains to scratch for your puny profits, the Wasps bring tyranny and war, and they *fly* – either in themselves or in their machines. That makes all the difference in the world, for while your people grub in the earth, they will look to the heights as they hone their swords. So, I will return with you now and tell my people what I have seen – for all they will not want to hear it. I will try to convince them that the Wasps must be fought, in such ways as my people are wont to fight. I will not go to war to save Helleron, but I will go to war to save my own people, whether from Beetle-kinden or Wasp-kinden, or whoever dares raise a hand against us.'

Thirty-two

After Salma had gone Che was left only with the bitter taste of the harsh words she had exchanged with him. The harsh words she had given him, in fact. He had smiled through them, shrugged them off.

She had told him what a foolish thing he was doing, going out into the city right under the eyes of the Wasps, actually seeking them out, and he had freely admitted it. She had pointed out that he hardly knew the woman: some short days of shared imprisonment, a few words and a chained dance. He had nodded amiably.

'Do you think you're invisible?' she had shouted at him. 'There's a whole city full of Wasps out there!'

He had shaken his head maddeningly. 'They are at the palace, and they are waiting for a Mynan rebellion. You heard what Kymene said. They will be watching the ground, not the air, and they will not be out on the streets in force if they want to tempt the Mynans to rise up.'

'But they will be watching the ground from the air,' she had insisted.

He had shrugged again, equally maddeningly. 'And I shall see them before they see me, because I have better eyes, and I am a better flier than any Wasp alive.' His expression suggested it was all so simple.

She had become angry with him, but it was only because she could not understand why he was taking such risks, such needless risks, just for Grief in Chains.

And at the end she had run out of words to throw at

him, whereupon he just smiled and shrugged again. 'It's just something I have to do, so if it can be done, I'll do it.'

'You know this Aagen is a close friend of Thalric, that you'll almost certainly run into Thalric himself when you go after him. Salma, we've only just been set free ourselves.'

'That's because we had friends who cared enough to come after us,' he said, infuriating in his reasonableness. 'Who does *she* have?'

'Who do any of them have? You can't set every slave in the Empire free!'

'No, just one.'

And then he had gone. Wearing Mynan garb, and heavily cloaked, but still looking like nothing other than a Dragonfly noble from the Commonweal, off he had gone. She watched from the doorway of their hideout until he was out of sight, and then she watched some more in case the power of her gaze might, by some mechanics quite unknown to her, draw him back.

A hand fell on her shoulder and she knew, before she turned, that it belonged to Achaeos. For a moment she let it rest there, and then he said, 'I can tell you why, if you wish, but you won't believe me.'

She turned round, stepping away from him. 'I suppose it's magic.'

'Yes,' he said, and there was a slight smile on his face, so she was not sure whether he was mocking her or not.

'I don't . . . I can't believe in magic. There is always an explanation, always.'

'And if magic *is* the explanation?'

'Magic doesn't explain anything. In Collegium there are papers, studies from years going all the way back to the revolution. They've done test after test and there's no such thing as magic.'

'That's like a man who lives in a world without wind denying the existence of a sailing ship,' Achaeos replied.

With a great display of diffidence he seated himself beside the sentry at the door, who shuffled sideways and made more room for him than he needed. 'It is because magic – the magic that I myself have grown up with – is blown by winds that your tests take no account of. Winds of the mind, I mean, like confidence, belief. Look, the sun is out, yet I have my cowl up because my people are not fond of it. If I were to tell you a story now of strange deeds and ghosts, or somesuch, would I scare you?'

'That depends on the story.' The sentry now had made enough room for her to sit down next to him. 'Probably not.'

'And then tonight, in the dark of the moon, when the world is quiet and yet full of odd sounds, you prepare to take your rest, and the story recurs to you, and you cannot sleep for the fears preying on your mind. Magic is like that. I simplify, of course, but magic breaks into the world where doubt leaves a gap for it.'

'That doesn't make sense. Not to me.' Yet just for a moment the idea made her feel queasy, as though there were a chasm yawning at her feet.

'Perhaps not, but your friend has been enchanted. This dancer was a magician – or at least the sort that the Butterfly-kinden have amongst them.' He spoke the name with a certain distaste that, oddly, made Che feel better. She wondered if it was mere jealousy at this wondrous dancing woman that everyone seemed to like so much, or perhaps it was something more than that. Perhaps it was even what Achaeos was telling her: that the woman was a magician, that she had cast a spell on Salma.

She did not believe it, but at the same time she had to know.

'So what has she done? Not that I—'

'Not that you believe she has done anything, but what *has* she done?' finished Achaeos with an arch glance. 'She was desperate, I imagine. She was weak, surrounded by enemies. It is a simple charm that her people practise much, but it is one of powerful attraction. Her captors were proof against it because they already owned her. But then she saw your friend, and saw in him something that might help her. As a slave, with nowhere else to turn, she touched his mind. That is all. Perhaps some of it was just the Ancestor Art, for there are ways to catch the mind through that, but those charms fade. To last so long, through such separation, she used her magic.'

'But I didn't see her use any . . . or do anything . . . or . . .' Che stumbled to a halt with the sentence.

'And you knew what to look for? She danced for him, yes?'

'She danced.'

'But in her mind she danced only for him. In his mind that was so as well. *That* was the incantation, no green smoke and no words of power. A dance is quite enough, and your friend was caught. Not unwillingly, I suspect, for I know Butterfly-kinden have charms of a physical nature.'

She caught that hint of derision again, and recalled: 'She said, "Night Brother", when . . . when I woke from the dream. You have the same eyes, you and she.'

It was a moment before he spoke. 'Yes, well, it is said that we were kin long ago. Children of the sun, children of the moon. And we *hate* them,' he added, almost cheerily. 'For their light and their wonder, we hate them.'

'You hate all sorts of people,' Che pointed out.

'Oh, for all the wrongs done to us, we have hated your people for five hundred years. But the Butterfly-kinden, the weakest and most ineffectual people in the world, we have hated forever.'

He took one last look about these rooms, which he had rented so recently. He had experienced such a run of emotions here, he could almost feel them in the walls. What sights, what thoughts. Aagen shook his head but it would not clear. Instead it took him over to the balcony, where the open shutters were admitting the rain.

Thalric's plans. Always a dangerous game and Aagen was still unsure of what his colleague had achieved, in the end. Thalric was an old friend, but he was Rekef too. It was known that the Rekef had no friends, not really.

Out there, lanced steadily by the rain, Myna lay quiet. Aagen knew the city was not expected to remain so. The resistance were gathering, their leader now returned to them. Thalric had said they were reckoned to strike soon. Aagen knew that of the men passing through Myna for the warfront, a good thousand were still close at hand, within reach of the city walls. There was going to be a great deal of killing in Myna very soon, or so the men at the top reckoned. Aagen was very glad that he would be out of it.

Thalric had now done his work here and was going back to continue with whatever plots he had boiling away. He, Aagen, could meanwhile return to the relative simplicities of war.

He was glad to be a friend to Thalric, because if any man needed a friend it was him, but at the same time he could wish that Thalric had never met him in Asta or co-opted him in this business here.

Her feet had moved across this very bare floor, a dance for him alone, bounded by the chains she wore and by the confines of the room. He shivered at the memory.

I have done a terrible thing.

He could never tell Thalric what had transpired. There was no one he could tell. Yet it was such a thing that told itself, a cloud hanging over him that spoke of his guilt.

He went through his requisitioned rooms towards the door. Only a short way to go now. He had his gear packed, and shockingly little of it now. His heliopter was back waiting for him at the airfield, stocked with new parts and with his stoker already standing by to pipe up the engines.

There was nothing else keeping him here. One last bowl

of wine, perhaps, though it would not dissolve the memories, and then he would go.

That was when he heard the slight sound from the other room. When he turned, there was a man out on the balcony. He was a Dragonfly-kinden, and in his hand was a Wasp-made sword. For a moment neither of them moved, and then Aagen approached him slowly, one hand turned palm out in case he needed to call his Art. He saw the other man notice that gesture, tense to dodge the sting if it came.

'Who are you supposed to be?' Aagen demanded.

'I don't need to fight you,' Salma told him.

'I know you,' the Wasp said belatedly. 'You're Thalric's prisoner. Well, at least you were. If I were you I'd still be running.'

Salma was now balanced on the balls of his feet, waiting for a strike that would turn this into bloodshed. 'Just give me what I want,' he said. 'We don't have to fight. There's been enough blood already in this city.'

'What do you want?' Aagen asked him, though he had a fair idea already.

'I've come for her,' the Dragonfly said, and took a quick step sideways, even then expecting the blast.

It did not come. 'I thought you had,' the Wasp said. 'I thought it must be that. Come in.'

Salma's mouth twitched into a smile, but it disguised only suspicion. 'In?'

'At least come out of the rain. Your kinden have sense enough for that, don't you?' Aagen clenched his fists, and it came to Salma, in a moment of almost vertiginous culture shock, that for the Wasp-kinden a clenched fist meant peace and an open hand death.

Aagen turned his back, as simply as that, and headed into the next room. If he had wanted, Salma could have killed him right then, but he was too surprised to take the man on. Instead he padded after him, sword still drawn. *He can open a hand faster than I can get this blade clear of my belt.* It made Salma lament for his own sword, lost like his robe and everything else he had owned.

'Grief in Chains,' he insisted, as the Wasp sat down heavily on the bed there in the next room, looked at his hands and then up at Salma. There was a wine jug and a bowl on a shelf above him, with another jug lying empty under the bed. Salma guessed that the Wasp artificer had been its solitary beneficiary.

'I had her, here,' Aagen said. 'She danced for me.'

'What have you done with her?'

'And then Thalric came, and said she was mine. He gave her . . . no, the Empire gave her to me. Can you believe it?'

Salma's hand clenched about the sword's hilt. 'I'm taking her,' he said. 'She's no one's slave. Where is she? What have you done with her?'

'I set her free.'

For a moment the words failed to find any meaning in Salma's mind. Then: 'You . . . killed her?'

Aagen looked up at him, uncaring of the sword. 'I set her free. I gave her freedom. I let her go.'

Salma stared at him, and something inside him squirmed with rage. The feeling horrified him because he knew what it was. It was that he had come here to take Grief in Chains, and take her for himself, and he had been thwarted. In that moment he was a slaver, a slave-master, as much as any Wasp-kinden – as much as Brutan or Ulther. The recognition of that part of what had driven him here made him feel ill, and he lowered the blade. 'You just . . . ?'

'Oh, not turned her out of doors. I know better than that. She is such that, law or no law, some man was bound to seize on her,' Aagen replied. He fetched down the jug and bowl and poured out the last of the wine. 'Will you join me? You've never drunk with a Wasp before, I'd wager. Nor I with a Commonwealer.'

The shift, this change in understanding, made Salma feel dizzy, and he knelt across from Aagen, one hand to his head. When the bowl came to him he took it gratefully, taking a swallow of the harsh, dry liquid just to bring himself back to reality.

'Have you heard of Mercy's Daughters?' inquired Aagen. 'They are a sect in the Empire.'

'I thought the Empire didn't tolerate sects.'

'Not officially, but these are healers, and they often follow the armies, tending to the wounded. Often they provide a dying soldier's last comfort. Any officer who speaks against them most likely loses the loyalty of his men. So they persist, these women, although sometimes they are punished or driven away. I saw a Butterfly-kinden amongst their ranks once before. Her kinden has a gift, an Art I think, for healing.' Aagen took the bowl back, drained the final dregs. 'Well she has gone to them. If she can be kept safe at all, they will do it. They head off with the army.'

Salma cast his mind back along all the plans that Stenwold had unveiled. *With the army* must mean to the city of Tark, he realized, where the vast majority of the Wasp forces were heading.

'I'm going to go after her,' he said, only realizing the truth as he said it. *Not to take her, not to own her, but to save her from the war. To give her the choice.*

Aagen studied him for a long time, and something in that look told Salma how very hard it had been for the man to let her go, and what hidden strength had allowed him to do it.

'Good luck,' the Wasp told him. 'I hope that, if you deserve it, you find her.'

'You're not like other Wasps.'

'Aren't I?' Aagen smiled, but it was a painful smile. 'No doubt you've killed my kinsmen by the score.'

'A few,' Salma allowed.

'Well, next time you shed my kinden's blood, think on this: we are but men, no less nor more than other men, and we strive and feel joy and fail as men have always done. We live in the darkness that is the birthright of us all, that of hurt and ignorance, only sometimes . . . sometimes there comes the sun.' He let the bowl fall from his fingers to the floor, watching it spin and settle, unbroken. 'You should fly now while it's still raining. People never look up that much in the wet.'

Hokiak himself came to deliver their supplies to Stenwold, arriving like visiting royalty in a sedan chair borne by four of his Mynan servants.

'See you fell on your feet, then.' Once inside he looked around at all the resistance fighters while leaning on his cane. 'Wouldn't of put money on it. This lot wouldn't trust their own mothers half the time. Mind you, a lot of sand's blown by since then.'

'I hope we haven't been bad for your business,' Stenwold said.

'In my line of work, ain't no such thing. We can sell 'em capes when it rains, an' buy 'em back at half the price when it's dry. Business is always good at Hokiak's.' He gave a wheezy little laugh. 'I got your horses, too. Them's waiting for you outside town.' Hokiak watched the supplies being checked over by Khenice, the old fighter whom Stenwold only just remembered from his first visit here, when they were all of them a lot younger.

'Got a runner out there, too,' Hokiak added. 'You want her for Tark, to go spy on the Waspies. You let her know what's what, and she'll be on it. Her name's Skrill, and she's a squirmly little creature, but she'll do for you.'

'Everything's accounted for,' Khenice reported. 'Look's like you're set to go, as soon as your man comes back.'

'When he does, yes.' Stenwold fought off a sinking feeling, knowing that Salma was still absent on his madman's errand. *I have taught these youngsters badly, that they are so bold.* 'You've been a good friend, Hokiak.'

'Ain't got no friends. Just got customers and business associates,' the old Scorpion muttered, shrugging it off. He did not look at Stenwold when he said it, though. 'Mind, can't say for sure which one *you* are, so maybe that makes you as near a friend as I'm like to get these days.'

Totho had watched Che for about as long as he could bear to, as she conversed in low tones with the Moth-kinden. It was not right, this. It was eating at him. She had met the man only once, some fleeting business at Monger's place before the Wasps seized her. Now it was just as though he was some long-lost childhood friend. Totho neither liked nor trusted him. The man's featureless eyes, his skulking manner, the way he kept his cowl raised up so much: it made him look like an assassin.

Stenwold was packing up his own kit when Totho approached him. 'I need to speak with you, sir.'

'Go ahead.' Stenwold had his toolstrip still unrolled, and Totho's eyes flicked over the surprisingly extensive collection there.

'It's about the Moth, sir.'

'Achaeos?' Stenwold's hands stopped moving.

Totho knelt by him. 'I don't trust him.'

'Totho, you had valid concerns before. We didn't know him from Finni, as the Flies say. If he was going to sell us to the Wasps, though, he's already had his chance. As I understand it he did good work for us, there in the palace. He's no Wasp agent, whatever else he is.'

'Then what is he?' Totho asked. 'Why are the Wasps the only . . . the only ones for us to worry about? What about his own people? They'd love to see Helleron burn, and you know it. They hate us.' He was not sure what he meant, by that 'us'. 'How do you know he isn't just . . . worming his way into your confidence. They're subtle, they're clever, everyone knows.'

Stenwold smiled. 'Well yes, they are that, and I can't swear to you that there's no chance of what you suggest. There's every chance, in fact, whether Achaeos becomes a part of it or not, that his people will not be our allies in this business. I have to trust Scuto to scent that out for me. As for Achaeos, though, he has earned his place amongst us until proved otherwise. I'm certainly not going to drive him away because of the colour of his eyes.'

Totho bit his lip and made to get up, but Stenwold stopped him with a gesture.

'Yes, sir?'

'You spoke to me earlier, before we met Chyses and the others. You recall?'

Against his will, Totho's eyes flicked across the room towards Che. 'Yes, sir.'

'Not "sir", not "Master Maker" – just "Stenwold", please.' Even as he said it, Stenwold knew that it was a faint hope. 'I want to apologize for my reaction then, really. I've no right to judge, least of all regarding a man's heritage.' *After all, I myself have been raising Tisamon's halfbreed daughter all these years.* 'I will not stand in the way of any man that Che favours. Unless he's a Wasp, possibly. Or a Scorpion.' With a wry smile that Totho failed to catch, Stenwold sighed. 'But I won't promise her to anyone, either. I know it's a custom, and even though I'm not her father I know I could, but I won't. She has a mind as fine as anyone's, and it's hers to bestow along with the rest of her. You understand why I'm saying this. I'm not blind, Totho. I have seen the way things have fallen, since the rescue.'

'I . . . understand, sir.'

And after that discussion it was just a matter of waiting until she was alone. Totho, who had gone into the palace of the Wasps without shuddering, and clung to the hull of the fixed-wing, starting its engine even as it fell, barely had the courage for this. He had no other path to take, though, that would not lead him further from her.

Achaeos was elsewhere, or at least Totho could not spot him there, which he supposed was no guarantee. He had found Che standing at one of the upper windows, staring out at rain-dashed Myna. She was worried about Salma, he knew, and he supposed he should be, too, but there was only room in his head for so many worries at a time.

'Che—'

She turned, gave him a weak smile. 'You really don't have to come to see how I am. Or did Uncle Sten send you?'

That 'Uncle Sten' – a child's abbreviation – cut him sharply. He knew that there were only a few months between their ages, but Che always seemed younger than him, certainly younger than Salma or Tynisa. 'No, I . . . I just wanted to talk . . . but if you don't want to . . .'

She was looking out of the window again. 'I can't understand the man,' she said. 'I can't believe he'd just go off like this. He thinks they can't harm him. If they catch him now, they'll kill him. The Wasps have no patience with escaped slaves. We witnessed that ourselves.'

Silently, Totho sat down close to her, within arm's reach.

'And all for a woman he's barely met,' she added. 'I know I shouldn't believe this but . . . it really is like he's under a spell or something.'

Quite, Totho thought, then said slowly, 'There are ways to . . . catch someone's attention that aren't Art or magic. The Spider-kinden are renowned for it, weaving their webs, making people believe all sorts of things . . . As are other kinden, too . . .' He made this last observation as pointedly as he could but she did not take the hint.

'I don't care about the woman at all, but I hope *he's* safe. He never did take things seriously enough.'

'Che—'

'Yes?' She turned to him. There were spots of damp across her face and for a moment he thought she had been crying. It was just the rain, though, blown inside past the lop-sided shutters.

'I . . . When you were captured . . . We've known . . . For a long time, we've known each other . . .' His voice, to his own ears, sounded like someone else's, some stranger rehearsing a conversation like an actor going over his words. But this *was* the performance. This was *him*. 'What do you think of me, Che?'

She blinked at him, and she smiled slightly, and his heart leapt, but the hook had not caught. He was no Spider-kinden, no sly Moth mystic, to set such snares.

'I'm sorry,' she said. 'You're right. *You* did as much as anyone, and I've been so wrapped up in myself, I never thanked you. For coming to rescue me.'

'It's not—'

'Totho, I know you sometimes feel like an outsider. I really don't care about who your parents are. You've always been a good friend, ever since in Mechanics when you helped me with my notes. I know sometimes you've not felt right, what with Salma and Tynisa fighting so well, and being . . . being who they are. Believe me, I've felt the same. You can't imagine how it felt, growing up with Tynisa there and always in her shadow, but it's different now – that's all behind us. You're as much a part of this as anyone.'

'But—'

'But you're more than that, to me,' she told him, and he found that he suddenly couldn't breathe. It was not hope that clutched him so. He felt the words about to emerge as though he was himself a seer.

'You're like a brother,' she said. 'You're family, almost. Because you've always been there.'

He wanted to say more. He wanted to warn her about Achaeos, to demand, in fact, that she send the man away. He wanted to shout at her, or get his crossbow and put three bolts into the Moth-kinden, wherever he was, and then demand to be taken seriously.

But her words had stripped his strength from him. They had pierced him like knives. So he left her there, still awaiting Salma's return.

Thirty-three

And there Che waited, with the rain slanting across the ruined window, for Salma to come home.

We held on to each other so long. All through their joint captivity. *And now we're free he's off on his own, doing mad things.*

This was only a ladleful of the whole bowl of worries and thoughts that beset her. There was Achaeos, of course, and he frightened her because he was different, alien, and because of the way she felt when he looked at her or touched her hand. Beyond that there was all that Tynisa had confessed: how the haughty Mantis-kinden killer was not only, somehow, an old friend of her uncle's, but Tynisa's own father. That Tynisa, the golden child, was a halfbreed after all. Through the fog of this, Totho's words had barely penetrated.

And then she gasped, and almost let out such a loud cry that the entire Empire would hear, because there was suddenly a bedraggled figure atop a building across the square, and it was Salma. She saw him wearily let himself down, half-climbing, half-flying, and dash across the square out of the rain, and she hurried down to the ground floor to meet him.

'Salma!' She hugged him. 'You're safe!' And then, a moment later, 'You didn't find her.'

'I know where she is.' Salma looked exhausted. 'Can someone get me dry clothes, do you think? I've been playing dodge with the Wasp patrols for far too long in this foul weather. I think in the end they gave up because, no matter what they did once they caught me, they'd never make me feel more uncomfortable than I already am.'

By the time he had some dry clothes on, made of the same Mynan homespun that they were all wearing bar Tisamon, Stenwold had come over to him.

'The rain's easing. Dusk's on its way. I want to be moving out when it gets here.'

'No argument here,' replied Salma. 'This is a good city to be out of.'

'We'll collect the horses beyond the city wall,' Stenwold explained.

'We're meeting your messenger there. The one going to Tark?'

'That's right.'

'I'll be going there too.'

For a moment neither Stenwold nor Che realized exactly what he meant.

'I don't need you in Tark,' Stenwold explained eventually, but Che was wiser than he was in this.

'The Wasps have taken her away with the army,' she said. 'Grief in Chains.'

'In a sense. She's gone with them, anyway.' In his mind, Salma recalled the parting words of the Wasp artificer. As Salma had stepped back onto the balcony, Aagen had said to him, 'She has changed her name, of course. They do that often, her kinden.'

'What name does she go by now?' Salma had asked.

'Now? Who can say?' There was a twitch to the man's expression, some melancholy emotion rising behind his eyes. 'When she left here she called herself "Aagen's Joy".'

And Salma realized that in all his life, privileged as it was, he had never really known envy. Not until then.

'I will go with your man to Tark,' he explained to Stenwold, in a tone that brooked no argument. 'If you have work for me there, then give it to me and I'll be your agent. But it's to Tark that I'm going.'

Stenwold sucked his breath through his teeth like a tradesman costing a job. 'I can't change your mind in this? Tark will be more dangerous by far.'

Salma just shook his head.

'Then yes, you *can* do my work there. Give me a short while to think. By the time we set out, I'll have it.'

He turned, leaving only Che's horrified look.

'Salma, it's an army, a whole army of Wasps,' she hissed. 'They'll kill you if they catch you. Torture you, perhaps.'

'Then they had better not catch me.' He opened his arms to her, held her against his chest. 'We've been through the wars, you and I, but we'll have our time together, when this is done. I'll keep my skin safe and I'll trust you to keep yours. I'll be all right.'

There was much packing and preparation for them to do, and Kymene's people were checking their route out of the city. For those without a mind to stuff bags or pore over maps it was a time of unexpected idleness. Perhaps to avoid Che's recriminations, Salma had taken himself high up, to the top floors of a derelict building where the boards were rotten and the footing unsure. In stalking him here, Tynisa had been as silent and stealthy as when she and Tisamon had mounted their midnight raid on Asta, but still, somehow, he knew that she was coming.

'I've never been a man for arguing with friends,' he said softly. She had got here partly through her natural sense of balance and partly through her Art, which had allowed her to go hand over hand up the walls when the upper floors had been too frail to support her. Now she stretched a leg out, testing the strength of a beam. The floorboards it had once supported were perishing to beetle-grubs and time, but the footing she found was solid.

'Totho couldn't get up here, nor Che or Stenwold,' Salma went on. He was sitting in a nook, beneath a roof that was peppered with holes. One of the shafts of wan sunlight touched his face, and made it more golden still. 'The Mantis or the Moth wouldn't care where I went or what I did. Which just leaves you. You've got some words for me, no doubt?'

His resting place was close to where the beam met the wall, and she took a few steps along it, shifting her shoulders slightly to stay level. 'What game are you playing now, O hero of the Commonweal?' she asked him.

'No idea. I'm still waiting for someone to tell me the rules,' he replied.

'Che says it's because of some *dancer*.' She put a lot of venom into the word, more than she had meant.

'Well, my people are great patrons of the arts,' he told her flippantly and she yelled, '*Will you be serious for once in your cursed life?*' and heard the words jumble and blur into the echo all the way down to the cellars. She might just have called the entire Empire down on the resistance, but for all that she could not have kept the words in.

'I was a slave,' he said simply, not rising to the bait at all. 'I was a prisoner. They took the sky from me. They made me serious, I assure you.'

'Then why are you going? Why not stay with us? With your friends, who ... with people who love you? Don't tell me it's just some great crusade to free the Empire one slave at a time.'

'I won't tell you that, no.' His face, in the sunlight, was beautiful. She was itching to punch it.

'Che says that she, that *woman*, used her Art on you, or worse.'

Salma shrugged, no more than that.

'You love her more than you love us, is that it?'

He looked at her sadly. 'Perhaps love means different

things to different kinden,' he said softly. 'I cannot ignore her.'

But you can ignore me? She found that her hand had gone to the hilt of her new rapier without her meaning it. As soon as she realized, it took a great effort of will not to draw the blade.

'Salma . . .'

He stood up abruptly, in a brief flurry of wings, to land within her sword's reach on the beam, facing her. The muscles in her arm twitched and in her mind, rising from a thousand years of buried heredity, came the words, *Challenge him.*

'No . . .' she said to herself, staring at his face.

Challenge him. It is the only way you will win him. Show him your skill. Defeat him.

She was trembling. The voices of a host of Mantis-kinden had clawed their way free of her ignorance and her Collegium upbringing. Salma just watched her patiently. Part of her was amazed that he had not taken up his own sword. *Fight!* howled part of her mind. *Fight me!*

She jerked, the rapier rattling in its scabbard, and abruptly she had lost her balance, teetering on the beam. Instantly he had stepped in, arms about her to steady her, and for a moment she let herself rest against his chest, the voices in her head banished.

'I'm sorry,' he said. 'I'm still going. I have no choice.' Once he was sure she was steady, he stepped from the beam and let his wings carry him gently downwards, leaving her to make her own halting way.

With the Wasps still waiting for the resistance to rise against them, leaving the city without being seen was easy enough, tucked away amidst one of Hokiak's caravans, with a few coins paid to the guards to forestall too detailed a search. The last thing the Empire expected of its enemies just now was for them to leave. Once beyond the walls it was Khenice who led them: a line of hooded travellers who might be no more than a band of locals out to slingshot moths or gather night-growing mushrooms. They left as the sky was darkening, but there was light enough from the west by the time Khenice found their rendezvous point.

There was nobody there, nor any horses, but the old Mynan told them to wait. It was only a minute or two before a voice from the gloom startled them.

'If you're not those I'm waiting for, I'm going straight home and selling the horses.' It was a voice strangely accented, and the figure that stepped out in front of them was stranger still. Che let her Art-eyes adjust to the darkness, and what had seemed at first like a very lanky Fly-kinden was revealed as something quite other.

Skrill, as Hokiak had named her, was a halfbreed, and part of her blood must be local Mynan, for she had their shade of skin and hair, and something of their look. Her face was thinner, though, and her ears were back-sloped, long and pointed, with a nose and chin almost as sharp. Her build was the most disconcerting aspect of her, though. She was very small in the body, like a Fly-kinden or child indeed, but her limbs were overlong, not grotesquely but certainly enough to notice, so that despite her lack of height the strides she took would match a tall man's. Her movements were jerky, either a quick dash or standing very still. Beneath her cloak was a cuirass of metal scales, padded with felt for quiet movement. The packroll slung across her back had the two ends of a bow protruding from it, and there was a Wasp-issue shortsword baldricked up enough for the hilt to be almost hidden in her armpit. Beside her high-pitched voice there was little of the feminine about her, and her angular features rendered her androgynous.

'Don't stare at the lady,' she chided them, for that was

what they had been doing. 'Now which one of you great lords is Master Stenwold Maker? I hear you've a job for me.'

'And a companion too,' Stenwold agreed, beckoning Salma over. She looked the Dragonfly up and down.

'I reckon I don't mind that at all, Master Maker.'

Stenwold took both her and Salma aside, while Khenice began building a fire.

His flier was ready for him in the airfield, Thalric knew. His possessions, so few, were already packed. He knew he should leave the palace, and Myna itself, before Colonel Latvoc decided that his refusals qualified as disloyalty. In truth, he would have departed two days ago, if not for the visitor.

Thalric now stood by the workbench of the interrogation room and thought hard about that encounter because it had brought on him a sense of creeping discomfort that he had yet to shake off.

It had seemed reasonable enough when a Wasp officer of middle years had arrived asking for him. The face had seemed vaguely familiar, but the number of such men that he had met was in the hundreds so he had thought nothing of it.

In the small room commandeered as his office, he had been finishing his report for the colonel when the man came in. After a brief glance up he had returned to it, saying, 'What can I do for you, soldier?'

'Oh Major, surely you can do better than that.'

The use of his true rank had snapped his head up, thinking that this must be a Rekef matter. The officer was not standing to attention like a soldier should, and that face was becoming maddeningly familiar . . .

And then it had struck him like a physical blow. It was his own face he was looking at. Not an identical copy, which would have caused comment, but it could have been some extra brother he did not know about and the voice was one he knew as well.

'Scylis?' he had said softly, and the Wasp officer nodded with a smile that was most un-Wasplike.

'Well done, Major, although I did rather make it easy for you.'

Thalric remembered looking in vain for the edge of a mask, the sign of make-up. This was the first time he had clearly seen any face that Scylis had chosen to put up. There was no mask, nothing but that living face. It had sent a shiver of horror through him – horror at the unaccountable.

'I really could have used you three days ago,' he had said to disguise his shock. 'You do pick your moments to turn up.'

'And meanwhile your operation in Helleron is wondering if you're still alive. I decided I was best suited to tracking you down. Travelling as a Wasp officer within the Empire has its benefits. I might even consider it as a retirement option.'

Thalric had carefully not asked where Scylis had obtained the armour he was wearing.

And then there had been the gift, for Scylis had not arrived empty handed. He had been in the city long enough to learn which way was up, politically. He had brought in a prisoner for interrogation.

The prisoner was behind him now, stretched out on the bench. Because of the shortness of time available, Scylis had consented to let Thalric watch him work. The procedure had chilled him, he who had himself interrogated countless prisoners for the army or the Rekef.

When Thalric asked questions, it was about troop movements, the identities of agents, supply lines and the plans of other spymasters. His methods utilized a trained artificer and the devices that hung above the workbench, folded like an insect's limbs.

Because he was not Apt, Scylis worked by hand. Spiders almost never were, assuming he truly was a Spider-kinden at all. He worked like an artist and, amongst the questions regarding names and places, he simply sought the details of everyday life, preparing himself for the role he would be playing. His voice was soft and patient, almost sympathetic, but behind it Thalric had recognized the glee of a man rejoicing in the skill and the power he wielded. It had been a glee enhanced by the fact that Thalric was his audience, and Scylis could witness the effect on him that his ministrations were having.

At the end of it Thalric had given him his further orders and he had gladly accepted them. He had entered the palace as a Wasp officer, but by the time he was back in the city he would have another face entirely.

Behind Thalric, on the workbench, the body of Khenice waited for disposal.

At some point in the night Che sensed that she half-woke, some footfall beside her bringing her to the very brink of consciousness. Opening her eyes she saw something pale beside the rolled-up cloak that was her pillow and she identified it merely as a folded paper before passing back into troubled slumber. It seemed to her, some time later, that yet another crouched by her, but she turned over, resolutely determined not to be woken, dreaming only that whatever paper had been left beside her was now being opened and read.

And then she was being shaken, only gently but she snapped out of her dreams with one hand fumbling for her sword. The paper, had there ever been one, was gone.

'What is it? Is it Thalric?' she gasped, but then she recalled she was a prisoner no longer. They were in the shadow of the Darakyon, with the lights of Asta visible now to the south, and just last evening Salma had gone to follow the army to Tark with Skrill as his guide.

Her eyes finally obliged and the night grew pale for her – and there was Achaeos kneeling beside her, his hand on her shoulder.

'What is it? Is it my watch now?'

'Your sister is still on watch,' he said, which, because they were plainly not sisters, oddly touched her.

She sat up, looking about. 'What is it, then?' Tynisa was indeed sitting alert on a hummock near the forest's edge and, without her Art, Che would never have been able to see her.

'I need to take you somewhere,' Achaeos whispered.

She eyed him suspiciously. 'Oh yes?'

'I cannot say where it is, what it is, only that it is something that I need you to see.'

'If I knew in advance, I wouldn't go, is that it?'

'It is.' He said without shame. 'Will you come with me?'

And in that was weighed the question: how far did she trust him? Was there some slaver or Wasp agent waiting there within the dark wood? What did she really know about this grey-skinned man with his strange beliefs and his unreadable eyes?

She rubbed her own eyes, stood up and threw her cloak over her shoulders against the night's chill, then buckled on her baldric, the sword tapping against her leg like some familiar trained animal. She had been separated from it too long.

'I will trust you,' she decided, and he led her to the edge of the wood.

Tynisa watched them approach cautiously. 'Che, you shouldn't go with him if you don't want to,' she said.

'It's all right, I . . . I want to.'

'Well just shout if there's any trouble.' There seemed more to this warning than Achaeos taking liberties or even servants of the Empire lying in wait. Che frowned, but even as she opened her mouth to reply a shadow was looming beside her, making her squeak with fright.

'Are you ready?' asked Tisamon.

'We are,' Achaeos replied.

'He's coming too?' Che asked, and the Moth nodded so very seriously.

'We need him. We would not be safe without him. Not even I.'

'Achaeos, what's going on?'

'I cannot tell you. Until you yourself have seen, you would not understand.'

Even to her enhanced vision, the Darakyon was dark. She wondered that Tisamon, padding ahead, could see anything, and she saw him keep one hand out ahead of him, brushing the bark of the old trees, as though he was making his way by touch combined with some other sense she had no concept of.

She decided that she was not fond of this forest, or forests in general – at least at night. It was filled with the sounds of small things, and not so small things, and at every step she made something, somewhere nearby, twitched. Achaeos's hooded form was making its way resolutely ahead and being left behind would be even worse.

And then Tisamon had stopped and she saw his claw was on his hand, though she had not seen him don and buckle it.

'I have returned,' said Achaeos, and he announced it to the air and to the trees. 'You know me, and your power marks me still.'

He had gone mad, that was clear enough, and she glanced worriedly at Tisamon. She saw him cock his head and it was a moment before she identified this as the reaction of someone *listening*.

'I have brought her because I wanted her to see you,' Achaeos continued and then, after a pause. 'My reasons are my own.'

It seemed to her that a sudden breeze gusted through the trees, and shook the leaves a little.

'I have no more favours, and besides,' Achaeos said, 'what could I offer, who am already bound?'

Che shook her head, reaching out to tap his shoulder, as if to demand the reason for this performance. The wind was becoming more insistent, gusting and then falling in irregular patterns. Unexpectedly, Tisamon's hand encircled her wrist, drawing her hand away from the Moth's shoulder.

'Whatever you can ask of me, ask it,' said Achaeos, but his voice trembled as he spoke.

And she *heard*. The rustle of the trees, the whisper of leaves, insects scraping in the night. A hundred natural sounds, but together they formed a voice. If she listened very carefully, they were a voice.

Heart and soul, blood and bone, mind and will, what would you give?

A whimper escaped her, and had it not been for Tisamon's hand on her, she would have slid to the ground.

You return to us, little neophyte, with your prize and your temerity. What will we ask? Go and grow. Become great. Don Skryre's robes and learn the secrets. Go to the ends of the earth if you will. But always know you are bound, bound to us, to our destiny, go you ever so far. One day, in a shadow, in a mirror, in the face of the waters, you shall see us, and we shall ask of you, and that time shall be soon.

'Achaeos?' she said, her voice reed-thin with fright.

'You see them?' His voice was soft, like that of a hunter who dares not take his eyes from his prey.

'See? No, but I can hear. There are voices, Achaeos. Who else is here?'

'Your eyes can cut the dark like mine can, Che. I want you to *see*.'

She looked around wildly, but there was no one there and, besides, nobody, no ordinary human being, could have given that voice life.

Tisamon, the composite voice of the forest spoke, and

the Mantis let go of her and straightened up. Still there was nobody visible between the boles of the dark trees.

Tisamon, it said again, *you have been altered since last you passed within these halls.*

It shocked her that the Mantis, the most intimidating man she had ever met, gave a soft exhalation of fear.

You were Tisamon the Hollow Man when east you went. Now you are Tisamon of the Purpose. But your purpose is clouded to us, Tisamon. As clouded as it is to you yourself. Do you mean to send the girl into a better future, or weight her with the past?

Tisamon made no answer, but she saw his teeth were bared, his eyes fixed on something ahead. She followed that riveted gaze, and *saw*.

She collapsed then, hiding her eyes from them. There were so many of them, a score at least, and they were hideous. They were composed of smooth chitin and barbed spines, and knotted bark and thorns and twisted briars, and yet they were human beings, Mantis-kinden features as like to Tisamon's as to be family. And their eyes were huge, and they stared and stared.

She had only a brief glimpse of them before she wrenched her head aside, but the image, the sight of them, would stay with her for all her remaining days.

Then she felt Achaeos's hands on her shoulders, heard his voice, low and comforting, and she found that she clung to him because she had nothing else.

'What are they? Why did you bring me here? *Why?*'

'This is the ghost story in the night, Che. This is the dream that is there when you wake. This is the worst of dark magic. And I want you to believe, Che. You must *believe*.'

She now had her face pressed into his chest, for fear of what she might see beyond him. 'I can't believe. I can't have a world with such things in it. Please—'

'And tomorrow you will tell yourself they were just men

in costume, or that you saw them unclearly, or that you merely dreamt them, but I want you to remember this, Che. You must remember that what you have seen is real, and cannot be explained away.'

At last she dared to meet his eyes. 'But why?'

'Because this is *my* world, Che, and I want you to see it, to acknowledge it. We are the people of the twilight, of the Lore Age, before all your gears and levers. Though we fail and dwindle, we have some power yet. We are the keepers of those secrets that the world yet retains.'

'You want me to . . .'

'I would share my world with you, if your mind could absorb it. If you could just for once tear away the veil of doubt that surrounds all of your people. I may hate machines, and either destroy them or leave them, but at least I cannot avoid the fact of them. Che, please look. Please.'

And he was begging her and that was what finally persuaded her. He, who could have forced this on her, was a slave to her will in that moment.

She looked past his shoulder, clutching hard to him as her eyes picked them out again between the trees. They were speaking for Tisamon only, now. Their voice was a soft rush that she could not pick out words from. Even now they were not clear: they shifted before her, merging with the trees and each other. Che shuddered as every part of her mind except one demanded that she look away.

She made herself look. With Achaeos's slim arms about her, with him almost as her shield, she forced her eyes until they saw, they truly *saw* the abomination that was the Darakyon. Hideous tortured ghosts splayed on the rack of history, had they not been occupied with their living kinsman, their faceted gaze would have flayed her. Instead she felt she was looking into the very soul of Tisamon's people, ripped out and hung in the air like smoke and cobwebs. They were tall and proud and callous – and lost and sad.

'What did this to them?' she whispered, for the pain contained in those crooked things was infinite, as was their power.

Achaeos's voice was very soft, very solemn. 'You did,' he said. 'You did and then we did.' And he would not explain further.

Thirty-four

The Wasps had come to Helleron. At first Stenwold thought the city was under siege, for from the east they saw only the tents of the Empire's soldiers, their gold-and-black barred flags and armoured automotives. Even as they watched, an orthopter in imperial colours ghosted down silently, wings spread to catch the air.

They approached carefully, circling to the south, and from there it became apparent that matters were very different.

There was a very sizeable Wasp encampment outside Helleron, all the men and materials that Stenwold had already guessed at, but beyond them the city went on about its business just the same. There were caravans of goods, roads cluttered with people, the perpetual entrances and exits that turned the money mills of Helleron. The same tent city of traders, foreign buyers, slave markets and hawkers took up where the Wasps left off and yet nobody seemed to care that there were two thousand soldiers from an enemy power camped at the wall-less gates.

'They have surrendered,' Achaeos said bitterly. 'The moment the Wasp army got here, they laid down their weapons.'

'I don't think so,' Stenwold said. 'What we're seeing here is not an occupied city. Look, people coming and going as they please, no guards, no sentries or militia. This is Helleron just as it always was.'

'A thousand Wasps don't just turn up here to see the sights or go to the theatre,' Tynisa said.

'Our answers will be found inside,' Stenwold decided. 'We have to meet with Scuto.'

It was strange, entering that city again, for it held so many memories. Flight and fight for Tynisa and Totho, betrayal and capture for Che. Tisamon must be recalling his countless mercenary duels, all those years counted out in meaningless exercise of his skills. Achaeos tugged his cowl over his face and hid his hands. There were a few Moth-kinden in Helleron, but they were despised.

There were Wasps, too, within the crowd. Not many, and doing nothing more than talking to traders or passing on their way, but there they were. They were in armour, in uniform, rubbing shoulders in the weapon markets with Ant-kinden who regarded them suspiciously. Wasp quartermasters could be seen taking up provisions for their men, while Wasp artificers debated with Beetle machinesmiths over the quality of their wares. None of them spared a glance for the incoming train of riders. It was all so strangely unreal.

Stenwold found them stabling for the horses and paid over the high prices Helleron demanded, and then they went to seek out the poor quarter of the city where Scuto had his home.

'I don't understand it any more than you,' the Thorn Bug said. He was perched on a bench in his workroom, with quite a crowd there. Stenwold and his companions had been joined by almost a score of others who were obviously Scuto's agents within the city. They were a motley and disparate pack of rogues, Che decided: Beetles, Flies and Ants, halfbreeds, an elegant Spider-kinden in fine silks, even a scarred Scorpion-kinden whose left hand was now just a two-pronged hook of metal.

'They arrived here, what, a tenday ago, bit by bit, and

they're still trickling in. As my lads can tell you, there was a real panic at first. The magnates all mobilized their retinues, and the Council hired every mercenary they could put their hands on. It was knife-edge stuff all the way for a day or so, but the stripeys, they just sat there outside, pitching their tents. Then word got out that it was something else they were here for, but not the fighting. Some news arrived from the south saying there was an army marching on Tark that made this bunch look like the boys who clean the dunnies. Then the word was that this lot were only here to buy. They had pots of gold, Helleron mint and their own tat coins, and they were after weapons, supplies, all sorts of kit. Some reckoned they were going north – to go kick the Commonweal again maybe. People was talking maybe like they could be hired, as a mercenary army. They wanted to send them against Tharn, and this lad's folk.'

Achaeos, silent and pale, looked from Stenwold to Scuto's grotesque features.

'And that's all I know and there they are. There's been some fighting, mostly Tarkesh Ants having a go at them. They ain't exactly shy about drawing blood, the Waspies, but they pay out in good coin when the Council of Magnates asks 'em to. And there they sit, making the city rich, and here we sit, wondering what the plague the buggers really want.'

'I'm missing something here.' Stenwold looked down at his fists. 'We all are. There's no help for it but I need to talk to the Magnates.'

'It's not like they'll listen to a word you've got to say, chief,' Scuto put in helpfully.

'The Council as a whole, no, but there are a couple of them who know me of old. They owe me favours. I'm not saying they'll take that as seriously as Tisamon here might, but it still counts for something, and information's free to give. In the meantime, all of you, spread your nets as wide as you can. I want to know what the Empire is after. Helleron could depend on it. The entire Lowlands could depend on it.'

He turned to his own band as Scuto hopped off the bench and began giving out orders. 'We still have our parts to play, now or later. So I want most of you to stay here, wait for me, until the picture's clear.'

'But you want me to go to my people?' said Achaeos.

'I do indeed. Will you speak for me?'

'I will not.' The Moth folded his arms. 'I will speak for the truth, though, and that will serve you just as well. I am not your agent, Stenwold Maker.'

'Then don't do it for me, and certainly don't do it for Helleron. Do it for the Lowlands, Achaeos. Do it for your own people, by all means, but the Moths were a wide-sighted people once and surely they can be so again. They must see that, piecemeal, we are all food for the Empire, to fall beneath her armies, be taken up by her slavers. There are a hundred age-old slights that draw their boundaries across the Lowlands. Your people hate mine. Tisamon's hate the Spider-kinden. The Ant city-states hate one another. If we cannot stitch these wounds together, even for a little while, then we will fall.'

Achaeos, who had obviously had a snide remark already poised, thought better of it. 'You are right, of course,' he said. 'I shall go to my people and tell them all I can. I am no great statesmen of theirs, no leader, but whatever I can move with my words, it shall be moved.'

And it seemed that he was finished, and Stenwold was turning away from him, until he said, 'And I wish your niece Cheerwell to come with me.'

Scuto's voice still sounded in the background, parcelling out wards and fiefs of the city to his men. About Stenwold and Achaeos, though, the Moth's words echoed loudly.

'No!' Totho shouted. By sheer instinct he had his sword half out of his scabbard, and that changed everything.

Tisamon was instantly on guard, his clawed glove on his hand, and Tynisa found she had half-drawn along with him. Stenwold was holding his hands up, aware that Scuto had stuttered into silence, staring at them.

'It is out of the question,' he said to Achaeos. 'How could you even ask such a thing?'

'Because it will *help*,' Achaeos said. 'Since I am to tell them that they must aid your folk for the good of us all, I wish to present her to the elders of my race, Master Maker. It will help. They must see her.'

'You can't even begin to think about it!' snapped Totho. 'Not Che, not any of us!'

'They'll kill her,' put in Tynisa.

'They will not,' Achaeos said. 'Do you really think we know nothing of hospitality? Do not judge us by the laws of *this* forsaken place. If I bring her to Tharn with me she will be safe. Welcome, I cannot guarantee, but safe she will be.'

'The answer is still no,' said Stenwold firmly. 'No more debate on this. I will not risk my niece—'

'Uncle Sten.' At last Che's voice broke in, and it had enough steel in it that they all stopped and looked when she spoke. 'Do you remember the last time you tried to keep me from harm?'

He stared at her, thinking of that long chain of happenstance that had taken her from the *Sky Without* to the cells of Myna. 'Are you saying that you . . . want to go?'

Che swallowed, balling up her courage. 'You have been a scholar, Uncle, among many other things. Tell me how many of our kinden have walked through the halls of the Moths? Do you know of *any*, in this day and age?'

'Che, you cannot know, none of us can know, what might befall you there. Every place has rules of hospitality, and I mean no insult now when I say that every place breaks those rules from time to time.'

'I trust Achaeos,' she said. 'And if I can do something

to help, rather than just sit here and hide my head, I'll do it. You don't know, Uncle Sten, what I have been through since we parted at Collegium. I've been a fugitive and I've fought, I've been a slave and a prisoner. I've been on a torturer's table and I've even struck Wasp officers. I'm not just Cheerwell the student who needs to be kept out of harm's way. I'm going with him. I'm doing my part.'

Stenwold gave out a huge sigh that spoke mostly of the way the wheel of the years had turned while he had been looking elsewhere. He heard Totho insist, 'You can't let her!' but even he knew that by then the matter was out of his hands.

'Go,' her uncle told her. 'But take all care you can. You're right. Though you're still my niece, my family, you are a soldier in this war, and risk is a soldier's constant companion.'

After nightfall Achaeos took Che out of the city by the quickest way, and then around its periphery, anxious to remain in Helleron's shadow as little as possible. Soon they were passing the massive construction yards that were labouring over the last stretches of the Helleron–Collegium rail line – the Iron Road as they called it – which pounded out their metal rhythm every hour of day and night to get the job done.

Then they were heading towards the mountains. Outdoors, Che's vision faltered after a distance, so that the ground before her feet was lit in shades of grey, but the mountains beyond still loomed as black, star-blotting shapes.

They had been on the move for some hours now, and they had no equipment with them for scaling such slopes. Even if Achaeos knew some secret path up to his home, Che was not sure she would be able to make it.

'We may have to rest at the foothills,' she warned him.

He did not seem to react at first, but seemed to be

looking for some specific place in the scrubby, rising terrain. If she looked to the north and the east, Che could see the lights of the mining operations, Elias Monger's amongst them no doubt. She wondered if Achaeos's people would be raiding again tonight, and who had now inherited Elias Monger's share.

'We will be there later tonight,' said Achaeos. It was already dusk.

'I don't think I can manage that.'

He turned at last, his pale eyes gleaming in her vision. 'You cannot fly, can you? I know that some Beetles can.'

'Few, very few, and that only badly,' she confirmed. 'I would . . . I would so like to fly and I wouldn't care how clumsy I might look. I've not been good with the Art, though. I only started seeing in the dark after the . . . after I dreamed . . .' She had to force herself to say it. 'After you spoke to me that night, before we reached Myna.'

'You have more skill than you guess,' he said. 'Beetles endure; even *my* people know that. Think what you have already endured, and tell me your Art did not help you. However, you will not need to fly to Tharn. Simply find me a little brush that is dry enough to burn, and I will summon some transportation.'

'Summon? Is this more magic?' she asked him.

'I would prefer to say yes, and take the credit, but, no, this is a mere trick.'

When they had enough suitable material to burn, he began to lay it out in a pattern that she was too close to make out, lighting each pile of dry grass and broken wood in turn until they were surrounded by an irregular ring of small fires. A shiver ran down Che's spine: despite his words this felt like magic to her.

And then she felt something in the sky. Felt, not heard, for it made no sound, but the wingbeats were enough to make the fires dance and the warmed air gust across her. She reached out for Achaeos and clutched his sleeve as the stars above them went dark with the passage overhead of some enormous winged thing.

And then it dropped lower, and her eyes caught it in all its pale majesty. It was a moth, no more, no less, but as it circled down towards them she saw that its furry body was larger than that of a horse, its wingspan awesome, each wing as long as six men laid end to end. It had a small head, eyes glittering amongst the glossy fur behind frond-like antennae that extended forward in delicate furls. As it landed, the sweep of its wings extinguished most of their little fires.

'We of Tharn cannot always fly so high. We are sometimes weary – or injured, of course.' He grinned at her. 'This was to be my plan after I left the stables where you met me, but other things then intervened.' With a smooth movement and a flash of his own wings he was up on the great creature's back, holding out a hand for her to join him.

She walked up to the moth's side, behind the enormous sweep of its wingspan, putting a hand on its thick fur, feeling a warmth within that most of the great insects lacked. She took Achaeos's hand and, with his help, clambered up onto the creature's back. It shifted briefly on its six legs, adjusting to the extra weight. There was no saddle, she saw, but there were cords run from somewhere amongst its mouthparts, and Achaeos had clutched these like reins.

'You must hold on tight,' he said, and she put her arms about his waist and did her best to grip with her knees.

He made some signal with the reins and, in a single lurching movement, the moth flung itself airborne.

In that moment Che was sure she was going to slide off, bound back from the powering wing and then tumble to the ground however far below. She clutched at Achaeos so desperately that she could feel the hard line ridging his side where her stitches still held.

Then she began to anticipate the rhythm of the insect's flying, and it was not as she had expected. Instead of the manic fluttering, the almost random blundering of its little brothers, the giant's wings had a slow and sombre beat, each downturn propelling the moth forwards and upwards into the air, It was a patient and tireless rhythm that reminded her of being out in a rowing boat with Stenwold once, when she was very young, with her uncle pulling on the oars with his unfailing strength. She slowly loosened her hold on Achaeos so that he could breathe again, and looked about her.

She was too far from the ground to see more than the red lights of Helleron's distant forges, too far out from the mountain to detect its slopes. Above there were only stars. Achaeos and the moth and herself were the only other bright things in the world, coursing through the cool, still air, higher and ever higher. She leant her head on Achaeos's shoulder. It was so silent up here. The insect's wings made no sound, and the flight was gentle enough for there to be no rushing of air in her ears. It was so different from the fixed-wing she had piloted, or the ponderous bulk of the *Sky Without* or the Wasps' clattering heliopter.

How wonderful it would be to fly like this, she thought. Ever since childhood she had coveted this moment, that was being given to her now so casually. She could not say why she craved it, for Stenwold could not fly, nor could Tynisa. Che had often looked out of her bedroom window at the clouds or the stars, and at Fly-kinden messengers on their frantic errands or slow-droning fliers coming in towards the airfield, and she had known that here was something she would always want, and never have.

And then the slopes of the mountain came into sight, and she realized that she was now seeing Tharn.

She had pictured, perhaps, houses built slantwise on the slopes, or even caves carved into them. She had known the Moth-kinden were an ancient people, and that these places that were their last homes had also been their first. That fact had never meant much to her until now.

The lowest slopes that she could see were cut into steps that were tens of yards wide, deep with waving crops, where water trickled from one artificial plateau to the next in delicate, dividing streams. Here and there were shacks and huts for the fieldhands, but this was not Tharn. Instead Che could see Tharn on the upper slopes. For a sheer height of over one hundred yards the side of the mountain had been worked into a city.

They met in a darkened room again, the back room of some dingy Beetle hostelry where the guests were obliged to bring their own lamps. Thalric was glad of that, anyway. He had no wish to see his own face leering at him out of the gloom.

The figure that was Scylis found a chair by barely more than starlight, but then Spider-kinden always had good eyes, Thalric knew. He heard more than saw the other man pour a bowl of wine and sip a little.

'Progress?' he said impatiently.

Scylis swallowed and made a disappointed noise. 'Abysmal vintage, this. Given my current short commons I'd ask you to find something better, but I'm afraid your people's taste in wine is even worse.'

Thalric hissed through his teeth. 'Time is short, Scylis.'

'I know it is, Major, but never fear, all is in hand. I'm well in with Stenwold's divided little band. With this face I'm closer to Stenwold than his shadow.'

'I thought you were intending to go all the way with them disguised as Khenice.'

'I didn't think that would convince, and in my position the least suspicion can be fatal. So I found a better opportunity – a perfect opportunity that fell right in my lap. They had so much on their minds that they never wondered why poor Khenice left them without saying goodbye.'

'Who?' A cold feeling came over Thalric, though he was hard put to place it. 'Whose . . . face are you now wearing?'

'My secrecy is my life, Major. Do you think I would trust you with my life? Would you trust me with yours?'

'Then what have you got for me?'

'You've been admirably patient this last year, Major, in putting your plans into operation. Now you're like a child who has been promised a toy. Very well. I will show you where Stenwold's man has his den. He has mustered quite a force of malcontents there. You should, I think, move on them. Use local muscle if you're worried about the look of it. Thirty decent fighters should do it.'

'Hiring thirty men without word spreading will be difficult.'

'I leave that in your capable hands,' Scylis said. 'You won't catch all of them, because about half are out on errands at any given time. I will leave you details of where and to whom, for those I know about. A few will slip past, but you'll at least cut off the head. The top man is a spiky little grotesque called Scuto. Kill him, if you can. Kill all of them, if you can.'

'And what about you? If you won't tell me who you're dressed up as, you could get caught in the middle.'

'If that happens then I deserve to be,' Scylis said dismissively. 'Let me look after that. I'm very good at it.'

'Anything else?'

'They're hoping the Moth-kinden hermits will help them out. I can sour that, I think.'

Thalric nodded. 'We've already sent men to them. They're now in hand.'

'I wonder.'

'You doubt me?' Thalric asked.

'I doubt your understanding,' said Scylis. 'They're not

just mountain savages, you know. They're a clever pack of quacksalvers, the Moths, and nobody ever quite knows what they're after. I would make them a priority, if I were you, since they are adept at breaking up just the sort of plans you are relying on.'

'Then do it,' he said. 'Prevent any alliance with the Moths, by whatever means.'

'And Stenwold Maker?'

'Can you take him alive?'

'Probably not, as things stand.'

Thalric considered. 'I have my men looking out for him. If only I can get *him* to the interrogation table . . .' He made up his mind. 'We'll kill his people, and we'll break any of their links with the Moths, but if there's the slightest chance of a live Stenwold Maker in my hands at the end of it, that's what I really want.'

Thirty-five

Tharn was a city placed on its side. There were windows above windows, doorways above doorways, and it was not mere blank stone that separated them. It had been carved, every inch of surface. At first the detail was so much as to defeat the eye, but as the moth swooped closer it proliferated and proliferated further. There were twisting pillars and fretwork, friezes and statues, a whole history of pictures and close-chiselled commentary. Lines of robed figures performed obscure devotions. Battles were caught in mid-blow, the stylized figures of Mantis, Moth and Spider, and other races she could not name, locked in conflict. There were figures of beasts and abstract arabesques and things she knew were simply beyond her knowledge to identify. The Moths had made the face of the mountain their book and their history, and it was grand and vast, stern and awful, and it was so sad that she felt tears catch at her throat. A thousand years of carving were on this lonely mountainside: the work of a people who had once stretched out their hand to control half the known world, and were now dismissed as mere mountain mystics by those who had usurped their place.

'How you must hate us,' she whispered timidly in Achaeos's ear. He looked round at her, surprised.

'I did not think . . . you see this now as we see it. Lost glories and better days.'

The moth had picked out a mottled wall as its destination and was flying in narrowing, slowing circles as it readied itself to alight. She saw that the mottling was, in fact, the flat-folded wings of other moths and that the creature was intending to roost vertically. There was a ledge at the foot of the wall, and the insect found purchase close enough that Che was able to half-clamber, half-fall onto the solid stone. Achaeos helped her up as the insect clambered towards a higher resting place above them.

'Will I even be able to get myself from room to room in your city?' she asked him.

'You are not the only earthbound guest who has come here. For visitors, there are places set aside close to the edge,' he explained.

'Close to the edge?'

'Why of course,' he told her, smiling. 'Tharn is a city, not just this façade. In building it we have delved all the way into the mountain.'

'But . . . the sun . . . ? How do you . . . ?'

'The dark is no barrier for us. Nor is it for you,' he reminded her.

Beneath the mountain, in that darkness that was not darkness, the mind played tricks. Although this circular room's walls were picked out in subtle shades of grey, so that the inscriptions and carvings that twined across them were clear to her sight, her mind still knew that they were black as night, and never intended for her eyes. Her ears strained, and by straining, heard.

'Achaeos,' she said uncertainly. 'I can hear music.'

'It's just the sixth hour.' He had been pacing, seeming more nervous now within the halls of his people than he had been in the city of his enemies.

'The sixth . . . hour? I don't understand.' She heard it more clearly now, and it seemed as though, deep within the mountain, a chorus of high, sweet voices was singing words she could not quite disentangle.

He halted, turning towards her, a smile starting that had

been lacking since they left sight of the open air. 'But of course you cannot know. This is my home, so I think of its habits as my habits. Forgive me. Children of my people are given to choirs whose voices announce the changing of the hours. This is the hymn to the sixth hour of night. I remember singing it myself, when I was only seven or eight years. I still recall the words.'

'It's . . . beautiful.' And it was: beautiful and solemn, like all this place, and racked with sorrow. 'But don't you have clocks?' She suspected even as she said it that they did not. No mechanisms, no devices, no artifice here. They were an alien people to her.

But Achaeos replied, 'Of course we have clocks. Water clocks fed from the mountain rains which keep the best time we need, but we record the hours for many reasons, ritual and practical, and by these voices everyone may know how the night passes.'

'I would assume most people would be asleep,' said Che, and corrected herself even before he opened his mouth. 'But of course not. Night is when your people are most busy.' And he nodded.

'That is why the Skryres will shortly hear us,' he agreed. 'I'd hoped to have more time to prepare our case, but they have already known that I was coming, and why, and with whom, so we must brave it out.'

'These . . . Skryres.' She stumbled over the unfamiliar word. 'They lead you? They are your statesmen?'

'More than that. I am a seer, and thus I have started on the road of knowledge. They are not near its end, for no one is, but they are so far along it that I cannot even imagine what they know: of men's minds, of the universal truths, of the Art and the forces of the world. We are not ruled by the strongest or the richest, or those who can talk most smoothly. We are ruled instead by the wisest and the most terrible. Che, you must be careful not to offend them.'

But it is you who are afraid, she realized. She wanted to ask him what these Skryres might do if he failed to move them but, even as she stood up to go to him, a door opened seamlessly in one wall, carvings sliding into carvings, an age of history being devoured. A robed Moth-kinden stood there, older than Achaeos, though she could not judge by how much. His pale eyes narrowed when they saw her.

'It is true then,' the newcomer said in a hard, quiet voice. 'You have been corrupted.'

'That is not for you to judge,' Achaeos told him sharply. 'I will put my case before the Skryres.'

'How fortunate,' said the stranger, 'since that is what they wish also. You are to come with me.' His nose wrinkled at the thought. 'Both of you.'

The capacity of Che's vision could just encompass the room they were taken to, and then led to the centre of. In the heart of the mountain was an amphitheatre, stepping up and up in tiers, the steps themselves worn smooth and rounded by the councils of antiquity until at the very last it rose to terminate in high walls, disappearing out of sight into the lurking darkness. There were lamps up there, which surprised her at first: dim, pale lamps burning coldly blue and shedding only the faintest of pale radiance.

The seats were burdened with the Moth-kinden, for in the room sat several hundred of them at least, a crowd in Beetle terms but a multitude amongst this more reclusive people. They could not, she decided, all be the Skryres, yet they all looked alike to her, grey-skinned and white-eyed, all robed as Achaeos was, their heads close together as they whispered. She did not need to speculate on what had caught their imagination. Slim-fingered hands picked her out as she entered, pointing as they followed her progress across the floor. She saw blank eyes flash angrily, and sudden fierce gestures. The assembly of

Moths stared down on her with loathing as cold as the lamps above them.

The fear that had already been quickening in Achaeos took hold of her now. She was in a strange place and she had somehow assumed that all these people would be like Achaeos or Doctor Nicrephos, the only Moths she had ever known. She knew that they disliked her race, so she had been ready for shouting, perhaps, or rough shoving, the way her own people would show hostility. Not this, though. Not this cool distaste lancing through her, as though she were nothing more than the insect itself, a grubby beetle crawling beneath their glare. She wanted to stretch out her hand for Achaeos, as the only comfort she could hope for, but he was beyond her reach, fighting his own monsters.

We were their slaves once, she thought helplessly. *Before the revolution we sweated for them, built for them, smithed for them.* They had clearly not forgotten. Here, beneath this massed gaze of contempt, she was nothing but a slave again, daughter of a lesser people, fit only for brute work or for their amusement.

It was the force of their attention and their Art, like a physical thing, compressing and limiting her to make her the thing they believed she should be. She looked back and forth across that unforgiving crowd for any relief.

They could have me killed right here and never care.

Then her gaze met a face whose eyes had pupils. There were soldiers there as well, a mere quartet of them to guard this angry host from the intolerable fact of her. They were neither help nor comfort though, for their arrogant looks held her in even less esteem. They were Mantis-kinden, dressed in pale armour of leather and metal. Their forearms were jagged with spines, and each bore the same gauntleted claw that Tisamon wore. If the order came then these would be the executioners. It was for these, then, that the lamps were lit. Mantis eyes were good but they could not manage the deepest of darknesses.

As mine can. Irrationally, this thought gave her some small hope.

From a dark doorway across from her more Moths began to emerge. She could tell, ignorant as she was, that these must be the Skryres and therefore all the others mere spectators. They wore robes of a differing cut to their kin, no finer cloth but the hoods peaked high, and the drape of their skirts folded and flowed like water. On their brows they wore pale metal, coronets or diadems for some, ornately inscribed skullcaps for others. Although she found it difficult to judge Moth-kinden ages, she could see that most of these men and women were very old. Some even had wrinkles, or grey in their dark hair, which would have spoken of five decades in a Beetle but here could mean, she guessed, a century or more.

They did not sit down, however old they were, and though some held to carved staffs, they all stood straight as lances. Their stares did not reveal the same hostility as the others, but something beyond that, and Che felt she was being evaluated in ways she could not guess at.

A man whose skullcap dipped in a sharp widow's peak above his nose rapped his staff once on the floor, and by the time it echoed each and every Moth there had fallen still and quiet. All their eyes were fixed on Che still, with no more love than before.

'Come forth, advocate, and speak,' the Skryre demanded, and in her innocence Che thought he meant Achaeos. She looked to him, waiting for him to explain it all, to transform their hate into something warmer, but his own attention drew her to a newcomer coming in by the same way that they had entered. It was a Moth woman, not much beyond Achaeos's age perhaps, and she carried a ceremonial staff, gold-capped, on which winged insects of all kinds chased one another, layering over each other in an eye-twisting tide.

'Make your accusations,' the Skryre said, and Che now realized that this was the advocate, and the situation was worse than she had thought.

'Tharn accuses the man named Achaeos, who stands now before you,' the advocate announced. Her voice was low, but it carried all the way to the upper walls, lifted by the elegant architecture of the place. 'Achaeos, neophyte and raider, fell wounded in battle with the Hated Enemy. He was seen to flee, as should be done, but the next dusk did not find him back in his proper place. Instead, our eyes and ears within the Forging City heard that he had chosen his own path and committed himself to the cause of another. He sought then to leave for eastern lands, for he claimed some greater enemy awaited him there. See how now he skulks back having leagued himself with the Hated Enemy. He has even brought one of them to our very halls. He has clearly lost his way in the temptations of the outer world and been corrupted. He is lost to us and thus Tharn can have no home for him. I call for his exile, his exile or his death, whichever his courage prefers.'

The thought made Che cold that, while Achaeos was worth accusing, worth the bother of a trial, she herself was considered nothing. She would live or die by no merit whatsoever of her own. She was now at the mercy of Achaeos's words.

'You have been accused,' said the Skryre who had spoken before. 'Achaeos, once a son of Tharn, what can you say to this?'

'I had not expected such accusations,' Achaeos said hotly, but Che heard his voice tremble. 'What I have done has been for Tharn. Would I have come back here, if I was guilty of all this?'

'Such things are said by all who come here,' chimed the advocate's voice behind them. 'How can a single neophyte weigh the good of a city while cut off from our counsel and pursuing his own ends? There are many who leave yet try to return, believing a few meagre words may heal this rift. This is no adequate explanation.'

'You disappoint us,' the Skryre said to Achaeos. 'Speak of your fall from grace, Achaeos.'

'There is a foe now gathered at the gates of the Forging City that will threaten even our halls of Tharn,' Achaeos said, but Che could sense that he was losing both his composure and his train of thought. 'I have seen them myself, seen their armies: a race of the Apt in countless numbers, flying where they please. They are at the gates of the Lowlands now, and it may seem a wonderful thing to you all that they have their swords at the Enemy's throat, but those swords are whet for *all* of us. They know no allies, no equals, only enemies and slaves. I have seen this. I have uncovered this.'

'What is he asking of us?' the advocate said, and Che, sick of her voice, wanted to turn round and hit her. 'Can he be asking for us to aid the Hated Enemy now that they are at odds with some cousin-race of theirs? He has been swayed by them. He has been lost to them. He even brings them here as his allies. Look at this coarse creature he chooses as his companion! He cares nothing for Tharn now. His loyalties lie elsewhere.'

Che turned on her then, but managed to keep her temper in check. All about them, across the tiers of seats, Moths had stood up suddenly. She realized this was their way of shouting, of heckling. They would not speak out of turn in front of their leaders, and so they merely stood to show their opposition to Achaeos, their support for the advocate's words.

'I defy that!' Achaeos cried. 'I am no traitor to my people!'

'He would not be the first, either. The Hated Enemy have their tricks and ways to seduce even our best. They offer their promises of opportunity, their gold, their devices that cannot be comprehended. Who knows what has called him from the true path, but it is certain that he is lost to us.'

'We are under deadly threat!' Achaeos said desperately. 'And you cannot ignore that. Whatever the Enemy might do, whatever *I* might do, there is an Empire out there that cares nothing for a thousand years of history, that seeks only to write its own name in our dust! We have resisted the Forging City for a century, but if we stood alone against this Empire we would not have one more month to live in freedom!'

'Enough, Achaeos,' interrupted another Skryre, a woman who seemed perhaps the oldest of them all. Achaeos bared his teeth, but could not manage to speak as she walked carefully forward. The single sound in all that echoing chamber was the rap of her wooden staff on the stone floor.

'We do not credit your words,' she said simply, and a shudder went through Achaeos that chilled Che to witness it. 'The world cannot change so swiftly, and these newcomers, these men of black and gold, are the enemies of our enemies and have so far shown us no harm. You are condemned, either exile or death, unless you would submit yourself to us.'

Achaeos seemed frozen, and Che could not understand what the woman meant. *Submit,* she urged him mentally. *Exile or death, what could be worse?*

The woman reached out a hand, claw-thin with age, and Achaeos shrank away from it. He seemed like a cornered beast without means of escape, broken.

'Achaeos,' she continued, and there was something kindly in her voice, some kind of sympathy. 'We are not unjust, as you well know. We give you this chance to show us, with no masks or lies, the truth of your words. Or else we must wonder what you would hide from us, and the advocate's judgment shall stand.'

This time, Che could not stay silent. 'Let her!' she hissed, and her voice rippled disapproval across the audience of Moths. 'Let her do it, whatever it is!'

He cast her a look that was filled wholly with guilt. Not fear, but guilt.

She thought she understood, then, what it was that he could not show them. 'Then let me,' she said, and his look turned to horror, and almost every one of the Moths around them was again on his feet, so that a great wave of disapproval fell crashing over her.

But she endured, as her race always had. 'Whatever you want. I'll do it. I can show you exactly what the Wasp-kinden are like, better than Achaeos here, better than anyone.'

'Heed not her words. She has no leave to speak here,' said the advocate from behind.

And Che decided that she would actually strike the woman, had even taken two paces forward, when the Skryre, the old woman, spoke. 'What is this prodigy?'

Around them, men and women were resuming their seats, aware that there was something here they had, in their animosity, passed over. Even the advocate looked uncertain.

'Come here, Beetlechild,' said the Skryre, and Che turned and approached her slowly. Her blank eyes were nested in wrinkles but their gaze was steady as stone. 'You would submit, would you? Submit to what?'

'Whatever you were going to do to him,' Che said. 'Your Art or your . . . whatever it is you do.'

'No Art, Beetlechild. Art alone cannot lay a mind bare. Do you understand me?'

'I think I do.' She stood before the woman, bracing herself, and only then did she realize that the old woman was no taller than she. A moment before she had seemed towering.

'You cannot do this,' one of the other Skryres said softly. 'She is the Enemy.'

'It is an abuse of our power,' added another. 'We will suffer for it.'

'And yet . . .' A third, the skullcapped man who had spoken first, came forward. Abruptly his hand was on Che's chin, dragging her head around to look at him. 'What can she believe? What can she understand? There is something in her beyond her kind's blindness. I feel no fear in her, or very little.'

That 'very little' felt like a great deal of fear to Che, but she stood, steadfast, and waited, and when they simply exchanged looks, she said, 'Do it. Please, just do whatever you want, whatever you need.'

'What are you, Beetlechild? What path do you walk?' asked the old woman.

'I am a scholar of the Great College,' Che said with pride.

'It has been known.' The old woman nodded sagely. 'Not within living memory, but it has been known for such a one to seek knowledge amongst us. To have an open mind. I will examine her. I will pay the cost for it, if cost there be. I do this of my own will.'

There were dissenting looks from some of the other Skryres, but they held their peace.

'Think of nothing,' said the old woman, and placed her cool, thin hand on Che's forehead.

Think of nothing? came the instant riposte from Che's thoughts. *Nobody can think of nothing. It cannot be done . . .* And while she was distracting herself with such tautology the Moth woman entered her mind.

Che was not sure what she was expecting. Perhaps a cold force reaching into her brain, talons ripping there, digging for what they sought. She felt nothing, except . . .

except after a while it was as though there was a babble of voices at the very edge of her hearing, and all of these voices were her own . . .

And she snapped back to the moment, for the Skryre had drawn her hand away and Che could not even tell how much time had passed. She swayed, abruptly dizzy, those blandly hostile faces swimming all around her. The hard floor of the chamber struck her knees a moment later. Then she was lying on her side, feeling the entire mountain of Tharn revolve gently with herself as the hub. She struggled to sit up, at least, casting about for sight of the Skryres.

The old woman stared bleakly at her, and for a moment Che thought she had failed whatever test had been set her.

'You have been into the woods of the Darakyon,' the Skryre announced. 'And you have seen there what your people have not ever seen before. Achaeos has much to answer for in this.'

Che's heart sank, and she looked helplessly across at him. His face was set expectantly.

'You have seen the Empire of the Wasp-kinden, and you have seen that they devour everything that falls their way. They have no friends. They leave no place untouched. They believe only in conquest. That is what you believe, but what is a Beetlechild's belief, to us?'

There was more to come. Che could tell from the tone of her voice.

'But you have seen, and you believe.'

For a moment Che thought she meant the Wasps, but it was more than that. She felt a current of shock course through the watching audience. She could not understand what was meant, until . . .

They mean their magic. Surely it cannot be that important that Achaeos has shown it to me. She assumed then that it had doomed them both.

Instead it had saved them.

'Achaeos, you have not been true to your kinden, and we do not condone what you have done. However, you have not earned exile, not yet,' said the Skryre. 'Against our judgment and against our interests, you have found something worth studying. The accusations are stayed, for now.'

He sagged visibly in relief, and Che would, anywhere else, have gone to comfort him. She was still pinned by the gaze of the Skryre, though.

'What of the Wasps?' she asked.

'You come late into this battle,' the old woman told her. 'They have already sent their emissaries to us. They have explained their plans, for the Hated Enemy. We have treated with them. They are a vile people, but they may have their uses.'

'But—' Che began helplessly.

'But now you have spoken to us, and we must return to our counsels,' said the Skryre. 'We shall deliberate and chart our course, and consult the omens. And you shall meanwhile wait for our word.'

And the Skryres turned as one, and disappeared into the darkness whence they had come, and all about them, one by one, the Moths were lifting off, their wings flickering darkly, casting wild shadows from the lamps as they ascended, so that only the Mantis-kinden guards were left. Only then did Achaeos take hold of her sleeve and draw her away.

They had found Che a place to stay, and she suspected it was that part of Tharn where they usually housed foreigners. One wall was a lattice of carved stonework in the form of interlacing trees that framed an open doorway. The balcony beyond was edged only by a low ledge and she did not feel safe at all on it.

She had been grateful for the sunlight even though she had slept fitfully and badly in it. The back-to-front lives of the Moths were beyond her ability to get used to. Now the sun was casting the mountains' shadows across all the land that she could see, as though dusk was pouring out from the Moths' high kingdom and spreading over the world. The air, which had been chill before, was now becoming bitter, but there were Moths passing by, children even, going sandalled and in thin garments, heedless of a cold that they must have been used to since birth.

She sat close to the fire, on a rug woven of a soft fabric that Achaeos had explained was moth fur. She tried to imagine these serious people shaving the giant moths with great ceremony. At least it brought a smile to her face.

There had been no word yet from the Skryres, none at all, and she had seen little enough of Achaeos. When she had come to this place he had thanked her haltingly, awkwardly. She had not realized just how shaken he had been, having come back as the hero only to be treated as a criminal and a traitor.

He had left her there to sleep, but now she had been awake some hours and there was still no sign of him. Instead there were Moth servants, and occasionally she saw a Mantis, or one of the Spider-kinden. In place of the hostility that had blasted her earlier there was now a strange diffidence. They did not know what to do with her, but she had passed some crucial test. She was no longer the Hated Enemy. Neither she nor they, it seemed, were quite sure what she was.

Even as she thought this there was a fluttering at the balcony. Achaeos was there with the wind tugging at his hood and robe. She ran to him, changed her mind halfway, and ended up meeting him just inside the doorway.

'Where have you been? Have you heard anything new?'

'The Skryres deliberate still,' he told her. 'Or if they've finished I've had no word. I have been . . . talking with a great many people, though. A few sought me out, with their own concerns about the Wasps, willing to nock an arrow if need be. There are others, more I regret, who would rather the Skryres had come to a different decision concerning me. I have been going about my kin trying to calm waters . . .' he smiled weakly, 'and stitch wounds.'

'Enemies? Who was that woman?' she asked him. 'What did you do to her, to make her hate you that much?'

He did not know who she meant, but when she added, 'The advocate, whoever she was,' he was quick to correct her.

'It was nothing personal. I know her distantly, but we have hardly crossed paths. It is simply a role that someone must perform. I have done it myself. The advocate must accuse, must attack as fiercely as possible. The accused is supposed to resist these accusations with the truth. I did poorly because I was not prepared.'

'But they wanted to do to you whatever they did to me. Did they read my mind, really?' She was clinging to her rational heritage as best she could, but amongst this alien people, she could easily believe that magic lurked in every corner.

'They did. It is the last defence of any, according to our law. The Skryres see all truth.' He broke from her gaze then. 'My motives are not so pure as I had told them. If they had seen . . . they would have cast me out. They may yet do so. My own people. I knew I was going beyond what they expected of me but . . .' He went over before the fire, kneeling on the rug. 'They were right, of course. I had been around foreigners too long. It alters the way the world appears.'

'I'm sorry if I've—'

'You? You saved my life. More, you've done more to swing the balance here than I ever could. And perhaps a new way of looking at the world is no bad thing.' With an awkward gesture he suggested she join him by the fire. It was strange, she thought, seeing him do anything awkwardly. All these old races, the faded inks of history, had such a grace about them. Ants were the lords of war in the Lowlands, but no Ant could fight like a Mantis. Beetles dealt and traded and brokered in every city, but they were grubby peddlers beside the elegance of the Spider-kinden, steeped in centuries of political devices. And whilst her own kinden loved lore and learning, and had founded the greatest institution devoted to knowledge in the whole world, still they did not possess the Moths' reserved air of deeper understanding that pervaded this whole city.

And here now was Achaeos, who was all things: a raider, a scholar, a sorcerer – if he could be believed – and a rescuer. Since that first moment of seeing him in the stables, with his desperate, wounded defiance, she had romanticized him. Then he had travelled across all those dangerous miles for her, and the glowing image she had built of him, like any dreaming schoolgirl might, had been borne out. And here he was, as confused as she, coming to terms, just as she was, with a world larger than he had thought existed.

'We trade our debts, we two,' he said softly. 'You aid me, I aid you. Now I have, like a fool, brought you to a place where both our lives hang by a spider's thread and, here in my own homeland, you saved me.'

'We don't need to think of debts,' she told him. 'We . . . know each other too well.' Even as she said it, she was not sure whether that was true.

'I have a service I can perform for you. It may come to nothing, but you have said you have had little progress with the Ancestor Art.'

'It's no secret,' she agreed. 'I suppose there are always some like me.'

'Of course, but amongst your people, where you have your thousands and more, it passes notice. Here each man and woman counts, for we are fewer than you think. We have ways of aiding meditation, of raising the mind to the correct state.'

'You're serious?' She was wide-eyed now. 'If you think there's even the smallest chance that it could work I'll do it, whatever it is. Please, Achaeos, you can't imagine how long . . .'

He nodded. 'You should sit and face the fire. Close your eyes, or stare into it, just as you prefer.'

She did so. When she closed her eyes the dancing of the fire came through her eyelids, more as the warmth that passed over her face than light itself. 'What do I do next?'

'Nothing. Relax and let your mind go . . . where it will . . .' His voice seemed uncertain, but she kept her eyes shut.

His hands dropped onto her shoulders, making her start, and she realized he must be kneeling behind her. She steadied her breathing, tried all the meditative tricks her tutors had once given her to take her mind off the here and now.

She felt his fingers trace a path over her shoulders, and then dig in, his thumbs firm against her shoulder blades, and he began to gently knead the flesh there through her tunic. A shiver went through her, and her concentration went to pieces, but his hands seemed to hold her pinioned, as though she was manacled like Salma had been by the Wasps. She wanted to say something, tell him that he was not helping in any way, but his hands seemed to be smoothing calmness into her very muscles, prying and easing about her neck and working down her spine. They moved with infinite patience and delicacy, like an artificer deconstructing a machine piece by piece – save that now she was the machine.

The Mynan homespun cloth was scratchy under his touch, though. Its coarseness scraped against her back. His fingers eased past the collar, between the cloth and her skin, searching across her exposed shoulders. She saw, with a catch of breath, how this would normally be done and, before her nerve could fail her, she took hold of her tunic's hem. Her arms felt oddly leaden but she was able to drag it halfway up, muffling herself within it. His hands paused for a moment, fingertips trailing. She was shocked by her own daring but equally she knew that this was how it was meant to be.

He removed the garment from over her head, slid it up her arms and cast it away into the unseen room behind her. She felt an instant chill across her belly and breasts, and then the fire's heat straight after. Her back felt numb but comfortably warm.

His hands settled again on her bare shoulders, and she could not suppress a sharp intake of breath. The hands began to work again, from the start, slowly and carefully smoothing and clenching their way across her skin, levelling out the knots and aches that had been with her since Myna, pulling and working over her shoulder blades and along the curve of her back with infinite care. How could she meditate when her whole mind was taken up with those hands? Delicate hands, but with an archer's strength in them. They were slowly kneading their way into her very mind. She could not possibly concentrate, with her body so loose and distant, and with him so close.

'Lie down,' he said in her ear, and she found herself lying full length on the rug, its soft weave pressing against her cheek. He was straddling her hips, his hands still engaged in their dulling progress, now rubbing and squeezing at the bulge of her waist. She had forgotten to concentrate, but instead she lay there with her eyes closed, being eased away from herself, drifting out towards the very far shore of consciousness.

And it seemed gradually as though there was a third presence in the nebulous darkness of the room, somehow beyond the walls, or on the far side of the fire. Something vast and undefined, beyond anything her mind could grasp, and yet it knew her, and loved her as it loved all its children.

And she felt his hands on her shoulders once more, trembling, and then his breath on her neck, and his lips brushed her ear, and kissed her cheek. From the depths of her drifting daze she heard him say, 'I am lost to you. I am drowning in you. Help me.'

With sluggish motion, revelling in every sensation of it, her skin against his, her skin against the softness of the rug, she turned over to face him, and heard his breath catch in quiet wonder. At last she opened her eyes to meet his, and even in their blank whiteness she read a longing, a yearning that chimed in perfect accord with her own.

She tugged at his own tunic, drawing it from him by measured degrees, seeing again his lean frame, the fateful scar on his side, mostly healed by now. She drew a lazy finger across it and saw him shiver. He was the mystic, but in that moment the tide that carried her was the heartbeat of the world, and she drew him along helpless with her.

'Achaeos,' she breathed. She was still adrift on the dizzying sea of his touch, of his spell, whatever it had been. She was so full of love for him that tears ran down her cheeks until he kissed them away, and she drew him down to her breasts and lost herself to the universe, and to him.

And towards dawn she woke, and found him still sleeping beside her, one arm softly holding her to him as though he feared she would be gone.

Gently, she eased herself from beneath it and got herself dressed. The fire was now embers but she felt none of the night's chill.

She went out onto the balcony, spread her wings and flew.

Thirty-six

There was little enough goodwill left amongst the thirteen magnates who governed Helleron. If Stenwold, coming with his apocalyptic warnings, had been a stranger to them, he would have been thrown out onto the street, or worse. As it was, one of the two councillors whose marker he supposedly held had made it clear that he neither remembered nor cared to meet anyone by the name of Stenwold Maker.

There remained one honest man in the city, although, after all the time and effort it took to wheedle his way through the man's lackeys and subordinates, Stenwold was ready to wager that it was just the one, and his name was Greenwise Artector. If his family, as the surname suggested, had once earned their bread by designing buildings, now their wealth came from owning them: renting them by the tenday to the swarming hordes that came looking for new hope on Helleron's teeming streets. Whole warrens of the poor quarters were now in Artector hands. It suggested an uncertain moral basis on which to place trust, but Stenwold was without options, and at least the man agreed to see him.

They met in a chocolate house three avenues away from the Councillar Chambers. It was the latest vice amongst the very rich, Stenwold understood: drinking chocolate, brought from the Spiderlands at vast expense, was apparently the mark of a gentleman. Stenwold prudently left it to Greenwise's tab.

Greenwise Artector was a man only a few years Stenwold's senior. His slighter waist was a corset, his fuller head a wig. When they had first met, the younger Greenwise had dyed his hair grey and drawn on wrinkles for the then current fashion of sagacity and wisdom. Now truly a man of that age, he shammed youth now that the tastes of the cultivated had changed. He wore even more finery than Stenwold remembered: his coat was elaborate red brocade slashed with cloth of gold, and the sword he sported had a hilt of rare metals and precious stones, and had surely never so much as left its scabbard. After all, he had other people to draw weapons for him. Three of them hovered at a discreet distance, near the chocolate-house door, Beetle-kinden brawlers with mace and crossbow and mail shirts visible beneath their long coats.

The general expression on Greenwise's face was the only thing about him that had not changed; it was what had made Stenwold deal with him initially and what brought Stenwold to him now. It was built of world-weary cynicism and a wry humour, and that reflected an honesty of a sort.

'You're a troublemaker, Sten,' grumbled the magnate. 'Every time you're in town we find bodies lying in the alleys. One might almost think you make a living as an assassin, or at our age perhaps just broker for them. True?'

'Hardly.'

'A shame. It would make you a useful fellow to know. These days a man could be glad of a trusty hired killer.'

The face of Tisamon occurred in Stenwold's mind but he quickly repressed it. 'I'm just a concerned citizen, Green.'

'Of Collegium, though,' Greenwise noted.

'And if Helleron suffers, where is Collegium then? And the reverse is equally true. We devise what you profit by, remember. No new device nor advance in metallurgy, no talented technologist or mining engineer is seen in Collegium that does not come to Helleron in time. And I have seen the accounts of the Great College, and I know that the magnates of Helleron ensure that we are well provided for. Don't think I've not seen your name included there.'

'Not so loud. If I get a reputation for charity I'm ruined.' Greenwise shrugged. 'You called and I came, Sten. Since you've been of service to me in the past. What can I do for you that won't bite too deeply into my own interests?'

As succinctly as he could, Stenwold laid out what he knew of the Wasps' future intentions, the gold-and-black vision he had seen, with their soldiers garrisoned in every city, their flag flying from every spire.

'And now they're here right on your doorstep,' he concluded. 'And they may be talking peace and profit with you now, but they mean none of it.'

Greenwise nodded. 'I'm glad you came to me with this, as I happen to agree with you, but if you'd brought it before the Council, you'd be lying at the bottom of a mineshaft by now. The Wasps have recently renegotiated the Treaty of Iron. Which is to say that some of their diplomats came before the Council with a new treaty, and we all signed it with big, strained smiles. They have naturally restated their avowed intent never to set foot in the Lowlands with armed force or hostile intent.'

'But how does that work when they're currently marching on Tark?' Stenwold demanded.

'Ah well,' Greenwise said dryly. 'Surely you must know that Tark is not a city of the Lowlands?'

'Since when?'

'Since this new Treaty and the map drawn up on page thirty-two. Turns out those lying Ants have been claiming to be Lowlanders all this time, when in fact they're actually part of the Dryclaw or the Spiderlands or something. Can you believe the cheek of them?' There was not a trace of humour on Greenwise's face. 'It's just as well the Wasps are going to give them a slap, we all say, for such pernicious falsehood.'

'And so the Council just signed Tark away?'

'With the aforementioned smiles. Because everyone was thinking about all those swords and automotives and explosives and flying machines we sold them. What if they find fault with them, and want to bring them all back for refunds – bring them all back point first?'

Stenwold nodded glumly. 'And how long before they do that anyway? Haven't the Magnates at least started to talk about raising a standing army or improving the city defences?'

'It was mentioned,' Greenwise admitted. 'Specifically it was mentioned that if we started rattling our sabres and building siege weapons then the Empire might wonder why we're keeping back some of our stock in trade, rather than selling it to them, and after that there might be trouble. Besides, have you any idea what most of my peers think the Empire's chief export is? Money. And they think that because of the way these Wasp-kinden have been spending it recently. Everyone's had a nasty shock, but you'll find that both shock and common sense are soluble in a sufficient concentration of money.'

'Easy for the Wasps to spend what they have taken by force from others.'

'Well, pirated gold is still good gold in this man's town.' Greenwise sipped his bitter chocolate thoughtfully. 'You want Helleron to turn away their money? Helleron takes *anybody's* money, and the moment we stop is the moment we breed enemies. We have never taken sides and never will. That way we have grown rich stoking the fires of other people's wars, and never, ever having a war of our own.' He shook his head. 'Oh, when we were both young I could jeer at the rich old men who practised such trades. Now I'm one of those rich old bastards, Sten, and it's a bloody business all round. Two years ago I went north, do you know that? To what used to be the Commonweal, apparently, though I never visited there when it was. Your black-and-gold boys are all over it now. I know you're right, Sten, but nobody would believe me, let alone believe you. And if I wouldn't shut up about it, I might find my properties burned down, or my servants attacked, or worse.'

'The Wasps would do that openly?'

Greenwise gave him a pitying smile. 'Why should they need to, when my profiteering peers would gladly do it on their own initiative?'

'I think I understand.'

'I'm sorry, Sten. Until the Wasps actually start looting parts of this city nobody else here will take a blind piece of notice, and even then, they'd have to loot somewhere fashionable for anyone to care. Until then, well, the Wasps are just sitting there spending their money with us, and if they wanted to cause trouble they could have surely done so by now. But I know they're ... waiting, Sten. They'll swarm when it happens, whatever it is, but until then they're our best friends and best customers.'

'So what *are* they waiting for, do you think?'

'Some say they're after the Commonweal again, but as I told you, they're well entrenched north of here already. They don't need to sit on our doorstep for that. Others say they'll go south, give the Spiders some bother, or Tark, or even harass the Scorpions of the Dryclaw. Anywhere so long as it isn't here. You know the mentality.'

'I do.' *I've missed something, though.* Sitting there, where the rich and powerful took their ease, Stenwold felt shackled and helpless. Something was eluding him, and he had a keen sense that time was running out, the hands of the clock sweeping towards the last hour.

He stood. 'Thank you for at least talking to me.'

Greenwise shrugged yet again. It was a frequent gesture that seemed characteristic of him now, and had not been so evident before. 'Good luck, Sten, and one more thing . . .'

'Yes?' Stenwold felt a sudden tension, and his hand strayed near his sword hilt.

'We were followed on our way here. So watch yourself, as you leave.'

With Greenwise's warning in mind, Stenwold left the chocolate house cautiously. At first there was no hint of trouble, for this was a wealthy area, with guardsmen and private militia all over it. Then his eyes met other eyes fixed on him, belonging to a lone Wasp-kinden across the street. There was no pretence at subterfuge: just a man, a little short of Stenwold's years, in a striped tunic and unarmed. As soon as he had Stenwold's attention he came walking over, smiling as though meeting a friend.

Stenwold realized he had seen this man before, but his mind failed to place him – the realization coming only with the introduction.

'Master Stenwold Maker of the Great College?' the Wasp said, stopping just out of sword reach. 'A good day to you. My name is Captain Thalric of the Imperial Army.'

'Yes, you are, aren't you.' For as soon as the name was mentioned, Stenwold recalled seeing this man in the Assembly chambers. He had been standing beside that smooth statesman of theirs as though he was some menial, but Stenwold had seen through it. 'You're the one who turned my niece into a slave.'

Thalric actually smiled at that and Stenwold felt anger rising in him. *Steady yourself. It's supposed to be they who have the tempers.* A fight here would end badly for whoever started it.

'She was technically not a slave but a prisoner of war. A captured spy, if you will. I understand that you yourself put her into that line of business.' The Wasp spoke mildly but it was obvious he was angling for a response.

'What do you want, Captain?' Stenwold asked him. 'Are you come to bribe me, perhaps? Offer me a rank badge to serve your Empire?'

'What would be the point? You wouldn't accept,' Thalric replied, still smiling, but it was a complex expression, that smile. There was both mockery and melancholy contained within it. Stenwold had an odd sense that there were other things the man wanted to say, but could not feed them past the filter of his duty.

'If you've men here, to make an end of me, then you had better summon them, Captain,' Stenwold said, hand now resting on his sword hilt. The crowds buffeted them both constantly. A single passing killer, a blade beneath the ribs? Stenwold tried to hold himself in absolute readiness, as if he were Tisamon or some other professional designed for such business.

Thalric's smile was wintry. 'Your voice has fallen on deaf ears all these years, Master Maker. My people tell me you have buzzed your tale in the Assembly for over a decade, and were simply brushed away for your pains. The discovery of your murdered corpse, on the other hand, might speak most eloquently, and remind them too readily of all your living words of warning besides. No, it is nothing so sinister that brings me here, Master Maker. I merely wanted to see you, speak with you. We have been enemies for a long time, since long before each knew of the other's existence. The game is nearly done now. Only a few days until the world looks very different. I might then not have another chance to see my adversary.'

'I did not think Wasp officers were allowed to be so indulgent,' said Stenwold, innocently enough, but to his surprise a muscle twitched in the man's face, a nerve touched.

'They are not.' Thalric looked away. 'They are not, lest they fall. Will you drink with me, Master Maker?'

'What?'

'One drink. No poison, I promise, although I hear trying to poison Beetles is an uncertain business.'

'You want . . . to drink with me?'

Thalric stared back at him, saying nothing, just waiting, and in the end it was sheer curiosity that made Stenwold accept.

Stenwold chose the drinking den himself. It was only four streets from the chocolate house, but a different character of place altogether, a vice den where rich dilettantes came to spend their money. Whilst a Spider-kinden woman danced and undressed in tired and practised stages, he and Thalric shared a jug of sharp and acrid Forta Water that made their eyes sting.

'I will not speak of the superiority of the Empire,' Thalric said. 'I've beat that drum quite enough.'

'And do you still like the sound of it?'

The Wasp gave a short laugh. 'You'd try to recruit me, would you? Master Maker, nobody ever understands that I have only one love, and that is the Empire.' He said it in such a way that Stenwold saw that 'nobody' included those of Thalric's own party. He remembered the story of infighting at Myna that Kymene had told. 'No, I just wanted to see you, to gain your measure, as no doubt you are similarly gauging me.'

'You strike me as an unusual man, for one of your race.'

'I try to be anything but. Perhaps that is what makes me unusual.' Thalric drained his bowl without flinching, and poured some more. 'Your niece is a remarkable woman.'

'She said you were going to torture her.'

'And?' Thalric raised an eyebrow.

'And I can read between the lines. You could have done so. Perhaps you would have, if she had not been freed.'

'I would have had to, eventually.'

Stenwold frowned. 'You're not a happy man, Captain.'

'Nor are you, Master Maker. I may have only now met you, but on paper I know you very well. College scholar, artificer, traveller – so what brought you to this sordid trade?'

'You mean *your* trade.'

'I do, yes.'

Stenwold had his own bitter smile for that. 'You did – perhaps not personally, but your Empire. I was in Myna at the conquest. I realized the future then.'

'A hazard of ambition is to make enemies,' Thalric acknowledged. 'Would it make things easier for you to know that I was part of that conquest. I was much younger then, of course.'

'We all were, Captain Thalric. But you're not here for Helleron.'

'Am I not? If you don't already understand, you can't think that I will tell you.' And there was a glint in Thalric's eye that chilled Stenwold through and through. 'Would you join me in a toast, now, Master Maker? It is a Lowlander habit, and I adopt it in deference to the . . . current allegiance of our surroundings.'

'Name your toast,' Stenwold said.

Thalric had been about to say something cutting, a needle-comment to bait him with, but at the last moment something twisted in him, that part of him that had clapped Aagen on the shoulder, and had once been Ulther's protégé, and instead he said, 'Everything is going to change, Master Maker. The old will be swept away, the new will march in. The Lowland cities are no different to two score others that now serve the Empire. You have striven mightily against us, against the apathy and cupidity of your own people, and at last it has come to this. We meet now, because even if you stabbed me through the heart right here and now you would still be too late to turn aside the course of history. But I admire you, because at least you have tried. Because you also believe in your people, however misplaced that belief may be. So let us have an old toast, while we still can. To absent friends.'

Stenwold stared at him, thinking of Marius and Atryssa, so long dead now, but with him still, and he could almost see reflected in Thalric's eyes some kindred loss, more recent but no less deep. He raised his bowl and clicked it against the Wasp's own, and they drank.

Once Stenwold had gone, Thalric's aide came to him, his face a mix of concern and disapproval. 'Do you want me to follow him, sir? What was that all about?'

Thalric drained the last harsh dregs from his bowl. 'It was an indulgence,' he said, mostly to himself. 'And we already know where he is going.' He had held Stenwold Maker up enough, he felt. By the time the man arrived, it would all be over.

Stenwold's head was spinning, but not from the strong drink. First his maddening conversation with Greenwise, highlighting that elusive cog missing from the machine he had been building in his mind. *Why were the Wasps here? What were they waiting for?* Then the baffling conversation with Thalric, a man racked by a confession he could tell nobody. The thought of Wasp fighting Wasp in Myna recurred to him and he could make nothing of it.

Greenwise Artector had confirmed only what Stenwold had already known. The Wasps were waiting, were looking elsewhere but Helleron. If so, why come here at all? Two thousand soldiers with vehicles and supplies was an investment the Empire would not make without reason. Was there some incursion they were here to put down?

In a few days . . .

Those were Thalric's words, and not given as any revelation, just something said as a matter of course. Clock hands counting down, and yet for all this the Wasp had dropped no further clue. But there had been an apology, had there not? Unspoken, but there had been a heaviness to Thalric like a doctor coming to relatives with bad news. Something had been eating at the man. He had gone away with his bad news unsaid, and yet . . .

Stenwold was no Helleren, and he had come here expecting the city to be under attack, yet that was not the case. Thalric had been telling him, whether gloatingly or just unconsciously, that their move, when it came, would . . .

There was a queasy feeling growing in Stenwold's stomach. The strong drink boiled there: not with any poison but a horrible suspicion, growing and growing. Here in Helleron there was one matter that the next day or so would bring to fruition. A commercial matter. A profitable matter. Something that would change the face of the Lowlands forever.

As soon as he had the idea, it put its jaws into him and shook him, and desperately he began to run, pushing through the streets of Helleron because he had questions, desperate questions, for Scuto.

He had to know more about the Iron Road.

Thirty-seven

When the Ant-kinden burst in it was a moment before he could speak, leaning against the door jamb of Scuto's extended shack and gasping for breath. At last, and with everyone on their feet and staring at him, he got it out. 'Marre's dead.'

Scuto swore, baring pointed teeth. Totho, who had been carefully watching him at work, asked, 'Who's Marre?'

'She was that Fly-kinden you sent to talk to the Moths, wasn't she?' Tynisa said to Scuto.

'Yes she was.' The Thorn Bug stomped over towards the newcomer, a big-framed Ant in plate-reinforced chain mail. 'How do you know, Balkus? Are you sure of it?'

'I saw the body.' Balkus spoke jerkily, still catching his wind. 'Arrow in her. They found her out on the slopes.'

'The Moths have made their choice, then,' Tynisa said calmly.

'We don't know that,' Scuto insisted, but he was now looking hunted.

'Che's with them!' Totho said. '*I knew it!* I told her not to go, and I told Stenwold not to let her go!'

There was a rising current of concern among the dozen or so of Scuto's people waiting for his instructions, and eventually their chief held his spiked hands in the air. 'Shut up, the lot of you!' His lips twisted over his teeth in frustration. 'Speak to me, Balkus.'

'Don't know more than that. I was out in the Sarnesh

quarter, trawling for rumours like you asked. That was the rumour I got. The guard had her down as just another dead Fly with no connections, but I knew her. A single shot, right up under the ribs. Someone must have got her in flight.'

'Oh bloody loose wheels and knives!' Scuto shouted at the lot of them, or maybe at himself. 'Everyone get your weapons. Everyone who wears it get into armour. Now! Someone help me.'

He looked to Totho, but the halfbreed was obviously not inclined to be anybody's arming squire and so it was Balkus took down a breast- and back-plate that had been cut and twisted, welded and burned until its ruined, punctured contours matched Scuto's own deformities.

Tynisa, whose blade was always on her hip and who had no armour to wear, watched the men and women of Scuto's service get themselves ready for war with the speed of long practice. Two Fly-kinden strung bows whilst another racked up the tension on a crossbow. A Beetle-kinden man and woman were strapping each other into matching suits of part-plate backed with tough canvas. Another brace of Beetles wore artificer's heavy leathers. The one-armed Scorpion had looped something like an apron over his head, and a layer of metal and leather over his chest that left his back bare. There was a Dragonfly-kinden woman, only recently arrived, buckling on bracers and greaves, and then contorting herself to string a bow as tall as she was. Finished with Scuto, Balkus the Ant had slung on a baldric of wooden boxes, and began testing the action on a blocky, bulky thing she recognized as a nail-bow, whilst beside him another Ant from another city was shrugging into chain mail, taking up a shield whose device had been defaced with plain black paint. Tisamon stood ready from the moment Balkus had burst in, but there was a second Mantis with them now, an angular-faced woman who had so far kept her distance from him. Now she had a rapier in her right hand, and in her left another ground down for balance, with forward curving horns for trapping a blade.

'What is going on?' Tynisa demanded of Scuto, who now had his armour on, little more than slung over his shoulders and held in place by his own thorns.

'There's a lifespan to any band like mine in the information game,' he said, checking the action on a repeating crossbow. 'Don't matter how good you are, things come to the crunch point sooner or later. The point where, no matter how careful you are, the enemy knows enough about your gang to make a move. When that happens, it happens all together. I've seen networks wound up in a day, a score of men and women disappearing, dead or captured or turned traitor.'

'But this might just be—'

'It might just be anything, miss,' he said, although his eyes held no hope in them. 'But we got to be ready 'cos if it's coming, it's coming right away.'

But when the door burst open at that very moment she saw that he had not meant 'right away' as in that very moment. He had meant sometime that day, or the coming night, or the next day.

There was a Fly child in the doorway, his face completely wild with fright. 'Scuto! Scuto!' he was bawling. 'Men's coming! Bad men! A whole load of 'em!'

'Bows to the wall!' Scuto snapped out as the child fled, door slamming behind him. 'We'll take their first charge and then we're getting out of here. Rendezvous is the Merro on Shriek Street!'

He slammed the door closed and put his bow to one of the small windows. Other archers and crossbowmen were finding positions about the walls of Scuto's workshop, some at ground level, others powering upwards with brief wing-flares to find vantage points in the sloping roof.

'Tell me you've got a back door,' Tisamon said.

'Sure I do, but anyone putting their head out now is going to catch a whole load of crossbow.'

'Give the word and I'll go out there, open the way for the rest of you,' Tisamon suggested.

Scuto spared him one look and saw he was serious. 'Behind the bench. There's a mechanism. Sperra!'

A Fly-kinden woman looked back from sighting down her crossbow. 'Chief?'

'When I give the word, let this madman out,' Scuto told her.

'They're on us!' shouted one of his men.

'Give them everything!' Scuto bellowed, and the shack resounded to the sound of Balkus's nailbow roaring. Tynisa staggered away from the man, seeing the firing chamber flare and flare as he loosed off his bolts with the sound of thunder. She could hear nothing of the bows and crossbows, nothing of the enemy, whoever they were, outside.

She tried to get to a free window, saw one higher up, and began to climb to it, hands flat against the cobbled-together wood and metal, her Art giving her grip. Even as she did, a hole was punched abruptly through the wall, a jagged knot of daylight appearing in the wood. Another came a moment later, and she caught the flash of a heavy-headed crossbow bolt, four feet long, as it powered across the room and knocked an identical hole in the far wall.

She got to the window, putting as much of her body behind the protection of metal as she could. Outside was a scene of panic and confusion. In such a ramshackle part of the city there was no real open space. Instead the attackers were already on the hut and had made their charge from mere yards away. They had paid heavily for those yards, though. A dozen of the dead carpeted the mud and cobbles, their bodies studded with end-inches of crossbow bolts or the slender wands of arrows, or the exploded-looking holes that Balkus's nailbow bolts made when they tore through flesh. There were more of them still alive out there, but they had taken what cover they could and showed no signs of pressing their attack.

Tynisa looked at the fallen. They were mostly Beetles, Ants, or halfbreeds of the two, wearing an ugly mismatch of metal and leathers. She knew the type. Sinon Halfway had kept plenty of them on his books: the lowest of Helleron's mercenary classes, the strong-armers and thugs of which the city had an infinite supply.

And seeing that composition, and the hurried scowls of the others as they risked glances out from cover, she knew what they were waiting for. By that time, it was already on them.

One of the Fly-kinden, up at the roof, was suddenly jerking backwards, falling from his vantage point in a trail of blood. Tynisa saw the end of a blade drawn back through the arrowslit, and then there were iron hooks tearing at the workshop's roof, ripping out a jagged section all of two feet across.

By now Tynisa was on her way herself, hands and feet gripping the irregular wall, moving up towards the slant of the ceiling.

A bolt of golden fire spat through the hole, scorching at one of Scuto's Beetle henchmen. Then the first Wasp soldier pushed his way in. He was not in uniform, his armour painted over in other colours, but he was a soldier of the Empire nonetheless. Tynisa recognized that well enough.

Even as he cleared the roof he took a nailbow bolt directly in the chest, plummeting, spinning, to the ground a dozen feet below. There were more of them, though, and another hole soon gaped in the ceiling at the building's other side.

'Now, Scuto! Now!' Tynisa was shouting, and Scuto obviously agreed.

'Time to go! You, Mantis, head out the back! Everyone

else, wait till he's in action, then a serious barrage and we go. I'm rearguard with Balkus!'

The Fly, Sperra, flew straight across Tisamon's face and spent a precious second hauling at the mechanism. A moment later half the back wall slid aside and, in the moment before it reclosed, Tisamon was gone through it.

Tynisa had reached the closest hole in the roof by then. Still clinging with her Art by one hand and both knees she dragged her rapier from its scabbard. The dark, heavy blade seemed to shudder in her hand, and when the next Wasp appeared, already putting his hand towards her, she struck.

She had been aiming for the armpit, where his armour ended, but the perspective tricked her. The narrow blade struck the metal plate over his breast and pierced straight through it, punching a diamond-shaped hole with a seamstress's precision and lancing him through the chest. It drew from the wound without resistance, and the Wasp died halfway through the gap.

Below her, the soldiers of Scuto's army gave off their round of shot, and Tynisa knew that Tisamon was out there exercising his skills and teaching the thugs of Helleron why the Mantis-kinden had been feared since before the revolution. She saw Scuto kick open the door and his people flood through it. There were Wasps inside now, entering from the other roof-hole, and three of Scuto's men were down already. Tynisa saw a pair of imperial soldiers dive, blasting with their stings at the fleeing men and women. Then one was abruptly arching away, the Dragonfly woman having put an arrow through his ribs. Tynisa braced herself, and leapt for the other one.

She had hoped to put her sword into him first, but instead the point passed him by, so she struck him bodily, one hand dragging back his hair, knees locked about his waist. He shouted out, and then fell from the air, his wings unable to keep both of them up.

They separated as they hit the floor, and Tynisa took most of the impact. Even as she sat up, holding her head, he was standing over her with sword in hand.

But the rapier was still with her and, stunned as she was, it took his blade aside and ran him through the thigh. She stumbled to her feet as he fell, and finished him with another lunge.

Scuto was shouting at her: 'Get out! Out out out!'

He was at one of his workbenches at the back. Her head still ringing, she could not work out why.

'I'll guard you!' she said.

'You bloody won't!'

A hand grabbed for her arm and she nearly put her sword into Balkus, who backed off just in time.

'We have to go!' he shouted. Through the slot of the door she could see a savage melee as Scuto's band tried to fight its way clear. Her sword twitched, and she felt it wanting to join in. Then she realized what Scuto was doing and she nodded sharply to Balkus and ran outside.

It was a bloody business out there and Tisamon was the vanguard. He had cut a swathe through them as they came. A dozen of Helleron's street vandals and enforcers were already down, and he drove another dozen before him, desperate to stay out of his reach. His claw was never still, and any man who came close enough to try it had his own stroke caught and carried, and the Mantis blade passed his guard before he could dodge it. As she watched, a crossbow bolt flashed towards him and then exploded as he cut it from the air.

There were more than mere street thugs on the attack here. Wasp soldiers were shooting from overhead, or dropping on them from the sky. Tynisa ran one through even as he fell on her but there were now pitched skirmishes all about her. She saw two Fly-kinden rolling on the ground, knives out, and could not tell which side either was on. The Ant-kinden with the blank shield was fighting with brutal economy. His shield had three bolts embedded in it; one that had passed on through his arm. His sword trailed blood as he ripped it across the face of a Beetle bruiser. The Dragonfly had abandoned her bow and wielded a long, straight sword in both hands, spinning it about her head and lopping stray hands off. Tynisa went to aid her, but the blast of a Wasp sting suddenly scorched a circle on the woman's back and she fell to her knees. She rammed her blade into the gut of the man she was fighting, even as he put his shortsword down past her collarbone. Beyond her the Mantis woman danced and stabbed with her rapiers, taking an Ant-kinden through the eye and then turning to cut a swooping Wasp from the air. Her face was all the while without expression.

Tynisa lunged forward, her rapier splitting chain-mail rings to kill a halfbreed man who was about to stab Totho in the back. Then three of them rushed her together, a Wasp and two of the hired help. The rapier danced. It was not actually tugging at her arm and yet, when she moved it, it seemed that it was by some mutual consent that it caught her opponents' blades and cast them in all directions, tangling the Wasp with the man on his left so that she could parry and bind the third man and whip the red-gleaming rapier's point across his throat. Then Scuto's huge Scorpion had his hook in the Wasp's back, dragging the man in to split him with a monstrous axe-blow, and abruptly the final one of the three was fleeing, dropping his sword. Tynisa had to fight the urge to go after him, for there was an exhilaration in her, a fierce, beating joy that sang in her ears, and she knew it was her Mantis blood, and that Tisamon must be feeling just the same.

Balkus's nailbow exploded again. He was standing with his back to the workshop wall, tracking flying Wasp-kinden with his eyes narrowed, choosing his shots with care. A moment later he crouched in order to slot another of his wooden boxes into the top of the bow. Scuto appeared in the doorway beside him, loosing his crossbow over and over until it was empty.

'Go!' he shouted simply.

And they were going. Tisamon had done his work well and most of the hired rabble were dead or fled. Under the barrage of the Wasps, the survivors of Scuto's people made their desperate escape. Some of the imperial soldiers had already darted inside the workshop and were busy ransacking it for Scuto's papers when the device he had set exploded, incinerating everything less durable than metal within the shack's walls.

It was Tynisa who intercepted Stenwold as he returned to the ruined workshop, and brought him instead to the low dive that Scuto had chosen as a fallback retreat. He was brimming with news but she gave him no time to explain it, simply leading him through the crooked streets of Helleron towards the blue lanterns of the Taverna Merro.

Inside, in the back room, were the survivors: Totho and Tisamon, the former with a long, shallow wound now bandaged on his arm; Balkus the nailbowman, and a slightly singed Scuto; Sperra the Fly-kinden, currently playing doctor to the worst wounded; the one-handed Scorpion, known as Rakka and apparently mute, grimly sharpening the blade of his axe. One of the Beetle artificers had survived, and the Mantis-kinden woman; both were badly injured, having been burned by the Wasp-kinden stings. They had been joined by some of Scuto's other agents from elsewhere in the city, who, seeing the damage at his headquarters, had found their way to other safe-houses, and thence to the Merro. Many had not come home at all.

'Hammer and tongs!' said Stenwold. 'What happened?'

'What always happens. They rooted us out.' Scuto hissed in pain as Sperra put a cold sponge to his burns. His armour still hung off him, the breastplate blackened where it had turned away a sting bolt. 'I've had a half-dozen and more of my people dead in every quarter of the city. We're bust, chief. We're cooked. The operation's over.'

There were perhaps a dozen of them, in total, with a similar number unaccounted for, but more than half of Scuto's people were confirmed dead.

Stenwold sat heavily on the floor by a low table. 'You know what this means?'

'They're going to do it, whatever it is,' Scuto agreed.

'And I know what. Or at least I can't think of anything else, so—'

'Hold it there, chief,' Scuto told him quickly. 'Totho, you remember what we talked about, about Bolwyn.'

The artificer nodded. 'I do.'

'We're not secure, chief. You know why. They knew where a whole lot of my people would be, all over the city. There's a spy here, and there's no way of knowing just who.'

Stenwold looked at his hands. 'This is all sounding far too familiar.'

'Isn't it just,' said Tisamon. 'Just like Myna, back before the conquest.'

'We can't ever leave it behind us, can we?' Stenwold abruptly slammed a fist into the tabletop. 'So what do you suggest?'

'You've got a plan,' Scuto told him. 'I know you.'

'Calling it a plan is an overstatement,' said Stenwold. 'However, consider merely that I've got one.'

Scuto managed a harsh smile. 'Then you don't tell *anyone*, you don't even tell me, until we're ready. At least then they won't know in advance where or when we're moving.'

'What about the Moths?' Tynisa asked. 'What about Che?'

'Why?' Stenwold looked round at her. 'What about them?'

'I sent my girl Marre to chase 'em up, 'cos your girl and that fellow had been such a long time. Balkus saw Marre dead with a Moth arrow in her.'

Stenwold felt as if a cold stone was sinking in his chest. When his agents were attacked, it was war. But when his flesh and blood were attacked . . .

'Can you spare anyone to go . . . ?'

Scuto looked down. 'This is it, chief. This is all they left us.'

'I'll go.' Totho stood. 'I can't fly or anything, but I can climb if I have to. I'll go wherever you tell me your people go in order to meet the Moths.'

'Totho—' Stenwold began, but the artificer cut him off angrily.

'No, this time you're not stopping me. I'm going – and I'm going to save Che, because she should never have gone in the first place. And Stenwold, even if you say no, I'm still going. You'll have to chain me to keep me from it. *You* know why.'

To Stenwold's mind's eye came, then, a moment's vision. The Prowess Forum, the Majestic Felbling taking its stand across from old Paldron's lot. Now Salma was going off to the war at Tark, and Che was lost, and Totho was heading into still more danger. Tisamon had said it best. Stenwold had become the thing he hated.

'I won't stop you,' he said. 'So go.'

'Tell me one thing,' Che said. 'You said your people had a special way to wake the Art. Does it always work like that?' Her smile got even broader when his cheeks darkened with embarrassment.

'Usually . . . just the massage.' Achaeos shrugged his pack on his shoulder, the bow sticking up above one ear. 'I . . .'

He looked so uncertain just then that she hugged him, and he kissed her forehead in return. They were ready to travel now. They had been told that the Skryres were to give their judgment. That word was all they were waiting for.

It came more swiftly than they had hoped. An old Moth, who must have served the Skryres for decades, poled his way over to them, his staff clacking on the stone floor. His expression suggested that it was a crime to have him thus awake in daylight, and that Achaeos was a fool for adopting the patterns of outsiders.

'The Skryres have made their decision?' Achaeos asked him.

'They have,' the old man said. He took a deep breath. 'And they have decided to make no decision.'

There was a pause before Che said, 'They have decided what?'

The old man barely acknowledged her, spoke instead to Achaeos. 'The emissaries of the Wasp Empire have made many promises, which may yet be fulfilled. You have brought many warnings, which also may yet be fulfilled. The omens have been cast, and the world holds its breath. The Skryres, in their wisdom, will wait, and let the lesser people below us enact their petty plots. They will reach their decision when the omens change, or when fresh knowledge comes to them.'

'Then what are *we* two supposed to do?' Achaeos demanded.

'What you wish,' said the old man, sublimely unconcerned. 'However, if it is fresh information you seek, you could leave Tharn to go and find it, and take' – a dismissive gesture – 'your baggage with you.'

Achaeos smiled thinly. 'Well, I shall find you the fresh knowledge, then. I will find something to prod them into action, shall I? And if not then, one evening, you will look out of the mountain and have the fresh knowledge that a Wasp armada is at the gates of Tharn, and perhaps *then* the Skryres will decide to act.'

The old man curled his lip and left them.

Che clutched at Achaeos's sleeve. 'What are we going to do?'

'Leave here, as he said. If I can find something to convince them, then so. If not, I'll do what I can with my own two hands.' He turned to her. 'We can leave now freely, you realize.'

'I . . . I'm not sure. I only . . . It was only for a little while, last night.'

'All we have to do is step off the mountain,' Achaeos told her, 'and then you open your wings. It's as simple as that.'

She held to his hand as they took the leap, and he was a far better flier than she could ever be. She lumbered in the air, the curse of her race. Rather than glide down, she simply fell rather more slowly, with him keeping pace with her all the way, pulling her up whenever she faltered.

And then they were at the foot of the mountain, and she could only look back up, at the great slopes, and at all the intervening clouds they had passed through. She had not noticed, in that lurching descent, the chill air grow warm with the approaching land or the great spectacle of Helleron spreading itself out below.

Next time I shall fly properly, she told herself, and she hugged Achaeos fiercely, because he had given her a gift beyond counting – and love as well.

They had come down near where their fires had brought the great moth to them, at the base of the foothills of the Tornos range. Che's infant power of flight was too weak to take her any further and it was still a walk of some way to get to Helleron. The going was rugged at first, but Che did not care. The mere thought that soon, if she wished, she would be able to rise above this difficult terrain and coast along on her own wings was enough to sustain her.

Beside her, Achaeos was in a thoughtful mood, but there was also a faint smile on his face.

He is thinking of me.

And how strange, after all this time, to be thinking this. She had been in Tynisa's shadow so long, watching every caller's face turn to eye her beautiful foster-sister, ignoring poor, hardworking Che, who had done everything to follow in her uncle's footsteps. Now, unbidden, this man had looked on her and found her fair.

And with that thought a hand caught her and dragged her from his side.

'Achaeos!' she cried, fumbling for her sword. Whoever it was had his arm around her neck, clutching at her tunic. Achaeos had a hand to his dagger, but it remained undrawn.

'You keep away from her, you bastard!' growled a voice in her ear, and it was a voice she recognized. Her hand fell away from her sword hilt.

'Totho?'

'Are you all right, Che?'

'Of course I'm all right. What are you doing?'

'We're betrayed, Che,' Totho said desperately. He had a sword in his other hand. Twisting her head she saw his eyes were fixed on Achaeos furiously. 'We're betrayed,' he said again. 'Scuto's place is gone. Most of his people are dead. They knew just where they all were, even the messenger Scuto sent out to this bastard and his people. Who knew, Che? Who was able to set us up?'

'Totho, he's been with me . . .' But it was not quite true. There had been time enough when he had been away from her side. *I won't believe it.* Her voice shook when she said, 'Totho, Achaeos is not a traitor. He's been trying to help—'

Achaeos had strung his bow, as calmly as a man might tie a lace. The string was back, the arrow nocked.

'Achaeos, don't! Look, this is a misunderstanding!' Che said desperately. She felt Totho's grip tighten on her. He was mostly behind her. That arrow could cut into herself as easily as him.

It could be meant for me.

'Please!' she cried out to both of them, and then Achaeos ran forward, and Totho brought his sword back, and at the last moment the Moth kicked off and was in the air above them.

She head the swift, tearing sound of the arrow, the thrum of the string in the same instant, felt the shudder of its impact, deep between Totho's shoulder and neck. With a startled sound the artificer fell away from her, his grip dragging a moment before it went slack.

Thirty-eight

'Captain.'

Thalric turned from his reports. This close to the knife-edge his agents had little to tell him anyway. He knew there were Rekef men who spent their entire lives focused on paperwork, but he had always needed to be where it was happening, ready to put his own hands to the plan and force it into place.

He saluted. 'Major Godran.' The salute was a mere formality, for both men knew who was in charge.

'All quiet last night,' Godran told him. 'No move at all.'

He hasn't worked it out, Thalric mused. He had expected rather more from Stenwold Maker. *If he stays blind for long it will be too late for him to stop us anyway. Which will be all for the best, of course.*

'Do you want me to double the guard tonight?'

Thalric considered that. Matters were delicately poised, but he could not risk being heavy-handed. 'No,' he decided. 'If Stenwold's people see where we're looking, then we'll as good as have told them what's going on. Unless we hear that he's taking action we'll remain discreet.'

He regarded Godran. The man was regular army but he had served in the Twelve-Year War alongside the Rekef Outlander. He was reliable.

'Your men are ready to move in force?'

'Every one of them,' Godran confirmed. 'They've been

kicking their heels for a while now, and they're keen to see a fight.'

'I'm not sure "fight" is the best word for it,' said Thalric. 'We've both seen how things lie. It will be butchery.'

Godran shrugged. The thought did not bother him. He was, Thalric considered, a good servant of the Empire.

Does it bother me, myself? His instant reaction, that of course it did not, rang hollow.

Let me be honest. It does not matter whether I like the idea or not. The Empire commands.

Che screamed, pure grief and loss exploding in her, searing out all other feelings she had ever felt. As Achaeos landed she was already charging him with sword drawn. She almost had him, too, but he twisted past her blade at the last moment, grappling with her face-to-face and shouting at her. The blood in her ears was so thunderous she heard not a word he said. She fought and fought, and it took both his hands to keep her blade from him, and then she punched him in the jaw, just as she had with Thalric, sending him reeling.

And she stood over him and her face was murder.

'Che!' he yelled. 'Look!'

Instinct made her follow the pointing finger. The sword fell from her suddenly nerveless grip.

There was a body there. There was a pale arrow slanting up from it. The body was . . .

For a moment it swam before her eyes, but it was not Totho's. The face, the form, the clothes, the sword. It was a slender, wicked-looking blade, not Totho's Collegium piece or even a borrowed Wasp weapon.

It was the body of a Spider-kinden woman, of middle years at least, although it was as hard to tell with that race as it was with the Moths. She stared glassily at the sky and the set expression remaining on her face was, horribly, the resolute one she had seen on Totho's own so often.

'The spy?' She had seen Bolwyn's face blur in that very same way. There could be no doubt. 'Hammer and tongs! You . . . you knew. How did you know, Achaeos?' She thought it must be his magic, until his racked expression betrayed him.

'You . . . did know, didn't you?'

'Oh I knew. It's just . . . I haven't been honest with you – in one way.'

She felt only confusion. 'In what way?'

'After we passed the Darakyon . . . which was when I knew that I . . . I truly loved you.' *When I admitted it to myself*, he added inwardly. 'Then I knew Totho was my rival. He hated me and it was easy to see. So I . . . I wanted to discredit him.'

'Your rival?' For a moment she simply did not understand. 'You mean for *me?* Totho?'

'Yes, he was,' Achaeos confirmed, and memories were tugging at her, giving her the belated suspicion that he was right, and that she had been told in terms clear enough, had she wanted to listen.

'I went through his pack one night. He was off on watch and I am good at not being seen. I found . . . a letter.'

She still could make no sense of this, and so he went over to the Spider's body and searched until he found it. Mutely, he passed it to her, and she folded it open and read.

Dear Cheerwell,

Please forgive me. I had always thought that I was a man of courage but I suppose this shows otherwise. You must remember, when you think of me, that I have fought for you. I came all the way to Myna for you. Even though they all did, do not forget that I was among them. I shed Wasp blood there in the palace, and it was for you.

I wish I had more I could give you. I have tried to give you all I have, but I understand why you do not wish to take it. I have no prospects. My blood will make sure that I will never rise to high rank or be a great man. I have no grace, either. I have always been the worst of us, the most unfinished.

I have loved you since those classes we shared at the Great College, and my cowardice is such that I have never said it. It seems so long now. I have lived with this burden. To be sent away is only a relief.

I still love you and I hope you will think of me fondly. I will continue helping your uncle's cause. By the time you read this I will be by Salma's side, on the way to Tark. I'm sure we will see each other, some time again. Do not be angry with Khenice for letting me leave unheralded. By the time you read this I shall be long departed. It is better that way, though it may be the coward's way. It is the only way I can bear.

Please forgive me for this last cowardice, this letter. I have not the heart to tell it to your face.

Yours

T.

'When I read it at first, I thought he had changed his mind,' Achaeos said carefully. 'I thought he had decided not to go. But later it seemed strange that he would keep this letter. And of course, they had been talking at Myna about the spy, the face-changing spy, and my people, too, know of that old order. And slowly I began to wonder, what if that letter had been left, and then found by another? What if your friend had gone, but his shoes had been filled so quickly that nobody realized. I cannot even remember when the Mynan woman left us, the guide. She made no ceremony of it, but I had thought that was simply their way, sullen people that they are. But if she had found that note, and seen her chance, then we would never have realized that Totho had gone. Instead we would only have thought that our Mynan guide had turned back for home . . .'

'You couldn't have known,' she said. 'Not just from that. You couldn't have been sure.'

'But there were two other things that made me sure. Where was his crossbow weapon? But, of course, if he was who I suspected he now was, then he could no more manage a crossbow than I could. But most of all, I saw the way he was holding you.'

'What do you mean?'

'He . . . She was holding you so I couldn't shoot her, so that if I loosed a shot, I would hit you instead. The man who wrote that letter would never have done that.'

Che just stared at the letter, and tears rose unbidden. Her lip trembled.

'I . . . am sorry,' the Moth said awkwardly, 'I have not served you well.'

She realized that she could hate him for this. She could make the absent Totho a martyr, the man she would have been with, if not for Achaeos. This was hanging as an option in her mind, and its sole purpose was to cover the shameful way that she had treated Totho before he left.

'Please,' she whispered, and held out her arms to him, and Achaeos held her tightly as she wept.

Magic was concentration, and the pain was savage and sharp. She dared not even touch the arrow. Scylis – Scyla as she truly was – had lost all of her masks when it drove into her, and she fell to the ground in nothing but her own body, all her disguises breached. In that moment of shock and agony it took all she possessed just to play dead.

When the Moth came over to her, she thought he would finish her off, but he had been more interested in that cursed *letter* than in making sure. She had lain there, dressed as her own corpse, and let him rifle her possessions and go back, so that the two of them could act out their little drama together. But it had given her time.

She had been hurt before, though never this badly. There were tricks, of the mind and of magic, to stave off the pain, to lock it away. The sands of her time were running out, because the Moth was no fool and sooner or later he would make sure.

It was a wretched effort, and yet it nearly killed her more surely than did the arrow. The force of will required made the arrowhead grate and contort inside her, but she rolled over, as the two of them stood embracing, and she cast off her skin behind her. Had they looked, had either of them even glanced just then, they would have seen two dead Scylas, and the game would have been up.

She shuddered, realizing she had no strength left for magic, but there was still the Art, the innate heritage of her people. She seldom called on it, with all the tools already at her disposal, and yet she had spent her due time in earnest meditation all those years ago, when even she had once been young.

She now called upon that Art that so many of the elder races owned, and felt herself fade and blend, the light sliding off her, the shadows cloaking her, the colours of the earth and the stones embracing her. It was a hunter's Art, for ambush or sudden strike, but here and now its camouflage was her one weak chance at life. When they finally had eyes for anything other than each other, they looked over and saw only one corpse.

It could still have failed. If he had taken the time to cut her throat with his dagger then he would have found the flesh beneath his blade parting like mist. He was true to his kinden, though. He came with his bow and stood over her body, and he sent an arrow through that illusory forehead and into the ground. Just to be sure, as he must be thinking.

After they had gone, she stirred herself from hiding,

feeling the shaft that was buried in her stab and grate. *So much*, she thought, *for turning them against the Moth-kinden*. She had killed the Fly, Marre, just to keep the Moths out of this fight, and so to strip Stenwold down to no more than the tattered remains of Scuto's people. It had been easy, given her skills, to slip to and fro, and never have one of them wonder where solid, stupid Totho really was. It should have been a simple matter for her to kill the old man's niece. Then Totho would have come back weeping to Stenwold with the terrible news, and the Moths would reap the blame.

She did not know, as she pushed herself to her feet, if she would last through this. The best of her training was deployed in keeping the pain at bay, but it was still a long walk to Helleron.

But if she reached Helleron, if her blood lasted that long, then she would find Thalric and she would enjoy what last revenge she could. For Stenwold now had the Wasp's secret. He had admitted as much, and she believed him. She would let Thalric know that his enemies were onto him. She would make sure that Stenwold's little pack of clowns would have a reception waiting for them, when they made their move.

They made their camp without fire, as they had for two nights, the two who were sleeping tucked close together by necessity, and the one who was left on watch shivering the hours out.

When Totho had caught them up, his explanations had been scant, and Salma had not pressed him further. From the Dragonfly's expression he had guessed more than was admitted by Totho, and possibly the whole of the story. Salma had good eyes, Totho knew. He saw many things.

They were closing on Tark now, less than a tenday away. They had been keeping thus far to the well-used road but they had begun to encounter travellers with disturbing stories. There were soldiers ahead, soldiers that the better-travelled identified as imperial Wasps, who were turning the wayfarers back. Others, arriving from Tark, had seen dust on the horizon from a vast horde cutting across the Dryclaw. One Fly trader, tacitly a carrier of illicit goods, had been treading the same paths when he had seen them, and was able to give them a better account. A whole Wasp host was on the move, men marching along with Fly and Wasp airborne scouts, automotives, pack animals and war engines. They had Scorpion guides, an entire clan of them, leading them the best ways through the desert.

Until they had this eyewitness testimony, Stenwold's speculations had not seemed entirely real. Now it was unclear whether they would reach Tark before or after the Wasp army, or maybe at the same time. Certainly the enemy outriders were already on the road ahead of them, isolating the city.

'But Tark is an Ant city-state,' Totho had protested. 'Ants fight. It's what they do best. To try to take their city is madness.'

Salma had just shaken his head. 'The Wasps have run into Ant-kinden before. Near the Commonweal borders there's an Ant city, Maynes, which the Wasps seized and used as their staging post to attack us. The Wasps have ways of defeating even Ant-kinden.'

The next day's close put them within sight of Wasp soldiers. Half a dozen of them had staked out a bridge and were obviously ready to challenge anyone wanting to cross. They took turns to glide up into the air, circling lazily.

Skrill sucked her breath through her teeth. 'You, Beetle-boy,' she said. It was what she had taken to calling Totho. 'You're not the flying kind, I'll wager, but can you swim?'

'A little. Not a whole river's width.'

'Can you swim it if you hold on to something?'

He nodded dumbly.

'These here, they're to stop reinforcements, goods, supplies getting through, not people. His Lordship here's got wings. He can pick a slice of the river and fly, and water's nothing to stop me. This is the most fordable point of the river, though, and I know that 'cos this is where they put the bridge. So if we're crossing, or if *you're* crossing, it's here. Got me?'

Totho and she put together a makeshift raft, big enough to float their packs across, with his legs providing the motive power.

'Now, I'll shadow you across the river,' she said. 'Your Lordship, you can meet us on the far side.'

Salma nodded, and swung into the air with his sword drawn, disappearing overhead.

Totho had no night vision whatsoever. The Wasps had a fire lit in the bowl of a metal shield laid on the bridge, though, and torches burning at either end. The night was chill and the guards had pulled into the bridge's centre and the burning shield to take up the warmth.

He crept to the edge, balancing the raft across his shoulders. He had stripped to his waist, and his boots hung across his neck by their laces. Skrill flitted past him, a shapeless, cloaked ghost, still fully clad, but although he could hear the water ahead of him, he heard no splash.

He lowered himself into the river gently. The raft bobbed but rose again, and he began to push it out, feeling the sluggish current begin to manhandle him towards and under the bridge. He could not see Skrill, and it was too dark to try. Only the fires of the Wasps gave out any light at all.

The river bed fell away from under his feet and he began to kick awkwardly, splashing a little but trying to keep his feet below the surface. The bridge was now passing smoothly overhead and he could hear the murmuring voices of the Wasp guards. He was doing his best to keep a straight course but the insistent current was pulling him out from under the bridge's shadow now. By the time he was halfway across the stream he was in the open. The red light of the fire crackled above him, but little of it got as far as the water.

The opposite shore was getting close. He could not yet see it but the sound of the water rippling alongside it told him enough. He risked a glance over his shoulder.

There was a Wasp at the bridge railing, staring down into the water. To Totho it seemed the man's eyes were full on him, and it could only be a moment before he noticed the bulky shape moving in the water.

Then the soldier clapped a hand to his neck irritably, as if stung by some small insect. He turned to make some comment to his fellows, then abruptly his legs gave way under him and he collapsed.

Totho turned his gaze away and concentrated on gaining the far shore. Skrill loomed before him, removing a long pipe from her lips and stowing it away in her cloak. By some trick of her Art she was actually standing on the water, rolling with the swell like a sailor on the deck of a ship.

As he reached the far shore and she quickly helped him lift the raft and packs clear of the water, Totho looked back. The Wasps had noticed their fallen comrade but their attention, as airborne soldiers themselves, was now fixed on the skies, Three of them were lifting off, swords drawn, hunting in high circles over the bridge.

From then on the road before them was clear all the way to Tark, and Totho could only hope that the others were having as smooth a journey.

When Che had finished telling their story there was a stunned quiet for a moment.

'Totho?' Stenwold said at last, feeling hollow.

'We have to assume he's now with Salma, like his letter

says. So when you hear from Tark, you'll hear from him. We have to assume that.'

'What alternative do we have?' Stenwold agreed.

'The lad'll be fine,' Scuto said. 'Look at you all. Why the long faces?' He leapt to his feet with a whoop. 'Don't you see it?' he shouted. 'We're clear of the spy! Now you can tell us what's going on, and we can sort it out. They've had us in a lock today. Now we'll have them right back, right, chief?'

'But I failed,' Achaeos said. 'The Skryres will only wait.'

Stenwold looked up at him, an odd light in his eyes. 'And I have just what they're waiting for,' he said. Achaeos cocked an eyebrow at him. 'It's time to open everyone's eyes,' said the Beetle. He looked across the ragged band that was all that was left of his operation in Helleron. 'Achaeos,' he began.

'I'm here.'

'When I'm done talking, you'll want to get back to Tharn by the quickest way possible and tell them what I plan. I hope it will be enough to tip the balance.'

He stood before them now just like a lecturer at the Great College. The sight brought a fond but painful echo of familiarity to Che and Tynisa both.

'The Wasps are not here to attack Helleron – not yet,' Stenwold continued. 'They are attacking a much greater target. They are attacking the Lowlands as a whole. We're all guilty of thinking like Lowlanders, not like Imperials. We were seeing the war city by city, because we know the Lowlands is divided. They see the war as a whole, because they fear the Lowlands becoming united. Scuto, tell me now about the Iron Road.'

'What do you want to know, chief?'

'When will the first train run?'

'In a tenday, give or take.'

'But when will it be ready to run? When will the track be laid, the engine ready?'

'The engine's ready now,' Scuto said, mystified. '*Pride*, she's called, and a beautiful piece of engineering. She'll run as soon as the last track's in place.'

'She will indeed,' Stenwold confirmed. 'But not at Helleron's behest. Tell me more about the *Pride*. What's her capacity, if you crammed her with passengers? How does she run?'

'She's got the latest engine from the College technologists, chief. A *lightning engine*, it's called. The absolute knees, I can tell you. Really advanced stuff. As for capacity, they reckon five hundred, with all the luxury you can eat, but . . . you mean people stashed in the cargo trucks as well? And ripping out the seats, all of that?'

Stenwold nodded.

'Then . . . Pack her to the gills, shoulder to shoulder, every carriage, and she'd haul around . . .' Scuto's fingers moved in quick calculation, and then slowed, a nervous look coming into his eyes. 'Around two, maybe two and a half thousand men, maybe even more. She's got a lot of carriages.'

'All the Wasps camped at our doorstep, on a rail automotive that will take them to Collegium faster than anything else. *Collegium*, not Helleron. Two thousand men, say, carried swiftly to the very heart of Collegium, swarming out with sword and sting, attacking the Assembly, attacking the College. The Lowlands needs to join together to stave off the Empire, and that union can only start with Collegium. Only in Collegium are all races and citizenries welcome. Only in Collegium are such ideas as a fair and free unity of the Lowlands mooted and practised. If the Wasps take the *Pride*, they can sack Collegium before the city's allies even know about it. They can take control of the Assembly, instigate martial law. Even if we sent a Fly-kinden messenger at this very moment, he'd not race the train there if it left within two days. Even if we sent a fixed-wing the Assembly would still be debating the story when the Wasps arrived.'

'Bloody spinning wheels,' spat Scuto. 'So what's the plan, chief?'

Stenwold sighed heavily. 'We attack the site. We destroy the *Pride*.'

There was a close, dead silence. They were his agents, but many of them were men and women of Helleron. What he was proposing would mean a death sentence here in this city if their involvement were ever known.

Scuto glanced from face to face, holding their eyes until he had exacted reluctant nods from all of his own people. 'I reckon you've made your case, chief,' he said at last. 'I don't think any of us is happy with the plan, but we all know Collegium. Enough of us studied our scrolls at the College, even. Now it's time to pay for that privilege.'

'And I now see why you want me to go back home,' Achaeos put in.

'Tell the Skryres of Tharn that Stenwold Maker of Collegium wants the Iron Road smashed, the engine destroyed. Tell them I ask their help, their raiders, for that very cause. No tricks, no traps. Whoever you can fetch, come with them to the south of the engine sheds at dusk. Fly now.'

Achaeos rose, gave him a little bow and then squeezed Che's hand. 'I'll bring them or else I'll come on my own,' he announced. His wings unfurled, glittering in the light, and then he was gone, the hatch of the fallback in the ceiling slamming behind him.

Dusk came too soon, with a finality nobody was happy with. They made a ragged band, the wounds of the Wasp attack still unhealed. They had resupplied, taken everything that Scuto had laid down that might be any use to them. Stenwold had donned his hardwearing artificer's leathers, a crossbow across his back and half a dozen hatched iron grenades carried in a bag at his belt. Beside him Scuto was in his warped armour with another sack of the dangerous toys, and a brand new repeater as well. There were spare magazines of bolts dangling from his spikes and from the straps of his armour.

Tisamon wore no more armour than his arming jacket, that had seen so many deaths and yet bore so few scars or scratches. He had found a similar garment for Tynisa, buckling it for her up the side with care, awl-punching new holes in the straps where they were needed so as to fit her slender frame. Stenwold looked at his adopted daughter, at Tisamon's daughter, and knew that she had passed out of his hands. Not into her father's but into her own. She was steering her own course in the world from now on.

And then there was Cheerwell, his niece, his flesh and blood, and in the time that the Wasps had taken her from him, she had grown up too. She stood by Scuto, wearing artificer's armour like her uncle, and with a toolstrip on one hip balancing the sword on the other. She buckled a leather helmet on, protective goggles riding high on her forehead, and he barely recognized her.

Behind them the mobile remnant of Scuto's agents was ready. Stenwold knew Balkus well enough: the Ant was a mercenary rather than a loyal agent but he owed Scuto and he took his debt of honour seriously. Then there was Rakka, whose right hand had been forfeit to imperial justice and who had not forgotten or forgiven. Sperra the Fly carried her crossbow and a kit of bandages and salves, in case the chance came to use them. Beyond her there were a grab-bag of Beetles, Flies, Ant-kinden and one halfbreed, Scuto's last surviving agents from the city, now drawn together here for safe keeping. They bore crossbows, swords, grenades and a piecemeal approach to armour. One of the Beetle-kinden had a blunderbow, its flared mouth already loaded with shrapnel. Another wore most of a suit of sentinel plate, massively bulked with metal, and carried a great poleaxe late of the city guard armouries. These were not soldiers, but they had as much skirmishing experience as any Wasp regular.

'I think we're ready, chief,' Scuto said quietly.

Collegium stands or falls on what we do today.

'Let's move out,' Stenwold said.

They were close enough to the rail works to hear the hammering of the industrious engines that were still producing the track, and the shunting and grinding of the automotives that shipped it down the line, ever narrowing the gap between the works begun in Collegium and those started here. How many yards were yet to cover? Each hour whittled that intervening distance away. The launching of the *Pride*'s pirated maiden voyage could be tomorrow or the day after.

The *Pride* itself was kept apart from such gross scurryings. It was aloof from mere industry. When it moved, it would make its first run from Helleron to Collegium and revolutionize the world. Progress would be advanced, with all the virtues and vices that entailed.

And we are here to stop it. The idea still seemed mad to Stenwold, but he had come to this insanity through ineluctable logic.

The *Pride* sat on its sidelined rails under a great awning that shielded it from what mild ill weather the season might throw at it. A lesser engine might be consigned to a shed but the *Pride* was too great and grand, and its engineers required its flanks bared to bring their machines close enough to service her. She was a new breed, hulking and hammer-headed at the front, but capped with silver worked into beautiful and ornate designs, as though she were some great bludgeoning weapon made for ceremonial purposes. Behind that solid nose was the engine itself, the 'lightning engine'. Stenwold had never seen one, and knew nothing about them. He had an uncomfortable feeling that Scuto was little better informed but it would be the Thorn Bug's work to destroy it, either by explosives or by simply overcharging and detonating the engine itself. It was a truly vast piece of engineering, twenty feet in length, its slab-like sides wormed through with ducts and pipes, coils and twisting funnels. A five-foot rod stood proud of the roof, glittering slightly in the darkness beneath the vast awning. Behind that monumental engine was the engineer's cab itself. Where more primitive devices would have, say, a wood-burning furnace for steam power, Stenwold could not even guess what controls and fail-safes a lightning engine would require.

There was no sign of a watch, no sign of a guard. They had come south of the engine yard to get the best look, but even then it was a difficult prospect. The yard was a pit dug ten feet down and more than ten times that across. There were spoil heaps, tool sheds and lesser engines scattered around it. A dozen sentries could be concealed there.

Stenwold knew that nobody would move and nothing would happen until he gave the word and, once he gave it, the entire business would unfold without any chance for him to stop it or change its direction. It would leave his hands like some apprentice artificer's flying machine, and whether it flew or fell would not be his to determine.

He found that, at this stage, he could not bring himself to give the word.

And then Sperra hissed ''Ware above! I hear fliers!'

Thirty-nine

The whole band of them scattered, crossbows dragged up towards the dark sky, but a moment later it was Che's voice saying, 'Calm! Quiet! It's Achaeos.'

They clustered again, and saw the first shape come down a little way away. There was a waxing moon that gave a wan light and there were lights enough across the engine yard behind them, but even then it took Stenwold a moment to pick Achaeos out of the shadows.

He was about to go to greet the Moth when the other figures came down, and he stood, paralysed for a moment with the fear of betrayal, and then with sudden hope.

There were at least half a dozen other Moths, all with bows in hand, and a brace of Fly-kinden wearing cut-down versions of the Moths' hooded garb. There were two Mantis-kinden as well, male and female in studded armour, as tall and arch as Tisamon ever was. There was a Dragonfly maiden with a longbow, and a Grasshopper-kinden with a pair of long daggers glittering in his hands. All of them were in shades of grey, mottled and patched so that, between the moonlight and the shadows, they might stand in the open before wide eyes and yet be near invisible.

'Hammer and tongs,' Stenwold said, some small piece of the weight on him lifting at the sight. 'Your Skryres saw the light then? Or the darkness, however you want.'

Che pushed past him to fling her arms round Achaeos, and then suddenly looked back at Stenwold guiltily, but at that moment he could not care.

'When I arrived back at Tharn, these men and women were already waiting for me,' Achaeos said, one arm about Che. Even he sounded a little awed by it. 'I now find myself their captain. The Skryres ... deliberate, still ... Tharn has as yet taken no stance on the Empire.'

'Then who *are* these?' Stenwold asked, and then the word welled unbidden in his mind. 'Arcanum ... ?'

Achaeos glanced back at his cohort. 'They have said nothing but that they will fight the Wasps, Master Maker. Some Skryre has clearly made a personal decision on this, and called upon his or her own agents. Yes, they are Arcanum, Master Maker, and they are with you. For this one task only, Stenwold Maker, they are with you.'

'So how're we going to do this?' Scuto asked, still sizing up the newcomers.

'We have scouted this place before,' Achaeos said. 'It has been guarded, always. Now the Helleren guards are gone.'

'Easier for us, surely,' said Balkus from over Scuto's shoulder.

'No, for it means our coming is known,' Achaeos said.

Stenwold had to agree. 'All killed or bought off, or perhaps they were withdrawn on some magnate's orders, some merchant-lord bought by the Empire. So where are the Wasps, Achaeos?'

'There are some inside the machine itself,' the Moth explained. 'And we have also seen four sentries hidden about this place. We think there are more and that this is a trap.'

'And we know it is a trap, and therefore we can do something about it, so the trap snaps both ways,' Stenwold said.

'If you wish to do this thing we will follow,' Achaeos said. 'Everyone here with me is sworn to it.' He grimaced, squeezing Che just the once and then letting her go. 'It will be a fight, Master Maker. We have seen two score

Wasp soldiers lurking close to here, surely waiting for a signal from the sentries. Their main camp is close as well, no doubt by design, so they will be able to reinforce almost immediately. How long will it take to destroy the engine?'

Stenwold glanced at Scuto, who shrugged expressively. 'Ain't easy to tell. Never had a crack at a beast like this before.'

'Then it will be a fight,' the Moth said sombrely. He looked pale and very young, and then Stenwold looked over the other faces there. Apart from himself and Scuto, and Tisamon, and the Grasshopper-kinden brought by Achaeos, they all looked so young to him.

'If anyone, I mean *anyone*, wishes to go now, then go,' he said, and of course none of them moved. They were all scared, except a few like Tisamon who had death running like blood in their veins. It was pride and fear of shame that kept them here, and he wanted to shout at them that dented pride might heal where mortal wounds would not.

But he said nothing, for they were now *his* people. They were here for his plan, to live or to die as chance and their skills dictated.

'How can we best use you?' he asked Achaeos.

'We will be able to strike without their seeing us. We will have the first cut of the knife,' the Moth said. He glanced at the female Mantis, whom Stenwold guessed to be his tactician of sorts. 'What we will do,' he explained, 'is attack the Wasps in the engine – and the sentries, those we have found. You will see it happening, and at that moment you should run for the engine. The alarm will sound, I am sure, but there will be confusion. My people, and those of your people who are not destroying the engine, will have to hold off whatever the Wasps produce, until the task is done. That is our plan.'

Stenwold nodded. 'I have no better one,' he conceded.

★

Achaeos and his war party melted into the darkness that for him at least was no darkness. Stenwold gestured to the others to keep low, and advanced to the lip of the works pit. There was a spoil heap below, so getting down there and over to the *Pride* itself would present no problems. Getting out again with a whole skin would be another challenge altogether.

He had started counting, and realized that he was counting towards no number he could guess, and so he stopped. The night was cool, with the faintest breeze blowing from the east, and silent beyond all measure. He could hardly believe there were two score Wasps lurking within spitting distance.

They must be holding their breath.

'There!' Tynisa hissed. Stenwold had seen nothing, but he was so keyed up he responded on her recognizance.

'Go!' he hissed.

'Sir!' one of his men called, and Thalric snapped out of his reverie. The night was quiet, and no signal had been called.

'What is it?' he demanded.

'I saw something by the engine, sir.'

Thalric mounted the bank and stared. His people were not night creatures, but the gas lamps burning around the *Pride* were bold enough.

'I don't see anything . . .' he said, but then he did, and a sentry got off his whistle at the same moment.

A shadow. It had only been a shadow between the light and him, but then a man had fallen out of the *Pride*'s cab. One of his ambush party. The attack had started.

'Move out, the lot of you!' he shouted. 'Light airborne, secure the engine. Infantry—' Even as he spoke he saw men surging down the side of the pit and across the engine field. 'Take them down.' He pointed. There were a dozen of his men in the air already, wings springing to life to propel them towards the engine with all the speed they could muster. Another dozen were surging past him, more heavily armoured with spear and shield. Thalric took one more brief look at the intruders and thought he spotted Stenwold at the fore. In these small actions a good commander should lead his troops, and Thalric respected him for that.

'You.' He turned on the Fly-kinden messenger at his heels. The youth was staff, not local, wearing imperial livery over a leather breastplate. 'Go to Major Godran,' Thalric told him. 'Tell him to bring up three . . . make it four squads at all speed, and tell him to send in the automotive and the spotter.'

'Yes, sir.' And then the messenger was gone, darting into the night as he headed for the main imperial camp. Thalric, who had been surrounded by two dozen men and more a moment earlier, was now on his own.

Stenwold was no runner, and the fleeter members of his party were outstripping him before he had made half the distance to the *Pride*. He had heard a shrill whistle that spoke of at least one sentry the Moths had not found in time. Ahead of him fleet forms were flitting past the lights that festooned the *Pride*'s awning. He saw brief motes of gaslight on steel, heard grunts of pain, cut-off cries. Tisamon and Tynisa had the vanguard now, bearing down on the engine with murderous speed, but they would be unable to do anything with it once they got there save shed enemy blood.

A Moth raider flashed overhead, a confused image of grey cloth with white eyes and a drawn bowstring. Stenwold, his breath already failing him, saw most of the others had passed him now. He risked slowing down to save his strength, glancing right and left.

To the left the engine works were mostly clear until a pair of coupled carriages made a dark, curving wall on a veering section of track. To the right the darkness was mounded and humped, two spoil heaps forming almost perfect cones of debris. Past them, as he ran, he saw another rail engine, a midge compared to the *Pride*'s great bulk, and he caught movement through its windows: there were men running along the line of the vacant engine's far side.

Ahead there erupted full-scale fighting all of a sudden. He saw the flashes of Wasp stings, the cries of the wounded. He was close enough to see one Moth-kinden flung backwards against the *Pride*'s unforgiving metal hide, the smoke of his burn-wound bright under the gaslight. One of the Tharn Mantis soldiers leapt into the air with her wings unfolding, cutting down the leading Wasp even as he tried to slow his charge.

'To the right!' Stenwold bellowed. 'Che! Scuto! Tis and Nisa! Get on to the engine! The rest with me!'

Having ordained it, simply stopping was a difficult thing to do, skidding in the grit and gravel, while trying to bring his crossbow up. There was a squad of Wasp soldiers running straight for them, well armoured and formed into a wedge, shields high and spears levelled. Even as he got a bolt to the already-drawn string, two missiles had flashed past him to stand quivering in the Wasp shields. The wedge was coming at a brisk run. Stenwold reached into his pouch for a grenade.

He was deafened the next moment, because Balkus had opened up with his nailbow, three quick detonations that echoed across the whole sunken field. The point of the Wasp wedge was abruptly collapsing, two men falling backwards with holes punched through shield and armour. Balkus was kneeling now, fighting to clear a jammed bolt. Another crossbow bolt picked off a soldier near the rear as Sperra leapt into the air to shoot down on them. For a moment the wedge was broken before re-forming. Stenwold saw Wasps passing spears to their left hands so as to free up their stings.

Put in his place, perhaps greater commanders had all the time their genius required to weigh the balance of the moment, but Stenwold was no soldier and so he simply shouted 'Charge them!' Even as he said it, he had the grenade lit with a flick of his steel lighter, and was hurling the hatched metal ball ahead of him.

It struck a shield, rebounded and fell at the nearest soldier's feet. The man had only a moment to see what it was before it ripped apart, sending out shards of metal that scythed him down and cut across his fellows. Stenwold, in the lead, felt one jagged fragment skin his own shoulder.

And then they were in. He had his sword out and in a second he was in their midst as they tried to pull together. He got one man in the armpit where the armour did not reach, who clung to Stenwold desperately as he fell. Beside him the Beetle-kinden in the sentinel armour slammed his poleaxe down, buckling a shield and breaking the arm that carried it. Balkus's nailbow roared twice more at point-blank range and then he slung it over his shoulder and dragged a shortsword from its resting place, fighting always with the neat economy of his race.

Che was still running for the engine, seeing that there was a great deal of fighting there, and too many bodies. She saw, through that darkness, that they were mostly Wasps, but that three Moths lay dead, and any one of them could be Achaeos.

I must not think like that. Even so she could not stop thinking like that, but her legs knew what to do and carried her onwards.

There were Wasps there now, and they were turning to face the newcomers. An energy bolt sizzled past her, over her head. Another lanced towards Tynisa but she sidestepped it nimbly, and then she and her father were in.

They had been seconds ahead, those two, just steps ahead. Che could not believe her eyes, despite all the evidence of Myna. She had never seen Tisamon fight before, and never realized her own foster-sister could come so close to matching him.

They gave the Wasps no chance, no time. They charged from the darkness into the harsh artificial light and they drank blood, or that was how it seemed to Che. Tisamon danced with his claw, as though it and he were two separate things, attacking from separate vantage points, but linked in the mind like Ants of the same city. Tynisa was never still, never where their swords drove at. The rapier in her hand could not be stopped or parried or ducked. Each thrust moved with her victim, followed and followed until it had run itself red in him.

Scuto just passed between them, barely sparing them a glance. He vaulted up into the engineer's cab at the back of the *Pride* and then came straight out again with a Wasp's sting searing over his shoulder. His assailant cut down at him, but the shortsword clanged off his breastplate, and then Scuto seized him, hugged him close, a dozen hooked spines tearing into the twisting soldier, scratching his armour. Che found that she wanted to stop clear of the action, not for fear of the Empire, but for fear of Tisamon and his daughter, lest their deadly skills should not discriminate. She forced herself on, and her sword lodged itself in the back of the man Scuto wrestled with.

She felt it scrape against his mail and then plunge into his flesh. It was a shock that went right through her. Her first life's blood truly shed. It was a horrible feeling, a knowledge for the worse.

And she had no time, no time to adjust. Scuto was already hurling the body away, leaping back up into the cab and holding a prickly hand out for her.

Inside, as the killing went on without, they stared.

It was the face of the lightning engine, and neither of them had ever seen anything like it. The central panel was blurry glass, and behind it there were coiled pillars that sparked and danced and glowed like lit glass themselves. Either side were dials and levers, pull-chains and toggles, and it all meant so little to her. She could see from his face that it meant even less to Scuto.

'I wish we had Totho here now,' she said sadly. 'When I did my mechanics, this sort of thing was just being thought of. I know only the . . . the basics.'

'Good,' Scuto said. With a brutal movement he brought the butt of his crossbow down onto the glass, but it barely chipped. 'Founder's mark!' he spat. 'Must be a foot thick. Can't even trust grenades on that. You reckon you can overcharge this thing?'

Che looked over the instruments, in the familiar situation of being their best expert on a subject she knew little enough about. 'Let's try,' she said. 'Let's just try.'

Scuto risked a look out across the engine field. 'Try fast,' he advised. The Wasp wedge had fallen. A pair of survivors was running, and Balkus was already slotting a new magazine into place atop his nailbow to loose at them. Stenwold glanced around, seeing a mess of dead men. Here were Wasps, fallen in close order, attacked from all sides, bodies one atop another. There lay one of Scuto's Beetle-kinden with his face charred, and beyond was a dead Fly, blank eyes fixed upwards.

Everyone's eyes were looking upwards in the next moment, as energy bolts started to fall around them. The next wave was here already, swooping down on them with extended, fiery hands, and lances levelled. Balkus loosed smoothly, sending bolt after miniature bolt ripping into them, spinning the flying men off balance, punching them right out of the sky.

'Cover!' Stenwold shouted, as one of his Ant-kinden

fell trying to reload his crossbow. Sperra was already in the shadow of the lesser engine, frantically turning the winch of her own weapon.

There was a flurry of motion above even as Stenwold cast himself behind the uncertain shelter of an earth mound. He then dared to look, and saw that the entire sky had become a battleground. The Wasp squad was wheeling and passing against some of Achaeos's people. The Dragonfly flashed through the melee's centre, a better flier than any of the others, turning even as she flew to slice an arrow through the air that caught an unsuspecting Wasp in the back. The male Mantis-kinden caught an enemy by the belt and carved his claw into the man, two brief moves and then releasing the limp body. Then a bolt caught him in the side and he dropped. He hit the earth still living, but a Wasp had dropped with him, driving his sword into him before the stricken Mantis could recover from the fall. Stenwold shot the victor in the chest as he made to get back into the air.

Someone was shouting a warning but he could not catch the words. A moment later he did not need to. From the side of the Wasps' camp the clashing of gears told him everything before the monstrous shape of the automotive came into view. It was a squat, armoured thing, an ugly, riveted box with a front like a sentinel's helm and narrow slits to look onto the outside world. Its four legs arched up like a spider's and moved it in sudden jerky steps that covered a great deal of ground. There were two great crossbows mounted beneath its blunt nose that were loosing even as it appeared, and on its back a mounted ballista – but it was more than that. Stenwold threw himself down again even as the jagged outline became clear. There was a shield bolted to the weapon to protect the crewman but he had spotted the great wooden magazine beyond it. A repeating ballista, a truly modern weapon. Seconds later began the harsh clack-clack-clack of it as it flung its bolts one after another.

It would soon smash them to pieces, he realized. They had to destroy the thing before it got into its stride.

Within his first two steps from cover his courage left him. He saw the Beetle sentinel cut down by the crossbows at the engine's fore, collapsing back in a chaos of armour with twin spines jutting through the metal plate over his chest. One of the Tharn Fly-kinden tried to dart overhead, but the ballista winched round smoothly, and the bolt hit her so hard that for a moment she was dead still in the air as the missle passed straight through her, and then she dropped.

The automotive lumbered on, gathering pace. There were other Wasps ranked behind it, another squad at least. Stenwold took a grenade out, wondering how thick this machine's armour was but knowing there was only one way to find out.

He lit the fuse and counted – a ballista bolt flew past him as he did – and then threw, and he had the range perfect for once. The grenade struck, and as it struck it exploded. For a moment there was fire and nothing else in his view, and then the automotive was there again, rocking back on its spindly legs. The front had been dented by the impact, and at least one of the crossbows below it was ruined, trailing its bow arm uselessly, but after a second the monstrous thing was forging ahead once more.

'Destroy it!' he shouted impotently, with no means of doing so.

There was fighting behind the automotive now, for two or three of the Moth contingent had dropped there. Stenwold saw the Grasshopper with the two knives making bloody work, leaping and dancing and scattering bodies aside. The ballista wheeled back to face the machine's stern, showing Stenwold the back of the bowman's armoured chair.

'Now! Go now!' he shouted, and ran for the advancing automotive without knowing if anyone was following him.

Achaeos slashed once more at the man he was fighting, his long dagger striking sparks off armour, then he was in the air again, spiralling away. Two or three bolts of energy passed him, and he glanced back to see the Wasp soldier barrelling after him, hand extended and face furious. Achaeos threw himself into a loop that left the Wasp spinning in the air and stabbed out as soon as he was in arm's reach, jabbing the man in the leg. As the Wasp turned to follow him one of Achaeos's fellows sped past and hooked the man around the neck, clinging on grimly as Achaeos looped back and put his blade in twice, three times, until the Wasp dropped out of the sky. He and his comrade then flew their separate ways across the battlefield.

Achaeos's warriors were split up now, each acting on his or her own. That was the way they worked, in both raids and warfare. Nobody realized that the Moths ever went to war, but it was midnight skirmishes like this that brought out the warrior in them. He sheathed his dagger, shrugged his bow from over his shoulder and loosened the drawstring holding his quiver closed.

He saw the automotive wade ponderously across the battlefield, the murderous artificer's device atop it pivoting back and forth, constantly spitting death. Passing over, he saw that some few were even attacking it, and that one of these was Stenwold.

Stenwold was undoubtedly going to die. The fat old Beetle was making almost as much heavy going as the machine itself and the weapon was swinging round towards him like the head of some blind god. Nobody believed in gods, of course, but the artificers had created them anyway.

Achaeos reached for his Art, that trancing Art he had

used on Che what now seemed so long ago, and dashed past the slit of the ballista. The first shot spun past him, and the second, and then he felt the shock of contact as his mind, his gaze, caught the artillerist's.

He dragged on that contact, as his wings took him up and back, and he knew that, for precious seconds at least, the man's gaze would be drawn with him, the weapon itself swinging away blindly.

Thalric was trying to make sense of the battle, and there was precious little sense to be made. It was the cursed Moth-kinden and their allies. They had taken the fighting everywhere, whereas Stenwold's sorry lot could have been contained. The fighting at the *Pride* itself had been over a moment ago, and now it was back on, another squad of the light airborne coming down to root out the attackers. Meanwhile the automotive was making steady progress, despite fierce resistance. When it got to the *Pride* the night would be as good as won, but he knew that there were no certainties this night. Stenwold had mustered more allies than he had ever expected. Even the smashing of Scuto's ring seemed hardly to have broken the Beetle's stride.

Major Godran was now by his side. The man picked to lead the invasion of Collegium, he was peering towards the *Pride* with any captain's concern at the fate of his vessel.

'Will you look at that!' he choked. He was pointing at the skirmish around the engine, and Thalric saw it too. What a one-sided affair it should have been, the Wasp soldiers stinging down, then dropping with drawn blade to take on so few defenders. What a one-sided affair it was, indeed. There was a Mantis-kinden there who moved like light and shadow both. The stings of the Wasps could not find him, and when they closed to sword's reach, they died. There was no more subtlety to it than that. Thalric's eyes could not follow it, but the man seemed to have a lethal aura about him, as though even the air he moved through was fatal to his enemies. He was holding them off. He was more than holding them off. He was slaughtering them.

The automotive continued to manage a slow crawl across the field. They needed something more than that now. Thalric looked for the only useful flier they could mobilize, a spotter blimp with a pair of winched repeating crossbows mounted in its belly. He located its pale bulk overhead, but saw instantly that it was in trouble. There were Moth-kinden attacking it, gashing the gasbag and clinging onto the small gondola as they stabbed at the crew. That particular gambit had died before it even entered the battle. There would be no help there.

Which left one thing.

'I'll take a squad in,' Thalric decided.

'Are you sure that's wise, Captain?' asked Godran.

'No choice, Major.' Thalric rapped his fist on the armour of a sergeant. 'You and yours, with me!' he said, and kicked off into the air.

Stenwold was halfway to the automotive, with another grenade in his hand, when he saw the ballista cupola wheel back towards him. Even as he saw it he was directly before it, seeing the arms tensioned back, the power in this weapon of bent steel and twined horsehair enough to split him in two.

And yet it did not shoot. He stared at the head of the bolt, metal sheathing it for a full eighteen inches, and then it lurched aside, tilting up at the stars. He lit the grenade, throwing it even as he did so.

He thought the fuse must have been cut too short, because he was punched from his feet almost instantly, the wash of fire singeing his eyebrows and fragments of metal gashing his armour and his scalp. A moment later he saw the cupola rock back with the impact. Then four men were dashing past him. One, the Beetle with the blunderbow, was cut down by the remaining fore crossbow, almost falling onto Stenwold's legs. Rakka the Scorpion was already past, long-hafted axe raised high, and Balkus and Sperra were following close behind. Stenwold saw Sperra leap into the air and launch a bolt at the bowman behind the ballista, but it merely rebounded from the weapon's armoured housing. Then the ballista was sweeping around, trying to pick her out of the air, its tireless mechanisms throwing bolt after bolt at her. In the confusion, Rakka gained the side of the automotive.

The huge man had only an axe and, even as he raised it, Stenwold could not understand what he meant to do. Then the Scorpion brought it down where the leg closest to him met the machine's housing.

It seemed a futile gesture but Rakka was stronger than Stenwold realized, a strength augmented by surging tides of Scorpion Art. The axehead bit deep into the leg's casing, buckling the pistons and gears operating within. When the automotive took its next step, that same foreleg made only half the gain, slewing the entire machine round.

A sting blast scorched across Rakka's bare back, and the Scorpion howled in pain. Balkus returned the shot, the chamber of his nailbow flashing again and again. Rakka now had the axe up once more, every ounce of his strength focused on that single point of the machine. With a wordless battle cry he brought it down once, and then twice, even as a second bolt of energy impacted between his shoulder blades. The leg had canted to one side with the first stroke, its joints abruptly frozen. The second blow must have cut almost through it because, when the automotive took its next step, the damaged leg snapped off entirely and the machine tipped forwards, back leg waving in the air, its nose grinding into the dirt.

'Clear it!' Stenwold shouted, rushing ahead. Balkus was meanwhile helping Rakka away, whereupon Stenwold lit his last grenade and hurled it at the ballista's cupola.

It bounced, but he had overshot, and so it struck the sloping hull beyond the weapon and rolled back. Then it thundered to pieces and in its wake the ballista became a shredded splay of metal around an open hatch.

Stenwold looked for Balkus and saw the Ant lowering Rakka's body to the ground before snatching his nailbow up again. Even before Stenwold could call it, he was rushing forward, stepping up onto the tilted hull. He levelled his nailbow down the hatch and emptied it at the crew as they tried to climb out.

There were more Wasps out there, at least another two squads that had been following up behind the automotive. Stenwold felt old, weary to his bones, his heart like a hammer pounding in his chest and his lungs raw. He was past all this. He should be safe in some distant study with his papers, like all good spymasters. He squared himself up, advanced to the cover of the wrecked automotive, waiting for them.

But they were not coming closer: instead they were fighting. He could not tell who they were fighting save that it was armoured men, not Achaeos's raiders. Then he *could* tell, and could not quite believe. They were Helleren militia, men with pikes and crossbows and chain mail. They were not as mobile or as savage as the Wasps, but there were more of them, and they were giving a good account of themselves.

His first thought was that it was Greenwise who had sent them, but how would he have known? The obvious answer then came, that there had been enough commotion in this place to attract *someone*'s attention, and when the guardsmen had arrived they had taken the closest combatants rushing towards the embattled engine as their enemies.

*

Thalric came in high, fast. He saw the Mantis-kinden duellist spin, dance, another two men falling back, and dying as they did so. There was a chill in the Wasp's heart. He was better travelled than most of his race, so he had heard tell of Mantis Weaponsmasters, the last scions of a truly ancient cult. He could not really believe it but here was the very thing.

He would have no second chance now. He watched the swift passes of the Mantis's claw, the step of his feet, the rhythm of his fight. Thalric was no novice himself: his Art-sting was second nature to him, stronger than it was in his fellows, and he himself more practised with it.

As Tisamon lashed out at another of his soldiers, Thalric chose his moment and loosed, the golden energy of his bolt streaking ahead of him like a falling star.

Impossibly, the Mantis was already turning away from the bolt, twisting away from it even as he fought. Thalric saw it strike, though, lashing down the Mantis's side as the man finished off the last of his opponents, throwing him against the *Pride*'s hull and bouncing him backwards to where he collapsed.

Victory soared in Thalric's heart and he stooped on the *Pride*, determined to finish this. He heard a voice, and it surely must have been Cheerwell Maker's voice, cry out, 'Tisamon!'

Thalric landed ahead of his men, sword in his right hand and his left spread open to unleash his Art-fire. The Mantis was hunched about the wound, struggling to rise. One blow and it would be a simple matter to break into the engine room and dispatch whoever was inside, dispatch Cheerwell, if it was her.

The idea hurt him, but it was for the Empire. It was *war*.

He looked up, and Tynisa descended on him from atop the engine. She led with her sword, and she shrieked something as mad as the rage-racked look on her face.

His blade was coming up, and he was falling back, but too late, too late.

The point of the rapier lanced for his chest. It struck the banded imperial armour and pierced it with the slightest bending of the blade, but the plates slowed it enough that when it met the copperweave beneath it merely scraped down the links, severing them one after another, drawing a line of agony down his chest that was nevertheless only skin deep, until it ripped free of his ruined armour and stabbed him through his thigh.

He dropped to one knee with a cry of pain and lunged forward with his own blade. It caught her in the belly but it was a weak blow, dulled by shock and hurt, and it skidded across her arming jacket before it drew blood, slicing along her waist and then bloodying her arm on the backstroke. She reeled backwards and he saw her fingers open, and yet the rapier hung in her hand still, refusing to be dropped.

He stood, fell to his knee almost immediately, but already loosing his sting at her. It melted a fist-sized dent in the metal of the *Pride* as she lurched out of the way.

'You killed him!' she screamed at Thalric, and he fell back and rolled as she lunged at him, the rapier's tip drawing a line of blood across his scalp. He came up swinging, forcing her back, left hand pulled back for another shot.

Tisamon lurched to his feet. They were both deadly still in that moment as he levered himself halfway up, and then forced himself to rise the rest of the way. One arm was wrapped about his burned side, but his claw hung ready for battle, steeped in the blood of two dozen Wasps and not slaked yet.

His bared teeth might have been a grimace of pain or a smile of anticipation.

Faced with that sight, wounded and battered and with this monster on its feet again and standing like an executioner, Thalric felt his nerve falter. He had feared before, but it had been a rational fear. Now he kicked backwards, wings flickering in and out of his back, putting a distance between himself and this mad killer and his even worse daughter. Then his men were there, rushing into the fray, and he watched Tisamon and Tynisa take them on. Both injured, both more ragged in movement than before, and yet they held their ground. Thalric gathered himself, looking round for the automotive which surely must be there by now.

It was burning, he now saw. Three legs were rigid and one gone entirely, flames licked from within its cabin, gusted from its eyeslit. Beyond it he could see a slow trail of fire in the sky where the spotter blimp was drifting downwards in ruin.

Che pulled another two levers and turned one of the crank wheels, feeling the power within the engine start to vibrate the footplates beneath her. She was almost there, she knew. The glass-fronted chamber was almost incandescent, with Scuto peering into it through two layers of cloth. She could feel the whole of the *Pride* shaking, and she knew its inventors had never intended such intense stresses on it.

'Almost,' she said, and gave the wheel another three turns, bringing the supercharged elements within the engine's long body closer and closer. She could only imagine the lightning crackling one to another, faster and faster until it was lightning no longer, but pure motive power.

'Che—' Scuto began nervously.

'Just a little more,' she told him.

'*Che!*' he said. 'No more! We have to go!'

'Why?' she asked, and looked up from the controls.

He was only half there, or so her eyes told her. The half of him furthest from that window was dark shadow, the rest was invisible in a sea of light. Not heat, she realized, pure light, and yet the thick glass was running like ice on a warm morning, limned with a molten glow, streaking the metal beneath it to puddle like wax on the floor.

'We have to go!' he said again desperately, and then with all his might, for those close to the *Pride*, he yelled, 'Everybody clear of the train!'

Tynisa heard the Thorn Bug's wild cry. She saw the surviving Wasps were already being routed, those few that could. She looked at Tisamon and saw him ashen even in the moonlight, swaying.

She caught him, got his arm over her shoulder and her arm about his waist. He barked with the pain, but there was no time, no time. Behind them white light was streaming from the *Pride*'s cab, and from the very seams of its engine housing.

There was a Wasp ahead of them on one knee, the very man who had shot Tisamon. She readied her rapier, hoping to cut him down before he could loose his sting or cut at them. For a moment she met his eyes, seeing pain and bitterness and a certain resignation. Then he was gone, his wings casting him high into the sky.

And she ran, and Tisamon ran when he could and she dragged him when he couldn't.

And they fell. She looked back then, at the *Pride*, which was leaking fire at every rivet hole.

She saw it explode.

Except it was not that, not quite. The roof of the engine chamber burst open with a thunderous peal and a bolt of lightning shot straight *upwards* at clouds that were forming even then, spewing out of a vortex above the stricken *Pride*, enough to blot out the moon.

And a clear second later, the lightning lashed down, a stabbing spear of blinding white that struck the *Pride* square on and blasted it to pieces. She was blinded by it, seeing white only, and deafened because of the thunder that rumbled on and on in the sky.

She realized then that she had not seen Che get clear of the doomed engine before the bolt struck.

Forty

Tynisa awoke slowly, knowing pain. She had shifted position, and sleep had cast her out of its welcome embrace at once. The world was now contracted to a dull throb in her side, a slightly sharper one in her arm. But of course, though the latter cut was shallower, she had worked with that arm, fighting that last squad of soldiers beside her father, and then she had been running, his weight bearing down on her, and there had been that cataclysmic explosion of light and metal . . .

And she remembered precious little more. Her strength had not lasted much past that moment.

She had no idea where she was. *Perhaps the Wasps caught me!*

That forced her to open her eyes. The room was dim, lit only by windows high in the walls. For a moment she thought she was back in the resistance shelter in Myna, but the architecture here was different, only the mood was the same.

She propped herself up on one elbow, discovering that someone had cleaned and dressed her wounds. To one side there was a woman she recognized vaguely as one of Scuto's crew who had fought alongside her. She was still asleep, or unconscious, and there were blotched bandages neatly wrapped about her head and chest. To Tynisa's unprofessional eye the woman looked in a bad way.

Beyond her was Tisamon. He slept, too. Tynisa sat up, feeing her side twinge, the stitches pull, but hold. He lived, then. His bare chest rose and fell, and she saw the extent of the burn that he had taken, a shiny blemish across his skin from waist almost to collarbone, all up one side. But he lived: she had not known, in those confused last moments, if any of them would.

She looked to the other side, and saw a Moth's back as he knelt beside another pallet. Somehow she knew it was Achaeos, and realized this because he no longer held himself quite like others of his race. Something had opened up in him.

She shifted round, and as he turned at the sound she saw that he was tending to Che.

The girl was awake, but she had dozens of tiny wounds, small patches of bandage across her face and shoulders and body. Tynisa gaped at the extent of it.

'Is that what the . . . the explosion . . . ?'

There was a chuckling cough from near the foot of Che's bed, and Tynisa saw that a second row of pallets had been laid toe to toe with her own row, and that Scuto was there. He lay, improbably, on his front, and she saw his back was a war of blisters across the blasted landscape of his spines.

'I'm afraid that scattershot was me,' the Thorn Bug said. 'We'd only got a second, and I just grabbed 'er up and jumped. Sometimes I forget my own shape, you know. All shallow, though, and they'll heal good as new, mind, 'cos Beetles is tough buggers, but they had to cut her armour off 'er before they could prise it off me.'

'And . . . ? How did we do? Who did we lose?'

'Enough,' said Scuto soberly. 'Rakka's gone. Pedro and Halyard Brighter. Archedamae, who took a hit when we got out of the workshop, she died while we were fighting at the *Pride*. More, more and more. Easier to name the survivors. Balkus didn't get scratched, the bastard, but Sperra's all cut up. You've seen Hadraxa to your right, and she's not so good. All in all I've got five left, including me. That's the Helleron operation. I mean, we did our bit, in the end, made it worth the chief putting us here, but we paid for it. The lad's lot there, they took their cuts as well.'

Achaeos just nodded. Tynisa saw that he held one of Che's hands anxiously in both of his.

Thalric gritted his teeth as the field surgeon dealt with his leg, the heated needle passing deftly back and forth as Thalric bit down on the softwood bar and winced.

'You were lucky with this one, sir,' the surgeon announced, and Thalric knew that he had dealt with many less lucky men before this particular job. 'A little off and the big blood vessel would have been cut. Dead in minutes then, sir.'

And there were two suits of armour riven before that blade even bloodied me. Not quite true, of course. In the way of ripping both his prized copperweave and the regulation imperial light cuirass, it had drawn a pretty scar from his nipple to his navel, but he had taken worse than that and still fought on.

Beside the failure of the previous night, any injury short of death was light work. There was a blank scroll waiting for him, and what he wrote there would go to Colonel Latvoc or General Reiner or some other Rekef official, who would decide just how much he had lost the Empire by his failure.

The Wasps were already packing up their camp beside Helleron. There were impatient delegations from the Council of Magnates, who were becoming more difficult to fob off with misdirection. They wanted to know whether it was the Empire that had destroyed Helleron's *Pride*. Telling them that they, the Wasps, had been trying to save it only posed further awkward questions. This setback might claim Thalric's career. It might even claim his life, politics being what they were, but it would barely dent the Empire's ambition.

He had often wondered how he would take an occasion like this, when his star had fallen but the Empire still peopled the night sky with its lights, and he was both surprised and relieved to find he took comfort in that. He could be lost, but he was only one small piece of the machine, and the machine itself would go on forever. To the south the assault on Tark would be starting any day, if it had not begun already. Tark would fall as Ant cities always fell to the Empire, with a bloody, brutal, no-quarter fight, but overwhelmed by an enemy more numerous, more mobile, broader of thought, and ruthless of purpose.

And Helleron? Thalric would return home with the balance of his two thousand soldiers, but either he, or his successor, would be back with five thousand, or perhaps he would counsel fifty thousand. The Helleron Beetles were already telling themselves that the entire Imperial Army was at Tark – for the news was finally breaking here – but the men who were in sight of Tark's walls were only the Fourth Army, supported by a few Auxillian battalions and some detachments of the Engineering Corps. The Empire had plenty of armies to spare, as Helleron would discover.

As the surgeon swabbed off the stitched wound and closed his toolbag, Thalric began to compose his report, without emotion or fear.

Stenwold gathered up those who could travel. After the two days that had passed, that included Che, Tynisa and even Tisamon, although the Mantis was still pained by his wound and kept his chest bare, his arming jacket slung open over his shoulders.

'Now comes the time,' Stenwold told them simply. 'We have struck a small victory against a great enemy, not for Helleron, or Collegium, or revenge, or justice, or anything so small. We have done it for all the Lowlands, so the Lowlands retains a chance to lock shields against the foe.

'But of course it is only one blow struck. There is now war in Tark as you know, and the Empire is sending more troops westwards, I guarantee it. We must carry the word ahead of them. Unity or slavery, these must be our watchwords, for they are no more than the flat truth. The future of the Lowlands: unity or slavery. The unity, if we achieve it, will never last. The slavery, however, might lie on our shoulders forever.

'So I myself am bound for Collegium, which is the best soil we have for unity to grow in. Collegium is already allied with the Ants of Sarn, and that net can spread. If Tark does fall, as I fear it will, it will serve as an example, burning letters ten feet high that state: *The Empire Must Be Stopped.*

'And there will be danger aplenty, for the Wasps will have their agents in Collegium and Sarn and Merro, and all the other places, and they will be preaching to the great and the good of all those places that the Empire comes only to attack their enemies, not them. They will tell each city to rub its hands as its ancient rivals fall, and in this way they will seek to eat the Lowlands bit by bit, and they may even succeed.

'Ours will not be a war of swords, but of words. The swords are there, but we must convince the hands that hold them to draw them from the scabbard, to let them flash defiance in the sun.

'I have sent messengers already, to Collegium, to Sarn, even to the Spiderlands, whose denizens have always worked against Lowlander unity in the past. There is no hand from which I would not take help at this point. I would write to the underground halls of the Centipede kingdom or the Mosquito Lords if they were anything more than a myth. Perhaps, if matters grow much worse, I will do so anyway.'

He looked over his audience, battered and bruised as they were. His niece and his adopted daughter, and her true father; the ever-faithful, durable Scuto, and Balkus the mercenary Ant-kinden, who had not been paid and yet was here; Achaeos, forever inscrutable, here amidst his traditional enemies; Sperra the Fly-kinden, who had insisted on being carried from her convalescence to hear his words.

He thought of that other fellowship, so long ago, of dead Marius and of Tisamon's lost love.

Not in vain. He swore it to himself. Each sword raised against the Empire, each word spoken, would be added to the scales. He would rally and rouse, he would wake the sleeping, open the eyes of the blind, to gain those swords for his cause, and in the end, if the scales did not tip, if the tide of the Empire drowned all the lands he knew of, then it would not be because he had spared an ounce of effort in resisting it.

'Will you come with me to Collegium?' he asked them all, and not one face, not even Achaeos's, told him 'no'.

The first shots were yet to be loosed but, when Salma and the others came within sight of Tark, the Wasps were already there. Their camp half-encircled the city's walls, and it seemed incredible, impossible, that so many had come so swiftly, and making their way through the desert's fringe.

Skrill shielded her eyes, tracking down the banners and the symbols, the machines and the formations. 'I see serious artillery. Wall-pounders and leadshotters are the least of it. Looks like Bee-kinden Auxillian engineers from Szar, if I'm a judge; Cricket diggers from Delve; some wild-boy Wasps from the hill tribes for shock value; even Maynes Ants under arms there, guess they know how much Ants like killing Ants. And there's a whole row of somethings under canvas, autos or the like. Cut me open, that's the whole Fourth and then some. Bloody flux!'

Salma and Totho simply took in this sight in silence.

They had never seen so many men of war in one place, let alone their equipment, machinery, earthworks, slaves, mounts, camp followers and sutlers.

Neither had Tark, they realized. Neither had anywhere in the Lowlands, ever before.